KINGDOM

OF THE

TWO MOONS

ALEXANDRA THOMASHOFF

Disclaimer:
This is a work of fiction. All characters, locations, and businesses are purely products of the author's imagination and are entirely fictitious. Any resemblance to actual people, living or dead, or to businesses, places, or events is completely coincidental.

Last Unicorn Press

For you, the star-crossed love of my life. Forever.

And for all the readers who needed fantasy and books to survive reality. Because I sure as hells did.

TRIGGER WARNING

This book delves into complex and sensitive subject matter that may be deeply distressing for some readers. It includes explicit depictions and discussions of sexual assault, graphic violence, domestic abuse, mental illness, and suicide. These topics are explored with the intent of telling a compelling and impactful story but may evoke strong emotional responses.

The narrative also features a dark romance theme, incorporating elements such as kidnapping, manipulation, and dubious consent. These themes are central to the plot and character development but may be unsettling or triggering for those sensitive to such content.

The intention behind addressing these challenging topics is to portray a raw and realistic exploration of human emotions, trauma, and resilience. However, we understand that not all readers will feel comfortable engaging with such material.

If at any point during the story you find the content overwhelming, we encourage you to pause or step away. Your mental and emotional health is paramount.

Please take care of yourself while reading, and if any of the topics resonate with personal experiences, consider reaching out to a trusted friend, counselor, or support service. Engaging with difficult content can be a powerful but also emotionally taxing experience, and it's okay to prioritize your well-being over completing the story.

Thank you for approaching this book with an open mind and understanding.

The world has changed since the chains broke.
The time of contempt is over.
I can feel it in the whispers of the wind.
Taste it in the tears of the sea.
Read it in the curling smokes of the eternal fires.
Danger is looming.
Madness on the threshold.
Foreign troubles that have been unlooked for too long.
I can hear the hooves of the dark riders.
The hounds have been summoned.
Unless silver blood is spilled
and timeless lips bend down to quench their thirst
and be forever remedied.
Hear your fate, oh dweller of worlds!
Find what waits and always has.
An earthborn child of ancient blood.
A girl who carries within her the light,
she is the only one who will end the blight.

Prophecy given by Kalleandara, High Oracle of the Islands of
Mists in the Lands of the Undead

MAP OF THE FAE WORLD

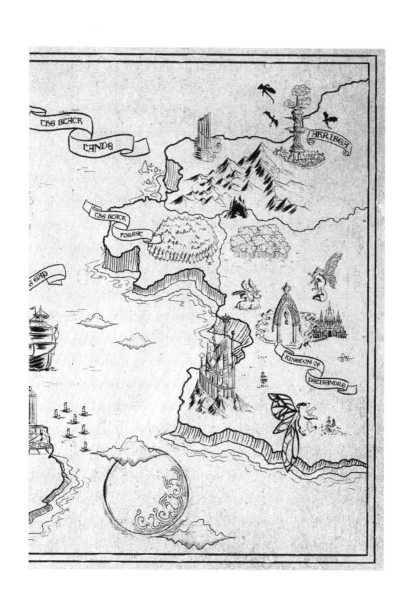

GLOSSARY

HIGH FAE:

All fae with strong inherent magic.

Angels: Celestials. Feared among all the fae because of their wrath, inability to feel, and their cruelty. Winged elves with terrifying powers and the ability to jump from world to world, open up portals, or close them if need be, and take their inherent magic with them. They had been hunted to near extinction by Palisandre and the witches.

High elves: Elves gifted with outstanding power and magic among the elves, usually born to become rulers.

Witches: Allegedly born out of an alliance with demons from the Abyss. Elves with long, sharp, silver canines and long, silver claws, known for their hunger for power and blood. Matriarchal societies. If a male is born, he is given away to die in the woods. Some of them are said to have survived and turned witchers, destined to hunt down the very mothers who abandoned them.

Nefarians: Elves with leathery wings and long, sharp talons. They have dark, demonic magic flowing in their veins. They came from another world, and as with the witches, are believed to be yet another offspring of an alliance between demons and elves. They are believed to have been extinct in the fae world, but some claim a few escaped, hiding in the Black Forest.

LESSER FAE:

All creatures of lesser strength and few magical powers.

Elves: Although there are only a few high elves among the elven society, they consider themselves superior. They all are shockingly beautiful and have sharp, pointed ears. They are well-known for their outstanding architectural skills. They love aesthetics and are often cruel and cold-hearted, especially when they age.

Most elves can live to be a thousand years old, an age otherwise only witches and angels are known to reach.

Sirens: Folk of the deep sea, of rivers and lakes alike. All societies have heard myths of sirens, sitting on rocks, luring sailors and fishermen to death with their voices. Those myths are not true. They are remarkably civil and disinterested in enthralling anyone for food—or at least those at the Dark Lord's court are. Some colonies still thrive in the depths of the oceans, subservient only to the mer-queen. Some legends claim some stayed behind in the human world before the angels closed the gates and magic disappeared from there.

They usually have lush bodies, the color of their skin and hair ranges from coral tones over deep sepia to light aquamarine. Sometimes their skins are striped, or covered in patches of semi-transparent, shimmering, soft scales. They can live on land and water, but as soon as they immerse themselves into water, their hands and feet become webbed, their necks lined with gills. Their eyes are turning all black to make them able to absorb every little bit of light down below. Their ears have the shape of shells. They smell of salt water and seaweed.

Like all mer-folk, their societies tend to be matriarchal. The women hunt, the men become soldiers. A lot of sirens abandoned the lakes and steaming rivers of Palisandre when the elves turned cruel under their king.

Dryads: Dryads used to live in all sylvan woodlands, alongside unicorns, taking care of the forest and its plants, sprites, and all wildlife. Every dryad is bound to her tree and every tree is bound to the queen of their forest. Their colonies had been almost hunted down to extinction by the elves and later further diminished under the bloody reign of the witch queen Gatilla.

Their skin colors range from sap-laden spring foliage green to ebony. A lot of them have colorful hair, which is adorned with leaves, pearls, and flowers. They are skilled hunters and infamous for their stealth and wrath when someone attacks their home. Some of them have horns. Queen Calianthe of the Emerald Forest is known to be the last dryad queen in the fae world.

Some of them had been famous for being the best healers of the fae world.

Fauns: Fauns love all kinds of sins and shenanigans. They love to dance under the full moon, drink wine, and take part in all forms of sexual escapades. They have a taste for pleasure and war, which makes some of them the most dangerous enemies among the lesser fae. Among them, crimson-horns show exceptional bloodlust.

Fauns usually smell of earth and have beautiful, large horns and hooved feet, as well as large, round ears. Apart from that, their upper bodies appear mostly humanoid. Fauns live everywhere and, given their tremendous appetites, often are great cooks and, therefore, well-liked, even among the elves.

They don't live in tribes or colonies and only sometimes pledge themselves to a leader of their choice. Only rarely do they show traits of magic in their blood.

Prologue

MELODY

Jump.

Just jump. Then it's over.

The icy cold wind cuts from below, deep into my bruised and throbbing skin.

Just one more step and it's over. You're almost there. Just one more tiny step.

No more Lyrian. No more being locked away for days. No more beatings. No more threats and a life I cannot bear.

I watch the deep, gray waves waltz below. The impact would shatter my body, I think. The cliff I'm standing on is so high I would just die, the water below like concrete from this height. I hope I won't feel a thing.

Just one more tiny step. My last resort.

Small rocks come loose under my shoes as I stare down into the beckoning depth, feeling its lure in my bones, in my very blood, like a song.

The abyss always knew my name, even when I was still a small child. Always used to call to me. Like the wind.

Just then a gust comes up.

It whispers around me, telling me about foreign lands and creatures. About emerald forests and lilac woods, of milky turquoise streams, of horses with horns and feathery wings, and of dragons, their scaled hides glimmering like rainbows under the sun. I can almost smell the exotic fragrances, the flowers, the sap of the forests, as if those places truly existed.

I stretch out my arms and lean forward, into the wind. For a moment, I imagine myself having wings. That they catch the breeze as I jump and carry me, not down, but away. Somewhere safe. Somewhere good.

It would be so easy to give in. Easier than to go back. To keep going. To keep fighting. I can feel my body reeling forward, my balance tipping.

I feel myself falling.

At the last moment, I startle back, breathing hard.

Not today. I can give up any other day. But not today. First, I will try to find another way. I will fight some more.

I turn and run back the way I came from, through the crooked, moss-covered willows with their bent branches. I swear the ocean's call is following me back to the mansion as if some ancient sea-good is disappointed to have been once again cheated out of claiming my soul.

BLAIR

Blair Alaric *loves* the human world. She loves ice cream, loves the way it tastes, the colors it comes in, like flowers of the elven forest. She loves their clothing too—the neon-hued sneakers she's wearing with a skintight plastic dress that flatters her lush body. Face it, even the best dressmakers of Palisandre can't provide a thing like that.

Oh yes, she fucking loves the way that tight, short-as-sin piece of synthetic silver clings to her in all the right places, showing off her ample cleavage, only to end shy of her navel. Setting off the silver piercing there she got from a shady corner parlor.

The young man inside her seems to love it too, nuzzling her neck from behind, one large hand encircling her nipple, the other grabbing at her waist. He's pounding into her from behind while he keeps whispering all those terribly filthy things in her ear. He's so good that she almost tears the washbasin from the wall as a wave of release breaks over her. She has to bite the inside of her cheeks so as not to let the whole club know why exactly the door has been locked for almost thirty minutes now.

A tiny moan escapes him at that. She watches him in the battered mirror. The way he tilts his head back, exposing his throat but not stopping his thrusts, spurring her right towards another climax. *Good boy.*

He's probably high as hell right now, judging by the smell of his sweat and the way his eyelids flutter. But she doesn't care. Not her problem.

As long as he fucks like this. Let's face it, this is the best sex she's had in weeks. The best sex since…

She hates the fact that she still thinks about the fucking angel every time she orgasms. To hell with that vain bastard Caryan.

Too bad he's going to kill her the next time she sees him.

Too fucking bad.

Her second climax eddies away and suddenly she really wants to tear that fucking washbasin from the wall just to let off some steam. But then the man grabs her waist with two hands, squashing her impulse as he goes over the edge.

Right, he deserves it.

As soon as he is done, Blair steps out of his embrace, rolling down the hem of that ridiculous idea of a dress, and reaches for the toilet door. Not waiting for him, she stumbles back into the club full of twitching humans. The music's pounding hard against her bones and over mirrored pillars, melting with her blood.

With her soul, *if she has one.*

She takes a moment to drink it all in, soak in it. The dancing, the giggling, the music. The music especially. *The Abyss,* how much she loves music—no, not loves, *needs it.* It glitters through her veins like a thousand twinkling stars, makes her blood hum, makes her very soul sing with… *joy.* A feeling she hadn't known until she arrived in the human realm a year ago and a melody caught her ear.

Music…

A thing long banned in the witch territories by Blair's cruel aunt, the witch queen Gatilla herself. Just another attempt to suck any joy from the witch lands. Anything worth living for. If you could call it living in the first place.

Since Blair got her hands on a smartphone and some headphones she's gone nowhere without them, music in her ears from the moment she gets up to the moment she closes her eyes to sleep. Most of the time moving her body to it as if she'd been born to dance. As if her very core is a song and only rhythms and notes can express what she truly feels. All those emotions she hadn't known she was capable of having. What lies beyond all that darkness and cruelty and emptiness in her.

For the first time in her whole life, she feels like *more*. More than the cruel witch she's been raised to become. More than the ruthless warrior. And more than... well, the ghost she's turned into since Caryan left her side.

She's been nothing but a shell since the night her aunt died. Since Caryan and she broke up, she fell apart. It doesn't matter that it happened more than fucking twenty years ago. It tore her in half, a cut so deep that, on some days, only her rage and darkness and pain keep her going, keep her together. She knows it makes her pathetic. Weak.

But she's become mortal enough to cry.

Maybe this is why she's feeling that kind of belonging. Those songs the humans write, so full of pain and heartbreak, she knows they understand what she's feeling inside.

Nothing a fae would ever comprehend. But listening to music, to voices out there sharing her kind of torment... it doesn't heal her wounds but at least it soothes them. Makes even the darkest hours bearable so that, in those moments when she so much as thinks Caryan's name, she can at least keep breathing.

Like now, she focuses back on the music. On the notes and rhythms.

It helps. It makes her feel something else. Something other than the emptiness and crack in her heart.

On some days, she even catches herself smiling. On others, a shy part of her dares to imagine what she could be, could one day become, if she was to ever leave her past and the fae world behind.

If.

It is a dream, nothing else. Because she has to return to the fae world. *Soon.*

But it's a nice dream, nonetheless. And music's brought all that to the surface. Music and the sweet little human world.

Blair has no idea how she's going to live without music once she's back in the fae realms. Oh hells, it will be bad. She's not sure she would be able to charge a mobile phone with her magic, but she will sure as death try. Even if a dark part of her knows it won't work.

Well, she's not sure she will survive without music anyway, so it won't matter.

She swallows hard. Usually, she manages pretty well to block out the fact that she has to go back at some point. But there are moments where it is especially hard. Moments like this, when she's surrounded by people who just party their heads off because, fuck it, why not?

In moments like these, she wishes nothing more than to be a human. To shed her immortal skin. To just walk onto that dance floor, slide amid those sweat-slicked, delicate bodies of adorable humans with glitter in their hair and glow sticks around their wrists, and reduce herself to the beats. Just knock back some drinks and dance, dance, dance until her legs give out and be back at it the next night.

For a heartbeat, her sight turns blurry before she swallows the hint of emotion. Smothers it. Locks it into the endless, black void inside her, reminding herself why she's here in the first place. She's got work to do.

With a last, longing glance towards the dancing throng—people writhing as if to worship a forgotten king—she pushes her way through the crowd that flocks the bars. Wild, colorful lights flicker over her, confusing her witch senses. That's probably why she only notices the man when he grabs her wrist.

She keeps telling herself that it's not her despair that sometimes makes her lame. Distracted. Negligent.

She swivels around, briefly caught off guard, suppressing the sheer reflex to pull free and send him flying across the room. And wreak havoc on that club. She clenches her teeth, just in time, reining in her violent instincts—a painful reminder of just how different she is to them.

Abyss, she almost killed him with a flip of her wrist.

Humans—so delicate. So breakable. So... ridiculously weak, but sweet.

She also suppresses the instinct to snap her long, sharp, silver canines right in his face as a warning. Well, a good thing those teeth are currently hidden by the magic coming from an enchanted bracelet that camouflages her pointed ears, silver claws and teeth. The latter the trademark of the witches.

She knows the young man means no harm. Humans rarely do.

She snaps at him nonetheless. "You might not want to do that again." *Or I might bite off your head and call it an accident.*

He quickly lets go of her and pulls his hand back, as if he could hear what she didn't say. But it's shame coloring his absurd cheekbones and not fear. "I—I'm sorry," he stammers, scratching his neck. "It's just—I don't even know your name."

Blair tilts her head, her long, wine-red hair gracing her hip. Then she arches a brow. "Your mom taught you to be polite, asking for a girl's name *after* you've screwed her in a bathroom?"

Sarcasm—another adorable trait all fae lack but that she's adopted over the year she's spent in the human world.

He frowns at her, blushing even more violently before the corner of his sensuous mouth twitches up. His eyes light up while he runs a hand through his messy, blond hair. "Nope, I guess my mom would have told me not to fuck a girl in a bathroom in the first place."

Abyss save her, those dimples. As she's said—weak but adorable. Her fury eases a little. It's not their fault they are so clumsy and naïve. Not his fault she is an emotional mess. Certainly not his fault that the thought of Caryan ruined her second orgasm, and not for the first time. That this young man is all she wants to be, with his round ears and easy smile.

She pouts her full lips, crooning, "Huh, too bad. You'd have missed out on so much fun."

"Yeah. Want a drink or something?" He gestures to the bar, hope shining in his eyes.

Hmm, maybe she should keep him for a while. But she can't. She's got work to do. She tells him so.

He frowns, obviously confused. "Oh wow, can I... I don't know... at least get your number?"

7

That's the thing about human lovers. It's such fun to fuck them.

Granted, they can be a little unreliable as lovers, but there is no denying they are terribly cute when they are nervous—and they always are, even the older ones. Not afraid or arrogant, but insecure—something no fae would ever be. Especially no fae man, let alone an angel. The arrogance of a fae man is unbeatable. An angel is the very definition of that word.

Humans even fuck differently. Kind and gentle and generous. Fucking her as if she's the answer. A revelation. Never bored. Never just out of sheer need and drive instead of real affection.

There's never violence. No, they rather tend to freak out when her teeth come near their necks. Once, she whispered to a man that she would like to try his blood—well, that didn't end well, and she hasn't done that since.

She sighs. She could drag him right back to that bathroom for round two, trying to forget about Caryan and her mission and about fucking everything else.

No, she can't, she reminds herself.

She steps up to him and gently pats his cheek, careful not to bring her sharp, silver claws anywhere close to his delicate skin. "I would love to, but I've really got work to do."

He frowns, then blinks a few times before even more red starts to creep over his handsome face. Oh yes, now he's thinking she's a hooker. She should go. Find that wolf shifter, a creep nicknamed Fenrir, who uses this club as his hunting ground, and flay him alive—literally.

She needs to get a hold of him and torture the information she wants out of him. Others sang his name after she'd finished with them, said the guy has direct contact with Lyrian, high elf and magic harvester. Lyrian, with the girl, Melody, in tow—the actual reason the witch queen Perenilla has sent Blair to the human world in the first place. She needs to find her and bring her to the fae world. Then her mission will be accomplished. Fun over.

She nips that thought in the bud.

"My treat, sweetmeat," Blair purrs instead, before turning on her heel and vanishing deeper into the club. Her acute sense of smell chases after the peculiar stench of wet dog among all those humans.

She smiles when she picks up the trail on the upper floor and walks straight up to the bar.

Time to play. Show him who's the real shark in the water.

"Please."

Please. That word always passes their lips in the end. Blair doubts a sadistic, murderous prick like Fenrir ever used that word before.

She leans closer to the body hanging upside down from the ceiling, held by chains she put around his ankles. He tries to wriggle away from her—and fails miserably. Blair flashes him a grin. She can't deny that she delights in the fear that crept into his haughty face the moment he learned her name. She's drinking it in now.

Raw fear when she dropped her glamour and revealed what lay under the magical façade she'd put on. What really lurked behind the long, blonde hair and brown deer-eyes she'd taken on just for him—Fenrir's target group.

He let out a whimper when they arrived in his psycho-hut in the middle of nowhere—this was the cabin he used to kill all those girls in, for fuck's sake—and she eventually dropped the act, along with her glamour. Revealed her shocking amber eyes, long, deadly, silver canines, and matching, sharp, and utterly deadly, silver nails. Oh, yes, and her red, wavy mane, flowing down her body.

The Scarlet Death—that's what she is. That's what some call her. One of the most feared witches in the whole fae world. And beyond, it seems.

So feared that even Fenrir, the wolf shifter who was banned from the fae lands because he couldn't control his bloodlust, almost shit his pants.

This little piece of filth fled his execution, carving out a living in the human realms like so many others of his kind. A wolf without a pack is either a dead wolf or a crazy one. Since there is no alpha around to control creatures like him, he's turned out to be the latter.

Here, he's just another unleashed carnivore who preys on young women with no one around to stop him. Shit, without the angels guarding the worlds, all kinds of monsters have started to roam all too freely, too unchecked, and the humans are utterly helpless.

Well, until now. She would end him and Lyrian and his shady trade along with it.

Oh, she'd gladly wipe them all from the face of the Earth.

Maybe it isn't too bad to be a monster sometimes, as long as you are the biggest one in the aquarium.

"Where's Lyrian?" she asks, not for the first time.

"I don't know where he lives, witch."

Blair licks her lips in annoyance. Lyrian, the underworld god of the fae in the human world. A necessity for those shunned ones to hide their fae features, but a perverse one.

"I know you're one of his best deliverers," Blair drawls, studying her nails and the dried blood under them. "I know that keeping your existence hidden in the human realm requires a bunch of dirty, shady work to trade for harvested magic. The kind Lyrian sells. So tell me where you delivered all those people to. Must have been a lot over the years. I'm sure you have a secret meeting spot. Not easy to get rid of so many and harvest them. Even harder without anyone noticing. Must be somewhere secluded. So where?"

Fenrir only whimpers again. Blair rolls her eyes before she punches him straight in the face. Bones crush, followed by a nasal sob.

But the heat is getting to her, making her impatient. Not that patience has ever been her strong point. But it takes a lot not to lash out and go for Fenrir's throat straight away.

She needs to get to Lyrian—the elf she's been hunting and searching for more than a year now. He's barely more than a rumor. But all the scum she's tracked down and tortured so far have led her to Fenrir, and Fenrir would finally lead her to Lyrian. She is so close.

She can feel a tingling sensation in the tips of her fingers. The ache for bloodshed announcing itself… a prickling before she gets to the real deal.

Over the last year she's gleaned so much information on Lyrian—the worst kind… what he did to the ones he hunted and how he did it and so on—that her whole essence burns to end his life.

It's become personal for her.

After all, Lyrian is hunting her kind—all fae, witches included. Admittedly, the girl she is to retrieve for Perenilla—Melody—has become nothing but a side mission. But killing Lyrian… sometimes she dreams about that at night.

It hasn't been easy to get on Fenrir's tail. But once she found out where the wolf shifter's hunting grounds were, all she had to do was dress up in that flimsy thing and look blurry-eyed and drunk.

She let him buy her another drink. Let him guide her to his car. He didn't even look that bad. Nothing to suggest he was a creep who got off on raping girls before killing and eating them.

But even worse, he frequently wipes the memories of the police clean with more magic. He literally erases the girls from the memories of their families and friends, as if they never existed at all.

"Please," Fenrir breathes again, the sound more like a pup whining. Blood clogs his nostrils, making his breathing hard.

Blair wriggles her long nails in front of his eyes, tracing one along his cheek, leaving a gaping cut in its wake. "Did they say the same to you when you raped them?" Blair's voice is sweet and thick like honey, but she knows her eyes are not. Her eyes shine with unveiled hate and disgust. Utterly lethal.

Normally, she tortures her prisoners quickly to get the answers she needs about Lyrian and his whereabouts, but she's been taking her sweet time with this one. Carving him up slowly, bit by bit. She's let him hang here from these chains, head down so he has to swallow his blood while she works on him, over and over.

"Please, witch. Please, just kill me."

He is no longer begging for freedom. Just for death. She must be doing something right after all.

"Do you think you deserve it? The sweet oblivion?" She shakes her head to answer her question, running her tongue over her silver teeth before she leans close to his ear. "You know, if I had more time on my hands, I'd take you to one of the oracles and throw you into the cracks of time and space, broken and wounded as you are, so that you would feel like this forever. Luckily for you, I don't have the time, so I'll just drain you. Give you a taste of your own medicine. After all, that's what you do for Lyrian—trade live goods on the sly, right?"

When he looks at her, confused, she clarifies, "Collect fae so he can drain them."

"I told you—I don't know where Lyrian lives—" the shifter starts again, but she cuts him off with another punch to the face.

"Oh, drop it, fleabag, because it's getting ridiculous. I *know* every tiny dirty little bit you did, you piece of shit. And I know that you *know* where I can find Lyrian. There's nothing you can do to prevent me from getting my hands on him. Tell me and I promise that I will let you off the hook."

It is indeed ridiculous, but she's purposely let him draw this out. Partly because she delights in torturing him. But the real reason she's left the bastard hanging there the whole day, left him rotting in the unbearable heat of this tiny wooden cabin in the middle of the desert, is that she went to find a crystal flacon to store his magical essence in.

She *needs* his magic before she goes on, since what she'd stored in her bracelet is already used up, and she can hardly run around in her witch form. She could bind the shifter's magic to an object, but that would take up more time she doesn't have. Easier to decant it into a vessel.

That the bastard deserves every second of it, and far worse, sure makes it much more enjoyable.

But now she's got the flacon, she doesn't need to play with her food much longer.

"In case you were wondering what Lyrian does with all the people you bring him, there is your answer," Blair purrs while she runs her nails over the assortment of carefully selected knives, laid out before her on a table.

Better to bring across the truth, because there's a good chance this prick, like most fae, still has no idea how black magic works, despite the fact he collected fae for Lyrian. Judging from his stubbornness, this dimwit has no inkling what she's been working up to so far and how exactly this is going to end for him.

"This is exactly what I'm doing here—I'm harvesting your magic, just as Lyrian did. Draining or harvesting magic is a slow, excruciating procedure. You have to carefully drain the magic out of every fiber of a fae. It takes a long time and a lot of patience. It's all about carefully placed cuts and peeled-back layers, or the magic would just dissolve, you see. It's easily considered the peak of the dark arts of magic. Because magic, once freed, is a terribly fleeting thing. Prone to bind itself to the strongest fae around. You have to be quick to gather it up before it dissipates."

Blair smacks her lips as she picks up a crescent-shaped knife. "But you're lucky. Since I'm Gatilla's heir, I know very well how to harvest it."

It is satisfying to watch pure, undiluted fear enter the wolf shifter's eyes as the penny drops.

She laughs. "Uh, just as I figured—you, moron, had no clue, right? You probably thought I'd just play around a little bit and then finish you. But no, the best part is yet to come." She leans over him, the knife catching the light. "Just so you know, we're getting to my favorite part—your organs. I have to take them out while you're still alive."

"Wait, witch! Wait! I'll tell you where I think Lyrian is."

He tells her everything. Of course he does. And all the while, Blair watches him with a cruel smile plastered on her face.

When he's done, she asks, crooning, "Was that really so hard?"

He pants, sweat glistening on his forehead. "Will you let me go now?"

"Let you go? Oh, boy. Did I forget to mention? We're playing my game now."

"But you *promised* you would let me off the hook."

"Yeah, I did. And I will. I didn't specify when though, did I? And whether you would still be alive. I'm afraid I do indeed need your organs first. They won't work for my purposes once you're dead."

Blair makes a show of glancing up at the metal hook in the ceiling holding his chains. Then she puts the knife away.

Fenrir lets out a sigh of relief.

She turns back to him. "That was just for show. Do you know what I found to be the fastest way into a man's heart?"

She pouts her lips and reaches for a crowbar.

"Tearing a hole through his ribcage."

BLAIR

Blair once again camouflages her sharply pointed ears and silver canines with the magic she's taken from the wolf shifter. It's now contained in a tiny crystal flacon on a chain around her neck. It will last for a few more days before she will have to refill it with someone else's essence. There's no natural magic in the human world that fae can draw from, leaving them more or less vulnerable. The only side effect of the human world Blair doesn't like. Shifters, like Fenrir, are still able to change forms, but they are not able to wield or summon or the like. Only angels can take their inherent magic with them when they jump from world to world.

But Fenrir's essence will last until she finds Lyrian and ends him. And should she still need magic after that to stay a while longer for whatever reason, she can just harvest Lyrian himself.

Her pink Porsche Panamera flies over the rain-slicked street. She left the desert shortly after midnight, heading north, cabin door wide open. Let some desert scavengers feed on the body.

At some point in between, the rain kicked in, and instead of seizing, it only got worse the further up north she pushed. Now dusk is already approaching, although the monotonous storm gray of this area barely suggests it. It's as if, up here, there's no sun at all.

A strange place on Earth. Depressing. It reminds her of the Blacklands, the wastelands the witches call their kingdom. Fitting for Lyrian.

The whole drive, Blair's been pondering how best to proceed. There is no denying that Lyrian poses a threat, even to her, and that there will be some of his henchmen around she will have to deal with in order to get to him. Lyrian *is* dangerous and obviously in possession of so much magic he can hide from even *her* senses. It's been almost a year since Blair climbed out of the waters of the fae gap, and she has not felt a trace of him, not even a bristle of incongruous power, though one of her talents is just that—sensing accumulations of power in a range of hundreds of miles.

She's attracted to it, like a moth to a flame.

But Lyrian she didn't feel, which is strange, but she'll find out why. How he does it. One step after the other.

First thing, she's got to find his hidden domicile up here. The wolf shifter wasn't able to give her the precise location of Lyrian's house.

Lyrian, paranoid as ever.

Blair isn't worried, though. She doesn't think Lyrian, no matter how much magic he's gathered, will be able to truly harm her—not here in this world, where his elf powers are practically useless. Save for his reflexes and speed. He can't even wield a spell while she still has her witch's silver claws and teeth to fight with.

But what about that girl? Will Melody be with him? Or has he hidden her away somewhere else? No. If the wolf shifter could be trusted, Lyrian was using her special skill—to sniff out magic—to help him harvest. So Melody will be close to him.

Blair curses silently.

Melody. The half-blooded girl the new witch queen Perenilla wants so desperately because of just that—this special talent of hers. To use it to find some ancient elven relics. Objects the high elves stored their magic in long ago. They hid them away under the dark reign of Gatilla, so that if the witches came to slaughter them, their magic couldn't be harvested and added to the witch's reservoir under Gatilla's amethyst tower, Windscar. That morbid tower where Blair was raised and honed into a predator.

The memory of those dark times pushes up unwanted, and she

clenches the steering wheel, fighting it. It bubbles up nonetheless. How many nights did she stare at those polished, purple walls? How many times was she chained to the pillory outside on its landing platform and left there night after night until hunger and cold almost drove her mad? How many times was she flogged for talking back, for so much as batting an eye at an order from her cruel aunt, or kicked out naked into the snowstorm when she was still a child?

Too fucking many.

Sure, Perenilla isn't half as bad as Gatilla. But she is hell-bent on changing that. She even had the collapsed amethyst tower rebuilt further east of Akribea and called the new one—made of polished onyx—Cloudcleaver.

For now, Perenilla's bad enough. But with the relics adding to her current power… it doesn't take much to imagine what she will become. Let alone what Perenilla will do to the girl… will *make* her do in order to find them. And what it means that Blair will deliver her up. Ignoring the consequences…

Blair's hands tighten even harder around the steering wheel. So hard that the material starts to bend under her fingers like molten wax.

Delivering the girl up to Perenilla… it doesn't sit right with her for all the wrong sorts of reasons. She's never cared much about rules, but she cares about these humans.

She knows she's not supposed to. Knows she can't ignore an order coming from her queen. But sometimes Blair can't help but wonder what she would be like if she had been born a human. If she had grown up in the mortal world. She might have gone to school, taken her place in the world for granted. Maybe traveled the world or got a real job, as they called them. Had an apartment. A cat. A fucking TV. Eating ice cream out of the tub while binge-watching some stupid soap with her friends.

Oh hells, she would have *friends*.

She would be nice and laugh and joke. She definitely wouldn't rip a girl out of that to put her into a world that is cruel, ancient, and raw. Give her to creatures who will make her serve and suffer.

Better Perenilla has her than Caryan, she tells herself, not for the first time. It sounds hollow.

Blair forces herself to focus on the rain instead. On her mission. On her fucking breathing. She cranks up the music, and Eminem jumps to life in her car, cleaning out his closet and doing a damn fine job at it. Oh, how much she can relate to all the anger in his voice...

As darkness falls, she reaches an accumulation of houses and stops the car in front of the only bar in the deserted greenery. Alarmingly close to the fae gap, and she still isn't feeling a thing. *Weird.*

She gets out, her sneakers getting wet as she strolls toward the battered door with a blinking neon sign saying *Open.*

Blair hasn't bothered to change her outfit since that night in the club. Just patted the shifter's blood off. Sloppily, she realizes, as she looks down at herself and finds some dried stains still there.

It's not the blood that's a problem, but her dress.

Not changing into something else might have been a bad idea, because *everything* stops when she enters. She can hear it—their breathing, damn, even their heartbeats—stopping before picking up. All the men ogling her and the dress that clings to her curve-gifted figure. Her lush waves of wine-red hair. Her eyes gleaming in an unnatural, shocking amber.

She suppresses a grin and might even be swaying her hips, just a little. These mortals, devouring her with their eyes. She should be used to it by now, but *Abyss* save her, she isn't.

These humans, fawning over her beauty, are unable to sense the danger in her, the wrongness that should make them shrink back in horror. So they don't. They're solemnly haunted by the desire to see her again. Unable to see that she is a beautiful, fully grown, flesh-devouring monster. Her teeth so sharp she can open up their skins like a razor blade.

On a deeper level, she knows that fae beauty is different from mortal beauty. Elemental. Painful to look at, even with her glamour up.

And she *is* a looker, even among the fae, so can she blame them?

She slips into a booth at the far end. From here, she can overlook the bar, waiting until the humans recover and get back to whatever it is they were doing before. The table in front of her is filthy, covered by a patina of grease. Probably beer and frying fat judging by how sticky the laminated menu is. Not to mention the heavy, sour scent of old sweat that hangs in the air. Blair licks her teeth so as not to cringe.

Sometimes the acute sense of smell is a burden, especially in the human world. She envies those mortals who wear the cheapest, artificial crap on their skin and still are able to call it perfume, while it smells like some sort of detergent they use to wipe the floors with. Not to mention all those other smells they seem to be immune to.

A shy waitress pads closer and Blair orders three extra-large burgers with fries, the meat still bleeding, and some red wine, before she props her sneakers up on the bench opposite her, listlessly following some silly game where a lot of humans chase a ball over a field like dogs.

As she said, silly but adorable. In the way pets are adorable.

Her red wine arrives, and Blair tastes it, pulling a face. Watery and already off. She downs it anyway and orders another one.

The staring only intensifies when her burgers arrive. The whole bar turns to her, the stupid game forgotten, as if to see whether a woman like her is truly able to eat this much.

Blair grins at them while she takes a hearty bite. She wolfs down the three massive portions of food in record time, before she makes a show of licking the remnants of sauce and meat off her fingers.

Then she sighs theatrically. Abyss, she *loves* their food. Pizza and instant noodles and vanilla sauce straight out of the can.

She orders one more burger before she leans back on the hard, wooden bench, thinking of how best to find Lyrian because the bastard sure as fuck won't be running around here blurting about his whereabouts. He will be hiding like the creep he is.

At that moment, the door flies open, and a dark-haired girl strides in. Her face has the angular beauty of a mortal, but there's something else there aiding her attractiveness. A delicate face, dark eyes, and full, red lips. Her skin looks dewy, but at the same time lacks the absurdly picture-perfect, smooth skin of the fae. Her long, dark hair is lush but without the oppressive mass and shine of all fae that can be suffocating. And it vies with the moon white of her skin. She's taller than the average human, slim, athletic, dressed in all black. A leather jacket hangs on her shoulders, rustling with every movement. Black boots hug her ankles.

Blair sits up straight, her eyes following the girl through the bar. There's something off with her. With her demeanor, the fluid way she moves.

The girl doesn't so much as glance toward Blair as she slides onto one of the barstools at the counter, which is also odd. Blair's sitting right in the line of sight of anyone who enters, and she is definitely something to look at.

But the denizens of the bar sure as fuck ogle the girl as much as Blair. Because something about her *is* odd, Blair realizes.

It's something that sets even the humans' underdeveloped instincts off.

Blair squints and smells the air. The effect is not a magical glamour, or Blair would feel it on her. No, this girl possesses about as much magic as a stray cat, but the same grace when she moves. Like a fae. All instinct and fluidity.

It should be enough to light up Blair's own instincts. But it is only when the girl dips her head back and the light hits her face at a certain angle that Blair's hackles rise.

Fuck.

How could she have not seen what is so obvious? This is *the girl.*

Must be.

The half-blood. Melody.

The daughter of that haughty, murderous, silver-blooded elven princess Ciellara. The last silver elf who infiltrated Gatilla's court. Who Blair wished someone would impale on a stick, so she wouldn't have had to keep up with her yappery and arrogance all day long.

Sitting at the bar is her half-human daughter. Must be. They look so alike.

Blair stares at her, so focused that she barely notices the shy waitress shoving the fourth burger over to her, as if afraid her hand might make a good side to her dinner. If Blair wasn't so distracted, she would have congratulated the waitress on her appropriate intuition. Instead, she ignores her and keeps staring at the girl like a raptor who's spotted a mouse.

A strange-looking mouse.

This can't be a coincidence. Witches don't believe in chance. And the girl she's been searching for has just walked straight to her. But then, in the middle of nowhere where you can count the people living here on one hand, it might not be so odd after all.

Eventually, Blair grabs her burger and sinks her teeth into it, savoring every bite while she keeps watching the girl. Melody sits with her legs crossed, swirling her glass of the same cheap, warm, red wine.

Blair almost laughs when she tilts the glass, drinks, and scrunches up her face just as Blair had done, apparently coming to the same conclusion. The wine tastes like shit.

The girl orders some ice and throws two cubes in it before emptying the glass to the dregs and ordering another one.

Blair takes a sip of her wine, washing the slightly tangy, rancid taste of cheddar and old meat away while at the same time liking the idea that she's tasting the very same flavor on her lips as the girl.

Fuck. The girl she's been hunting for a year. Combing through every city from north to south. And now she's sitting right in front of her.

Melody glances at her phone before putting down money. She slides off the stool and walks straight toward Blair. Blair briefly thinks she will head straight for the bathroom through the door next to Blair's table.

But when she passes Blair, the girl's eyes meet hers—depthless, dark eyes—and she whispers, "Run. Lyrian's coming for you."

Then she's through the door and gone.

21

Those six little words clank through Blair. *What the hell? Lyrian, coming for me? Bullshit.*

Yet Blair jerks up, her senses straining. Her fae hearing picks up the sound of another door opening. She smells a waft of wet, moldy breeze that tells her there must be a second exit back there.

Fuck, fuck, fuck.

She slams a hundred-dollar note on the table and heads after the girl.

She opens the first door. Washrooms to her right. The girl's scent betrays her, and Blair stumbles through an inconspicuous door to her left, outside into the rain.

Right on time.

Blair catches Melody's wrist right before she can get into a black, sleek sedan. She wrenches the girl back, pushing her face-first against the wall of the bar. One hand slides around the girl's neck, the other over her lips.

Melody fights her, trying to throw elbows and land kicks, which Blair parries easily.

While she keeps the girl's slender body against the wall, Blair feels how delicate she is. How breakable. One wrong move and Blair could snap her bones.

It is not fair, the useless voice in her head whispers.

Blair tries hard to block it out. But she can't help but notice the smell of desperation that clings to the girl, going down to her very essence as Blair leans in, parrying another elbow blow that came pretty close to her temple.

Fuck, how old is this girl? Maybe twenty? Twenty-five maximum. Reared by a monster.

It's not my problem, she reminds herself, but that useless sympathy stirs in her anyway. Everything reminds Blair too much of her own fucked-up childhood.

Too bad Blair has been ordered to bring her to Perenilla, or she would have mercy. Would let this rare half-fae go.

The girl bites down hard into the palm of Blair's hand. Blair lets out a violent hiss, her sympathy vanishing into thin air.

Ouch. This half-human thing *bit* her.

"Don't fuck around or I'll kill you right here," Blair snarls, bringing her head close to Melody's neck, her bleeding hand sliding to the girl's right arm as she tries to slam her elbow back another time, pinning it to the wall.

What a little fighter.

The girl's voice comes breathless, desperate. "He's coming. He's coming for you. He knows you're here. You need to let me go!"

"Keep dreaming," is Blair's only response.

The girl manages to get a leg free and kicks hard against Blair's left knee. Blair bares her teeth against the searing pain.

Little bitch.

Melody must have damaged Blair's knee more than she thought because it gives way when she tries to step back, her fae healing not able to knit joints and fibers back together so quickly.

The girl takes advantage of it and twists in Blair's grip. Those wide, brown eyes stare directly into Blair's, the look in them haunting. It is what makes Blair hesitate for a second. Makes her *really* listen this time.

"Lyrian *is* coming. He sent me to find you. He's going to kill you. I'll lead them away, but you need to run! Now!"

The truth hits Blair in the face then. *Lyrian is coming. For me. He knows I'm here.*

The girl doesn't wait for her reaction but shoves her and makes for the sedan.

While Blair watches the girl flee her senses pick up a cloud of undiluted, dark energy pushing closer. Fast. *Something* that has managed to veil itself from her senses until it came that close.

Shit. She halts, watching the girl jerking the gear into place and reversing, as Blair's magic strains to identify what exactly is coming her way.

An army of renegade fae. Enough to kill her.

The girl wasn't lying.

Blair tests her knee again, and this time it holds. Without losing another precious second, she sprints off to her car while the black sedan shoots down the rain-wet street and is gone.

A few minutes later, Blair steers the Panamera in the opposite direction, the car flying toward the fae gap a few miles from here.

But that black wave—it's on her heels. Drawing closer by the second. Way too fast. Lyrian must have gathered an army of renegades around himself. Things have gone sideways here, but Blair won't think about that now.

Not when she spots a bunch of wolves running through the woods next to the road, way too fast and big to be natural wolves.

More shifters.

She pushes the gas pedal, and the Panamera roars, but those furred and fanged beasts keep up, undoubtedly fueled by Lyrian's magic.

Shit, I'm doomed.

One wolf jumps, landing on her car with a solid thump, denting the roof.

Long talons scratch the metal, trying to hold on, but failing as Blair yanks the steering wheel around, sending the car sliding.

A black mass of fur rolls off the hood, but another silvery one has already taken his place, running and jumping, its deadly claws missing Blair's window by a hairsbreadth.

Instead the wolf hits the back window and shatters it, sending shards raining over her as she jerks the steering wheel to the right.

Another one down. But at least a dozen more coming.

Blair floors the gas, the landscape and the wolves chasing her turning into a blur of green and brown. She can already smell the sea which connects the two worlds—the fae world and the human world—with each other. And the fae gap a bit off the coast. All she needs to do is get there.

The only problem is the elevated coastline.

No, that's not the *only* problem, she corrects herself. A heavy thud shakes the car. Another wolf has landed on the roof of the car, denting the metal before huge, sharp claws tear it open like a tin can.

If Blair could summon her magic, she'd send all those furry

mutants into the afterlife, but she can't because her magic doesn't work here.

The claws miss her head by an inch when she veers off the road again, bumping over open fields of grass now before sliding back onto the road. But the wolf's holding on, and more are jumping toward her, the one on the roof so close she can smell his rancid breath.

She throws one last glance at the pack that's trying to encircle her before she steers hard to the right and... off the cliff.

If they want to kill her—fine. But no fucking way will they get her magic.

The car is flying. She can only pray to gods she doesn't believe in that her body will survive the collision with the water. That these wolves can't swim.

She turns back in her seat to see the pack pausing at the cliff, fangs flashing. But not following. The one on the roof must have either jumped off at the last minute or is tumbling to his death.

Blair throws a last, melancholic glance at the smartphone next to her in the passenger seat. All the music stored on it will die along with her. Music she will now never be able to show to Aurora and Sofya.

Because she will never see Aurora or Sofya again. Will never be able to say goodbye.

It's her last thought before she mashes her eyes shut.

Then, her world shatters as the car collides with the surface of the ocean.

MELODY

My heart hammers in my chest like mad as I pelt down the rain-slicked road. I take another breath, trying to calm my nerves. My trembling fingers.

A woman.

In all these years, I've never hunted a woman.

A strikingly beautiful woman. Her burning amber eyes are still on my mind, matching her strange aura. That dense fog of grayish black, laced with streaks of emerald-green and purple.

Horror sluices through me at the memory of what Lyrian does to his victims—and what it makes me for delivering them up.

What the hell has she wrought to deserve Lyrian's wrath and hate? She looks barely older than me.

I let her go. As I let so many others go.

The only reason I sometimes tell Lyrian who and where my targets are is that they are bad too. Their auras are a solid black, almost like Lyrian's own. I figure the world will probably be a better place without them. They are murderers, or worse, I know.

Not that the end justifies the means.

Lyrian tortures them in a hall next to the woods. Far enough away from the mansion that I can't see it from there, but close enough that their screams and pleas keep me from sleep.

Why Lyrian does it? I asked once. All I got for an answer was to be thrown into the bunker for two nights.

The woman from the bar is dark yes, but not dark enough, by far, to kill her. Not nearly bad enough that I want her blood on my hands.

It is all I can do—spare the good souls.

Even if it costs me.

Lyrian makes me pay every single time I let someone escape. It gets worse each time. Last time I let someone escape, he had the bloodhounds—at least that's what I call Hunter and Kayne as a reference to their ugly faces, bald heads, and towering masses of flesh and muscle, and for their unrelenting ability to chase me down wherever I go—beat me up and leave me without food for three days straight.

In the distance, the first flicker of lightning splits the sky, followed by thunder that growls like an earthquake. Electricity runs along my skin like an undercurrent of power.

I shift the car down a gear, flooring the gas, accelerating as the familiar tingle of a panic attack bristles along my bones. It is the only thing I know, the only thing I've ever known: to conquer anxiety with madness.

I don't care whether I die. Never have.

Dying might be a hell of a lot better than what Lyrian would do to me. What Hunter and Kayne would do to me.

The moment my car cuts past their SUV, they make a full spin and come after me. They've been trailing me from a distance like they always do. Ready to sweep in to collect their target.

The only reason they don't go with me is that I once told Lyrian I can't track down my targets properly with them in my space. So they keep their distance now. It's the only resistance against Lyrian I've ever succeeded at.

The lie cost me, but I paid that price gladly. Two weeks trapped in total darkness. Continuous beatings. Lyrian waited for me to relent, waited for me to break. Eventually, the bastard gave up and ordered his henchmen to hang back a little when they followed me.

Of course, Lyrian didn't believe me for a second. He knows

why I want space. He knows I let people go. He knows I lie to him, again and again.

I clench my teeth hard to suppress my tears.

Yes, dying would definitely be better than facing what he will no doubt do to me.

I crank up the music, my lips moving quietly along with Margot Timmins' otherworldly voice, begging darkness to be her pillow, to take her hand and make her sleep. Then I open the windows, letting my dark, long hair stream unbound and rain pelt my face.

I go even faster, the car cutting through the landscape like the brushstroke of an angry painter.

Moments like this almost feel like flying. The only moments where I feel free, unbound, untethered.

I breathe in the cold air, heavy with sap and gravel and wet concrete. But it is the lighting that wakes something in me. Lashing the sky with the promise of deluge and decay.

I like storms, always have. They remind me that even the sky needs to scream sometimes. And not just me.

It's something other than this suffocating, inescapable solitude, expanding everywhere around me.

And I tried to escape it so many times I've lost count. But Lyrian and his brutal henchmen, Hunter and Kayne, always manage to track me down in the end, no matter how fast and far I've gone. Twice, I even made it so far as to dump the car in a stretch of forest, escaping on foot and checking into a hotel miles away two days later. They found me in the middle of the night and dragged me back to Lyrian in chains.

I fumble a cigarette out of the pack and manage to light it with one hand, taking a long drag of smoke.

Escape. For a while, I tried it constantly. Every job Lyrian sent me out on was another opportunity to run.

Lyrian, my *keeper.* I've never come up with another term for him. The strangely thin man with white-blond hair who took me in after my parents died. Not that I remember them.

Smoking is just another form of protest. It's not that I like it. It's just something that calms my nerves and pisses Lyrian off. That is all my so-called life has ever been about really—trying to escape and piss him off.

Hunts like these that Lyrian sends me out on are the only hints of freedom I have left. The only freedom I have ever known. Because I'm nothing but a prisoner.

It's my special *gift* as Lyrian calls it—my strange ability to track people down, no matter where they are hiding—that makes him keep me, I know. This *gift* he forces me to use to find people for him, for his dark purposes.

And I let her escape.

I fucked up again.

Lyrian is bad. So bad, in so many ways, that his aura is a solid, dark, black wall. Nothing I've ever seen before. Seeing auras is, well, another *talent* of mine. I learned early on that other people can't read the same energy fields, or see the aura's colors unraveling over a person's very being. Every sentiment wavering there, in the periphery of their bodies. Every thought and craving, ranging from innocent blue to the deepest, thickest gray.

Gods, my punishment will be bad.

Another panic attack stirs and threatens to rise. To consume me and leave me crushed.

I can't. Not now. Not here.

I fight it, trying to push it down and into the void inside me. *Later.* Later I can cry and cower somewhere, curl up on the floor of my room until my body rids itself of even the last remnant of adrenaline. *But not now.* I can't afford it. I need to get through this. I need to go on, or I know, deep down, that Lyrian will make my already hellish life even worse.

He is the kind of man who, if he ever learns about my attacks, will only make me suffer more. He hates nothing more than weakness. I've certainly learned that the hard way.

I clutch the steering wheel so hard that my knuckles turn white. I need to get out; I need to get away from him before I totally lose it. Sometimes it already feels like I have lost it—as if I'm standing on the threshold of a total collapse. The panic attacks so heavy and unrelenting that they go on for hours, crippling me in every sense.

I try to breathe against them. Against my right ribs while I recite my mantra.

You will have a life one day. A real life. Maybe a house on the beach, and sunshine, somewhere far away. A dog maybe. You'll find a way to escape.

I keep telling myself those things, over and over and over. It's the only thing I have left. The only thing I ever had—hope.

I ignore the car in the rearview mirror. The bloodhounds' stern, hungry faces. I try to think of anything that is not related to Lyrian... that is not what awaits me once I arrive back at his property.

David. I always think of David in my darkest hours, and my heart aches.

An ordinary name for an ordinary boy. Handsome and kind, his aura unusually bright. A farmer's son. Blond. Blue eyes.

I met him in the bookshop in that *town* where Lyrian let me go when I was still a teenager. David also liked to read. We became something like friends, if I ever had one. Then a little bit more.

A boy I one day found tortured and unconscious, handcuffed to the very same steel table and chair I'd been shackled to so many times.

That was years ago, but the picture of David there—unconscious, head lolling, eyes swollen, lips cracked, multiple ribs broken—has burned itself into my memory.

Lyrian didn't kill him that day, but the message was clear: never get close to anybody again.

Sometimes I lie awake at night and wonder what has become of him, of the brash but kind sixteen-year-old boy who would now be twenty-two, like me. I wonder whether he ever recovered from what Lyrian did to him. Wonder whether he still lives here or left town like everyone else halfway sane, to get a real life in a real city. Maybe he went to university to become the surgeon he dreamed of being. I wonder how he spends his evenings. Whether he has friends with whom he goes to bars and clubs and cafés. Not that I know anything about such a life.

I sometimes wonder whether he still thinks about me from time to time.

Probably not.

In those dark moments, I allow myself to imagine how I would have turned out if I'd been allowed to be *young* and relatively unburdened. Whether I would go to clubs and parties. Have friends of my own. Who would I be? What would I be like?

A dangerous thing to think.

I flick the cigarette out the window and watch the endless line of trees pass by.

One tiny jerk of the wheel and it would be over. I would not have to go back. I would not get beaten up by the bloodhounds and thrown into the dark cell for days in a row. It would just stop.

I would just stop.

I take another, steadying breath.

I've always believed dying for someone you love would be a beautiful way to leave. At least it would have a purpose then, my death. Now no one cares. Lyrian would lose a tool, but nothing more.

So I shove it down and steel myself.

It will pass, I tell myself. The punishment will be bad. *But it will pass eventually, and you will survive.*

I keep telling myself that over and over, ignoring how hollow it sounds to my ears as I pull up in front of the huge mansion. Nothing but night-shrouded nature and trees covered with moss and lichen around me. I cringe as the tires of the sedan behind me slither to a halt on the gravel and Kayne and Hunter get out of their car. Their faces are sinister, their lips slim lines, promising violence.

I don't even try to resist when they drag me out of my car. Don't try to kick or land an elbow strike when they grab me by the arms, pulling me, not toward the mansion, but toward the inconspicuous, gray concrete building a little off to the side of the impressive Victorian building.

"Enough fun for tonight. And that bitch is already dead, sweetheart," Hunter grunts into my ear.

Horror runs down my spine like icy water. "How do you know?" I snap at him.

He gives me a grin, drinking in my shock before he points to a tiny little device in his ear. I've never seen him wearing it before. "Radio frequency. You think we're the only ones on Lyrian's payroll? Ask yourself whether it was worth it, Melody—infuriating him like that. Because I'm telling you: it was for shit."

I hiss at the last part, snapping my teeth at him, ready to rip his throat out. I would, if I was any closer, I realize with a kind of shock.

Hunter stares at me, a little wide-eyed, before he growls, "Wicked little thing."

Then he hurls me inside the bare, windowless room. The door closes fast, leaving me in total darkness once again.

It's the same. The same I've survived a hundred times before.

I keep telling myself that as the walls close in on me, as they always do. When the trauma I've come to know so well over the years flares up again. The anger. The desperation. The fear. It all washes over me in a feverish deluge. So achingly familiar.

And still, its effect never ceases. It always leaves me strained and exhausted.

The bitch is already dead, sweetheart.

Those words play over and over in my head. So I hadn't been able to save her, but led them right to her. All had been for nothing.

Moonlight leaks in through the tiny window, falling on the ground. Sometimes the night sky is the only thing that lets me know I'm not yet dead.

That there is still beauty out in the world.

Even if my body and soul feel like falling apart and I can't piece them back together.

I lean my head against the wall, curling my knees to my chest, trying to calm my ragged, uneven breathing.

I jolt up as the halogen ceiling light flicks to life. A second later, the door opens, and Kayne swaggers in, grabbing me roughly and pulling me up, handcuffing me to the metal chair. Lyrian comes striding in after him, and I wonder whether I will ever get used to his strange look, his strange clothes, the inhuman coldness on his face.

Today, he's wearing a blue silken damask tunic that reaches almost down to his ankles, the sleeves and collar embroidered with golden ornaments, the color matching his pale blue eyes. Lyrian is exceptionally tall and lean with long, almost white hair that falls far beyond his shoulders. A heavy chain and various bulky, golden rings shimmer on every spindly finger.

He loves extravagance. It is obvious everywhere, from the house to the eccentric furniture to his bizarre clothes. I've never seen any other human walking around in attire like his. Oddly enough, though, no one else seems to pay much attention to his strange appearance.

He stares down at me as if I'm a cockroach that's just crawled out from under the fridge. I feel the urge to spit at him.

"Where is the woman?" His voice cuts the air like a knife.

She's still alive? I don't let my surprise or relief show on my face.

Instead, I jut my chin up stubbornly, looking first at the massive necklace of rough-cut azure he never takes off, before I meet those hard, cold eyes I learned to hate so early on.

"You never told me it was a woman," I reply as indifferently as I can.

"Does it matter?" he snaps. He's tenser than usual, the fog of his dark aura coming in slow ripples, like a heavy, sullen mass. As if you'd thrown a stone into hot tar.

"It matters to me," I retort. I try hard not to flinch when he grabs my chin and compresses my face with his eerily long, but surprisingly strong fingers. Bruising me. He has to be in some mood to show his temper so much. *Who was that woman?*

"Because she's one of your kind. A weak little female. Easier to kill than a bad male, huh?"

"It's not easy. Never. And you are the one killing them!" I seethe between clenched teeth.

"Keep telling yourself that. But we both know the truth. You're a little monster."

The words hit me, and for the first time, I wish I *could* be a monster. Powerful. Able to rip his face off with my claws.

I snap my teeth at him, remembering how it felt to sink them into the flesh of the red-haired woman, to taste her blood.

In that moment, I feel something inside me opening its eyes. Something unholy. As if there is indeed a monster prowling under my skin. Something that would be all talons and fangs, biting and clawing, was it to ever come out.

A creature of instinct and little else.

Lyrian curls his thin lips slightly—in surprise or disgust, I can't tell—but he lets go of me. "No one would have taken you in when your parents died. No one would have cared for such a rebellious, wild *thing*. You would have been living on the streets like the animal you are if I hadn't taken you on, fed you, taught you all you know. I was generous, was I not? I even bought you all the books you wanted and your canvases to paint your silly landscapes on. All I want from you is this tiny little exchange. And you? You lie to me, and I am tired of it."

His voice is so cold I feel a shiver going right through me. But at his words, something in me snaps. "You never let me have a life!"

"No life? I spoiled you!"

"You lock me away and worse! Don't pretend that mine was ever a normal childhood. I know how other children grow up."

The words spill out, but I'm too sick of it all to care. Too sick of Lyrian and his control. For a brief second, I think that he will make Kayne discipline me, but instead, he just lets out a long, loud laugh that reverberates within the close walls.

A cruel, mocking echo.

"Ah, yes, of course—you *know*. From your silly books." He scowls down at me before his lips tear into a slanted smile. "No, now I know—it was that little boy you were seeing—what was his name again? Something so ordinary to the ears it hurt."

I clench my teeth at the mention of David. At the lurid image in my head that flares up again at his name. Of his blood-crusted lips and swollen eyes.

As if Lyrian senses my thoughts, he probes on. "The boy you ruined your pretty, young skin for."

He bends down to me again, his sweet breath making my stomach turn. This time, I do flinch away when he stretches out his finger to trace the almost invisible scratches on my cheek left there by my nails. I manage to avoid his touch.

He lets me but keeps smiling coldly down at me, clearly remembering how I stood in that doorway and dug my nails so deep into my face they left bloody scratches from my forehead down my cheeks to my chin.

My only words were *If you kill him, I will kill myself. Do you understand?*

It had left scars, but if I wore makeup, no one could see them at all. Not that I care.

I did it to save David's life. I also did it in an attempt to shed my own skin. As if it could turn me into somebody else. A free, happy person.

But it hit Lyrian on a deeper level and showed me just how much he needed me. It changed our relationship, even if only slightly.

I try not to let my face show anything as I say coolly, "I never asked for any of this. If you don't want me, why don't you let me go?"

He pulls his hand back as if burned and straightens up abruptly, the fine fabric of his vest rustling at the movement. "Unredeemable and stupid—so typical of your *kind*. You do know what a contract is? You owe me, and I will not let you go until you've paid me back for my kindness." His expression is frighteningly neutral, but his tone is lethal.

Another wave of panic and nausea stirs in me.

Never show fear. Never cry in front of him.

I force myself to look him in the eye. In those surreal pale-blue eyes in his skull-like face, his skin like old paper.

"I told you what would happen if you disappointed me again, and yet you did. I told you I would consider giving you to Hunter and Kayne, let them make a woman out of you."

I ignore Kayne's greedy leer at this remark, ignore the sickness roiling in my bones at the sheer thought.

I remind myself that I know all of this too. The pain, the punishment, the threats.

I remain as calm as *they* trained me to stay—Kayne and Hunter, who trained me to undergo cross-examination and to fight because Lyrian told them to.

I say, "Then do it. I've listened to your threats over and over. You've threatened to hand me over to them since I was thirteen. Maybe it's time to make good on that promise."

He showed me—drummed into me—not to show fear. Lyrian himself taught me how to lie, even under extreme pressure. Taught me to never show any weakness.

His eyes narrow and he raises his hand. At that, Kayne steps forward and backhands me so hard my head snaps to the side. Coppery blood fills my mouth, dripping over my chin.

This is also routine. They have their ways of hitting me so they never break my bones or shatter my teeth—or at least, it's never happened so far.

I blink against the onslaught of pain. The dizziness. Then I lift my head toward Lyrian and spit blood onto his silken tunic. "You don't even have the guts to hit me yourself. Come on, do it. Just once. Or are you not man enough?" My voice comes out dead. I glower at him, dare him to do it.

He looks at me, and for a brief second, it appears as if he's truly considering it. But instead, he just smooths down his vest as if the stain isn't there. "You'll regret that," is all he says. "Now I'll leave you to your punishment as the pathetic creature you are."

I watch him leave. The door closes behind him, and only Kayne stays with me. For another bizarre second, I fear that this time, Lyrian will indeed make good on his threat. But Kayne just looks at me for a while before he unchains me.

Then he also leaves, closing the door behind him, leaving me in total darkness once more.

BLAIR

The iron-tipped whip digs deep into Blair's skin, tearing the wounds that already gape there even wider. The metal clashes with her magic as it hits her blood, blocking it. At least for a while. Blair grunts, clenching her teeth so hard she wonders why they don't turn into powder.

But no fucking way will she scream. No fucking way will she give Perenilla the satisfaction. This woman is so much like her aunt.

Blair looks up to meet Sofya's pained stare, then dips her chin to a silent nod. Daring her to swing the whip another time. *Do it. Get it over with. Or Perenilla will delight in your pain too.* But Sofya looks back at her blankly, her hand not moving. Her long, whitish-blonde hair dancing in the cold wind.

Blair turns her head to see Aurora, the breathtakingly beautiful, dark-haired witch, between the other witches. Her face is a mask of agony so deep Blair feels a dark flame in her jumping to life. The face she thought she'd never see again. She's never met her natural mother—she died giving birth to her—but Aurora has always taken her place. Aurora and Sofya, her two mothers. To see Aurora in so much pain—pain caused by Perenilla, who is forcing Sofya to whip her…

It makes Blair get back to her feet, a crazy grin plastered on her face. "Come on, do it! Do it for me!" she barks at Sofya, trying hard not to sway from the blood loss as she holds her mother's blue stare.

Don't give her the satisfaction.

Sofya scrunches up her perfect face before she brings the whip down one more time.

The crack reverberates from the high mountains around them like an avalanche.

And again.

And again.

Blair doesn't look once at Perenilla, who's following the whole scenario from the stone throne four witches have carried up from the throne room to the landing platform. The spiral tower, Cloudcleaver, made of polished onyx, reaches further up into the sky to her right, indeed scratching the clouds.

Taller than Gatilla's Windscar ever was.

The huge, newly built tower also has an even bigger reservoir in its base. Cavern-like halls, deeply embedded in the stone the tower was built on. The new reservoir is the biggest storage unit for magic the fae world has ever seen. Brutally harvested magic for the witches to draw from, amplifying their inherent power.

"You disappointed me, Blair Alaric, oh, heir of your great aunt Gatilla," Perenilla speaks up when it's over, her voice ringing over the soaring wind. Mockery drenches every word.

Blair glances over at her without turning her head. Somehow she managed to keep standing. Still manages to keep her head high and her shoulders back while she pushes back the nausea and the pain that threaten to overtake her. Only iron will and honed discipline keep her from wiping out.

Perenilla's even risen from her throne for her pretty little speech. The thin, raven-haired and ashen-skinned witch looks more like a noon wraith in her fringed robe than a queen though.

She looks small amidst the ring of the black coven that stands gathered around the throne—thirty-three of Perenilla's closest and most powerful witches. All of them pledged to her. The ones who govern the reservoir's magic, deciding who can draw from it and how much.

Blair's coven—the red coven—in their black riding leathers and crimson cloaks, form a semicircle on Blair's left side, Perenilla's sentinels in their long, black robes billowing in the wind on her right. The robes are a clear statement of their station. Those witches never get their hands dirty. That's what Blair's red coven and the other covens are here for.

That's what she's become: Blair Alaric, the Scarlet Death, the former great heir, wing leader of all covens, now barely more than Perenilla's personal cutthroat. The red coven, whose reputation for mercilessness and cruelty once sent enemies running, now degraded to being servants at Perenilla's beck and call. And all the witches, merely more than starved scavengers picking through the ashes, looking for bugs because there's no meat left to feed on.

At least Gatilla let them fly over the border to harvest once she started the war against Palisandre. Perenilla insists they limit their hunts to their dead lands, so as not to provoke any of their numerous enemies.

They can't afford to lose another member.

Blair meets the gaze of every robed witch.

Every one of them considers her a nuisance at best—a threat to Perenilla's throne, the root of all evil, at worst. Sometimes Blair wonders whether the sheer loyalty of Sofya and Aurora and the witches of the red coven has prevented her from having been backstabbed with a knife so far. Not that she's ever done anything to earn it.

No, quite the opposite.

She's such a fucking failure.

Perenilla's voice booms again over the platform, amplified by magic. "You were sent to the human world to bring the girl from the prophecy to me."

Melody. The girl Caryan so desperately wants. Perenilla doesn't have to say it, everyone here knows Kalleandara's prophecy by heart.

"Yet you dare to return empty-handed. I should let you rot in the oubliette."

Blair's strength falters, blackness wavering in her peripheral vision. For a second, her knees buckle. She digs her claws into the onyx beneath her, leaving deep scratches in the polished stone before she makes it back up to her feet. Cold sweat runs down in rivulets under her torn leathers, mingling with her blood that's soaked her shredded clothes. The pain is almost too much, but hells would she cower in front of Perenilla. She'd rather bite off her own hand.

"I had to flee. The human realms have been left unchecked for too long, and dark beings have been allowed to thrive. Lyrian has managed to gather an army which ambushed me when I almost caught the girl. I had no choice but to run."

"You could have fought." Perenilla's dark eyes glitter with obvious disgust and hate.

Go ahead, bitch, hate me. But I hate myself harder.

Blair holds her gaze before she grinds out, "They were too many of them."

"You could have fought nonetheless. Yet you chose to come running back like the coward you are, Blair Alaric. You chose to tuck tail instead of fighting for your kind. The ongoing war has become a threat to our existence. That girl could change the tides of that war. It is your responsibility alone to find the means to win it. Yet you failed me. You failed all of us."

Blair can't help it—that hollow laugh that escapes her throat. Yes, she failed. Yes, she fucked up in more ways than possible. No, she can't explain that this very girl saved her sorry life. But *this* statement is ridiculous. "Mine? Why in the Abyss's name would it be my responsibility alone?"

Perenilla's eyes only darken. "Aren't you the heir of your great-aunt? And haven't our ties with Palisandre been broken under her reign? That delicate truce severed before we witches had a chance to recover from our tremendous losses?"

"Those losses came because we killed the angels after we already lost so many witches to the Demon Wars!" Blair's temper snaps before she can leash it. "Palisandre suffered similar losses."

"Yet elven children are not as rare as witchlings," Perenilla snaps back, her silver canines bared. "It was your aunt's insatiable greed for power. Because she decided to enslave the last angel and started a war to harvest the magic of high elves with his aid. Because she couldn't get enough. It was her hubris that made this world fall apart. That tipped the balance of magic once and for all. That made all the portals to the hells burst open and wreaked havoc on this world. Plummeted us into misery."

Perenilla's voice is strained, her whole body shaking with anger, her whole being bristling with a challenge Blair more than aches to meet.

Abyss help her, she bares her teeth right back at the queen. "You can't blame this on me."

"Caryan is her dark creation, if I am not mistaken. She worked on him with magical ink and turned him into the blood-sucking demon he now is. She bestowed on him *the curse* and made him a living weapon. He is the reason we need to keep harvesting magic to prepare for another war. Palisandre never forgave us, and ever since, we've been paying the price. We have been banned from their lands. Our trading routes cut off. Our numbers have been depleted to this tiny circle. Another war could wipe us off the face of this world, once and for all."

Blair wants to bite out a sharp retort—but it gets stuck in her throat, along with a cracking in her heart. It's true. She did nothing to stop this when she could have back then.

Gatilla enslaved Caryan. She inflicted it on him—the *curse,* enabling him to suck up magic from any creature he drank from and adopt their magical gifts and talents. He managed to break free and turn against her. He absorbed all her magic and, merging it with his own, became immortal. The dark irony was—immortality was something Blair's aunt always tried to achieve. But she ended up dying before she could, felled by his hand.

Blair could have stopped her aunt before Gatilla could elevate herself to such an unfathomable station. Could have prevented that last, devastating war.

Or she could have killed Caryan once he was freed and still weak before the magic merged with his own.

But she did none of those things.

Because deep down, she feared her aunt and craved her praise.

Because she fell so hard for Caryan. Then she fell so hard.

Traitor. Traitor. Traitor, that ugly inner voice keeps hissing. She failed her mothers so unforgivably. Failed the witches. Failed her black coven. She could never atone, only try to protect them.

If they knew, Blair, they would abandon you. Curse the day you were born, the callous voice continues. The voice that keeps haunting every waking and dreaming minute.

Fucking useless voice.

But they must not know! No one, ever, Blair shoots back. Because the truth would harm Aurora and Sofya. And whether they love her or not, Blair will do everything to keep them safe. Anything. If she has to die for them, she will do so without a moment's hesitation.

So she's got to play along because silence makes you look weak. And weakness gets you killed.

"And that makes me complicit?" Blair asks in a voice she knows makes people want to throttle her. She juts up her chin, looking down her nose at Perenilla, just as her aunt had taught her to.

As an answer, Perenilla nods to Illistra, the current wing leader of the black coven and one of Perenilla's thirty-three. An ugly witch with short-trimmed hair. A woman in the body of an ogre and with the brain matter of a squirrel, but it's Illistra's physical strength that is unmatched among the witches. No one challenges Illistra in hand-to-hand combat.

The hag steps forward with a grin and rips the bloody whip out of Sofya's hand.

Then she shoves Sofya aside like a curtain. Sofya stumbles.

A vicious snarl escapes her mother's lips. "I'll claw your eyes out, Illistra," Sofya growls, her clawed hand curled.

But other witches hold her mother back before Sofya can launch herself at her.

"It is a pleasure to finally punish the rabble," Illistra drawls to Blair, her small, mean eyes glittering with ancient bloodlust.

There is no warning before the whip cracks through the air.

Blair raises her arm to block the most severe damage. The lash is merciless though. It cuts open Blair's arm and splits part of her right hip, the iron digging in so close to the bone that Blair grits her teeth to keep herself from screaming out.

Illistra's grin only widens as she swings the whip again.

This time, Blair reaches out and catches the tip midair. The delicate skin of her palm splits in half as the arrow-shaped end pierces it. Blair forces her fist to close around it, ignoring the pain as the iron tip bites deeper into her flesh.

"Don't you dare whip me, witch, or I'll peel your skin off and eat the strips," Blair barks, as she yanks the whip towards her with enough force to send Illistra stumbling.

"Oh, that I want to see, Blair," Illistra answers with a matching snarl and a brutal yank back. One that brings Blair closer, just as Blair estimated.

She doesn't hesitate. She charges. She moves around Illistra, wrapping the whip around her massive neck, once, twice, before Illistra can do so much as blink.

Blair, still holding the whip's end, places one booted foot in Illistra's back for more leverage. Then she pulls. The straps go tight.

Illistra coughs, her face turning into a ripe shade of red.

"Want to see what, Illistra? How I cut off your ugly head with some leather strip?" Blair hisses at her ear. Then she pulls even tighter. The leather of the leash starts to cut into Illistra's flesh.

Illistra reflexively drops her end of the whip and Blair grabs it. Now, with both ends in her hands, she pulls the straps *really* tight.

Illistra's face contorts in pain, a soundless howl escapes her throat before she falls to her knees, blood running down her neck in rivulets.

The crowd has fallen utterly silent. For a moment, even the howling wind seems to halt and watch.

Perenilla stands again, her face frozen by cold rage, but her grayish eyes glisten dangerously. "Enough. Let her go."

"Really? Just when things are getting interesting," Blair drawls, her voice dropping to pure ice.

At her feet, Illistra is slowly dying.

"You heard your queen," Perenilla warns.

"She's putting on quite a spectacular show, don't you agree?" Blair doesn't so much as cut a glance at the queen.

The crowd draws in a sharp breath, followed by a ripple of murmurs.

Perenilla's voice cuts them all off as it once again booms over them. "Are you disobeying my orders, Blair Alaric? I should have all witches of your coven punished for this."

Blair lifts her head. "I'm merely reminding you that it was *us*, your red riders, who helped fill the new reservoir after Caryan imbibed all of Gatilla's magic, along with the magic of the old reservoir, my queen."

"I warn you, Blair—" Perenilla starts again.

But Blair cuts her off, turning to look at all of them—at each pair of eyes—as she says, "It is *us* you sent out to harvest to refill *your* reservoir. To cement your power. Us who you sent to hunt down high elves. My red coven who lost witches to the high elves' swords."

Finally, she turns back to Perenilla. The queen has her arms outstretched, her fingers splayed, shaking with strain.

Another wave of murmurs washes over the crowd as dark, raw magic begins to twine through the air around her like a snake encircling its victim before it chokes it mercilessly.

Something as wicked and dark and warped as Blair's soul. But as it sizzles around her, Blair can't help but notice its anger. She's never heard of magic having emotions, but damn she can feel fury bristling right in its essence, lacing every wave, burning right down to its dark core. Something that has been broken too many times and never healed, only held together by rage. Something that feels all too familiar to herself. *Interesting.*

That doesn't mean it's not going to kill her.

It hisses and writhes around her. A raging beast that has finally been released from its cage. Eager to shred and tear and lash at everyone and everything in sight. Can she blame it? Is she any different?

Blair swallows once, holding perfectly still.

She is going to die. This wild, arcane magic is going to crush her to dust.

Wide-eyed witches of all covens stare back at her when she looks over them one last time. Witches who once flew under her command, who fought by her side, who ransacked whole villages at her order. Some of them glower at her or bare their silver canines, impatient to see Blair being finally ended. Some others though...

Their eyes are shining with pride. Hidden, but still there.

And *hope*. Beautiful, precious hope.

Blair's own eyes find Aurora's in the crowd. Her mother's warm eyes are wide with shock. The witch silently shakes her head, as if she can deny what will inevitably come next.

Blair's head snaps down to Illistra at her feet as the witch lets out a last, pain-laced breath. Blair leans over her. "I did this for my mothers, Illistra. You owe me your life now, because the wind itself knows I could let you die. You will protect them when I'm gone," she whispers so quietly only the ugly witch can hear.

Then she lets both ends of the whip slide out of her bleeding palms.

Illistra draws in precious air but Blair no longer watches her, turning her attention to Perenilla and her stolen magic all around her.

She is going to die.

She will face it like the warrior she is.

She meets Perenilla's eyes. "Shall we start? I think the crowd's tired of waiting."

But to Blair's surprise, Perenilla says, "Yield now, Blair Alaric. I will give you one last chance and bestow pardon on you if you kneel and apologize."

A pardon. Why?

Blair can't stand the naked plea in Aurora's eyes as she glances back at her. The plea to kneel. To grovel. To subjugate again. Can't stand to see her mother's desperation. Blair knows her death will devastate her mother.

She draws her gaze back to Perenilla once again, the magic

around her growing denser and denser by the minute. Slithering over her skin, licking up her fingers, twirling tighter around her, as if she's fallen into a pit full of tiny, deadly snakes.

Why don't you bite? she asks it.

Why don't you bite, Blair Alaric? You are a witch, after all, it seems to whisper right back.

Blair stares at the warping shadows. *Is that real?* No. You can't talk to magic. But then, dryads and nymphs do that all the time, don't they? When they ask the world for rain or a good harvest.

So she asks, *What do you want me to do?*

Silence greets her. She closes her eyes, and Abyss, just then, the magic whispers again. Over and over and over. *Take me. Claim me. Wield me.*

I can't. You're not mine.

I am no one's anymore. But we both want the same. Vengeance.

I'm not strong enough, Blair argues, but all the magic chants is, *Free me. Unleash me.*

I can't. I'm just a witch... Blair contradicts.

Just a witch... just a witch. The magic cuts her off with another chant, sung by a thousand different voices and none at all. Soundless. She knows only she can hear it. *Just a witch. Just a teeny-tiny witch.* Mocking.

If you don't have anything useful to say, fuck off, she shoots back, and with a last, grounding breath, opens her eyes again and draws them back to Perenilla. She knows what she has to do.

Her mind slides to a calm and cold place. Her voice is bright and clear as the first snow as she says, "I won't apologize for what we did for you. I made a mistake, and I hereby accept my punishment. But my aunt's actions are not my hereditary sin nor that of the red witches."

The crowd starts to scream, hissing and snarling and cheering, those primal sounds vying with each other.

"Well, then stare down the execution, Blair," Perenilla cuts through all of them.

Blair braces herself for the pain, for the magic to rip into her.

But a scream to her right sends her reeling. Sofya is on her knees, the tornado of dark magic swirling around her. Her mother's breathtaking face is torn in pure agony. "No. Stop this!"

"I said you need to yield and apologize or there will be an execution. You demanded the execution, Blair," Perenilla responds, her voice like ice.

"No! Please." Blair falls to her knees, but Sofya keeps screaming and screaming and screaming as the magic starts to slowly tear her apart.

"No! Stop it! Stop it!" Blair's screams cut through the turmoil, through that hateful, deadly tornado around her mother. She's no longer saying the words to anyone. She just *needs* this to stop.

She mashes her eyes shut like she did when her car collided with the water. "*Stop it! I do anything. Anything, but stop it!*"

Suddenly, Sofya's quiet. Utterly quiet. So are the rest of them.

No. I can't. Blair can't look and see Sofya's torn body. Can never look at Aurora's shattered heart.

She will kill Perenilla. She's going to kill her for this. She's going to stop all of it! A fiery determination smothers every other thought or instinct in her, filling her up.

But when she opens her eyes, Sofya is still in one piece. Her bright eyes are huge, but her face is bereft of pain. The magic has paused, swirling but softer, as if suspended in the air. Hovering. Waiting.

Blair glances at Aurora, who's wearing the same expression. Shock. Horror. Then at Perenilla, who has a strange look of frustration on her face. Her pale forehead is glistening with sweat, her whole body trembling as if she's *trying* to crush Sofya, but...the magic won't obey. *It is fighting her...*

"I hereby pardon you, Sofya Merrygold. In the name of what you witches did during the years of darkness, what you did for all of us, I pardon you," Perenilla says, lowering her arms eventually. The magic is gone in an instant. "Now, bring Blair Alaric to the dungeons. She might want to spend some time down there and think about what she's done and how terribly she failed."

Perenilla turns on her heels and strides away, not once looking back as the robed witches grab Blair. She's hauled to her feet, still stumbling from the blood loss, leaving a gory trail all the way past the reservoir, down and down into the very black heart of the tower.

MELODY

Two days. They leave me in the bunker for two solid days.

When the door finally opens, I blink into the gray daylight, willing myself to walk away with my head raised high, although my body is shaky with hunger and exhaustion. But most of all rage. Pure, deep, visceral hatred.

In the beginning, when I was still a child, I would cower in the corner and cry, beg, try to find a way out, try to somehow break that fucking door open.

I thought of my parents then. Of the idea of my mom and the image I barely remembered. Of how her arms must have felt around me.

I also thought I would go crazy.

Now I work out. Try to sleep, drifting in and out of nightmares until the panic ebbs away. Trying not to go crazy. But every time I feel more broken. More shattered.

I make it to my room upstairs in the main building without shedding a tear, my face so impassive I must look dead from the outside.

The mansion is vast, embedded alone in the middle of a forest and hills covered by nothing but more trees. The property alone is the size of a small national park. Lyrian bought the whole valley. My room is small compared to the others, and utterly barren, but at least it has a window from which I can see the forest.

As soon as I'm alone, I retch into the toilet. Not that I have much food in me. I meet my reflection in the mirror as I brush my teeth. My skin is ivory white, but not just because of my frequent sun-starved days or the relentless rain.

No. I have no color in this place—never have, never will—save for the regular bruises on my body.

It is only when I'm in the shower, under the stream of water, away from Lyrian's all-seeing eyes, that I allow myself to cry.

I crouch on the tiles for a long time before I get up and eventually turn off the water. I change into fresh clothes—black running gear—and head out the door. Rain hits me. There's barely a day when there is no fog or at least a slight drizzle.

I start to run—toward the hills, through the evergreen forest, through those strangely crooked oaks and willows, their branches covered by moss and their trunks so crooked they look like ancient creatures, bending to the relentless wind.

The shore is forty minutes from the mansion. I easily find the path that twines through the woods, would find it even with my eyes closed. I have run here since I was a child, following its lure until I stood at the very edge of the cliff, the ocean waltzing hundreds of yards below.

I stop now, my lungs burning from the sprint, my muscles protesting from exhaustion and lack of sleep. I step to the very edge like I always do, thinking not for the first time of spreading my arms and jumping.

It's my way out. If I can't bear it any longer, it is my way out. That's my deal with myself.

But not now.

Not like this.

Not without fighting.

Yet every time I stand here, the Abyss seems to call to me. Beckoning me to take one more step and jump. Sometimes I even dream about it, of the water calling my name.

I ignore it and turn away and, slowly this time, make my way back.

☽ ✴ ☾

It's almost dark when I reach the mansion. I go straight up to my room where a tray with bread and butter awaits me on the floor in front of my door.

I eat it out of sheer necessity. I need my strength. Need it to escape one day.

I wolf down a few bites before I step toward the window, to the empty canvas standing there, and start to paint.

Painting. Sometimes it is the only thing that allows me to hold on, that can give me joy. Makes me forget for a while about my miserable life. Of who I am. Where I am.

☽ ✴ ☾

Later in the evening, there's a knock at the door. Kayne walks in uninvited with a dress draped over his arm.

I glower at him, my lips curling back, baring my teeth. Sometimes I dream of ripping his throat out with those teeth. Strange, lurid dreams, I know, but maybe my past has indeed made me an animal. Half wild, just like Lyrian says.

As if he can sense something in me, the colossus takes one step back before he declares, "There's a function. Lyrian wants you to accompany him."

"Does he now?"

"Don't play games, Melody. You know it will only get worse." When I say nothing, he adds, "And you should wash that paint off. You know how he hates that."

He leaves the dress on my bed, though not without another indiscreet swipe over me that makes me clutch the brush in my hand tighter, wondering how it might possibly pierce his skull. Everything is a weapon. Wasn't it Kayne who taught me exactly that?

One day… one day I will wipe the soil from Lyrian and his bloodhounds. It is that thought, that anger, that fuels me. That prevents me from falling to my knees and weeping for what Lyrian has just done to me again.

But the truth is, I've been feeling on the verge for a while now. Closer to breaking than I've ever felt. I'm just so tired.

When Kayne's gone, I look at the dress. An expensive little thing. Nothing less when I have to appear next to Lyrian, who loves luxury over everything else.

A function. Along with my tracking activities, the functions Lyrian likes to attend are possibilities for me to escape for good. Not that I ever succeed. But I need to try. I need to get away. I can't stay any longer. I need to seize every opportunity I can get, be it ever so tiny. I can't just give up and accept my fate.

I swallow down my tears, along with my hopelessness.

When I'm sure Kayne has gone for good, I grab the dress and walk to the bathroom to undress. You never know with Kayne. But he was right in one regard: When I look in the mirror, there's paint everywhere, in my dark hair and all over my skin. I step under the shower one more time and scrub it off, trying to get it out of my hair, but there's still some left in the strands when I get out.

Oh hell, Lyrian will be furious.

I spend a long time getting ready. It takes a good deal of time to cover up the nasty violet-and-bluish spot Kayne's hand left on my face. Not to mention the bruises from the handcuffs. But then I've had a lot of practice over the years. Eventually, I put on the black dress. It's a skintight, half-translucent thing, showing off every inch of my tall, slim body, leaving no room for imagination. I clench my teeth. I hate it. I feel naked.

A dark part of me wonders why Lyrian sent such a thing for me to put on in the first place. Probably because he knows how uncomfortable it will make me feel. Another punishment.

Then again, he does love to brag, even about me, as if I, too, am a trophy. He delights when people want what he has. Apart from that, he is so vain everything around him has to look perfect. So I'll play along, if only to buy myself another chance to run away.

BLAIR

Blair stands in her cell, the ripped fabric of the silver dress she's still wearing stiff with dried blood. She no longer feels the ice biting her bare skin. A human would long since have died from the cold. A human like that girl…

Blair's mind keeps wandering back to her. *Melody.*

She saved her. Not that Blair deserved that act of mercy.

Why? Why did she do it?

Witches know no mercy. Mercy is a coward's trait. Compassion, another deficiency. It's something that haunts Blair—why the very girl she has hunted for a year, chose to spare her. Because she's a human with a soft, human heart?

Blair knows it was a sacrifice. Because a man like Lyrian won't let a kindness like that go unpunished.

And now… Caryan has found her.

Last night, Aurora snuck down here. A stolen moment to tell Blair that Sofya was alright, to bring Blair some medicine and the rumors that Caryan had caught the girl. A seer told them so.

Melody. Ciellara's daughter. The daughter of the woman who almost killed Caryan that fatal night at Gatilla's tower.

Her daughter, born to continue her mother's legacy and finish the task her mother didn't accomplish. To kill Caryan.

Melody, the girl from Kalleandara's prophecy. *The girl who will end the blight.*

Blair didn't expect the task of finding the girl would bring the past rushing back in a deluge. The time in her aunt's tower. A time of so much darkness, only lightened by the moments she and Caryan tangled in the sheets in some languid nightly hours.

And now this girl is in Caryan's cruel hands...

A fact that could change this world all over.

Blair's officially failed. The witches. Her people.

She leans her scarred back against the wall, her teeth chattering so hard her face aches. But a dark part of her heart aches even worse. A part she doesn't want to examine too closely. A silly, useless stir of emotion. Definitely nothing she wants to acknowledge. But it bubbles up unasked, again and again like a burning itch until she can no longer ignore it.

It is pain, she realizes. Pain about the knowledge that she's not only failed her people—she's also failed that girl. A girl, as desperate and lonely as Blair has been.

Blair turns and looks out through the tiny crack in the wall that serves as a window. Outside, a storm is howling, and rain patters down as if the sky itself is weeping.

Blair doesn't know what would have been worse for Melody—if Caryan or Perenilla got hold of her. What would be worse for this world?

She huddles against the wall and pulls her legs up close to her body before she closes her eyes. She normally likes storms, but tonight she can't help but feel that it's full of ghosts.

Raging.

Howling.

Just as that magic, locked away even deeper below than she. In an even darker place, where no light is ever going to reach it.

BLAIR, TWO YEARS BEFORE GATILLA'S DEATH

Blair's long, wine-red hair had come loose from her braid during the long and draining flight back on their phantom wyverns—half-solid beasts, looking like real ones, summoned by magic, untouched by the cold or rain or wind as they cut through the night, close to the fae moon, violet up in the witches' territories. Blair's face was raw from the biting, wintery cold, and she could no longer feel her fingers in her leather gloves when they finally started their descent back to Akribea, the capital of the Blacklands. Its infamous landmark Windscar, the amethyst tower, punctured the impenetrable fog like a spear.

Blair rode at the front; Aurora, her second, to her left; Sofya, her third, on her right. The rest of the thirty witches of Blair's chosen coven, the red coven, fell into formation, where they'd flown loosely before. They always fell back into their roles when they neared the tower, because her Aunt Gatilla could be watching. Or someone else might report any slight lack of discipline.

If her aunt ever caught wind of such acts of frivolity, she'd make short work of them all.

Bloodlust. Cruelty. Brutality.

The three principles the witches lived by. Her aunt's three favorite words, not Blair's, and she knew her aunt would rip her tongue out with her silver nails if Blair ever said that out loud.

Blair stifled a yawn, then schooled her face into its usual mask of arrogance and superiority. She held on tight to the scales of her wyvern as it plummeted down from the sky on her silent command. Blair didn't know how it worked, the unspoken connection between her and her summoned, magical creation. It wasn't like she controlled the creature. It certainly acted on a will of its own, although the rational part in her told her that this couldn't be real.

It was magic, nothing else. No matter how much she wished her wyvern to be real. Hoped those half-leathery wings would become solid. When Blair leaned in, though, it *wasn't* just her wishful thinking... she could feel the beast's heat seep into her body, smell her scaled hide, and the blood she consumed daily.

Yes, her wyvern *ate*. Magic shouldn't need to feed on anything but its creator. But all the wyverns did.

Also, Blair knew in her core that her wyvern was a female. How she would look if she were solid. Rainbow-colored scales and wings where sunlight would shine through. Her head adorned with beautiful, spiraled horns.

As always, her stomach shot right into her throat as the world started to tilt. Her wyvern spread her leathery wings wide at last, riding the wind currents before she banked and landed smoothly on the tower's platform, which was coated by a treacherous layer of ice. Conditions like these had cost two witches their lives in the last century.

Blair's knees almost gave out from exhaustion and cold, from three weeks of relentless, arctic torrents, as she slipped from her wyvern's back. She dismissed the beast with a negligent wave of her numb hand, fingers almost too stiff to move. Gods, she was drained. Days full of snow and bloodshed, nights full of slowly eviscerating the bodies they collected and storing the harvested magic in vessels before collapsing on bedrolls on cold stone ground, their tents tucked into caves they found in the deadly ravines.

But it was where they were safe. Where no one could reach them.

It was this ability that separated the witches' magic from all other high fae—the talent to summon a hell beast and ride it. It was what made them so utterly dangerous.

Blair heard the other witches touching base behind her, probably as chilled to the bone and tired as she.

Patience was frail these days, and tempers were high because the strain of their missions barely outweighed the amount of harvested magic. Or food.

Their rotations consisted of three weeks in a row. Her coven had three days off for Blair to inform her aunt about their movements, feed the harvested magic into the reservoir, and recover before they'd be sent back out. It was Blair's inherent talent that made her commander of all the aerial units, her talent to feel accumulations and density of magic. The witches went wherever Blair's instinct guided them.

This time, she and her coven had been assigned to harvest the last villages at the border to Avandal, where some hard-assed fae carved out their miserable existence, feeding on crops and the occasional mountain goat or snow hare.

Easy prey, those scrawny, thin creatures, the little magic in their veins barely worth the effort.

There wasn't much left in the Blacklands, barely enough for the witches to still their hunger and fill their bellies with blood. These cycles of hunting had become longer over the years Blair had been flying for her aunt, the villages and targets becoming more and more distant. And dangerous.

Blair tried not to think about the witch they lost to an avalanche. Ysadora. A witch around Blair's age—a little more than a hundred years old. She'd been hit by a mass of snow and plummeted into the chasm.

Her death meant a punishment for Blair. Maybe for her whole coven, but not if Blair could prevent it. It had been her mistake, choosing to fly the sharp and narrow formation of rocks because a snowstorm had broken loose and she deemed them safer tucked between the ancient, cruel stone than flying higher over the peaks.

Whipping. Probably. Maybe they'd been banned from flying for a week.

Normally, Blair couldn't wait to leave the claustrophobic halls of the amethyst tower Windscar, from where her aunt, Queen Gatilla, ruled the kingdom of the witches.

More than two days indoors had already made her restless. On edge. Made her itching to get back out there. Riding the wind, reddening the steel of her sword, and getting a belly full of hot blood—those were the things a witch lived for.

Ambushing Palisandrean villages close to the border was the real deal. Ransacking those rundown settlements—left mostly unprotected because Palisandre would not spare its precious soldiers to guard some lesser fae farmers and a few scattered cattle wranglers—was the highlight of the year.

Those raids were the only fun the witches had—picking some of those men and using them for their needs before sinking their teeth into their throats. Fucking and looting before leaving nothing but death and destruction behind.

It was what Blair had lived for.

Yeah, normally she couldn't wait to leave again.

But things changed.

Now she found herself secretly hoping for a ban. Anything that would let her stay here a little longer. She told herself that the reason for her change of heart had nothing to do with the black-winged angel Caryan. Knowing it was a lie. Her heart made a treacherous jump only thinking his name.

She lifted her head and took a few deep, steadying breaths to calm herself for the encounter with her aunt as she crossed the frost-swept platform, untying her snow-encrusted braid and running her nails through her hair in an attempt to detangle it.

It was an honor to serve her aunt, she reminded herself, not for the first time. An honor to be commander of all the riders, of all aerial units. An honor to lead the red coven—the deadliest one. Blair was their head, their wing leader. She would one day become queen.

But as she crossed the platform towards the heavy stone doors with the spiral staircase leading deep down into the cold belly of the Fortress, all she felt was exhaustion and cold in every fiber of her being.

And a thrumming need, more of an ache, that started to build underneath her skin. An ache that was constantly there, setting her on edge if she was away for too long and intensifying to the verge of consuming pain the instant she got back and felt Caryan's presence. She knew that amount of desire was unhealthy, so strong it was soul-eating.

But she couldn't help it. Just as she couldn't help the fact that these missions had started to feel like some kind of punishment for something she hadn't yet committed.

That all of her just wanted to stay a little while longer this time.

The insides of her palms started to turn sweaty at the prospect of seeing the angel again. Abyss, she was nervous like a fucking youngling. But she longed for him. Had longed for him every single day she'd been away. Burned for him with every part of her body. She hadn't changed her clothes in order to keep his smell on her for as long as possible. She hid it under a wall of magic, though, so none of the other witches would pick it up on her.

If her aunt ever found out, she'd be the blood and meat that fed her wyvern. After she'd been tortured for a week straight.

Hells, she'd be doomed. Not even her mothers could know that she and Caryan were sleeping with each other. Not when he was her aunt's slave. Her aunt's lover. Her dark creation.

Her weapon.

Treacherous heat pooled in her core as she picked up the faintest whiff of his elusive scent in the corridor. Along with jittery excitement thrumming along her bones, making her dizzy. They'd been fucking for five years now and still, she felt nervous every time.

Never ever had it been like that with a man. Had she been like that. And deep down, she knew she shared some form of connection with him beyond the physical.

It was so wrong, though. So dangerous. But how could something so wrong feel so right?

She had known she loved him since the moment she set eyes on him.

She had seen angels before they had been hunted down. She

had heard stories about them. About their beauty, outstanding even among the fae. About their power. Their wrath.

But Caryan was no normal angel, if there even was such a thing.

No. She knew in her bones that he was different even from them. And it wasn't just his mesmerizing, ever-changing eyes. No, everything on him was a pure force of nature. Made of undiluted, otherworldly, dark power that sang to her very soul.

The moment she saw him she'd felt the tendrils of fate twirling around her, closing tight.

She'd reached the huge, double-winged door to her aunt's council chamber.

"Do you want me to come with you?" Her mother's voice sounded behind her, startling her. Not Aurora, but Sofya. Always blonde, beautiful Sofya, who was reckless and brave.

Blair turned and met the deep-blue eyes of the white-haired witch, her hair the color of moonlight on a lake. "Go have some mead in the hall. I'll do this alone."

"You know you don't always have to lay your head on the block, Blair. Not alone. Let me be with you."

"What happened to Ysadora was my fault and mine alone. I'm your wingleader."

"I'm your mother."

"You are my third, flying under my command. Leave. It's an order." Blair's tone had changed, turned cold and distant.

Every other witch knew better than to jut her chin up, but Sofya had never been that way. Her eyes shimmered with determination. "I will stay with you."

Blair's hand shot out so fast, her silver claws digging into Sofya's neck, drawing blood that even Sofya seemed surprised about it.

Blair pulled her nearer so that her silver teeth got close to Sofya's tender skin. "Do not question my orders, ever, Sofya."

She pushed her mother back and turned on her heel, striding through the double-winged iron door without looking back.

Blair stared at the violet wall opposite her with her hands clasped behind her back. Gods, how many hours of her not-so-mortal life had she been staring at those walls? At the suffocating, monotonous, violet stone, hewn and forged and polished by the enslaved dwarves her aunt kept deep, deep below the tower in the mines.

Too many.

Today, it took a solid hour until the door to her aunt's chambers opened. Seven of her aunt's closest witches poured in, their heads hidden under heavy hoods, their robes' hems gliding over the shining floor. None of them so much as acknowledged Blair's presence as they sat down at the long, black table. It was an honor for a witch to be recognized by one of the seven, and Blair hadn't earned that honor yet.

Not in almost a century of serving.

Nor with her cruelty or the name she'd gained from it—the Scarlet Death.

It took another half an hour before the door on the other side of the room, leading to her aunt's private chambers, opened and her Aunt Gatilla came striding out, followed by Caryan. He walked close enough to her to make it clear he belonged to her, as her aunt demanded.

His short, black hair was messy, his remarkable eyes black, save for his irises. They were a bright red, tinted by her aunt's blood, Blair knew. The rest of his too-perfect face was void of emotion.

Blair sometimes wondered how he could bear it. How he found the strength to go on. Bow to her aunt. Fight for her. Serve her in more ways than Blair wanted to think about.

She pushed the thought away and kept her face impassive while Caryan took her in.

No feathery wings—he rarely had them out. Just black battle gear clinging to his strong, tall body, accentuating every rip and pane of sculpted muscle. But the sheer feeling of his gaze on her was more than enough to make Blair's knees turn weak. Make her heartbeat pick up a notch. The slight incline of Caryan's chin told her he had heard. He knew.

A warning flashed in his eyes before he looked away.

Blair straightened when her aunt finally took her seat at the head of the table. Blair had always believed her aunt was the less good-looking version of herself. Gatilla was beautiful, by human standards, with the same symmetrical face, alabaster skin, and luxurious, dark-red cascade of silky hair, but Blair was outstanding. Outshining her aunt in beauty.

Yet, the longer she took in her aunt, the more she started to think differently. Her aunt possessed features and a demeanor that made her not beautiful, but alluring.

That made everyone fall silent when she spoke. Made everyone pause and look at her when she entered a room. She had that kind of presence. Of dominance.

And Blair couldn't help but feel suddenly ordinary.

It didn't help that her aunt's scent still clung to Caryan like an assault. She knew exactly why her aunt had taken so long and why his black hair was disheveled.

It took everything in Blair not to scrunch up her nose, not to snarl and bare her teeth at her aunt.

It was ridiculous. It wasn't as if Caryan had a choice. She had never been jealous in her life. Not once. Not even a hint.

But now the full wave hit her like an avalanche. Like that avalanche that had made Ysadora plummet from the sky like an angel with shredded wings.

"Blair," her aunt eventually addressed her, her features limned with disdain as if Blair was a stain on her embroidered damask tunic.

Blair made the fatal mistake of looking at Caryan again. Foolish. Her treacherous heart skipped another beat before she caught herself.

"My queen. Caryan," she answered along with a bow.

Caryan. What in the hells? The angel lifted his chin the same moment she realized her mistake. Icy claws raked down her spine and her heart started to thunder with real panic.

"My commander. You will address me as my commander, witch," Caryan corrected, his tone like a lash of lightning.

Even the seven lifted their heads to look at the angel, vulpine smiles on their faces, their eyes hungry.

So they did respect the angel enough to acknowledge him. *Fabulous.*

Blair made herself hold his stare, longer than was wise for anyone. But she'd messed up. She needed to clean up her mistake. There was no backing out of this now. They had to keep up appearances.

She lifted her chin and sneered. "You are not my commander, angel."

Her aunt flitted her blazing eyes to Blair's, and Blair knew it was a test.

She added, baring her teeth, letting her eyes shine with outright disgust. "We witches bow to no one except our queen, angel."

"On your knees, witch," Caryan purred, a smile soft as silk on his lips.

"Make me," Blair growled back, but in truth, she was holding her breath. No one ever outrightly challenged the angel and walked away from it.

A moment later, black magic filled the room, her own rising in answer.

"Enough of these antics. You will address him as your commander from now on, Blair." Her aunt's sharp voice cut through the room, her command leashing Caryan's power until it collapsed.

Commander. This was something new, yet Blair knew better than to question her aunt's decisions. She had barely survived this mistake.

She schooled her face once again into a mask of indifference as Gatilla waved an impatient, heavy-ringed hand, and ordered, "Report."

Caryan's eyes betrayed nothing as Gatilla's silver nails slashed over Blair's cheeks when she'd finished, leaving deep, violent cuts all the way down to her collarbones, even cutting through her riding leathers.

"A witch. You lost a witch. A blood price must be paid. Every witch of the red coven is going to receive ten lashes."

"It was my mistake, my queen—and mine alone," Blair said, keeping her voice carefully neutral.

"Is that so? How noble," her aunt mocked, her poison-green eyes flaring.

Blair would pay. She would do anything to spare Sofya, Aurora, and the others. "I chose to fly through the gap. I will take the punishment."

Her aunt sat down and leaned back in her chair, her long, still-bloody claws clicking on the table. "Negligence breeds indolence. And indolence breeds madness," her aunt recited. Words that defined her aunt's whole, bloody reign. Words Blair had grown up with.

Blair dipped her chin in a nod. "I understand, my queen. Please let me atone for my deeds."

"Very well. Thirty lashes then," her aunt ordered, her cruel eyes taking in the cuts in Blair's flesh with a dark kind of satisfaction.

Thirty, not the average twenty. Blair knew then that this was more a retribution for her previous insolence—for addressing Caryan the way she had—than mere punishment.

Her aunt turned to Caryan. "Go, get the pale elf. He will administer the punishment."

She got up and strode back to Blair. Blair didn't flinch as she lifted her hand again and patted Blair's unharmed cheek.

"After all, pain must be delivered by a measured, loving hand to truly take effect. Mine would be the wrong one."

Her aunt smiled as the door swung open, and Caryan returned with Riven, the pale elf of Palisandre, following on his heels. As always, the similarity to Caryan struck Blair. They could be brothers, twins even, if it wasn't for the deep despair etched into Riven's beautiful face and the bottomless sorrow in his remarkably lilac eyes. An elven prince Gatilla had enslaved and in whose suffering she seemed to take special delight. Such soulless, dead eyes.

"Well, elven prince," Blair's aunt crooned. "Take my niece up to the platform and flog her. And when you and she are done, you will bring her back down. We have matters to discuss concerning the war."

Blair's outright confusion must have shown on her face, but she no longer cared to hide it. Caryan's dark eyes told her nothing, and her aunt didn't even bother to look at her again. She blurted, "What war?"

"The war against Palisandre. Caryan will be your general, Blair. You will do as he says. Take a night to rest. You will gather your coven. Tomorrow night, we are going to paint their cities red."

BLAIR

For a moment, Blair is still back there. For a sweet moment, she is still that girl, so eager and proud to do her aunt's bidding. To be Caryan's secret lover, his secretly chosen one. The one he favored over her aunt.

For some precious, dreamlike seconds, her body feels whole again. Filled with pride and purpose before she blinks to her senses, remembering where she is. *No, leave me dreaming!* Sleep is the only time she comes close to feeling alright these days.

The months after her aunt's death, after she and Caryan parted, she barely left her bed. She took potions to keep her mind in sweet oblivion. Reality had felt like being underwater. Not dead, but unable to breathe, flooded by despair and agony. Only when Aurora and Sofya came to force her out of bed every morning did she go, and even those waking hours were a blur. Only fractions of them are left. Scrapes and bits, all a mere collection of shards, like herself.

In those waking hours, she played along. She played her role. *You only have to make it through the day so you can crawl back into your bed,* she told herself. Her credo. Her deal with herself. *Only one more day. One step at a time.*

She made it. She doesn't know how, but she made it. Basic instincts kicked back in and slowly, so slowly, her bloodlust returned. She was a husk, but a hungry one. And an angry one. So one day, the fire found a home in her, the pain, the darkness.

She returned from the Abyss, snapping and biting and hissing at everyone and everything in her way.

It was only in the human world that she felt she could start anew. Be something other than this shell. Something more.

And now she's back here, more doomed than ever.

She gets up when she hears steps coming down. Perenilla stands on the other side of the bars, her two bodyguards—mercenaries, more male wolf shifters, who've lost their pack—in tow. The same kind that had hunted her down in the human world. The witches killed so many of their alphas, the remaining wolves are now ganging up, selling their services to *anyone*—even to the witches—with all rules out the window, turning into ruthless, savage creatures with few morals and even less qualms.

"Blair, I must say you look..."

"Beautiful? I know. Can we move on now?" Blair drawls, bored, pretending to examine her nails.

"I was actually going to say a little pale," Perenilla answers sourly.

"Oh, that. It's probably just my skin that's hanging from my bones in scraps. Nothing good makeup can't fix, don't worry," Blair hisses, looking fully at the queen, the iron bars like a magic-blocking wall between them. "But to have my queen come down here in person—I should be flattered."

Perenilla might have pardoned Sofya, but there's been no news about Blair. Not that Blair expects the queen to let her live after her performance up there. Not that she knows why she spared Sofya either.

She's pondered it during her nice stay down here. Either Perenilla needs Sofya as leverage or it would have just looked bad to kill her after what Blair dared to say. Perenilla is more of a politician than a witch, after all, having been raised at a court in Palisandre. But that was long before Blair's aunt started another war. Before she became the tyrant she was. And a thing like that—a witch living anywhere outside the Blacklands—became an unthinkable thing.

Perenilla says, "You're actually funny, Blair. Or rather, your incapacity for diplomacy is."

Blair bats her lashes at her. "Is it this charming trait of mine that has kept you from having me executed so far, Perenilla?"

"That's *my queen* to you, Blair."

"Does it matter?"

As an answer, one of the shifters draws back his lips to reveal cruel teeth, flashing them at Blair in warning. He is currently caught in some state between fae and wolf, with predatory teeth and claws on his fingers instead of nails. Not to mention the sheer amount of hair on his arms, or rather, *fur*—definitely more *dog* than human.

Blair scrunches up her nose before she flashes her teeth right back at him. "Oh, really? Don't fucking bark if you can't fucking bite, fleabag."

"Careful, witch. You smell too delicious. We might just take a bite out of you."

"Yeah. Come in here and see how that goes."

"Seems the witch is a bit needy," the other one drawls with a leer, his gaze snagging on her breasts. "Too much time alone down here."

Blair's brows twitch up before she rakes her gaze over him, letting her disgust reflect on her face. "Keep dreaming. Ever taken a look in the mirror? Well, you should. They don't lie, but you're lucky they don't laugh either."

Both of them blink in obvious confusion, and Blair throws her head back and laughs. "You don't get it. Too complicated? Too many syllables for you?"

Another growl rumbles up their throats and gone is the leer from seconds before. "Watch it, witch, or—" the seconds one warns.

"Enough!" Perenilla cuts both of them a sharp look and they fall silent.

"Now who's a good boy?" Blair purrs.

Perenilla's gaze flits to her. Her nostrils flare, the only indicator of her anger. "That goes for you too."

Blair just shrugs, going back to scrutinizing her nails. "It's not my fault. Stupidity always makes me break out in sarcasm." She glances back up at Perenilla, sucking on a canine. "Sorry, but they could really use a shave. And a bath. I wonder how you can stand that reek of wet dog. They have some nice pet shampoos over there in the human world."

She grins at the way Perenilla pales before a flush creeps up the queen's throat, working its way up to her cheeks. That's the disadvantage of growing up in Palisandre. All those staunch rules and etiquette.

Blair steps closer to the bars, making a show of sniffing the air, her fingers curling around the metal. "Or maybe… that smell turns you on. So animalistic. All I wonder is—do they do you doggy-style or missionary? And are they in their hum—"

"Shut it, witch-whore," the other mongrel growls, while his companion's shifting further into his wolf form. Ribs crack as he transforms into a large wolf, growling at her.

Blair just grins at him. *Good luck with those iron bars.*

Perenilla smooths down the fabric of her robe, hectic spots of redness still covering her cheeks. But she recovers enough to ask, "Is this really what you want to talk about, Blair, before I leave you to your miserable fate?"

Blair taps her lips with a long claw while she peers up at the ceiling. Then her gaze snaps back to the queen. "No, there's indeed another thing that bothers me."

"Then speak."

She hesitates before she leans in, as if sharing a secret. Perenilla, after a moment, leans in too, as Blair whispers through the bars, "Are wolf tongues as rough as I imagine them to be?"

Perenilla jolts back, glowering at her. "Believe it or not, I want a better future, Blair—for all of us."

"Do I get bonus points if I pretend that I care?"

"Aren't you weary of living in a wasteland day in, day out?"

When Blair doesn't answer, Perenilla lets out a long sigh. "You do care, Blair. I know you do. I want to change things. I want to turn them to the better."

Blair just lets out a hollow laugh. "If this was true, you would have changed things long ago. Changed this whole wasteland of a kingdom into a lush land of abundance as it once was. Instead, you milk the last essence out of everything magical just to gain more power."

Just like her aunt.

But then her aunt would have had her butchered straight away for her insolence. Obedience had been everything. If you broke the rules, you'd signed your death wish. Gatilla's justice had been swift and merciless. But Perenilla...

Blair tries to ignore the strange memory flaring up of what exactly happened on that platform. She's been churning it over and over in her mind. That black tornado of magic... What it said to her. Perenilla's stunned face.

Had she spared Sofya or...? Or had the magic... refused to obey her?

No. It can't be. Magic has no will of its own. But then, it also doesn't talk to people.

Maybe it hadn't, and Blair just went a little bit crazy from the blood loss.

She scrutinizes Perenilla's face as the witch retorts, "I could indeed return those lands to their former splendor, but spending magic on that now seems rather unwise. It is interesting, though, to note how little the war and its outcome seems to affect you, Blair, when you seemed heartbroken as I almost killed the beautiful Sofya."

Every bit of remaining warmth in Blair's face dies. "I would have butchered you like a lamb if you killed her."

"Would you have? Interesting. To me, it seemed you could barely keep yourself on your feet. Almost like when your aunt died. I wonder, was it really the loss of your *beloved* aunt that shook you so badly, or was it that maybe—" Perenilla makes a show of scrutinizing her own, long silver claws now before she drawls "— that the angel disposed of you like a used, dirty rag?"

Blair feels a wave of ice coat her veins. She makes herself snarl, "Nonsense!"

"Nonsense, huh? You know, when I decided to keep you after

your aunt died, I was surprised to see you serving me so well. How obedient you are. And I must say useful. Until now, it seems. Such a disappointment. You could have just brought me the girl, and nothing need have changed, Blair. There would have been no need to bring up the past."

"As I said—I didn't expect Lyrian's army," Blair bites out.

"Maybe you truly didn't. But you know that the girl is of utmost importance in this war. You also know that Caryan has been searching for her like mad, which makes me wonder... perhaps you purposely left her to him, thinking you might win back his favor and save your own hide?"

"Bullshit!"

"Resorting to such crude language won't save you from the truth, Blair. Not this time, not with me. Because I know what you are, Blair Alaric." Perenilla's voice has fallen dangerously low. "You are a traitor, after all."

The queen steps up to her, bringing her gaunt face as close to Blair as if she wants to kiss her through the bars. "Awww, so taciturn for once? Did you really think I didn't know your dark little secret, Blair? You were there the night Caryan killed your aunt. You were there, in that very room, with your aunt bleeding out, and yet... yet you didn't do anything as they butchered her. No, you ran like a coward! Now tell me what all your witches will do to Aurora and Sofya if they learn of that? Those two women who practically raised you. Tell me, what will they make of that? Once they learn what a big traitor and failure you are?"

Blair blinks a few times against the truth, against the lump in her throat and the sting of panic clutching her heart. *How the hell does Perenilla know that?* Everyone is dead except for Caryan, Kyrith, and Riven.

Perenilla's thin lips tear into a cruel grin as Blair reads the answer from them. Ciellara. Sure. The elven bitch ratted her out before she kicked the bucket.

Perenilla's washed-out eyes follow Blair's train of thought before she says, "Yes, the last silver elf. Did you think she didn't talk when I sought her out in the human world, Blair? You thought the king of Evander did you a favor when he cut her in half, and let her die with her secret. But she told me, Blair, before Regus found her. What a burden it must have been to keep this from your mothers all those years. You and the feared angel, what a story. Not even your aunt knew, did she? I wonder, did it give you a feeling of triumph over your aunt when you screwed him, Blair? Did it make you feel special? You must have been tired, being cold in her shadow day in and day out."

Blair stays silent, too shocked to even breathe. Her words seem far away, as far away as the rest of her body.

"Huh…" Now it's Perenilla who taps her lips a few times with her forefinger. "You know what truly interests *me*, Blair?" Blair does nothing as Perenilla runs her long, sharp nail over Blair's cheek, leaving blood in its wake before the witch sucks it off. "How did it feel when he eventually killed her so you could advance up the line? Was it a dark sort of triumph? And did you tell him to do it, too fine to make your own hands dirty?"

"You know that's not how it was!" Blair bleats.

Now it's Perenilla who throws her head back and laughs as if she's heard a truly funny joke. "Oh, yes, I know, Blair. Because I know you. And you just don't have it in you. I waited for years for you to stand up against me. To challenge me for the throne and claim your heritage, but you never have. You've stayed calm and quiet, performing your little, childish rebellions to anger me, but you've never, ever truly thought of acting against me. It is heartwarming, in some way, and touching to see how utterly wrong your aunt was for thinking she could groom you into her successor. I know you really loved him, Blair. And I know you couldn't stop him because deep down, you hoped you'd rule together one day and have little angel-witches running around your feet. How bitter to learn that he used you and moved on, not even caring enough about you to kill you."

Blair can't breathe. She just can't gulp down air. Magic alone keeps her heart beating, keeps her alive and standing, when it feels as if the ground beneath her feet has opened up, as if, again, she's tumbling back down and down into the hole she clawed her way out of.

"If you know, why haven't you killed me?" Somehow, she manages to form the words. To utter them.

Perenilla looks at her with a smile that is half pitying, half evil as if she couldn't quite decide what to feel.

Because, somehow, Blair has become pathetic enough to be pitied instead of executed.

"As Gatilla's direct heir, you still pose a threat to me, even if you never act on it. If I had smothered you unprovoked, it would have raised tempers. So I watched you and waited, but you… you were so broken and full of self-loathing. I realized that all I had to do was lean back and watch a while longer, that Gatilla's big heir and hope of the witches would do it all by herself—deconstruct herself, bit by bit. Because the truth about you is that you're nothing but a dreamer, Blair. A dreamer and a failure. But the others don't know that. To them, it will look like betrayal. Like you committed treason. They will want to see your head roll."

Blair doesn't know how she keeps standing. Why her body just doesn't let out. All she wants to do is curl up on the ground and drink so many potions she will never see daylight again. Secretly, she's been waiting for an ambush all these years. There are enough witches who remember Gatilla with Blair at her side and still bear a grudge. Women who would gladly push Blair off a cliff, make it look like an accident. She's always wondered why Perenilla never killed her openly, squashing Gatilla's heir in front of their eyes. Now the truth is finally out.

The queen's face smoothens into a mask of contempt as she watches everything settle in Blair like dust after a storm. "Yes. There's nothing more effective and shattering than seeing that the beacon you so fiercely believed in is nothing but a hollow dream. I just wonder what they will do to the women who raised you. Whether they'll blame them. Whether their heads will roll too. What do you think?"

It is that searing hot spear of panic that pulls Blair back. That tethers her to the ground and back into her body. That makes the black, devouring hole under her feet close, flushing out her anger instead. *Aurora and Sofya.*

"What do you want?" Her voice comes out raspy, as if she hasn't spoken in weeks.

Perenilla just gives her the hint of a smile. "You know what I want, Blair. I want that girl. I don't care what you do, but bring her to me and I shall forget about your failure. About your cowardice. I shall let you and your *mothers* Sofya and Aurora live. A promise, given by me, here and now. Ambush him once he sets out with the girl to find the relics."

Blair sucks in a sharp breath. The promise of a fae is an unbreakable thing. They can't lie. There's no way they can break a promise they've made without dying a cruel death. Yet an ambush… three witches against Caryan. Impossible.

She says, "This will never work. At least give me the red coven for an attack."

Perenilla shakes her head. "No, Blair. I won't spare any other witch for this. I can't. There is a war coming, and there are only a few of us left anyway. This is down to you."

"What do you expect me to do? Throw myself at him alone? You might as well kill me here."

"Use the ties you had. Maybe he has not forgotten."

"You can't tell me you expect me to just waltz up to him."

"I do, Blair."

"And then what? Seduce him? Beg him? You don't know him like I do."

"I do not care what you do. But I do expect you to do *everything* in your power to get me this girl. Because you want to save your mothers, after all. And now, this conversation is over."

Blair nods slowly. She has no choice. She either brings the girl or dies trying, because there is no alternative.

"I know you have a sense of reason, Blair. Do not disappoint me again."

MELODY

A helicopter waits for us. Always the helicopter for the rare occasions Lyrian leaves the property at all. He hates driving. It is a one-and-a-half-hour flight over nothing but vast, endless forest to another big mansion that lies alone in a valley, frighteningly similar to Lyrian's own. Most of the events he attends are in similar secluded spaces. I figure it is everyone's wish at those parties to be as private and exclusive as possible. Why, I have no idea, but the events sure *are* strange.

I've never found out what it is exactly that Lyrian does for a living and what has made him so insanely rich, made him hide away from the world, but my work as a type of bounty hunter must have something to do with it. Nothing came up when I once sneaked into Hunter's office and ran his name through an internet search. Same goes for the property of his—it showed up nowhere. I wonder whether Lyrian has another identity, or whether people like him simply don't exist in the normal world.

I wonder whether I exist at all, like on paper. Whether I have a birth certificate.

Probably not.

I look back into the room, a replica of a Victorian ballroom. It's filled with blackness radiating from auras so thick it is suffocating to just move through them. The sort of blackness I hunt.

So many evil, loathsome people. Not all of them, though. Some bring along their wives, but their light auras are so tiny, swallowed by the omnipresent black that feels like wading through a bog. Not for the first time I ask myself how they can stand it—living among such horrible people? Sharing a life with them. A bed.

I shudder and down a glass of champagne, leaning against one of the marble columns. When I was a child, I hid under the banquet tables, eating the fallen leftovers. Those parties were always an opportunity to taste something other than bread. Or I would sneak off into one of the rooms of those mansions, hiding under beds, praying Lyrian wouldn't notice my absence and that someone else would take me in. I imagined nice, loving parents who'd hug me and let me sleep in their bed, until Kayne and Hunter dragged me away, hissing and scratching and kicking.

Now I just get drunk, or at least pretend to, because the bloodhounds are watching.

No one ever speaks to me, though. No one ever pays me much attention apart from occasional, leering looks down my body and at my face. I imagine the sole reason I'm here at all is that Lyrian doesn't want to leave me alone at the mansion but doesn't want to spare Kayne and Hunter either. He's fucking paranoid.

I take another flute of champagne from a tray carried by a waiter with white gloves. I sip it listlessly, the champagne more medicine than anything else, to dull the void in me while I watch Lyrian gliding effortlessly through the crowd, smiling and laughing and offering handshakes. So different from how he usually is. So different from the ice-cold monster that hides underneath his slick façade.

I startle when I feel a gaze on me, like something licking down my spine.

When I turn, I find a man looking directly at me from across the room. Involuntarily, I stiffen. My instincts register something my eyes need more time to comprehend.

He is tall, slender, not in a suit like everyone else here, but in black trousers and boots and a shirt that yawns wide open, made of a fabric in a shade of midnight blue that seems to melt into his ivory skin. His hair is dark, with an almost bluish tinge, his face shockingly symmetrical and utterly handsome—edgy, with high, gaunt cheeks and a sensual mouth.

But it's not the mocking symmetry that's tugging at the painter in me, nor all the jewelry on him, glistening cabochons set in gold that catch the light in a stunning range of colors from deep indigo to azure—but his ears. His ears are delicately arched and on top of them sit golden caps in the form of wings.

Elven ears.

My heartbeat quickens as if I've just spotted a predator.

An elf. Like in one of my books. Unreal. There are no elves in the real world.

I must be going crazy.

I quickly look away, but I can still feel him watching me, still looking exactly the same when I glance back at him a moment later. I scan the crowd, but no one else seems to notice him or to give him so much as a second glance.

What the fuck?

I've probably had too much to drink. I feel the sudden need to hide, the need for fresh air. I briskly walk out of the room, too startled to look back.

Only outside, on the terrace, when my eyes search through the huge windows for Lyrian somewhere inside in the crowd, does my heartbeat return to normal.

I've had too much to drink, eaten, and slept too little. My eyes were playing a trick on me.

But when I finally make out Lyrian in the crowd, I notice something entirely else. Something I've never witnessed before: Lyrian's strange, cold eyes are on the man, too, and for the first time in all these years, there's... fear in them.

Before I can dwell too long on whatever reason the man's presence seems to affect Lyrian, I turn and start to run toward the edge of the terrace.

At the balustrade, I stop and drop my glass. It shatters on the marble tiles. I carefully choose a large, sharp shard—a cheap stand-in for a knife, in case Kayne and Hunter come after me, but better than nothing.

Oh, I would fight back this time.

Not wasting another second, I slip out of these ridiculous high heels and jump off the veranda, my bare feet touching soft, mossy grass, cold and soggy from the never-ending rain. Then I sprint off as fast as I can. I'm a good runner. Very tall, slim, and athletic from all the long runs I've taken since I turned six, desperately pushing, trying to understand the edges and boundaries of Lyrian's property.

Keeping to the shadows of large hedges, I bolt over the meadows, closer to the seam of a forest that borders it. The ground under my feet shifts suddenly when I dive into the protection of its canopies. It changes, turns hard and solid and treacherous.

Soon my bare soles hurt, stones and thorns digging into my flesh. My lungs ache as if they are on fire. Low branches slap me in the face, leaving scratches on my cheeks and arms, but I barely feel them.

All I can think of is my escape, the tiny window of freedom that's just opened up. It occurs to me that I have no idea of the terrain. No idea of the property's layout. I have only the memory of an outline in my head, the land I saw from above from the helicopter. We were heading south. There was a street somewhere.

Still, I have no clue where the hell I am.

But that doesn't matter. I can make it. I feel it, for the first time in my life—that I will escape for good.

I push deeper and deeper, probe further and further into the thicket of the trees and bushes. I lose my last sense of orientation when darkness enshrouds me so thoroughly I can barely make out my surroundings. It sends me stumbling more often than I'd like.

Just the faintest sound of occasional cars somewhere far in the distance above the rustling of leaves gives me any sense of my location. The road I saw from the helicopter. I must stay away from the road!

I veer sharply to the right. More stones bite into my bare flesh like nails, but I ignore them. Eventually, the sound of the street grows quieter, and soon all I can hear is my blood rushing in my ears. My own heartbeat, thudding and feverish. The sound of my feet on the ground. My vision is blurred from sweat and rain and exhaustion.

I don't know how long I've been running when I finally sink down to my knees, desperately gasping for air, every inch of me strained, every muscle protesting. The strip of fabric that is my dress is soaked through, clinging to my skin like a layer of ice. Tears well in my eyes so unexpectedly I'm not sure I know where they come from. Whether it is just the rain.

I close my eyes, trying to calm down, trying to calm my ragged breathing and push back the exhaustion a little while longer. I've made it this far. I need to go further.

I brush back a sweaty strand of hair, then get up. Only to stop dead in my tracks.

Right before me stands the man from the ballroom. His gaze holds the same, gloomy shine as he looks at me with a cold, calculating expression.

What the hell?

He can't have run like me. No. There is no trace of exhaustion on his body. Not a drop of sweat. Not a strand of hair out of place. Yet I got far away from the mansion—or have I been running in circles?

For a second, desperation clutches my throat so tight I can't breathe.

No! No way. I haven't. Can't have. He isn't real.

Again, my sleep-deprived mind is making up strange things.

He is not real.

But then I hear his voice, as real as it can be, melodious and deep as he asks, "Are you trying to run from me?" His words cut through the surreal, sudden silence, as if the forest, too, has stopped for a couple of seconds to listen.

I stare at him, at the eyes that shine through the fallen darkness like frozen violets. Surreal, stunning eyes. For a moment, I don't understand his question. Then the meaning hits me—the latent threat in them—and I instinctively take a step backward.

I jut my chin upward and ask, sounding as unafraid as I can, "Why would I?"

He tilts his head slightly, almost curious at my tone. Clearly not used to it. "I wonder—from whom are you running then, if not from me?"

What a weird question. What a fucking weird conversation.

But I'm arrested by his gaze, drained beyond the point of a breakdown. That's probably why I answer automatically, "From Lyrian."

He seems to consider this. Then he glances down to my bare, savaged feet. I seize the moment and sprint off to the right. I will outrun him. I will never turn back. To no one. Real or not real. I run until my lungs hurt more than ever.

A hand grabs my wrist and I'm brutally wrenched backward, caught in a sprint. I scream when my arm twists, and I'm hurled to the ground.

How? I didn't hear any steps behind me.

Before I can think, I've clasped the shard of glass in my palm tighter. Driven by sheer instinct, I lash out, putting all the fluidity and speed I can muster into the movement. The shard catches the moonlight before it slashes into finely woven fabric and skin.

There's only air, where a split second ago there was this man and his shirt.

Impossible.

I stare, breathing hard.

When I swivel around, I find him standing right behind me.

Unmoved. Untouched. His lips curled in faint amusement.

I must have gone mad. Fighting my own demons made flesh. Beautiful demons, I have to give him that.

"Let me go or I'll hurt you. I don't want to. All I want is to get away from here," I say, hating how my voice trembles, betraying me.

He angles his head as if weighing my words. "I'm afraid I can't."

Not hesitating, I lash out again, aiming for his neck this time.

Lyrian taught me that when you fight, you have to be ready to kill, or it makes no sense to fight at all. If you are not prepared to kill, you are predestined to die.

There's another blur of movement, white skin flickering in the darkness, and the shard once again cuts nothing but air.

Then it all happens too fast for me to react, and I'm standing with that very shard held to my neck, so close I can feel the cool glass pressing down on my delicate skin.

How he's done it, I have no idea.

But he's standing so close now I can see his eyes in the gloom, can feel his breath brushing my lips. They are indeed still bright, as if they are radiating from within in a simmering, dark purple.

It is beautiful and terrifying at the same time. I almost forget about the shard at my neck. That I'm pinned against a tree.

"Don't do that ever again." His voice pulls me back. It is laced with an inhuman calmness that slithers along my bones. Then he lowers the shard and throws it somewhere behind us, deep into the forest.

"Why—why is Lyrian afraid of you?" It is all I can muster. I'm still numb. Dazed from the exhaustion, from the surreality of it.

"He has every reason to be," is all I get in return.

Yet there's the weight of truth in his words. A threat. A hint at brutality. Only then do I notice his aura. It is dark, but not too dark. The same midnight blue as his shirt, laced with black and purple tendrils like the aura of the wine-haired woman in the bar.

My eyes come to rest again on his pointed ears. On the rubies and emeralds that dangle from long, obelisk-shaped gems in his lobes. At the golden wing-shaped cuff that covers the peak of those ears.

I say quietly in a way that sounds almost like a plea, "You don't need me. I mean nothing to Lyrian."

"You are wrong. You mean everything to him—you are his life."

I follow him wordlessly through the darkness. I should ask where he is taking me, but I just can't muster the courage. Instead, I watch his movements, so graceful and quiet through the forest that he looks almost feline. Inhuman. Like his ears.

I shiver in my flimsy dress, the air cold and biting, but I barely register it. I feel too numb.

I was about to escape. I would have made it.

I ask again, "Why is Lyrian afraid of you? Really?" The question churns over and over in my head.

"Not *of* me." A clearer answer this time, and yet he's still told me nothing.

I push on. "I saw it in his eyes, the fear when he spotted you."

To my shock, he lets out a quiet chuckle—a rolling, sultry sound. "I just stand for someone Lyrian is very afraid of."

"Who?"

"Someone on whose behalf I am looking for you."

My stomach tightens. Every instinct screams at me to run again, but it would get me nowhere. He is much faster, much stronger than I'll ever be, I just found that out.

"Are you real?"

That earns me a sidelong glance with raised eyebrows. Then another chuckle, deeper this time, as if he finds the whole thing funny. "Do I not look real to you?"

"You have elven ears."

Now he snarls, curling his lips back, exposing two *fangs*. He doesn't seem to notice what he's doing, but I keep my gaze trained on those long, sharp teeth.

"That means I am not real?"

"In my world, yes."

"This is not *your world*," he replies, matter-of-factly.

I ignore his remark. "Why was no one else looking at you? At that party?"

He stops so abruptly I almost bump into him. He turns to me, scanning my face—for what, I don't know—but my heartbeat quickens involuntarily. His eyes start to gleam as if he can hear it. He probably can.

"Lyrian never told you, then. And probably never showed you *his* true self either."

"Told me what? Showed me what?"

"About us. About the fae gap," he says calmly, unfazed by my sharp tone.

"The fae gap?"

"Have you never wondered why he lives here, in this—" he makes a sweeping gesture with his hand, disgust limning in his features "—remarkably remote area with its particularly enticing climate? Why he chose this nowhere land to carve out his miserable existence?" I'm surprised by his bitter tone as he goes on. "Why all those creatures you hunted down were here, never more than three hundred miles away from his house?"

Creatures. Not men. Not people. Lyrian used the same term to refer to me.

And he knows. Knows I hunt them. What else does he know?

"What is this fae gap and where is it?"

He snarls again, but not angrily, or at least not at me. Then he looks down at me as if he has just realized something about me, because his face softens. "It is the only portal left to our world, to the fae world. Everyone who wants to cross to the human world or back must do it here."

"And at the party... why didn't—"

"Why did no one seem to notice my pointed ears?" he finishes my question. As an answer, he taps his earrings. "Magic. A spell. It camouflages my appearance to the eyes of those who are not meant to see them, glamours them. And to all unfae creatures in general. To them, I look like a normal man in a normal suit." He smiles at that, as if the idea truly amuses him. An utterly devastating smile that makes him less scary. *Unfae.*

"Normal? So no one can see your ears and—"

"And?"

"Your beauty?" I add quietly, blushing against my will. I quickly look away, sensing that he can feel my embarrassment.

His widening smile tells me does. "Do you pity them?"

There's teasing in his words now. I scowl at him. I won't forget that he just brought that shard to my throat. That I am once again a captive thanks to him.

"Why would I?"

His tone stays too soft when he says, "Because they can't see what you see and indulge in the sight of me."

"Be careful or people might think you're a little self-obsessed," I bite out.

He laughs now, a soft and honest sound I like despite myself. "I know how handsome I am, but it never hurts to hear it."

I decide to ignore this. "But why can I see your true form when others can't?" Why am I meant to see it if he said *to all unfae creatures in general...*

He moves so fast I don't register it before his fingers brush against my tender skin, over the still purple swelling hidden underneath my makeup. From the gentleness of his touch, I know he can see everything there. I shiver when his fingers glide down my cheek, stopping just above my lips. An unfinished motion.

His tone is sweet as honey, his eyes liquid, as he whispers, "Have you never wondered why so many men stare at you? Women too, I suppose? Because the fae blood runs through your veins as well as through mine."

For a moment, there is only his touch. Only the feel of skin against skin, the heat of his body close to mine. So unfamiliar.

Fae blood. What the hell? I have gone mad, for sure.

I take a step back, and he slowly lowers his hand. When I lift my gaze, the same gentleness he applied now lies in his face. That and something else entirely.

I'm not sure I trust my hearing when he says, "You are as beautiful as they said you would be. But, for now, let's go."

"Where?"

"Back to Lyrian's house."

I shake my head reflexively, knowing that the terror in my eyes is showing because the hint of what I just saw in his eyes gives way to pity.

"He will hurt me. He'll hurt me badly. I can't." Only a whisper comes from my lips now.

"He won't," he replies, still soft.

"How do you know?" My voice is louder now, shriller. I take a few steps back. I will fight. Fight until the end. But I will never, ever go back to Lyrian.

His answer is not angry, but calm and firm. "Because I will not allow it."

"You can't take me back to him."

"I won't bring you back to Lyrian."

All the things he's told me. All the things he hasn't told me. I read them in his face.

"What? Why are we going back then? Where are you taking me?"

"I'm taking you to the High Lord of Darkness," he says, and I hate the remorse in his face.

I can't bring myself to ask what that means. He holds out his hand to me, a silent offering—a silent *threat*, because it means that he will force me to come if I don't obey.

I glower at his hand as if it's a poisonous snake.

He says, his voice suddenly solemn, "I hereby swear that no harm shall come to you from Lyrian's hand and neither from mine. And that I will always protect you."

I stare at him, wide-eyed, as a strange prickle runs through my body, as if something has just been branded right underneath my flesh. I wonder whether I imagined it. But that strange sensation, it stays.

"And that... High Lord of Darkness?" I ask, my voice coming out a little bit breathless.

His remarkable eyes flicker, as does his aura. "I will do everything in my power to ensure that my king will not hurt you either."

I look back at those violet eyes, unsure what to make of that statement. I can always tell when people are lying, thanks to my *talent*. Their auras betray them. He's speaking the truth. Despite my better instincts, I nod once and follow him through the woods. Not that I have much of a choice.

"Can you at least tell me your name?" I ask his back.

He pauses briefly, then looks back at me over his shoulder. "Oh, darling, I thought you'd never ask. I'm Riven."

MELODY

I follow him back to the main road where a car is waiting for us. Reluctantly, I climb in, pulling my legs up close to me. Riven turns on the heat as soon as we drive off, as if he can hear my chattering teeth. We don't exchange another word, though I find myself glancing at him from time to time. At those delicate, strange ears. Those big, yet elegant, white hands with gold and gems heavy on his fingers. I watch him from behind my curtain of long, dark hair. His surreal long eyelashes. The way they almost touch his cheeks as he glances down the shimmering road.

We spend half the night speeding back over rain-wet asphalt, way too fast, but I'd hardly mind if we hit a tree. That we don't is probably down to his fae reflexes.

The first gray of morning stretches over the horizon when we finally arrive at Lyrian's house. As soon as we do, I sit up straight, trying to brace myself for whatever horror comes next.

The High Lord of Darkness, Riven said. Whatever the fuck that means.

The lights are on in the huge mansion when we pull up in the driveway and stop in front of the massive stone fountain with two ugly putti pouring water from jugs.

Riven frowns at them. "Grotesque," is all he says before he kills the engine and gets out.

I follow suit. The morning air is cold, sobering, but I hardly feel anything anyway. I stare at the huge doors as if they will swing open by magic. Riven steps up next to me, his eyes holding the same warmth they held when he touched me in the woods.

Involuntarily, I look down to my naked feet.

"I promised," he whispers one more time and again holds out his hand.

I surprise myself when I take it. Feeling his warm fingers around mine is strangely soothing. Reassuring. Together we approach the house. We enter through the front door, which is normally locked, but now is not. *Weird.* Part of me expects the bloodhounds to come cutting around a corner, guns at the ready, but they're nowhere to be seen either.

Instead, the massive, winged doors to the living room are closed. Riven pauses there, letting go of my hand before looking me up and down.

I promised, his eyes seem to say once more.

Instead, he asks, "Ready?"

Hell no!

But I nod once. If not over, then through, right? He gives me one more second to gather myself before he pushes open the door. Lyrian never allowed me access to this room, but now we stroll into the opulent living room as if it's ours.

Lyrian is standing in front of the fireplace, the fire crackling there the only source of light. He is still in his evening attire—an embroidered silk coat of azure and mantis-green that reaches down to his boots with oddly pointed ends that bend slightly upward at the tip. He's holding a tumbler of whiskey in his hand, and by the gleam in his eyes, I can tell it isn't his first.

Those pale, cruel eyes widen ever so slightly when they settle on the stranger next to me, then on me in tow.

It is only then, standing in the middle of the room, my gaze trained on Lyrian, that I notice two other men standing in the shadows, motionless as statues. Not Kayne or Hunter—there is still no trace of them—but two other men clad all in black with combat boots on their feet. They are as tall as Riven. A third figure sits in Lyrian's armchair, his face hidden in the shadows.

The last one breaks the silence. "Finally. It took a while."

His voice is deep, sensual, and somber. It sends a ripple all over my skin. I feel the sudden need to see his face, to step closer, as if his voice is, in truth, calling to me, to my very blood.

I swallow against this strange sensation.

Riven straightens involuntarily as if he too has felt that irresistible pull of... power. He answers casually, "She made it quite far."

The man in the chair still doesn't look our way as he says with a negligent wave of his hand, "You may go upstairs with her. This might take a moment longer."

The High Lord of Darkness... that must be him... the way he speaks. The way the ripples of power come flowing off him with every word. Despite his disinterested tone, I can feel the latent impatience underneath. From the look in Lyrian's eyes, I know he can feel it too. They glide to mine, as if to plead for help.

I would laugh at that if I wasn't so terrified myself.

Would spit into his face, asking, *Really? Me? Are you fucking kidding me?*

Instead, I look away and follow Riven upstairs to my room. He pauses in front of the door, letting me enter first before I hear his steps behind me.

I try not to notice how his huge, powerful stature towers in the room. I keep my head down, not wanting to witness the way he takes in my bed, my easel, my paintings that lean everywhere, against walls and cabinets, covering every free space. The only things that bring color in here.

"You might want to gather the things you would like to take with you," he says too gently.

We're leaving, that's what he's telling me. I look around the room, my bedroom, but whatever I thought I would feel is not here. No relief that I'm finally leaving. No terror of what the future might hold. No, I feel nothing at all.

Mechanically, I grab a bag—the same bag I once packed for my escape, before I discovered it slowed me down—and start to fold my clothes inside… all black. I've never worn anything other than black in my life.

When I'm done, Riven is still standing, unmoved, but his eyes are resting on one picture leaning against the wall. Of two people. Arm in arm. Smiling.

"My parents. Or what I think my parents might have looked like. I never met them, but I needed a picture in my mind, so I made one."

Made one and placed it here so I could imagine them watching me at night.

I don't know why I'm telling him this.

To my surprise, he retorts, "They didn't look like that. Your father, well, you're quite close, but your mother didn't look like that."

More questions start to form, but before I can ask them, an inhuman scream cuts through the air. *Lyrian.*

"Melody, don't!" Riven says, reaching for me, but I'm already out the door.

I storm downstairs, pushing the double-winged door open. I don't know why. But I need to know what made Lyrian scream that way. I need to know what fate awaits me once they take me.

What I see freezes the blood in my veins.

Lyrian is suspended several feet off the ground, held up by the outstretched arm of the man who'd been sitting in the armchair before. His hand is closed around Lyrian's throat.

There is a lot of blood. It's dripping from Lyrian's neck, seeping into his fine tunic, the carpet. Blood that drips from the Dark Lord's chin. From his *fangs*.

At the sight of me, Lyrian starts pleading. "Take her! Take her! You can see in my blood that I spoke the truth! I kept her for you, my lord. Your Highness. I hid her away, for all these years, just for you when the time was ripe! I'll give her to you in exchange for my life. One life debt for another."

There is little human in the snarl the Dark Lord lets out when he says, "Liar."

Rage leashes his aura, and I swear the room is darkening with shadows.

"We can't lie, my lord—you know—"

"Do not tempt me, Lyrian. Benignity is not a virtue I am known to have. Your breed has been allowed to thrive for too long."

"Please, my king. You know the prophecy. The curse if you kill me—" Lyrian starts again, cut off once more by another growl that makes my insides turn cold.

"I don't care as much about curses as you might have heard. I'll claim her, but you—if you ever once so much as *interact* with any other fae, I will personally skin you alive, Lyrian. You have already been banned from the fae lands, but I hereby strip you of any belongings, any rights and declare you an outlaw. Prey for *anyone* who seeks bloodshed, or redemption."

Lyrian falls utterly silent. The Dark Lord loosens his grip around his neck, and Lyrian tumbles inelegantly to the ground, clutching his sore throat, fumbling for a necklace that is no longer there but in the hand of the Dark Lord.

I watch, spellbound, as he crumbles the object of gems and gold in his fingers, as if it is a piece of paper, until nothing but ash sifts down.

The effect is instant.

The Lyrian at his feet is no longer the Lyrian I know, but an aged, shrunken version of himself. His cheeks are gaunt and sunken, his sharp features even more distinct, with hollow eyes and pointed ears.

The necklace was a glamour. And Lyrian... is an elf too.

After this, the Dark Lord's head turns to me.

My heart stops for a few precious seconds.

Raven-black hair offsets his pale, almost entirely white skin, those cruel cheekbones, his chiseled chin. He is even more beautiful than Riven, if that is possible. He is the most beautiful man I have ever seen.

But his eyes...

His eyes are even more extraordinary than his face.

They are all black, save for his irises, which gleam an undiluted, deep red. But the color isn't static like in everyone else's eyes. No. The pigment in those eyes seems to move, almost like the waves of an ocean at sunset, bundled into two marbles.

They are frightening and at the same time utterly, indescribably beautiful.

I can't help but stare. Mesmerized.

Until a cutting voice startles me. "Lower your eyes, slave, for this is the High Lord of Darkness you're looking at. You're never to look one of us in the eyes unless called upon to do so."

Slave. I flinch at the word. At the harsh tone. My head snaps to the other huge man, who's stepped up to me so quietly I didn't hear him coming. Handsome. Blond hair that reaches down to his shoulders, striking green eyes, and sharp, hard features glower at me.

Again, fangs flash where his canines should be. He has them bared at me. An animalistic hiss emanates from his throat when I don't obey. "Lower your eyes or I'll teach you manners, girl."

"I'm no one's slave," I reply as coldly as I can, straightening my shoulders and lifting my chin, not willing to show any of them how scared I truly am, although they definitely can hear my wildly thundering heartbeat.

The hateful grimace on his face stays as he declares, "You are now, since Lyrian Elderberg has just sold you off. So lower your eyes or you'll regret it. This is the last time I'll tell you."

I barely hear the last part. *Sold you off.*

My eyes flit to Lyrian, who is still cowering at the Dark Lord's feet, his expression so rattled and shaken I wonder whether he understands any of what's happening here. He doesn't seem the least bit surprised by their fangs, by just having been bitten. No. If anything at all, he just looks broken.

Maybe it should satisfy me on a deep, dark level to see Lyrian like this, but all it does is stir my diffuse fear, confusion, and rage.

It's this rage that makes me step forward, up to him, looking down on him for maybe the first time in my life. He flinches slightly, as if he's afraid I'll strike him and crawls backward. I clench my fingers into a fist. Maybe I should.

Instead, I ask, "You sold me? You fucking *sold* me as if I was your fucking property? After all I did for you? After all you've made me do?"

Fury makes my voice tremble. I should have known. Riven warned me. Told me that Lyrian kept me for this sole reason. I have been nothing but a life insurance. I don't know why it matters so much. It shouldn't. I know it shouldn't.

My eyes fill up with tears of rage and shame and helplessness nonetheless. I try to swallow them down. I can't start crying in front of Lyrian, in front of *them*, but the indignity of being sold like a *thing*...

"My, my, Lyrian. I must say you have withered." Riven's voice is a silken purr. He saunters over to my side, his hands in the pockets of his trousers, looking down at Lyrian with a cruel smile on his lips. "But I suppose staying holed up in an area like this for more than a century takes its toll."

He clicks his tongue as he surveys the room. "But you could have renovated. It smells like a grave in here."

"Please," Lyrian says. He is trembling with fear, I realize. "The Dark Lord spared me."

In a flash of motion, Riven's hand closes around Lyrian's thin throat, his teeth dangerously close to his face. Despite myself, I marvel at the grace of his immortal strength, the movement smooth as silk. I envy it, how easily he manages to scare someone like Lyrian. Another part of me is frozen in terror at the undiluted rage in his voice.

"Spared you? Oh no—he condemned you, Lyrian. Do not make me ponder what that means."

"Please, my lord. I'll do anything." Lyrian's gone stiff as a stick.

As quickly as Riven came, he withdraws his hand and straightens, casual and careless again. His voice is almost gentle as he says, "Please what?"

"Don't kill me."

Riven considers him with a gaze as if he were dirt he would kick aside with his boot. "Ah, groveling. The most sincere form of manipulation. I almost forgot how much training you had, back at the elven king's side in Palisandre. Before you ran and started this— flourishing trade." Although Riven's voice is still soft, his eyes are not. Those eyes burn with a dark fire.

"Please…" Lyrian starts again.

Riven holds up a finger. "None of that. No more pleading. It is tiresome. And pathetic. You are far too desperate. To be kept alive, you should be trying to keep me entertained. And your king, of course." Riven's smile becomes a vicious, dark thing. "What about this? Normally, I would make you bow, but given that you're already on your knees, I'll make an exception. Kiss our king's boot and then crawl back over here and kiss mine."

Lyrian keeps staring as if he can't remember where or who he is. His face, for the first time since I've known him, is blank. Vacant. Bereft of the cruelty, of anything.

"Go on. Do it before I change my mind and decide to decorate this lovely carpet with your innards," Riven chimes lightly, as if he hadn't just delivered a death threat that makes the blood in my veins run cold.

Lyrian startles out of his stupor. I hold my breath as Lyrian— the cruel, cold, arrogant Lyrian I know, who's tormented me all my life, starts to indeed crawl over to the Dark Lord like a dog.

Riven clicks his tongue and points to the ground. "Lower, Lyrian. Your head should be touching the ground, so low that I don't have to see your ugly face anymore. You know what this is supposed to look like. You have watched it so many times in Palisandre."

Lyrian lowers his head to the floor, so close his chin touches the carpet as he moves to the Dark Lord.

"Oh, and make it memorable, Lyrian," Riven croons after him. "After all, this is your new king in front of you, and you certainly don't want to upset him. He is not as forgiving as I."

Lyrian doesn't look up to the king as he whispers, "My king, it is my sincerest pleasure to serve you." He lowers his head and presses his pale lips to his leather boot. Then he crawls back.

Riven watches him with raised eyebrows as Lyrian pauses in front of us. "No flattery left for me, Lyrian?"

Lyrian flinches before he says, "Of course, my lord. You look as fresh as the morning dew on a rose petal."

"I was speaking of flattery, not poetry, but go on now." Riven waves a lazy hand, and Lyrian leans forward to bring his lips to Riven's boot.

I hold my breath. But somehow, to see Lyrian humiliated like this feels better than hurting him would.

Riven lets out a sultry chuckle when Lyrian stays on all fours, his head still lowered, as if he can't bear meeting anyone's eye. "Groveling suits you, Lyrian. One might almost assume you have been born for this." At the last sentence, Riven finally glances over at me. This moment... I know Riven did this for me.

I flash him a grateful look before my eyes drift back to the Dark Lord's, still a churning red but darker now. I feel a twist in my stomach when I find him studying me in return, his gaze so intimate it could burn a hole in me.

I blush at his stare but keep looking back at him, at the swirling shadows all around him. Spellbound.

Too late, I notice the blur of movement behind me. Someone grabs my long hair, pulling my head back. The blond warrior, suddenly next to me, his green eyes vicious slits.

I spin out of his grip to face him. He raises his hand too fast for me to comprehend, too fast for me to dodge... but then it's suspended, mere inches from my face. His palm is already open where it would have connected with my skin and no doubt split it open a sliver of a second later. I feel the gust of wind in my hair provoked by his movement.

But there is no collision. No slap. No pain.

The warrior just stands there, in this position, hand raised, as if he has been frozen.

Only then do I feel the wave of power flickering through the room, those dark shadows that have been gathering in the corners, now swirling everywhere around us. Soft as the night, but just as deadly.

The Dark Lord has just stopped the blond man from slapping me with his power and an invisible command.

His voice follows a second later, calm, but cold as he says, "Don't, Kyrith."

Kyrith.

My heart is in my mouth. Hammering. Slowly catching up. My eyes search for Riven's. I find them wide open, as if he too forgot about Kyrith. Kyrith's face to my right is still an angry mask, still motionless, his eyes still narrowed to slits, and his fangs exposed when I glance back at him. He still can't move. He looks like he is going to kill me with his gaze though.

He manages to growl, "I warned her."

"I take it upon myself to discipline my slaves." The Dark Lord doesn't look at me again when he declares, "We're leaving."

$$\supset \cdot \complement$$

I follow them outside and to the forest. The Dark Lord is leading the way, Kyrith trailing behind him, followed by the quiet but beautiful man with red hair and Riven walking next to me. We take my path through the woods, the path I've run a thousand times, until we reach the cliff. The cold wind's soaring up from below, the Abyss again beckoning, the ocean churning.

This is the very cliff where I stood so many times as if something was calling me.

I finally dare to glance at Riven, who is carrying my bag. I know he reads the question in my eyes, the panic, when he says, "This is the fae gap. Now, we jump."

And with that, he grabs my arm and together we go over the cliff.

11

RIVEN

Melody fell asleep as soon as they entered the fae realms. Riven feels the familiar rush of magic in his veins at his return, his own magic singing at the reunion.

He has been away for too long.

The human world is a funny thing. Those weak little creatures that populate it, so tender and fragile without magic.

He looks down at the woman he carries in his arms. Her dark, long hair falls over her shoulders, covering most of her face, brushing his forearms. Her beautiful half-fae face glistens in the moonlight as they emerge from the waves and wade toward the shore to the stretch of neutral territory between the three kingdoms—Avandal in the north, the Emerald Forest bordering it, the range of those absurdly high trees and the mist that surrounds them visible in the distance.

The Kingdom of the Two Moons—Caryan's kingdom—spans over the whole southern continent to Riven's left.

Melody stirs slightly in his arms but doesn't wake up. Riven finds it hard not to look at her. He's never seen a human half-blood before, and he doubts any of them ever have, not even Caryan. But that is not the reason for his staring.

The girl, bound to Caryan's fate through Kalleandara's prophecy.

The girl they have been searching for since the day she was born.

The girl he's been dreaming about for years.

When they finally found her last night and Caryan sent him after her, he had been so sure it was to kill her.

That Caryan ordered him to bring her to him instead...

Riven doesn't allow himself to ponder the consequences of this. Not now. Not when the others are around, too easily picking up even the smallest shift in him. Their acute sense of hearing and smell are more often a nuisance than useful.

Not to mention Caryan himself. He will feel every emotion in him through the bond that connects them, all the more if he is close.

None of them can shield themselves from Caryan since they accepted the *curse*—the bond to Caryan. But if Caryan is distracted enough, he does not pay them too close attention.

So Riven shuts down his instincts for now and retreats to a dark and quiet place within himself. He can think about this later.

He looks back down at the girl in his arms, her weight not more than a tiny bird's to his fae strength.

So strange to finally hold her. She looks exactly the way she looked in his dreams. When he found her in the woods, he couldn't resist touching her.

A mistake. Because the effect of that touch shook him. An echo of it still sears the underside of his skin like a burn, as if it has been branded there. Maybe it is the rare kind of light she seems to emanate—a hint of the silvery blood flowing through her veins. The light of the moon and the stars, they whisper.

Melody, half-human, half-moon elf.

When Riven glances up, he finds Caryan looking at her too, his eyes still tinged red from Lyrian's cowardly blood. It must have tasted rancid, like the rotten bastard's soul, but Riven hasn't had the nerve to ask. He hasn't had the nerve to ask about Caryan's rush of anger that rippled through the room when he had swallowed the first drop of Lyrian's blood either.

What did he taste that made their leader release that feral growl?

It's so rare to see Caryan angry. Rare to see him with any emotions at all. Through their bond to him, they sometimes feel what he feels, or at least a fragment of it. But back at Lyrian's house, Riven felt a bolt of hate jolting through the bond right into him, as hot and searing as lightning. It was painful. Riven knew Kyrith and Ronin felt it too. No one would bring it up though.

Caryan looks away again as they walk on.

All of them are strangely quiet, save for Kyrith, who gave Riven a hard time when he took Melody's hand for the jump off the cliff and who held her as soon as they hit the water, bracing her fall with his own body to spare her bruises. He's been carrying her ever since.

What are you now? Her knight in shining armor? Carrying a mortal girl? Since when have we sunk so low?

Riven ignored Kyrith as he does most of the time. It is enough to feel Kyrith's temper and moods through the bond. To answer them is more than he is willing to do. Kyrith is one of the most feared fae warriors of Palisandre. His power is impressive, and Riven has heard stories about the white-haired warrior and his cadre. Yet he wonders how his former comrades dealt with Kyrith without the constant wish to throw their commander off a cliff. And that was before Caryan brought him back to life on a battlefield and offered him a fresh start.

Kyrith had been an animal before, and it has only gotten worse.

He is a ruthless bastard.

Kyrith passes him now, glowering down at the girl. Riven finds his lip curling in a silent warning.

"You look like you're going to fuck her as soon as we're out of sight."

Riven exposes even more of his fae canines which have now turned into vicious fangs since Caryan offered him the curse. Only the woman in his arms prevents him from trying to rip Kyrith's throat out straight away.

Kyrith sees his chance and uses it. "Didn't know you had a soft spot for mortal girls. That's why you love to wander the human realms so much. A penchant for scum."

"She is no mortal; she's half-fae," Riven replies coolly.

"Makes it all the more fun. They don't break so easily."

A growl comes out of Riven's throat, one that no longer holds much civility. A face he so rarely shows these days, but one that reveals his deadly nature. A face he tries to avoid when looking in the mirror. Tries to forget. A face of black flames, burnt corpses, ashes, and ruins.

Riven is glad Melody is still sleeping, or she would be even more afraid of him than she already is.

"Try to touch her one more time, and I'll give you a taste of your own medicine, Kyrith."

"Now that sounds like fun."

As if on cue, dark flames start to singe the tips of Kyrith's white hair—demonic flames no water or ice could douse. Stench fills the air, followed by a sharp hiss from Kyrith's throat.

"I'll fucking kill you—"

"You needed a trim anyway, Kyrith. It really brings out your cheekbones, you know," Riven purrs, but his voice is laced with silky menace. He meant every word he said—he would reduce Kyrith to dust without so much as batting an eye if Kyrith so much as looked at her the wrong way again.

"You—"

"Enough now." Caryan's voice ripples through them, a command humming in their blood they can't ignore even if they want to, smothering the black flames in Riven's veins and leashing Kyrith's attempt at retribution.

Riven is glad for that. The Dark Lord is the only one who can put a lid on Kyrith, handle him. Riven knows that Caryan's command to stop Kyrith from hitting the girl needles Kyrith, makes him hate her even more deeply than he already does.

Kyrith loves Caryan, more than the warrior has ever loved anyone else. Not in a romantic sense, but not the way all of them love each other like brothers either, even though the bond to Caryan is stronger than anything Riven himself has ever felt before. But Kyrith has never once in his life respected anyone. Not in his old life, when he served the king of Palisandre. But he looks up to Caryan with undiluted awe and respect. That he did something Caryan didn't tolerate hurt him, Riven knows.

That is probably why, after a moment of silence, Riven says, calm again, "She is not her mother, Kyrith. You have to see that."

"Her blood runs in the girl's veins," Kyrith blurts.

"She hardly knew her. She is not like her. She doesn't deserve your hatred. She is a girl who grew up with that monster."

"Like calls to like."

"*She is not like us,* you blanched, dimwitted brute," Riven spits back. Why did he even try?

Kyrith hisses at that but says nothing more. Caryan doesn't turn back to them, but Riven knows he has followed every word.

Riven glances toward Ronin, the red-haired former witcher, who's as quiet as Caryan. Ronin's eyes meet Riven's, a silent communication confirming that he, too, felt Caryan's strange surge of emotion in Lyrian's house and doesn't know what to make of it.

All talking stops when they eventually reach the border of Caryan's kingdom. The two Trochetian horses, powerful and rare demons from another world that can take on any shape their owner desires—currently in the form of two black, sleek sports cars—are waiting where they left them days ago.

One door opens on a silent command, and Caryan gets in, as Ronin and Kyrith walk over to the other demon. Riven's glad to ride with Caryan. He carefully puts Melody down on the backseat—the demon shifting slightly to create the space that hadn't been there before to accommodate her too—before Riven gets in on the passenger seat.

He leans back and closes his eyes for a moment as the door seals shut.

He's tired and he wonders whether Caryan is tired too. But when he glances at his king, Caryan looks as alert as ever. Riven exhales and closes his eyes again. It is a long ride back after a long night already.

When Riven opens his eyes the next time, the Fortress—as the citizens call the huge modern complex of concrete, glass, and magic, enthroned on top of a hill overlooking the town Niavara below—gleams in the darkness, as if alive from within. A beacon in the night for so many.

Home.

The word settles deep in Riven's bones as he sits up in his seat. Every time he returns, he can't help but think that this is the first real home he's ever had. Khalix, the desert lands on a continent far west of Palisandre, never felt that way to him, although he grew up there. Not to even mention Palisandre. He certainly never felt as if he belonged there. But Niavara—the town, the Fortress, the whole continent, being at Caryan's side—has become a part of him. And vice versa.

Sometimes it is hard to believe that only twenty years ago, before Caryan took over the whole deserted continent and declared it his kingdom, making Niavara the capital of the lands of the two moons, there'd been nothing but wasteland and elven ruins.

Niavara itself had been merely a few crumbling stones. Just another town that had been abandoned, its name long forgotten after the veils between the other worlds had started to tear, allowing all forms of dangerous creatures to seep in through the rips. The rumors claimed that all the city's inhabitants fell victim to a raid of specters hundreds of years ago. Demons had feasted on their souls before they moved up to the fallen city Avander with its once-famous harbor, before the angels finally swept in to kill them.

Old stories of old times. Long before the angels became extinct themselves.

Riven clenches his teeth. They—*his kind*—had hunted the angels down, not thinking they might need their special talents once again because those rips became more and more as the balance of magic tipped further.

More monsters came in every year. Monsters that could easily kill high elves.

They arrive at the Fortress. Both demons shift into the shape that earned them their names—black horses with slick, leathery skin; sharp teeth; eerie red eyes; and taloned claws instead of hooves; long, dark tails swishing behind them—as soon as they climbed out.

Leaving the demons behind without another glance, Caryan starts to walk up the stairs, Kyrith and Ronin trailing behind. Riven follows last, Melody still in his arms.

Once in the throne room, Caryan pauses. "Leave her in the dungeon. And put on some iron handcuffs on her."

Riven looks down at her. She looks so pale and thin, more like a ghost. "Is that necessary?"

Caryan turns to him at that, his eyes dark and depthless. Ronin and Kyrith both pause too, watching. Ronin's amber eyes flash in a warning. Kyrith crosses his arms, waiting.

Barely anyone ever questions anything Caryan tells them. But Riven and Caryan's bond is different, due to their time together at Gatilla's court.

He pushes, "She is no fae, Caryan. Neither her heart nor her body is yet fae. She has never been in touch with magic."

"You heard me."

"She is still soaking wet," Riven presses.

Caryan bares his teeth at him. A warning.

Kyrith grins before both he and Ronin walk away, probably to find some company for the night.

Riven nods once. He turns on his heels and walks out in the other direction, towards the dungeons. At the end of the hall, he pauses and says very quietly, "She is no threat yet. Give her some time to adapt."

The words are barely audible, but he knows Caryan heard them by the sound of footsteps halting on the other side of the room.

They are still facing away from each other, at a distance of at least thirty yards. The conversation no more than a murmur.

Eventually, Caryan turns. "I do not care what she is other than my slave. Do it." At that, iron handcuffs appear around her wrists, so tight they cut into her skin.

Riven sucks in a breath. Caryan stares him down, daring him to object, but Riven carries on toward the dungeon. Dumping her wet and cold like that in that icy cell, leaving her to Caryan's mercy—it doesn't feel good. But he has no choice.

A command is a command. Trying to fight it would mean his death.

MELODY

I don't know what happens after the jump. After hitting the ice-cold water that seems to drain all life from me. After the darkness pulls me down.

All I remember is the sensation of freefall. That I am underwater, but that I am still able to breathe. That the cold is too bad to bear.

And then the darkness claims me, and I think that's what dying must feel like.

My skin feels raw and feverish when I wake up, curled up into a ball, my head still numb, as if someone drugged me. And... iron handcuffs around my wrists. I jolt upright, pulling my legs up to my body while I wait for my eyes to adjust to the darkness. Where the hell am I? What did they do to me? Maybe they did drug me. Maybe they *glamoured* me?

It is dark. Dim. Cold. The floor underneath me is ice-cold and biting. I get up shakily, the ground still a little unreliable as I look around.

I'm in a cellar... or some sort of dungeon. The single door is barred by huge, broad columns of steel. A cell.

I am trapped. In an iron cage. Manacled.

Locked away, again.

Reflexively, I run toward the bars. I put my fingers around them, yanking them hard as if I can somehow tear them apart, make them budge at least a tiny bit.

But nothing. *Of course* nothing.

Tears stream down my cheeks. My breathing comes sharp and fast. Not again. Not again, *please.*

It is too much. Too much like my past. I shudder against the feeling of the walls closing in on me like they always do. Of the feeling of too little air.

Of being trapped in darkness.

At least I knew Lyrian wouldn't let me die.

Breathe! Just breathe. But I seem unable to get down enough air.

I sink onto the floor, my bare shoulders leaning against the cool walls. I cry until my tears subside. My body is still shaking from fear or cold or desperation, I don't know anymore. It doesn't matter. There is nothing left in me, not even hope, just a never-ending, gaping void.

Something catches my eye in my peripheral vision. I jerk my head up.

Gleaming crimson eyes watch me—a demon in the night.

I reflexively swivel backward, as far away as the tiny cell will allow, only to bump against the other wall.

The High Lord of Darkness. The color in his eyes flickers slightly, the red like burning embers as they take me in. I try hard not to think of where the red comes from.

How did he get in here? The cell door is still locked.

He takes a step towards me. He is huge, I realize. Taller than I, which is saying something since I am well over average height for most women. But his stature is towering in the tiny cell. I shift even further back, as far away from him as possible, until my left shoulder hits the opposite end of the cell. I wish I could melt into the wall. Hide. Turn invisible.

There is nothing left in me to pretend I'm not scared to my very essence.

My heart startles as he takes another step toward me. I look up at him then, into those mesmerizing eyes, too numb to remember that Kyrith warned me to never look him in the eye unbidden. Too numb to remember that I am a slave now.

But once more, I find myself unable to look away.

Shadows limn his face, casting his cheekbones and his soft, sullen mouth into stark relief. Even with his red eyes, he is mercilessly beautiful. The kind of beauty that hurts when you look at it.

Only after a while do I realize that he's holding something out to me. A glass bottle with clear liquid in it.

As if he can feel my suspicion, he says in his deep, sensual voice, "Water."

I just gaze at his hand. At those elegant, pallid fingers and the tattoo that stretches up from his wrist almost to his fingertips. Tendrils of ink mixed with gold form strange symbols I've never seen before. They seem to move... or is it just in my mind?

I focus back on the bottle.

I wouldn't dare take it from his hands if I wasn't so thirsty. But I am. With one last glance at his face, I take it and unscrew it. I gulp the water down so greedily that some of it runs over my chin and down my collarbones, seeping into my dress.

I hadn't realized that those iron shackles around my wrists had dissolved, or when; leaving only deep, angry rims in my flesh.

Only when the bottle is empty do I glance back up to him. Again I find him watching me in return. I get up when he takes a last step closer. This time, I stand my ground, although it takes all my willpower not to shrink back.

Don't show fear. No tears. No fear.

I repeat that over and over in my mind, but it doesn't prevent me from flinching when he lifts his hand. I blush, hating myself for it. For shuddering when his fingers raise my chin. Now, so close, I avoid his eyes, trying to concentrate on a point past him in the darkness. My thundering heart blocks out every clear thought.

I stiffen when his fingers brush back my long hair, away from my neck, as gently as if he were my lover.

When he bends slightly down to me.

"You need to relax, or it will hurt," he whispers right into my ear, his breath on my neck.

He's going to drink my blood. How much? All of it? Will he kill me? Suck me dry? Every inch of my body goes taut as the meaning of his words echoes through me.

Such nonchalant words. As if they mean nothing. As if I mean nothing.

To him, I probably don't. I'm nothing more than a slave, and who the hell knows what these vampires do with their slaves?

I turn rigid as his fingers around my chin tighten ever so slightly, as if to lock me into place. His lips brush against my vulnerable skin then. I try not to think of his fangs as I brace myself for the pain.

But he doesn't bite me.

Instead, he waits, suspended, his breath over my feverish skin, his fingers stroking my cheek now. His voice is nothing but gentle when he says, "Relax."

Why is he so patient with me? Why not just get it over with?

As if to answer my silent question, he straightens, lifting my chin again. When I glance up, I'm surprised to find his eyes no longer that aggressive red, but a bright, calm blue that makes him look entirely different. Not *so* scary anymore.

How does this work? Can he change his eye colors by will or is it influenced by something else?

If it works like auras, he probably can't control it.

Suddenly, I wish to ask. To know. Those glittering blue eyes are the most beautiful I have ever seen. Just what the ocean must look like under a full moon. Silver ripples where the light meets the waves, oscillating like a thousand diamonds, surrounded by the darkest of nights.

Only when he says, "I'll be careful. I won't hurt you," do I realize that I'm shivering so hard that my whole body trembles.

He won't hurt me. All I manage is a shy nod. He waits a moment longer before I feel his lips there again, right on my pulse. I close my eyes, force myself to believe him, to trust him. I have no other choice anyway.

His fangs pierce my skin then and my whole world narrows down to the feeling of them in me.

It doesn't hurt when they penetrate my flesh. Instead, there's a strange heat rushing through my body, as if every cell has been set on fire. I shudder as he drinks me in, but no longer from fear. I barely register how my fingers dig into the fabric of his shirt, that he has moved even closer, his huge body pinning mine against the cold wall, pressing hard against me.

Then, all too soon, I feel him pulling back, only absently feel him running his tongue over the wounds his teeth have left. He takes a step back from me, the red blood in his eyes intermingling with streaks of burning gold.

I look at my blood dripping from his lips. And despite all instincts, I find myself wishing that he would carry on. For a brief second, I have the sensation that he... might be feeling the same.

Desire glitters in his aurum eyes. Before they widen slightly, and he looks at me with some kind of... horror.

His features harden involuntarily, the gold in his eyes giving way to a vicious black as he regards me now, spreading through the red-like tendrils of ink.

As if I... disgust him.

Despite my fear, I blush with shame. Maybe it's my blood? Or my... appearance? I don't want to know what I must look like to him with my wet, half-torn dress and uncombed hair. Filthy. My eyes red-rimmed from crying. How could I ever think that he...

I can't finish the thought. Can't think it without dying of shame and confusion and exhaustion.

I am a slave. Food for him, nothing more.

I don't know why it matters to me. It doesn't, I tell myself. It's a lie.

I can't look back at him. I keep my head lowered, willing my hair to fall all over my face to hide from him.

When I look up again, he's gone. Vanished into thin air.

)·(

I slump against the wall, my heart pounding too fast, as if it wants to break free of my ribs. My head's still hazy from what just happened, my thoughts diffuse, my body just so cold.

There's the solid jolt of a bolt.

I look up to find a spindly woman with ashen-brown skin and long, silver hair that reaches almost down to her hips standing in the open cell door. She wears a long, kaftan-like dress that shimmers in shades of deep-sea colors, setting off eyes smooth and bright as river pebbles.

"Melody," she says as if my name is a foreign word for her, her voice laced with an accent I've never heard before. "I am Nidaw. I have been sent for you. Please, come. The Dark Lord told me to take care of you."

The Dark Lord. I slowly get up, silently following the woman through the corridors of this dungeon that undoubtedly serves as a prison. As I walk, I try hard not to peek into each cell we pass, try not to listen to the weeping or hushed whispers in foreign tongues somewhere in the cold, dim darkness, desperation so thick in the air it's palpable.

At the end of the corridor is a flight of stairs. I brace myself for what might come next. I'm still barefoot, but so is Nidaw. When we reach the top of the stairs, the uneven cobbles under my naked feet end abruptly, and my soles touch onyx marble, which is occasionally crisscrossed by golden veins, the stone surprisingly warm under my feet. So is the air. A gentle, warm breeze envelops me as we walk on, carrying the faintest smell of jasmine and wisteria as if wafting in from a nearby garden—the total opposite to the underground.

I look around, wide-eyed. Everything is dipped in a soft light from backlit alabaster plates that stretch from the ground up to a ceiling so high I can't see the apex.

Despite the horrors of that dungeon, I can't help but marvel at the design. I have no idea what I expected, but more likely a medieval castle matching the underground prison than... *this*. Definitely nothing so modern. So... tasteful.

It looks like a designer complex, where an architect was allowed to live his dream, and money was clearly no issue.

Nidaw leads me down the hallway and pauses in front of a huge, beautifully carved double-winged door made of some dark wood I have never seen before.

There is the metal head of a creature, half lion, half dragon, adorned with curled horns, embedded in the wall next to it.

When Nidaw steps closer to it and says, "I am here to bring Lady Melody on behalf of the High Lord of Darkness," its dark eyes sparkle blue with sudden life.

It answers, "Be welcome, Nidaw. And you too, Melody."

I stare at the head, which has gone back to slumber, no sign that it had just spoken, its eyes two holes again.

Nidaw takes me by the arm. "Come now, girl," she says gently, ushering me into a vast hall, the ceiling a gold-painted dome.

The floor here is forest-green marble, polished to perfection. Embedded in the middle is a huge rectangular pool, several steps leading down into steaming, perfumed water. Candles burn in every corner, providing light, but at the same time offering more privacy than lamps would have.

Before I can take everything in, four more women who look similar to Nidaw have stepped up to me and started to roll my loop dress down my body. I try to wriggle out of their reach.

Nidaw mutters something like, "Human modesty," before she looks straight at me with those serious riverstone eyes. "You will get fresh clothes, girl. But first, you *need* a bath."

The way she says it makes me self-conscious all over. The servants' long fingers with sharp, dark nails start to tug at the fabric again, impatiently now. But this time, I don't resist. I must look bad.

I let them undress me, too exhausted to argue, although there is something unnerving about being the only naked person in the room. I let them guide me toward the bath and down the steps into the hot water. They enter with me, still in their tunics, which they have knotted around their very slim bodies. They start to scrub me and wash my hair with lavender and golden soap. I let it all happen, I'm too tired to do otherwise.

I let them lead me out again when they deem me clean enough, wrap me into a towel, and eventually guide me over to a marble table with a mirror where Nidaw already awaits me, perched on a velvet stool.

Those bony fingers push me down onto the stool next to hers, and she starts to detangle the mess of my hair with a golden comb shaped like a swan.

I meet her pale eyes in the mirror. "Where are we?"

"In the Twilight Kingdom," she answers tersely.

"No. I mean—where is it?"

Nidaw pauses, looking me up and down as if to size me up. "You are from the human world." She grimaces a little at the word *human*, as if it is an insult.

I nod, but Nidaw keeps looking at me in that strange way before she resumes brushing my hair.

"How long was I asleep?" It's bothering me, not knowing what day it is and how long I've been *away*. More than I let on.

Nidaw just chuckles lightly, an unfamiliar sound, like the hum of bees, before she says, "An hour, maybe two. Not long, don't worry. It's the magic that makes you so tired."

"Magic?"

Nidaw laughs again at my incredulous tone, as if I made a joke. "You don't have magic in the human world, I forget that. Magic is everywhere here. It's just another form of energy. The human world has no magic, and we can't use magic in the human world except if we bind it to objects. But here, everything is held together by magic."

I look at Nidaw's long, claw-like nails, and at the beautiful but strange color of her skin. Her pointed ears are shaped slightly differently than Riven's, I notice. Hers are pointed too, but have one more curve instead of a straight arch, which makes them look almost like the spiraled silhouettes of beautiful seashells.

"Can you *perform* magic? Like a witch?"

Nidaw shakes her head once. "No. I am only a river siren. We can just ask nature for magic, or plea to magic itself for help. But the high elves and the witches can."

"Are you also... a slave?" I dare to ask the question.

Nidaw angles her head at this but doesn't meet my eyes. "I am a servant, not a slave," she states eventually, but not unkindly.

"So you are here out of your free will."

Nidaw's slim eyebrows raise in question. "You make it sound like that is so unbelievable."

"No. Maybe... It's just... The Dark Lord and his men are very frightening," I admit quietly, looking down.

She stops brushing my hair. It has already been dried by a warm, balmy wind.

Nidaw clicks her tongue once. At that, two of the four sirens who washed me, who I assume are also sirens since they look like Nidaw, emerge from the shadows, a bundle of black fabric in their hand. At another tongue-click from Nidaw, they put it down and disappear as soundlessly as they came. Nidaw gestures for me to pick it up. *Clothes.* Neatly folded and incredibly soft, made of silk and cotton.

I carefully step out of the towel and slip into some wide, long, black trousers and a loose, black shirt whose sleeves reach my elbows, with a cut like that of a kimono.

Nidaw sizes me up with her ancient eyes and then nods once. "Very well. Come now, I will show you to your room."

MELODY

My bedroom is in a separate wing. We step out into the same hallway we came from, and walk down in the other direction. It ends up in a patio surrounded by sleek, modern marble colonnades, with a fountain in its middle, framed by hip-high bushes of rosemary and lavender. Blooming teardrops of wisteria run along the outside walls, climbing up the modernistic, subtle sandstone façade.

All in all, it looks like a contemporary, tasteful interpretation of an ancient Roman villa, or maybe an occidental palace, where the water provides coolness against the no doubt singeing midday heat. Here, outside, the air is still hot and dry when it is not cooled by the cold stone walls inside, the winds carrying an arid taste as if the place is in a desert.

When I look up, I see a crimson sky with the normal whitish moon and another huge, gleaming, red ball next to it.

I stare until Nidaw tugs at my sleeves. I ask, not moving an inch, "What is that?"

"Those are the two moons."

"*Two* moons?"

Nidaw nods and points with her sinewy arm toward the sky. "Yes. You are in the land of the two moons now. The white one— this is the moon from your world, or rather, a reflection of it. You can only see it in the Two-Moon realm when its image falls through the sea and the ripple within that connects our worlds."

"And the red one?"

A knowing smile plays around the siren's narrow lips. "This is the blood moon. Welcome to the lands of the High Lord of Darkness."

With that declaration, Nidaw tugs harder on my sleeve, and I follow her onward through another corridor and another patio, a smaller one, but, like the first one, fragrant with jasmine and lavender. Finally, we take a small flight of stairs.

"These are the servant and slave quarters. You get up every day at six, and then we will gather in the kitchen to start preparing food. After that, I will give you some more tasks, but we will see about that tomorrow. The kitchen is behind a door accessed through the second patio we crossed. You can hardly miss it."

Nidaw keeps talking as she opens one of the simple doors in a long corridor, and we enter a similarly simple chamber with a bed in front of a huge window that leads out to the front side of the complex we're in. From here, I can see that the building lies on a hill in the middle of a white desert. At its foot, there are lights of a city made of buildings with flat roofs. A town.

"Do you live here too?" I ask quietly, before Nidaw can leave me.

The siren stops in the doorway and nods once. "Yes. All the servants live here."

"But…" I hesitate, not sure whether I should ask. I decide I don't have much to lose anyway. "What if I want to leave?"

Nidaw's expression darkens. I feel a lump in my stomach as she shakes her head. "You can't leave. You are a slave, and slaves are not allowed to leave."

"And you?" I can't help my tone, the hurt in it, the sharpness.

She lifts her chin, but says, "I could, but it's not advisable to go to town, especially not at night."

"Not even for you?"

She shakes her head again, but her face softens. "A lot of the creatures who decided to follow the Dark Lord—they're his spawn. They have the curse."

"You're here and *not* cursed, right?" I push her, only then remembering that I don't see any fangs on her, but rather two rows of sharp-pointed teeth. Anyway, I need to know more. If I want to leave this place, I need to find out as much about it as I can. The sooner, the better.

Nidaw sighs once, as if she isn't sure she should tell me all of this. Her pale eyes flit to the window, to the glistening town below.

Then she says, very quietly, "No, I am not. But in those realms under the Dark Lord's control—the fae who've been brought back to life—the curse made them wild, wilder than usual, and stronger than they were before they were reincarnated. Especially when they're still *fresh* or *young*. Those the lord reincarnated recently. They need to learn to control the curse, their new thirst for blood. They're usually controlled by the high lords, but they're not always around. And without them, they can be unpredictable. There is some measure of anarchy."

"This is the curse then? The Dark Lord reincarnates the dead, and they grow fangs and have to drink blood afterward?" I ask carefully, not sure I have it right.

Nidaw nods once, her expression grave. Her eyes quickly wander to my neck, as if she can see what the Dark Lord did there. Maybe she can. Maybe the mark is still there. The skin there starts to prickle, and I resist the urge to touch it.

Nidaw nods, too quickly this time, and a little frustrated. "Yes. The Dark Lord—he is a necromancer. Some who live here and drink blood are fallen people. The Dark Lord usually finds them on the battlefield, and offers them the curse. If they accept, they are alive again, but they need to drink blood. And as I said, the high lords can control them, but still, they are not the way they were before. Not always, at least."

Not when they're hungry, she seems to imply.

She grabs my chin with her long-clawed fingers splayed on my cheeks. "So whatever you do, girl—never go to town at night, do you hear me? Never! Promise me. Right now." Her pale, washed-out eyes seem to burn themselves into mine.

"I do. I won't. I promise," I say a touch too quickly, remembering that Lyrian said fae can't lie. But as I do, I wonder whether giving a promise you're sure to break is considered a lie. And whether Nidaw knows that humans *can* lie.

But it seems to placate the siren. I exhale when Nidaw lets go of my chin at last. To change the topic I ask, "So there are lesser fae and high lords?"

"No. There are lesser fae, higher fae, and high lords."

"And... what's the difference?" I ask carefully, not sure if it is considered rude to ask.

Nidaw squints slightly, licking her sharp teeth, but then says, "Lesser fae are all the folk with a little magic in their veins. Like me. Occasionally, there are some who are born with more magic or special talents, which makes them higher fae. And then there are high lords, the most magically gifted creatures in this world, along with the witches."

"And who are the high lords here?"

"They're the king's inner circle—I assume you met them already. Lord Riven, Lord Kyrith, and Lord Ronin." As if she's already said too much, Nidaw turns back toward the door. She pauses after she's taken a step, obviously struggling with herself. "Try to obey, Melody. Humans here usually don't live long. Neither do slaves."

It doesn't escape me that she's avoiding my gaze at that. Then she turns on her heel and vanishes into the night.

After that declaration, I sit on the bed at the open window and watch the blood moon and the stars for a long while, absentmindedly rubbing the bite mark on my neck. I'd looked at myself in the tiny mirror over the basin after Nidaw left. There is nothing left of it, no trace, not even a bruise.

The moon looks like it is aflame, encircled by a deep-red halo that tinges all the darkness around it in permanent semi-twilight. Despite my inner terror, I can't help but marvel at it, can't deny how beautiful it is. The artist in me wants to paint it. Preserve it. I catch myself wondering when Riven will show up to return the duffle bag he was carrying for me.

He is a high lord. He has fangs, too, so maybe he's also cursed? Nidaw doesn't have fangs. He must be.

I look up at the other moon—my moon, the humans' moon. How pale it looks. And peaceful in comparison. Harmless.

I shudder against all the thoughts in my mind, running wild.

The portal is the sea. The sea right in front of Lyrian's house. Lyrian was using me to hunt down fae who crossed the gap to the human world. Lyrian himself is some sort of elf—maybe. Maybe he is something else entirely, since *everyone* here seems to have pointed ears. But then again, does it matter what he is other than a monster?

And I? What am I? A human and a slave. In the fae world. A slave of a vampire lord.

Part of me still believes I'm in some sort of weird dream. That I will wake up and...

find myself right back in my room, stuck with Lyrian and the bloodhounds.

No. No! Anything is better than being back with Lyrian.

Slave.

Humans here usually don't live long. Neither do slaves.

Maybe I'm wrong. Maybe I'd be better off with Lyrian.

I bury my face in my hands, wondering for the thousandth time whether I've just gone crazy. Maybe I have, after all. For sure. But what if... not? I pinch the skin on my thigh hard, so hard it is almost unbearable. Part of me waiting to snap out of some very dark dream at last. But nothing happens.

It's real then. Or I am mad.

Again, Nidaw's words cut through my mind, no matter how hard I try to ignore them. I have barely ever lived. I want to see the world, go somewhere where the sun shines on a reliable basis, and where the water isn't storm gray, but a deep, glistening azure. I made myself a promise, but now I am a slave. All over again. In a world I know nothing about.

A new wave of despair and panic threatens to rise, to swamp me, and bury me underneath. I shove it down and get up.

Quietly, I sneak to the door. It isn't locked, and I open it slightly. My ears strain to pick up the faintest noise in the corridor before I open it a touch wider. Without a second thought, I slip through.

The hallway is dark, the indirect light that illuminated it before has disappeared. I take a few steps, and wait. Then I start to run, silently and barefoot, figuring I might as well be fast.

Occasionally, I pause in the shade of an alcove. Listening. There are distant noises outside, but not too close. Are there guards? Someone who watches the slave quarters? I guess I'll find out soon enough. But I discover no one as I venture back through the first atrium.

Footsteps.

Instinctively, I duck behind one of the lush rosemary hedges when someone enters the patio, walking right towards me. My heart stops for a second. Then I force myself to move. On all fours, I crawl along the hedge, reaching the shadows just as a cloaked figure passes, disappearing into the very hallway I just came from.

Shit, that was close.

I don't allow myself a moment of relief. I don't stop long enough to think what would have happened if I'd been caught either.

I cross the patio in a few steps before I push open another door. Silver and copper pans gleam in the dark. Metal treacherously clinks in the breeze that comes in along with me. The kitchen. The perfumed smell of herbs hangs heavily in the air as I bolt down the rows of silvery stone that cross the huge room like railway tracks. Briefly, I consider looking for a knife, given what Nidaw said about the cursed fae in town, but quickly discard the idea, remembering how well my stand-off with my makeshift blade in the woods went.

With a last sprint, I cross the remaining yards toward another door at the end. I stop again there, catching my breath. Then I push it open slightly, peeking into a vast room beyond.

Red moonlight falls in through windows that stretch from the floor all the way up to the enormously high ceiling. More sleek, polished stone pillars line the room. The walls are made from white marble fractured by massive golden veins that seem to consist of pure gold.

My eyes flit to the doorway at the other end, leading out onto what looks like a veranda.

Without thinking, I head toward it, cutting across the large hall until I reach the door. It swings open, and soft, featherlike air embraces me.

I make my way toward a marble railing as the déjà vu hits me. Just hours ago, I sprinted for my supposed freedom from that party. I would run again.

I reach the railing, ready to jump over it, only to stop dead at the last moment. The wicked layout of this complex on its hill has confused all my calculations.

There is no meadow… only a gaping abyss opening up in front of me.

14

RIVEN

Later in the night, a blue-haired nymph rocks up and down on Riven's body, her stunning green eyes ablaze. Yet Riven finds his mind drifting back to the girl in the dungeon. Melody. The way her eyes shone when he found her in the woods. The way her skin felt when he touched her.

The nymph squeezes her thighs tighter against his hips as she climaxes before she collapses on top of him. When Riven looks up, he spots Caryan walking past through the vast hall where they usually spend their evenings together, drinking and fucking. Neither Ronin nor Kyrith seem to notice, too absorbed in similar activities.

Riven gently pushes the woman off him and gets up. He grabs his clothes and trails Caryan out of the hall and along the corridor to Caryan's private rooms. He follows Caryan in uninvited and enters. Caryan's quarters at the top of the Fortress never fail to impress him, with its high walls and a huge open front that looks out over Niavara, the two moons looming over the blue mountain range in the distance, the blood moon casting the peaks into a crimson fire.

Everything is airy and high, with a huge terrace leading out into the night.

It's clearly been built for creatures with wings. You could spread them out anywhere without tipping something over or having to tuck them in tight. Magic seals the windows up here, not glass, allowing Caryan to pass in and out as freely as the wind.

But Riven's favorite part is the terrace leading out into the balmy night. From here, it is as if you stand directly under the stars.

"If you wanted an audience, you should have asked for one," Caryan snarls, keeping his back turned to Riven.

But Riven knows if Caryan didn't want him here, the door would have slammed in his face, or Caryan's power would have blocked him like a wall.

"And you should have showered first. You smell of seaweed."

Riven chuckles quietly at Caryan's remark. All folk of the water—nymphs, mers, and sirens—smell unmistakably of tang and salt, a smell Riven likes and which reminds him of tossing floods and glimmering corals.

Caryan turns to him, his ever-changing eyes shifting between red and some mild blue Riven hardly ever sees on him—he doubts many others have at all.

Caryan allows him to see it, Riven knows. This is how they stand for a while, wordless, the room doused in the dirty red twilight shed by the blood moon.

"What do you want, Riven?" Caryan asks eventually, but his voice has whetted itself to an edge. Caryan knows very well why he is here, feeling everything over the bond.

Riven clears his throat. His voice is solemn, no trace of humor left as he asks, "Do you believe in Kalleandara's prophecy?"

The girl who ends the blight. The blight—a reference to Caryan and his curse.

And Melody, the very girl.

Caryan just shrugs—a strange, human gesture—while Riven drops his clothes in his hand to the ground. There is no point in getting dressed now to keep up any rules of civility. He walks over to the bar built into the wall, pouring each of them a glass of ruby brandy. He saunters back to Caryan and hands him one.

Shoulder to shoulder they stand and look out over the city, until Caryan eventually decides to give him an answer.

"Prophecies hold a certain truth. I have learned that over the years."

There it is—the fact that Caryan is older than all of them. Older than any fae has ever been. He was made immortal by Gatilla. Riven has no clue how long he served Gatilla before Riven himself was forced to join her court. Gatilla reached an age no witch or elf should ever be able to, no doubt due to her stolen magic. She made herself immortal, or at least thought she had. Until Caryan proved her wrong when he found a way to circumvent it—when he sucked all the magic out of her. Her supposed immortality went with it, transferred to Caryan.

But that Caryan cannot die naturally does not mean he cannot be *killed*, as far as Riven is aware.

Riven watches Caryan take another sip from the glass, that strange blue still in his eyes. Whatever the reason is, Riven knows it has something to do with that girl. "I am not sure that answers my question," he says quietly.

"What do you want to know, then?" Shadows curl off Caryan's powerful shoulders, dancing in a breeze like smoke.

"Do you believe prophecies hold true in general or can they be changed?"

"They point out the inevitable. But I think you should go to bed now. We need to go to the borders tomorrow," Caryan answers casually before he turns away, striding towards the double-winged door that leads to his private chambers. Too casually, dismissing him. It stirs a strange kind of slumbering anger in Riven.

Riven steps into the shadows. Only to appear right in front of Caryan again, blocking his way.

A flicker of fury—maybe also disbelief—flashes across Caryan's features before his face turns arctic. Black power rips from him, licking up Riven's bare skin, ready to strike.

Riven just inclines his chin, forcing himself to keep his face schooled in careful indifference. Only years as the cruel enforcer of Palisandre and the years at Gatilla's court after that make his heart rate stay calm, his breathing even.

He will pay for this, he knows. But he will pay gladly.

He pushes, "They say she ends the blight. The blight is you."

Caryan's eyes shift, the blue replaced by a blazing amber promising violence.

Yet Riven continues, "Does she mean your end?"

"What exactly is your question, Riven?" Another growl. A concession, though. Something Caryan has granted him, those deadly shadows still curling, waiting. Suspended. *For now.*

"Why bring her here then? Why not hide her? Hide her from anyone, even from you? I could do it. I'll take her to the end of the world if you want me to and never return." He means every word. He would do *anything* to prevent Caryan's certain death. Even if it breaks his own heart.

A second passes between them, unspoken. The embers in Caryan's eyes dim like fire without oxygen. "The prophecy says she will end the blight, but we do not yet know in what way she will end the blight—or me, if you will. I brought her here to find out."

"No, you brought her here to find what only she can find. To gain more power. You brought her here to retrieve those relics. The elven artifacts. You want to use her talent, just as Lyrian did."

Caryan's teeth snap right into his face as fast as a lash of black lightning. He growls, "Not. Like. Lyrian." Just as fast as he came, Caryan pulls back, and all that unholy magic with him. When he speaks again, his voice is slick as ice, so at odds with the black fire that still dances in his eyes. "Very careful, Riven, or I'm going to draw some more blood tonight."

Riven pushes on regardless. "Then do it. But it needs to be said—keeping her here is tantamount to suicide."

"I'm not going to warn you a second time," Caryan seethes. His upper lip curls back, baring his fangs to their full length.

"She is a half-blood, Caryan!"

Half-bloods. So rare among the fae. Most of them are born with no magic at all, yet some… Some bear magic that is even more devastating than the magic of a high fae or a witch. Along with unique talents and skills. This is what makes them so feared.

"Her magic can be cataclysmic. And you don't even know what else slumbers in her blood."

"Hold your tongue, Riven." Power fills the room, wavering in the corners and bristling all around them, charging the air like a thunderstorm. Abyss save him, keeping his ground when Caryan is like this feels like weathering a storm. A deadly storm that will crush you and drown you and spit you out broken.

Riven flashes his teeth back. Hells, never has he overstepped so far. "No. It needs to be said—what you are looking for can't be so valuable to risk having her here. You're putting everything at risk. Everything you've built."

"And everything can crumble to dust with the next war, Riven. I need those relics to win it." Caryan's voice is pure ice, streaks of black lightning now sizzling through the air. Ready to strike and maim and burn.

Riven ignores them. "You don't. I have already spoken to leaders of other courts. We can get their support. I can win them over. They will have our back if we offer them something in return, side with us instead of Palisandre. I have also been successful in infiltrating the elven kingdoms, we—"

Caryan cuts him off. "Having them at my back gives them the perfect opportunity to drive a knife in. I have seen this game too often."

"You can't risk your own life, Caryan! Her very mother almost killed you!" Riven waits for Caryan's magic to cleave him. But the surge of power ripples away and subsides, and Caryan's eyes turn dark again. Riven doesn't know what is worse—that Caryan doesn't punish him or the vacant expression on his face.

"I told you that prophecies point out the inevitable. Even if the girl means my end... I can't escape my fate."

Riven feels his own heart in his chest breaking, as if something keeps piercing it again and again, prying it apart. Shattering it. His voice breaks, too, as he murmurs, "I can't allow it."

"Can't allow what, Riven? You can't outrun your destiny, or mine for that matter."

"We must be able to do *something*."

Caryan only slowly shakes his head.

"Send her away! Send me away with her! I beseech you!" he tries again, desperation tingeing every word.

"You know the paradox of a prophecy—of fate? You don't know in what way it will be fulfilled, Riven. You don't know which of those steps you take are planned and which are random. But fate always finds a way, no matter how much you bend it, or even outsmart it. It will catch up, even if you try to run away with her." Caryan's voice has a finality that creeps like ice under Riven's skin, makes him shiver from the inside, turning it dead.

"That's not true. Meanara changed fate when she saved your life. There is always another way. Please, Caryan. Let's go to the great oracle again. Let's ask Kalleandara for another way!"

"I have already done that, Riven. She told me that it is sealed, was sealed the day Meanara decided to cure me."

Meanara, the great healer of Avandal. Riven just stands there, arms slack at his sides, unable to find words. Caryan has already consulted the oracle. His last scrap of hope swiped away.

And burnt to ashes.

It only makes it worse when Caryan adds quietly, "My fate won't include you, though. Nor Kyrith or Ronin. You will live, I made sure of that. The oracle promised."

Riven can't help it. Can't help but fall to his knees then, resting his forehead against Caryan's thigh, allowing his eyes to drift shut. "You can't, Caryan. There must be a way…"

Caryan gently runs his fingers through Riven's hair. "Go, Riven. Sleep. Even we must sleep. It's been a long night. And I need you ready tomorrow. Darker times are approaching."

With this, Caryan steps away from him, turning his back and walking out of the room into the next one. The door closes behind him with a saturated thud, shutting Riven out.

Riven stays there, on the floor, on his knees. If he was a mortal, he would weep. But fae can't cry, so he waits for the tightness in his chest, in his heart, to ease enough that he can breathe again.

125

He will find a way.

He will not allow his closest friend, his brother, to die. He can't.

He grabs his clothes from where he dropped them on the floor and puts them back on before he ventures out, back into the quiet halls.

He will find a way.

And if the girl is the one to kill Caryan one day, he is going to find out how... and prevent it.

The cold air bites his skin as he enters the dungeon. But when he walks up to the cell where he carefully laid Melody down some hours ago, he finds it empty.

So Caryan allowed her out after all. *Strange.* Caryan isn't known for mercy, or pity.

Yet... he should have known by the blue in Caryan's eyes. Melody somehow caused it, Riven knows. In his experience, the blue indicates the moments Caryan comes closest to feeling *something*. And the girl made Caryan feel something after all these years.

Riven runs a hand through his hair. Yes, he *should* have known. As he should have known so many other things, damn him. That Caryan always planned to keep her in the first place. Riven, as Caryan's right hand, should have anticipated it. Sensed it. But he had been so focused on finding her that he never even entertained another possibility other than that Caryan would eliminate her immediately.

Riven lets out a long breath while he keeps staring at the empty cell. He was a fool.

But that Melody managed to trigger Caryan, in whatever way... maybe it's a key. A clue, a hint to follow up on. He will take everything into consideration to cheat fate. To save his brother.

He turns and walks away, ignoring all the hushed, pleading voices from the other cells, following him up the stairs.

He stops in the hall where he dropped her bag, the black duffle bag containing all her belongings. So little. He tries not to remember the reek of desperation that clung in every fiber of her loveless, barren room. In the linen of her bedsheets. In the curtains. In the colorless carpet. The scent of distress. Of panic. Of undiluted fear and desperation, so dense it felt like acid in his nose.

No wonder she tried to fight him, to run from him in the woods. No wonder she didn't want to go back to Lyrian's house.

Whatever Lyrian had done to her, it was terrible. It was hard to follow Caryan's wishes. Not only because of what Riven just said to his friend. Not only because bringing the girl here means fulfilling Kalleandara's prophecy, knowing her presence will affect Caryan's fate, but also to do this to her—bring her here and dump her in the middle of a cruel fae court.

She deserves some calm, some peace, some happiness, and being a slave here…

He clenches his teeth, unwilling to pursue that train of thought.

Duffle bag in hand, he walks straight to the slave quarters, following the faint trace of her scent up to a tiny room.

But when he opens the door, the room too is empty.

BLAIR

Blair sits on the landing platform, legs dangling off the edge, the cold wind soaring up, cutting into her face. To her right, the new mighty Cloudcleaver reaches like a spear, penetrating the clouds.

She's been sitting here for two hours, trying to get her head straight while she watches her mighty wyvern circle the tower. The beast's screeches tear through the wild currents and the hungry, moonlight-drenched quiet that's lurking beneath, her luminous rainbow-body unbattered by the occasional hailstones.

"Yeah, I've missed you too," Blair mutters.

Hells, her wyvern is so beautiful that whenever Blair watches her flying, it takes her breath away and a sentiment close to… tenderness is clefting her heart. Not for the first time Blair thinks how different she looks to all the other wyverns with her unusual iridescent scales, her two white, twirling horns, her rounded snout and a tail that ends in three long whips of silken strands, the three deadly tips shaped and sharp like dagger-blades hidden under their feathery plumes.

A creature made to inspire beauty and awe instead of bloodshed and death.

At least at first glance.

Next to her, the other wyverns, most of them massive beasts with thick, leathery skins and tails tailored to maim and kill, look more like instruments of war. Beautiful and terrifying in a different way.

Blair sighs, flexing her claws. It usually works—coming out here to detangle that mess of her mind and the ridiculous beating organ behind her ribs—but not this time.

Instead, she's just started shivering from the relentless cold. The wind is so icy it can bite the flesh from your bones. Perenilla owns these lands in the north, but she doesn't want to waste any magic to make the weather a little kinder, so this stretch of land is merciless, the landscape around Akribea nothing but dead, burned soil, covered by hoarfrost and haunted by snowstorms and blizzards.

Blair aches for the human world.

In the human world, she'd just turn the music louder and dance it off. Or go to a club. Or get her brain fucked out. She grinds her teeth.

There's nothing worth living for here. No sun. Just rain. Cold, icy rain that might quickly turn into ice.

Abyss, she hates every second of it. So much has changed since her aunt died. And at the same time, nothing has.

She closes her eyes, baring her teeth, the cold biting her lips like a cruel lover.

It's true what Perenilla said—she *did* stand beside the carnage. She did *nothing* while Caryan killed her aunt. Slaughtering her aunt's seven witches along with her.

Blair's never thought back on it since the moment she ran out that door and sprinted down that collapsing staircase, escaping sure death through a window.

As if a part of her died with her aunt that night.

Why did Caryan let her go? Because he was too badly hurt to do anything else. He sure as the hells had been in no state to chase a witch on her wyvern through a storm. But no one would care for the full truth, would they? All that matters is that Blair stood apart and watched her aunt being slaughtered.

It would be considered nothing other than treason.

Even now, with the scene playing over and over in her head,

Blair doesn't know why she didn't act. Didn't defend her aunt. Her own blood. The woman she owed so much—not love, witches don't love. But they do feel respect. And gratitude.

Treason—so this is the reason Perenilla keeps her around. Knowing that tiny calamitous detail about her. One word from Perenilla's mouth and Blair is as good as dead. Since fae can't lie, it's enough to just state those fact as facts.

Fuck, how could she not see that coming?

Blair doesn't turn when she hears the familiar rhythm of Aurora's steps behind her.

"Are you alright?" her mother asks, resting her hand on Blair's shoulder.

"Why wouldn't I be?" Blair snaps and dismisses her wyvern with a wave of her hand.

"Because you've been sitting here since you left the dungeon, and I can smell the blood all over you," Aurora answers calmly, her white nose already turning red from the biting cold.

Blair clenches her fists against the need to hug Aurora, to feel her body against hers. Soak in her mother's reassuring warmth. She wants to tell her how much she missed them. How she thought she'd never see them again. Instead, she digs her sharp nails so deep into the palms of her hands that they pierce flesh.

She says as lightly as she can, "You know me—pretty face, dark, badass soul."

"Come inside with me. Let me see to those wounds, Blair," Aurora retorts gently, as if she can see right through the act.

"We need to leave soon," Blair says as if she hasn't heard the words. She doesn't deserve to have her wounds healed. She doesn't deserve any of Aurora's kindness. She's drawn them into this mess. She's doomed them.

"Where?" Aurora asks.

"We need to find that girl I failed to capture in the human world."

A suicidal mission.

Hells, she can't allow anything to happen to them, yet Perenilla's order is clear—Sofya and Aurora must go with her.

"Why only us?" Aurora asks, frowning.

"Because Perenilla doesn't want to spare more witches and we happen to be the chosen ones," Blair snarls. She's just so fucking angry at herself. She needs a way to get Aurora and Sofya out, even if she knows Perenilla plans for them to die along with her. But if they return, Perenilla might let them live, deeming them no longer a threat…

Maybe.

Dark times when all Blair can do is hope.

Aurora looks over her shoulder, then leans in closer. Not that anyone is around, but at this court, you never know. "We can't, Blair. You can't be serious. We don't even know what the prophecy means."

Blair frowns. She's never heard her mom speak like that before. She's always believed both of her mothers fiercely loyal to their queen.

"We do know that the girl has the talent to find the elven relics."

"But you know what will happen if Perenilla gets her hands on them." Aurora's eyes simmer with justified fear.

"I *do* know," Blair barks back, her teeth snapping toward her mother.

To her credit, Aurora doesn't flinch. She holds Blair's gaze, challenging. "Then we can't."

"And what do you suggest? Just say no and ride off into the sunset?" Blair barks, not caring to hide her sarcasm. She needs this anger. Anger is better than the void of sadness that tries to swallow her whole. Better than the fear for Aurora and Sofya that threatens to suffocate her.

"Kill the girl. Kill her straight away. When she's gone, no one gets the magic. Not Caryan, not Perenilla. It's lost forever. Eventually. As it always should have been."

The truth hits Blair, although she can't say why. She's killed so many. Men and women alike. It has never mattered to her. But that girl, that woman—Blair owes her a life debt.

That girl, for some reason beyond Blair's comprehension, *cared* enough for her to save her. Blair looks back out over the unfertile lands fading into nothingness. "It's not so bad, you know, the human world. You're free. Can you imagine how that feels? No one whips you or throws you in a dungeon. No one there to behead you or burn you to cinders either."

The words get swallowed up by the wind, Blair's voice so low she hopes Aurora hasn't heard them.

But Aurora frowns, her amber eyes burning. "That is a deadly thing to say, Blair."

"It wasn't me who started it."

"Killing the girl is one thing, Blair. Perenilla might forgive you one day. She will come around to see that it is better she's dead than in Caryan's hands."

"Bullshit," Blair snaps. "As if that bitch wouldn't love to see me burn."

"Blair, please. Don't say such things."

"I know, I know—it's *dangerous, boo-hoo*. But what of it? It's true. I'm over a fucking hundred years old and I have never been free in my life. I've been over there often and it's… it's different. You would like it, to no longer be shackled by these archaic rules," Blair says, the words tumbling out of her before she can hinder them. But she wants Aurora to understand. To see that future as a possibility for them too. She doesn't know how much more time she has with them.

And she could see the three of them so clearly, so beautifully— getting ice cream and manicures together. Doing fancy Sunday brunches in cafés and movie nights in pajamas, one of them grabbing rancid Chinese food on their way home.

It would be easy. Light.

They would be happy.

Aurora just stares at her and Blair blinks back to reality. Aurora, two hundred years older than Blair, is the closest thing to a friend Blair has ever had. To family. Not that they are friends. Witches have no friends. They have no lovers. They sleep with each other.

Some do, or with men, but they never *love*. It is a need, a relief, a satisfaction. A necessity.

Nothing more.

"You know that you would be accused of treason if someone hears you talking like that. Running away is not an option. Besides, it would never work."

"But what if… what if I can make it work?" Blair asks quietly. Aurora leans in and tucks a strand of Blair's crimson hair behind her ear. Then she says softly, "Only cowards run. So we won't. And you're Gatilla's heir."

Blair's head flies up. "Yeah, I know I am. And so what?"

"A lot of witches still look up to you. Why do you think Perenilla hasn't yet dared to turn against you?"

"It's a fucking burden, Aurora. A burden I'm not sure I want to carry. My heritage is something Perenilla has made me pay for every day since she's been in power."

"I know, but you must not call it a burden, Blair. You should see it as a chance. You are meant for more. Do not throw that away so lightly."

They would turn away when they see that their beacon is nothing but a hollow promise. A coward—*you're nothing but a coward.* Perenilla's words struck home. Her aunt made a mistake in making her heir. Blair never had any interest in stepping into her aunt's shoes, in claiming the throne. A dreamer. That's what she is.

There is pleading in Aurora's voice, and the same timid flame of hope shining in her eyes—a flame that refuses to die—that makes Blair focus back on the conversation, makes her swallow her fury, her despair and relent. Makes her say, "You are right."

She can see Aurora's delicate shoulders sag with relief as she entwines her icy fingers with Blair's. But if Blair had a human heart, it would break from what lies ahead of her.

"I'm so proud of you. Come now, Blair. Let me see to your wounds, please."

16

MELODY

"Please don't jump. Not even the Dark Lord himself would be able to breathe life into a rather unsavory mess of bones and flesh."

I swivel on my heels toward the familiar voice, only to meet violet eyes, sparkling with dark amusement.

Riven stands there in the shadow in front of one of the large windows, clad in an elegant black tunic, one hand in his pocket, a whiskey tumbler in the other. "It's good to see you woke up so quickly. Most sleep much longer after their first contact with magic," he says. "Now you certainly want to tell me what exactly it is that you're doing *here* at this late hour?"

I just look back at him. There's no point in denying that I've been trying to escape.

He casually saunters closer, not once taking his eyes off me. It makes me feel like prey in front of a deadly, sleek predator. Reflexively, I draw back. I meet hard, cold stone pressing into my lower back.

Riven stops halfway to me, his gaze sweeping over me only once before it comes to rest at my neck. A frown enters his face. "Please... don't. Let's keep that lovely neck of yours in one piece. He will not be too pleased if you meet such an ignominious end."

His expression has become serious, the teasing, dark amusement from just a moment ago, wiped off.

"You mean if *his food* tumbled to its death? Maybe that's better than what awaits me here." I can't help my tone.

A muscle feathers in his jaw and for a moment his eyes lose their shine. "I'm serious," he adds, dead stern.

"Oh, so am I," I snap back. However nice he's been to me, he's also the one who brought me here. Maybe I'm being reckless because he is also dangerous. Underneath his elegant and well-mannered façade, a different kind of danger radiates from him like a pulse. A quieter kind, but lethal all the more.

A danger that made Lyrian break out in cold sweat. A danger that made Lyrian grovel on his knees with a snip of his fingers.

He cocks his head to the side. "I see. Do you know what we do to slaves who try to escape?" His voice has fallen to a quiet purr, more feline than human, the sound traveling down my body. "No? Nidaw didn't tell you… she probably should have. But allow me to flesh it out for you. We flay them. Fifteen lashes. The *first* time."

I stare at him, unable to move when he draws closer. He towers over me, as tall as the Dark Lord. My heart skips a beat before it starts to hammer.

"Please don't tell him." I'm not too proud to beg. I wouldn't let myself beg Lyrian for mercy, but I would beg Riven.

"You want me to *lie* to the Dark Lord." It's not a question, but rather a statement. Mocking again. When I don't answer, his full lips curl into something close to a smile. "You are too adorable. But you already know we can't lie."

They can't lie—so it's true what Lyrian said at his house. I stash the information for later. *If* there is a later.

"But you can withhold things, can't you?" I'm not sure; it's a stab in the dark. "I'll give you something for it. Whatever you want," I add quickly.

"Do you think you possess anything of interest to me?" His words sound pejorative and cruel, and I remember the way the Dark Lord looked at me in that dungeon. Disgusted, yet hungry.

I retreat out of instinct, or at least try to. Again, there's the balustrade pushing against the small of my back and no escape. A breeze comes up and I smell him, a beguiling mixture of woods and moss and lilac. He's so close I can see the black kohl under his eyes, the elegant curl of those absurdly long lashes, a touch of gold dust on his eyelids, on his cheeks, the diamonds and gemstones still dangling from his beautiful arched ears.

He doesn't at all look like a vampire. Rather like an elven prince, save for the fangs that flash behind his lips when he smiles and the vicious gleam in his eyes. A predator playing with his food.

"My blood, maybe?" I force the words out. *What else can he want? What else can I possibly give him?*

I close my eyes when he lifts his hand. His fingertips trace the curve of my chin a moment later, the way he did in the woods, before he tilts my head back.

His words shape over my skin, gently, coaxingly, like a lover. "I can't say I'm not tempted. I'm sure you taste rather... exquisite, Melody."

At the sound of my name from his lips I open my eyes. His burn like lilac stars. My heart startles again and a flush creeps up my throat, heating my skin.

"But I must decline with this warning. Don't offer your blood to *anyone*, ever."

He pulls back, but his fingertips stay on my cheek. Yet there's no jolt from his touch, so different from when the Dark Lord touched me. In that dungeon, my skin was electrified everywhere. To a point where it is painful. It rattled me, while this here... it terrifies me in a different way.

"Why?" I make my voice sound cold.

His fingers slide down my skin, brushing over the mark where the Dark Lord's teeth buried themselves. I freeze at the touch, at the flicker that suddenly flares up at that very spot like a warning.

He says darkly, "Because it might be your death sentence. We are slaves to sanguine hunger and tremendous appetite. Only a few of us can master enough self-control to stop after a few sips. Besides, the Dark Lord most certainly won't appreciate it if I sucked his property dry. Not when he has already marked you."

He laughs quietly as he suddenly pulls his hand back, as if all of this is somehow funny. But the humor doesn't reach his eyes. "But I mean what I said—stay as far away as you can and be vigilant. The same goes for contracts with fae. Never enter into a bargain with a fae. And never make promises."

I feel a twist in my belly. "Why not?"

"Because such bargains are the reasons mortals are stolen away. They always come with a sting in their tail. And promises will most likely be used against you, since no fae can break them once made."

"But I'm no fae," I say carefully, thinking about the promise I made to that siren Nidaw.

He narrows his eyes. "You're half-fae," he corrects me.

Half-fae. Again, that term. I don't know what to say. What that means for me. What that means for my parents. If this is true, one of my parents must have been an elf. The fact that I know so little about any of it hits me hard, but I swallow it down for now.

"Well, whatever. I can lie, you know," I add viciously, inclining my chin. Something I have over them. But the actual reason I'm giving my trump card away is that I need to know whether breaking my promise to Nidaw would indeed result in something unpleasant.

He angles his head as if he's seen me in a new light. "My cheeky little pup, so full of surprises. I must confess I've never even entertained that possibility."

I raise my brows. "No? Not even when I told you how good you look?" With that I try to slink past him, but he steps in my way, looking down at me.

"Maybe I was straight-out lying," I add.

He licks his teeth, tilting his head, obviously annoyed. "You weren't."

I just shrug. "Some say vanity is a weakness."

He says, full teeth flashing, "It's an indulgence, I grant you. Now tell me that you weren't lying." He grabs my wrist so fast I can't follow. Wrenching me close. His eyes briefly rest on my lips, and it does something to me. The way they rove over my face then.

Keeping my voice light, I offer, "I could. We can make a bargain."

He bares his teeth at me again and it takes a lot not to recoil. Not that he would let me.

"I hate to repeat myself, but I will for your sake. Bargains are off-limits, Melody. I mean that. Make as many promises as you like since you obviously can lie and it won't have any consequences for you. But never, ever make a bargain."

"Why? It's not like I'm selling my soul, right?" I'm pushing him, I know I am. But I need to know more. If I'm stuck in this world, I must learn as much as I can about it.

He relents. "It is like selling a shard of your soul. You bind a part of you to someone else. You can be forced to do things you do not want to do. Such a contract only dies once its terms are fulfilled, or one party is dead. So believe me when I say, do not. Now, go and get some sleep."

I notice the pain in his aura and wonder what kind of bargain he'd once struck. But I don't dare ask.

He lets go of me and steps aside, but then adds like an afterthought, "And Melody—don't get caught. Do not get yourself into trouble... please."

I pause at the last word, only to walk away briskly. Too aware that I've just turned my back on him and not liking it at all.

But then I stop, halfway, turning back to him. "You *promised* to protect me." My words are barely a whisper, but I know he heard every word.

I want to know whether he meant it, in the woods. Whether he indeed *must* hold to his promise.

Darkness sweeps over his face, but he dips his elegant chin once. A half-finished nod. "I did. But I can't always be around. You will find your belongings in your room. I took the liberty of bringing them."

One look at his boots and I know then. Know that he was the hooded figure who walked through that patio. Not a watchman, but him. A strange, new sensation coils through me at that. A different one.

He came to look after me.

Before he can see the flicker of emotion on my face, I turn and hurry back to my room.

$$\supset \cdot \subset$$

I lie on my bed and watch the two moons for a very long time. Despite my exhaustion, sleep won't come, so eventually I get up and go over to the black duffle bag sitting next to the bed like a foreign object. Like I myself, lost in another world.

I gingerly open it to find some of my old clothes and my paints and brushes, as well as some paper I managed to stuff in there. Everything has miraculously survived the sea water, and I wonder whether Riven put some kind of glamour on it, or whether the sea here just follows different laws. Either way, I'm grateful.

I take them over to my bed. There isn't enough time to paint, and I don't have any canvas anyway, so I start to draw Riven's face.

I must have fallen asleep, because when I wake, a silvery sun gleams on the horizon, the desert land enshrouded by morning mist, and I'm lying curled up next to my drawing.

17

BLAIR, TWO YEARS BEFORE
GATILLA'S DEATH

It was deep into the night, and Blair was still trying to clean her wounds while she waited for them to close fully. It took too long, thanks to the iron slowing her healing to the rate of a lesser fae. Every form of metal was bad. After Nefarian steel, which was utterly deadly, silver and iron inflicted the worst damage.

Blair closed her eyes and gritted her teeth against the pain as her fingers pulled another ribbon of shredded fabric out of a wound. Her aunt hadn't allowed her to take off her flying leathers and silken shirt before Riven whipped her.

She still saw the pale elf's pained face in her mind. The remorse on his remarkable features the moment he went up to the platform with her and his elegant fingers unfurled the whip. His teeth, bared against the command. But he had no choice. He couldn't resist Gatilla's order, even if he wanted to.

None of her slaves could.

Blair blinked a few times, trying to shake the image off. Hells, she wasn't too fond of the elf. All the less because Caryan had taken some liking to him. He had been the one to enslave the elf in the first place and bring him here. Why, Blair hadn't yet found out.

Blair had taken the lashing without a sound. Without a plea or scream. Without any reaction at all, just as any witch would have done. After that, she'd returned down to the council chamber and sat bleeding through the whole meeting.

War. They'd be flying to war against Palisandre.

It was deep into the night when wing beats filled the air and Caryan appeared through her window. He leaned against the wall, his powerful arms crossed in front of his body, no trace of the mighty, black wings from a moment before. He'd dismissed them the moment he set foot in here as he always did. Blair once asked whether she could touch them, but he denied her. She never dared to ask again. Afraid of another rejection.

She found his dark eyes resting on her naked, still bleeding back. She got up from the chair and slowly walked toward him, dropping the towel already stained red with her blood as she went.

He just kept looking at her in that stoic way of his. His eyes, still and dark and ancient, and his irises faded to a gloomy red. A horizon announcing doom.

"Addressing me as Caryan, Blair? You're getting reckless," was all he said when she paused in front of him.

She resisted the urge to crane her neck. She already felt small but having him looking at her like that made her feel tiny. Young, but in a bad way. He had that effect on her. Always. She always tried to look alluring around him, to say something witty and sharp.

In the beginning, she even tried to make him laugh or smile. But Caryan never smiled, let alone laughed, which only made her feel more stupid for even trying.

Being reprimanded didn't make it any better.

She covered it as she always did—with teasing. "My commander. Seriously?"

His remarkable eyes shifted into a prickling amber that promised a challenge, not unlike her own as he took her in.

So fucking beautiful.

"I mean it," he retorted, unmoved. "Leash your temper."

"Oh, I mean it too, believe me," she crooned right back.

"That you bow to no one?"

She grinned at his tone. Hells, he was still pissed. She could see the dark tendrils of magic coming off him.

She stretched out a hand to touch him, but he caught her wrist in midair.

"It's been three fucking weeks," she whispered when his face stayed stern, no trace of softness. No, he was ancient and cold. If she was fire, he was eternal stone under a glacier. And still, she burned and burned and burned. Three fucking weeks without seeing him. Touching him. Tasting him. It almost drove her mad. It was that way since they started sleeping with each other and the fire hadn't ceased. Quite the contrary. All she could think about was him.

Whenever her aunt sent her away, it made her restless, nervous, and aching.

He kept her locked in place when she tried to yank her hand back. With an effortlessness that made a completely different form of heat pool between her legs. Fuck, she needed him everywhere.

He just tilted his head slightly when she attempted to wriggle free a second time. "Sometimes I wonder what will get you killed faster—your stubbornness or your temper."

She cocked an eyebrow. "My temper? I thought you liked that about me."

"I can't deny a certain attraction."

"I need to touch you," she said then, no longer caring that her voice had fallen to a whispered plea. Unashamed of how plaintive she sounded. It was true. She needed him more than she needed blood, food or even water. And the thought that her aunt would be sending her away earlier than planned… that she won't even have two more nights with him, made her want to cry.

"Please, Caryan…" she whispered again when he kept holding her. Before him, she'd never begged for a thing in her life. Certainly never for a man. Hells, she'd never let herself be under a man before, but now that was what she lived and died for.

Letting go of her wrist, as if he could hear every dark thought she'd ever had, he said, "Then get down on your knees and beg for it."

The night was waning. The moonlight danced over his perfect face, his honed, sweat-slicked angelic body when they finally parted. He got up, as always. Never holding her. Never staying through the night. He went to the window, gazing up at the moon.

She swallowed down her pride, her hurt, and just watched him, memorizing every detail of his chiseled body, although she already knew it by heart. Every ridge and pane.

It truly hurt to look at him.

Next to him, even she felt common. Average. It was a kind of beauty that made you ache.

She sat up eventually. Slowly, so slowly, her mind came back to reality. To what her aunt declared before. *War.*

"So it's truly going to happen. We are going to war with Palisandre?" Blair asked, still not quite believing it.

"Those lands are drained of their essence. It's the only logical next step to acquire more magic."

"She already has enough magic as it is."

He glanced at her. "Greed and the thirst for power are insatiable."

Blair frowned. "You make it sound as if you agree with her."

"I don't. I just have been wandering the grounds of this world for too long." There it was again, the fact that Caryan was so old it was hard for even her to grasp.

She didn't like the change in his tone though. His voice was lush with menace and marvelously unsentimental.

"We don't even have an army," she said, feeling foolish already for even trying to talk him out of this.

"Gatilla thinks we don't need an army with these runes on my body. She finished them the night before."

Caryan didn't look at her as he said that. He merely stretched out his right arm where the gold-and-black runes Gatilla gave him writhed over his skin like a beautiful, strange kind of snake. He looked at them as if they weren't part of his body though.

Blair got up and carefully walked up to him to look at them more closely. It was a language so old it was long forgotten by the world. Symbols, drawn and inked into his flesh with the help of Ciellara, the silver elf— the only one still versed in the dark languages. When Blair asked her once, she said those runes came from the depths of the black hell, the last of the nine hells, itself. That those words had been whispered in the tongues of the devils when the fae had still been as fragile and mortal as humans.

Before magic spread over the lands.

Silver elves themselves were more legend than anything. Books said they had been hunted down to extinction like the angels, too feared for their strange powers and the never-dying knowledge of the worlds that flowed through their blood. Books Blair read as a child. Books that sounded like fairy tales, talking about the other worlds. About the nine hells and the Abyss. Vivid stories that came along with a glossary of hellish beasts.

Ciellara, the last silver elf in existence. She'd spent her life hiding away from everyone when Gatilla found her. A secret daughter of Evander, evil tongues hissed in shadows and dark corners. They said she'd brought shame over her house, over her father Regus, the right hand of the former king of Palisandre, when she refused a mating bond.

Blair didn't know whether that was true. But Ciellara was hunted, had been hunted, and would be for the rest of her life.

With silver elves, secrets never died. And secrets were dangerous. Deadly.

Her aunt had offered Ciellara shelter in exchange for the runes. Gatilla had her working on Caryan, carving wild, raw magic into his skin with a needle made of monster bone, ink from the hells, and infernal fire from the dwarfen forge deep below, close to the hot and living core of this world.

With those runes, Gatilla and Ciellara turned Caryan into an abomination.

But the tattoo on Caryan's body—seeing it with her own eyes,

144

Blair couldn't deny that, apart from the unholy power it was brimming with like a heartbeat, it was also breathtaking.

Horrifying. Mesmerizing.

Blair bit back the need to ask how Caryan had managed to bear the pain. It was said that there was no greater pain than infusing a body with magic. One tattoo took an eternity. And Caryan had *a lot*.

Blair swallowed.

The endless hours he'd spent in the darkest, hottest core of the amethyst tower, chained to the altar. Only to be taken apart and pierced together anew by that unholy magic. Forged anew. Bit by bit.

Gatilla put him through hell. And he still came out unbroken.

Someone other than Caryan would have long ago gone mad from the pain. It was dark, dark magic. Some before her aunt had tried to do the same but failed. Black heretics. Feared and utterly skilled mages and witches. But the result had always been madness for the receiver of such runes. Had always ended in a fatal bloodbath, the dark creation usually killing everyone around, including the heretics themselves.

Blair was grateful that Caryan was alive, the forgotten gods help her, but the truth was—he shouldn't be. It shouldn't have been possible.

She carefully touched his skin, the runes there. She hissed and pulled her hand back at the singeing pain the touch evoked before the runes dispersed like a swarm of bees, slithering away from her hand as if they didn't wish to be touched.

A sinister kind of power sizzled through the air then.

Blair drew in a sharp breath as she sensed the magnitude of Caryan's unfettered power for the first time. As if it had been hiding from her senses all that time and only now revealed itself.

No, not he. Her aunt. Because she held the reins of his power, controlled it.

But when had Caryan grown so powerful? When in the last two years? And that was even without him having access to the reservoir.

It was so strong, so endless, it knocked the breath from her lungs.

Finally, she said, "Palisandre has cellars and cellars full of weapons forged of Nefarian steel."

No matter how powerful Caryan was, she still didn't want that war. And no matter how powerful, they still had brought the angels down with Nefarian steel. Caryan might be the strongest fae in existence, but he was not immortal.

He offered her his profile as he answered, "Not anymore. There is no Nefarian steel left in this world, your aunt made sure of that."

"What? You can't know that for sure."

"I do, as a fact, know for sure." She sucked in a sharp breath at the reprimand.

"Well, even if that is true, there is always some secret stash of someone clever who likes to trade. One arrow is more than enough to kill you."

His eyes flickered when he looked back at her fully. As if he would weigh his next words carefully. "Maybe. But I'm immune to Nefarian steel."

A confession.

Her eyes widened. She wanted to ask—because of the runes? But she kept quiet because it would ruin the moment.

So she clamped down on her damn curiosity and asked instead, "How do you feel?"

It was the closest she ever got to talking with him about what Gatilla had done to him. She'd once before asked him and he said nothing. Just nothing. She'd never asked again.

His face was severe in the dim light, the candles accentuating his cruel beauty. Desire undid her so hard she could barely breathe. She needed him again. She resisted the urge to run her fingers past the sculpted muscles of his abdomen and down. Shit, they had one night, and she didn't want to spend it talking about war, selfish as it was. No, all she wanted was to stay in his arms forever and let the world pass them by.

She thought that, again, he'd leave her without an answer, but he finally said, "It feels strange, I must admit."

She could imagine. No more torture. No more pain. Just all that power.

She leaned in and whispered against his naked chest. "We can't go to war. There will be too many casualties." Gods help her, she remembered her mother's vivid stories about the Demon Wars all too well. She couldn't risk their lives. She couldn't allow anything to happen to them.

"Another war is coming inevitably, Blair. Whether you want it or not."

"We struck a truce with Palisandre." She sounded almost defiant.

"I've waged more wars than I can count. A brittle alliance can never be mended. It can only break, and it will."

"Gatilla's been planning that for a while now, hasn't she?" She didn't bother to keep the bitterness from her voice. The spite.

"She has."

"You could have told me."

"I couldn't. She forbade it," he answered dryly.

"You could have found a way." He could have left something for her to see. To find.

"It won't have changed anything." The casual frankness of his answer felt cruel.

So cruel she took a step back from him. "Maybe it would." It sounded childish.

All the more as he retorted, "No. It would have been all the same."

He was so unfazed, so free of remorse, that she let out a warning snarl, baring her teeth at him. He was right, but this was wrong. She deserved to know. The gesture would have sent every other man fleeing for his life, but Caryan didn't so much as spare a side-glance at her.

As if she was nothing more than a nuisance. A fly on his food. Gods, she'd love to throw something at him. The bottle of wine she'd had, that chair. Or probably, most likely, herself.

"Do not, Blair." His voice was a cold, but subtle, silken warning before he turned his powerful back on her, the runes twining and untwining, ever-changing, dancing over his shoulder blades.

She hissed. "Fuck you." No one, not even Caryan, turned his back on a witch.

All he said was, "You know what the most tiresome truth is you learn when you gaze into the Abyss of eternity? It's that everyone is so predictable."

Blair felt as if something tried to crack her open. "I'm not." She felt like a child the moment she said it. But fuck him. Fuck this. She was tired and bloodless, and she just learned they'd be flying to fucking war tomorrow. "You know what? You're a fucking ass sometimes!"

He whipped his head to her so quickly, his pupils flaring open. Despite her anger, she took a step back, banging into the desk behind her. He stepped closer, watching her in that cold, assessing way of his that always made her feel as if she was a book and he was reading all her ridiculous little secrets.

His sullen mouth pulled into the shyest hint of a smile when he noticed her startled heartbeat. Her breathing. For a second, she glimpsed the yawning fissure deep inside him. Before his face shuttered.

"Careful, Blair."

Two simple words laced with hundreds of years of violence. It was always that tone of his that sent a thrill through her body and bones. A dark king's voice.

"You look scared," he drawled.

She was. Sometimes he *did* scare her. Even now, although she'd had him over and in her for the better part of a night.

But the look in his eyes was just so deadly.

It scares me that I love you, that's what she also wanted to say. *That I could lose my mothers, could lose you.* It got stuck in her throat.

Her eyes widened as he trapped her, keeping her against the desk.

"Are you?" he asked. Oh hells, the bastard knew her all too well.

She leaned in, taking his lower lip between her teeth, and bit down until she tasted his blood filling her mouth.

Then she whispered right into him. "Just fuck me."

MELODY

I shower in the tiny open shower that looks too much like it comes straight out of the human world. But then, so does the rest of the place.

After that, I put on the fresh set of clothes someone has left for me before I venture down those long corridors.

Everything looks different during the day. Brighter in the sunlight that falls in through the huge windows. Peaceful. *Sunlight.* For a second I don't trust my eyes. It leaks in in thick, buttery columns and I gingerly stretch out my hand, pale and bruised, but beautiful in the new morning light. I marvel at the warm sensation on my skin, so much better than I could have ever imagined it back in my bleak room. As if my whole body came alive for the very first time. And against my will, against the lump in my stomach and my nervousness a smile spreads over my face. *You will not be afraid. You will have a life one day.* For the first time, those words feel true.

Finally I force myself to move on. Doves sing in the lemon and persimmon trees that grow in the courtyards and sparrows bathe in the water of the fountains, ruffling their feathers.

Again, I briefly pause to watch them. I would love to linger, love to soak up some of the warmth and sunshine, but I'm already late.

I head straight to the kitchen as Nidaw instructed. A lot of other women are already gathered. They look similar enough to Nidaw, with the same deep-sea-colored skin and bright eyes, that I assume they are sirens too. But it's the color of their hair I stare at too often. It reminds me of the sea and its corals, ranging from the palest sea foam blue to Tyrian purple.

They ogle me in return as I enter, mainly my telltale round ears and the still barely healed wounds on my wrists. I quickly look down, suddenly ashamed of my difference, and try to smooth my hair over my ears and hide my hands behind my back.

It is a long day that follows. And I learn what it means to be a servant in a fairy palace. First, in the kitchen, I cut vegetables before Nidaw sends me away with a group of women to clean some of the rooms, each one more luxurious and overwhelming than the next. Velvet-covered furniture and heavy rugs made of silvery silk. Shiny, long curtains of cobalt blue damask sway in the breeze and double-winged doors made of black wood mark the entrances. There are scenes carved into the material, so detailed and exquisite the fingers that made them must have been those of very tiny creatures.

I sweep out huge fireplaces and mantelpieces made of another stone I've never seen before, brushing past columns and statues of the same gold-veined, fascinating material that seems to change its colors in accordance with the time of day. I realize that what looked like bleached bone last night now ranges from a shy Isabelline in the morning, to a fiery orchil around midday, only to fade into an ashy heliotrope in the afternoon.

The other women keep watching me, mostly vigilantly. It is only later in the afternoon that they eventually seem to forget about me, and start to talk quietly with each other in a tongue I can't understand. And I finally have some time to orient myself.

I try to memorize the rooms, the layout of the palace, and potential escape routes. I've already figured out that the slave and servant quarters are located on the very edge of the building I'm in, a huge complex on its own. But when we are done with one room and I follow the women onward, I lose track again of where we are.

Occasionally, in the hallways I see other fae hurry by. Some have hooves and horns. When we walk back through one of the patios, I spot two green-skinned, blue-haired men bent over the lush hedges of herbs, translucent pixie wings on their backs catching the light in all the colors of the rainbow.

☽ ⋅ ☾

The days are too long, and I can't help but feel that Nidaw's giving me particularly exhausting tasks to drain me. When they are over, my back aches worse than after a round of combat training with Kayne or Hunter, and I'm so tired all I can do is wolf down the food someone left in my room—fresh mint tea, a broth, some honey-glazed goose meat, some walnuts, and a piece of chocolate cake with a flower on top, all lovingly arranged—before I slump onto the bed and fall asleep.

It works. To exhaust me, make me so tired I can barely walk straight, giving me no time to think. But when I glance in the mirror in the morning, I'm no longer so pale. I touch my face. *A half-fae,* Riven said. But my ears are round, and I don't look at all like *them.* I don't have their perfect skin and waves of colorful hair. I look ordinary with my brown eyes and human skin.

But then, better than I ever have. Still slim, or thin, yes, lean with muscles but no longer on the verge of starvation. Some life has crept into my eyes, a rosy color into my cheeks and lips.

Perhaps because I'm no longer constantly hungry. Maybe because my nightmares have vanished, too, as if by magic. The same as my panic has faded down from a wildfire to simmering embers as if something in the Fortress kept them at bay.

Something that sweeps through the corridors and fills the very heart of the complex as if it is a part of every stone, every wall, the fundament itself. A presence that fills the corridors and brushes up my skin like a caress sometimes. Curious. Gentle.

Something soft like dew and night. A dark twin to the balmy breeze outside.

But I'm too tired even for this thought.

☽ ⁑ ☾

On my fourth night, I step out of the shower. The day has been hot, the warm desert air wafting in and out of the palace through its open windows. Even now, so late, it has not lost its heat.

I get out naked, not bothering to use the towel, but rather letting the water and the wind cool my overheated skin. I love it, the hot, arid air, soft as a murmur. I've stayed winter-pale from all the time inside, the brief crossings of the patio in the mornings not enough to bring the slightest tan. Though that doesn't prevent me from marveling at the gleaming, relentless sun every time I look out through one of the palace windows, sometimes over the city, sometimes at a raw stretch of stone and undulating dunes, or the range of blue mountains in the backdrop that are watching over everything like a sentinel.

The nights are equally magical, especially the few hours before the moons rise. I've never seen so many stars before. So close. So bright. As if you could stretch out your hand and pluck them from the sky.

I'm too focused on the darkening horizon and the town that shimmers like a puddle of glowing lights underneath to notice that I'm not alone. My instinct alerts me… too late though. My nose catches Riven's elusive scent a second after I spot his violet eyes.

I shiver from the way he's looking straight at me, although I'm totally naked.

"That's not very gentlemanly at all," I say with all the bravery and harshness I can muster.

"Is it not?"

His form ripples out of the shadows as if he is a part of them. And again I'm struck by how similar he looks to the Dark Lord. But at the same time totally different. I don't know why it matters so much. I also don't know why every time I fall asleep, I have the Dark Lord's blue and gold eyes in my mind. Why the fact that I know he's somewhere close makes my heartbeat quicken and, absurdly enough, calms me on a deeper level.

I push the thoughts away, grabbing the towel from where it hangs from a rack on the wall and wrapping it around me. Trying hard to ignore another thought as it sluices through me—that I'm a slave now and that Riven probably can do whatever he pleases with me.

As if Riven knows what I'm thinking, he purrs, "My little treat with her lovely cheeks all flushed. Now, aren't you perfect?"

I scowl at him, knowing that he's mocking me.

"I see you still choose to ignore the rules for a slave," he drawls, silky menace lacing into his words as he approaches with this otherworldly grace I would never manage to capture on paper. Not in a thousand years.

Today, he's wearing a loose shirt that offers glimpses of his body beneath at every move, thanks to the fabric turning partly translucent whenever the light of the single candle burning on my nightstand hits it at a certain angle.

I swallow at the landscape of rigidly sculpted abdominals and rippling muscles, flashing at every step.

Heat stings my cheeks, and I look away. "Other people knock, you know," I mutter.

"But then I would have missed such a delightful sight." His voice has fallen to a gentle murmur—a lover's voice—as he leans down, right to my face.

He smells of wine and herbs and rain and lilac. Beguiling.

I jerk away and glare at him, forcing down my shame. He's just seen me naked, for fuck's sake. And now he's toying with me.

"Why are you here? Certainly not only to see me naked," I hiss.

His gaze softens unexpectedly when he looks down at my wrists, at the wounds the handcuffs left there, so tight they cut into my flesh. The strangest thing is that they have barely healed. "Indeed, it wasn't only to sate my desire for something distinctive, mind you. The Dark Lord sent me to look after you."

"*Look* after me?"

"And take care of those wounds."

He gently reaches for my arm. But when his cool fingers touch my skin, I yank it back.

"I'm fine," I snap. I certainly don't want his pity. I'm also not sure I can stand anyone touching me. No one ever did without hurting me.

"Those cuts are infected from the iron. You need to treat them," he retorts, unfazed, producing a tiny can out of his trouser pocket. "This is an ointment. Apply it."

He holds it out to me, but I don't take it.

"You don't trust me," he states.

I'd laugh at how astonished he sounds if my ribs weren't so tight, squeezing my heart, and my lungs. As if I had any reason to trust him. "I don't trust anyone. You could tear me to pieces and eat me alive if you wanted to, right?"

I don't add *You do that to girls like me, don't you? Eat us alive,* even though it's probably true.

He just watches me with the same curious look he had in the woods, his eyes a sparkling violet. They don't change their color, but I almost expect them to.

His answer comes slowly, along with a frown. "Probably."

I swallow. At least he's honest, although I hate the way it speeds my heart. I chase my first question with another one. "What are you?"

He takes another step toward me, closing the distance I just opened up between us without realizing it. As if this is a dance, I retreat once more.

He purses his lips as if he finds me amusing. "You could ask *who* I am instead. Wouldn't that be polite?"

"Depends—are you going to lash me if I don't?"

"Prickly." He inclines his head ever so slightly, glancing down at me. Gods, he's tall.

"I told you to obey, which you certainly aren't at the moment. It's rather unwise." His voice holds no anger though. It strikes me that he is simply pointing out a fact.

"Then why not just discipline me?"

I know *this* is dumb, speaking to him like this. Provoking him like this. But hells, I spent too long with Lyrian. Faced too many punishments. I would not be afraid again.

His eyes darken as he watches me. "I don't believe in such things."

"In violence?"

"For one. But these are the rules. I didn't make them. I can't abandon them... simply bend them. It would be wise not to provoke anyone else like you're provoking me. Or I won't be able to protect you as I promised." He adds the latter part like an afterthought, his voice unbearably gentle.

I weigh whatever lies in his face, in his aura. Then I ask a shade more conciliatory, "Who are you?"

"I'm Riven Caedmon, High Lord and Prince of the Enchanted Forest," he answers in a way that makes him sound almost human.

"And *what* are you?"

A smile curves his lips. "This is an interesting question we might save for later."

I probe on nonetheless. "You're a high lord and also a vampire. Are you an elf or a vampire now?"

He sketches a brow. "We all are and aren't *vampires* in the way humans imagine them. And every fae has pointed ears, not just the elves."

"You don't drink blood and sleep in a coffin?" I'm too aware of the sarcasm ringing in every word.

His eyes flash in a warning. "Bold. No, no coffin. But as you already figured out, some other clichés certainly hold true." His smile widens into one designed to show his fangs.

I suppress a shudder.

"The Dark Lord made you a vampire," I push, refusing to balk.

"Yes, Caryan did." He lets out a sigh, looking suddenly exhausted. Then he sinks onto my bed and leans forward, running a hand through his ink-black hair, leaving it messy. It makes him look almost boyish.

"Caryan?" I ask carefully.

He waves a hand in a dismissive motion. "The Dark Lord, my king, or just *Your Highness* to you," he says.

I try the name in my head. *Caryan.* The vampire with the ever-changing eyes. The casualness with which Riven uses the name of the king surprises me, though. At Lyrian's house, it seemed that there was a strict hierarchy between the Dark Lord and them, laden with respect and submission. But now Riven's speaking of the king almost like a close friend.

I don't know why it is so hard for me to believe that anyone could be close to such a frightening—*man.*

I ask quietly, "And he *made* you because you *died?* They say he's a necromancer."

I'm not sure I have any right to ask. Not sure it is clever. But Riven takes it with a shrug. An utterly human gesture, strangely at odds with his usual grace and predatory demeanor.

"You've already picked up a lot here. I forgot how much servants talk. Well, normally Caryan offers the *curse*—" he seems to struggle with the word, as if it holds another meaning for him "—to people who have already died or are on the threshold of death. But with me, it was different. We go back a long way and—let's just say I accepted without having lost my life before."

His voice has turned grave, as if this burdens him. His aura shifts too; the midnight hues grow darker, gaining depth. He leans forward again, bracing his elbows on his thighs.

I slowly approach and sit a healthy distance away from him on the bed. There's no more denying that every joint hurts from the day's work and I need to sit.

Damn it, right now, I'm more tired than scared.

"Is that a bad thing?" I ask after a while.

He raises his head, looking at a point in the middle of the room. "Some people think it is."

"Some people who mean a lot to you?" I ask carefully, plucking it from his aura.

A muscle ticks in the curve of his jaw. "They used to. They were my people. I was a prince of my lands, my court, once to become king. But it's a long and complicated story. Let's just say I would be king if it weren't for my various... attributes."

"But you said you still are an elf..."

"A high elf," he corrects me, but not unkindly. "The difference between an elf and a high elf is their inherent power. We are rare, though. And to answer your other question—I still am a high elf. The fangs don't change that."

I stare at him, at the darkness that has gathered around him in thick waves. I'm not entirely sure I understand what he is telling me though.

"But why did you accept then? The... curse? You said the Dark Lord gave you a choice."

He gives me a sidelong glance. "So many questions already, and you have barely arrived. I wonder why," he muses quietly. But the darkness in his aura stays. And for some absurd reason, I don't like it at all—to see him sad like this.

"Why not?" I ask as nonchalantly as I can. Then I stand up and walk over, stopping right in front of him. I like how he seems surprised by this, how his pupils widen ever so slightly. How he has to lean back on my bed to take me in fully.

I try to ignore how this turns his shirt semi-translucent again, enough to see *everything*. A body, honed to perfection. The light dances over every dip of his sculpted chest, the ridge of his abdominals, the sensuous curve of his strong collarbones, as if it, too, likes to touch him.

I ignore the rush of heat in my body as I lean over him and whisper, "Who wouldn't want to hear the pretty boy story?"

It's almost comical to watch the incredulous expression flick over his stunning face. My bet is that no one's ever spoken to him like this.

Dangerous. So dangerous.

He says, "I'm serious," but I swear his voice is a touch hoarse.

I slip between his long legs. "Oh, so am I. You're eye candy, and I want to hear the sob story." I raise my brows at him, smiling at his still slightly shocked expression.

What the hell am I doing? Flirting? But as crazy as it might be, it feels good. For a moment, I'm more than a slave. More than a prisoner. More than a *thing*.

A stupid, stupid idea.

"My volatile, little villain. Now I know that you can lie, I never know when you're serious." His voice is troublingly sincere as he looks up at me through his long lashes, searching my face. As if this really bothers him. And in that moment, I know I'm going to paint him like that. His head tilted slightly back, his throat exposed, his eyes half closed with that lazy expression.

"That's what makes it fun."

"For you," he grumbles.

I bite back another smile, sucking in my lower lip. His eyes follow the movement.

"I'll admit that you surprise me," he remarks, almost thoughtfully.

"That a good or a bad thing?"

"A dangerous one, I guess."

At that, he sits up. His movement is so fast and fluid, I take a step back. And just like that, he's standing in front of me again, and I'm trembling with a feeling I barely understand.

"You're hurt…" he starts before he cuts himself off. Then he tilts his head, looking at my face more closely. "No. You're… afraid."

I look away at that.

But his sudden closeness startles me. Scares me. Even if it's not in the way I'm so schooled in. He leans down to me, his breath brushing over my suddenly feverish skin.

His voice drops to a whisper—low, soft, and intimate—as he says, "You don't have to be afraid of me. I will always be careful with you."

I feel a tug deep down in my belly as his lips touch my neck then, merely a brush, a second before he pulls back, as if he's caught himself.

As quickly as he came, he withdraws and straightens, casual and distant. And I wonder whether I just imagined the heat in his words, the brush of his lips.

Of course I did. I look so ordinary next to him, he would never notice me. Would never be here if the Dark Lord hadn't sent him here to check up on me.

I take another step back, wrapping the towel tighter around myself, suddenly too self-conscious.

He adds, "To answer your last question: there were several reasons I accepted Caryan's offer. But the most important one is that I would go anywhere Caryan goes. No matter what." A graveness has snuck into his voice.

Just then, I spot a deep, golden band weaving through his aura. "You love him," I whisper.

A smile graces his face, and warms his eyes, heartbreaking in its beauty. "I do."

"Are you and he—"

"Lovers? No. Not in your sense." He straightens the fabric of his shirt, and I quickly glance away again. He goes on as if he hadn't noticed. "I've been to your world a few times and I've found that humans only have a few, strictly set rules when it comes to their understanding of love. Here, it's different. We don't have a human heart, Melody."

I startle when he lifts his hand to tuck a loose strand behind my ear.

"We don't love like humans. We don't *feel* like humans in a lot of ways, or behave like humans, for that matter. We don't have so many emotions, but we have bonds. And sometimes a bond to someone can be stronger than anything else, made for eternity."

I don't know what I read in his face, in his aura, in his words. What to make of all the hues there, swirling. Only the bond to Caryan, solid and static, like a golden anchor in their midst.

But his words sober me up. "You live *forever*?" The thought scares me.

"Not really. But compared to humans, it certainly seems that way. Some of us reach a thousand years."

"How old are you?"

"Two hundred and thirty-two," he says, and my eyes widen. He laughs at my incredulous expression. "I know—immortality and its serene youth. But by elven standards, I'm still young. Now, I think I've answered enough of your questions. Let me see to those wounds. After all, I too have someone to obey." Again, he holds out his hand, ready to receive mine.

"Caryan," I say.

He smiles at me again, gut-wrenchingly handsome, before he winks at me. "Who else might an elven prince serve?"

I let him take my hand and we sit down again. He opens up the salve tin and starts to gently apply the ointment. I try to sit still, to not pull my hand back, although instinct tells me to do just that. No one ever touched me like this before. He is far gentler than I would have been with myself.

"You said you steal humans away. And... keep them as slaves." *For food. For sex.* It gets stuck in my throat before I can say it. I've overheard the servants talking about that. Noticed their pitiful glances wherever I went. Heard their uttered words, which they supposed were too quiet for me to catch. *Slave. Sex slave. Blood slave. Vampire food. Another stolen one. Poor human. Won't make it long here.*

All those words stalk me. Haunt me. "Is this why I'm here?" I finish. I've been dreading this question for too long anyway.

Riven curls his lips slightly, a line forming between his eyes. "It's true. We do take humans sometimes. As I told you, when we take them, it's usually because of bargains they made with us. We take them for various reasons, but you're not here to serve as food."

"But the Dark Lord drank my blood," I say quietly.

"I imagine you are rather delectable," Riven counters in a raw, deep voice that makes me pull my hand back as if I'd burned myself. But he is faster and locks it into place. He laughs softly, and I realize he's just been playing with me. Just as I played with him before.

To cheer me up.

I throw him an admonishing look. "Very funny."

161

"Isn't it just?"

"Why did he do it? To make me a vampire too?"

Riven lets out a true laugh at that. A sound so deep and rumbling I just watch him. I wonder whether he knows how different it makes him look. How his eyes sparkle even more.

After a moment, he turns serious again. "Oh, those mortal clichés. No, that would require more than just a bite, including a blood exchange and a blood oath. You would need to pledge yourself to him."

"Why did he do it then?" I look down at my hand, still in his. His fingers have gone back to performing circular motions over my wrists. The wounds there, to my surprise, are almost gone.

"To get a taste of you—literally. He has a special talent all of us lack. If he drinks your blood, he can see everything you are and were and what made you become who you are."

I stare at him. "What? What does he see? He can't really see *everything,* can he?"

"It's hard to explain. He sees incidents that happened to you. In your life. Usually major things or events. It's pretty much the way your memory works too. The bigger the impression events leave on you, the more alive they still are in you, and the more likely it is that they'll show. The same goes for recent events. Things that don't lie too far in the past are more likely to show up. The more intense, the more likely it is that Caryan will see them."

"He can't control it?"

"No. I don't think so. All I know is that it's random—what he sees in your blood and what comes up. These scenes or sequences come in the form of flashbacks. He sees it the way you saw it when it happened to you, through your eyes."

That's why he drank Lyrian's blood—to see what Lyrian kept from him. I don't want to know what he saw in my blood.

I stay silent for a long while, unable to put into words what I feel. The Dark Lord has seen me and my life and my most personal moments. I can't shake off the feeling of embarrassment, shame, and nakedness, as if I'm made of glass. I'm angry, too, I realize. Angry about this intrusion, this uninvited trespass.

He stands up, finished with my wrists, and looks me over one last time. "Sleep now. It's been a long day."

He turns and is heading for the door when I say, "Wait. Please."

He stops, turning back to me.

I swallow before I raise my gaze back to him. "If he doesn't want my blood—what else does he want from me?"

"I cannot tell you for sure."

"You said I can trust you." I don't know why it matters so much whether I can trust him. But it does. As if a strange, new part of me wishes for nothing more than to trust him. It's a dangerous line to walk, I know.

He seems to consider this.

"Did he forbid it?" I probe on.

"No. He didn't, Melody. He wouldn't do such a thing to me. It's only that I'm very much in the dark about Caryan's true motivations myself," he says after a pause.

"But you're—you're his friend."

The shadow over his features seems to grow even further. Something like pain flickers in his eyes before he looks down to the floor.

He doesn't say anything else though. He doesn't need to, because I see everything too clearly in his aura. Pain. Loss. Sadness. Desperation. Anger.

It hits me then. "Is this… is this why you did this? Made the promise, in the woods—to protect me?" My voice comes out strained, while my mind still tries to fully catch up to what that means. *Protect me from the others. But also, maybe even more from Caryan himself.*

The sad smile that curls the edges of Riven's lips is confirmation enough. It makes my blood run cold.

"Caryan can be unpredictable. I certainly learned that the hard way."

An answer that is not an answer at all. I don't know what to say. *Caryan can be cruel. Is cruel.* And Riven has accepted that because he knows no way to stop him.

No other way than death.

I watch how he walks out the door without turning back.

MELODY

I don't see Riven for the next week, nor Caryan. Only rarely do I spot the other high lords, Kyrith, and the red-haired, quiet one. Ronin, Nidaw called him. Whenever they walk down the hallways, there's a sudden tension in the air. Servants lowering their heads, bowing and parting, or falling to a knee, keen not to glance in their direction or draw their eyes. I match them, carefully trying not to stand out in the servants' crowd, until they pass, carefully trying not to stare at their blood-covered swords, remembering my last encounter with the blond, Kyrith, all too well.

This week, I learn more and more about the structure and the way of things around here. I learn to keep my head down, only to look at someone through the curtain of my long hair. I learn that to look someone directly in the eye at the wrong moment will be understood as a sign of challenge or aggression, especially if they have a higher rank. It seems part of their fae communication, as it does when they pull back their lips to expose their sharp, pointed teeth and hiss at each other.

I get hissed and growled at a lot before I manage this new form of language, glad my round ears seem to save me from serious trouble when I do the wrong thing.

One night, after another dreary day of scrubbing the floor on all fours and polishing tiles and statues, I almost sleepwalk to my room, looking forward to a hot shower to ease some of the tension in my sore muscles, along with food and my bed.

But Nidaw awaits me when I enter, standing in the middle of my room. "No sleeping tonight. One of the high lords has requested that you serve at the equinox festivities," she declares, gesturing for me to follow her back out.

We take the familiar route to the baths I'd been washed in after I arrived. Two other servants are already waiting.

"What are the equinox festivities?" I ask while they strip me down and pull me toward the steaming bath as they did on my first night. I don't resist this time. I'm too tired to mind my nakedness.

Nidaw steps to the edge of the bath. "Two weeks of nightly celebrations."

I say nothing as the servants grab sponges. I also accept being scrubbed down without protest, even when my skin itches afterwards and feels raw. I'm so exhausted I can barely move anyway. *Two weeks.* I wonder how I'm going to survive them without collapsing.

My body is stiff and aching, but when I finally step out of the water, I feel strangely restored, as if I've slept for a few hours.

"Healing water, from Avandal," one of the girls explains, reading my face as they towel me dry and then guide me over to the vanity, where Nidaw waits, perched on that velvet stool again.

Only then do I notice the silvery glimmer and glitter all over her dark, ashen skin, her pearlescent hair laced with matching silver filaments.

"Are you celebrating too?" I ask, watching her in the mirror while she detangles my hair.

Nidaw doesn't look up when she says, "All of us are, even with the coming war."

"The war?" My eyes widen and Nidaw bites her lip. "What war?" I ask before the siren can decide not to talk to me at all.

"There's war in this world. It started fifty years ago in the northern realms but has now spread all over. It reached our borders this month."

"That's why I saw the high lords with their swords bloody," I gather.

Nidaw's lips become a slim line, but she nods once, curtly. "Yes. That's why they are not much around these days," she confirms with another meaningful glance toward me. Something I don't understand.

When my hair is done, I want to get up, but Nidaw's claws push me down again. "You too—it's a tradition that we dress up and so will all of the servants, including *you*."

With that, she pulls out a golden thread, matching the one she's wearing in silver, and starts to twirl it through strands of my dark hair. When she is done, she forms some tiny stars out of the thread with a talent I find hard to put into words. Then she places them all over my hair as if my head is the night sky I so often watch from the window.

It's nothing short of beautiful.

Nidaw gets up and brings me a long, black dress—so similar to the one Lyrian gave me that fatal night weeks ago.

I take it shyly, only slipping into it after realizing that all of the servants are wearing the same style of dress. That too seems to be part of the tradition.

The servants step forward, their long-clawed fingers pulling the fabric into place before they start to dust my milk-white skin all over with golden powder. Finally, my whole body shimmers with a gentle, warm glow as I regard myself in the mirror. Some patches look solid gold. Some, like my collarbones, are only lightly dusted. Other parts, like my cheeks, have streaks that accentuate my face strangely, but beautifully.

When I'm done, I find even the servants looking at me differently, as if I've transformed into one of them, as tall and slim and beautiful as they are, my hair hiding my human ears.

"Now—let's go," Nidaw offers, obviously content with her work.

I follow her, more than a little nervous, as we venture into the main hall. Exotic music's now drifting through the corridors, reverberating from the high stone walls. Eerie, haunting voices, singing a chant, underlined by a beat that sounds almost electronic—nothing I've ever heard before but something that thrums across my skin and along my bones.

"Remember to keep your head down," Nidaw says as a final warning before we slip through the kitchen and into the ballroom with the huge terrace I ventured through on my first night here. I barely recognize it, though as my gaze sweeps over the room.

It's been transformed into a twilight revelry, unlike anything I've ever seen before. *Almost* naked, painted bodies flash everywhere, lit by a thousand candles.

Some fae stand, some lounge in chairs and on low benches that have been carried in. There's a lot of naked skin on display, lithe figures with skins in all ranges of the palette—from sapphire to topaz green to a subtle amethyst. Gold and silver dust covers the bodies, flickering and glittering in the light, the wild colors singing to the painter in me.

In the semi-darkness, I spot hooves and curled horns coated with gold and adorned with jewelry, and the same sort of filaments I wear in my hair.

In a corner, there's the group of sirens singing to the strange music, next to two naked men playing on harps and two fauns beating various drums. The air's heavily fragranced with the smell of jasmine and orange petals that some green-skinned men with those beautiful pixie wings crush under their bare feet to disperse their scent. Others burn incense that blurs the outlines of the room, the brown wood smoke curling in the air like filaments.

Everywhere in between, servants glide through the crowd, carrying plates stacked with goblets of wine and laden with overripe fruits and other strange delicacies.

I know some of these flavors from the faun cook who slips me some things to try when no one's looking. Today it was a raspberry so delicate and sweet that tears filled my eyes. And a tiny bird, its skin honeyed and crackling with fat, stuffed with crushed nuts and pomegranate seeds.

I watched the cook and Nidaw eating them, too, bones and all, spitting out the beak.

Nidaw seizes my arm to steer me back to the kitchen. There, she orders me to grab a plate of food and follow the other servants. I obey, taking one of the trays laden with macadamia bread, adorned with a ball of cinnamon butter, sugared violets, and those bittersweet cocoa-coated, summer-ripe raspberries, and venture out. I struggle to find my way between swaying bodies, trying hard not to bump into anyone while I avoid faces, just as Nidaw told me to.

But a moment after I step out of the kitchen, several heads turn to look, and a murmur goes through the crowd. Some even gape at me with their mouths wide open.

Everyone seems to stare at me, bathed in candlelight.

A wave of heat and sensation crushes over me, and I fight not to look up. Fight my suddenly racing heart and sweating fingers. I want to run straight back into the kitchen and hide.

Do I look so alien to them?

I doubt it. Doubt my round ears show through my long hair at all.

Maybe it's my smell? *Maybe I smell human?*

I force myself on, concentrating solemnly on my task, and eventually, everyone turns back to dancing, conversing, or other things. Only occasionally someone still points a finger and whispers.

Times runs differently while I serve, on and on, round after round. Watery red wine that smells of cloves and lemons, powdery wine that looks like champagne. Then dove confits on a bed of bursting figs coated with maple syrup. It is only when the light dims and the strange music fades into a deeper, darker and slower rhythm, that the smell of sweat and sex is suddenly everywhere, thick and heavy. Bodies start to move rhythmically in corners, and my ears pick up the softest sighs and moans.

I hurry back behind the bar, as if the marble counter might shield me from the world. Only from there do I allow myself to take in the room, the dimly lit, meandering figures.

I *feel* someone looking at me.

The need to turn around and see who's watching me is suddenly so overwhelming, as if something's calling my very blood.

I turn. It's not Riven's gaze on me.

My heart stops for a few moments.

Dark, loose shirt, dark pants. Combat boots. Cruel cheekbones. Black, callous eyes.

But it's the hungry look in them that makes my heartbeat return faster and harder than ever.

He's back, then.

Caryan.

He sits next to the other high lords, astonishing women by his side. Yet he's watching me from across the room with an intensity that burns right into my innermost being. In this moment, I know that no man has ever looked at me like that before, and maybe never will again.

I feel naked.

Stripped down. Brutally.

Claimed.

Consumed.

Turned over.

Vulnerable in a way I can't describe.

Only slowly does my sense of reality kick back in, and I look away. Closing my eyes against the already familiar undercurrent that flickers in the air, that clearly comes from his presence, and that *should have* warned me if I'd listened.

Suddenly too restless, I need a break. I need to get away, to get out for a moment.

I disappear into the kitchen, eager to busy myself there, piling more food I've never seen nor tasted before on trays the cooks conjure out of thin air, until Nidaw shoos me back outside.

The night ventures on as I carry more plates, the tinge of sex and lust becoming even more oppressive. I try hard not to look at the flashing skins but at the floor ahead, where tails curl and feet and hooves threaten to block my way. People lounge on cushions and low sofas, licking golden dust from collarbones and sipping wine from bellybuttons. I'm so absorbed in the task of blocking it all out that I almost bump into the chest of a tall man.

I don't dare to look up, only whisper my apologies, when a familiar voice drawls, "There you are. Bring some elderberry wine and whiskey over to our table for all of us. Oh, and mix some lavender ice in one glass for the Dark Lord."

Kyrith's vicious voice rakes down my spine like a slick, cold tongue.

I only nod, not daring to look up or over to them, to the niche where Riven and Caryan are probably still lounging. Not daring to remember the expression with which Caryan beheld me earlier.

$$) * ($$

I return with what Kyrith requested, trying hard to steady my shaking fingers. I gently put the tray down on the glassy table in front of them, trying hard not to glance at Caryan, who's sitting right in front of me. Or at the stunningly beautiful blonde woman with pistachio-colored lips next to him, staring daggers at me. Another woman with cerulean skin is straddling Riven. A breathtakingly beautiful satyr sits right next to Ronin, his hand on his bare chest, delicate fingers playing with a thin, golden chain around Ronin's neck.

My peripheral vision picks it all up, whether I want it to or not.

It's Kyrith's voice that startles me once again. "Look who we've got here. Why don't you get down on your knees when serving the Dark Lord?"

His words are so drenched with hate, mockery, and cruelty that they cut through all my senses while I fumble with the bottle. He stands to my right, in my blind spot.

I sink down onto my knees as I'm told, right in front of Caryan, and start to pour elderberry wine into glasses. Kyrith's evil laugh makes me shudder once more.

"So docile. The very opposite of Lara, don't you think?"

A laugh ripples through the crowd, especially from the women, while I struggle to keep my hand steady. *Lara. Who the hell is Lara? Another human perhaps?*

"Why don't we see how far your docility goes? Since you're already on your knees, you could give our Dark Lord a little demonstration. Make yourself *useful*, so to speak. Like a good slave," Kyrith mocks, not yet done with me.

Another round of laughter spills over me, but I can feel the sudden tension, can feel everyone looking at me now, as if they haven't caught a glimpse of me before.

Everyone can hear my racing heart, I'm sure.

Instinctively, I glance up at Caryan, only to find him looking right back at me, his irises like shaded onyx, circled by a rim of gold. Depthless. Unreal. His expression would be a mask of boredom and latent disinterest if his eyes weren't as ravenous as earlier when they took me in.

I glance down again, blushing violently as Caryan says, "That's enough, Kyrith."

"Why? If you don't want her, why not give her to me, my king? I promise to make a woman out of her. Teach her how to be a good girl, so she'll be fun when you get her back."

"As far as I remember, she's still mine," Caryan answers casually, but there is an edge to his voice now, followed by a subtle prickle of power that runs through the room, whetting itself as it goes.

"It's just a little fun. Come on. You could use some. It's equinox after all, and you must admit, after what was done to her, she doesn't look too hard on the eye. Some might even call her beautiful with all that gold on her. Mistake her for something other than half-human scum," Kyrith goes on unperturbed, seemingly ignoring the warning. The charged air. He bends over me and twirls a strand of my hair in his fingers as if to make a point.

I stop dead. The marks on my neck bristle at the touch. It takes all my self-discipline not to pull back, not to drive my elbow into Kyrith's nose.

I truly consider it and maybe would have done just that if there weren't a growl coming from Caryan's throat, so deep and frightening that it makes my blood freeze in my veins.

Kyrith laughs it off, but I know he, too, feels the effect of Caryan's power, because he lets go of me as if I'm hot iron.

Caryan's voice is leashed lightning as he snarls, "Take your hands off her."

"I was just kidding, my king," Kyrith says, but his voice sounds a little shaky. Betraying him.

"Were you just *kidding?*"

I can't read the shadows in Caryan's eyes when I dare to glance up. Liquid night fills his eyes before shadows erupt.

Bones crack. Kyrith screams.

His right hand, the hand that just touched me, is fractured, his fingers disintegrated and at odd angles.

Caryan's still lounging on the sofa, but his voice has taken on a horrible calm. "Next time you decide to speak like that to your king, or touch something that's mine for that matter, you'll find yourself without a head. Now go and see a healer."

There is a primal dominance in every word. And for a second, everyone seems to stop breathing.

When my eyes shift to Riven's, he gives me the slightest raise of his eyebrows, utterly unfazed by the violence. A gesture that seems to say, *the bastard deserved it.*

Caryan waves a hand. "Help yourself to the drinks." An order, not a suggestion—a king has spoken—and they all scramble to their feet, reaching for the bottles and glasses as if they can't oblige fast enough.

I watch them, still kneeling. The darkness of Caryan's magic is like dew on my skin. My fear, a wild sea within me.

Caryan leans forward, bracing his arms on his legs, and says to me, "Come over here."

I tremble, willing my heart to calm. I hoped I'd be beneath his notice. Quick to forget. Not interesting enough.

I don't trust my knees when I get up and approach him.

"Closer," he orders.

I step even closer until I'm standing between his long, spread legs. He looks at me and then says, more quietly now, his voice deep and raw over my suddenly feverish skin, "Even closer."

I move until I'm climbing on top of him, straddling him, my senses swamped by his sudden proximity. At the feeling of my body connecting with his.

Until his voice is nothing more than a murmur shaped by his lips against my neck. Cold, as if he feels none of what I'm feeling at the closeness. "Good girl. And now—amuse me."

Amuse me. How? I have no experience at all.

One sidelong glance over to the woman who's straddling Riven tells me enough of what he expects me to do. I blush deeply when I spot another one who's settled between another man's legs and is performing some up-and-down movements with her mouth, moaning softly every time she takes him in deeply.

I quickly look away again.

Amuse me.

I have no clue how to seduce a man. How to hide my inexperience. I've never been with a man before. Only with David, but that—

I force myself to place my hands on Caryan's chest, trying hard to ignore the sensation of lightning and heat that jolts through my palms, as if I've immersed myself into an electric current.

It's almost too much, almost painful.

He leans his head back against the sofa cushions, watching me through lashes nearly as long as Riven's, his voice cold with cruel amusement as he whispers, "More."

More.

I lean over him, shaking all over. All I manage to do is let my long hair fall into my face, shielding myself from his knowing gaze. As if I can hide behind it.

I wish I *could* hide as I let my fingers slip under the seam of his shirt, finding surprisingly smooth skin. His heat and power crawling into me. And then, tracing his sculpted collarbone, with fingers trembling even harder than before, I open one button of his black shirt. Then another one. Exposing more skin, smooth and white as marble, stretching over chiseled muscles.

I fail to rein in my trembling as the third button follows. The last one. His shirt gapes open, revealing a torso that looks like that of a statue. A god forged of marble right under me.

I close my eyes against the sensation of his scent that engulfs me when I lean forward, closer to his neck. He smells like something wild, uncontained. Like a forest, like moss and sandalwood and pines and citrus and wet gravel, as if I've fallen into a magical, evergreen, enchanted forest. A scent that seems to speak directly to my soul.

It's too much, too overwhelming. His closeness. His power, writhing through me like a living creature. His scent; swamping all my senses.

I no longer know what I'm doing when I gently let my fingers glide over the bare stretch of naked skin, down over the hard, muscled plane of his belly.

I forget that I'm a slave. Forget about where I am. Forget about everyone else.

Suddenly, all that matters is his touch, his scent all over me, around me. The whole world narrows down to the feeling of skin on skin.

I glance down at his face. At his lips specked with flakes of gold. Finding that the black behind his silver-rimmed lashes has morphed into liquefied gold as he beholds me.

Then something feral enters his gaze as he whispers, "More," in a way that shifts me all over. His voice, deep and husky, almost a moan.

I bring my lips to his neck. Kissing the golden trace of paint on his exposed throat. His unringed fingers roam over my body before they dig into the naked flesh of my thighs where my dress must have slid up. Unrestrained now, as if he is no longer able to keep his hands passive. Bruising me. It sends another rush of heat through my veins that merges with the hum of his power.

I gasp slightly when I feel him pressing hard against me, when

I feel myself spreading my legs further, terrified by my own reaction.

But my senses are dizzy, flooded and unstable, as if I'm riotously drunk.

I shift a little to breathe more kisses onto his chest, my hands gliding further down to the seam of his pants.

He grabs me by the wrists and stops me midway.

For some precarious moments, we are face-to-face, his eyes on my lips, before he says, "That's enough. You can go now."

His voice is iced over, the total opposite of just moments before. But the same lucent, blazing gold still swims in his eyes, betraying him. The way they were when he drank my blood. *It makes no sense.*

"Did I do something wrong?" I whisper, my eyes wide with shock and fear. I need to ask. Need to know.

"No, you didn't. Now go to bed," he replies, even more coldly, as if he can't get rid of me fast enough. As if I'd done *everything* wrong. *Again.*

Then he raises his head and says to no one in particular, "Get me a real woman."

I scramble off him and away, my face burning hot with shame and fear and a swirl of emotions I can't name. I don't dare to look at anyone, not even at Riven, as I turn away. I try hard not to run through the crowd before I finally slink into the seclusion of the kitchen, the feeling of his hands around my wrists lingering like molten metal. Tears are streaming down my face even before I reach the deceptive security of my chambers.

Get me a real woman.

His words burn into my mind, echoing over and over.

I don't know why it matters so much. I should be grateful for having been dismissed.

But when I curl up on my side, watching the eerie blood moon, all I can think about is the feeling of Caryan's skin under my lips, of his scent all around me, of his hands around my wrists, on my thighs.

Get me a real woman.

I bury my face in my hands and cry until darkness and sleep claim me.

20

RIVEN

Riven watches the whole scene, his teeth clenched so hard they hurt as Melody cowers on the floor in front of Caryan, scented with fear, her whole body shaking so violently she tries hard not to spill any of the elderberry wine as she pours it into glasses.

Something strangely possessive stirs in him. Along with it, the daemonic power slumbering in his veins opens its eyes.

It takes all his willpower not to get up and shove Kyrith's face into the wall. Not to release a gust of shadowfire on him. Just because it isn't his call to make, but Caryan's. Yet, as that brazen bastard Kyrith has the nerve to bend down to her and touch her hair... it takes all of Riven's self-control not to incinerate Kyrith with half a thought.

He doesn't allow himself to dwell on this. He's never been protective before, not in the way that keeping her safe feels more instinctive and not even remotely like a rational decision.

Last night, when she stood before him, looking at him with those eyes, wrapped only in a towel... when he almost kissed her neck...

He digs his fingernails so deep into the armrest his knuckles turn white, long, black talons threatening to take form.

Relief floods him as Caryan eventually puts Kyrith on the leash, chaining him through the invisible bond between them. A brutal yank in their very bones only they can feel, followed by an unmistakable rumble of power in Caryan's growl that washes over the whole ballroom. A deadly, night-kissed flood that makes everyone draw in a sharp breath.

Kyrith chooses to ignore both. *Stupid bastard.*

Riven tries not to chuckle when Caryan shatters his hand and Kyrith bleats like a lamb.

But what follows afterward makes Riven's throat dry out. Caryan doesn't let her go. No. He orders her to step closer.

To crawl onto his lap. The words he whispers to her make the hair in Riven's neck stand up.

Amuse me.

Melody shakes even harder, the smell of fear so clear it is palpable. Riven barely feels the touch of the woman above him, no matter how hard her lips and tongue and skilled hands try to steer his attention away from them and back to her.

He can't block out what's happening right in front of his eyes. Can't block out Melody's feverish heartbeat, or her smell.

Why is Caryan doing this? Riven knows he's grandstanding— to show everyone here that Ciellara's daughter is his slave and that he can—and will—make her serve in his bedroom if he wants to. A part of Riven understands the message it carries to the outside world—to show his people that the daughter of the woman who almost killed him is his property now.

That those days are over, once and for all.

But she is still a child. Traumatized by Lyrian, who did gods know what to her.

But he can't stop it, can't speak out against it. All he can do is watch.

It's a new kind of torture.

He closes his eyes, trying hard to focus on the water nymph's touches. He forces himself not to watch how Melody kneels over Caryan but to concentrate on the lap of the woman above him, her hips demanding his full attention as she grinds her body against his.

He isn't in the mood, though. Not with this tension hanging

between all of them, the air thick and charged with Caryan's nightmarish power.

It's only when he hears Caryan say coolly, "That's enough. You can go now," and then, "Get me a real woman," that Riven allows himself to look across again, only to see Melody, ashen-faced, her eyes silver-lined as she hurries out of the room.

As if on cue, Sarynx saunters over, the blonde elf waiting for Caryan to rise, and the two of them disappear from the room. Eventually Riven lets himself feel again, succumbing to the revelry around him.

Later, the orgies are still going on in some dark corners; in others, people are already sleeping, hair ruffled and limbs entangled, when Riven finds himself once again venturing toward Caryan's private rooms. He knocks and the door opens for him, Caryan's magic obeying its ruler's will.

He finds Sarynx sprawled naked on the couch, making no move to cover herself. If anything, triumph glitters in her cerulean eyes. Caryan stands in front of the huge window, wearing only trousers. The air still smells heavily of sex. A *lot* of sex.

Riven ignores the blonde elf, who loves nothing more than attention and power and undiluted admiration from men and hates Riven for the fact that he doesn't lust after her the way Kyrith does.

He never has. He never will.

"Leave," Caryan growls at Sarynx, and Riven likes the way she—who looks at everyone down her nose, except for Caryan himself—scrambles to her feet, collects her clothes, and slips out the door, not even taking the time to get dressed again. She rushes past Riven, not without throwing him a lethal glance. He would almost laugh if it wasn't for the somber mood he could feel surrounding Caryan like a void, twin to his own since Melody stormed out of the room crying.

"I had the feeling you wanted to talk to me," he says, helping himself to one more glass of vermilion wine before he approaches Caryan, watching the ever-shifting gold-and-black tattoo sliding like a snake over Caryan's body. It's made up of the runes and beautiful symbols that Ciellara tattooed there, which shift and rearrange themselves like a living creature, wandering over his body as they please—or so Riven suspects, although he's never asked Caryan about it.

Sometimes he even has the feeling that the tattoo reacts to his presence, because, as soon as he nears, it always seems to draw closer to him, gliding to the place nearest to Riven's body, which is currently on Caryan's right side, the tattoo now stretching from Caryan's neck down his right arm and right flank.

"Then your feeling betrayed you," Caryan responds coolly after a heavy silence. "But since you're already here, tell me whose idea it was to have her serving at the celebrations. Yours?"

Riven stills. "I'd never have put her in harm's way. You know that." *Definitely not in such a tasteless manner. Definitely not after I swore that oath to her.*

The oath—he meant every word. The moment he said it, it felt like the most natural thing to do. It was the only way to truly protect Melody from himself.

He would die for her. Would rather die than harm her—that's what it meant.

That realization hits him somewhere deep in his bones. He pushes it away.

He has other problems.

They spent the whole last week combing through Caryan's kingdom, tracking down the spies from Palisandre that had started to infiltrate the lands, coming in over the border to the Emerald Forest, where the wall of wards around Caryan's kingdom is the weakest. Tracking down his own people and cruelly killing them— that's what Riven has been doing the last few days.

Even more had come since the rumors spread that Caryan had found the girl from Kalleandara's prophecy and brought her here.

They'd taken rotations, one high lord staying at the castle while the other three hunted down the spies, which was also unusual. Normally, Caryan sent them and didn't go himself, but this time he did.

"Who then?" Caryan asks.

"It must have been Kyrith. I should have known. He's hell-bent on giving Lara's daughter a hard time, Caryan. I would have intervened, yet I thought it was your wish."

"My wish?" Caryan's head snaps to him too quickly, his eyes black as ebony, his voice suddenly full of barely restrained rage. Rage Riven so rarely sees in him. "Why would that be my wish?" Caryan snarls and a wave of dark, biting power pours over Riven like a deluge.

Riven grits his teeth. "I thought you might have decided to… make a statement."

His words and tone are collected, not showing any of the rage he felt at that party when he saw Melody appear, even though he thought her long in bed, safely tucked away from all of this as he promised. He failed her, didn't register that Kyrith had ordered her there, made her wear a dress like that, and paraded her in front of everyone to show that Ciellara's daughter was here now. A slave. Caryan's slave.

"A statement?" Caryan's tone is like ice, his expression incredulous.

"To the right hand of the king of Palisandre." *Ciellara's father.* A snub to the whole of Palisandre. A provocation. A demonstration of power.

Caryan looks at him then, really looks at him for the very first time today, no doubt feeling Riven's emotions. "You think I need to resort to such blatant methods? That I am so desperate for their attention?"

"I thought you did it to draw them out. To intimidate them. But how can I know what you are thinking, Caryan, when you don't share any of your thoughts with me when it comes to the girl? Why not leave with her immediately and look for the relics?"

Caryan's eyes flare in a warning. "My motivations are none of your concern."

"None of my concern? I'm your right hand. Palisandre is readying its army. Every week we catch more rogues at the border. You know that *someone* managed to slip through the wall of your wards, but we haven't yet found him. Someone invaded your kingdom, Caryan! And we don't know what the witches are going to do once they learn you've found the girl. And now *everyone* has seen her. So if they don't know already, they will. It's going to catalyze recent developments. Everyone will try to get her. And they won't stop. We're running out of time. So I'm asking you—what are you waiting for? Why not set out with her now and search for the relics?"

"You seem to have forgotten your place recently," Caryan snaps, flashing his fangs.

Riven lifts his chin, although Caryan's voice makes an intrinsic part of him want to lower his head in submission. "I'm asking you as your right hand, Caryan. Household chores as a slave can't really be the position you had in mind for her. And you can't just proceed as if there's no threat."

"That's exactly what we're going to do—proceed as normal. And now this conversation is over." Caryan turns on his heel, striding away.

Riven says, "Caryan—please. If you won't talk to me as your right hand, then at least talk to me as your friend. Please don't lock me out."

Caryan pauses at the plea in his voice, turning back to him.

"Please," Riven pushes, "tell me what you're really waiting for. Why stall?"

"You said it yourself—someone infiltrated my kingdom. I felt them slipping through holes in the wards. I want to find them first and eliminate the threat."

"But the longer we wait, the more time we're giving everyone else to prepare an attack—" Riven counters.

Power rumbles through the room, crawling up the high walls. "Enough of this! I won't expose her to danger after I searched for her for so long. I won't have her leave the seclusion of the Fortress. I won't allow anything to happen to her, do you hear me?"

Riven stills at the unusual rage in Caryan's voice. He's never seen Caryan like this before. He nods once and the dark power slowly retreats, pulling back into Caryan.

Caryan *is* different; it's not just his imagination. He's more withdrawn than ever. More on edge than ever.

And it's not just the rare, light blue in Caryan's eyes, nor the blazing gold in them when Melody knelt over him, something Riven's never seen before.

Or what just happened between them in that ballroom— Caryan and that girl, both so absorbed, forgetting the world. *Something* was going on between them that Riven felt in his blood. Only for Caryan to send her away moments later, using harsh words, as if he wanted to chase her off.

And that Caryan decided to wait, for her protection, instead of setting out for the relics…

"You got your answers, Riven. Now leave me," Caryan orders, and all Riven can do is obey.

21

BLAIR

A black, hooded cloak hides Blair's features from the little people who frequent Akribea's streets at night. The cold has swept the town empty. Frost is gnawing on windows, icy wind crawling in under doors. Her fingers are already numb from the flight down here.

The ground is muddy and dirty from snow and rain, treacherous ice coats the bridges, her boots soaked and heavy. She pulls the cloak even tighter around herself, not to hide, but against the cold. There's no reason to hide. Not here. There are only a few witches left anyway, too old to live in Perenilla's tower and serve. And very few other fae have stayed, despite the threat of being murdered or harvested. Who survived Gatilla's reign in the first place. The ones who haven't left are creatures with barely any magic worth slaughtering for.

And anyone who sees her will know better than to utter a word.

Blair looks up and bares her teeth at the sentinel of the collapsed tower rising to her right. The ruins of Windscar, the amethyst stone black in the absence of light, looming over the town like a warning.

Lights are on in only a few of the formerly elegant, now-rotting townhouses as Blair ventures on. Once richly ornamented façades are now crumbling, most of the windows broken or missing altogether, the doors under impressive portals scratched and unhinged, clattering in the wind.

But the worst is the wind itself, which howls through the empty buildings like the lost souls from the Abyss.

Akribea is a ghost town.

As Blair ventures on, she remembers the stories Aurora and Sofya told her when she was still a small child. About what a flourishing metropolis Akribea had been when they were young and came here to study at the great university of witches, open to all races and teaching all subjects. Not only dark magic and methods of harvesting, as it is nowadays.

The streets then were brimming with students and merchants and art shops and markets, beloved by elves and everyone else alike. Aurora's and Sofya's stories are so vivid in Blair's imagination that it's as if she'd seen it herself. Artists painting and playing instruments and taverns where bards sang lewd songs and Aurora and Sofya danced all night long.

Blair clenches her teeth at the gaping hole in her heart. *Music.* Dancing.

All fae love music and dancing. *Everyone* loves to party and dance and sing. Hells, how she misses it every fucking minute. She can only imagine how it must have been for her mothers, for everyone here, when Gatilla suddenly took over these lands, long before Blair was born, and everything fell into darkness.

One of the first things her aunt did as queen was ban all forms of art and music. Those things she viewed as distractions, keeping the witches from focusing on brutality and training.

Taverns and bars closed, along with shops and cafés. Trade dried out. Fae started to move away—first in a trickle, then in a flood, because they could no longer make a living in this kingdom. That was when the *harvesting* began. Her aunt considered everyone who left a traitor.

After that, Gatilla built the reservoir. Then sent the witches throughout the kingdom to track down all fae with magic worth stealing in their veins and butcher them too. Then she sent them *beyond* their borders.

For a brief period of time, as Palisandre approached to strike a truce and ask for help to kill the angels, it looked as if things would eventually stop. And they did. Until her aunt managed to enslave Caryan and turned him into her weapon.

The last remnants of a once-glorious kingdom finally perished when Gatilla initiated the devastating, final war—the Witch War—leaving only ashes and ruins behind.

Blair cuts a corner and rats scurry away from her gaze into the dark. She sucks at her teeth, again thinking about what Perenilla said—about her aunt backing the wrong horse.

About Blair being a dreamer.

About why she did nothing to prevent her aunt from being butchered.

Because she'd been just that—a coward. Naïve. Foolish. Waiting like a love-sick puppy until Caryan made the decision she never dared to make herself.

The truth was, even as Caryan's blade cleaved her aunt's bloodless skin, she hadn't been sure which side to choose. She'd stood there and stared and stared and stared. And then she ran because, by all means, she had been afraid. Terrified.

She betrayed her coven. She betrayed Caryan when she didn't help him. She betrayed them all.

She pauses, the wave of self-loathing so bad that, for a moment, she can barely breathe.

If only they knew, Blair, that ugly, hideous voice in her head chimes on and on like a chorus. So similar to the reservoir's magic.

Yeah, if only they knew, she bites back.

What she did was bad, sure, but it isn't even the worst of her betrayals.

No. She's done so much worse. Things even her mothers are unaware of, thank the Abyss.

In the days after Gatilla's death, the second-oldest witch, Drusilla, had taken command and ordered Blair and the thirty-three covens of witches to attack Avandal, the capital of the Kingdom of the Seven Rivers, and its healing spring. Drusilla, an old and vile witch with a humped back, had heard rumors that Caryan was hiding out at the temple there to heal and decided to nip the problem in the bud.

The night before the attack, Blair had flown straight to the temple on her phantom wyvern, to a beautiful healer by the name of Meanara.

That winter-haired elf had been the only one awake, sitting on the stairs and watching the stars. So Blair told her about the attack. Told her to warn her queen. To hide the women and children. To ready their troops.

Blair hadn't done it for Caryan. Well, maybe a tiny part of her had.

Maybe not.

The angel would probably kill her anyway. Whatever. *Fuck it.*

But she's definitely done it for Avandal.

Blair had never been to the glorious cities of Palisandre, but she'd been to Avandal several times, disguised as a lesser fae, before they installed the wall of wards around it. If she ever had the choice to live somewhere else, it would have been Avandal.

She fell in love with it. With the city itself and the seven magical rivers that gave the kingdom its name, running like steaming, glittery silvery-blue veins through it. With the streets made of stone so white the entire city glistens and gleams, even at night. And its people, the kindest she's ever met, drinking tea at various tea houses, while harpists and flutists play on every corner, and the constant fragrant perfume of wisterias and jasmine fills the air.

She couldn't allow the city to suffer the same fate as Akribea.

The night of the attack, many witches died. Blair made sure to send the witches of the covens close to her to places she knew would be mild and barely protected. The other ones, the cruel, bloodthirsty witches like her aunt, she sent right into the epicenter as she had agreed with Meanara. The latter covens were called the wild ones, even among the witches. It had become a form of sport among them to impress her aunt by surpassing each other with cruelty. Killing women and children and eating them had always been off-limits among the witches, until Blair's aunt came to power. Blair couldn't allow that either. Honestly, it made her fucking sick to her stomach. She just couldn't, whatever that made her.

A lot of witches fell, especially the wild ones. Drusilla eventually had to stop the attack and retreat. There had been so many casualties on both sides.

But Drusilla considered the attack Blair's failure and threw her into the dungeon to rot there forever. And maybe Blair would have, if Drusilla hadn't died miraculously a week later.

Blair rubs her temples. There is nothing to deny—the deaths of most of the wild ones hang on her shoulders. Yet Blair never regretted it. And never would. But she wonders what fate keeps in stock for her. Whether all those deeds have finally come back to bite her in the ass.

She stops in front of an inconspicuous house, knocks three times loudly, and four times quietly. A blond elf opens the door, his green eyes shining and wide. One of the few men who still live here, if you could call it living. He's a high elf. She feels the magic in his veins. A high elf who fled his impending execution in Silvander, the capital of the Enchanted Forest, but never made it to the human world and somehow washed up here a few years ago.

She's the only one who knows about him and his heritage, though, because her talent is sensing strong magic. To all the others, he might just look like any other lesser fae and not the high elf he is.

And he has proven useful in enough ways for Blair to keep his secret.

Though in all these years, she's never asked what he did to make his kind want to kill him. But then, she doesn't care. He's one of the best blacksmiths this world has ever seen. He's quite good in bed, too, but this time, Blair's here for a new blade.

"My ruby, I haven't seen you in a long while," he drawls, cocking an eyebrow.

She bats her long lashes, smiling innocently. "Sassy. Are you calling me that because of all the gems I bring you? Or because of the color of my hair?"

"Can't it be both?"

"Give me the best you have," she says more sternly, putting five huge rubies on the desk.

He disappears into an adjacent room, only to return with a sword like she's only ever seen Caryan carrying. Old, glistening runes are embedded in the shaft, flaring purple as she touches it.

The smith says, "Made from mithral ore and sealed with ancient spells. I called it Heartbreaker, because it's said to never miss the heart."

How fitting for me.

She unsheathes it, weighs it in her hand. Light as a feather, but much, much deadlier. "Sweet. I'll keep it."

"I'm afraid it will cost you a little more than a few shiny gems this time," the blacksmith says, crossing his muscled arms in front of his chest, a charming smile tugging at the corner of his lips.

Abyss, she doesn't even know his name, or his age. He could pass as eighteen but might be much older than her. And fuck, his dimples remind her of that human man she's screwed in that bathroom.

"You're a pervert," she retorts dryly. "Short of women these days?"

His lips spread into a cocky grin. "Maybe I just missed you, my ruby."

"Always a charmer. But first I need something more."

"More?"

She gestures with one silver claw past the heaps of dried wolfsbane and bowls containing blood moss to a faded map nailed to the wall. It's taken her several visits to figure out what that bleached, old map showed. Then the penny dropped.

Places of power.

He follows her gaze and his expression darkens.

She says, "I need to open up a portal."

"You will need more power for this, I'm afraid. Even you, witch. Even at a place of power."

"Stick to your steel, blacksmith," she warns. "And give me that map."

Three witches and a place of power to draw from—where veins of wild magic cross. They would amplify her own. It would have to do. It would have to be enough to open a portal, to bring Sofya, Aurora and her back to the human world. Enough to never return.

She's been awake for the better part of the night, thinking about what she said to Aurora. About getting them all safely to the human world when she remembered the blacksmith's map. A fucking epiphany.

When he's done carefully taking the map off the wall and folding it in a strip of soft pig hide, she says, "Now, run me a bath, because I'm freezing my ass off. And then we'll see about your other qualities, blacksmith."

Later, she stands in front of the window in his apartment, which occupies the upper floor over his shop. She likes it here—the whole building is always warm thanks to the fire in his forge.

"Who did this?" His voice is hoarse as he looks at the remnants of the scars the iron-tipped whip left—cute mementos all over her back that will only disappear with the help of a very, very talented healer, thanks to the iron.

She looks over her shoulder. "None of your business."

He steps up behind her, sinking one hand into her long hair and pulling her head back, his large canines scraping her neck. She closes her eyes, a moan escaping her as this feeling evokes the memory of totally different teeth sinking into her.

Fuck. No, not again. Not now!

To hell with fucking Caryan.

"You've already had me," she whispers. "Twice."

"You said you'll be going away," he groans into her ear, his calloused hands starting to circle her nipples again.

"Touching a witch unasked is a dangerous thing," she snarls, but he keeps his hands there.

"I know, but I like to play with fire. You better hold on."

With those words he slams his remarkable hardness into her all over again, driving in so deep she almost sees stars.

She grabs the edges of the table, her nails shredding wood, the material groaning at the impact before it gives way under her fingertips. She stifles a cry when he pulls back out and drives into her again. And again. Even deeper.

She arches her back as he licks the sweat off her neck and shoulder blades. A guttural moan escapes his throat, which drives her over the edge. She goes limp, collapsing on the table. He grabs her hips as he keeps pushing into her in ruthless, sharp thrusts.

And just when she thinks she's too tired to keep standing, his calloused hands find the spot between her legs.

The forgotten kings of the Abyss spare her. *Elven lovers.* Not as rude and irreverent as angels, but just as potent and thorough. She comes again, this time with a cry that makes him come too. She collapses on the table, him on top of her, spending himself inside her.

Afterward, she takes another bath, soaking in the hot water and watching the flickering candles throw shapes of monsters crawling over the wooden ceiling.

He steps up to her, a long sword in his hand, black as the night, cabochons embedded in its pommel.

She sits up straight, looking up at him wide-eyed. Meteorite ore. A material from another world. The only thing that could cut even through celestial magic, not to mention every other form of magic.

"Where did you get this?"

"I traded it," he says. His voice is as rough as his hands, his eyes clarion, catching the flame.

"It can't be. They are gone. The portals closed... the weapons destroyed."

He shakes his head. "The weapons from back then were destroyed, yes. But they came back. They're lying low in the Black Forest."

Her mind catches on the word *they. Nefarians.* Hellborns. Sub-breeds of an elven race from another world. Basically high elves who formed bonds with shadow demons from the Abyss. Connections so deep the demons' magic left traces of it in their own bloodline, causing the offspring to be born with huge, black, taloned membrane wings and claws.

Legends say they were born after the angels had come to this world. That they are the result of a power imbalance because the angels were too dominating. Too powerful, so the demons intervened, merging their bloodline with that of the high fae.

Blair read a similar theory once about where the witches came from—from an alliance with demons, high fae, and dragons, but no one really knew, and most of the books were written in languages long forgotten.

She frowns at the black sword in his hands, brimming with danger. Meteorite ore is deadly for every fae, not only angels, and her own being wants to bare her teeth and hiss at it.

The Nefarians entered this world back then through a portal, bringing meteorite ore with them, knowing its value and how to craft it into weapons. They allied with Gatilla and the elves from Palisandre and traded the ore for a place in this world as they rebelled against the angels.

And swept the soil clean of them.

Afterward, though, her aunt and the elves broke their word and hunted the Nefarians down almost to extinction because they feared their aerial units and strong warriors. Some of the surviving Nefarians fled back to where they came from, and with the portals closed, Blair never thought it possible that they'd return one day.

Everything made of meteorite ore was destroyed before the Witch War, her aunt made sure of that. Abyss, Caryan himself had led the raids on Palisandre's armories, cleaning them out one by one. Due to the toxic energy meteorite steel emanates, one that weakens magic in its direct proximity, Palisandre kept them at the outposts and never in the cities. Big mistake.

Water splashes as Blair rises, foam dripping over her lush figure as she holds her hand out. The smith obediently puts the sword in it. Blair weighs it in her hand. It is heavy—heavier than it looks—as if its dark nature adds to its heft.

Shit, that elven bitch Ciellara cut Caryan open with a thing like this. With one of the few blades secretly stashed away that remained in this world. Ciellara let her moon magic flow into that sword as she tried to cleave him in half.

"And you know this for certain, that the Nefarians are back?" she asks, guiding the sword a few times through the air. She swears the blade starts to sing a dark song.

The smith nods once. "It was a Nefarian man who gave it to me."

"I don't want to spoil the moment and ask why you went to the Black Forest. It's not for innocent elven boys." She holds his gaze, his bottle-green eyes.

He just laughs quietly. "You never asked what I used to do, Blair. Maybe I'm not so innocent after all. But I went to see the seer dwelling there. You might want to seek her out too."

She angles her head, her long, soaked hair swaying. The predator in her rears up its head. "How do you know my name?" she asks sharply.

"I wanted to know who you are. The seer told me your name is Blair."

"Why?" Her voice has become strained.

He takes a step back from her, as if he's sensed the danger suddenly coming off her. Her magic starts to whisper through the room, ready to rip into him like her phantom wyvern.

"You never cared to learn mine, though."

She snaps, "Skip the banter. Why give me this sword?"

"Because I have the feeling you'll need it in the near future." His voice is calm, fearless, and he holds her gaze unperturbed. He's brave. Bold. She might have asked him for his name, his heritage. About his former profession. But not if she's going to leave this world forever. Which she is. Not when she's not sure whether she's going to kill him.

"What did you do to get it? It's…"

"Priceless," he finishes for her. "It depends how much your life is worth to you."

He chuckles at her puzzled expression, and she flashes her teeth at him. He doesn't flinch. The smile stays, only his eyes darken a shade.

"Some would call fearless boys like you stupid."

"I'm not so much a boy, Blair, however I look. I think I've got a few more years under my belt than you. And have stared down creatures that are much more wicked and ancient than you."

And walked away from it. She tries not to dwell on it.

"And what in Abyss's wrath did you do to get this sword?"

"I saved a Nefarian's life—I was there for business, and I found him half dead. I collected herbs and cured him of a deadly wound. He gave me his sword as his sign of gratitude."

"That was kind of you," she says, meaning it.

He brushes it off with a casual shrug. "You'll never know when enemies might turn into allies. But what I do know is that no one ever forgets an act of mercy and kindness."

"What do you want for this sword?" She's already talked to him too much.

"Nothing. It's a gift for you."

"Why?" She frowns.

"You don't remember me, do you? I was there the night the witches attacked Avandal. I'd been living there for quite a while, hiding out from the assassins after Palisandre put a bounty on my head. I saw you at the temple that night, Blair. I saw you warning Meanara."

Blair gapes at him. He even knows the beautiful healer's name. How is it that she didn't pick up his scent on the wind that night?

"I'll never forget what you did for my kin. Neither will I forget what Caryan did."

My kin. He said he was from Palisandre, so he must have some family in Avandal.

But Blair's mind catches on Caryan's name. She snarls, "What *did* Caryan do?"

"You've never heard, I see. Interesting. Caryan stayed there for two years. He brought back every single man and woman who fell that night at the slaughter in Avandal. Avandal suffered no losses because the angel brought them all back. That is why it took the angel two years to recover—because he spent so much of his energy bringing back all those souls."

Blair stares at him, her eyes wide. Caryan did *what* in Avandal? Of course, she hadn't heard because she'd been too busy sleeping and hiding from the world.

She doesn't want to ponder what it means, though, that a lot of *cursed* creatures are now running free in Avandal, stronger and more vicious than they were back then. How could the witches not know about this?

The blacksmith says, "You have a good heart, Blair, no matter what they say about you. About the witches. You have a good heart."

She brings the blade to his throat so quickly all he can do is blink. She steps out of the bathtub, keeping the point of the blade at his throat, watching him retreat with every step she takes forward like a shadow dance, until his broad shoulders hit the wall.

She sneers when she spots fear in his face for the first time.

"Don't ever make such ridiculous assumptions again, friend of Avandal. I would also strongly advise that you never breathe a word to anyone about that night, or I might come back and cut you into tiny slices before I eat you for dinner to prove to you how good my heart truly is."

"I would never breathe a word to anyone, Blair Alaric. But I do wish you to come back one day."

She narrows her eyes. "You're a fool."

With that, she lowers the blade, only to lash out with her clawed hand, cutting his abdomen before licking his blood. She keeps looking in his eyes the entire time, the slashes on his skin gaping wide open, as if a wild animal has attacked him. *Good energy.* She almost spits it out because it tastes so disgusting on her tongue.

"Don't you see what your true nature is, Blair? Why you like the taste of rotten souls so much but shun the good ones?"

She hisses at him, her claws around his broad throat, her lips only inches from his.

She allows her powers to stir, to flare up in her like golden, deadly curls of wildfire. Let it gnaw at his skin like aurum frost, like tiny hellhounds, ready to rip into skin and tear him apart. Let it shine through her amber eyes.

To his credit, he doesn't budge. Makes no move to fight until she lets go of him. She turns on her heels, grabbing her clothes from where they fell to the floor and starts to don her riding leathers and, at last, her dried red cloak.

He's still standing there, watching her every move, when she eventually turns to him. "Never push me again, blacksmith."

With this, she sheathes the two new swords in the scabbard on her back and walks to the door. She reaches for the doorknob but pauses, turning to him one last time.

I shouldn't care. I should just walk out and forget about it.

To fucking hell with it.

"What utter fools you fae are. You have no idea what you have brought upon Avandal, accepting the curse."

"Caryan offered help in the darkest hours. Without him, Avandal wouldn't have recovered. It was an act of altruism."

That is not like Caryan.

She throws her head back and laughs. A vicious sound. "An act of altruism? Can you hear yourself? Have fun waking up one day and finding out how terribly wrong you've all been. You know Caryan can control the creatures he brought back—his spawns, right? He and his high lord lapdogs. All he has to do is give them the command to shred their own people apart with their teeth... and they will. He has no mercy, the same way I have no mercy."

The blacksmith's face doesn't falter as he says, "Maybe. And maybe he will never do so, Blair. I guess all we can do is wait and find out."

"Naivety's a fool's blessing. Thanks for the fucks," she says, opening the door and disappearing into the night. The bad taste in her mouth lingers.

MELODY

Someone is watching me. Hungry predator eyes.

I jerk awake. Two gleaming red marbles watch me from the corner of the room. Sanguine gems, streaks of blue and gold leaking into them.

I sit up straight, staring at the sentinel, the outline of a man in the shadows. But when I fumble for the light next to my bed and switch it on a moment later, the figure is gone.

Outside there's the faintest sound of heavy wings soaring in the skies.

I feel drained. After the incident in the night, I fell back into a restless slumber. I've forgotten my dreams as I always do, but I know it wasn't a nightmare that woke me.

I look pale, dark circles under my eyes when I get up in the morning, meeting my reflection in the mirror. When I return to my bed after a brief shower, I find the drawings I left sprawled all across the floor stacked in a neat pile next to the bed.

I stare at them for a long time. The top sheet shows Riven's stunningly beautiful profile. I wonder who put them there like that. Who has come to watch me while I slept?

☽ ✳ ☾

Today is the same as all the others during the equinox festival. In the morning, we spend hours preparing all the food for the festivities later. Two weeks, Nidaw said. My head swirls at the idea that last night might repeat itself. I don't allow myself to think of any of it. Of Kyrith. Of the Dark Lord. Of the feeling of his hands on my skin.

I banish every thought of him, but useless shame crawls up my body nonetheless.

I focus on the task of cutting food and crushing herbs, doing my best to distract myself.

It's easier here, in the hustle and bustle of the kitchen. It's also the kitchen I like most. I truly enjoy watching the cooks conjure meals that look too fairy-like and fantastic to be true. I particularly like one of the chefs—if the fae call them chefs in the fairy world— a huge satyr with two massive, black gayal horns that protrude from behind his large, round, furred ears, fierce and terrifying. He has shiny black hooves, dark skin, intriguing blue eyes, and ink-black hair he wears in dreadlocks braided tight to his head, three golden earrings dangling from his earlobes.

Whenever he notices me watching him create one of his magnificent dishes, especially the sweets, he slips me something to try. This time, it's a slice of a dark fruit that has a soft texture and glistens like licorice but tastes like a chocolate pudding in my mouth.

He laughs heartily at my wide eyes. I smile back at him shyly, and he slips me another before he stalks away, barking orders through the halls.

I'm licking my fingers when I catch Nidaw watching me from the other end of the room before she orders me over into the hall where last night's celebrations took place.

When I enter along with the other servants, there's no trace of any party left. The whole room is as immaculate and clean as it could possibly be, with the floors shining, all the furniture and cushions gone, not one stain to be found anywhere.

For a brief second, I find it hard to believe that it happened at all, that the high lords had been lounging right over there.

I must have been staring a moment too long because Nidaw says, "Magic." The siren has suddenly appeared next to me, following my gaze.

I turn to her, startled. Nidaw rarely speaks to us servants during work time. "So why do we need to clean at all when magic can do this all?" I make a gesture with my hands, and to my surprise, she chuckles.

"It's not *our* magic. It's the Dark Lord's magic, so it's up to him whether he spends some of it on cleaning up."

When I frown, she explains, "The fae world adapts to its ruler. It's subject to his wishes, his ideas. He can bend it to his will—starting from this—" she gestures to include the whole building "—architecture, to even the temperature outside."

"The temperature? So the Dark Lord turned it into a... desert?"

"No. It was a desert when he took over. He didn't change much of it save for a little rise in temperature lately, yet he could—if he wanted to," Nidaw finishes.

I can't help but notice the gleam of awe in the siren's eyes at that. There's always a warmth in her voice when she speaks about him, and adoration.

"You once said you like him—the Dark Lord."

Nidaw smiles at me with her row of slightly pointed teeth, then nods. "Yes, we all do."

"I thought he can be—cruel?" I ask quietly.

Nidaw's smile falters and turns wistful for a second. "Every ruler is also cruel, Melody. He has to be. But he was also the one who offered us a new home where we are safe after we lost ours. When no one cared for us lesser fae, apart from spitting on us. He never treated us any worse than he treats any high elf. This is why we love him."

"So you don't mind *the curse*? Apart from not being able to go to town at night, I mean?"

I try to ask as lightly as I can, but Nidaw narrows her eyes anyway, clearly not pleased that I'm bringing up the town again.

"No. A lot condemn him and what he represents. Yet it's not in our nature, the nature of the water folk, to judge. We believe that, in the world, there's no right or wrong. There's never only light, nor is there only darkness. One can't exist without the other. They're interdependent, do you understand?" Her voice is gentle, kind, kinder than she's ever been.

I want to shake my head, to tell her that I don't understand, but Nidaw goes on.

"It's always chance, Melody. Chance and choice. It's in our hands, always. We're not creatures without will, no matter what they tell us about our future, our fate. Don't forget that it hasn't been written yet."

With that, she takes my hands and holds them in hers. "You are a part of this world, as you can see. Magic likes you; it welcomes you. It wants you here, home." She touches my chest, as if to make a point. The question must be so obvious in my eyes that Nidaw chuckles again. "You have elven blood in you and, now in contact with magic, your fae blood is reacting to it."

"How do you *know* I'm not fully human?" That Riven knows, well... he obviously knew my parents but Nidaw...

Nidaw tilts her head at me. "Did you never notice in the human world that you were different? You also wouldn't have tasted chocolate in the fruit if you were human," she says with a glint in her eyes.

It was a test, then. I push the thought away into the line of so many others I don't want to think about—the fact that a lot of fae here seem to be watching my every step.

Instead, I say, "But my ears."

"Your ears, your teeth. From a distance, they look *almost* pointed, have you never noticed? And your canines, not as large as elven ones, but not human either."

I don't know what to say. What that means for me. What that means for my parents. If this is true, one of my parents must have been an elf. The fact that I know so little about any of it hits me hard, but I swallow it down for now. Like I always do.

"And besides," Nidaw adds knowingly, "you'd have already died if you were human. No human survives exposure to raw magic for long."

"But why… why am I here?" My voice drops to a whisper. I *will not* allow myself to contemplate what Nidaw has just revealed. Not now, when I need so many more answers.

Nidaw lets go of my hands. "Because there was a prophecy, given by the greatest of the oracles this world has ever seen. By Kalleandara herself." Her eyes widen with fear and awe as she speaks the oracle's name.

"What does it say?"

The siren shakes her head to cut me off. "I know that this is why you are here. Fate brought you here."

"But—"

"No buts. Remember what I said? About chance and choice. Fate is inevitable, but we—the siren folk and the nymphs of the sacred springs of Avandal—we don't listen much to prophecies, because they're always cryptic, always vague, and one can only interpret them. But no one, not once in history, has ever been able to predict the future correctly, not even the high oracles, even if they claim they can. It always comes down to choice and chance in the end."

At that, she puts a hand to my heart. "Listen to it, Melody. I know you have the gift to see a creature's true character. Use it wisely and be glad for what you are. Half-breeds are so rare, but so special."

"Why? Why are they special?"

Nidaw just taps my chest again.

With that, she steps back and leaves me behind, more confused than ever.

$$\supset * \complement$$

Later, when the same taciturn servants come and wash me and dress me up like the previous night, all I can think of is the evening ahead of me. The closer we get to the celebrations, the more nervous I become.

My skin itches even more than last night when they dry me off, and I have the feeling it's not just the scrubbing. I try hard not to scratch as they apply some flower-scented oil before they start to paint me gold again. Then Nidaw is back at my hair. This time, she takes some of the upper strands back and braids them into two buns she adorns with silver lacework, the rest of my hair falling loose down my body.

"Stop fidgeting," she says, as she spins me around to face her. Then she applies some thick, black kohl around my eyes before she dusts my lips with golden powder.

Those golden specks on Caryan's lips, mirroring the gold in his eyes. The laughter, the humiliation.

The beautiful, blue-skinned woman on top of Riven. His head tipped back, his sensual lips parted.

I can't think about it. Won't.

When I look in the mirror, I'm frightened by my own reflection. The woman in there is a stranger.

"Adorable," Nidaw says behind me, as if she somehow read my mind, gently combing one last time through my hair.

I look down at my hands, then say quietly, "You all are so beautiful here."

It's true. There is no one who is close to *normal*-looking, not by human standards. Here, I feel like the ugly duckling compared to the elegant way they move, the way they carry themselves, straight-backed and heads high, with their long necks and sculpted bodies and natural grace.

Nidaw's hands pause at my neck. "And so are you, Melody. Look in the mirror. You look just like your mother."

My mother?

"You knew my mother?" I ask, suddenly breathless.

Nidaw gives me a warm smile. "I did. She was an outstanding beauty, and you take after her. When I first saw you, I briefly mistook you for her."

I don't know what to say.

"Was she human?" I barely dare to ask the question, not sure I can stand the answer after what Nidaw told me about humans who came to this world.

"No. She was an elf. A daughter of Evander," Nidaw says, as if this should mean something to me.

"Wait—"

More questions suddenly burn on my tongue, but Nidaw's already striding away. The two servants hold me back, their nails sharp as they sink into my skin when I try to wrench free, leaving half-moon marks in my skin.

I relent, my heart pounding fast as the sirens help me into the same dress I wore yesterday.

Eventually, I make my way back to the kitchen, more lost in thought than ever.

More lost than ever.

MELODY

The evening unfolds like the previous one. A lot of wine, syrupy delicacies and glasses garnished with pink cricket salt. The crowd is too beautiful to be real. Too beautiful for me to ever become used to.

I glide among more lithe, painted bodies and elaborate dresses stitched with fantastic motifs, not daring to look toward the lounge where Caryan and the other high lords were sitting last night.

It's only when we serve the dinner course—rabbits stuffed with dates and hazelnuts and some other things I can't name but which Chef sneaked me—that I glance over, only to find Caryan is not here.

My heart skips a beat.

Will he come? Does it matter?

Instinctively, I find myself reaching out to search for his power, trying to *sense* it. A strange part of me is relieved when I feel him close. As if knowing he's close calms me. *What the hell is wrong with me?*

I shake my head as if to clear it, grabbing another tray that comes straight out of the kitchen before I head in for another round. I'm tired from the long days and lack of sleep, too tired to spot the man in front of me—Kyrith's blond, shoulder-length hair, and angular face. Too busy looking at the ground again for feet and petals or other things that have found their way on the floor.

I bump right into him, like yesterday. The tray in my hand comes loose and hits the floor. Glasses shatter and everything is awash with shards and spilled liquid.

His hand slaps me so hard I feel my lip burst. I taste blood in my mouth. I fall to my knees. Bracing myself with my hands, splinters plunge into my skin. I swear, grinding my teeth against the pain, my head dizzy, still catching up.

"You spilled wine on me, you useless whore," Kyrith growls at me. He grabs for my hair.

Before I know what I'm doing, before I realize my own, newly won speed, I've drawn the dagger that dangled from the hilt on his belt and sliced down his forearm in a neat cut.

Blood spills as he pulls his arm back. I slide backwards, away from him over the floor. The crowd parts, gaping, making room for me... and him. My heart lodges in my throat as I take in his hateful gaze, transfixed on me.

I've to fight my way out of here. Or die trying.

My hand curls around the dagger as he comes for me. I throw it and it lodges in his shoulder. He flinches but doesn't stop, rage flaring in his eyes.

I'm dead. I know it when he growls, "You!"

A moment later, something barrels into him, driving Kyrith into the wall at the very far end of the ballroom. The stone cracks and fractures as his body collides with the stone.

For a second, I glimpse Riven, holding Kyrith by the throat, both surrounded by a wall of dark fire.

I blink, and Kyrith...

Is right before me. Riven's hand holds nothing but air.

"Get me the fucking whip!" Kyrith growls, and I know I'm not going to survive the whipping. Not me, a half-fae something. Not when Kyrith does it.

"No whip."

The whole party pauses as a wave of power shakes the room so violently I mistake it for an earthquake. Or thunder. More glasses tingle, tumbling to the ground, plates following.

Not an earthquake, I realize slowly, as the crowd parts, heads lowered, some bowing, others falling on a knee and making obeisance. It's Caryan who has spoken. He's appeared out of nowhere behind Kyrith, stepping out of a ripple of purest night. Although he looks calm on the outside, I can see his aura is a black storm.

"Take her to my quarters, Ronin," Caryan says without taking his eyes off Kyrith, who stands right before me, frozen mid-motion like once in Lyrian's house.

Everyone's gathered to look at him, at Kyrith, then at me on the floor, when the red-haired high lord steps in. I feel him lift me up by my shoulders before he takes me by the elbow and gently steers me toward the hallway.

I let him, my head still dazed from the slap. Blood is dripping everywhere on the stone floor, leaving a lurid trail. I'm not sure whether I cut myself on the shards or whether it's Kyrith's. I don't really care.

In the hallway, Ronin's voice finally startles me. He says, "I don't need to tell you that, if you fight, the result will be much worse than what Kyrith just did."

"Don't worry, I've learned that already."

"Not well enough, it seems," he replies, gesturing for me to lead the way, as if he doesn't want to walk behind me. As if I could somehow be the dangerous one. *Funny.*

I obey, my face throbbing in pain with every step, with every violent beat my heart performs in my chest. Ronin guides me down a corridor I've never been to before and finally pauses in front of a huge, double-winged stone door. The head of a creature that is partly dragon, partly lion, with horns and long teeth, is embedded in the wall next to it; an exact replica of the one Nidaw spoke to on my first night here.

Its eyes flicker to life with bluish flames when Ronin stops in front of it.

"I'm bringing the Dark Lord's slave."

"You mean the Dark Lord's *lady*," the head corrects him.

"The last I heard, she was still his slave," Ronin snaps at the head.

But the head just replies cooly, "I'm rather rarely mistaken, Lord Ronin," before the blue fire in its eyes expires and one side of the door swings open as if by an invisible hand.

I enter a huge room, larger than all the others, apart from those where the celebrations are held, the walls so high I almost can't see the ceiling in the dim light. They are made of the same foreign, dark and gold-veined stone as in the hall, but the floor is different. It's a dark, matte, ashy wood that looks like velvet and is just as soft under my bare feet. The front of the room is opened, and the warm, dry, still-heated desert wind blows in.

Two other massive, winged stone doors on either side suggest more rooms, but they are closed.

Caryan's quarters.

I pause in the middle of the room, feeling lost, my arms wrapped tightly around myself, braced against whatever awaits me.

Ronin's face is hard and his amber eyes cold when I look back at him. He has two swords strapped down his back and is not in an outfit for celebration but for battle—boots and clothing reinforced with leather on knees and elbows. He looks like a warrior, despite the fine features of his face that seem almost feminine. Another glance at his eyes, and I know nothing good is in store for me.

I attacked a high lord. They will whip me. At least. Will Ronin do it? The iciness in his eyes makes me hope not.

He leans against a wall next to a modern, wooden bar, stocked with beautifully cut decanters and liquids that dance in the scarce light, his arms crossed, his gaze trained on me like a weapon.

I keep my head low, but I can still see his aura. Feel it rather. It's pure pain. A loss so deep it has cut right through him like a ravine, splitting him in half. And anger. The furious red wafts wrap around the core of sadness as if they can hide it from the world, from himself too. Hold him together.

He frowns, as if he is hearing an invisible voice. "You stay here and touch nothing."

He's already crossed the room toward the door. It swings open and then shuts me in.

I allow myself to let out a shuddering breath. My face still hurts badly. I don't want to see how I look. Tears well in my eyes, and I blink them away. It all feels too much like life with Lyrian. The pain, the violence. My helplessness. That I can't fight it because everyone here is stronger and faster than me.

I hate it. Hate to be locked away day in, day out.

More useless tears stream down my cheeks unasked, until I wipe them away. Crying has never helped me, has only ever made things worse, so I try to guide my attention toward my surroundings to take my mind off the inevitable.

At least this isn't a cell, it isn't the dungeon. *Not yet,* my inner voice snaps, but I shut it down.

Touch nothing. This means that there must be something around worth touching.

I slowly walk up to the bar, looking closer at the shimmering liquids held by the bottles. If I drink something, will it numb me? Numb me enough to make it easier to handle the pain?

But I don't dare to reach out for one of the decanters. Instead, I stride toward the double-winged door to the left. It swings open.

"I assume my master's lady likes to read, so enter," another ornamental head, twin of the one embedded in the wall outside, says, the same bluish flame dancing in his eyes.

It takes me a moment to respond, to snap out of the surprise. "Thank you. How did you know?" I ask, and the door chuckles. It actually *chuckles.*

"As I said to Lord Ronin before—I'm rarely mistaken."

I nod, whispering another thank you as I enter a room similar in dimension to the first, with the same wide front, only with bookshelves stretching from bottom to top. The three walls are filled with the colorful spines of books, indirectly illuminated by a warm light that seems to gleam somewhere behind them.

I step closer, carefully touching the back of a book so old I'm afraid it will fall apart in my hand. But the strange words on its back seem to burn from within in a dampened, eerie green, in a type of writing I've never seen before, turning brighter at my touch. As if the book's calling me, impatient to be opened.

"The section in your language is down the room. There's even some literature from the human world." A voice behind me, so close, though I heard no one coming.

I swivel around, only to find Caryan standing in the doorway, his eyes red and scary. He, like Ronin, isn't dressed in celebratory attire but all in black. Battle gear, I think, though I spot no weapons on him—this is all I glean before I lower my head.

Maybe you don't need a weapon when you are one yourself.

He steps into the room, and I feel the already familiar pulsing of his power as if it's reaching out to me, running up my body. In response, my blood rushes in my ears. I sling my arms around myself again.

Caryan pauses next to me, and it's all I can do not to run, not to retreat even a step when he reaches out and takes the book I was drawn to off the shelf.

It seems to nestle into his hand, as if it likes his touch, before it falls open and reveals pages with more of those signs and symbols that gleam blue in the light.

"Some of them can be dangerous for the wrong person to touch," he says.

I try to find my words while his power brushes against my skin once again, even stronger than before because of his proximity. It's dark, coming off him in a wavy black mist. But what had been a storm full of black lightning before has ebbed to something gentle and velvety that wraps around me now. Soft like the night, longing for the silvery light of the moon and the stars.

I study the symbols, trying to focus on them instead of on his scent which engulfs me—the invisible twin to his magic. Something in me flares up then. A strange kind of... recognition, as if—as if I could decipher this text if I spent a little more time with the book.

"Those are runes. Old runes. One of the elder languages," I say, surprising myself with the knowledge. *Woah. Where did that come from?*

But the book starts to wave its pages at my words, like a bird flapping its wings. Caryan stretches out his hand for me to hold it.

I glance up at his black eyes, his irises still red but waiting, and I gently take the book from him, placing it on my open palm. The book ruffles its pages one more time as if satisfied before nestling against my skin like it did with him. I can't help but reach out with my other hand to gently stroke its back like I wanted to before.

"What—what does that mean? That they're dangerous for the wrong person?" I whisper, still watching the book.

"Some of them like you, some don't. They tend to get barbaric when someone they despise touches them," Caryan answers in a tone I can't decipher. "But this one seems to have taken a liking to you, so keep it."

"A present, for me?"

"It's about silver elves. You may read it one day," he retorts in the same ambiguous way I can't interpret.

"Thank you," I whisper. I don't know what else to say. I've never gotten a present in my life before.

I don't dare to look up at him again, not when he's this close. Not when all my blood seems to hum with his very presence, his scent wrapped everywhere around us, his power brushing up against something under my skin. Instead, I look at his collarbones showing through his V-cut shirt. *Stupid.*

Involuntarily, my whole skin flushes with heat at the knowledge that his skin is only inches away from mine. That only yesterday, my lips had touched that very spot.

What the hell is wrong with me?

I look down to the floor quickly, my eyes tracking the patterns of wood.

"You are shaking," he says.

I bite my swollen lip so hard it hurts, but fight for the strength to ask, "You're going to punish me, right?"

Better to have it out. He knows anyway, can sense *everything* about me. My treacherous, feverish heartbeat, the rush of adrenaline, the heat coming off me. All the confusion, my thoughts running so wild and in despair. And all those other things that make no sense to me.

Better to focus on the brutal part.

I need to get it over with. *I will survive.* I keep telling myself that, over and over, like a mantra.

When he doesn't answer, I glance up again, only to find him scrutinizing my face, the red in his eyes streaked with hues of midnight blue now. He's so utterly beautiful, no matter how cruel he is, I will always find him beautiful, I know.

But to my surprise, he asks almost gently, "I am?"

"You are angry with me." My voice is no more than a hush.

"I am?"

I cringe. This is a game. A cruel joke, like Lyrian played so many times on me. Telling me he was not angry and then making Hunter and Kayne pay me back for weeks.

I feel Caryan's anger too keenly, see it in his aura. Something pulsing under the midnight veil of fog, ready to break free. Something red and violet and violent, burning in dark flames.

When I dare to look up at him again, I find his eyes resting on my split, swollen lip before they flick up to mine. I whisper, "Sorry," and look down again, chastising myself, wondering when I will ever get used to this—to being a slave. Or to his eyes, to the golden veins that have started to leak back in, mingling with the red and blue.

He retorts, "I am not."

"You are. I can see it all over you, in your aura," I say too quickly. I bite the inside of my cheek. *Stupid.* Maybe I'm just utterly damn stupid.

"I didn't know you had that gift," he admits. "Well, then let me be precise: I am angry. But not *at* you."

I want to ask *who else are you angry with.* Instead, I say, "I tried to stab a high lord."

"With his own dagger. After he slapped you. I don't know the last time anyone managed to cut Kyrith's skin open. In front of my whole court, that is." His voice is genuinely admiring, almost surprised. "I'm sure he won't forget that anytime soon."

"That's exactly what I'm afraid of."

"You don't have to be. He won't touch you again, I made sure of that."

My heart stops at the sudden darkness in his tone. In his aura. I remember how Caryan said that Kyrith would find himself without a head the next time he so much as touched me.

Next time you decide to speak like that to your king, or touch something that's mine for that matter, you'll find yourself without a head. Isn't that what he said last night? That he would *kill* him. Kill Kyrith, because he touched *me*. Something that is *mine*. That's what I am, his *property* and nothing more, I remind myself.

But it doesn't match the gentleness, still in his voice when he asks, "How do you feel?"

Lost. Hurt. Helpless. Angry. Confused.

I recoil at the sudden movement of Caryan's arm. And just as in the dungeon, I hate myself for it.

I hold my breath as tender fingers probe over my raw skin a moment later.

"Look at me," he demands, and I do, feeling the strange rush of sensation when looking into his eyes, of being, for once, allowed to see what I long to see. More blue, more gold, but subtle, just a little gleam of red in the background like a sunset in a dream.

I can't help but think that there's something vaguely familiar in his features. As if I've seen him before. Somewhere. It *was* in a dream. *He* was in a dream. But before I can grasp that thought, that revelation fully, it slips away again.

I swallow at the way his eyes drink in my face. Resist the strange urge to lean into his touch.

My gaze falls to my hands again. "Why am I here?"

"Because of an arrangement with Lyrian," he answers too neutrally, evasively.

"Why am I *really* here?"

He hesitates for a second, irritation flickering over his features. "Because you're unique to this world."

My mouth goes dry. I swallow, then ask, "You've never seen a half-blood before?"

"No, not a human half-blood." His hand brushes back my hair to reveal my round ear, the curve of my cheek, the shape of my neck; gently, before he pulls it back. But his eyes keep roving over my skin with some kind of rapt curiosity. "I must admit that even I have not. I think only a few ever have."

I don't have it in me to ask whether this makes me a special trophy. Something... extraordinary to keep and show around. Is that why he wanted me? Why he *traded* me?

The question burns in my mind, along with so many others. What about my mother... my father?

But I'm not ready to ask. Not now. Not here.

Not when I'm all alone with him.

Eventually, he says, "Go. Sleep. It's already late."

I turn to get away as quickly as possible when the sound of his voice makes me pause midway. "And Melody—"

I glance over my shoulder. "Trying to run would be foolish."

My heartbeat stutters. Does he know? Did Riven tell him? "Because you're going to flay me. Got it."

"Because monsters roam this realm," he counters, ignoring my remark. "Monsters that come straight out of the nine hells."

24

RIVEN

A cracking sound, so hard it almost shakes the thick walls of the training rooms. Followed by a bone-grinding growl from Caryan's throat. Even Riven startles at the brute force with which Caryan has driven Kyrith into the wall, the stone giving way and fracturing under Kyrith's body.

Caryan's fangs are only slivers away from Kyrith's throat, pausing a second before he sinks them into his flesh. Brutal, without mercy, as if Caryan wants to rip it out.

Kyrith's face is a mask of pain, but he doesn't make any sound. Doesn't fight it until Caryan eventually lets go of him, but not without grabbing Kyrith's throat again, along with the wound there, and hurling him across the room into the opposite wall. Kyrith collapses on the floor like a mass of dead flesh.

Riven stares at his friend. It's time that Caryan disciplined Kyrith, but he's never seen Caryan *this* angry. He's even taken the damper off his magic, and the power in the room is flaring so thick it's almost suffocating.

For the dark kings of the Abyss's sake, it has no beginning and no end. It takes all of Riven's own magic to move against it, not to be crushed by it like a ship buried under the weight of the ocean.

Caryan strides over toward Kyrith, who's still lying curled on the floor, every visible part of him bleeding. Kyrith lifts his head, blood dripping over his chin, looking up at Caryan like a dog at his master, pain shining on his face so bright and clear it's gut-wrenching.

But Riven knows it's not the physical pain. Kyrith's a hard bastard. He can handle shattered bones. It's the fact that he has upset Caryan so much.

Riven almost feels pity. Almost, if the thought of Melody on the ground doesn't make him want to send another kick into Kyrith's already cracked ribs.

Caryan wipes the blood off his chin with his sleeve before he says, calmer now, "I know you hate her because she looks like her mother, Kyrith. But you can't punish her for that."

"I treated her just like we treat slaves. She dropped and spilled everything. A slap was the least—"

"First you dare to speak to me like that in front of others. Now you dare to lie to my face. You ran into her deliberately, Kyrith. Do you think I can't see it in your blood? Do not tempt me." Caryan's voice cuts through the air like a knife.

Riven isn't sure, but he thinks he sees Kyrith blush under all his cuts and bruises. Kyrith opens his mouth and, briefly, Riven expects him to apologize.

But instead, Kyrith straightens up as far as his broken bones allow. He stares right into Caryan's face, a challenge bristling in his own forest-green eyes. "Tell me why, Caryan? Tell me why you brought her here! She will be trouble. She already is."

"She's nothing of the sort, and you know very well why she's here."

"The elven relics. How could I forget?" Kyrith snarls bitterly. "But why not use her now, Caryan? Why wait? Why not get her to find them *now* if you're so keen to, with all those spies clambering over each other to get their hands on her too? Why let her work her ass off like a servant? You know exactly why all those spies are coming here."

Riven stares, surprised to hear Kyrith throwing this in Caryan's face. Granted, he's been unwilling to believe that Kyrith, of all people, would be astute enough to figure things out. Or that he had the spine to confront Caryan.

"You're in no position to question my actions." Caryan's voice is like slick, solid ice, his eyes gleaming deadlier than ever.

"For fuck's sake, am I the only one who sees the truth?" Kyrith's eyes flit to Riven's before they settle back on Caryan's. "She can be dangerous, and you know it! But for some reason, you and Riven pretend she isn't. You mustn't trust her!"

"She isn't dangerous, Kyrith." Riven says because that is what Caryan expects him to say. And no matter what happens on the inside, between them, to the outside they have to stand in unison, like a wall. He is still Caryan's right hand.

"You mean she is not *now*," Kyrith barks at him before he looks at Caryan. "But we heard what the future holds, Caryan." He braces himself against the wall, flinching against the pain, but he manages to stand. His gaze is still trained on Caryan, determination burning in his eyes.

Riven winces. Not that he likes Kyrith much, but this can't end well.

Caryan growls at him, power rippling through all of them. "Don't you dare strike such a tone with me. Stand down."

"No! You deemed her mother harmless, and look where it got you, Caryan! She almost *killed* you! You can't be so blind. You know the prophecy. You know what her daughter will do, *can* do. She will be your end! To me, that means she'll do the exact thing her mother didn't manage—kill you. Do you expect us to stand by and watch?"

Riven feels a crack running through him at that. There is pain shining in Kyrith's voice, in his face, so much a reflection of Riven's own that, for a second, it makes him empathize with Kyrith. Makes it hard to stand by and keep a cold face.

But the sentiment dies when Kyrith carries on, pleading, "Kill her, just kill her, Caryan—or let me do it! Please."

A vicious snarl escapes Riven's own throat.

Kyrith's swollen, blood-encrusted eyes snap back toward him, turning into mean slits. "That's exactly what I'm talking about! That sort of mercy is reckless. What's wrong with you? You—you two seem to have a soft spot for her. For some fucking reason! Snap her neck and it's over, Kalleandara's prophecy gone! Fuck those relics; you'll win the war, with or without them, and you know it, Caryan!"

"You're overstepping your mark *again*, Kyrith. Back down now, and I'll let you get away with it." Caryan's voice is such a low growl that Riven feels the hair on his neck stand up—a final warning Kyrith chooses to ignore.

"If I didn't know any better, I'd say you *like* to have her here. You don't treat her like a fucking slave, but like a princess."

"That's utterly ridiculous," Riven cuts in.

"Is it?" Kyrith barks toward Riven before his eyes glide back to Caryan. "Don't pretend we can't see the way you look at her. Why not make her your whore, huh? We can all tell how badly you want to fuck her. It's so fucking obvious it—" Kyrith's voice cracks in the middle of the sentence, and the second part almost sounds like whining when Caryan slams him against the wall once more. Only Caryan's hand at Kyrith's collar keeps Kyrith upright. Keeps him from slumping to the ground like dead weight.

"Touch her again, Kyrith, and I'll flay you alive. Circumvent my commands one more time, and I'll banish you from my court, throw you to your people and see what they do with you. Do you understand? You'll spend the night here and think about what you've done."

With that, he lets go of Kyrith's tunic. Kyrith slumps down like a sack of grain.

Caryan turns on his heel, and Riven, with one last glance toward Kyrith, follows him out. The door closes shut behind them and locks Kyrith in.

Riven and Caryan stand in the quiet hallway for a moment, the mild sounds of the festivities drifting through the open spaces, carried by the wind like ghosts of better times. Such a hard contrast to the violence. Riven looks at Caryan's knuckles, which are bruised and cracked from the blows he dealt Kyrith. Caryan doesn't seem to notice, although they must hurt like hell, even if they will heal fast, especially when he just drank Kyrith's blood.

Blood laden with strong magic.

Steps sound, and Ronin comes running down the hall, the witcher's moves fast as lightning. "I brought her to your rooms, my king," is all Ronin says, following with a shallow bow.

The quiet warrior, discreet as always, doesn't utter a word or a question about Caryan's bruises or the heavy scent of Kyrith's blood all over them.

Caryan just turns away. Riven wants to go after him, to beg him not to go and see Melody while he's still in this mood. But Ronin's hand closes around his arm, holding him back. Ronin shakes his head only once.

Riven meets the amber eyes of his friend. The witcher who can feel more than most others, who has the exceptional talent of being at the right place at the right time, to do the right thing at the right moment—a gift from his heritage, no doubt.

It's an instinct Riven's learned to trust, so he obeys and lets Caryan go.

25

BLAIR

Blair slides off the back of her phantom wyvern and the summoned, glimmering beast with rainbow scales vanishes into thin air. She strides toward some rocks, looking for the entrance of the seer's cave. Only her witch senses can detect the strange power lurking within those natural walls, telling her that something is hiding here in the first place.

A natural, tiny little cave in the woods, situated on the outskirts of the Black Forest and the Kingdom of the Witches, marked by the Nordriff—the range of high-peaked mountains that cuts through the continent like a ravine. High, snowy cliffs alternate with abysses—almost unconquerable if you can't fly over them.

A reason Palisandre hasn't yet dared to attack the witches.

The cave itself lies at the bottom of one of the many nameless, snow-swept mountains. Eventually, Blair finds the entrance, a tiny hole between a crack in the stones, almost invisible to the eye.

She has to duck because the ceiling of the den is so low. But a long tunnel stretches out in front of her, connecting the entrance with one large, cavernous hall at its end.

Inside it smells damp, and faintly of venison and dried herbs that grow in the border forest that merges with the Black Forest. The only difference between the two forests is magic. While the trees in the border forest are green, shielded from the icy winds by the mountains, and the streams crystal clear, the trees in the Black Forest are huge firs and such a dark green they look almost black, growing densely, their branches reaching so low they block out all light. The ground is barren, and the streams are muddy and brown and treacherous, with a lot of strange, hungry creatures lurking in there.

The Black Forest has become a zone of anarchy, where wild, packless wolf shifters, and worse creatures roam.

Blair shudders at what the blacksmith told her. About the Nefarians hiding out there. Nefarians, like the angels, are so feared because they can fly and attack from the air. A little like the witches on their phantom wyverns, but with more stealth. A strange breed.

Blair shakes the thought off as she reaches the hall, a floor of pressed soil covered with carpets made of spun wool. A fire crackles in a corner, and she identifies remnants of burnt goat stew. Wild goats, apart from deer, snow hares and other fae, are the only animals that still roam these territories since the great cold came.

Blair sneers at the smell, longing for human food. Then she spots the seer lying on a makeshift bed on the ground next to the fire. A slim bundle of torn linen.

"Get up," Blair says, nudging the bundle with a booted foot.

It stirs, and Blair raises her brows as an excessively slim young woman with hair the color of corn and huge, pointed ears sits up, flinching away from Blair and her silver claws. Wide, pearl-like eyes look up at Blair, the seer's tiny, slim body cowering.

"Please don't harm me, witch."

Seers. Outcasts. No one quite knows what they are. A mood of nature and magic. Shunned mainly because people don't like hearing about futures they don't want to have.

Blair crouches next to her bed—or rather the moth-eaten cloak stuffed with straw or dried weeds of some sort. "I want you to tell me where Caryan keeps the girl from Kalleandara's prophecy. The girl who ends the blight. Where can I find her? Tell me and you don't need to fear me."

The girl angles her head up to her, her pale eyes widening. Hells, she looks skinny with hunger and half-frozen. Blair looks around but can't find any clothes; the girl probably goes out into the cold in these rags. How she will survive the next winter, Blair has no idea.

"That girl is the one who saved your life…" she whispers, and Blair flashes her teeth at her.

"Come, seer, don't test me."

The girl flinches, trying to push herself into the wall and further away from Blair's sharp teeth and nails. She wonders what the blacksmith wanted here. Why he sought this scrawny thing out.

"The Dark Lord will look for the first elven artifact. He will go to the holy mountain Silas. But she… she will die there."

Now it's Blair who stares at her. *Will I be the one to kill her?*

"Why? Why will she die?"

But the seer only shakes her head, a little desperate. "I can't see. It's veiled."

"Try."

"I can't."

"You better try harder, or I might change my mind about hurting you."

The girl just shakes her head again. "I can't. The veil around the holy mountain won't let me."

"Who kills her then?"

"I can't see that either."

Blair runs her tongue over her teeth, annoyed, and gets up, pacing back and forth before she stops. She swivels to the girl who just sits there and watches her, legs pulled close to her body. "She can't die. She's the one who's going to kill Caryan."

"Is that what you want, witch? To see him dead?" the seer asks so nonchalantly Blair wants to slap her.

"It's what the prophecy of Kalleandara says," Blair blurts.

"Is it?" the girl muses.

Only then does Blair realize the girl's sober tone is not meant to mock her but that she's simply curious.

"Is it not?" Blair asks back, snapping her teeth toward her in a warning.

"Remember, witch, we are hardly ever what we seem. Even rarer what we dream."

"I asked you a damn fucking question, seer. I suggest you answer it if you want to keep your miserable hide."

The girl shrugs, utterly unfazed. "I don't know. But the prophecy says that she will end the blight. Nothing more, nothing less."

"Caryan *is* the blight."

"Maybe he is, in a sense, maybe not, but... what of it anyway? What has this to do with you, other than a broken heart?"

"I have no damn broken heart!" Blair hisses, showing the full length of her elongated, silver canines. But how many nights has Caryan's name played in her head like a song on repeat when she tried to sleep?

The girl looks back at her, playing with a strand of her whitish, pearlescent hair and some twigs and leaves that have caught there, saying nothing. Blair wonders how old this creature is. Older than her or as young as she looks?

"It also says madness is on the threshold, that the hounds of war have been summoned," Blair goes on, her voice still sharp, her brows raised. "Has he gone mad? Is he going to start a war?"

"Maybe," the girl offers.

"*Foreign troubles that have been unlooked for too long... An earthborn child of ancient blood, who carries within her the light; she is the only one who will end the blight,*" Blair recites.

The girl just shrugs again.

"You don't believe the oracles?" Blair snaps.

"I do and I don't. They're so vague and so moody. They can change their prophecies all over. All it takes is one tiny decision, and everything turns out differently. Sometimes it's the tiny things that make the biggest difference. Like an act of kindness, or mercy."

"Is that what you told the blacksmith, along with my name?"

"I told the blacksmith where to find the wounded Nefarians. He wanted to know your name. That was all he came for. He said he dreamed about you. I see he gave you the sword the Nefarian gifted him." The seer's eyes rest on the black sword on Blair's belt.

"Why are the Nefarians back?"

"Maybe they were never gone in the first place."

"Stop being cryptic, seer! Or you're going to end up as a treat for my wyvern."

"The Nefarians still live in Khalix, the desert lands in the west. The forgotten continent."

Blair stares at her, truly shocked. "What? There's nothing there anymore. Nothing but dirt and dust. And we know. We flew there once and checked. The city hewn in stone is vacated, not a soul there left."

"Yes, you did fly there once, I know. And you saw nothing because Khalix and the City of Sky and Stone are hidden under a glamour."

"No way. There is no one powerful enough to hide a whole godsdamn city from the rest of the world."

"Oh yes, there is, Blair Alaric. You always knew how powerful *he* is, because you're attracted to accumulations of power."

"Caryan," Blair whispers, a part of her unable to believe it. "Yes."

"But why? Why would he let them stay? Help them?"

The seer lifts her whitish brows. "An act of altruism, maybe?" she suggests, repeating the very words the blacksmith gave Blair.

"No. What does he want from the Nefarians?" Blair snaps, scowling at the creature when she just shrugs again.

"Fucking tell me!"

"You know him better than I, Blair Alaric, don't you?" she just asks back.

Blair flexes her clawed fingers, contemplating for a moment to cut the seer's neck and make this woman her dinner before she relents. Not her fault Caryan's everywhere she goes, in every breath she takes. She pulls her head back and lets out a long sigh, feeling her fury ebbing and giving way to bone-grinding exhaustion. All this useless fury about what Perenilla made her do. In truth, she's tired. Just so fucking tired.

She stalks over to the kettle that dangles over the fire and peeks inside. Empty. Boiled down to the dregs. She sighs again and looks to the girl. "Are you hungry?"

The seer just shrugs. Blair looks back at her one last time before she stalks away.

She returns two hours later with a dead boar around her shoulders. She'd let her phantom wyvern's claws close around the unfortunate grazing beast. It didn't feel a thing before the wyvern's claws snapped its neck. Then Blair had flown to the border forest, collected berries she wrapped in her cloak, and dug out some roots she found with her acute sense of smell.

She crossed a merchant's path on the edge of the Black Forest on his way to Silvander and bought some boots, dried herbs and a leathery skin filled with honey wine from him. She glamoured herself to pass as an elf. If word spread that a witch had passed into Palisandre, all hell would break loose.

It's a pity though that the elves had woven glamour-stripping spells around every major town. Otherwise, the witches would have long infiltrated the elven courts.

The glamour ebbs off as she soars back through the sky. Her wyvern screeches like a real one as its huge, clawed feet touch down in front of the den. To Blair's surprise, the girl comes running out, her eyes wide as she takes in the whitish beast, half-translucent and half-solid, its rainbow scales glimmering in the moonlight.

"She is beautiful," the girl remarks, her voice full of awe.

Blair squints. "How do you know it's a girl?"

"I just know," the seer retorts in that unnerving manner of hers. "Can I... touch her?"

Blair nods once, frowning as her magical creation nuzzles its snout against the seer's outstretched hand before disappearing into thin air on her command.

"It's just magic," Blair mutters under her breath, stalking back into the den.

Later, they sit by the fire, the girl with her new shoes on and huddled in Blair's cloak, spooning the boar stew with roots up like a hungry wolf.

Blair eats little of hers to leave more for the seer. She'd sliced the boar up, skinned it, and showed the girl how to prepare its hide, how to preserve its meat with salt she found in a burlap sack in a corner, along with some clay pots and weed baskets. How to cook out the fat and keep it too. Things she learned from Aurora and Sofya.

She grabs the wineskin and takes a hearty swig before she passes it to the girl, who takes it and drinks, scrunching up her delicate nose. "Ugh. That stuff is strong," she mutters.

"Not strong enough," Blair remarks, running her claws over the ground.

"Where did you find all the ingredients?" the girl asks, gesturing to the stew in her hand as if she hasn't heard.

"My nose. And my claws."

The seer eyes them as if seeing them in a new light. "I wish I could be like you," she admits very quietly.

"What happened to you?"

"My father wanted to… use me for dark purposes. I escaped, and since then, I've been hiding out here."

A growl of thunder rumbles outside and Blair looks toward the corridor. *Great.* Now she will have to stay the whole night or get soaked. She's careful to hide her annoyance when she looks back at the girl though. She stretches out her legs, settling deeper into the mattress. If she has to stay, she might as well get comfortable.

"I am… I've always been so lonely," the seer adds, like an afterthought, taking another mouthful of wine before she hands the skin back to Blair, who matches her.

She leans her head back and closes her eyes for a moment, listening to the rain. Then she says, "So have I."

When she looks back at the girl again, she finds her studying her face.

"You know, when I was a child, I used to summon that

phantom wyvern in a baby form and play with her. I wished she'd one day become real, so I'd have a..." Blair cuts herself off. What the hell is she doing here? Must be the mead, going to her head.

"A friend," the girl says.

And for a second Blair finds it hard to breathe. "I still sometimes wish she was... real."

"You could go to the Abyss, ask one of the beasts dwelling there whether it wants to be yours."

Blair stares at her before she finds her speech again. "Going to the Abyss would be suicide. And I don't have the power to harness a demon." Unlike Caryan. Does the girl not see that? Does she want her to die?

But the seer just shakes her head. "I wasn't only talking about demons. But... demons, not all of them are evil, you know. They will sometimes join someone if they want to."

"They're fucking lethal. That's what they are," Blair contradicts, horror in her voice.

The girl just drains another bowl and some color's creeping back into her gaunt cheeks. "Aren't we all, if we want to be?" With that, she rolls up next to Blair, placing her head on Blair's thigh, the blonde hair spreading wide.

Blair just watches her, spellbound. Unsure.

The girl turns her head to look up with sleepy eyes before she whispers, "Nothing's ever written in stone, Blair, not even a prophecy. It always comes down to choice. Your fates are linked, Blair. The girl's and yours."

"What's that supposed to mean? Speak, seer."

"I cannot see more, because I do not know, Blair Alaric. I told you all I know. But remember, you don't have to be the witch from the story—the one who hid her heart so it would always stay broken and finally turn into stone." Then she turns back, her breathing becoming deep and even.

Blair just looks at her, too afraid that, if she moves, the girl will wake up. But the longer she watches, the more the seer looks like *the* girl. Like Melody. Her hair is no longer light, but dark. Her face no longer so sharp, but softer. Her body no longer so bony, but long-limbed and muscular.

She still looks that way, still asleep, wrapped in Blair's cloak, when Blair leaves at the first gray of morning, not looking back.

26

RIVEN

Riven finds Kyrith slumped against the wall, his hairline encrusted with blood, his lips caked with dried crimson, his nose broken, sweat slicking his whole body. He barely looks up when the door opens and Riven steps closer to him, avoiding the puddle of dried blood.

Riven holds out a glass bottle of water. Eventually, Kyrith drags his gaze up at him, then squints at the bottle in Riven's hand.

"Just another fucking thing Caryan took from the human world."

"They're good for the environment," Riven counters with a cold grin.

"Fuck you."

"Unlike your language, Kyrith. It seems the word *fuck* is something you brought from them and seem to like quite a lot."

Kyrith snarls but stops when exposing his fangs obviously hurts him. His healing process is being slowed down by the masses of blood Caryan drank from him.

"Came here to finally kill me, Riven, because Caryan ran out of patience with me?" he grumbles but snatches the bottle from Riven's hand and downs it in one solid swig.

Riven regards his fingernails in the low light. "Agreed, there is no shame in a capricious murder now and again."

"Then stop stalling. Burn me but make it quick. Not that you'd ruin one of your manicured nails using your hands for once," Kyrith spits.

"Actually, I'm here because I took pity on you, but go on and I might change my mind," Riven says, bringing his wrist to his teeth and cutting a gash before offering it to Kyrith.

Kyrith looks surprised but eventually takes the offer and starts drinking. The effect is instant—his bruises heal and every wound, every crack, every tiny cut, starts to close and is erased within seconds—this rapid healing, faster than their normal fae healing, just another gift from the curse.

"Thank you," Kyrith grunts eventually, leaning his head back against the wall. "But why?"

"Why what?" Riven asks coolly, watching his own flesh close up before he pulls the sleeve of his black hunting shirt back down.

"Why take pity on me?" Kyrith asks, spitting saliva and blood into a corner.

"Because I know why you did it—for the same reason I do the things I do."

"You fucking know that she's a threat. If you love him, if you love any of us, then stop it," Kyrith hisses.

Riven sighs at the teeth bared in his direction. "For someone who looked so battered a solid minute ago, you're pretty ungrateful."

"I'm always straightforward and that's exactly why you like me."

"Do I like you?"

"Fuck you!" Kyrith mutters.

Riven sighs again. "Always going in hard with the charm. You know, some diplomacy might have saved your sorry ass, and you might not be sucking blood right now—to put it in your words. Ever thought about that?"

This shuts Kyrith up. The mention of why Kyrith had been dead… before Caryan found him and offered him a second chance. Good. A Kyrith whose blood-fresh magic's humming might shatter Riven's nerves.

A moment of unusual silence draws out between them. Riven waits until Kyrith breaks it. "I never regretted it, though—the gift from Caryan, you know? Not once in my life," he says quietly, almost to himself.

When Riven says nothing, Kyrith looks up to him, his own eyes shaded by darkness. "If I got the chance again, I'd do no different. I'd do the very same again, just to be at Caryan's side."

Riven shrugs. "It's not such a bad thing."

"Isn't it? To leave my people, who I fought alongside for centuries. My cadres. My friends."

"You realized you were fighting for the wrong things, Kyrith. Ultimately, it was a good decision to change sides."

"Yeah? Will it be when Caryan dies in the end? Will it all be worth it then?"

Riven doesn't answer. Instead, he sinks down next to Kyrith, leaning his back against the wall, the stone soothingly cold and solid against his shoulders.

Next to him, Kyrith runs a calloused hand through his thick, whitish hair. "He already has enough power. He doesn't need those fucking elf relics and their ancient magic. With the girl gone, he'd make sure no one else could get them either. We both know that, Riven. We've always known that. That's what I was saying. Why start down that path when he has a choice to turn away? Why not kill her, for fuck's sake? Or, if he's suddenly, for some weird reason, turned sentimental, why not hide her away somewhere safe? Why bring her here?"

Riven closes his eyes, suppressing every hint of emotion that pushes up from his own innermost being. He knows too well that Kyrith's immaculately accurate senses would pick it up immediately. He learned this the hard way when he served Gatilla, and became well versed in hiding his emotions.

He forces his voice to be controlled too, smooth as wet stone, and calm when he says, "Have you ever wondered what happens when Caryan has taken over the world? What happens when he's reached everything Gatilla made him aspire to?"

"The world will yearn to kneel and offer their necks. I can't wait to see the day," Kyrith growls, pride and admiration resonating in every word.

"Maybe it will. But madness and greatness are two sides of the same coin. Imagine—for just a single moment—imagine an immortal high king."

Riven barely dares to speak the words. Barely forces them out, but it's his part in all of this. He will always choose Caryan's side, always support the decisions his king makes, and if this helps Caryan's cause, he will gladly play along.

He feels Kyrith studying him in the dark and turns his head to meet his gaze. He continues. "He might indeed go mad. He might grow tired and weary."

"He wouldn't. He told us several times that he can't feel anything. That he has no fucking emotions, because he's a fucking fallen angel," Kyrith contradicts, shaking his head, but Riven feels the weight of his words sinking in.

"And that makes it better? Who'll stay his hand? Caution him?"

"You, Riven. That's what you do all the time, right? You're the only one who gets through to him. If he listens to anybody, it'll be you."

"And if not, Kyrith? Caryan's changed. What if he grows so cold that even we can't get through to him anymore?" Riven pushes on.

Kyrith shakes his head as if he wanted to deny that Riven said the words, rubbing his eyes. His teeth are bared as if in great pain. "You can't tell me he'll accept dying because of that," he growls.

The anger's not directed toward Riven but toward fate and the prophecy. An anger Riven understands too well. He fights hard not to open up. It would feel so good to share his own worries with someone for once. But it's his burden to carry, for Caryan's sake. He's always done so.

Anything else would be betrayal.

"It's his choice, Kyrith. And maybe he's tired already. He's so old. Only the ancient gods know how long he served Gatilla and what he did before."

"I know that," Kyrith confirms bitterly.

"Maybe this is what Caryan wants. What if she's the only way he can die? Can you imagine that burden—to have to live forever? Maybe this is why he brought Melody along. Why he keeps her around."

"He can't die." Kyrith's head jerks up. He glowers at Riven, eyes full of loss and despair. "We can't allow that!"

"You can't stop the inevitable, Kyrith," Riven finds himself saying, realizing he's repeating the very same words Caryan told him. The very same words he hates so much that just saying them burns a hole in his soul. Seeing his own demons reflected and thrown back at him, laughing in his face. "The wheels of fate are already in motion, and they have been for a long while."

Riven stands, putting a hand on Kyrith's broad, strong shoulder.

"It already started that day when Lara almost killed him. When the healer, the elf Meanara at the temple in Avandal, decided to help him instead of letting him die," Riven explains, and understanding enters Kyrith's green eyes. "When Lara escaped into the human world and met that human and shortly after bore Melody. A new era dawned then, along with it a new prophecy."

"We took the first step when we started looking for Lara's daughter in the human world twenty years ago," Kyrith says breathlessly, his eyes wide in shock and realization.

Riven nods slowly. "Yes."

"Caryan always planned to bring the girl here. All those years."

Riven nods again.

Kyrith stays quiet for once. Then he shakes his head, rubbing his eyes again, head low. "So it's not just me who thinks he's always behaved strangely about that girl. That feverish searching, us turning every damn stone in the human world. As if she was an obsession."

It's Riven's turn to say nothing.

Kyrith's eyes are bloodshot as he mutters, "All of that so he can die?"

"Maybe."

But Kyrith shakes his head. "Nuh. I don't believe that's all. Come on, you saw it too. He wants to fuck her, wanted her at that party. Badly. For a fact, I've never seen Caryan like this. And she's a slave. Why not just take her?"

"We don't know—"

"I know what I saw, and you know it too. I knew for sure when he broke my nose for mentioning it."

"She was shaking all over, Kyrith. You smelled her fear, it was everywhere. I'm glad he let her go," Riven points out, his teeth clenched at the last words.

"Oh, come on. We both know that's not what I'm talking about. It was fucking crazy what went down between them, with Caryan's eyes turning that gold. I've never seen him like that. And yeah, the girl was afraid, but there was more on her side too. There was some weird shit going on, as if—as if they had some sort of connection beyond my understanding."

Yes, I saw it too. Felt it. Witnessed it.

He says, "I don't know what it is exactly that we saw. Felt. Maybe it was indeed that she is his destiny. That she's the one who will kill him in the end and he knows it. Even you have to admit that this makes a weird relationship."

Kyrith looks at him for a long moment, that relentless flame dancing in his green eyes; the flame that makes him such a dangerous enemy. Made him a legend on the battlefield, when Kyrith still served the King of Elves. Maybe it's that Kyrith is too much—too much power, too much loyalty—maybe the truth is Kyrith doesn't know how to handle himself sometimes.

But Riven sees a kind of gratitude in the warrior's eyes— gratitude that Riven's shared a part of that knowledge with him, even if Kyrith would never say so.

"You've known all this for a very long while, huh?" Kyrith eventually says with a heavy sigh.

"I have. For twenty-two years, to be precise, when Caryan started searching for her. And believe me, I'd have done anything to change it, but it wasn't my decision. I couldn't have stopped him, no matter how much I tried. And ultimately, I deemed it wasn't my place to step between Caryan and her. It was his decision, to kill her or let her live."

Kyrith's whole expression changes into a mask of pain, worse than before as he gets up and gently places his two large hands on Riven's shoulders. "You could have shared, you know? You could have told us. You didn't need to carry this burden alone all these years." His voice is grave, his eyes as clear as a forest in the morning of a summer's day.

"I made a promise, Kyrith. A promise to Caryan. I gave him my word of honor to serve him to whatever end."

Kyrith nods. If there's something Kyrith understands, it's loyalty. It's the only currency Kyrith's ever traded in.

"Besides—" Riven allows some humor to enter his tone, even if it's forced "—it was actually fun to see you enjoying yourself around those humans. Especially the women."

"Oh, c'mon. Those trips to the human world were quite dreary," Kyrith snaps, but a little of the darkness in his face vanishes.

Riven raises a brow.

"Okay, okay—cut me some slack," Kyrith grunts.

"They loved you. They clung to your lips and other parts."

"You got me. They aren't too bad, those humans, I'll give you that."

"And what a dancer you are—I didn't know you could move your hips like that."

"Enough!" Kyrith growls, letting go of Riven's shoulders and shaking his head, though he's smiling to himself now. At the memory. Of the numerous times they hit the mortal clubs, searching every inch for Lyrian or his henchmen.

"No, you were the star of those clubs or discos, or whatever they call those pleasure dens. I think they liked you in black leather."

Kyrith laughs now, truly laughs, then pats Riven's shoulder. "You're a bastard. But yeah, they actually do know how to have fun. Definitely more than our fae women."

"Maybe their short lives make them daring."

"Must be it," Kyrith grunts his agreement.

Riven gestures to the door.

"I'm afraid I have to sit here some more until our master lets me out," Kyrith sighs.

"You do realize that everything reacts to Caryan's wishes, right? That includes opening the door so I could walk in in the first place. Which means I think you're free to leave. That is, if you let Melody be."

Kyrith frowns down at the last words. "Oh, don't worry, I won't touch her again, or Caryan will decorate the ground with my innards. He made that clear." Kyrith pauses. He runs his tongue over his teeth, deciding on something. "Listen. I know I was an ass. It's just—I didn't understand why he brought her here. When I let her get dressed up, it was to provoke him. To bring him to do *something. Anything.* Maybe get him to chase her off. Or set out to find those relics. I don't know what he's waiting for."

"I admit that I don't fully understand his motivations either," Riven says, peering up at the ceiling. "But I *do* understand why you did what you did, Kyrith. But she's still a girl, and she doesn't deserve any of it. She already had a hard time with Lyrian."

Kyrith's shoulders slump and he lets out a shuddering breath. "I know. She looks so much like Lara, though. I still remember that bitch and the sword in her hand, cutting right through Caryan like a damn butcher." He shakes his head, clearing the image.

"We all do. But she is different," Riven says carefully.

"I know. I felt it too—that light about her," Kyrith agrees, voice raw. Again, he surprises Riven with his answer. "I won't be too much of an ass anymore, I promise."

"Good enough for me. Now come, you need a bath. You reek."

MELODY

He wasn't there the following two nights for the celebrations. Neither were Riven, nor Kyrith, nor Ronin, although I kept glancing over to the corner where they had sat the other two nights, almost expecting them to suddenly walk in here.

Maybe I *should* be glad they aren't around. No, I should *definitely*. But a part in me feels empty when I still don't detect Caryan's power close by tonight, brushing up against my skin, that quiet, dark, yet soothing hum over me and all around, filling the rooms and my very soul. Without it, the whole Fortress feels hollowed out.

I'm mad.

I should be afraid.

I am. I'm terrified—and I'm not.

It's complicated, and the more I think about it, the less sense it makes to me. I'm not really afraid of Caryan, although I know that all the others are—even the high lords to some level. I saw it in their auras.

"They won't come," Nidaw tells me, having suddenly materialized next to me.

I jolt. "I wasn't—"

"You're looking. Constantly," the siren says with a strange, knowing side-glance toward me.

I chew on my lower lip, avoiding Nidaw's beautiful, pale eyes, hoping she can't detect the heat under my skin with her siren-senses. "It's the war, isn't it?" I ask.

Nidaw nods once. "You look very tired, girl. Go to sleep. And I think we can do without your help for the next two evenings."

I'm venturing back down the long, empty corridor toward my room, when the breathtakingly beautiful, blonde eleven woman I've seen next to Caryan comes sauntering along. Her long dress is made of two shafts of fabric connected in the middle, exposing most of her belly and her long thighs, making her even more beautiful. But then, I guess she could wear rags and still look breathtaking.

I step aside into an alcove to let her pass, but she pauses.

"Good to meet you, slave. My fireplace needs some cleaning."

I nod, earning a snarl when I look up into her stunning eyes. No fangs, though, just those elongated canines typical for fae.

She hisses, "Watch it, girl. I might not be as tolerant as some others around here. Come now."

I follow her into her room; a large, dark hall decorated mainly with daybeds alternating with tiny tables. Jewelry is strewn around everywhere, as are all sorts of cosmetics and dresses and empty wineglasses. It smells of exotic perfumes and oils. Heavy, velvet curtains are pulled shut, candles providing the only light, their wax dripping into the silken carpets.

As soon as we enter, she slumps down onto a massive bed, waving toward an enormous, marble mantelpiece before taking a large sip from the glass of red wine that has magically appeared in her hand.

I kneel in front of the fireplace, looking for fire irons, but find none. I turn to the elf. "There's no brush, or a shovel."

"Is there not? Shame. I guess you'll have to use your lovely hands," she croons, examining her long nails.

I have to bite back a snarl. "Do you have a bucket, or do you expect me to throw it out of the window?"

"You could eat it. Bite the dust—isn't that what you humans say? Because that's what you all do at some point. Wither away before you have lived. As if you were born already dead." She laughs about her own joke, but with a snap of her fingers, a bucket appears next to me. "Oh, and all of it, girl. Be meticulous, will you?"

I crawl deeper into the huge fireplace and start to scoop up charred wood and ash in my hands, throwing it heap by heap into the bucket. But every time I take another heap, it seems that more ash has appeared out of nowhere.

I turn back to look at her.

"Something wrong, human?" she asks innocently, looking insufferably pleased with herself.

"You're doing *this*."

"Doing what?" She blinks a few times with her long, blue lashes.

"You're summoning more ash, or however it works," I grind out, earning a shrill, bell-like laugh.

"Don't be ridiculous. Go back to work, you lazy creature. You should be grateful, you know. You'll not be his whore forever. You're nothing but a plaything. A wretched toy. Something he'll throw away when he's bored with it. There are so many women vying for his attention you'll be glad you can come close enough to kiss the hem of his cloak when he's done with you."

With another snap of her fingers, all the ash I've collected is scattered all over again, dusting even the floor around the fireplace. I'm covered in soot, my hands already sore from scraping over the rough stone.

I glower at the woman who offers me a feline smile in return.

"Is that what happened to *you*?" I ask before I can reconsider.

She sits up so abruptly that a little of the wine sloshes out of her glass and seeps into the silken sheets of her bed. "You know, I haven't yet decided whether you're just stupid or adorable for being so bold with an elf. Now clean it up."

"No." I get up, dusting my hands off on my dress, hiding how they are shaking at the sheer lunacy of what I'm doing here.

She gets to her feet too, pointing a finger at me, her eyes vicious slits. "You little piece of human filth. I should give you a taste of the whip. Soon enough you will beg me for household chores so he won't throw you to the wolves. Clean it."

"Or what? You'll punish me? I don't think he'll be too pleased about that. And you won't do it yourself, since it's likely he'll drink my blood and see in it what you did. Am I right?"

She stares at me as if I've slapped her awake, blinking at me. Then she curls her upper lip, flashing her large canines. "He'll probably peel off your skin in strips."

"Maybe. Maybe not. But the way I see it, I'm free to go."

I start to move, watching the blonde elf who looks like she wants to jump at me and rip out my throat. But she still stands rooted to the ground when I reach the door. Streaks of envy curl around her like thorned vines.

The door swings open as if it knows I'm there.

"I'll show him what you did when he comes in here to fuck me," the woman says to my back.

I pause, turning my head slowly, sniffing the air delicately. The same way my movements have gotten faster, my sense of smell too has become more accurate. I shrug. "You mean *if* he comes here. Which he never does. Because I can't smell him anywhere."

With that, I'm out the door.

I start to shiver as soon as the door has closed behind me.

What have I done?

What will Caryan do?

You won't be his whore forever. Is that what I'd become? Why he's keeping me. Why he made me kneel over him for everyone to see at that party.

My skin burns all over at the memory, but I swallow every sensation down. Smother every other thought that flares in my head, unbidden. Unwanted.

I won't go down that path. Not now. I don't plan to stay here long enough to find out.

I slowly walk back to my room.

There, I grab the book Caryan gave me, but it's fallen silent and motionless, no sign of it flapping its pages. I carefully open the first page, its paper waxen and foreign under my fingers. So old.

Runes. Runes of the elder language, that's what I said, right?

You might want to read it one day. Caryan's words. I'd been so nervous I didn't realize their meaning.

How'd I be able to read them? I, of all people here. A girl from the human world. *A book about silver elves,* he said.

I turn the pages, looking at those strange symbols. Strange, but so beautiful. But the feeling I had last night, that I could read them if I only tried long enough, doesn't stir. Maybe because I'm too restless.

Just as I'm about to close it, the text suddenly starts to make sense. I recognize words, then whole sentences, as if I've always known the language.

I flip through the pages. It's the history of the silver elves. Silver elves or moon elves inhabited these lands a long, long time ago. Most of them had been killed by a raid of specters from the hells. There are a lot of descriptions about various well-known silver elves, and at which courts they lived and worked, about their work itself.

I pause on the last page. It seems to flicker and suddenly words that haven't been here moments ago appear. My heart makes a leap, only to beat faster.

This is a message. A *secret* message. Written in the same runes. It takes me longer to make out the drawings because they're clearly handwritten, and the ink has already faded.

It says, *Unravel the truths, star-struck and moon-kissed one.*

And then below three places. *Library of Niavara. Archives of Evander. Ruins of Khalix.*

I stare at the drawings. What does this mean? That something *is* there? The truth? But the truth of what?

"What do you want to tell me?" I ask the book, remembering how it flapped its wings and wanted to get to me. I get a ruffle of pages in answer.

"You meant for me to find this," I say. "It wasn't about the book's content, but about that message." Again, the pages flap in agreement and I let out a long breath, gently stroking the book's spine.

Then I look to my right, at the lights that shimmer below at the bottom of the desert. *Niavara*, the town I can see from my room. Nidaw's words flare in my mind, and I touch the page. My mother had been an elf, a daughter of Evander.

My heart still beats fast in my chest. *You're unique to this world.* I look back down to that book in front of me, nestled in the sheets.

"You want me to go to Niavara?" I ask carefully. Again, it stirs, its pages humming in agreement. I suck in my lower lip. Why did Caryan give me this book? Because it called for me? There's no way he can read those runes, or can he? If he's old, *very* old, he maybe can. And why can I read it? "Can Caryan read you?" I ask the book.

It stays silent, the ink of the message fading back into oblivion. A no.

"So only me then," I say quietly. A gentle flap of a single page. I run a hand through my hair. I need to go to Niavara then. I close the book and carefully place it under my cushion before I get up and walk into the bathroom.

I turn on the shower and start to scrub the filth off my skin before I walk over to my bed, exhausted. But when I lie down, I can't rest. My mind's too full of all the things that happened. My mother... an *elf.* And my father... human. I, able to read runes. Runes I've never seen before. A half-blood. It still sounds surreal.

Instead of falling asleep, I find myself looking up at the eerie sanguine moon and the glittering stars around it. I grab one of the sheets of paper and start to draw. Before I know what I'm doing, what my own hand's performing, I find myself looking into Caryan's chiseled, picture-perfect face. But those eyes feel lifeless without their colors.

I get up and open the duffle bag, only to find all my colors dried out from the desert heat.

The next day in the kitchen, I peel violet and deep-yellow potatoes and carrots, their colors so vivid that I sneak two of them into my trouser pockets, determined to use the pigments of the flesh that stains my hands to make a paste.

The next night, before I leave, I ask Nidaw for some goose fat. Back in my room, having the evening off, I grind those potatoes and carrots and mix them with the fat and some water.

I'd need the biggest palette of colors one could possibly have to paint Caryan's eyes.

Since I don't have any color safe for the pastes of slight purple and golden ochre I just made, I take out one of the sketches I made of Riven's face and paint his eyes and some of the cabochons that dangle from the rings in his ears, until the picture looks so real I have the feeling he's indeed watching me.

BLAIR, TWO YEARS BEFORE GATILLA'S DEATH

Blair blocked out everything except for the heart song of the wind as she soared through the night-enshrouded sky, tasting mist and clouds that would soon be filled with the spray of blood and the acrid tang of murder. She ducked into a crouch over the massive neck of her wyvern as the half-solid, half-misty beast under her body spread her wings wide and arced down.

"Very, very quiet," Blair whispered against the wind screaming in her face. She knew her wyvern could hear her. Knew it in her bones, in the way the creature banked as she spotted the first fires in the watchtowers, just where Caryan had marked them on the maps.

Blair sat up tighter. Her body was still sore from the last night with Caryan. Still sore from what he did after she agreed to go to war for him and for her aunt. A punishment for her snarl. The tone she dared to strike with him before.

She'd known he wouldn't let a thing like that pass without retribution. She shivered when she thought of the feeling of his body against hers. But she pushed the memory away for now, treasuring that secret.

She glanced back over her shoulder to see her coven falling into formation behind her. The witches like a living swarm of night, silver nails and teeth glinting, the air alive with the beats of wings.

Apocalyptic riders.

Blair felt a stir of nervousness shadowing her impatience. Her eagerness for bloodletting.

To prove herself.

Surprise me, Caryan basically demanded. *You're predictable,* he'd said.

Oh, she wouldn't take that. She'd show him how wrong he was. She'd bring him the head of the cadre stationed here after they'd had their fun killing the high elves. The head of Kyrith, the famous mountain lion of Palisandre.

Yet… that tower was full of high elves. The soldiers stationed up here in the north bore inherent ice magic. *Wind wielders and blizzard summoners,* Caryan said.

Taking on a high elf was different than anything they'd done before—killing farmers or the occasional, unlucky high elf crossing their path. Here, there were at least a dozen high elves. Trained soldiers. Armed to the teeth.

Dangerous. They were dangerous. Witches could—*would*—die tonight.

Blair swallowed the lump in her throat and resisted the urge to turn around one more time and cast a last glance at Sofya and Aurora. She knew Aurora would be stern-faced. Her mother had cornered her that morning after battle brief, when Blair had donned her armor and weapons and filled her saddlebags.

"You can't be serious. You can't allow this, Blair. The witches barely survived the Demon War. Nor the fight against the angels."

"Are you questioning my orders?" Blair's voice had gone quiet as she stared her mother down like she would have any other witch of her coven. Yet Aurora hadn't backed off. Sofya and Aurora were like day and night, but not in that regard. Sofya was fire, but Aurora was stone. Both unbendable.

"No, I'm questioning your sanity."

"Watch it, Aurora, or I'll have you replaced."

Aurora hadn't so much as blinked. She held Blair's stare longer than anyone other than Gatilla or Caryan would have dared to.

Blair had lashed out and cut open her lip, yet Aurora still hadn't retreated. Hadn't even flinched.

"Impudence breeds madness," Blair recitet.

Aurora's remarkable eyes darkened. "You are not your aunt, so do not repeat her wicked words to me. You can't lead us into this war. Into a war that will cost so many more lives."

Treason. It was the first time ever that Aurora had so much as hinted at Blair's heritage. At her amber eyes and wine-red hair, the heirloom of Gatilla's bloodline—the strongest bloodline of all witch clans. Blair never particularly cared to learn about her heritage, but she knew that witches came from an alliance between demons of the hells and fae, and that the purple blood in her veins was a testimony to draconic blood. In her, like in her aunt, it ran almost pure.

"What do you want me to do?"

"Refuse. Lead us somewhere else. Stand up against her, Blair. This war has cost us too much. Witches will follow your lead."

"I should drag you right to our queen for even thinking such a thing," Blair snarled.

She should have punished Aurora then. Broken her nose, at least. Yet she couldn't bring herself to do it. She never could. She allowed such indiscipline, allowed that wildness to burgeon. If her aunt knew, she'd have all three of them cut open, dangling from hooks and bled to death while she wore her finest silk and sipped a glass of wine.

"Caryan knows what he's doing. Now step back in line," Blair said, but Aurora kept blocking her way.

"You can't be so foolish as to trust the angel. He is hers, Blair. Her weapon. Hers. He is ruination. To all of us if she unleashes him."

"He is as much hers as he is ours," Blair snapped back, her mother's words and their meaning, their implication, making her lash out again. "He's our only chance for survival. Our only chance against Palisandre."

After the Demon Wars had cost so many lives, they were too few. They needed Caryan's power. Her mother knew that, yet the look Aurora gave Blair then—it still ached like a scar.

Blair tried to ignore it. She also knew if she turned around now, some witches—Sofya, at least—would be grinning in anticipation, not sharing any of Aurora's qualms. That's when witches smiled— on the hunt. Right before a kill.

Her blonde mother was a pure witch, pure wildness raging in her heart, always eager for bloodletting. Sofya never backed off from a challenge. No, she threw herself at it, sword drawn.

They reached the outpost and Blair's mind finally cleared.

She gestured to the witches to disperse and take on the outpost as they discussed while she headed straight for the citadel's tower.

She sent out her magic—a wall of bristling, biting, red, fire-like energy—the second before her wyvern's massive claws tore the whole wooden roof away.

Screams had begun to fill the air when a white-haired elf suddenly appeared on the half-destroyed roof, and a wall of ice shot up to meet her magic.

His rough-spun clothes and wild hair suggested he'd been asleep moments ago. Yet he was already armed to the teeth, a long sword in both hands.

Blair silently commanded her wyvern to land right in front of the silver-haired high fae.

She drew her own sword from her scabbard on her back before she jumped down from her wyvern, landing smoothly in a crouch.

"Who of you is Kyrith, the white mountain lion of Palisandre?" she asked, blocking his blows with her sword while their magic writhed and clashed in the air around them like two massive beasts, trying to devour each other.

"In the flesh, witch," the elf snarled back. His sword came down so violently, it cleaved her sword in two.

Blair just raised her eyebrows, then threw the useless hilt off the tower. Shame. She'd have to use her nails and teeth then. But that way it was much more fun anyway.

She flashed a silvery grin. "How fortunate. I'm going level this outpost and then I'm going to leave with your head."

Kyrith turned out to be a particularly nasty bastard. He lashed out with his magic again before Blair could use hers as a shield. In a storm of ice and hail so thick Blair had bruises all over her body, he'd brought down the whole tower and summoned a gust of wind so strong it blew both of them down. They'd dropped from the sky in a free fall.

The asshole somehow managed to block his own deadly plummet before he could splatter on the ground. Blair would have been dead if it weren't for the claws of her wyvern catching her a few seconds before her body would have inelegantly plastered the ground.

Kyrith regained his footing fast and blasted another icy storm against her wyvern the moment he found his balance. Her wyvern had screamed and lunged towards him. Blair dismissed the creature a split second before a sharp cone of ice could have pierced her heart.

She didn't know whether a phantom could die, but she sure as death won't let herself find out.

"Touch her again and you'll burn," Blair growled, and a storm of her fiery, scorching magic once again collided with his.

It erupted in a bluish-red collision, before it collapsed. She flung out another wave, digging deep into her magic, letting it rush through her veins and shine through her eyes. Only then did she realize how long it had been since she'd loosened the leash, even a fraction. How good it felt.

But the coward didn't stay to block it. To play with her. No. When she swiveled for him, she found him sprinting towards the woods. The infamous mountain lion of Palisandre... running for his life like a coward.

Well, not so high and mighty after all, it seemed.

"Don't run, elf. You'll only die tired," Blair shouted after him, flicking debris and splinters of ice off her leathers while she made her magic follow him.

A channeled, spear-like flame rushed after him, piercing the night. She smiled. He wouldn't have a chance to scream before she'd skewered and roasted him like a pig.

All around her the night sky exploded with bursts of magic

from similar fights—witches against high elves, the air filled with cracks and snarling.

Blair paused to breathe it all in. It was beautiful in a macabre way. Crazy as it was, part of her had always been more comfortable in chaos. She allowed herself a split second. A split second too long, because that blanched bastard of an elf used it to summon some kind of ice-whip, which slammed into her flesh, hurling her through the air and into the wall of the castle.

How the fuck did he get here so fast? He must have teleported, because another second later, she was pulled back up to her feet, her head pushed so hard against the wall all over that her teeth ate stone and her jaw sang with pain. His body was close and unrelenting like steel, pressing so hard against hers she couldn't move. Her clawed hands somehow already pinned against her back. Useless.

"Game over, bitch," he snarled too close to her throat.

"I'm a witch, you fucker," she hissed. "Believe me, that one letter makes a big difference."

"I believe that dead, you're all the same," he seethed right back, ready to rip her throat out with his teeth, she knew.

"Yeah? I'd think twice about that if I were you. Might be a big mistake. Or probably not so big in your case," she said.

He froze as he felt the sting of her dagger pressing against the inside of his thigh. She'd flicked it free from her sleeve with a tiny twist of her wrist. He'd anticipated her claws, but not a knife.

She grinned. "Your favorite part might be an even better trophy than your head, and I reckon you even use it more often."

His answer was nothing short of a deadly growl, yet he didn't move a muscle.

"Right. Who's a good boy?"

"Shut your trap, witch."

"Why? Since we're obviously stuck here, we might as well get to know each other a little. Why don't you start by telling me what you did to get sent to a godsforsaken outpost in the middle of nowhere. Tell me, what did you do to piss off your little elven king?"

"Shut your mouth, witch."

She almost laughed at how on the spot she was. Almost. If her cheek didn't hurt so much, she would have.

"I'll rip out your throat before you can so much as twitch a finger," he hissed, accentuating it with another brutal shove.

"Will you?" She angled the knife at his groin slightly, so the tip bit into his skin. "I love a challenge."

"What about you tell me which outpost Caryan's planning on attacking next, and I'll let you live."

He knew Caryan, she could tell, by the way he used the angel's name so casually. *Strange.*

Blair let out a laugh, but it got choked by an icy wind that started to fill her lungs, smothering her fire, freezing her insides so fast she couldn't move.

A wildfire made of pure ice. What in the hells?

"So, witch. Which outpost? Dare lie, and your arm holding the knife will be the first to break off your body like a frozen twig. Snap, snap."

For a brief second, true panic stirred in Blair. She'd never been trapped like this. She tried to summon her magic, but the warrior's magic coated it all with a blanket of eternal ice. Her magic—it was muted, subdued. Silent.

"What in the hells have you done to me?"

"Don't like that much, do we, huh? Which one, Blair Alaric? Tell me before I run out of patience."

"Go to hell! Just kill me."

"You think your mighty aunt wants her only heir dead?" he asked instead.

She frowned. "Why leave me alive?" It truly interested her. Why stall instead of just finishing her off?

"I have my reasons, but my patience is running thin. Tell me, or I will deliver your head to my king. Your choice."

She believed him. As much as she hated it. Still, she made herself laugh. "Then go ahead, taste my blood, elf. And suffocate on it."

"I'm offering you a chance, you mad creature."

"What you don't understand is that, if you don't kill me, it will be my aunt's hands ripping out my innards."

"I see. Gatilla's famous generosity. Then don't tell your aunt. Go and only tell the angel, since it's his bed you're warming, judging by his smell all over you."

What the fuck? How did he...? How could he smell Caryan on her beneath all her magic? It shouldn't be possible.

Her voice sounded strained even to her ears when she asked, "You think Caryan will spare me?"

She realized the moment the question left her mouth that she had no clue how Caryan would react to her failure. Yes, she shared his bed, but Caryan was cruel and cold in a different way. Different from all other fae. He had no reputation for mercy. She didn't really want to find out whether this held true for his lovers, or whether she was going to be the exception.

Or whether he would just report her to her aunt because he was her slave after all.

A deep, dark part of her was afraid of the truth. Afraid to find out.

"Only one way to find out, witch," the elf blurted, reading her thoughts, so self-righteous she'd love to smack his teeth out.

"Fuck you."

"Tell the angel this is a gift for him. A gift he shall not forget. The way I know him, he will see reason," he seethed right into her ear before she was shoved so hard against that wall she saw stars.

By the time her vision cleared and she swiveled around to pierce his flesh, he was long gone.

MELODY

I gasp as I jolt awake. The red moonlight reflects off a dagger above me. A man towers at the foot of my bed, huge membrane wings flaring wide behind him.

What the hell?

Another is to my right. Instinct and training make me act, make me kick out and hit the solar plexus of the one to my right before I roll out of bed on the other side. I must have hit home because he sighs, dropping a long sword.

Not that he needs one, because long, evil talons emerge from where his fingers should be.

My heart leaps right into my throat, hammering like mad as I meet their shining eyes. Men—almost men—in some kind of scaled armor. Large, sharp claws protrude out of their hands and their wings. Huge, leathery wings, graced with a demonic claw at their apex, silvery veins shimmering through the thin membrane.

Wings. That explains how they got in.

I brush my lose hair out of my face—long hair is shit for a fight, but I didn't expect one—and meet their wide eyes.

Judging by their expressions, at least I surprised them too. *Good.*

The one at the bed reacts first. He lunges for me but is slowed down by the sheer size of his wings. I dodge and slam my elbow into his ribs, sending him careening onto my bed and into the other one. At least their wings are a disadvantage in a tiny room like this.

I don't wait for them to recover. *Everything is a weapon.* It was Lyrian himself who told me that. I grab the glass bottle of water that finds itself magically refilled every night on my nightstand and smash it against the wooden head of my bed. One end breaks, making a makeshift knife.

I sweep for their throats, but they dodge faster than before.

Then they attack.

Never let them get close. But they are fast. Like Riven in the woods.

The rest of the bottle is kicked out of my hand with appalling ease. Then one of them grips my throat, so delicate in his large hand. His eyes… they are a bright lilac. Like Riven's.

"Silver elf," he snarls right into my face.

I can feel his talons on my throat, ready to shred me open. But just as they close, his eyes bulge, widening with shock as the room explodes in a wave of darkness.

And in its middle, born out of it like something godlike forged out of purest night Caryan.

And I've never been more grateful that his gaze and the unleashed violence are not directed at me. Gods, he's lethal. His face is a mask of unyielding brutality, his eyes livid. All the ferocity swirling in his aura promises a long and painful death. Darkness writhes and warps through the air as his power fills the room and every space around him. It forms stakes that pin the men's wings to the wall, going right through flesh and bone.

The two men make no sound, only exchange a last glance.

Then, they each break something they must have been holding in the palms of their hands. The items crack.

One moment, they are here. The next, they are nothing but black dust scattered in the wind.

Caryan's onyx eyes slide to me eventually. The flare of his magic is almost unbearable. Biting and hissing.

I stagger back from him when he comes for me. "What were they?"

"Nefarians." He spits the word out as if it's something unpalatable, fangs flashing. "Are you hurt?" he asks then, his fingers grabbing my jaw. But gently. Carefully. His touch so at odds with his fury.

"I'm fine," I whisper and his eyes narrow. *Wrong answer.*

"Do not lie to me, Melody. Ever."

A warning. His magic slithers along my skin like a promise. Silken. And lethal.

"I'm not hurt," I correct myself breathlessly.

"I should have killed them very, very slowly," he seethes, lifting my chin. His eyes come to rest on my still burning throat. His eyes are black as the night, his irises the shade of the blood moon outside.

"They... why did they want to kill me?" I ask against the heat of his touch. Against the heat of his whole being, still shedding black, biting tendrils of magic. Against his simmering anger—a living thing, mingling with his power.

He doesn't answer but keeps scanning me for injuries.

"They called me silver elf," I push on.

"Did they now?" Another snarl.

"What does this mean? That I'm a silver elf?" It sounds silly, impossible even, but that's what they said.

Caryan ignores me.

I flinch back as his hands slide the fabric of my shirt up, the tips of his fingers tracing the ladder of my ribs, checking for bruises and broken bones.

"I'm fine," I snap, harsher than I should, but the trespass took me by surprise.

"You are fine when I say you are," he says right back.

I step back, trying to wrench out of his grasp, but tendrils of his black magic lock me against the wall, forcing my body to stay in place.

I gasp, staring at him, straining against the invisible shackles around me, but they only pull tighter.

Caryan says through gritted teeth, his voice carving across my nerves, "Do not fight me, Melody. I have no patience for this."

Maybe it's the adrenaline running too wild in my blood. But I feel anger boiling up, for once overruling my fear of him. I would have clawed at him if my body wasn't pinned.

"You have no right—" I seethe as he comes for me again, glowering at him when he cuts me off with a growl, fangs snapping right into my face.

The onyx in his irises turns into midnight-blue threads, spreading like tendrils of ink in black water. The effect of it makes him suddenly look like a predator on the hunt whose instincts have taken over.

"Oh, my little girl, I have every right in the world, believe me," he snaps. Then his hands trace my ribs again, his magic pushing my shirt up, bristling over my skin.

I freeze at the violation. Tears of anger and fear well up in my eyes, but I swallow them down.

An instant later, the shackles of magic loosen, and I have to fight against my knees to keep standing when he lets me go.

I glare up at him, not willing to submit to his bared teeth, sharp and honed, to his simmering eyes. "Fuck you!"

His hand shoots out so fast I only feel his grip around my neck when he pushes me against the wall once again. "Do not fight me again, ever. You are mine," he growls, a sound so low, so inhuman, it slithers over my bones and into my core.

Then his fangs pierce my flesh.

I don't feel the pain, barely feel anything before he pulls back, eyes wide. The same eerie alloy of gold and red suddenly simmer in them, lacing around the blackness. But the primal aggression, the sheer possessiveness of the act robs every remaining resistance, until all that lingers is my depthless fear.

I want to curl into myself. Hide.

He's still more animal than sentient being.

What have I done? I try to retreat, but he places a hand next to my head, blocking my way with his arm as if to say that he can force me to stay here. Can do *anything* to me.

He wants me to realize. To understand what I am to him.

He leans slightly closer, the gold weaving back in like filigree artwork, lacing those thick, black tendrils. His breath brushes my lips when he snarls, "Don't be fooled by my looks. I'm a monster, however human I might look to you. And I'm the very worst of them all. Don't make me lose control, do you understand? Do not push me ever again."

I hold perfectly still. Finally, he straightens slightly and lowers his hand, the blackness in his irises shifting into an ambiguous gray, as if he has made a decision.

Just then, Riven appears at the door, his lilac eyes wide with shock as I meet them.

30

RIVEN

"What happened?" Riven asks as soon as he trusts his own voice enough to speak. His tone is husky from the violence he just witnessed, from his own anger simmering under his skin, the cataclysmic magic in his veins still ready to surge. Abyss, he's never seen Caryan lose control that much. But then, he's never seen someone talk to Caryan like that and live long enough to see sunrise either. At least not after Gatilla, whose magical shackles had prevented him from killing without her explicit wish.

And yet, to see Caryan biting Melody like that—it flipped something in him.

It was pure dominance. Pure ownership. Pure... Caryan might as well have claimed her right before Riven.

The rational part in Riven knows Melody is his slave and that Caryan has every right to do with her whatever he desires, just as he told her. He knows Caryan bit her before.

Yet every fiber in his body screams at him to go for Caryan's throat.

He smothers those unfamiliar impulses and takes a deep breath, reminding himself that things could have turned out much worse.

Yet—if he'd come a minute earlier, this wouldn't have happened. He'd been at the border when Caryan had called him over their bond. He'd come as fast as he could, but—that one minute...

He should have been here. Should have intervened. He promised to protect her, always, yet he hadn't been there in time.

Nefarians infiltrated my kingdom. My court, Caryan says coolly, his voice sounding only in Riven's mind.

Riven can't help but notice the flicker in Caryan's eyes as he feels Riven's emotions. He doesn't know how Caryan interprets them. All Riven can do is choke those feelings further and let them fade slowly, the way he's trained for two centuries. Only because of that training, it works.

Another deep breath and Riven is calm again. Caryan shifts too. Gone is the half-feral angel from moments ago, replaced by the ice-cold king Riven knows so well. The king the world has learned to fear. The king who, even when he looks civilized on the outside, is much more dangerous than the creature of pure instinct he was just moments before.

We have a traitor in our rows, Caryan says, again silently over the bond so Melody won't hear. *I'm going to seal the Fortress. I'm going to find him. Meanwhile, I need you to stay with her and protect her. With your life.*

"I will," Riven says out loud because the mind-speaking works only one way.

Caryan's eyes rest on him a second longer, as if he, too, wonders about how easily that vow passed Riven's lips.

Then darkness ripples and he is gone.

Riven's eyes finally drift to Melody, who's been watching them vigilantly. His inner turmoil soars anew as he takes her in. She looks more vulnerable than ever. Her brown eyes are still wide with shock, her throat healed but smeared with blood. Her heartbeat is feverish, the air filled with fear and fury.

Those haunted eyes glide to him, then she runs into his arms and starts to cry.

Riven lifts her and carries her over to the bed, holding her until her tears subside and her body finally stops shaking. Eventually, she sits up. He gently brushes a strand of blood-crusted hair out of her face. She's still paler than he remembers her and dark rings rim her beautiful eyes.

"What happened?" he asks, more gently than he's ever been with anyone.

"There were two men in the room. They had wings and claws. I don't know... I fought them and, suddenly, Caryan was here, but—they crumbled to dust before he could kill them." Her voice breaks off and she frowns. "Caryan, he..." She shakes her head. "Nefarians... is that was those men were?"

"Yes."

"They were... frightening," she whispers.

Riven makes himself say, "They are."

Melody slides off his lap and stands. Her eyes, still restless, probe the room as if she expects them to return any moment.

Then she states quietly, "I'd like to take a shower," before she slips into the bathroom and closes the door behind her.

Riven lies sprawled on her bed, the sketch of him with purple eyes in his hands, when she returns. She's shockingly talented, the way she caught his and Caryan's faces. He already glimpsed her talent in the paintings in her room at Lyrian's house and was fascinated then. He'd seen a lot of the most talented artists at the court in Palisandre. But these are *more*. As if these sketches are alive, his own, violet eyes terrifyingly real, looking back at him like a mirror.

"You're very talented," he says, lowering the sketch to look at her fully.

Melody just stares at him, wrapping her towel tighter around herself, her eyes still glistening with vigilance. And shame, as she realizes what he's holding in his hand.

"I didn't plan for you to ever see that," she snaps.

"But I did. And I fascinated you enough that you drew me," he adds with an aloof smile that sends her glowering at him. Good. Anger is better than fear.

But then she turns her head, biting down on her full lip. To his surprise, she says, "It's just—I'd love to paint you, not just draw you."

"Oh, yes, your colors dried out, I saw. We can take care of that. One word to Caryan and—"

"No. No word to Caryan," she says, swiveling to him, then she walks over and tries to snatch the sketches from his hand.

He pulls them away too quickly and chuckles quietly when she almost stumbles over him onto the bed.

She pulls herself up onto her elbows before slumping down again and propping her head on her hands. But her face stays stern and her voice is almost a plea when she repeats, "Please, not Caryan."

"You don't want him to know that you drew him too," Riven muses. She'd drawn Caryan, several times actually. Riven wonders why.

He's still trying to figure her out. She and her *relationship* with Caryan, if he can call it such. But the way she drew Caryan, it touched Riven. Some of the sketches are of his profile, or just studies of his lips, or ears, how his hair curls around them. Others, though, they show him in private moments, when he wasn't aware anyone was watching, with his eyes closed, his throat exposed. They're almost… intimate.

And Caryan, on the other hand—

The gold in his eyes. The way he just lost control with her. There's more to it. More between them. It still doesn't make sense to Riven though.

And how had Caryan known she was in danger? A traitor among them—someone selling them out to the Nefarians, telling them which room was Melody's. How could this happen?

Riven runs his hand over his face, trying to ease some of the tension in his temples.

Caryan would call Kyrith and Ronin now, and they would start to take the whole Fortress apart. Thoroughly. Caryan would have everyone interrogated by Kyrith and Ronin and look into the blood of each resulting suspect. Riven would like to help.

He also knows he's the only one Caryan trusts enough to look after Melody.

"Why did they want to kill me?" Melody asks, startling him out of his thoughts.

"I can't—"

Before he can finish his sentence, she's jumped up from the bed and stands, glaring at him. "Oh no, don't give me this bullshit that you can't tell me, after all that happened. They almost fucking killed me, Riven."

"Melody—"

"No! I'm brought here to work as a fucking slave, and now someone breaks into my room—someone with wings and claws, damn it—and tries to slit my throat, and all I get is *I can't tell you.*"

He gets up and stretches out a hand, but she retreats, baring her teeth at him. Briefly, he's startled by this—by her fearlessness. It wasn't every day that someone dared to outright challenge him like that. Not many people have the courage, and he admires that. More than he should. *Much more.*

"They called me a silver elf. Is it because of that? Or because of the prophecy?" she probes on, her cheeks flushed, her eyes damning.

Riven stills, running a hand over his face. Hells, how much she's picked up. Of course she has.

He sighs, then slumps back down on her bed, bracing his elbows on his legs.

"Caryan said that I'm unique to this world," she pushes, pausing right in front of him.

"Because you are," he says finally.

"Why?"

"Because you *are* a silver elf."

She just crosses her arms in front of her chest, her eyes still livid. "And? What does that mean? Why are they special?"

He says, "Silver elves were unique in their gift to read and speak old, long-forgotten languages."

"*Were?*"

Riven grits his teeth. Abyss, Caryan would be furious that he told her. He says, "They were hunted to extinction. By those who wanted ancient knowledge banned and destroyed."

Melody takes a moment to let this settle. Her breathing still comes fast, her heartbeat elevated, though some of the fury seems to have ebbed out of her when she says, "That means I'm the last one? Like *really* the last one?"

"Indeed."

She briefly glances away to the window before her wood-eyes focus back on him with new intensity. "And what has all of this to do with Kalleandara's prophecy?"

Riven swallows hard. "I really cannot tell you, Melody."

"That's a fucking lie."

"It is not a lie."

"Right, or you couldn't have said it, I know. But it only has to be true *enough*, right?" she snaps. Her eyes shine with hurt that touches something deep inside him.

"I can't because it would mean a betrayal to Caryan. I'm his right hand. It would make me disloyal," he says, hoping she can understand. "I'm his friend too," he adds very quietly.

She looks down to her feet. After a while she asks, "What does he want with me? Why am I here?"

Riven draws in another long breath. "That you also have to ask him yourself."

Her head flies up. "He tells me nothing. And you... you said... you would *protect* me. That you don't know about his motivations. Was that also some nicely served semi-lie?"

Again, he lifts his hand to touch her, but she retreats another step, hissing, her eyes burning with betrayal. It slices like a knife to his side.

"It wasn't. He..." Riven starts but catches himself. Hells, this shouldn't be as hard as it feels. He shouldn't have so much trouble choosing between her and Caryan. But for some dark reason, it is almost painful. Not telling her the truth, to see her hurt like that...

"Is this why he *traded* me?" Her voice breaks, and he sees her eyes glittering like water. *Tears.* Such a mortal trait. Such a startlingly beautiful one, too. It briefly robs his breath.

"Caryan brought you here because of your heritage, yes," Riven admits after a moment. Abyss, how much more should he tell her.

"But why make me scrub the floors?" she spits, her jaw a hard line.

"Someone broke through his wards."

"Wards?" Her eyes are wide.

"Magical walls that surround his kingdom," Riven explains with a wave of his hand.

"And why can someone break through them?"

"Every wall has holes, no matter how strong the magic is woven, how immaculate. Although it takes years to find one."

"Years?" Melody asks, her incredulous tone matching Riven's dark thoughts. "So those... Nefarians have been—"

"Studying Caryan's wall for years and probing for a weakness, a way in, yes. Caryan felt it, that someone was prying but every time we went and searched we found nothing."

"Because they have wings," Melody says. "And you didn't expect someone with wings who'd just fly off."

Riven slowly shakes his head. "No. We didn't. *I* didn't," he adds bitterly, licking his teeth. He should have known. Should have at least suspected it, but he thought them loyal to Caryan, and if not to him, then at least to their leader. When he glances up, he finds her studying him closely. He looks away, out of the window as his throat works. He's glad he's kept the veil around his aura dense, pulled it up as soon as he set foot in the room, or she would read him like an open book. He's not sure he could stand it—being confronted with his past. A past he keeps locked away from even himself.

Not now.

Maybe never.

He runs a hand through his hair and finally meets her eyes again. "Caryan's waiting. He knows that someone invaded his kingdom. And has now infiltrated his court. He first wants to find out who and eliminate the threat."

"And all those household chores are to keep me busy?"

"It seems so," Riven offers.

Now Melody is the one to look away, swallowing hard. "And then?"

Her head snaps back to him when he doesn't answer immediately. Oh, he was wrong—her fury hasn't seized a bit. "Ah, right. You can't," she seethes.

"Melody,—" He gets up.

"Don't you dare touch me! Stay the fuck where you are!" She withdraws further as he approaches nonetheless, bumping against the skeletal remains of what used to be a desk. She glances over her shoulder. With a snip of Riven's fingers, it's as immaculate as ever. Even the glass of water that stood there is back, refilled.

"It was a long night, for all of us. Let's just—"Melody stares a moment at the restored desk before her head flies back to him, her whole body is trembling with rage.

"Let's just what? Put me back together like a piece of furniture? Tuck me back into bed and forget about it? Pretend nothing happened? Are you going to read me a good-night story as well?"

"Melody, be reasonable, please. You're tired and exhausted. You—"

"Reasonable? Don't be so fucking slick for once! So untouchable! You have no idea what it was like with Lyrian! You have no idea what it's like to be owned like a fucking thing!" With that, she lunges out and sweeps the water glass to the ground.

"Here. If you're so keen of fixing things, fix this." Her brown eyes glitter with a challenge. It snaps something in him that shouldn't snap.

"I have no idea? Do you really believe this?" His voice has fallen to a growl; he's stolen a step closer.

"Sure. Must have been nice to grow up like a prince," she throws right back, holding his gaze, unafraid. "Pampered and loved and adored."

He takes another step, baring his teeth. "Do not believe this, Melody. Do not believe that the few things I allow the outside world to see are the whole truth. That it's not hard for me to watch you suffer, day in, day out."

"Oh, must be pretty hard—watching me from your silken cushion, sipping your golden wine."

Gods damn him, that mouth.

His snarl tears the air like a knife slashing through a curtain. "I've been a slave for the better part of my life." His hands come to rest left and right of her head on the wall, his body pinning hers against that desk. She looks surprised but doesn't balk, doesn't break his stare either. He leans into her scent, her heat, ignoring both, his voice low, vicious. "First, I was forced to serve the king of Palisandre, then I was enslaved by Gatilla. I served in more ways than you might want to envision. I was forced to kill and maim, forced to serve her in her bedroom too." The words escape. Words he's never voiced before, but suddenly they tumble out, all on their own.

For a few moments, there is silence; and then Melody's face falls. All her rage is gone in an instant as she spots his aura that must have torn. And for a reason he can't fully comprehend, he lets her see it. Lets the veil around it rip and glide down further.

She just stares, and then her eyes widen. Compassion lies in them. Warmth and compassion he's never seen on a fae before.

"I'm sorry... I..."

He pulls back and straightens before he can do something he might regret, but his voice is still raw when he says, "You don't need to be sorry. You didn't know. And you were still a child with Lyrian. I was a young man. But do not believe it doesn't hurt me to see you shackled and afraid. That I don't know how you feel. But Caryan was the one who freed me. I owe him, Melody. I'm eternally grateful."

To his surprise, she leans in and hugs him. He's so stunned he just stands there as her arms wrap around him, her head at his neck, her scent everywhere in the air, even stronger than moments ago.

It takes a lot not to reach out and bury his hands in her hair. Not to run his hands down her soft skin, over her body, her shy curves. Not to treat her like she's his and trail his lips down the curve of her neck, lick the spot where it meets her collarbone.

Gods, he's never wanted a woman the way he wants her. It almost has him tripping.

He steps back and involuntarily, she lets go of him, dropping her arms, retreating herself. He hates the shame flushing her cheeks, the way she bites down her lower lip, looking everywhere but at him. He knows she believes that she'd made a mistake in touching him like that. And he hates that he lets her believe it, but it's the better way. The *only* way, he reminds himself. Anything else would be inacceptable.

He turns away from her and walks over to her bed, slumping down on it as relaxed as he can, letting none of his inner turmoil show on his face. All the thoughts that ravage his mind. That it's her bed he's lying in, Abyss doom him. That he has never spoken so openly about anything before, not even with Caryan. That he knows she's watching him because her eyes feel like a burn on his skin every time she does.

After a while she follows him and slowly curls up on the sheets, a healthy distance away from him, and it takes even more of his willpower to close his eyes, not to look at her but pretend he is tired. To make his voice sound disinterested and cold when she asks, "Who was Gatilla?" and he says, "One of the darkest figures the fae world has seen in a long time."

Only when he's sure she's fallen asleep does he allow himself to finally open his eyes again and watch her sleeping in the moonlight.

31

BLAIR, TWO YEARS BEFORE GATILLA'S DEATH

Blair strode towards Caryan's war tent. Her claws slashed through the heavy fabric of the flaps as she shoved them aside violently.

Then she stopped dead. Caryan stood there, his back to her, his powerful, male body totally naked. But Blair's gaze snared on her aunt sprawled all over his bed. The scent of sex and blood assaulting Blair's nostrils too late.

Blair blinked before she bowed her head and dropped to a knee.

"My queen. My commander," she gritted out, too startled and tired for much diplomacy.

"An interesting way to enter the tent of your general, Blair," her aunt chided, fabric rustling as she sat up, her eyes narrowed at Blair. A snake ready to spread her venom, strike and kill.

"Forgive me, but I have news that cannot wait a second longer," Blair answered dryly. Half true. True enough that the lie could pass her lips. She prayed that this was enough for her aunt not to probe further. *Keep them focused only on the essential parts*, that's what Caryan once told her.

Her aunt waved a hand. "Then, by all means, report, Blair."

Selective truths, Caryan also told her. What was she doing here? She should tell her aunt everything, shouldn't she? But this could put Caryan in peril... What Kyrith said, it changed things. She considered it on her flight back. The white mountain lion of Palisandre knew Caryan, even confirmed it. How? From where? Things she needed answers to before she spoke to her aunt. Fuck. She hadn't known Gatilla would come here, or she wouldn't have walked right into this trap.

Blair said, "The outpost is destroyed, my queen. No casualties on our side."

"Yet?" her aunt snapped.

Blair felt her aunt's magic bristling through the room. Impatient.

"Yet the mountain lion of Palisandre escaped."

"How?"

"He... ran when I attacked him. He can teleport."

Blair kept her eyes trained on the wood-paneled floor. Teleporting, so rare a gift beyond high elves. Some, like Riven, could step in and out of shadows, but it took up a great deal of their magic. But traveling through rips in the world and cover great distances without tiring, that was another thing entirely. Hells, she prayed this would be news enough for her aunt not to push, to distract her.

Blair found herself forgetting to breathe while she waited. Eventually, she heard the rustling of fabric as her aunt got up from the bed.

"This is definitely new." When Blair glanced up, she caught her aunt exchange a long look with Caryan. "It might reduce our odds in this war."

The angel nodded once, not even sparing Blair a glance before he surprised her by saying, "Not if he's fighting on our side."

"Explain, angel," her aunt demanded.

Caryan ran an eye over Blair then—his black-red eyes holding nothing but boredom and disdain—before he looked back at her aunt. "I've found a way to grow our army. Yet I need more magic for that. But then I'll gladly put my theory to test."

Blair could have sworn the silence that followed was laden with death.

Games. Dangerous games, the ones Caryan played.

Her aunt straightened her neck, adjusting the golden chains

there. "Very well, take as much as you need, angel. But do not disappoint me," she said finally.

"I would not dream to, my queen," Caryan said, the slightest hint of mocking in his words while he kept holding her aunt's gaze.

Blair caught her aunt's cold eyes glistening with menace before her lips curled into an amused, awful smile. A private game they were playing, Blair realized. Dangerous and fucked-up and private. She tried to keep her face passive as the scent of her aunt's arousal filled the room once more.

Eventually, her aunt turned to Blair, as if she'd all forgotten about her and only now remembered. "Blair, you reek of blood. Leave us and wash it off."

Blair didn't allow herself a shudder until much, much later when she'd long since bathed and was back in her tent, which had been moved as far away from Caryan's and her aunt's tent as possible.

She couldn't bear to hear them, even if Caryan did it just because he had to. She could barely stand him watching her aunt that way. With the same, dark promise in his eyes and words she knew so well and that made her blood sing and her legs weak.

She undressed completely and slipped between the silken sheets of her bed. No luxury had been spared for her war tent, just as she had ordered. It might well be her last night, so hells wouldn't she sleep in her silken sheets.

But sleep wouldn't come. She kept tossing and turning. Every time she closed her eyes, she felt Kyrith's magic suffocating her own, her own power slowly recoiling like a startled, frightened animal, trapped in the cage of her body.

She'd never felt more helpless. More vulnerable.

Abyss, she needed Caryan right now. Needed his experience, his wisdom, his unfaltering focus, the heat and hardness of his body. She needed to be held. She needed to talk to him.

Her aunt shouldn't be here.

And what Caryan said—a theory, to make Kyrith fight for them? How?

And Caryan... having just been granted free rein over the reservoir's magic...

Eventually, Blair threw back the sheets and got up, still naked, stepped outside her tent, and summoned her wyvern. She rode off into the night, with nothing but the wind and her wyvern all around her naked skin, her long, red hair flying unbound.

She couldn't deny that it was beautiful here. So different to the Blacklands. The air smelled of moss and camphor trees, was warm and soft and she could see the stars, clearer and brighter than ever.

No storms to veil them, to ravage these lands.

No, she realized with a cold kind of shock.

Here, she was the storm. Beautiful and haunting and terrifying. With rain in her eyes, ice in her heart, and chaos in her veins.

Craving nothing but lightning under her fingertips.

And one day, she was going to break loose. She would rage, the sky would split, and the wyverns would dance.

And this world would change forever.

MELODY

When I wake up the next morning, Riven's gone, the sun already up, so I hurry to brush my teeth, shower, and then run to the kitchen.

Later that morning, I return to the corridor that leads to the throne room… when a screech tears the air, followed by a slashing sound and a crack, as if something has just burst open.

I freeze. A slender, blue-skinned, turquoise-haired siren grabs me by the wrist and pulls me along with her into a different room, as big as the ballroom but darker, to join some other servants who're already crouching behind columns.

There, on a throne carved of gold-veined onyx with two beasts with long, vicious fangs forming the armrests, lounges the Dark Lord. The beasts are hewn in such an artistic form they seem to dissolve from the stone, ready to rip into the crowd that has gathered. But my eyes rest on a huge puddle of blood that stretches to a large double-winged door to the left and my heart jolts into my throat in answer.

Someone just dragged a body out.

My gaze wanders over the crowd, their faces rabid from the bloodletting and their eyes hungry. But below that, pure, undiluted fear paints their auras a deep, dark blue.

My mouth goes suddenly dry.

With a shudder, I look back to Caryan. A black-and-gold crown rests on his midnight hair at an insouciant angle, accentuating his perfect features. He wears black clothes that look like they're made for combat but at the same time strangely modern and human, just like his castle.

On the outside, he looks endlessly bored, indifference and disdain simmering in storm-gray eyes. But inside, he is still livid, his aura as furious and bristling as last night.

I shudder as my gaze falls on the huge sword that leans negligently against the throne next to him, discarded like an afterthought. Its blade glistens with fresh blood.

Riven stands slightly behind Caryan to the right. He wears a shirt of dark silk and a long coat made of heavy, black silk brocade, his hands casually in the pockets of his pants. As if he wants to show that he doesn't need his hands to kill. His aura, too, is swirling with fury.

Kyrith and Ronin flank the throne, two huge, silver swords slung across their backs. They're both clad in some kind of dark armor made of the scaly, shimmering skin of some creature I don't know.

Riven's face, like Caryan's, holds nothing but latent disinterest, while Ronin and Kyrith seem ready to shred the crowd to ribbons. The immovable masks of the Dark Lord's executors.

All of them watch the faun kneeling in front of the throne, dressed in a tunic of moss-green gossamer, a heavy scarlet cloak pinned at his shoulders. He carries a thin rapier on his belt, and his hooved feet are tipped in covers of liquid gold. Too late do I notice that the peaks of his huge, twirling horns are encrusted with a deep-red color, making it look like he recently impaled someone.

"Stand, spymaster." Caryan's voice booms through the room, followed by a wave of power that makes everyone present gasp for air.

The faun dips his head deeply, his horns touching the space in front of the king's boots before he comes back up to standing. "Thank you, my king. I have reason to believe that one of the servants' circles is behind the hostile infiltration attempts."

"Very well, my blade is still thirsting. Bring the creature and we'll see." Caryan waves an elegant hand and the massive door at the other end of the hall opens. Two guards, their horns the same deep red, drag in a pretty siren with blush pink hair and fine features. She'd be beautiful if her face wasn't so gaunt and her eyes so bruised.

My heart jumps. She's one of the girls who bathed and scrubbed me. A few meters away from her in the crowd of servants, I spot Nidaw covering her mouth with a hand, her eyes pained and wide with shock as the guards push the siren to her knees in front of Caryan.

The spymaster gestures with a hand whose tips are covered with long, golden claws. "Here she is, my lord. We've found evidence that she sent owls to the High Court of Palisandre. The letters were enchanted and burned themselves when we caught the owls, so we weren't able to retrieve their contents."

Another hush goes through the crowd. My eyes stay transfixed on the siren, who's now shivering the way I shivered in that dungeon. My throat tightens up as fear stirs in me, not for myself, but for her.

Caryan stands and comes down the few steps of the dais, stopping in front of her, that vicious blade still resting against the throne. "Rise," he commands.

The woman does, barely able to stand she's trembling so hard. Caryan takes her tiny hand and brings it up to his lips. The woman lets out a slight cry as his teeth sink into the flesh of her wrist. Caryan's storm-gray eyes shift into a menacing crimson as her blood flows from her into his body. He takes only a sip before he lets her go.

His voice breaks the crushing silence once again. "You wrote those letters to your aunt. You know that all contact with Palisandre is considered a crime warranting an execution. When I took you in as a servant, you were read the rules, and yet you chose to break them. To disobey your king."

The girl starts to plea heartbreakingly. It looks almost like she's crying, but no tears roll over her cheeks. She falls to her knees again, her forehead resting on the ground in front of the king's feet, her webbed fingers touching his boots. "I never meant to disobey the rules, my lord. It's just... my aunt. She raised me. She's old, my lord. Please, forgive me. Please."

I find myself holding my breath until Caryan says, "I will stay the execution this time, but disobey me again and your head will roll. Yet I won't let this infraction go unpunished. Whip her, fifteen times."

The last words are directed toward the spymaster, who nods once and pulls a long, leather whip free of his belt.

We flay them. Fifteen times.

Horror sluices through me as the two guards cut the siren's shirt open at the back, exposing her bluish, slightly striped skin. My throat has turned so dry I can barely swallow.

Caryan raises his head. "There is a traitor among you. And I do not deal kindly with traitors. Let this be a warning to all of you. This is an exception I will only make once. The next one who deems it wise to break my rules will find their head put on a spike and left outside for the crows and vultures to feed on."

With this said, he returns to his throne.

"No!" I whisper as the spymaster runs the whip through his fingers one last time, adjusting his position. "No!" I want to storm out to grab the siren, but sharp nails dig into the flesh of my arm, and Nidaw's face is suddenly next to mine.

"Don't, girl! That would only mean your certain execution. The spymaster and the guards are crimson-horns, the most dangerous of their kind. They'll kill anyone who interferes with their tasks. Once they shed blood, they cannot stop. They can only do so when the Dark Lord commands them to. *Forces* them to stop. They dip their horns in the blood of their victims and never wash it off."

Nidaw keeps digging her nails into me until her words register. Only when I nod slowly does she let go. Angry, bloody half-moons remain on my white skin.

A crack splits the room, followed by a heartbreaking scream. And every word, every thought, every feeling leaves me.

I watch numbly as the spymaster brings the lash across the siren's back again, another patch of her skin ripping open, the crack reverberating through the vast halls like a warning.

When I can't take it any longer, I glance back at Caryan, who looks sinister and infinitely bored. Riven's face behind him is a mask of glorious disinterest.

How can he not want to stop this?

"Come now, girl," Nidaw whispers into my ear, her long-clawed fingers tugging at the fabric of my clothes. "You've seen enough. Come now."

I let Nidaw sweep me away back to the kitchen, the siren's screams ebbing off with every step we distance ourselves from the throne room.

$$\supset \cdot \complement$$

Later, in the kitchen, Nidaw puts a pot of steaming water with herbs in front of me. Just then, the doors open, and some sirens drag the wounded girl in. Nidaw straightens from her place at the hearth and walks straight toward the girl.

I flinch when she slaps the girl so hard her head tilts to the side, her long, pink hair falling into her face.

"Stupid, stupid girl. What did you do?"

The girl, the fabric of her clothes still hanging in scraps along with her skin, just lowers her head. "I'm sorry, Nidaw."

"I brought you here to our king and you... you bring shame on all of us. You've been accused of treason."

"It was just—"

"Enough. We all heard it, loud and clear. You can be glad that he looked into your blood. I know he'd have killed you if it weren't for me, foolish girl. He spared you because of me. *For me.*"

The girl falls to her knees like she did in front of the Dark Lord. "Forgive me, Nidaw."

Nidaw glowers at her before she sinks down on her knees as well. Briefly, I think she is going to slap the girl again. But then she takes the girl's face in her hands, her eyes wide with pain. I understand then, the warning Nidaw gave me in the throne room.

She whispers to the girl, "How would I have lived with seeing you beheaded, huh? How would we all have lived with that? How could you be so stupid?"

I jolt up as the siren turns her head and points a finger at me. "This… this is all because of her. Her presence imperils us all."

Her face is suddenly contorted with fury so intense I feel my cheeks flame with heat. There's so much anger in her eyes, in her aura as she beholds me, as if she'd love to burn me with her gaze.

Nidaw grabs her by the shoulders and shakes her. "Stop it now, Everly, and never say that again, do you hear me?"

Everly finally lowers her head, but whispers loud enough that I can still hear her, "I'm sorry, Nidaw, but it's true. We all think it—all would be better if she'd never come here."

"I warn you, girl. One more word and you'll be sent to the prison, you hear me? Now, let me see to your wounds, silly one."

I drop my eyes to my tea, but my cheeks sting, and my heart hammers even faster than before and won't slow.

Because of you. All of *this* because of me? Why?

Because of those Nefarians who tried to kill me. Because I'm the last silver elf. Hells, they got interrogated and flayed because of me. But why? Can I really be so precious? All because I can read forgotten languages?

Her presence imperils us all.

I keep my head low as the sirens start to remove the scraps of clothing from Everly's deep wounds, applying an ointment that instantly seals the skin shut. Then I glance at Nidaw, who's taken the girl in her arms and keeps rocking her back and forth on the floor, both of them crying now without shedding tears.

I look away quickly, wishing someone had taken care of my wounds when the bloodhounds hurt me. I wish I had someone—anyone—who cared, the way they do for each other. But I don't belong here. No, I only make it worse.

To think that this… that *I* brought this upon them. I feel sick to my stomach.

Not to mention what Riven told me last night. He'd been a slave. Forced to kill and serve in Gatilla's bedroom. Is this what slaves do? Is this why Caryan made me kneel over him at the celebrations?

For a few moments, I feel like I can't breathe. That the walls are closing in. The room's suddenly too tight, even though it's vast. My heartbeat skyrockets. It makes me dizzy, my skin's breaking out in a cold sweat.

I startle as Nidaw gets up, sending all of us back to our tasks.

"Work is your friend. It makes you forget, so go!" she says as if she knew about the turmoil inside of me.

The punished girl gets to her feet. She's changed into a fresh set of clothes, and Nidaw shoos all of us out after putting a bucket with water and brushes into our hands as if nothing ever happened.

But it did happen. *All would be better if she'd never come here.*

BLAIR, TWO YEARS BEFORE GATILLA'S DEATH

It was in the morning hours, while mist and fog still hung heavily over the war tents, the biting scent of the long-smothered fires of the night still stinging Blair's nose, that she snuck up to Caryan's tent. Most of the witches had settled to bed by now, except for a few who stood watch. By now, her aunt would be sleeping too.

Caryan always slept alone.

Blair quietly slipped into his tent, but it was empty. His scent had long cooled. He hadn't been here in a while.

Her ride had cleansed her. Grounded her. She was ready for bed. And yet she was here.

She let out a long sigh before turning on her heel and stepping back outside, where she picked up a shy whiff of his scent and followed its trail.

Riven's tent. Her stomach tightened. Inside, there was the faintest sound of breathing.

She shouldn't.

She couldn't help herself. She brushed back the tent flap.

Caryan was lying on Riven's bed, and on him, sprawled over his chest—Riven.

Caryan looked up at her, Riven on his chest safe and sound asleep, almost like a child.

"So this is who warms your bed now?" she snapped. Her voice for once bereft of any emotion.

"It's not like that, Blair." If anything, Caryan sounded bored.

"No? To me, it looks a lot like *that*."

"I'll see you later," was all he said, and not for the first time did Blair long to dig her claws into his flesh until she reached bone.

She didn't move a muscle.

Caryan glanced at Riven before he met her gaze again. When he spoke this time, his voice had fallen so low that even with her fae hearing she could barely make out the words. "I mean it, Blair. I'll meet you later."

She left. The effect of the cooling night air and the wind in her heart gone. Vanished.

All that stayed was anger.

And loneliness.

She was just so alone.

He did come later. He must have bathed, because neither Riven's nor her aunt's scent clung to him, thank the gods. It was only his own scent, elusive, entrancing. Addictive.

Blair sat up on her bed and slid a little back from him, her teeth bared.

He just said, "You wanted to talk."

"Yeah, well, you know, I think I'm still too sober for this shit."

He frowned at the two empty bottles of wine next to her bed. He turned his head away, offering her his elegant profile, but she could see him bare his teeth; annoyed. It was the first sight of a feeling she'd seen on him in a long time.

"You shouldn't be drinking. You need sleep," he said.

She just threw her head back and laughed before she sucked the last remnants from the bottle. "If I can't be happy, at least I can be drunk."

His gaze shot back to her. "Do not act like a youngling, for once, Blair."

"Like a youngling? You fuck my aunt. You fuck Riven. Want to fuck my mothers too?"

"This is utterly ridiculous." More of his fangs showed as his upper lip pulled back.

"Is it? Riven's a looker. Maybe I should fuck him, too."

He growled. "You're acting like a prepubescent human."

She flung a dagger at him.

Caryan caught it midair with his bare hand, its tip stopping mere inches away from his left eye.

She flung another one. It crumbled to dust halfway to him, his shadows eating it up. Damn, he didn't even have to move his hands to wield his power. *Bastard.*

All he said was, "Get a hold of yourself."

"Oh, don't worry, I will. I just have to be dramatic first," she snarled, sending another dagger made of her magic at him.

He thwarted it with a wall of black, swirling magic. She shot to her feet, flinging more and more at him as she came for him.

He blocked every single one without so much as blinking. *Asshole.* Abyss, how immaculate he looked. And how much she wished to change that.

"You wanna play? Because I play better," she hissed. She lashed out with her claws when she reached him.

He didn't fight her. A dark part of her wondered if he would have if her aunt's magical shackles didn't make that impossible.

He merely took a step back as his dark magic formed misty, black shackles around her wrists, pulling tight and her body up until she dangled from the middle of the tent, suspended in the air.

Only then did he come closer. She growled and hissed at him, trying to make her own magic cut through the manacles. In vain. As if they were made of something else. Something her magic was powerless against. What in the sweet hells? Or maybe she was just too drunk.

"Fuck you! Fuck you, you fucking bastard. I almost got killed. Kyrith found a way to smother my magic and almost killed me, and you... you screw around behind my back!"

"I will say this only once: I do not fuck Riven."

"No? It sure as hells looked that way," she seethed through her teeth.

"He had a nightmare."

She kicked out again. He stepped back easily, his face blank, bored. Bereft of any emotion.

It was too much. She screamed at him. Screamed all the words she never dared to say sober and in the daylight. Screamed because she knew he'd already thrown up a shield to block the noise, or the others would have long since come running. Then everyone would finally know.

A part of her wished that. That it would just happen.

"I hate it! I hate this. I hate this fucking war! I'm tired and I'm scared as hells. I'm tired of hiding. I'm scared to want you, and I hate that I do, and—" Her voice broke off in tearless sobs. "Hold me. Fucking hold me. I want you to hold me like you held him." It sounded so miserable, but she no longer cared. Fuck that too.

For a moment, she thought he'd just leave her there. Leave her hanging for the better part of the breaking day... but then he stepped up to her, those shackles around her wrists loosening. He caught her and carried her over to her bed.

He held her for a long, long while, until her breathing finally slowed and her sobs subsided.

"We all serve someone, Blair," Caryan said eventually, putting his head back. Only then did she notice how tired he looked. There were dark circles under his eyes and he was even paler than usual.

"I want to be myself. Just once," she whispered, twisting in his arms and tracing his lips with the tip of her finger.

His eyes drifted shut. "And who would that be?"

"I don't know. That's what scares me the most—that I don't know."

She fell silent after that. Only after a long time did she whisper, "Why Riven?"

Why bring him here? Why him? For a moment, she thought Caryan was already asleep, but then he opened his eyes again.

She could feel his hesitation. She sat up, straddling him. "Please, Caryan. Give me something to hold on to. I need to know something about you. *Anything.*"

Maybe it was because he was tired, but he said, "He reminds me of someone I have lost. Someone very close to me."

"Who?"

His eyes closed again. She clenched her teeth, fighting her desperation.

But he finally answered, his voice quiet, "My twin brother."

MELODY

After the incident, Nidaw sends me to the laundry room where I fold bedsheets and pillowcases until my back aches so badly I'm not sure I'll be able to move tomorrow. But at least it makes me tired enough to keep my rising panic at bay, but not enough to dispel my dark thoughts. I try to push all the ugly fear down while I work. Try to forget how Caryan sank his teeth into me last night. His unleashed rage.

In vain.

I barely listen to the chatter of the sirens, the murmured, slightly hissed sounds washing over me like a soothing chant. I'm so absorbed in my sinister ruminations that I barely register when their whispers suddenly turn into actual words.

I glance over to them, wondering why they've suddenly changed their language to mine. Only to realize that they haven't. I can... understand them. Like those runes in the book. *Talents of a silver elf.* Maybe I should start to get used to it.

"In two days they celebrate Gatilla's death day in town. It's going to be huge, with fires everywhere and magnolia wine. And the Dark Lord will be there," the one with slightly coral hair whispers, covering her mouth with her hand as if she's just spilled a dangerous secret. *Gatilla's death day.*

Gatilla, the woman who enslaved Riven.

The other one looks at her, those teal eyes wide. "I thought we were not allowed to go."

"Didn't stop me last year," the coral-haired one admits with a wide grin.

"What? How did you get out?"

Her friend rolls her turquoise eyes before she juts her delicate chin toward an inconspicuous door to our right. "Everyone knows. You first get to the washrooms and then you take the first corridor right and walk straight out. There are steps that lead down the hill, and you have to cross the tiny stretch of desert, but then—you're right there."

I look down, and my heart starts to hammer even faster than before as if it wanted to escape my chest. An *exit*. I try hard to look bored so that they keep talking, hiding my trembling hands.

The other girl vehemently shakes her head, as if she's afraid of just thinking about the idea. "We can't. You know that the Dark Lord warded the whole Fortress and sealed it with spells," she whispers under her breath. "The wards are going to kill you if you don't know how to pass."

"Well, some soldiers *can* pass, and they're quite generous after sex." The siren smiles with her small, sharp teeth.

"But I heard that the crimson-horns are going to torture *everyone* they catch. You saw what happened to Everly."

"Everly was because of *her*," she tsks.

I try not to notice the pointed look she gives me. Try not to notice the hate burning in her aura. I quickly walk into another room to hide how bad I'm shaking.

The rest of the day goes by way too slowly. The silence of the Fortress is grating on me, making me restless; nervous. When Nidaw eventually releases us into the approaching evening, I run to my room as fast as I can, changing my loose shirt and trousers for my skintight black leggings and a fresh T-shirt. Before I leave my room, I grab my black ankle boots from where I hid them under my bed— leaving me without shoes would have been a good way to make sure I can't leave—and tuck them under my arm. I can't run quietly with them, but I'll need them out there in the unkind environment of the harsh desert ground.

A handful of moments later I'm already sprinting back to the kitchen, hellbent on using the tiny window of quiet between shift-end and the celebrations.

I already catalogued the rhythms of the staff, of the celebrations, so it's easy to time my movements right. The only thing I can't plan for are the guards. But no one spots me when I rip open the door to the laundry rooms and head straight for the door behind a few breaths later.

The corridor to the right. The door at the back, and then—

I slam into an invisible wall.

Wards.

I totally forgot about the fucking wards.

For a second desperation claws at me, ready to pull me under until I can't breathe as I stare at my freedom only one tiny step away. So close and yet so out of reach.

No! I won't be stopped by damn wards, or spells, or whatever. Not when I can taste the freedom on my tongue, the arid wind catching in my hair, the whisp of air and space as stare up at the endless horizon and at the sun that heats the ground right in front of my naked feet.

Only this invisible wall is separating me from *this*. From escaping.

I clamp down on my damn desperation and let the sudden fury rise in me. It quickly turns into fiery determination.

I will figure out those damn wards. I will get through this. No is not an option.

I carefully stretch out my hands and touch the smooth *wall* again. First, it's cool like stone, but then it suddenly starts to heat up under my palm, bristling and burning. *Ouch.*

I jerk my hand back, eyes wide at the prickle that ran through me. The inside of my hand is slightly red as if something bit me. *Out. You want out, Melody. You can do this.* Through that wall, I can see the desert waiting. *Freedom* waiting.

I take a deep breath and touch the barrier again.

This time I close my eyes and let the ward's magic hum through my body, directing it between my hands, more instinct than anything.

And some primal, alien part of me somehow recognizes its language, its magic, recognizes the spells with which the ward was woven. When I focus on it, I can see everything in front of my inner eye. An impossibly complicated pattern, gleaming otherworldly dark, bristling with black electricity and fire; sticky, like a spiderweb.

I know it's also deadly. One more step and it would burn me like a bolt of lightning. Reduce me to ash.

That slight burn on my hand has been a warning.

An intrinsic part of me knows this, yet... it's the only chance I have.

And before I know what I'm doing, I take another step while I mentally throw myself at those spells.

There is no collision. No combustion.

Those deadly tendrils disperse before they waver around me for a second, seemingly suspended. Then they regroup and come for me in dark arrows. Fast.

I'm dead. Panic threatens to consume me but I refuse to give in, refuse to step back but keep focusing on my own fury, flaring up like a wall of white flames around me, shielding me against the dark magic, catalyzed by my cast-iron will. *I want out. I want to rip them open.*

If they want to kill me, let them come—because I will fight back.

And I'm going to win.

Because I fucking won't die today.

Those white flames flare, dousing the arrows' brimming black power, their speed, and they turn back into sticky, black threads. Reflexively, I spread my fingers and *command* those tendrils to reform until they're snaking around my hand, still tame and no longer fatal. I gasp as it works, gasp at my own recklessness, as my body does it all by itself and I'm moving my hand, slowly twining and untwining the threads of magic.

I have no clue what the hells I'm doing but it seems to work. I'm not dead yet. Maybe another of my talents? But I don't have time to think about that because the air suddenly flickers and the barrier—gone.

I pull my hand back and let out a shuddering breath.

I did that. Well, some part of me did that. *Dwell on it later!* I slip through the door.

On the other side, I absently put my hand back against the stone wall of the Fortress and command the wards to seal the entrance again. The stone warms under my palm and I feel the magic that runs through it like veins through a body obeying; the gentlest of night-kissed shadows brushes against my cheek before the wall cools under my skin.

I glance up. I'm right under the sky, above me the beginning orange of a sunset already strewn with the first stars.

Freedom. For the first time in a long time, there are no walls around me, nothing but sky over my head. For a moment, I just stare, breathe in the vastness of the arid wasteland that stretches out before me. Then I slip into my boots and start to jog down the small trail of stairs that's been hewn into the reddish rock.

Only when I reach the last one do I look up to see the Fortress—the beautiful building made of stone, metal, and glass—elegantly and frighteningly enthroned on the hill.

With a final glance, I turn my head toward the city and run.

MELODY

Running has always been a matter of instinct.

But so has sensing danger.

I'm halfway to the city when the ground suddenly starts shaking, as if something monstrous is slithering underneath, so hard that I fall. I brace myself, my hands and knees scratching over the rough terrain.

As quickly as it came, it stops again, like a spent earthquake.

I take a few more steps. The trembling starts again. It's the only warning before the soil in front of me suddenly erupts. The ground gapes open, stones flying through the air.

A giant worm comes shooting out, its mouth a yawning hole filled with ring after ring of saw-like teeth, two evil-looking pincers right in front.

My heart stops before it starts to hammer.

The worm surges...

And misses me by a yard.

I'm already running for dear life. I saw no eyes on the creature, so my only hope is that it's blind. I store the information away. Not that this will be of too much help. I bet it can detect me by vibrations or even smell alone, but it might buy me a few precious seconds.

Behind me, the worm disappears into the ground again, the world reverberating from its thunderous movements. I wait until it's right under me.

Then I stop dead, trying not to even breathe.

Fear squeezes my heart, closing in on my ribs.

I *feel* the creature's senses zeroing in on me.

Again, that rumble, stronger than before, as if the worm is daring me to move. To give away my location.

It works. I stagger back. It's only a small movement, but enough to betray me. *Fuck.*

Against every instinct, I force myself to stay rooted, silently counting to three. Then I turn on my heel and sprint back the way I came, trying to make my moves as unpredictable as possible.

Kayne once taught me how to dodge a sniper in the woods. They hid behind trees, shooting at me. The essential lesson was to move randomly and unpredictably. So I had sprinted and slowed, zigzagging, dodging, pivoting, and running off in random directions.

I know I've failed when the worm comes shooting out right behind me, sending me airborne, flinging me through the air as if I weighed nothing. My cry gets stuck in my throat when I hit the ground hard. My skin rips open, my bones sing from the collision; the pain nearly robbing me of my senses. Dust fills my mouth, coats my tongue, for a moment blurring my vision.

Breathe! Just breathe and focus, die later!

When I turn my head, the worm's horrific brownish body writhes in the air, then comes surging for me *above* ground. Fast.

I'm dead.

I know I am when I stare down that gaping hole full of horrible, shredding teeth right in front of me. Its rotten smell slams into me while those bizarre, ghoulish pincers snap for my body. Desperation and panic claw at me.

No, I *won't* end like this! I can't! *Breathe! And get up!* my inner voice yells at me.

Those pincers close around me—

And again miss me by an inch.

I'm already on my feet again, throwing all my remaining strength into my legs. The Fortress is farther away than ever, so I veer right, running for the lights I've watched from my room on so many evenings. *The town.*

I don't turn back to see the massive body slamming back into the ground again.

Run. Run. Run!

I need to be faster, stealthier. There is that strange silence again before the rumble shakes the ground all over, more aggressively now, as if the creature's gotten angry.

Impatient with hunger. Probably spurred by the smell of my blood.

Again, I stop dead, panting heavily before sprinting off to the right. Again, I'm sent flying as those vicious teeth rear up out of the soil right underneath me.

I hit the ground, only to feel it sagging toward the massive hole that has opened right behind me, the tunnel ready to suck me in and bury me alive. *No! Not like this!*

My fear becomes wild.

My fingers dig into the soil, fighting the pull as hard as I can. In vain. I feel the lower part of my body being pulled down.

I mash my eyes shut, expecting certain death. Expecting to be shredded into mincemeat. The atrocious stench so immediate it's overpowering.

But suddenly—

It stops.

I gulp down precious air, my brain trying to catch up.

It stopped.

I'm still alive, still breathing.

I dare to open my eyes again. Blinking against flying stones and sand, I risk a glance over my shoulder. That ghoulish body of the worm and those pincers are so close behind me I could touch them. But the worm's not moving.

No, it's trying to... sense me.

Blind. It *is* blind. Relying solely on movement and vibrations. Unable to see what's right in front of it.

I can't believe my luck.

I pull myself out of the hole and scramble back to my feet. I bolt away, flinching against every aching muscle and bone in my body. The worm snaps its pincers once, probably realizing its mistake before it gives chase.

I don't look, I just run. Faster than ever.

My lungs are breathing fire, every muscle in my body protesting. A plan! I need a godsdamn plan!

There's a tiny hill of solid rock in the distance. I need to make it there. The monster might not be able to chew its way through solid stone. It's an idle bet. But all I have. The city is too far away. I'll never make it there.

The soil under me shakes and rumbles all over when the worm disappears once again.

I dash on, stumbling over rocks before catching myself, stopping despite every instinct. Sweat streams down my body, my whole being is trembling with stress and exhaustion while I wait out the already familiar, treacherous silence.

The wind carries laughter from the city, a cruel mockery to my ears. But I've got no time for tears or self-pity, no time for panic. *One. Two.* I wait one more second before I sprint off to the left.

I'm sent flying one more time, sprawling on the dirt. But as soon as I hit the ground, I hurtle to my feet. The short flight brought me closer to that rock, just as I planned. A few yards. A few more yards and I'll be safe.

I run harder than I've ever run, sobbing through my clenched teeth. The desert rushes by in a blur of red and brown. The worm chases me underground until there's silence again. I don't stop this time, knowing every one of my steps is telling that sinister creature my precise location.

I reach the rock. I jump, stretching out my arms, my fingers touching the solid stone as I try to find hold, try to pull my body up. I slip off. *No! No! Fuck no!*

I claw and kick at it, scrambling for purchase, grabbing onto it, pulling and trashing, fighting. My foot finally finds hold, and I manage to drag myself up.

I collapse onto a kind of flat plateau, gasping for air.

I made it. I fucking made it.

The worm shoots up from behind me, and I whirl onto my back. This time it's coming farther out of the ground than ever, exposing a rump that seems like it never ends, its terrible mouth shooting at least twenty yards into the air.

It's bigger than I thought. *Much, much* bigger.

I get up and watch with growing horror how the thing bends its impossibly long body, the mouth now like a black hole directly over me. Ready. Ready to devour and slice me into tiny parts, rock and all.

My ribs seize my heart, making it stutter into an uneven beat.

There's no more fighting. No more running. There's nowhere to hide. Nothing to make a weapon from.

I stare at the hole with its thousand rows of nightmarish teeth over me, hissing and churning, closing in; those horrifying pincers snapping and clicking.

I will die right here. All I hope is that it'll be quick.

I force myself to look away. To look at the sunset instead, at the last, breathtakingly beautiful crimson that seems to burn the sky. At the glittering stars and the two moons. I'd never see more of this world, nor of mine.

The worm's putrid breath slams into me, invading every part of me, but I still refuse to spend the last moments of my life staring down a nightmare.

Then, for a second, something erupts in silvery light all around me.

I roll into a ball, shielding my face with my hands. Through my fingers I glimpse the worm's massive body reeling back and *flinching*, as if blinded by something a creature without eyes shouldn't be able to see.

I blink once, twice, and the silvery light is gone.

Instead, there's something like blue and silver lightning dividing the sky. Then everything happens in slow motion: the worm's back-end collapses, leaving the other, now-severed end

291

strangely suspended in the air. Its deadly teeth are still hissing and turning as if the worm hasn't yet realized that its other half has just been extinguished.

It hovers for a split second before it comes crashing down on me, faster than before. It would have squashed me, but something swipes me up and drops me yards away, only to shoot back into the air and slice the worm into more pieces... and then some more.

It all happens so fast, I only see a blur of movement from afar before, suddenly, Caryan's standing next to me. His gaze is trained on the shredded pieces of the worm raining down from the sky.

Caryan lifts a hand, then closes his fist. The ground rumbles again, but differently than before. When he opens his hand again, the earth opens up in answer. Not to devour the worm but rather to push the other, still unharmed part of its body out. To my shock, this part is still moving, still very much alive.

But not for long.

Shadows creep in over the valley, whisper-soft against my skin, spreading over the ground, weaving through the air and sweeping over the desert, devouring light and life in their path. For a second, they even block out the moons and the stars and it turns pitch black.

For a moment, there is no sound, no light, just darkness.

Only pristine, primal darkness that devours all living things.

It's over in a heartbeat and the shadows pull back into their dark creator. Flakes of ash waft into my face—the only remnants of the worm.

I swallow hard.

Caryan just killed the rest of that monster with half a thought.

With his shadows. Shadows that can erase a monster like that worm in seconds, eating it up, reducing it to its very essence—dust.

I've seen the work of Caryan's shadows before. His magic. I saw what he could do with it—like shattering Kyrith's hand without having to lift a single finger. I know he can do much darker things if he wishes to.

But knowing it is different to witnessing it firsthand. *Feeling* it firsthand *is* different.

I sense the flow of his power everywhere, endless and mighty, writhing and ancient, singing around me through the air. A black, but beautiful melody through the world. What I felt on him when I touched him, what sometimes brushed up against me—I realize, with a kind of cold shock—was just a whisper of his raw, true power. A shard. A fragment.

No wonder he's feared.

Was he ever to release it fully, it might raze a forest, level a city. Destroy a whole world.

But I feel him calling it back, that tidal wave on the surface of an ocean of darkness. It obeys, pulling back into him, but not without one more brush against me, gentle and... *curious*, before being once again leashed and contained.

Only then does Caryan turn to me, his eyes as dark as his shadows, as if they're still shining through his eyes. They would be all black if it weren't for the golden ring around his irises, keeping the darkness at bay. His fangs are bared, the blue, glowing sword with which he cut the worm still in his hand. It's almost as long as my own body.

But for once, I don't look at his eyes or that sword, but at the huge, angelic wings that are protruding from his back.

Velvety, black feathers that look so soft I want to reach out and bury my whole body in them dance in a soft breeze. The last sunlight bounces off them, silvering their mighty arches, vying with the ink-black remnants of his magic that curl off them like living night and smoke.

Hells, he looks apocalyptic. And utterly, terrifyingly beautiful. An avenging angel who's just fallen from the sky.

"Are you mad? Do you so desperately want to die?" His voice is ice-cold, startling me out of my stupor. His anger, a living thing simmering in the air between us. But however lethal, I've never been happier to see him.

He is here. He came. He saved me.

My heart can't fully comprehend this possibility.

All I manage is a shake of my head.

I'm not dead. Not yet. Slowly, so slowly does this realization seep in.

He flares his wings once, shadows still whirling in their wake, trailing off him in waves now. His voice comes out more as a growl than words as he snaps, "No? Why do you break through my wards then and run out into the wild when I warned you about this? About monsters lurking and crawling here?"

My ribs are still too tight from the shock, and for a moment, relief is all I'm capable of feeling, although I should probably be terrified. Caryan's deadly, he's just proven that. *Again.*

And there will be consequences. It's that fact ringing in my head that makes me lift my chin, cutting through my dizziness. Sobering me up. "You warned me about yourself. You said you are the worst of them."

"And I told you not to push me, didn't I? I told you not to push your luck." His eyes have shifted to a flaming amber now, as if they are radiating from within.

It takes all my strength not to shiver, not to retreat from his sight, from those fangs and those eyes that seem to devour the darkness around us. Devour me. A part of him looks like he wants to do just that.

And gods help me, but right now he looks far more frightening than that fucking worm.

Maybe it's the adrenaline in my bloodstream, the crazy high from it making me daring, but I find myself saying, "Yeah, I guess I should consider myself lucky to be held as a slave in the middle of nowhere."

The growl that follows feels like a lash. The sound so definitely not human, I fight not to cower. To keep holding my ground and look him in the eye when he snarls, fangs flashing with every word, "Where would you rather be? Back in your world? Because your world was so—*enticing*?" Again, he's baring those vicious teeth fully, making a wild gesture with his hand. "Because you liked it so much? With Lyrian and his soulless lackeys?"

I shake my head.

The embers in his irises continue to singe me when he growls on, not yet done with me, his vast wings flaring wide behind him. "I saw in your blood, felt it—how much you *hated* that cold every single day. The relentless rain. To be locked away for days in that *cell*. I *felt* it. Your desperation! Your panic. Your nightmares! Now tell me, isn't this much better?"

It hits me like a whip—the fact that he's seen in my blood all the awful things Lyrian did to me. Without my permission. Only to throw that intimate knowledge right back into my face.

"Good. Because then you know that I don't want to be locked away anymore. I want to be free for once! Not to be at anyone's mercy! Bowing to someone's whims!" I seethe right back, all caution to hell. "Locked up and..." *Hurt, being threatened and punished,* I want to say but don't. Instead, I take a step back. "You're just like him."

His eyes flare and for the split of a second, I see horror flashing over his features before it all gives way to an icy, soulless cold. And I know he's going to slap me, smack me, whip me.

But then he sheathes the sword back into the scabbard on his back and speaks calmly, coldly, oddly collected, the ruffling of his wings the only sign of annoyance. "Get up."

I watch him walk away, those ridiculously magnificent wings tucked in tight behind him, that lethal sword strapped down his spine between them. Despite my anger I hurry to catch up with him, struggling to keep pace while my adrenaline levels dwindle. And with it, reality returns in stark relief. A secret part of me is afraid I pushed him too far. That he will just change his mind and fly off, leaving me behind for another monster to feed on.

Another part is terrified of returning with him to the Fortress.

I will pay. I know I will pay for this.

He's still furious, his aura a caliginous midnight river streaked with red. His whole being shedding heat and tension. He doesn't talk to me the whole way back, doesn't once turn to me, not even when he effortlessly climbs those stairs back up to the Fortress, keeping his wings elegantly above the ground.

And I, already tired, fall behind.

Hell, every part of my body aches. My bones, my muscles, every fiber.

We get in through the same door I sneaked through, the wards dissolving at the touch of Caryan's hand, a mere ripple in the air.

Caryan finally pauses in the tiny corridor in front of the stairs. I watch how he closes his eyes, rolls his shoulders once, and those wings vanish in the blink of an eye. He starts to walk up the stairs, again not waiting for me, his black clothes unscathed on his back, leaving no trace of what I just saw.

I follow him unasked, trying hard not to think of what exactly will happen next. Not while I trail him up the corridor that leads to his private rooms.

But my body is already tensing with the prospect of violence.

We meet no one on our way, but the music of the festival haunts me up to the huge door and the strange, talking head I actually have a fondness for.

"Welcome, my lord," the door says, swinging open. Although the head doesn't greet me this time, I have the feeling that it wants to but deems it better not to.

Caryan strides in, still heedless of me. Another door to my left, opposite the library, swings open, revealing a kitchen and a living room behind it. Kitchen counters made of a single block of moonstone greet me, glistening like his wings in the light.

Caryan walks over to a fridge to pour himself a drink while I silently come after him. I pause in the doorway, lost, my arms protectively folded around me. He still isn't looking at me as he takes a long sip. I watch the elegant movement of his Adam's apple as he swallows.

When he eventually turns to me, his eyes settle on me with predatory intensity.

I'm careful to keep the kitchen counter between us as he takes a step closer.

He pauses, the corners of his mouth pulling up into a cruel smile. "You look like you want to hide from me. Run from me. Again."

I swallow, hard. All the useless fury in my belly curdles into feral fear. *He knows.* The way his eyes shine, I know he knows.

"Do you want to run from me right now?" he asks, his voice deep and laced with cruel amusement.

"I do," I whisper truthfully, my eyes not once leaving the savage amber of his irises.

"Well—" he makes an elaborate gesture with the glass in his hand "—it would definitely be entertaining to watch you try now."

My gaze drops to my hands. I force myself to stay rooted to the ground as he prowls closer, steps soft as a whisper. His aura is still a storm, brimming with fury and violence.

His power brushes up against me, against my torn clothes, raw skin, and wind-wild hair. I swallow.

He's right. It was ridiculous, trying to flee from him.

He stops close to me. His scent is everywhere, entrancing and dangerous. Then my chin is in the cage of his fingers. He tilts my head so I look up into his eyes again, the rage in them still as hot as burning coals.

"Will you let me go after you're done with me?" I need to ask. Need to know.

"*Done with you.* What do you think I will to *do* with you?" he asks back, right into me. Lashes lowered. His gaze on my lips, on the echoes of bruises on my face.

My mouth goes dry. "I don't know."

"Don't lie to me," he snarls, his grip on me hardening. "Tell me what you think I *want* to do to you?"

I look down, startled, unable to hold his gaze. My body trembles with tension. Exhaustion. And more.

"Tell me, *Melody*," he says again, his power banking up against me like a wildfire.

It's all wrong. So wrong. Yet the sound of my name on his lips floods me.

"Hurt me." I can hardly force the words out.

His fingers trace down the line of my neck, pausing directly on my pulse, as if he could stop it. His voice still vicious and deep, his face so close, his breath a brush against my senses. "And why would I *want* that?"

"Because you're angry." I force the words out.

This time, it's not a question as he says, "Indeed, I am."

I close my eyes, nodding, biting down my lips so hard I taste blood. Every instinct in me is screaming to run. Moments pass between us. I say nothing, only looking up when he says with a jerk of his chin, "Take that off."

He takes a step back, pointing at my shirt.

I freeze, my eyes wide as I glance up at him. He's going to flay me. He's going to punish me for what I did. Of course he is. He warned me last time, and I was stupid enough to ignore it.

But I can't find the strength to move.

When I don't react, he repeats, "Take that top off. I won't say it again."

I look down to the floor and slowly start to peel the half-torn T-shirt from my raw skin. I pull it over my head, holding the scrunched-up fabric protectively in front of me as if it could shield me.

He looks at me, his gaze swiping indiscreetly over me in a way that makes me self-conscious all over. Absurdly enough, my mind goes back to those incredibly beautiful women at the equinox celebrations. My cheeks flush with shame, vying with the fear that has befallen me. Although I'm wearing a black bra, I've never felt more naked.

I will not be afraid.

I pull my shoulders back the way I did in Lyrian's house. Force myself to look him straight in the eye. *Fuck the rules.* Force myself to bear the bottomless depths in them.

I don't blink when he snarls, "I really should teach you manners."

"Then don't make me wait, please," I reply coolly, still not looking away. I would not yield.

I will survive. I will not be afraid. I will never be afraid again.

He tilts his head then. His fingers are cool when he touches me again, running the tips over the vulnerable stretch of skin where

Kyrith hit me. My flesh is still sore, still swollen. His eyes flicker with something dark.

His voice falls low, even lower when he asks, "Would you want that? That I hurt you?" He doesn't say it like he's angry, though, but gently. Darkly. There's something in his voice that runs down my throat like slow-dripping honey. As if he's my lover, asking for permission.

His words, his change of tone, do something to me. To my body. To my very soul. I shiver against it. Heat fills my blood. I know he notices; feels that shift in me.

What is this? A game? A dark one. One I don't know the rules of. Or maybe I do.

His eyes are a whirling dark now, as is his aura, but there are those gold and blue tendrils leaking in again. His gaze rests on my lips; his face unreadable when he says, "You're begging for trouble. I warned you, and yet you chose to ignore it. What am I to do with you?"

His magic still ebbs off him and around me like a dark mist, but it's no longer biting and hissing and snarling. Instead, it feels like dew and velvet and something night-streaked when it ghosts around my naked skin, twining around my ankles and wrists.

Caryan leans down as if to kiss me, so close his lashes brush my cheeks. I'm unable to shrink away as he whispers right into me, "Do I *need* to hurt you?"

His voice is like dark silk, gliding over my nervous, restless skin; twin to his magic that keeps twirling around me, sliding over my belly, under my pants, and up my bare legs.

All I manage is to shake my head, no longer sure what's happening. I feel as if the ground had been swept from under my feet.

All of a sudden, I feel so terribly, utterly young. Lost and fragile.

I know how to fight, but not here.

Not with these strange, new rules. Not against him.

I want to hide, but he's still holding my chin, staying so close. Not yet done with me.

"No? Then tell me what will keep you from running off, trying to kill yourself. Tell me what I must do."

His fingers tighten, digging into my bruises, making me flinch. Hurting me as if to remind me what he *could* do. So easily.

I feel my fear rising in answer, worse than ever before. I realize I've started to tremble. I only barely register that I've let go of my T-shirt, that my fingers are digging into his black shirt instead. Only barely register that I've wriggled free of his grip, leaning into him, hiding my head in his chest, breathing him in while tears well in my eyes, seeping into his shirt.

We stand like that for a while. I can't tell for how long. I can't tell how he will punish me for this impudence.

When he tries to step back, I only hold on tighter and whisper, without knowing where the words come from, "You were gone. You were just gone. You left me."

My voice comes out shaky. I feel him stiffening under my fingers but not pulling away.

He looks down at me, his eyes an indifferent gray, sizing me up—for what, I don't know.

He says nothing, so I ask too quietly, knowing too well it isn't appropriate—*it's uncouth*: "Are you going to go away again?"

It takes him a long time to respond. His voice is raspy when he says, "I won't be at the palace the day after tomorrow, but all the other nights I will."

My cheeks heat at the word *night*, although he certainly means nothing by it. Right, the equinox festivities in town. They are celebrating Gatilla's death day—that's what the servants said.

He shifts his weight before stepping back a little and freeing my body.

Without another glance, he turns his back on me and walks over to the kitchen. A bright light jumps on above, probably on his silent command.

He doesn't look at me when he says soberly, "Come over here, I want to see to those wounds on your arms."

I do, resisting the urge to pick up my shirt and pull it back over my head, but he barely looks at me anyway when I approach.

"Your arm," he demands.

Only then do I notice the patches of raw, bloodied skin where I'd skidded over the stony ground. He cleans my left arm first, then my right.

Eventually, he says, "Sit down. I want to see to those too." He juts his chin toward my naked belly.

I climb onto a stool, so he can clean those ugly cuts too. I stay silent all the while, not daring to look at him once, nor to flinch when it hurts. Not after what I've just said to him. It all feels so surreal—those words that I whispered. *Where did they come from? Did I mean them?*

But I *feel* their truth. I feel his physical absence like a hole in my body, as if a part of me is missing if he isn't around. Had always been missing. It scares me.

I don't dare to contemplate whether he might feel anything vaguely similar.

Of course he doesn't. *Why the fuck would he?* I bite my lower lip, hard.

My head is still dazed, swimming with too many wild thoughts.

Eventually, he steps back, and I watch as he takes a knife out of a drawer and cuts his own flesh, dripping his blood into a glass. After that, he licks the cut, and it closes up within seconds. He walks back to me and starts to apply his blood to my wounds. They're gone instantly as if sealed by magic, yet I gasp when I feel his fingertips on the tender stretch of skin right below my ribs.

"What—what was that in the desert?" I dare to ask as he rinses the glass. I watch his wide shoulders, the play of hard, powerful muscles beneath the black fabric, tense a little.

"A sand worm. But it shouldn't be here." His voice is grave as he answers.

"But why is it then? Nidaw said the land obeys you," I go on quietly, taking in my surroundings while he still has his back to me.

The first room is a place where he clearly holds official

meetings, but this feels more like his private rooms. The open terrace, the warm wind blowing in. There's a gray, modern sofa, and a chair opposite. A coffee table made of matte, ashy wood. And the kitchen—so, he eats *normal food* too? I haven't seen him eat anything so far, so he probably does.

Does he cook too? Does he maybe even *like* to cook? The thought sounds absurd, but why not?

I turn and look over my shoulder only to see another room containing a huge bed draped with dark silks. I don't know why I'm surprised that he, too, needs to sleep. Somehow, it feels absurd to imagine him lying down and closing his eyes like everybody else.

Caryan's whore, that's what the blonde elf called me. My mouth goes dry as I remember what Caryan said to me the other night. The way he said it. *You're mine.*

I shouldn't be thinking about it.

Heat flushes my entire body while I fight all those thoughts I haven't allowed myself to have. I haven't yet dared ask what he wants with me. And I don't have the courage right now—and probably never will, knowing me.

When I turn back, I know Caryan caught me looking. My heart skips a beat, and I know he can read everything in my face. I'm too unguarded around him.

I lower my eyes too quickly to read his expression, though, letting my hair fall over my face. My treacherous heart still flutters like a trapped bird in a cage, and it won't slow, despite my best efforts.

He says finally, "The land does obey me. But the sand worm comes from another world."

Another world. So the human world isn't the only other world. I'll think about that later. "And why is it here?"

He leans with his back against the counter, his muscled arms crossed in front of his chest. "There are a lot of reasons. But all of them have to do with magic and its delicate equilibrium."

Briefly, I think he will stop at that, but then he pushes himself off the counter and sinks down on one of the stools opposite me—

the sight so strange, so absurd, seeing the most beautiful man sitting in what looks like a human kitchen that I might almost—almost—laugh.

He doesn't seem to notice because he keeps his focus trained on the room behind me. "Magic is everywhere, like air. There are some of us who can access it, conjure it, channel it. Even carry it, naturally. Others steal it."

"Steal it how?"

"You saw the medallion Lyrian wore around his neck to hide his true appearance from the humans? It was stored magic, wrung from harvested blood. An artifact or relic. You can bind magic to it, even magic you stole from others. Elves tried it, others tried it, and it led to an imbalance that caused too much magic in some realms, too little in others. As a result, the land began to react, the veil between the worlds ripping open, and this is how those creatures come in."

"So Lyrian was…"

He frowns again, and I remember his expression when I said he was just like him. I wonder whether he's thinking about it now too.

"Lyrian was a lot of things throughout his life, but yes, he became a magic harvester in the human realms. The most successful one ever."

"Because of me," I whisper. I don't know what to do with the darkness that fills my heart. I dare glance up at Caryan.

He watches me back before he inclines his chin. "Yes, because of you."

His voice is void of emotion. There is no judgment there. It's just a fact, sober and rational, and I realize when I look at his aura, that he's indeed not judging me.

I don't know why it matters. But somehow it does—that he doesn't see me as a monster. Even if he thinks he is one himself.

He leans forward, bracing himself with his arms on the countertop, long, strong fingers splayed. The sleeve of his black tunic is still rolled up, revealing pristine white skin with bluish veins, beautiful yet brutal hands, and elegant wrists. Something shifts over his skin then. Something gold and dark snaking down his forearm.

The tattoo I once spotted.

He notices it too and rolls his sleeves down.

I suck in my lower lip. "Lyrian said that this portal where we—" I struggle with the word *lived*, because it sure as hell didn't feel like living so I just say "—where we *were*, he said that it was the last portal to your world."

"It is. Once there were no boundaries between the human world and the fae world. All the portals were open for every fae to cross freely."

"What happened?"

"They became too powerful in the human world, and we intervened. We closed all the portals save for this one. There are a few who can still open one to jump from world to world, but this requires a lot of magic and skill, and they are only temporary openings."

"We?" I ask quietly, sensing that there's more.

Shadows flicker in his already night-veiled eyes. "We angels," he says, but it seems to cost him some effort. "They called us wanderers of the worlds. It's what we were made for—to tear the veil of the worlds to pass through it, to rip it open or shut it down if need be, taking our power with us wherever we went."

I still at that, not wanting to imagine the aftermath should Caryan unleash his power on the human world.

Instead, I ask, "Called?"

"My kind has been hunted down to extinction," he explains darkly. "Well, almost. I am the last."

"Why?"

He frowns at the compassion in my voice, as if he doesn't know what to do with it. But his eyes flash in a warning.

"Because we are cruel beyond redemption."

MELODY

"Is that another threat?"

"I do not need to resort to threats," Caryan answers too calmly, his eyes never leaving mine as he gets up. I can see him frown, not at me, but like he heard something. He briefly glances away, as if something has caught his attention.

"May I go?" I ask quietly, slowly sliding off the stool.

Caryan's eyes dart back to me, refocused with new intensity. "I'm afraid you can't."

A shiver runs between my shoulder blades, and I stop dead in motion. For a moment, we look at each other, his eyes flickering with something unspoken.

Finally, he says, "I have to see about something. You'll remain here until I return."

My heart pounds at what that means. What that might imply. "No! Wait!"

He stops in his tracks, turning his face half to me, offering me his profile.

"Do not—please don't lock me in." The words tumble out of me, more desperate than I wish. "Please let me at least go to my room."

"I cannot, after what happened."

"I won't run away again." *For now. Not tonight.*

He retorts in a way that tells me he knows too well what I'm thinking, "I've not yet found who's behind the incident. Until then, you'll remain either in my presence or in one of the high lords's."

I startle at that. "So I'm downgraded from slave to prisoner?" I can't help it, the scorn in my voice. Fuck that he just saved me. Fuck that I almost died. Fuck that I'm so drained and tired I can barely keep standing.

"As I said, it's for your protection," he answers coolly.

"Why am I so important that you seal the whole Fortress for me?" I ask his back, because he's already turned away.

He pauses again, annoyance shining too clearly in his aura. I don't care. "Do not flatter yourself. Maybe it's not only for you," he throws over a shoulder.

"No? But it must mean something that you, as the king, come to save a runaway slave," I bite back. Pushing him. "Sealing the whole Fortress. Interrogating people."

He turns to me fully then, and I wish he wouldn't look as frightening as he did in the desert. To hell, or well, *hells* with it. "I know I'm the last silver elf."

His eyes gutter, shadows twirling from his shoulders and slowly coming for me. I realize he's still furious, however he just seemed.

I don't back off. I take a step towards him. "That's why the Nefarians want me dead. Badly enough to kill themselves. So, what is it I can do other than reading old languages?"

"Such a familiar tone," he purrs, but his eyes darken further at what I just revealed.

"I deserve to know, my *king*." Damn me, the last word *does* sound like an insult.

His fangs flash, but he finally says, "I don't yet know the full scope of what you can do. Yet breaking my wards as easily as tearing through a veil spun of sea silk seems to be yet another of your talents."

"And others can't do that?" I ask, surprised at his confession. At the fact that he told me *something*.

"Obviously not."

My heart staggers into an uneven beat as the reality of it catches up with me.

This is why he wanted me. Searched me. Keeps me. And what that means.

My eyes fall to the floor eventually. "So you're planning on locking me up and—forcing me to serve you?" I cannot stand looking into his eyes as I say it. *Just like Lyrian.*

"I would not necessarily force you," he retorts in a way that implies he would do exactly that.

My eyes fly back up to him; my anger winning out. "No? So I can just go? Seems to me that's exactly what I can't do."

He bares his teeth, and his shadows start to move again. I glower at him, at them, hiding my inner terror.

"As I said, not letting you leave is for your protection as well. You might realize that in time."

"Yeah? To me, it sounds a lot like a prison. Why not just put a collar around my neck."

"Do you want one?" he seethes back. His shadows reach me, bristling along my skin. "Because it can easily be arranged if you ask for it." He takes a step closer, and to my horror, as he turns the palm of his hands upwards, indeed a collar appears in it.

My eyes flare. He smiles then, truly smiles. It makes me want to run.

"Did it ever occur to you that others might treat you much worse than I?" he purrs softly.

"You torture people," I manage to say, but it comes out breathlessly. My eyes are still locked on that collar.

"I haven't tortured you, as far as I remember," he says back. *Not yet,* his eyes seem to imply, his shadows ghosting over my skin like wreathing, deadly, undiluted midnight.

I hold very, very still as they wander upwards, brushing up against my collarbone, my neck, my chin. Like a touch. Like a leash. Or a noose. Whatever he wills them to be with half a thought.

I say, "Maybe I'm more trouble than I'm worth."

He cocks his head at that, the movement pure predator.

"Interesting. Usually, people try to convince me that they're useful to me in one way or the other."

I shiver at the way his eyes dip to my face, my lips, and down over my sternum, snaring there before his face grows cold with sudden disdain.

I ignore the shame curling in my belly. Ignore my reflex to cover myself, my chest.

I say, as unfazed as I can, "How frustrating it must be to have everyone eager to comply with your desires. And boring, I imagine."

His eyes briefly widen with surprise. Yet, as he straightens, his face shows nothing but cruel arrogance. "You'd be wise to cherish my protection."

"And be locked away."

"Be guarded and safe," he snaps back. I can feel the last tether of his patience fraying.

"Hurting me when you feel like it is your idea of safety?"

"Careful, Melody." He glances down at the collar, still in his hand.

Horror lurches through me when I—for a brief second—feel it around my neck, the cold metal of the chain so tight it bites into my skin. Terrifyingly real. But then, it vanishes into thin air. As if it had never been there. I refuse the need to touch my neck, to make sure it is gone. I swear I still feel its echo like a soft burn.

The way his eyes glow and his lips tear into that lazy smile, he knows too well what I'm feeling. Thinking. What it did to me.

I should be terrified. I should back off.

But that collar—that demonstration of power. It makes me snap.

"You know what—bite me."

I think he will come for me. His eyes burning the color of his unholy magic. All black, drinking light, devastating in its force.

But all he does is snarl, "Then, by all means, leave. Saunter into your doom."

Shadows explode and he is gone.

RIVEN

"Cut off their hands and throw them back to the border where you found them," Caryan says, with one look at the elven warriors chained to the wall. None but one dares to meet his eye. Dares so much as flinch.

A statement. That's what the former king of Palisandre used to do to the witches. Sawed off their clawed hands before he threw them into the wind. That's what the new king, Lorvil, does to his prisoners before he throws them into the wild.

A game—whether their hands regrow quick enough for them to survive before an enemy or scavenger sniffs them out.

Usually, death finds them first.

Ronin steps away as Kyrith approaches, sword already in hand. None of the men lets out a sound while Kyrith severs their hands, one by one. Riven takes in the cruel sight. Well-trained warriors indeed. And strong ones. He can taste their blood in the air, their magic humming on his tongue when he licks his lips. Potent magic. High elves, probably from Western Palisandre. Riven knows none of them and neither does Kyrith.

"Send your king my regards if you make it," Caryan drawls, turning away.

"Wait, my lord. Please." A man with whiskey-colored eyes and long, dark-brown hair that falls over his back looks up.

Caryan pauses, then turns.

"We would like to pledge ourselves to you. We had enough time to think about it. I'm speaking in the name of my whole unit. We know you offered the curse to our kind before."

Riven's brows raise. That is definitely new. If Caryan is surprised, his face doesn't show. His eyes, just a touch lighter than his ebony wings. Kyrith glowers at them, Ronin's wearing his usual mask of contempt. But the witcher's eyes flash to Riven's briefly, equally surprised.

"We volunteered to come here. We wanted to offer ourselves to you, Dark Lord, our king."

Caryan frowns. "Why accept my punishment before you propose such a thing?"

The man lowers his head again in deference. "See it as a proof of our loyalty, my lord. A sacrifice. A testament of what we're capable of and glad to shoulder. Send us back once we're healed. We will be your spies, your eyes and ears. Or keep us here and let us serve under your command."

Caryan crouches down so he's at eye level with the man. "Why?"

"We believe in a future and this future lies not in the hands of the king of Palisandre, my lord. Besides, word has spread that you, your kingdom—they call it the kingdom where nobody dies. You have more adherers than you might know, my king. They operate in the dark, but they are there."

Caryan stands. "You will have to accept the curse. Swear a blood oath. It will force you to obey to my word."

"We will, my lord, if you regard us as worthy."

"I will decide on your fate when I deem fit," Caryan answers, then turns on his heel and walks out.

Riven follows him, leaving Ronin and Kyrith with the warriors.

As soon as they are alone and the soundproof doors shut behind them Riven asks, "Where the hells have you been? I've been worried."

He has been. When they returned, Caryan vanished, saying he

needed to see to something, leaving Riven and the others with the spies. A little longer and Riven would have left with Kyrith and Ronin to comb the area looking for him.

Then Caryan returned… with Melody's scent clinging to him. The scent of her blood and fear.

Caryan lets Riven's tone pass and says, "She ran off. I barely saved her from a sand worm."

Riven doesn't know what to say. What's worse—that she tried to run off again and nearly got killed, or the fact that a sand worm has shown up here? A monster that could easily kill elves. In fact, Caryan is one of the few creatures who could walk away from such an encounter alive, which was another reason Gatilla kept him—to fight against those dark scavengers that had started to impregnate their world and thrive in it due to the imbalance she caused.

"But how did she get out?"

"She broke through my wards."

Riven's eyes widen. Caryan's wards are some of the most ancient and complicated he's ever encountered. It would have taken a master of crafting magic a week or more to break through some of them. For her to just undo the magic…

Impossible. Or another of her *talents*. Not that Riven's ever heard of a talent like this before. It's a frightening idea to entertain, what she might be able to do with it.

She is so young though. Elves normally take half a century to even unlock the basic potential of their magic. To wield it is another thing entirely.

When Caryan turns and Riven sees his face, he knows his brother is thinking the same.

"A sand worm?" he says instead.

"There will be more." Caryan just looks tired when he states that fact.

The sight touches Riven, once again evokes those dark thoughts he fights so hard to push back—that maybe Caryan has slain too many such monsters in his long life. That he indeed is tired.

"And the blood?" Riven asks when Caryan doesn't offer

anything more. *Melody's blood.* He needs to ask. Needs to know whether she is alright.

"She had some cuts."

Riven watches him closely, but Caryan's eyes reveal nothing.

"Those Palisandrean soldiers—do they know who slipped through your ward wall? Do they know about the Nefarians? Are there more?" Caryan would know because he drank their blood. And even if Palisandre hates the Nefarians, it wasn't unheard of that Lorvil, high king of Palisandre, might bond with his enemies to pursue a greater objective.

But Caryan shakes his head. "No. Whoever slipped through wasn't from Palisandre. They know nothing about the Nefarians breaching my ward wall and invading my kingdom."

"They came for her then," Riven gathers. For Melody.

"Palisandre suspects that she's here. They haven't confirmed it though," Caryan says.

"But how do they know?"

"One of the oracles told them."

"I would have never expected them to change sides," Riven voices his thoughts. *The Palisandrean soldiers.* They even mentioned a sort of cult, right under the Palisandrean king's nose. If this is as large as they said it is...

Caryan turns his head to him. "Desperate times lead to desperate decisions. They're tired of death."

"I don't like them," Riven counters, his tone serious. "I don't trust them. Men who change sides so quickly tend to do it again."

"It won't matter as soon as they pledge themselves to me."

"It will. They can still go behind your back, still find a way to bend your commands in an unwatched moment."

"Then the leash must be kept shorter," Caryan counters casually.

"You can't control them all, Caryan. It's safer to kill them." Riven hates the words, hates their truth. But he loves Caryan more.

"They are powerful. We need their magic."

"This is madness, Caryan."

"It's power. Power I wield," Caryan snaps back at him.

"Someone from our own rows betrayed you, and you still haven't found out who," Riven says back, voicing the truth, knowing the danger.

Caryan turns on him, his snarl sending the lights guttering. "Do not lecture me on things I already know. Tell me rather whether Khalix has suddenly decided to turn against me? Whether the Nefarians there finally lost their minds to challenge me."

Riven shakes his head. "No. They haven't, or I would know about it. I have plenty of spies there. This attack had nothing to do with them. Those Nefarians that broke into the Fortress must have been renegades, who long broke bonds with Khalix." Riven lets a moment pass before he adds, "It might be the rebellion-group Shiera led. If that's the case, more will be coming."

"There *are* more coming, I can feel them. But where did they hide all those years?" Caryan's eyes flicker with coldness, but beneath it he looks drained. Riven can see it on him, the way he's paled even further, the way dark shadows rim his eyes—clear signs of the toll it takes on him to drink the blood of so many individuals and look into their memories. Even Caryan could only drink from so many a day without overusing his abilities. Without burning out.

"We never found any at the border, nor around the Emerald Forest. Avandal would never allow them in. So my only guess would be the Black Forest. That they searched for holes and flew back over the sea before we could sense them. I should have seen it coming," Riven adds quietly.

"Even you couldn't have known," Caryan says, turning away.

"I should. That's what I'm here for."

"No one could have guessed that they'd survive the Black Forest for years," Caryan retorts. "But it doesn't matter. I'm going to find the traitor and make him pay. Make an example to everyone. Make everyone else see what exactly happens if anyone deems it wise to go against my command. And then I'm going to find those Nefarians and scatter their ashes on the wind. I should have tracked them down and extinguished them from the very beginning."

"And... what if you don't find them in time? They're going to try again," Riven states gravely.

Caryan's eyes slide back to him, cold as death. "Let them. This is why I need you to watch her tonight. And the days and nights after. Watch her every step until I found out who wants her and how many they are."

"I will."

Caryan fully turns away from him. Riven, dismissed, strides back toward the door when a mumble makes him pause with his hand on the door handle.

"She said that I'm like Lyrian."

Riven swivels on his heel to find Caryan still with his back turned, seemingly lost in thought. Only after a while does his king turn his head, realizing Riven is still here.

They look at each other over the silence, a strange echo of emotion flickering over Caryan's face. Riven reins in his surprise before it can show on his own. He's never known Caryan to question himself, not his decisions, nor his cruelty. Riven knows it is not some sort of mercy for Melody's young age, nor for her humanity, because that has never stopped the angel before. Caryan is ruthless when it comes to the pursuit of his objectives.

Merciless.

This is new.

Until now, Riven believed that Caryan didn't care how she felt. That all that mattered to him was to keep her here, locked up, serving him if need be.

He says quietly, carefully, "I can understand why it must feel that way to her."

Caryan says nothing. He just stands there and watches Riven, his eyes gleaming in the dark like gems at the bottom of a very deep lake. Just as untouchable, as unreachable as the stars above. Farther away than ever. But still, he seems to wait for Riven to say more.

So Riven does. "It might help to give her a little more freedom, despite everything."

"Freedom? She already broke through my wards and tried to run away."

"She's young," Riven amends.

"She is reckless. She almost got killed." Caryan spits the words out as if they are something unpalatable.

"Fate wouldn't have allowed that."

"Do not hold fate against me. Do not be so naïve, Riven, not you, of all people. Fate is a vicious thing, but it too can be bent, shaped, twisted, and broken. It's no different from a living creature. I know that better than most."

Riven goes very still at the words, at their cryptic meaning. And at Caryan's tone. If he didn't know any better, he would say it affects Caryan—that she ran away.

"She's angry, Caryan. She is also afraid. She's been a prisoner all her life. Give her a little more rope and see what happens."

"She'll only run away again," Caryan growls, not meeting Riven's eyes.

"I don't believe that. Let me try. Let me protect her, watch her, as you ordered."

Riven forces himself to breathe while Caryan seems to debate his words. Too long, it takes too long. Every second, Riven can feel Caryan become more inclined to lock her up for good, cage her like an animal. It would break her. She would start to hate them in time.

But he suspects Caryan knows this. That a part of him, a part Riven hasn't yet managed to figure out, even toys with the idea for that reason. Be it the lure of Kalleandara's prophecy or something beyond Riven's grasp.

When he can't stand the silence any longer, he adds, his voice bereft of emotion, "Besides, as we agreed, whoever is after her is going to come for her again. They will be more inclined to make another move if she moves about, allegedly unwatched."

Caryan raises his chin, watching Riven's every breath. Riven endures it, silently praying to the ancient gods that Caryan will see reason. He hates how his hands are tied, how he can only watch the storm unfold.

Caryan turns away from him again eventually. But he gives a brusque wave with his hand. "Then by all means, Riven, we shall try it your way."

MELODY

A prickle all over my skin makes me look over my shoulder. Caryan's eyes rest on my naked shoulder blades. And for a second, I think I find hunger in them.

He leans in the doorframe, arms crossed in front of his chest.

I don't know for how long he's been standing here. Watching me. I shiver at the way he takes me in now. Me, in his bathtub, naked, a book in my hand.

He says, "You decided to stay."

"'Never run from anything immortal. It only attracts their attention,'" I quote, gently putting the book aside on a table. "That's what the unicorn in the book says. Or maybe I'm just tired of running."

He comes closer and I pray the bubble bath I found among an array of scented, gold-dusted soaps, and poured generously into the steaming water, covers most of me.

He frowns at the soaps as if he's never seen them before, then takes the book and holds it up. I found it in his library, in the section of my world. It's a used copy, well thumbed-through.

"*The Last Unicorn*," he says, reading the title. I watch his eyes, slate gray again, embedded in black. Then I scan his aura, still tinted by shed violence.

When his eyes drift to mine, I glance down, putting my arms

around my legs. "It was my favorite book. Someone read it to me when I was a child. Someone very close to me, I think," I say, frowning at myself, because a part of me knows there had never been anyone taking care of me, while another part knows *someone* was there. "Maybe I just imagined him," I whisper, suddenly unsure of my own mind.

"'We are not always what we seem, and hardly ever what we dream,'" he quotes.

I look up. "You know that book?"

"Quite well," he admits, still looking down at that title. Something flickers in his aura, but it turns into this indifferent gray before I can make out what it was.

He sinks onto a stool that has appeared out of nowhere, bracing his arms on his legs as he leans forward. I try not to look at the way the fabric of his black shirt clings to his body, vying with the whiteness of his skin. How his bluish veins shimmer beneath it like rivers under moonlit water. How the only color on him is in his lips, tinted like bruised plums in the little light.

Again, I wonder how I look in his eyes. Pale as him, my hair a touch lighter than his ink-black hair. Ordinary. Human.

I bite my lip and glance back down as heat flushes my cheeks. I cringe a little at my act of boldness, staying here. At the unwrittenness of the next chapter. Deep down, I feel too tender for it, like I'm falling apart. But I've always felt that way.

Rarely safe. Close to the edge. Close to losing myself. Anxious and agitated.

Tense.

And it always made me reckless. As it does now.

"I never intended to lock you in," he says eventually, into the laden silence. It sounds like another confession. "When you ran out today, Melody, you could have died. You *would* have died had I not found you in time."

His voice is so grave I look up again, startled by the sudden sapphire blue in his eyes, locked on me.

"Shame. You'd have lost your precious silver elf."

318

He looks like he wants to say something else but catches himself. "Do you *want* to die?" he asks instead, watching me very closely.

I wonder whether, if I said yes now, he would just end me. Drink me, all of me. Maybe I want him to.

I look away as he stands, towering over me. I think about his teeth on my skin.

"Answer me," he demands, a wave of his magic swamping me when I ignore him. When I keep my head turned away.

I hold on to myself a little tighter. "Sometimes I'm so tired. I'm just so… broken. I lived so long expecting to die every day that I no longer know how to imagine anything else. Anything a week ahead, or even a month. I wonder whether that will ever change?"

I don't know why I said that. I don't know whether he, as a real immortal, can do anything but laugh about me. But it's true. I feel stuck in this state, my whole body permanently expecting a threat. Danger.

"I didn't want to hurt you, the other night in your room," he says after a long while. He's been so silent I didn't even hear him breathing.

"I just thought…" He takes a deep breath but doesn't finish his sentence.

It makes me look at him, the fierceness in his gaze burning a hole in me. I want to know what he would have said though.

"Was that—an apology?" I ask, half-disbelieving, half-joking. But curious all the same.

He frowns as if this irritates him, and I wonder whether I pushed too far. Again. I doubt that a man like him, an angel, a king, has ever apologized for anything.

But then he asks, "Would it change anything if it was?" It's the raw tone of his voice that makes me flinch.

"I suppose. It's not like anyone's ever apologized to me," I say quietly, wondering what it means. "But I guess all I want are truths."

A muscle ticks in his jaw while he doesn't look at me, but at a point behind me. I wish I could read his aura now. Get a sense of what he's thinking. But it's still veiled behind that grayish mist.

"If truth is what you want, you shall have it."

He gets up and leaves without another word.

Later, when I slowly come out of the bathroom, I find Caryan with a glass of tawny liquid in one hand in his living room, right in front of the terrace. Now I understand the Fortress, the terraces, the way it was built. He could just walk out and plummet from the sky with his wings.

There's no trace of them now. He's changed into linen trousers and a linen shirt, the upper buttons opened to reveal more of his skin. I have the foolish thought that I've never seen him in ordinary clothes before.

A few candles burn in modern lanterns, the room soft with shadows. I shiver, but not from the cold. My hair is still damp, I'm wrapped in a towel since my clothes were gone when I got out of the bathtub. To find them gone filled me with something I don't want to ponder too closely.

Caryan turns at the sound of my naked feet on the floor. I pause in the middle of the room, feeling small in its vastness. As if I'm drowning.

His eyes rove over me. His lips blackened by the liquid in his glass.

I try to find my voice but can't. I just stand there, looking at him. A fawn before a lion.

I'm too tired to pretend. To bare, too naked after what I said to him in the bathroom. I wonder whether he, too, sheds his skin at the end of a day. Whether he wears the mask of the king, and if so, what he turns into when he takes it off? Who is he now?

His eyes darken, turning a glistening, tarry black, matching his lips as he saunters closer. Casually. So easily crossing the distance. So silently.

Darkness, treading light as a feather.

"I can hear your heartbeat," he says as if this is a way of greeting. "I can feel the heat of you, the rush of your blood through your veins like a brook in a forest."

He takes another step towards me. I don't move. As I said, I'm tired of running.

"Truth. That's what you want. Yet, when you asked whether that was an apology," he starts again, looking down at me through feathery lashes. "Would you like me to lie to you?"

"I don't know—can you?" My answer is a breath, not more.

Again, that smile on his lips. It's a fascinating sight. Terrifying.

"My astute little girl. If I could tell you many lies, would you wish me to, rather than the truth?"

Briefly I wonder whether he can. Whether this is what he's really trying to tell me. Because he promised to be honest.

Before I can answer, he says, "Do you wish me to tell you that I regret taking your blood so violently?"

My mouth goes dry. I forget where I am. Who I am. I don't know what the hell makes me shake my head.

"Good. Because I do not. Shall I tell you, rather, that I would like to drag my teeth across your chest to taste your beating heart?"

I'm unable to step back when he touches me. Unable to move at all. And I know I should. I should run. Should fight when he leans in and I feel his lips at my ear.

But all I do is close my eyes.

"Or that a part of me wishes to rip the flesh off your bones, bruise you all over, and leave you ravaged."

My heartbeat stumbles, and I know he feels it by the way his breath changes over my skin. I know he means it because I can sense his anger, buried somewhere deep inside him, clawing against his ribcage. But underneath, something even deeper and darker simmers.

"Or should I tell you how many nights we were under the same moon, and I was sick to know it, but could not find you?"

His words blur, so do the boundaries of our bodies. I can no longer tell what is real and what is not real. What is true and what is a lie. Again, I feel swamped, drunk.

I'm not sure that he whispers, "Shall I tell you that I kissed your hair when you slept?"

Not sure that I imagine his teeth grazing my pulse. The vague realization hits me then, far away and blurry, that he could open me and let me bleed out in his arms.

Yet he chooses to press a light kiss on my throat along with the words "Shall I tell you that I'll be careful with you? That I shall try to keep my horrors from you?"

A heavy darkness claims me, and I collapse into him. "Or shall I promise you that there is nowhere in existence you could run that I would not find you. That there is nothing I would not do to save you. That I would rip apart every world, every dream and every nightmare for you. I would even rip apart the hells."

I know it's magic, his magic, I recognize it even in sleep. Even in my dreams.

Because I always knew it.

39

BLAIR, TWO YEARS BEFORE GATILLA'S DEATH

They destroyed outposts night after night, striking randomly and out of nowhere. Palisandre couldn't predict a move, couldn't send reinforcements in time.

The truth was, Blair and Caryan chose the outposts after the accumulation of magic she sensed. The more powerful the high fae, the stronger the magic. They took them down one by one and bled them out, feeding their essences into the reservoir. They set up camp at the most remote mountain peaks or tucked away in caves and neck-breaking ravines, impossible to reach without wings or phantom wyverns.

It took a month until the whispers of a Palisandrean army being sent towards the Blacklands reached Gatilla's ears. Another week until war was openly declared and Blair found herself staring down into the valley, at the biggest army she'd ever seen.

The whole lush plain was crowded by rows and rows of soldiers in shining armor, setting up their tents and honing their weapons. Looking down on them, she couldn't help it: her heart sank. Her knees turned weak at the sight of so many high elves, at the throbbing wall of power they emanated. This was only a fragment of Palisandre's army, the most powerful kingdom in this world, and already the air flared and stirred with magic.

She'd known this would come. That this was what her aunt wanted—an outright confrontation for the whole world to see. What Blair and Caryan had been working towards during the last months. But seeing it was different.

A lot of witches would die.

A lot of soldiers would fall.

This was going to change this world forever. Change her. Forever.

She'd been so focused on the task of their mission that she'd managed to push it all back.

Time had been a blur.

She'd barely seen Caryan during those past months. Only in those hours they'd spent debating in the council tent, standing around the massive wooden table laid out with maps and protocols of his spies.

Had barely spent a night with him, thanks to her aunt sticking around. But she'd been too tired anyway for any clear thought. It had been worse than the harvesting they'd done before. Her magic was drained, night by night, from fighting high elves. She slept too little before she and her coven left again as the last ray of sun disappeared.

The full scope of what awaited them hadn't hit her until now.

Her gaze drifted back to the army down in the valley. One more day, maybe two, until they would attack.

And the world would bleed like never before.

40

RIVEN

Riven watches Melody sleep next to him on his bed. It was how Caryan came in, her in his arms, gently lowering her onto the silken pillows. His king vanished without a second glance at her, or another word to him.

Riven's been watching her ever since. The way her eyes move restlessly under her lids, the way she mumbles words as if talking to someone in her dreams, her delicate body still only veiled by a towel. Once, he found himself reaching out to her, as if to run his fingertips over the curve of her chin.

He shouldn't. Shouldn't be that much of a fool.

As if she sensed it, though, her eyes fly open.

"You… are not Caryan," she says.

"I cannot disagree."

She sits up, her eyes taking in her surroundings. He lit the candles for her, not sure whether she is able to see in the dark as fae can or not. They flicker in the color of his unholy magic, black with hues of lilac, mingling with the sanguine light the moon is shedding.

They make her brown hair shine in crimson hues, her red lips even darker, the color of her eyes like the leaves in fall.

He notices how her gaze catches on the tapestries hung on the walls. The only leftovers he took from his former life once Caryan freed him from his shackles.

"Those are… beautiful," she says.

"They are. I took them from the ivory halls of the royal palace in Palisandre," he agrees. They're the only flammable things his demonic flames haven't turned to ashes. The only remnants he wants to have around.

She glances at him, and he knows she sees the darkness in his aura by the way her eyes change. She looks back at the tapestries. "They seem alive, somehow."

"They are, in a sense. They were made by forest sprites. They say they wove the whole Newmoon Woodlands into five of them, capturing all its creatures and secrets within. It's a myth, though. A kind one."

"The Newmoon Woodlands?"

"The dryads' sanctum. The elves destroyed it and killed their queen when she refused to bow to the king. A lot of songs and stories sprang from that cruel event, as fae have a penchant for bloodshed and barbarity. One of them claims that a demon princess came along right on time, and with the aid of those forest sprites, turned them all into five murals to save them. As I said, a myth, but one I'd like to believe," he responds gravely. "Better than to think they did, indeed, burn down the forest and behead their queen."

She says nothing, just chews on her lips.

Riven leans forward. "Do you see now how cruel this world is? Or do you need some more stories to set a spark to your imagination?"

Her eyes fly up to him at his tone, at his words. "Thank you, I already know how cruel it is," she hisses. "It's not like I missed that scene in the throne room."

"Good. You shouldn't have. Maybe you understand now how lucky we are to find you still alive, not devoured by some otherworldly monster." She looks away as he continues, "I'm surprised, though, to find you still unharmed. Your skin not torn apart by the whip."

Her head snaps back to him, her eyes simmering. "You almost sound as if you wish it was."

"Maybe I do. Maybe some scars would carve some sense into

you," he growls viciously, and this time she flinches back from him as if he's hit her. As if she's never seen him before.

"Why not do it yourself? Or does your king not allow it?" Her eyes glow with fury and hurt.

"I would truly consider it if it kept you from such *idiotic* ideas in the future."

"Funny how he said something similar," she says, a smile on her face that looks as cold as the Winterlands.

Riven leans back, running a hand through his hair and over his face. Melody gets up.

"Where do you think you are going?" he asks, his voice still raw. But sharp.

"To my room." She heads for the door.

He gets up too. Before she's halfway crossed the room, he blocks her way. Although she is very tall, she still has to lift her head to look up at him. "Oh no. You are going nowhere. You and I are to stay here for the night, whether you like it or not."

"That sounds like *great* fun," she says.

To his surprise, she turns around and walks back to the bed. She sits down and pulls her legs up close, her long hair falling around her body, shielding her face. Riven follows her and sinks back into the chair, watching her.

"You're still pissed," she says after a while into the silence. "I can see it all over you."

"Indignant rather than *pissed*. Enraged, granted. Annoyed, perhaps," he retorts dryly, pursing his lips, his fingers drumming on the armrest.

"Really? Feels rather like sulky and sour to me."

"Well, babysitting is quite a waste of my talents." Riven scrutinizes his nails and adds, "And it gets rather tiresome."

"Yeah, what would you be rather doing? Day-drinking and seducing women?" She looks at him now, another challenge in her gaze. She's in some mood, provoking him like this but he's already seen her temper.

"Careful," he warns, reining in his instinct to bare his fangs.

"Or what? You'll singe my hair? Or rip into my throat like Caryan. Oh, you can't, remember. You made a promise not to hurt me."

He licks his teeth before he turns his head away, allowing himself a deep breath. "I did indeed."

"Regretting it already?"

His eyes go back to her. To his surprise there is pain in them, belying her sharpness. "My cheeky little pup, how could I ever, when you are so endearing?"

"Just trying to make babysitting more fun for you."

He leans forward, bracing himself on his legs. "I would know far more entertaining ways to achieve that." He expects her to back down, to blush. But whatever happened before, it must have stripped away her usual shyness, because she's holding his gaze, her face blank, her eyes cold.

He turns serious again. His voice falls low as he asks, "Why did you run away, Melody?"

"I don't know. Maybe I just don't like to be locked away, for one." She says it angrily but turns her head away from him at that.

"And where in the sweet hells would you have gone?"

"Away. To Niavara," she hisses, but her eyes are shining.

"Niavara is not for you," he answers.

Her head whips back to him. "Nothing here is for me. I'm weak and fragile. I don't belong here. It sucks." When he doesn't say anything, she says, "Come, deny it."

"I cannot."

She flinches slightly at his truth, as if this was an insult, but she catches herself. "Then go ahead, tell me how reckless, and foolish, and stupid I am. That I should be grateful Caryan found me first and keeps me like a pet."

Riven falls utterly still when he spots sudden tears welling in her eyes. Now she is truly crying. It's so rare to see a fae cry, he's forgotten how it looks. But every time she does, the sight arrests him anew, the cruel beauty of it. Like rain, pattering her skin, her eyes overflowing and wide. He feels the overwhelming urge to reach out to her, but that would be foolish.

"I will do no such thing," he says instead, his voice gentle.

She glances at him, vigilantly, as if she's expecting a cruel joke. "Why?"

"Because I don't think that you are foolish, or stupid, and I don't think that you should be grateful."

She seems surprised by his answer. "I thought you loved him."

"I do. But loving someone doesn't mean you always agree with the things he or she does. Why did you want to go to Niavara? There is no portal to the human world there," he says to make that very clear.

"I wasn't looking for a damn portal. What would I do in the human world anyway? I know barely more about the human world than about this one."

He hates how desperate she sounds. "What did you want there then?"

Melody bites her lips, clearly debating something. "I don't know... answers maybe," she admits finally.

"Answers?"

"Caryan gave me a book. In that book about silver elves, someone left a handwritten list with three places on the last page. One of them is the library in Niavara. I wanted to see whether I could find whatever is there. It was a message, for someone like me, written in the same language as the book."

Riven frowns, not showing his surprise. He truly thought she wanted to find a way home to the human world. And Caryan gave her a book. A test then, for her? Or something else? "I'm afraid there is no library there anymore. It was destroyed, more than two hundred years ago," he says. "Your book must be old."

"By specters, I know that. I read about the destruction of Niavara in that very book, so it must be newer. Someone left that message *after* Niavara was destroyed. That means whatever is there must still be there."

Riven's frown only deepens. There had been only one other

silver elf in the world before Melody. The only one for three centuries. *Her mother.*

She reads it in his face because she asks, "What?"

"It's interesting, that's all," he says quickly.

He can see she doesn't believe him. He concentrates hard on keeping the magical mist around his aura up and untorn while he holds her gaze. If she spotted the slightest hint there, she would do everything to get there, he knows.

But could it really be that Ciellara left a message for her in the book? Or maybe one of the acolytes that still lived in the archives of the great libraries, hidden away from the world, deep in the cellars did? A few of them still knew some forgotten languages, as far as Riven knows. Not that he's ever asked one, because they rarely came up from the depths and even more rarely spoke to anyone... or spoke at all, for that matter.

"What does this message say?" he asks.

Melody shrugs. "Just *Unravel the truths, star-struck and moon-kissed one.* And then three places. *Library of Niavara. Archives of Evander. Ruins of Khalix.* Do you know them?"

Unravel the truths. Which truths? And *moon-kissed and star-struck one*—clearly a reference to a silver elf.

Riven keeps his face blank as he says, "I do. Evander is a part of Palisandre."

"And Khalix?"

He swallows. "It's a desert city on the third continent to the east. I was born there."

Her eyes widen. "And... what is there? Is there a library?"

"Yes. One of the largest ones. It's a city hewn deep into a desert rock with massive, cavernous archives, but I wouldn't know what to find there."

"Can we... go there?" she asks carefully.

"No, I'm afraid not. Khalix is not on the best terms with Niavara," Riven retorts evasively. Not after the Nefarians broke into the Fortress. Abyss, Riven should be glad that Caryan hasn't yet decided to wipe Khalix from the face of this world forever—threat or no. "Besides, no one except the acolytes can enter the library. All archives are sealed to outsiders. Only those who swear themselves to the written knowledge are allowed access."

"Not even the queen or the king can go?"

"No."

She frowns, then asks quietly, "Not even… Caryan?"

Riven shakes his head. "No. They were sealed thousands of years ago with spells long forgotten, and ancient powers. Their wards have never been breached, not even by an angel."

Eventually, Melody looks away, chewing on her lip. "Gatilla's death party is in two days, right?"

Riven doesn't like the direction this is going either. "Indeed."

"It's in Niavara? You can take me."

"I can't take you, Melody. It's not safe. And besides, there is nothing left of that library."

"I'd be with you, would I not? And we could have a look. Makes babysitting a little more fun."

"That night in town." He shakes his head. "You have no idea what it is about. I cannot."

She gets up and walks over to him, stopping right in front of him. He has to lean back to look at her face, to take her in fully, her hair gilded by the moon and her skin glistening.

He wonders whether she can see what her presence is doing to him, whether his aura shows even though he tries hard to hide it. Because she leans in, over him, bracing herself on the armrests, her long hair grazing his elbows, that damn towel barely hiding her from his eyes.

"We could make a bargain," she says, her voice low. "You get whatever you *desire* and I…"

She's so close, her face over him, her breath brushing his lips. Her scent everywhere around him. He can feel her warmth, her heartbeat that has picked up just a notch. Abyss, she is beautiful.

"Will I? And what do you think I *desire*?"

She licks her lips, and he follows the movement of her tongue.

Her eyes rove over his face before she whispers, a touch shyly, "I don't know. You tell me."

"Didn't I warn you about bargains with villains like my kind?" He makes his voice sound cold. He sits up and she retreats instinctively. He follows her movement until they're both sitting on the bed, faces so close he can see the dark-gray rims around her brown irises. This brown, such an unusual color among fae, making it all the more intriguing. Like dark forest honey.

"You're not a villain."

Her eyes are wide as he reaches out and traces the curve of her cheek.

"Don't assume things you can't know. You might know what I did, but you don't know what I *am*," he drawls. A warning. He's indeed been careful to hide his aura from her behind a wall of gray magical mist from the moment he learned about her talent.

But she says, "I know that you're afraid you've lost your soul. Traded it for the darkness."

The way she says it makes him realize how much she can still sense on him. Or maybe he had been too distracted at times.

Her words make him unable to move though. His very fear lies bare. He's exposed. It unravels him, and renders him speechless.

It is she who reaches out to him now, who traces the shape of his ears and down over his cheeks. He holds perfectly still, watching her follow the movements of her fingers with her eyes.

It is she who pushes him down, who slides over him. She who kneels over him, looking down on him as if she knows every dark thought he's ever had, still only wrapped in that towel.

Her eyes flicker viciously. "Let's play a game. A truth for a truth."

"Then lead," he says before he can think better of it. Her presence and the absence of her clothes make thinking hard.

"Tell me what you want to do to me right now."

He swallows. "A lot of things."

"That doesn't count. The darkest of them."

He doesn't breathe. He can feel the magic of what he just

agreed to weaving around them, pulling tight. He made a deal. He has to answer. Truthfully. He's a fool.

"I don't think this would be appropriate," he says, his voice husky.

"I want to know."

"Melody, I do not..." He closes his eyes briefly, desperate for a way out as the magic around him pulls tighter, thick and heavy and unbreakable.

"Do not what?"

"I do not want to scare you," he admits, meaning it. "Please, ask me in another way."

"No," she says, her eyes never leaving his, the flames dancing in them relentlessly.

He reaches out to her, the magic making his throat ache to answer as he agreed to. "I want to have you in a way that erases all those who have touched you before."

"Like?"

He clenches his teeth against the power of the bargain pulling tighter and tighter. She won't let him out of this, and he cannot draw it out much longer.

"Don't be cruel," he says quietly, a plea in his voice.

But she just leans down, her beautiful lips only millimeters away. "Tell me."

He looks away, unable to bear her face, the look in it. Unable to ignore the burning in his throat, in his ribcage, in his very core either. The magic, growing stronger the longer he doesn't obey. It will burn him alive, from the inside out.

"Not the darkest, Melody. Anything but that—"

"That bad, huh?" Her voice is cold, but her eyes are not. They are wide and afraid.

"It is violent, I won't deny that. And it might sound..." He bares his teeth against the pain of it, of resisting. Gods, it will kill him. "I'll give you what you want, but do not force me to do this, I beseech you. I will go down on my knees and stay until they are raw if you wish me to. I will do anything, but not this."

"Anything." She ponders quietly, and were he not shaken by pain and fire inside, he would have chastised himself for this idiocy.

"You know I would never harm you in a way you don't wish me to. I made sure I couldn't, and even if I had not, I would not. Please," he forces out, his mouth slowly filling with blood as the magic keeps killing him from the inside.

"Take me to Niavara the day after tomorrow then," she says, her eyes going wide with shock as she notices the blood on his lips, more dripping over his chin.

He wipes it off with his dark sleeve before he breathes, "I will." His eyes drift shut as he gulps down precious air as the magic eases and vanishes. The deal fulfilled.

Melody still kneels over him, but her skin has turned glassy and pale, her face unreadable. That beautiful face limned by the night, her full lips, her straight nose, her ears that look like the perfect mixture of elf and human, startled and alert.

"What... where did that blood come from?" she whispers, her heart fast.

"The magic of that bargain," he cuts in, his voice rough, hard. "It would have killed me from the inside. Slowly bleeding me out."

In one fluid and fast movement, Riven is over her, holding her delicate wrists with his hands. "You owe *me* now, if I'm not mistaken." His voice has become almost a growl.

"A truth?" she asks coolly, but he can see her fluttering pulse under her skin. Hear it. Like the frantic wingbeats of a tiny bird.

"No, no longer a truth, since we changed the rules. A demand you will fulfill."

Now she looks at him with real fear in her eyes. But she doesn't yet know enough of the rules of this world. "Then tell me what you want." Her voice has fallen very quiet, lost its edge. She turns her head away from him, as he did before.

He leans down to her neck, breathing in her scent, her silken hair brushing his cheek. He could do anything with her. Take everything. He whispers against her skin, "Do you see now how dangerous bargains are with my kind?"

She flinches. He lets go of her hands when he hears her heartbeat stumble. When her fear tinges the air, oppressive and heavy. He's disgusted by himself.

He slides off her, lets her body free. She curls up on her side, still not looking at him, her hands clutching the sheets so hard her knuckles turn white as snow.

He gets up and looks down on her. "I could make you do anything. Call that bargain in anytime from now on, and you could not resist."

When she still doesn't look at him, he kneels in front of her.

"What do you want then?" she asks, her eyes lost, her gaze far away.

"What would *you* want?" he asks back gently, brushing a strand of long hair out of her face.

"Just say it. It's not like I've had my fair share of cruel encounters yet tonight."

Her words are mocking, but her tone doesn't go along. It's devoid of emotion, detached. He can't stand her resignation, as if she truly thought he would go through with his threat.

"I can be cruel. But not with you. Never with you," he says, making her look at him.

He can tell she doesn't believe him. And how could she, after what just happened between them? How could he possibly explain the way he meant what he said?

"Let's end this in a gentle way, shall we? Tell me whether you ever think of me at night," he orders, still stroking her head.

She glances up at him warily. "That's all? Just like that?"

"That's all."

"I do," she admits very quietly.

"Very well. Now sleep, my little love."

MELODY

I wake up with a vague sense of disorientation. Last night feels like a dream. The desert, the worm. Caryan whispering all those things into me. The only reason I know it was not a dream is that I never remember my dreams.

I'm in an opulent room, velvety curtains drawn. I blink against the shy daylight that comes in through a slit, dipping the room into an aqueous twilight. A bed, heavy brocades and silken sheets under my fingers. Tapestries and carpets cover a wall paneled with dark, shining wood. They show magical forests and creatures hiding in them. Badgers, their fur an eerie red, silvery foxes with shiny wings, deer with one horn between their antlers, and wolves with sable teeth. A bear with curled horns carrying a scarlet peacock in his mouth.

My gaze sweeps away over a landscape of sofas, a fireplace made of onyx—more magical creatures carved into it—fat pillar candles next to piles of heavy books on every scattered table.

So different to Caryan's purist, modern rooms. These are dark and artistic and lyrical. I could spend hours just looking at the tapestries.

Just then does the rest of last night come to me. The *game* with Riven—if I could call it that. I could feel the dark magic around us. Ancient and unforgiving. The way he begged me not to push. The way his lips became stained with his blood. Only then did I understand.

The magic hurt him. *I* hurt him. *I* made him bleed.

I suddenly turn around, only to find the other side of the bed empty.

I let out a long breath, horrified, shuddering as I remember everything else. His sudden, dark fury when I finally relented. The way he slid over me then. The way his body moved over mine. The feeling of his muscles pressing me into the mattress, hard. The way he held my wrists.

He'd been furious. I'd glimpsed the rage in his amethyst eyes. Rage I understood too well. Coming from humiliation.

How it felt when you were utterly at someone's mercy.

The fear of what someone might do. Not knowing how much farther he would go. The embarrassment of being unable to resist. The desperation.

I bury my face in my hands. I never wanted that. I just didn't understand how serious, how binding, a bargain was. How dangerous. How fatal.

I thought he'd pay me back, but he was gentle in the end.

I get up, suddenly restless.

I find an opulent bathroom with a bronze bathtub already filled with fragrant water, a toothbrush next to the sink, a beautiful hairbrush, and right next to it a steaming cup of cappuccino. A truce.

He forgave me.

Against everything, I have to suppress a smile, brush my teeth, and then take the still-hot cup with me in the bathtub.

☽ ☾

There's still no trace of Riven when I run down the corridor half an hour later. But I'm very fast, although my whole body still aches from yesterday's trip to the desert. Faster than I've ever been in the human world. My reflexes are quicker too, I realize, as Nidaw steps out right in front of me, and I slide to a halt, almost bumping into her.

She crosses her arms in front of her chest, her silvery eyebrows raised. I cringe.

"Do I want to know why you come running down the hallways as if chased by wolves?"

"I'm faster," I breathe. I can tell her, right? "Faster than I've ever been. I mean, in the human world. And I ran *a lot*." I felt it when I fought Kyrith. When I pulled the dagger out of the sheathe on his belt and sliced down his arm. I was impossibly fast for a human. Back then I blamed it on adrenaline, but...

"Of course you are. You're half-fae. Your strength and speed increase due to the exposure of magic. Probably your sense of smell too," she says, suddenly gentle, as if I'm a small child who just discovered how to walk, a bemused smile playing around her lips.

"That means I'm as fast as you?"

"I don't know, my little one. Only time will show," she says, still soft. "But what I do know is that you are late. Now come. We have work to do."

$$\supset \ast \subset$$

I cut vegetables until Nidaw shoos me and the others to clean some rooms I've never been in before. I notice the servants are strangely quiet around me. I do my best to ignore them, yet the day stretches out too long, seemingly endless.

It's only in the languorous afternoon hours, when the other servants start to bow deeply or even fall to their knees, that I notice Riven has entered. I'm still on my knees, on all fours, polishing the floor when he strides through the hall, only to stop right in front of me.

This morning, I thought he might no longer be angry with me, but looking up into his stern, set face now I'm not so sure anymore. He's just as breathtakingly beautiful as ever, frighteningly tall, his short ink hair just a touch messy yet his kohl-rimmed amethyst eyes are cold as they take me in. He reminds me too much of last night and it scares me.

I fear what he might do to me. Might he still decide to punish me? I realize that I expect him to, no matter how much I want to tell him how sorry I am. That I just didn't understand until it was too late. That I never wanted to harm him in any way.

But then he holds out an elegant hand, his lips purring, "Hello, my beautiful, little darling. May I help you up? You look a bit lost down there." His tone is gentle, his eyes a touch softer.

I get up without taking his hand, though, still not trusting it. He licks his lips, annoyed, his fangs flashing. And suddenly I'm too aware of the other servants listening. Watching—how I'm looking a high lord straight in the eye with my chin raised high.

When Riven cuts them a glance and snarls, "Leave us," they scatter in all directions, almost stumbling over themselves.

"Dramatic."

"Oh, one must know how to keep the gossip about you and me going," he drawls, looking back to me.

"Is there—gossip?" I ask, blushing against my will, but I refuse to look away.

His jaw is still set in that regal, elegant way, his eyes still blazing, but a smile plays around his lips now as he leans in and twirls a strand of my hair around his finger. A smile I'm not yet sure about either, as ambiguous as the sea.

"I'm sure there is. How else would they explain that you still smell of me other than that you came to my bed last night?"

"It's not like I had much choice," I grind out, fighting the embarrassment flushing up my whole body, although I know he's just toying with me. *Do I—still smell of him?* I resist the urge to sniff my hair.

"Oh, it certainly looked different last night," he purrs. "I remember that it was you who came to me first."

"I did it to win you around and take me to Niavara," I contradict, glowering at him. I would love to wipe the haughty expression off his face.

"Did you?" Before I can pull back and come up with a sharp retort, he's grabbed my chin. He leans down to me. "My sweet little villain, I know you can lie, but your eyes cannot."

This time I refuse to blush. "Maybe I'm just a very good actor."

He frowns slightly but lets go of me. "If you are, you certainly won't mind keeping up appearances a little longer. Attend the celebrations tonight, with me."

I have to look away to be able to say the next words, and they still don't come out as cold as I wish they would. "You can't really tell me that you want to be seen with a slave." A human. Whatever.

"Maybe I do."

I shake my head. "You just have to babysit me again and want to go."

When he says nothing, I look back to him, a strange pain echoing through my whole body. One that makes me long for my bed. For my sheets. Makes me want to slip under them and hide from the world.

"Can't it be both?" he asks finally, as unfazed and melodious as ever.

I suddenly envy him for it, all of them, for their fae hearts and fae looks, all as unbreakable as stone, laughing about a mortal like me and my silly mortal feelings.

"It can, but it's not," I state dryly.

"We can pretend," he counters.

"Sure. I can be a pretty slave for one night and then happily go back to being an ordinary slave tomorrow." He brushes an invisible fleck of dust off his black shirt before his eyes survey me again.

"It's entirely up to you whether you want to attend as an ordinary slave, although I'd much prefer you in something more exquisite. You're going to be with me, after all," he says, flashing me a cold grin that makes me all the more aware of how common I look compared to him. Not even the most beautiful dress will change that.

"Yeah, you know what—I don't want to go. Just have some guards watch my room, I promise I won't break any more wards, or try to run." I turn away but he grabs my wrist.

"Maybe I *want* you by my side tonight."

I let out a snort. "All those *maybes*. You don't."

He lets go of me and I turn away.

He says to my back, "A pity. I'm not allowed to leave you unsupervised, and I'd really hate to ask Kyrith to look after you tonight."

I swivel and glower at him. He just lets out a chuckle. *Bastard.*

"Just as I thought. I see you later, my little darling. Oh, and I think you're going to love the dress I had made for you."

He turns on his heel and strides elegantly away. Before he reaches the door, I pick the brush from the floor and hurl it at him.

He stops but doesn't stir as it hits the wall mere inches from his head.

"You know, you could at least have the decency to turn around when someone throws something at you," I seethe as he just walks on as if nothing ever happened.

He pauses and glances over his shoulder. His eyes glisten with dark amusement that somehow only makes it worse. "Why would I, when I heard you aim to miss?"

"Because I'm a human and can't aim?"

He looks genuinely surprised. "No. I can only speculate about your motivations, but I do like to think because you didn't wish to."

"Maybe I did," I say, still furious.

"Maybe, but unlikely, since your dagger had no problem finding Kyrith's shoulder, am I right? I do look forward to later tonight, Melody."

Then he's out the door.

☽ ✳ ☾

Nidaw enters later, slipping into the bathroom while I steam in the soothing waters, only to dress me in something totally different from what all the other servants are wearing. It's a loose dress made of silk, soft and semi-sheer, stitched with golden ornaments that hide my body just so, and so light on my skin that I feel naked. It hangs loose on me, only held by two pins at my shoulders, and cut so deeply at the back that I blush as I look at myself in the mirror.

The dress—it has the confidence of a seductress and the lightness of a nightgown.

I cannot, *will not* wear it. I catch Nidaw's gaze, shaking my head at the siren. "I can't wear this."

"You look breathtaking in it," Nidaw says with a questioning tilt of her head. "Lord Riven had it made especially for you."

"I know. But that's not me," I say quietly, self-consciously. Forcing myself to look back at Nidaw. I want to wear pants, something I can run and climb and fight in. Something I can hide a knife in. Definitely nothing that makes me feel even more vulnerable than I already do.

"It *is* you," the siren contradicts.

"I can't," I repeat. "I won't."

Nidaw clicks her tongue. "The high lord suspected you would say exactly that. And he said I should tell you that the dress is wild and beautiful—just like you are. That's why he chose it. But if you should not feel comfortable, you are free to wear whatever you please, he assured me. He wants you to feel comfortable," she adds the last part in a tone that makes it very clear that she doesn't at all agree with Riven and only says it because he ordered her to.

Riven said that I'm wild and beautiful? I don't know how to respond. Don't know whether I should believe it. But they can't lie, so…

I glance down at that dress. Then I look at Nidaw, who gives me a reassuring smile in return.

"Come, let's get your hair done first, and then you can decide," she offers kindly.

She sits me down at the vanity, painting my lips and eyes silver before she puts some magnificent peacock feathers in my hair, the color matching the azure and emerald glitter around my eyes and on my temples.

Eventually, Nidaw stands behind me as I look at myself one last time in the huge mirror next to the vanity.

The dress is indeed dreamlike. I want to strip it off. Want to slip into something less extravagant, something less revealing.

But Nidaw puts her clawed hands on my shoulders, meeting my eyes in the mirror. "You look like an elf," she states, proudness in her voice. "Like an elven princess."

"I am not," I respond quietly.

Nidaw frowns at me before she combs with loose fingers through my hair, as if to fix some stray strands. "You are not? Your mother was the daughter of a king. It may be time that you follow in her steps."

"What?"

Instead of an answer she takes my fingers and leads me to the door of the bathroom before whispering, with another knowing smile playing around her bluish lips, "But most of all—have fun, my little one. Life can be dire enough."

She ushers me out into the corridor before I can ask her more about my mother. Or tell her I've changed my mind about the dress.

MELODY

As I silently meander through the corridors, I wonder whether the fae ever ache after evenings of wine and celebrations. Are they ever hungover after they get riotously drunk? Do they ever fall into an exhausted sleep like I did the few times I stole wine from Lyrian's cellar?

I follow the sound traveling through the halls, along with the warm wind leading me out through a grand door and into a garden I've never seen before.

A surreal garden. Impossible. Full of green trees and the ground strewn with windfall apples. Surprisingly soft, plush grass under my bare feet, which could never exist in a desert like this if it weren't for magic.

A thousand fireflies dance between the oaks and willows and cherry trees, illuminating the moss-covered shingles of bark.

I stride through it, trailing after the sound of haunting music and laughter, until candles illuminate a path, two large torches flanking the entrance to a maze, its hedge higher than my head. I look around, unsure what to do. A man appears next to me, stepping out of the darkness. His skin is a pattern of white and black tattoos that seem to blur with the shadows, his hair the deepest blue in the flickering light, his face a masterpiece of classical beauty.

"Are you lost, my lady?" he asks gently.

"I'm no lady—" I start.

But he holds up a hand. "Indeed you are. Lord Riven sent me and wishes you the greatest of *fun*." His eyes twinkle as he speaks the last word, his sensuous mouth twitching. We both know Riven would never have used it. "I was sent to tell you that you might find him in the middle. He also mentioned that it shouldn't be a problem for you to find the right way if you just think of him."

Before I can say more, or ask for his name, he vanishes as if he was never here.

Fun. The same word twice in one evening.

I eye the maze, unsure, but then step into it. *Think of him.* Riven wants me to use my special talent to find him, so I will.

It's suddenly so easy to send my senses out and have them show me the way through the fallacious paths toward the laughing and dancing like a beacon. There are more torches lining the thick greenery of the vast clearing when I reach it. Everywhere, cushions and carpets are strewn in the dappled shade of oak trees and willows, their branches long and slim like ivy vines, shivering in the wind, hiding the naked bodies moving and writhing beneath it.

I probably should be used to the sight of openly displayed lust by now, but I'm not. I quickly look away, unsure where to settle my gaze. My eyes wander on, past naked men to my right, shining with gold paint and playing harps and flutes. I eventually make out Riven at the far end of the meadow. *Great.*

He looks so decadent and fluid in this atmosphere, as if he was born for this. Then I remember he probably was, as a fae prince. He's surrounded by breathtaking fae women. One of them has her delicate arms twined around his neck while he's laughing about something one of them must have said.

For some reason, my heart sinks.

I wrap my arms around myself and just watch him, too shy to approach. Unable to look away either.

The collar of his tunic is jeweled with shimmering onyx, an echo of his ink-drop hair. A ruff of pitch-black feathers hugs his pale throat. Black boots rise wide over his knees. Golden cuffs with serrated peaks cap his pointed ears, and heavy rings catch the light, each of them so big it covers his knuckles.

But the most stunning part of him is still his face, his features so similar to Caryan's they could be brothers if it weren't for the warm smile that fades when his eyes drift to mine.

He takes a step out of the woman's embrace, and with a last word to them, he comes over to me. Before I know what he's doing, he falls on one knee, his hands pushing up the fabric of my dress. He presses a kiss right on my naked hip.

"What the hell—"

"Forgive me, my love, but etiquette demands this," he interrupts, his voice smooth as polished stone.

"A little warning would have been nice," I hiss, ignoring the flush of treacherous heat as his fingers trail down my naked leg, slowly letting the thin fabric of my dress glide back down along with them.

"I'll make sure to warn you the next time I fall on my knees to kiss you," he retorts very quietly, so only I can hear.

I stare. His expression stays stern and formal, but I see the corners of his lips tugging up ever so slightly at my incredulous look.

He gets up and beckons to a pixie man with green hair and rainbow wings who's carrying a tray with wine. Riven hands me a glass of golden liquid before offering me his arm. I shyly take the glass *and* his arm, and he gently guides me through the crowd.

I try hard not to notice how everyone seems to steal glances at us. I hold on tighter while Riven steers us toward the long table in the middle of the yard, made of polished, turquoise stone and laden with impossible delicacies. Veal, still dripping with blood. Fat, dark grapes, so ripe they seem they might burst if you look at them too long. Stiff, whipped cream in the shapes of animals, rich and yellow like butter, dusted with gold. Edible flowers had been strewn in between all sorts of roasted things I don't know the names of.

"Eat. It's hard to worry over delicious food," Riven says, as if he feels my unease.

I look at the food, at all these enticing things I help prepare every day but only taste occasionally when Chef lets me. To help myself to it all—it feels forbidden. Like back at Lyrian's house, where I'd sometimes sneak into the kitchen at night when Lyrian wasn't around or was busy with other things. I'd ransacked the fridge, starved from either getting nothing or just plain bread and butter day in day out.

I don't stir, so it's Riven who takes one of the plates and starts to load it with a bit of everything. We stroll over to some cushions under trees, strings of gems interwoven with dried flowers dangling from the branches, dancing in a breeze.

Riven leans back, braced on his elbows, his throat exposed, his long legs outstretched.

I try not to look at him or marvel at how stunning he looks. Instead, I scrutinize the strange food on my plate. Eventually, my curiosity wins and I take one of the cream animals. He watches me as I bite off the head of a fox. It dissolves on my tongue, its taste citrusy and sweet, along with words *You will not know who tried to kiss you in the dark.*

Riven laughs at my wide eyes. "It's a game, a spell woven into it, whispering nonsense. What did yours say?"

I look down at my plate again, for some absurd reason remembering the feeling of his lips on my hip. It feels wrong to tell him, but also wrong not to, so I do.

He nods. "When I was a child, we imagined they held some meaning. Some truth, important to our lives. Some hint at the future."

I fully look at him then, trying to imagine him as a child. He looks barely older than twenty-five, and at the same time, he does. All of them do in some strange way. They look young and at the same time eternal. Ageless. Their eyes ancient.

I pick up a tiny cream bear and hold it out to him. "Your turn."

"Very well then," he says and puts it into his mouth.

I raise my brows at him. "And?"

"A riddle. *You can see your self in me, but you can never see mine, and in time, you can see no one at all.*"

347

"A mirror," I say. "Its silver tarnishes over time."

He tilts his head and looks at me. "Maybe. Or maybe someone who has forgotten how to love. Who can only ever find himself in others, until he can do not even that anymore."

His voice has fallen low again, and the way he looks at me changes. For a moment, there is no façade. There is no vicious glint in his eyes, nor the infinitely amused expression playing around his lips. For a moment, there is his real self, exposed, revealed. The grayish mist around his aura vanished, torn. Just like the other night, when he let me. When he told me that he'd once been a slave too.

Again, I try to make sense of what I see there, in his aura. He's talking about himself, and also not. There is pain and desperation, but also, somewhere, hope and joy. *Love.*

"If there's, indeed, truth in the saying, what would it be?" I ask, suddenly too aware of who he's really talking about as I spot the golden band again.

"Whatever we want it to be," he retorts, too casually. "Because it's just a riddle. Like a fairy tale. It's not real, so it only holds as much meaning as we give to it."

"But what if it is real?" I push.

"Then I would keenly wish it to be the mirror because what would life be without the ability to love? How empty, how dull. It must feel like a curse."

He's telling me something. Too much and, at the same time, nothing. I register somewhere in the back of my mind that the music's changed. People are starting to dance in a circle.

Riven gets up, too, holding his hand out to me, his somber mood wiped away.

"I can't dance. I mean, not real dancing. Not like *that*," I confess, mortified. Briefly afraid of what I've agreed to in coming here as I watch the swirling and spinning couples. Some move so preternaturally fast that the ground underneath them begins to spark and steam, leaving burned soil. How they exchange the mouths they kiss, along with their partners.

Riven gives me one of his smiles, so well-practiced and

ruthlessly polite. But it doesn't match the seriousness in his eyes when he says, "We'll take it slow."

I entwine my fingers with his when he steps up, his cheek at mine, his hand at the small of my back. Out of the corner of my eye, I see the disappointed faces of other women, envy all over their auras.

He follows my gaze. I stiffen. "You don't have to do this. You can just leave me here and dance with them," I say quietly.

"I do not wish to."

I watch our feet, my bare toes close to his boots. I should not ask, but I can't help it. "Why? Because we're still pretending?"

"What else would it be?" he asks darkly.

"I don't like this game, whatever kind it is," I say, more harshly than I should. But suddenly, being here in this dress makes me feel more vulnerable than ever.

"It's not a game."

"Well then, what is it?"

"I want you to enjoy yourself, Melody," he says, catching me gently when I make the wrong move.

"So, we're doing all of this just to make me feel... good?" Sarcasm rings in every word.

"I admit it might be a little bit selfish too," he whispers, close to my ear. "But yes, I would do a lot of things if they made you feel *good.*"

My breath hitches at the way he speaks the last word. I wonder what we're doing here. It feels dangerous.

"Should I tell you how pretty you look?" he asks as he spins me around.

Our eyes meet.

He turns me so my back is pressed against him, his hard body. Just then he murmurs into my neck, "I cannot. It would be a lie." I shiver at his breath over my skin, at his words running over it like slow-dripping honey. "Because you look breathtakingly beautiful."

If I didn't know fae can't lie, I would know he just did. *So dangerous.*

He spins me again until we're face-to-face. He smiles at the confusion all over me. Another private smile only meant for my eyes.

Then he leans into me and says with midnight smoothness, "Look at them. They can barely keep their eyes off you."

"Because I look human," I retort quietly.

"Oh, I assure you this is not the reason they're staring so unabashedly."

He spins me again, and I look over my shoulder to study his face. Heat flushes my neck when I find him glancing down at my dress for a second.

We spin again and he suddenly stops. "You still do not understand," he says, almost frustrated.

I shake my head, my heart beating a little too fast. No, I don't understand a lot of things. The way my skin feels more alive when he touches me, the way I feel differently. Bold, maybe, but in an entirely new way.

"They envy you because you are much more beautiful than they will ever be," he says.

I still cannot follow him. His eyes warm as he takes in my features. I look away. "They, you…"

"We are perfect, yes. All of us, blessed by eternal perfection. But perfection dulls the eye over time. It is our flaws that make us special. Our broken parts that make us unique." He traces the memories of scars on my face before he leans in again. "You are very beautiful, but you are also wild, and alive, and feeling. More alive and feeling than many of them will ever be." He says it with a touch of sadness. With a touch of melancholy. With a kind of longing.

And for a second, I don't care whether this is a game. I don't care what I am or who I am. Or was. A part of me just wants.

I let my gaze stray, afraid he can sense exactly what effect he has on me. Afraid of myself and what I want to do.

Black eyes catch mine. Under one of the willows lies Caryan, his head cushioned on a silken pillow.

The last angel. The face of dreams and nightmares.

He's wearing a long, loose, black hunting shirt that reveals a lot of his white chest. Two stunning women sit on either side of him, one undoing his pants while the other kisses his lips, which are ripe with the color of wine.

His eyes are barely open, but I can feel him watching me, his eyes glittering black as fresh tar through his thick lashes while he keeps kissing the woman. *A woman with skin as light as mine and hair equally dark and long.*

I try to shake the thought off...

But can't.

All the things he whispered to me suddenly run too fresh in my blood. Make my ribs cave in on my lungs. And just like that, it's as if I feel that collar again, cool and eternal against my delicate throat.

Horrified I tear my gaze away from Caryan, back to Riven. It takes everything I've got not to touch my neck to see if it's really gone. But I feel raw, my heartbeat stuttering, uneven, my breathing fast. Before I know what I'm doing, I've slinked past Riven and am running toward the hedges. Deeper into the maze, into its shade and dark niches.

Riven follows me. I hear him behind me. Only there do I look up to him. "Is Caryan... is he going to keep me forever?"

"Forever is a strong word, Melody," Riven starts, but I cut him off, still breathless.

"Do not... do not evade the truth to spare me. I deserve to know."

"I think so," Riven says gravely, his eyes losing their shine.

I can still feel the lingering touch of that collar that was never there. And yet the skin on my throat keeps burning with its otherworldly cold. "And if I don't obey whatever he wants me to do?" When Riven doesn't answer immediately, I take a step back from him. "I can never leave?"

"Melody," he says, reaching out to me, but I only step back further.

The blaring of a horn cuts through whatever he was about to say. His face looks tormented as he peers back over my head towards the center of the maze. "The chase. We cannot stay here," he says then, his eyes gliding back to me.

"The chase?"

"It's a midnight game. People will chase each other through the labyrinth," he explains somberly, then offers me his hand. A silent truce. Like in the woods. Like back in front of Lyrian's house, when he said he would protect me.

I take it.

"Who will chase whom?" I ask.

As if on cue, a tiny pink paper bracelet appears around my hand, a blue one around Riven's.

When we step back into the clearing, everyone has gathered, each one with a subtly differently colored bracelet around their wrist. "Your bracelet has a twin. But you don't find out until the person with the matching bracelet finds you, or vice versa," he explains when the horn sounds again. "But we won't participate. Just stay close to me and we'll get out."

His voice is serious, and he almost pulls me along, as if something about the game is dangerous.

The horn sounds a third time and at that, the crowd begins to run toward us like a herd of game chased by lions. We step back against a hedge to let them pass.

When I briefly let go of Riven's hand to flatten myself against the labyrinth's edge, some huge fauns grab me and pull me with them.

"Melody!" Riven shouts, eyes wide.

He's trying to get to me, but the fauns are like a stream, and I'm pushed by them. All too quickly I'm swallowed by the darkness we just came from. Only there do I manage to wriggle free, to step aside and let them pass.

But when I try to get back to the clearing, there's suddenly a hedge, sprouted out of nowhere before me, blocking my way.

The entrance to the center is gone.

When I turn, I'm all alone in the maze's path.

MELODY

I start running. But the labyrinth isn't like before when I found my way in. Now it's moving, constantly shifting. More hedges sprout out of nowhere, where there weren't any moments ago. Gaps, too, creating more corridors, leading only deeper and deeper. I keep hitting dead ends, no matter how hard I focus my senses on finding Riven.

I run even faster.

Occasionally, I rush past someone.

Giggles and hisses sound from behind a hedge, the thrumming of hooves over grass, the brush of bodies against the leaves and bushes.

As yet another tunnel with a pitch-black end awaits me, I feel the surge of my familiar panic.

I'm trapped. Trapped in darkness.

I turn, trying to calm my rising fear. *It's just a game. Just a game.* But I hate it!

I'm already sweating, my fingers cold, my heartbeat too fast. I cut around another corner, only to meet another dead end. And again. And again.

As it goes on, desperation crawls up inside me, clenching my throat. I freeze when I turn another corner, only to find two fauns, crimson-horns locked, hips moving in sync. I stare when one looks at me, hissing, his *fangs* bared, and I back out. Another hedge opens up behind me, sending me stumbling through.

More moaning. The smell of sex suddenly everywhere. Of blood too. My heart beats so fast it's humming. *What game is this?*

A fae game, I know. A *dark* game.

Around another corner, I spot Ronin bent over the naked body of one of the gold-painted musicians. His pants are down, and he holds the man by the hips, his head back, his eyes closed. He thrusts deeply into the harpist, heedless of me or anything else, as the man in front of him sighs quietly through parted lips.

The bracelets on their wrists match.

I pivot on my heels, a dark suspicion dawning in my mind of what this game is about. Of what happens if the hunter catches his prey.

In another corner, there's Kyrith with a nymph, his teeth and chin covered in her blood while the nymph's legs are closed around his waist.

Where the hell is Riven?

I run again in the other direction, more panic stirring in me, flooding my system. I won't get out of this. *There is no way out.*

I sprint faster when footsteps sound behind me, closing in.

I will fight. I won't be someone else's prey. This is a nightmare. I run and run, the burning in my lungs a painful, sobering reminder of when I tried to run from Lyrian.

Before he threw me into the dark cell again and things got bad.

The memory sends another jolt of adrenaline through me, swamping my senses, my barely controlled panic surging further. Tears start to stream down my cheeks as exhaustion kicks in.

No, I will go on. I will find a way out.

I will climb this fucking hedge. I try. It's too high, my fingers finding nothing to hold on to, as if the whole thing is slippery with some magic.

I give up at the third attempt, and more footsteps startle me. I run on, run for all it's worth. More corners, hedges, dead ends.

Eventually, I stop in a quiet corner, breathing too hard, my body trembling with fear. I'm trapped. I can't shake off the feeling that the labyrinth *wants* me to be found.

I cower into the darkest corner, begging silently for the labyrinth to hide me. To make an exception.

What if I scream? Will it matter to anyone? Will it attract attention? Draw my chaser? Where is Riven? He won't be able to find me if the labyrinth is preventing it or, with his speed, he would have already. Or maybe he already gave up on me, having seen that I'm not worth it?

I bury my head in my hands and start to cry in earnest while the damn hedges seem to draw closer and closer like the walls in that bunker. *I will not be afraid. I will not be afraid.* But the words sound hollow. The darkness is too much.

I don't look up when leaves rustle in a breeze. When a figure pauses in front of me, casting a long shadow. Someone to claim my blood, my body, with whatever sick desire.

But when I look up eventually, I find black eyes rimmed with gold, unreflective for once, and wings behind him.

Wings…

My whole stomach cramps. I slide backward as if I can somehow melt into the hedge.

"I won't hurt you, Melody," Caryan says, his power flooding me, dark and entrancing.

It's so much like the other night, so much like when he whispered all those dark things at my neck. Every word he said clanks through me with new ferocity, my flesh alive with burning fear.

He meant it. And here I am, a slave, an amusement, a fucking plaything. A wretched toy.

"I hate your games!" I blurt out, glowering at him, my body feverish and alert. "They're sick and weird and…" My voice is all wrong—too loud and breathless. "Everything here is weird, and so backward. Keeping slaves, whipping people for mistakes!"

The words tumble out. It's all I have left, to let him know what I think about whatever the hell he's going to do to me.

But to my surprise, he says, more gently than I ever imagined, "I know it appears that way to you."

He holds out a hand to me, and only then do I notice the green bracelet, his color not matching mine. He isn't my hunter then. "That's why I came to get you," he adds.

I stare at his hand. He's different. So different from the fury and anger when he found me in the desert. Different to last night too. Last night he was himself, I realize with a start. Untamed. Wild. And a little bit unhinged. Now he's—well, I don't fucking know what he is right now.

When I look up into his face again, his features have softened, the blackness of his eyes morphed into that resonating blue.

He has come to get me. Twice now.

I slowly edge closer, though I don't take his hand. He straightens and I stand up too.

"We have to fly back," he declares somberly.

I glance at his huge wings, then at him, unsure how it would work. "Can't we just… walk? It's your world, your labyrinth…"

"It's enchanted for the night. I would have to break the whole spell."

I try to ignore the surge of his power flickering up my skin once more. Try to ignore how his eyes draw over my half-translucent dress. About how that makes me feel.

As if my skin is too small. Aching. Raw.

Too bare.

The blue in Caryan's eyes turns into midnight hues. "This isn't for you. Riven shouldn't have brought you here." He seems to say it more to himself.

And there I feel it, a hint of his fury again.

"It wasn't his fault," I say too quickly.

Caryan's gaze snaps back up to me, his pupils flaring. "It wasn't? He shouldn't have left the clearing."

I startle at the sudden change in his tone. Darkness teems around him, his wings are suddenly night-kissed.

"It was my idea. I needed a break and snuck away." My words

come breathlessly. Panic of a different kind is stealing my thoughts. The image of David; pushing itself into my mind.

"I tasked him with the solemn duty of watching and guarding you. He knows better than to let you out of his sight, especially now."

"But he didn't do anything. It was I who left him. And he just… followed me. I know it was foolish to run, and I shouldn't have done it. I won't do it again, I promise."

"Won't you run again?" He tilts his head then, stepping up to me, his wings a monstrous wall behind him. Nothing could have prepared me for his tone, vicious and scraping as he leans down to me. "I wonder—how does it feel? To eventually obey to my word to protect him?"

Something in me recoils at the sudden anger and bitterness, all tangled up in his voice. My heart restlessly flutters in my chest as I look back up at him.

"Why don't you tell me how you want me to feel?" I whisper very quietly.

It's the intensity of his gaze that triggers me. Changes me. Makes me aware again of how he just looked at me in that dress. Is looking at me right now.

We are all alone here.

I want to run from him. To hide.

Another part of me, though…

All I can suddenly think of is the way he looked at me last night. The way he just kissed that woman. How she resembled me. And what… what would have happened if he *had* been my hunter?

Briefly, I'm afraid of my own mind. Of the way he can read my thoughts, sense the reaction of my body.

His eyes darken, shadows in them guttering in answer.

I quickly look back down to the ground. For the length of a heartbeat, there's only thrumming silence.

Again, he holds out his hand to me. This time, I take it and he pulls me up to him.

"Hold on tight," is all he says.

Then his strong arms wrap around me, clasping me against his hard body. Reflexively, I do the same, hugging his torso when he spreads his wings wide and shoots up in the air.

The world blurs, my senses swim with the rush, my panic, the height. Caryan's sudden closeness. His scent, invading me. The feeling of his hard, powerful body against mine... the land beneath us so small, so foreign, so insignificant.

Harmless. A star-strewn paradise.

I might be hiding my face in his neck. He might have tightened his grip on me ever so slightly.

A moment later, there's the feel of soft grass under my feet. I instinctively step away from Caryan, not daring to look at him. Too afraid that he can read my confusion all over me.

It's Riven's voice that makes me turn. Then my gaze falls onto four fauns kneeling on the lawn, their heads bowed, their hands tied behind their backs by Caryan's magic. A shiver rakes through me. One of them is the chef. He must be one of the fauns who grabbed me. I didn't look at their faces.

My heart lodges in my throat as I spot too clearly in their aura what they expect to happen next.

"Take her to your rooms, Riven," Caryan orders, his voice cold again.

The chef raises his head then, his blue eyes shimmering bright like the day sky. "It was a grievous error, my sire. We never intended any harm. It was just merrymaking. It is equinox and part of the tradition, after all. Please, let us atone."

I just stare as Riven gently takes my arm to steer me away.

Caryan says, "I made it very clear that the rules changed for the time being. I promised an execution to anyone who stepped out of line, so you will have it."

Caryan turns away from me, from us. I can feel his deadly magic rise, forming like a spear aimed at the chef.

I tear free from Riven's grip and throw myself over the faun, my eyes closed, my whole body locked up, bracing myself for imminent death.

For a moment, time itself seems to stop.

Then… nothing. Just the ragged breathing of the faun under me, matching my own.

I blink as a black wind of magic brushes around me, no longer carrying the promise of death.

When I dare to look at Caryan, I find his eyes wide and blazing, but… horrified.

The sentiment is replaced by a mask of Arctic ire. His voice is dead-cold when he orders, "Step away, Melody."

I glance at Riven, only to find him staring at me wide-eyed, his aura a storm of shock and terror before I look back at Caryan. "No. Please. Please, spare them. It was a mistake. I'm unharmed. He… he's my friend." Tears well in my eyes, my hands still curled around the horns of the faun under me, his head at an awkward angle, pressing into my belly. I dare not move. I dare not let go of him either.

Caryan's eyes are damning. Promising that I'm going to regret this.

I venture, "I offer you a bargain. Please, spare them, and I'll do whatever thing you want me to do." I say it without looking at Riven. I can't. I know what I'd see in his face. Horror. Grief. Destruction. But I know I won't regret it, not when it saves their lives.

I'm not sure Riven would—*could*—understand.

Caryan looks at me for a long while before he agrees, "Very well, a bargain it is. A thing called in anytime from now."

I hiss as something hot and sharp seeps into the skin of my left wrist. When I glance down at it, I find a black tattoo there. Two wings, folded around two crescent moons, burned into my flesh. It thrums. Thrums with a part of my soul that has been forged into it and caged there.

I force myself to not let my terror show on my face when I eventually let go of the chef and straighten.

"Do not ever court my ire again," Caryan says to the fauns.

The shackles around their hands loosen, but they stay kneeling, their heads bowed so low their horns touch the soft grass.

"You are dismissed. All of you," Caryan says with a last, long glance at me before he spreads his wings, their span easily twice my size, and shoots up into the air.

"What have you done, my little one?" Riven asks once we are back in the enclosure of his chambers. A warm black and lilac fire jumps alive in the huge fireplace as soon as we enter, and I sink before it, my legs pulled up tight against my body.

Riven hasn't spoken to me until now. We walked back in silence. I was numb, stealing glances at the strange tattoo.

I make myself meet his face at last, surprised to find only softness there. He holds out a tumbler to me, a liquid as black as elderberry sap in it. I take it, swallow and shudder against its taste, the way it fragrantly burns down my throat. A kind of distinct pain coming along with it, one that distracts from everything else.

I take another sip. "I know you're disappointed," I say finally, looking back at the beautiful flames, the black dancing with the violet.

"How could I be if you offered a bargain for such a noble reason?"

I frown up at him. "I'll admit that you surprise me," I say, quoting his words from a night that feels years back rather than mere weeks.

He gives me the gentlest hint of a smile. "Is that a good or a bad thing?"

I shrug before I get up. "A dangerous one, I guess." My eyes come to rest on his. My voice falls quiet. "Caryan has never done that before, has he—execute people for tiny mistakes? I saw your aura. The surprise there. The horror," I continue before he can answer me. I'd glimpsed it on that lawn, the moment Riven had been too distracted to keep up the veil.

Riven turns his head away, staring into the flames. "No, he has not."

"It is me, right?"

His jaw tenses but he doesn't answer.

"He still thinks that whoever was behind that incident in my room will try again, doesn't he?" I ask.

"They *are* going to try again," he retorts darkly.

"Why?" Again he avoids my eyes. "What is so important that they want me? Please tell me, Riven."

When his eyes slide back to mine, there is so much in them. "I already told you that I wish I could. Dearly so. But I cannot. You have to ask Caryan yourself, my little one."

"Why?" I ask sharply, unwilling to accept his answer.

"You know why. My hands are tied," he replies, his voice hoarse. Raw. Angry.

"He scared you, on that lawn. Caryan scared you," I push. "Why?"

Riven lets out a long exhale before he runs his fingers through his hair. "It scared me what he might do to you. I'm used to sacrifices, but you would be the one I am not willing to make," he says eventually. "Do you understand?"

I want to shake my head. No, I do not. Because no one will fucking tell me anything. But I swallow my anger and walk past him over to his huge bed.

If no one's going to tell me anything, I'll find out on my own.

I will go to Niavara tomorrow. Find whatever that book wants me to find.

BLAIR, TWO YEARS BEFORE GATILLA'S DEATH

It began with the beating of the war drums. The appearance Palisandre's army had given—an army still setting up; soldiers still readying themselves—it had been a ploy.

Blair jumped out of bed and donned her leathers, the screech of phantom wyverns already filling the night, the song of the summoned beasts a wild, wicked answer to the drums. She sprinted outside, braiding her hair as the first arrows came flying, piercing flesh and slicing tents. Ice-arrows. Fire-arrows.

Elven magic.

Aurora? Sofya? Blair's eyes scanned the disaster around her, but she couldn't find them.

Fear swamped her, ruthless and brutal fear.

Caryan. She needed to see him. She needed his guidance, his reassurance. His calm. His strength.

She was still looking when she felt a hand close around her wrist. There he was, already in his battle suit, his eyes dark but unfazed. He found her, as if he'd felt her panic.

"Cool your blood, Blair. I will be with you. Do as we discussed. Attack the front lines, try to take out the towers."

She nodded, but his words barely registered in her fear-addled mind.

He gripped her harder, baring his fangs. "You need to pull yourself together."

"I'm... terrified," she admitted.

Her breath caught as he put a hand on her neck and a warm, deep calm seeped into her, anchoring her. Grounding her.

"We will see each other tonight, but now, fight. There's no backing down now. No way back."

Her panic was gone, replaced by his magic. She was as calm as she'd ever been, and her mind so clear. So focused.

"I will," she agreed and walked over to her wyvern.

As the beast swung itself into the air, Blair threw out a mighty, burning shield of orange magic to block the arrows now raining down on them.

"Witches, fall into formation." Her voice boomed over the chaos, and she could feel disorder falling into order. Into a system.

More witches joined her.

"We are witches. Let us remind them what that means," she growled as her wyvern flew in a circle above. Finally, all the wyverns and their riders fell into formation.

"For the Blacklands!" Blair screamed, and all of them, a chorus of witches, answered, raising their swords, grinning up at her, teeth and swords glinting.

"For the Blacklands!"

The battle turned into an outright slaughter. Palisandre threw magic at the witches, who ripped into them like a burst dam. Blair lunged, slaying warrior after warrior, swearing at the slaughter and the tang of blood that coated her tongue. At some point, rain set in, the metal of her sword singing in the air, a melody to the screeching of her wyvern as its teeth and claws shredded flesh.

She knew then that war changed a person. Shaped them anew. Whatever dark creature she'd been before, she had turned even darker.

She readied her blade for another blow and breathed in the symphony of gore and blood and mud, trying hard not to think about her mothers somewhere on that battlefield. There were just so many high elves.

The army of elves they'd spotted had been tiny compared to what was coming for them now. Another trick from Palisandre—reinforcements waited but a day's march away and were pouring in minute by minute, swamping the valley.

Blair stood knee-deep in mud and gore, no longer able to tell the two apart. Fatigue had long since set in, but now despair started to weaken her blows, made her shields waver.

A lot of the witches had stayed back in Akribea, too far away to reach them in time. They were outnumbered. Defeat was inevitable.

Death was inevitable.

She knew then that all the witches she brought here were going to die tonight.

She readied her blade regardless as she stared down the impossible flood of soldiers coming for her.

A crack of dark lightning divided the sky, followed by bone-shaking thunder as equally black clouds collided.

For a moment, the slaughter stilled and everyone stared.

Then a horn blasted—their signal to retreat. Blair shouted commands, her wyvern banking and cutting sharp over the battlefield. It picked Blair up in its claws and veered right back to the mountain where their camp was set and where her aunt was standing at the very edge, her wide robes billowing, her red hair flowing around her dark crown like a halo of fire.

Wyvern after wyvern shook the mountain as they landed, wings flapping, witches dismounting. Blair didn't take the time to dismiss her wyvern when more bolts of dark lightning began to strike down from the sky. Celestial magic.

Caryan's magic.

Huge craters and burnt flesh and soil were all that was left where they met the ground. Palisandre had no time to react, barely time to retreat or throw up their shields as a shadow fell from the sky. Blotting out the sun.

No, not a shadow. An angel with black wings.

An angel who kept butchering every single soldier, surrounded by a tornado of blackest night and chains of darkest lightning.

And, as Blair stepped next to her aunt and gazed down at the carnage, she realized that the witches had just been a distraction. A prelude.

Caryan was her aunt's true weapon.

The only one she really needed.

45

MELODY

Riven is gone in the morning, but, again, there's a bubble bath waiting for me, along with that cup of perfect cappuccino that refills itself as soon as I empty it.

While I steam in the water, I try to ignore the tattoo on my wrist as best as I can, but I can't shake the feeling that it's watching me.

I scrub at it, but all that happens is that my skin flushes. I wouldn't be surprised if, should I dare to peel my skin, it just renewed itself.

I wash my hair, then get out and head for the kitchen. No one seems to notice me. I only catch Chef occasionally glancing my way before he quickly looks away again. It's only later that he comes up to me, catching my hands in his huge, clawed ones. He falls to a knee. Horror sweeps over me.

"No, please. Get up," I whisper, but he just holds me there, my hands clasped in his, his massive, beautiful horns almost reaching up to my neck even when he kneels, he's that huge.

The pearls woven in his braided strands of hair click with the movement. He takes one of them out. A black and shiny one that seems to brim with magic.

"Call me Arbor henceforth, because this is my name, and know that I am forever grateful. We do not have much, but I do have this," he says, putting the tiny, black pearl into my hand. "Swallow it, and it will dissolve, and you will be able to grow fairy wings and fly. But beware that the spell won't last long and that it will only work once."

"Thank you," I whisper, my hands closing around the pearl, but he bows only deeper.

"I would be your servant forevermore, obedient to your command, if I hadn't sworn fealty to my king already."

I say nothing. It would only make things worse if I told him that I saw what power does to people and that I don't want it. I know Caryan would not be pleased if he ever heard about this. Or worse, if he saw it in someone's blood.

So I just nod once, as if I understand.

I'm grateful when things fall into their usual order and I can go back to cutting vegetables, my mind still too adrift.

☽ ∗ ☾

Later that night, when the sun is already halfway down, Nidaw orders me and the blush-haired siren—Everly—to clean Lady Sarynx Maedavel's rooms. The blonde elf who'd been at Caryan's side. My stomach clenches at the prospect of another encounter with her.

When we enter the rooms, the ash around the fireplace and the bucket are gone, but the rest is as messy as it was. There are clothes and fine dresses strewn around everywhere, and so is the jewelry. Bracelets and pearls and earrings scattered all over the room, negligently thrown between flacons of luxurious oils and perfumes, golden glitter and burned-down candles.

We start to gather the things, collect and arrange them, folding fallen clothes, working wordlessly side by side. I occasionally glance at Everly, at her back, wondering whether she still has scars left there from the spymaster's whip.

"Come, tell me that I deserved worse," the siren says suddenly, catching me looking at her.

I jerk up from where I've been crouching to gather up some fallen rings. "I would never."

Everly watches me with her huge, pale eyes before she says, "She's my aunt, the one I wrote to, but she's practically my mother. She raised me. I haven't seen her for fifteen years. Since I left Palisandre. Since she sent me here to find Nidaw."

"I'd have done the same, I think," I say, meaning it. If I had a mother, I sure as hell would at least try to send her letters, all rules out the window.

The girl snorts, but then briefly smiles. A conspiratorial smile. "What's your name? Melody, is it?"

"Yeah, right."

"You saved Arbor's life, and the three others'," she says. "We heard. That was a kind thing to do. I'm sorry I was mean."

I dust my hands off on my pants. "You said it was my fault, that... circumstances changed."

She watches me curiously, her teal eyes wide. "You're the girl from Kalleandara's prophecy."

"Maybe. What does it say?"

She shies away, biting her lips, the inside limned with dark-bluish skin. "You don't know then," she states, her eyes darting around the room, as if she's looking for something.

I shake my head.

"I think I did you wrong, so I might tell you," Everly eventually decides. "It says war is coming and that you might change its outcome."

I don't know what to say other than, "How? How would *I* do that?"

Again, the siren chews on her lips before she shakes her head. "We don't know. No one really knows, that is the problem with prophecies. They stay cryptic, but we still believe in them."

"What does it say *exactly*?"

"That war is coming, and that you are the one who's going to end the blight."

"What's the blight?"

Her ears twitch. "We don't know that either. The seer didn't say."

A seer. I want to ask more, but Everly's growing restless, as if she's already told me too much. So instead, I ask, "Why did your aunt send you here?"

"So I could have a better life. A safe one. Elves can be cruel to us. They do all sort of things to us without consequence," Everly says, impressively lightly, finishing piling up some lacy underwear adorned with pearls and gemstones.

"And here, it is different?" I ask slightly surprised.

"Yes. The Dark Lord doesn't allow such things. If anyone harmed us without reason, there'd be a punishment. We're under his protection." There is awe and admiration in her voice. I remember that Nidaw once told me a similar thing.

Everly fishes a black, lacy negligee from the heap and holds it up to her body. "You think one of the high lords would look at me if I wore this?" She playfully pouts her lips and swishes her hips, clearly imitating the owner of the negligee, before her mouth tears into a wide, genuine smile, her eyes full with wicked amusement.

For a second, I'm struck by the quick change in her mood. By the familiarity of the gesture. By the *normalcy of it.* This is what it must feel like to have friends. Maybe I'd one day have friends like that. Be *normal,* or at least be whatever *normal* in the fae world is.

We look at each other for a second before we both burst out laughing.

"Which high lord?" I ask as she walks over to the bed to change the sheets.

I'm glad I have my back to Everly, glad she can't see me blushing violently when she says with a theatrical sigh, "Oh, I loooove Riven. All of us do. He's so eloquent and good-looking and charming. But…"

"But?" I ask, biting back my smile. If he knew, he'd be even more insufferable. But then, he probably knows already.

"I don't know, he seems to be more into curvy nymphs than stringy sirens. Unlike Kyrith, who's also attractive."

"Kyrith?" Now I do turn, throwing Everly an incredulous look.

The siren giggles—a silvery sound like wind bells. "Yeah, he can be so handsome and strong. You threw a dagger at him, right? That was so impressive."

I don't like how her eyes shimmer with admiration at that.

"What about the third?" I ask quickly.

"Oh, you mean Ronin. Sad that the witcher is not into women." She sighs again, as if it really bothers her. "And not to mention... the Dark Lord." She whispers the last words before she bursts out giggling again like a young girl.

I just stare at her until she asks, "What? Is he not that good a lover as they say he is?"

My heartbeat startles. *They. Caryan's whore,* that's what they called me. That's what the blonde elf, Sarynx called me.

I ask blankly, "*Who* says that?"

"All the women who've been with him do. They never get over him."

I bite down hard on my lip.

Everly pushes, her teal eyes shining. "So, *is* he?"

"I'm not... I'm not that."

"Oh." Her pink eyebrows raise. "I mean, that's curious."

"Curious why?" I don't know why I'm asking this. They probably all saw me that night in the throne room, kneeling over Caryan, and drew their own conclusions.

Everly shrugs. "Well, normally, the high lords... they don't notice most of us. We're just moments to pass their long lives."

I nod because I don't know what else to do before I ask quickly—to steer the conversation away from myself... but also because I'm just a tiny bit curious, "But you really... I mean... you *would*... with the Dark Lord?"

"Oh, of course I would. Who wouldn't?"

"It's just... he had you whipped, for one," I suggest.

"Oh, *that*," the siren says, impressively unbothered. "He saved my life that day. He had to follow his own rules, yet he decided to spare me in front of his whole court of high fae. I think that's hot."

"But you didn't mind the whipping?" I ask carefully. The

memory of the torn flesh and Everly's tearless sobs are branded on my mind.

But she just smiles with her small, sharp teeth. "Maybe it's *because* of the whipping. I think that's my new *kink*, that's what you mortals call it, right? I heard Kyrith use that word once, or twice."

I just stare, not sure she's serious.

Another smile blooms on her beautiful face and she goes on, more to herself, "It's... definitely. I know the Dark Lord's dangerous, but so gorgeous. Have you ever seen him with his wings?"

"Uhm, no," I lie, quickly turning back to stripping the sheets, feeling the tattoo on my wrist all too keenly.

"Uh, I want to touch them, just once. I imagine they must be incredibly fluffy. But they say the best that can happen if you touch an angel's wings without permission is to lose your hand, so I guess it'll remain a fantasy." She lets out another heavy sigh. "And his eyes... I wonder what they look like when he, you know, really fucks you. They say he's kind of a freak in bed." Again, Everly whispers the last part as if she's sharing a secret.

I say nothing, just trying to rein in my fluttering heartbeat.

Finally, the siren asks, "And you? Which one do you like?"

I'm done stripping the sheets and have to turn back to Everly to get the fresh ones she's put on one of the tables. "I don't know. I guess I never thought about it," I say quickly, hoping dearly she doesn't know I can lie. Hope she can't read the lie in my face.

I change the topic before she can probe on. "Are you going to Niavara today? For Gatilla's death?"

"No, we can't."

"Because the Fortress is still sealed?" I probe.

"For one. But, also, it's eerie, the town. It's people, they're wild. It's not safe for us, especially on a night like this."

I look at Everly's sharp teeth and wonder how dangerous the creatures there must be if it wasn't safe for her there.

I ask, keeping my tone a little bit detached, "Have you ever been to Niavara?"

"We go there once a month, to the markets, but only when one of the high lords is there."

"Is there a library, by any chance?"

"A library? Why would you want one?"

"Just... I'm looking for a book. Never mind."

Everly frowns. "No, not as far as I remem—"

The door flies open, and the beautiful blond elf, Sarynx, comes striding in.

Her beauty is so radiant it hurts. She's never looked better in an idea of a dress—almost translucent, stars sewn on it that seem to whirl around her body, gathering only around her breasts and between her legs.

Everly bows her head and falls to a knee. I just stand there until a vicious flicker enters Sarynx's eyes.

"You two would be long done if you'd stop chatting like agitated geese," she says, pursing her full lips.

Everly mumbles an excuse when Sarynx passes her, walking around the room as if she's looking for something. A vulture searching for a bone to pick. She stops in front of her dressing table where we have put all the jewelry we found.

"There's probably something missing," she purrs cruelly.

I see Everly flinch, shaking her head, throwing me a panicked look that says she didn't take anything.

"You two, come over here and tell me what you took."

"We didn't take anything, my lady," Everly says quietly.

Sarynx's cold gaze snaps to me. "You, maybe not. But you, human?"

"I didn't take anything either," I answer sternly.

"Oh, you cunning little liar. I will have you punished. Maybe I'll whip your new friend here," she says, drawing her eyes over to the siren, who flinches again at the prospect. "Why flinch, little siren? I thought that was your new... *kink*. Or is it different if it's not our king's hand who administers that punishment?"

Everly's cheeks turn as pink as her hair and she stares holes into the ground, as if they could open up and swallow her.

Sarynx strides up to her, lifting her chin with a manicured finger. "He would never make his hands dirty with you, little siren, but keep holding on to your ridiculous pining. Such a hideous pastime but fitting for dull minds like yours."

"As is eavesdropping," I say.

Sarynx's head snaps to me. She bares her teeth but lets go of Everly. "Watch your tongue, or I might cut it out one day. I don't care whether you are his latest whore, human." She comes for me, her teeth still bared.

"Try and see how that goes," I say with a hell of a lot more confidence than I feel. But her aura tells me she won't attack. Not yet.

Everly's eyes flash to me, surprised, but I'm too focused on Sarynx to care.

"Leave, siren, before I change my mind," she drawls, her azure eyes never straying from mine.

Everly throws me one last, apologetic glance before she runs for the door.

I don't blame her. I'm actually glad she went.

"You. Nothing but a feral girl with interesting talents. A tiny, snapping monster and a pain in the ass since you came here."

I take a step towards her. Maybe it's true. Maybe I *am* feral, because right now I want to sink my nails into her skin and draw blood.

"Maybe I am. But if Caryan still cared for you, he'd be drinking your blood. And if he was, he'd see *everything* you are, so maybe he's tired of that, and that's why you're jealous," I snarl right back at her.

I don't know where the words came from, but by the look on her face they hit home. I read all of it in her aura, and guessed the rest. But I should know better than making another enemy. Yet, I'm tired. Tired of her hate. Tired of her jealousy.

Sarynx's eyes widen, and for a second, her perfect façade falters. She hisses, "You'll regret that."

"I've long given up on regrets. So why not just get it over with right here? If you're so keen on putting a knife into my back, why not try it now?"

For a sliver of a second, I think she will, indeed, come for me now. But she doesn't, although fury burns stark and bright around her, like a firestorm, laced by yellowish streams of envy and ugly, grayish streaks of hate. But underneath... *fear.*

"You're afraid of me," I say, not believing it myself.

She raises her chin but doesn't deny it.

"You're afraid of the powers I might wield," I continue.

Her blue-painted mouth slices to the side into the hint of a smile. "Let's skip through the unpleasantness, shall we? You're sharp. Sharp enough to cut yourself. Yet have you ever wondered what Caryan will make you do? Do you know how he is when he wants something? Ruthless. Merciless. His path paved by corpses. Do you think he'll stop with you? Whatever it is you have that is of interest to him, he'll eviscerate it. Squash you in his palm and drink up your very essence, until you're nothing but a brittle husk. A ghost. If you stay, you're on the road to damnation."

I don't let my face show anything while I watch her aura. I wish so desperately to find a lie there, but there's none.

"If that's so, why do *you* stay?"

She lets out a laugh that sounds hollow and empty. "Because I have nothing he wants from me he has not already taken. Nothing more I can give or offer him. I understand what it takes to be with him. What it gives. But you? Have you? Do you even know what he wants from you?"

My blood slows. My stomach is suddenly tight, but not from hunger.

Her smile spreads into a knowing grin. "Maybe he doesn't know it yet, either," she muses, looking me up and down. "But the time will come. And once he does, there's nothing you can do. You can just beg that you're ready to give it. And should you ever decide to bite through the leash, he'll pull it so tight you will suffocate. Because he doesn't tolerate disobedience in any regard, little girl."

I swallow against the knot in my throat, the ache behind my ribs. My mouth is dry when I ask, "What should I do?"

She tilts her head and watches me with a mixture of disgust and calculation. "I don't know. Go find that library of yours—the one you asked Everly about—because I think there's a reason you want to do so. Call it a hunch or something else. And take it from there. Caryan's going to be distracted all night," she says in a sure tone.

I don't like to think about what she's implying. "Riven said there is no library."

"I believe he did, Caryan's ever-adoring minion." She laughs coolly. "It's true, there's no *library*. But the ruins of it still stand, slightly west of the main gate. And who knows what lies buried underneath all that sand. The famous library was once known for its cavernous underground archives. Built by the silver elves, a long time ago."

I don't at all like the cold glint in her eyes. A vision of the sand worm claws its way into my mind, but I fight it back. "He'll see everything once he drinks my blood. Why take that risk?"

She just shrugs her delicate shoulders, seemingly untroubled by any of it. Only her aura tells a different story. A part of her is terrified. Terrified he will find out, but she wants me gone more.

"Because we're both doomed in our own ways, and whether I like it or not, it binds us. But I think your disappearance means as much to you as it does to me. There'll be a horse waiting for you there, at the ruins. I'll arrange as much. And you may want to ride north. Now, excuse me, I need to prepare for tonight." *Escape.* She's helping me to escape.

She strides away, but halts, looking back at me over her shoulder. "Oh. I remember that your mother once mentioned those ruins too. Even visited them, I think. Briefly, before she ran from Caryan and hid from him in the human world."

Her words feel like a stab in my belly.

"She *ran* from him?"

"Of course she did. Why else do you think would anyone of us go to the human world? She went *because* of him. Accepted all the downsides it brings. The danger. Because she was terrified."

MELODY

Riven waits for me in the corridor to my room. He leans against the wall in the dark, muscled arms crossed, stepping in my way when I appear. I'm still so lost in my conversation with Sarynx that I startle.

"It's not too late to change your mind about going to Niavara," he says by way of greeting.

"You know I want to go," I retort, trying to keep the sharpness from my voice and my face blank. I'm going to run. I'm going to deceive him. My stomach twists into an ugly knot. Then I remind myself that it's *him* who keeps things from *me*. I make myself glower up at him, ignoring the ugly sting of betrayal behind my ribs. He just happened to leave out that part where my very mother ran from *Caryan*.

"I do, yes," he admits, as muscle flexing in his strong jaw.

He looks different today and it takes a moment for me to realize what it is. He's wearing banded armor, not his usual, lush attire. The gems on his body are gone, no rings on his fingers. Instead, he's got two vicious, double-edged swords strapped to his back.

He looks harder. Like a warrior. Frightening.

"You're expecting another attack in Niavara," I gather. I've thought about that, too—about the Nefarians wanting my head, preferably detached from my body. But they won't find me if I just disappear. I'd have to wear a hat to hide my round ears, sure, but then—I would just be a girl with a horse, somewhere out there in this world.

Boring. Unremarkable.

Absurdly enough, I'd probably be safer this way than anywhere else, even if I stayed locked away behind man-thick walls.

"It is very likely. But in Niavara, you never know anyways. Be on your guard," Riven answers evasively. He holds out something for me then. A bundle of clothes made of the same, strange material as his. Black, almost like leather. "I had this made for you. Wear it. We're going to ride," he declares.

I breathe a "Thank you," and take it.

He follows me to my chamber and enters with me. I look at the room. *My* room. It's been cleaned since the Nefarians attack two nights ago. Magic has restored every bit of damage. And yet, standing here again brings it all back in a rush.

I'm not sure what I'd have done after the attack if Riven had not stayed here with me. I'd probably have cowered somewhere, waiting for them to return and finish what they started. Again, that twist in my gut, in my heart at what I'm about to do.

And that silent question burning in the back of my mind, whether I'm ready for this world? Or would be ever, for that matter.

I know the answer to that, but ignore it. Because if I thought about it too long, I might as well put myself right into the cage Caryan designed for me, close its door and throw the keys away.

Not an option.

I spare one last glance at the drawings I made of Caryan and Riven, still stacked neatly next to my bed, then quickly look away and disappear into the bathroom to change.

I shrug out of my *slave* clothes and slip into the ones Riven gave me. They fit perfectly, almost like a second skin, black and shiny, reinforced with a pattern of black, inky scales on my elbows and knees. They smell of leather and fire and smoke.

I look at myself in the mirror. I look different in them. Like a warrior. Older. No longer like a shy, frightened girl.

I braid my long hair and then step back out to Riven. He's been looking out the window and turns when he hears me.

His eyes rove over me, lingering a second too long.

"What?" I feel a sting of heat, despite my anger.

"Nothing. It's just... it suits you," he says, his voice a touch hoarse. Then he steps close to me and shoves a dagger into a sheath sewn at my ribs. With a last glance over me, he says, "Keep it close tonight. Let's go."

He leads the way toward the dungeons, but then to the left, down another corridor, and there's the smell of hay and horses when I go down the steps, stumbling into a vast stable with stalls on the left and right, most of them empty because the horses have already been taken to Niavara.

I look at silver name plates on every stall, pausing in front of one that reads Stormhunter. The dappled stallion that stands in that box looks mostly like a horse, but also not. Two large horns protrude from his forehead, rising up high, just next to his ears. He's also much bigger than any horse I've ever seen in the human world. His tail is a lion's, swishing restlessly back and forth, his neck slimmer and longer, as are his legs, and his eyes are a pale, milky gray. Like the gray of my childhood.

"Not this one," Riven says and gestures to two horses next to Stormhunter. *Moonshine Meadow and Violet Daffodilspring* the sign reads.

"Is that a joke?" I can't help it, despite my tension, despite my own inner turmoil, I have to stifle a laugh.

Irritation flickers over Riven's features. "This is not funny, Melody."

"I don't know what about those names is *not* funny. Whatever. I *want* this one," I say before Riven can answer. There's an untamed fierceness in Stormhunter that attracts me. That calls my blood. "Hey..." I whisper, carefully stretching my hand out.

At first, the stallion scuttles back, but then he stretches his long neck and gently places his nose against my palm, becoming calm.

I smile at him. "Okay, so you don't seem to mind taking me to

Niavara?" And maybe beyond, I add silently. Maybe I won't need Sarynx's horse at all.

Stormhunter snorts. I take that as his agreement. Riven just watches me with his eyebrows raised and a slight frown, but he doesn't say no. Not that I would have listened.

I saddle Stormhunter quickly. There was a time when Lyrian taught me how to ride. I even had a horse of my own. Lyrian called him Roach because he couldn't stand him, like he could not stand so many other creatures, but I loved Roach fiercely, with all my tiny little heart. But that was before I got older and Lyrian realized the horse might be something I could escape on one day. Lyrian sold him.

My heart aches at the memory. Riding and cuddling with Roach had been the only almost-happy moments in my life. I shove the memory down and carefully lead Stormhunter out of his box before I swing myself up on his back. Riven is already sitting on a huge, black mare with silvery horns that curl down on either side of her head, her mane reaching down almost to her hooves in waves.

Just then the double-winged door to the stables opens and two guards appear.

Riven starts to say something just as I gently press my legs into Stormhunter's belly. As if the stallion read my mind, he makes a jump toward them, and I hold on tight, digging my fingers into his mane. He bolts past them so fast they can't do anything but stare after me, the fae horse swift as lightning and impossible to chase.

The horse gallops down the long, serpentine road that leads from the Fortress to the desert. His hooves move so fast all I can make out is a blur and a cloud of stirred, red dust behind us when I briefly glance back over my shoulder.

Riven's black mare finally catches up once we reach the flat desert ground, passing the spot where I was almost eaten by that oversized worm. But right now, on the impossibly fast horse, none of this matters. My dark hair has come loose of my braid, streaming unbound as I let go of Stormhunter's mane, stretch my arms out, and lean back into the wind until I'm lying flat on the horse, cradling that strange, giddy feeling inside me I realize is... joy.

I whoop and Stormhunter neighs in sync with me before he goes even faster. I lean forward, pressing my body flat against his as the world whips past. This is what flying must feel like. How Caryan must feel when he soars through the skies, riding the wind.

Moments like these I might come close to happiness.

The outlines of the town come into view—ochre-colored, rectangular buildings with flat roofs that people are using as terraces emerging out of the dust the closer we get.

We reach the outskirts as darkness falls and the blood moon climbs above the horizon, full and redder than ever, dipping everything in a scarlet twilight.

Stormhunter slows to a canter before easing into a trot alongside Riven's mare as we pass through the mighty city gate, its façade the same dark and golden-veined stone of the pillar in the Fortress. Huge figures in the form of naked fae with long spears in their hands flank it, sinister expression on their faces greeting everyone who comes through.

"Is this the main gate?" I ask.

Riven nods once. I look for the ruins Sarynx had spoken about to the west. I think I might, indeed, be able to make out some huge columns in the distance, the last remnants of a building that might have once been the library. *Later.*

Half-naked fae flock the ancient streets of the town. Torches burn in front of every house, along with fire that flickers in huge metal bowls every few meters. Smoke hangs thick in the air and the flames' shadows dance upon the walls. An eerie music follows us everywhere like a lure, drums echoing through me, wild voices beckoning.

Riven's riding next to me now, and a hush falls over the crowd when they spot us, throwing us long, penetrating stares. I keep my hair over my face to hide my human ears while the horses find their way through the swaying and chattering crowd, as if they know the way by heart.

I dig my fingers back into Stormhunter's mane as my eyes flick over fae fucking in corners, blood dripping from their lips and long fangs.

We reach a vast, oval-shaped open area that reminds me of a huge amphitheater in its shape, the buildings around it with their flat roofs forming the outer ring. Fires flicker everywhere, the ground under Stormhunter's hooves nothing but sand.

People are dancing around a high dais in its middle, dozens of steps leading up to a throne.

My heart leaps. On the throne on the dais is Caryan, surrounded by a lot of naked women. No wings to be seen today, but he seems to rarely have them out.

The music is even wilder here, unrestrained rhythms and deep voices. I spot a priestess on the right side of the platform, performing some kind of sacrifice judging by the slaughtered animals on the marble altar in front of her.

Riven dismounts from his mare and I follow suit, gently brushing the stallion's sweat-slicked neck as fae come running. They bow deeply to Riven before they lead the horses away.

I dive into the crowd, closer to the priestess, who is now singing, drawn by her voice.

The priestess is a lavender-skinned, tall woman with a lush body clad in nothing but a long, deep-red cloak, a golden tattoo of various stages of a moon's cycle gracing her forehead. Her eyes are closed. Her back arches and she lifts her arms to the sky the exact moment the fat, gleaming ball of the blood moon appears between them.

The crowd cheers as the priestess opens her eyes and grabs a crescent-shaped knife. Then she cuts her whole forearm open in one long and gaping slash.

The music quiets and her severe, alluring voice fills the air. "When the chains break, the world will rend into a new order. Darkness will reign, blood will drain. Long live our king."

I watch spellbound as her blood drips into a cabochon-rimmed chalice. She waits until the cut has sealed before she wipes the remnants off with a well-practiced swipe of a piece of cloth. Then she takes the chalice and starts to walk up the dais, her head bowed.

When she reaches Caryan, she falls to her knees, presenting the chalice to him with outstretched hands.

Caryan stands and takes it from her, downing it in one single draft. He then raises the cup high, his voice magnified by some magic, booming over the place. "This world is bent double from weeping. This world has been brought down to its knees. Depleted, compelled into a dark submission by shackles, by violence, by greed. But no more. It is time for a new dawn. A dawn of unity. A dawn of justice. A dawn of dominance."

An eerie quiet has settled over the revelry. Everything is silent. The crowd listens, awed. Spellbound. Electrified. Hanging on every word from Caryan's lips. I feel Riven close behind me as I stand among them, shivering as wave after wave of Caryan's dark power thunders over us, twin to the black lightning streaking over the red sky above us. I, too, am watching, arrested by the anger in his voice, by his fierce determination, by the very thing he is saying.

"No one ever expected an angel to set the world on fire. But I'm no average angel. I am the last. I am the most powerful. I wasn't born to be subservient. I wasn't born to kneel. I was born to make the world shake and tremble at my fingertips."

Again, thunder rumbles above, around, right through the crowd, his magic, breaking over the place like an avalanche. Black and mighty, its primal force so strong it brings the people to their knees.

"We are on the brink of war. A war bigger than anything this world has ever seen. We will stand shoulder to shoulder. We will fight shoulder to shoulder. You will bow to no one and nothing but me. I am your king. I will be your sword. I will make the sky scream. Together, we will bend the heavens and raise the hells.

"No one wearing a crown ever came in the name of peace. But I prefer times of precarious peace over a freedom in slavery. Let us fight. Let our enemies cower in the wake of our armies. If this is to end in fire, we will burn. Choke our foes on the dust of their scorched dreams. Smother them under the debris of their hubris. Let us dance in the ashes of tradition."

The crowd starts to cheer and jump as his power flickers through them once more, wicked, infernal, and ancient, driving them into a wild frenzy. Some start to rip their clothes from their bodies, others grab each other and dig their teeth into each other's throats, while others begin dancing to an even wilder, deeper, and darker music.

Kegs with wine and ale are rolled in and people fill wooden cups with it. I stroll, pushing my way through the crowd, through bodies grinding against each other, drinking blood from each other's throats. I watch fire eaters and acrobats dancing with two burning balls of fire on an end of a long chain, so fast they paint figures of animals into the night.

Although I don't look back, I know Riven's trailing me and staying close. I can *feel* him behind me. Feel his presence as close and physical as I feel Caryan's presence all over the place. As if there's an invisible chain connecting my soul with theirs. I don't want to ponder it. Certainly not now. Not after what Sarynx said to me before.

Not when I'm going to run.

When I glance up to the dais, I see a naked woman with moon-white skin and dark hair rocking up and down on Caryan. The same woman who kissed him last night.

The sight slices through me. Cuts straight through my wild mind to a place right behind my ribs.

I pause. I close my eyes then and, for a moment, let the drums and the voices and rhythms seep into me, right into my soul. For a moment, I become that dark thing that belongs to the fires, the smoke, the magic, as wild and violent as this world itself.

When I open my eyes again, I find Caryan looking straight at me, as if he can, indeed, make me out in the crowd. My heart startles.

He can't.

He probably can with his fae sight.

The woman still moves on him, arching her back, swirling her hips.

I bite down on my lip, hard. Again, that woman could be *me* with that skin, that long hair.

A dull ache fills me, reaching right down between my legs.

The way his hands are on her thighs. His lips on her throat…

I turn away, only to find Riven standing close behind me, watching my every move. The flames dance in his purple eyes and over his chiseled face. I thought he looked breathtaking in decadent attire, all the gems on him vying with his eyes. But he's never looked more beautiful than now.

Tall. Serene. Dark and dangerous.

I near him, carefully placing my hands on his chest, feeling the heat of him under my fingers through the scaled fabric seeping into my flesh. A shudder of premonition goes through me as he grabs my hips. A brief brush of his thumbs over my hipbones and a little bit down makes heat flush my very core.

I know he senses it in me by the way his amethyst eyes darken. He leans in and murmurs over my skin. "Careful. These nights are all part of a sacred rite. Tonight, Caryan's magic makes all of us wild. Makes it harder to control ourselves in *every* regard."

I should heed his warning. Maybe. But all I can think of is the feeling of his closeness and his hands on my body. Part of me wants to rip off those clothes and shred his skin.

He kept from me that my mother ran from Caryan. What else does he keep from me?

Maybe I'm one of them after all, because right now, it's hard not to bite him to taste his flesh. His blood. His lips. I sink my nails deep into his armor, all too aware that Caryan's still watching me. All too aware of Riven's hard body under my hands and how he felt above me. Painfully aware of Caryan's magic, reverberating through my flesh and bones with every heartbeat.

Riven lets out a hiss as my hands slide under his armor and my nails pierce the skin of his chest. "You do not want this," he growls.

"Maybe I do," I say, sinking them deeper into his skin, letting all my anger rush to the surface.

His eyes flare as he grabs my wrists, painfully strong. He spins me around so I'm pressed against him, my wrists now captured by his hand behind my back. "Tell me that you don't want this," Riven says again, but his words come cut off, breathless, his lips on my pulse.

I shiver from fury, from heat. "It's exactly what I want," I counter as I meet Caryan's gaze, the woman still straddling him, still moving up and down. I don't want to think anymore. I want to *feel*. More. Something other than this anger, this fear.

And this is dangerously different.

"Melody." Riven says my name like a warning, as if he's something to be warned about. His other hand catches in my hair, pulling my head back, making me arch into him. Forcing me into place before he pushes against me. Hard.

I swear the expression in Caryan's face shifts. Swear I feel all his lethal focus trained on me, as power, night-streaked dew and living, black lightning starts to slither along my skin and under it. I shiver as it runs along my waist, my belly. Flickering along the underside of my small breasts.

Magic, brimming with Caryan's very essence. However this works, it's *him* doing this. I know it in my blood as if he's touching me himself.

A strange, different kind of panic fuels me then. *What is happening here?*

But I keep my gaze straight, my chin up. Keep holding Caryan's eyes like a challenge. As if in answer, the magic morphs, turning unbearably soft, like river water. I gasp as it runs over my nipples, just as Riven's strong fingers let go of my wrists to splay over my belly, locking me into place as he thrusts against me another time.

Need, hot and searing, streaks down my spine, threating to make my knees buckle. It buries itself deep between my legs, thrumming there with an unfamiliar ache.

"Melody." Riven murmurs my name again, this time like a prayer against my ear. And it's the breathless, deep timbre in his voice, the desire in it, matching my own, that undoes me.

Another wave of *want*, stronger than before, sluices through me, hot and sharp and searing. So violent I can barely breathe. Riven pushes himself against me even harder at the same moment something sharp, like talons or teeth, scrapes over the sensitive peaks of my nipples, cutting through my senses.

I'm going to burst. To rip open and burn. And burn. And burn.

I suppress a whimper as Riven pushes his entire body against mine. I meet him halfway, leaning into him, desperate for more friction, cursing the layers of fabric between us.

But I need more. I need *him.*

It feels insane. This want. This desire. I've never been with a man before.

But I need him closer. *Deeper.* At the inside of my very being.

Riven lets out a growl that travels right into my core. He yanks my head back, exposing my neck and licks down the column of my throat.

That moment those teeth of smoke and dew and night clamp down my nipples, right under my clothes, one at a time, trailed by a night-kissed tongue and lips that suck at them, leaving me on the verge of pleasure and pain. *Caryan's magic.*

Riven's hand slides between my legs.

I might have cried out, but something pushes itself between my lips. Something velvety and dark as the night probing into my mouth.

My eyes fly up to the dais, to Caryan. I find him standing now, looking down on me. He's dressed again, no trace of the woman; his face utterly blank.

But by the golden glint in his eyes, I know it's still *him,* woven in between the inky plume of magic that still swirls around my nipples, who is now invading my lips. It's *him* in my mouth, gliding in and out in a slow, steady rhythm. A touch deeper each time he pulls out and pushes back again.

It's Caryan who's fucking my lips. My mouth. At the same pace Riven's fingers fuck me. The same pace with which he's pushing himself against me in hard thrusts.

It's too much. I can't take it.

I liquefy.

My legs shake and my body trembles as I come.

I would collapse if Riven let go of me, but his hands lock me into place, continuing while I fracture in his grip, watching Caryan through my lashes.

Another shove down my throat. Brutal this time. So deep it makes swallowing impossible.

I open my eyes wide. Caryan just looks back at me unfazed and cruel and ancient, his face still revealing nothing of what he's doing as his magic drives into me one more time.

Even deeper. Too deep. To a point where it just hurts.

Tears well in my eyes. I can't breathe.

He just keeps looking at me for a heartbeat longer.

Then darkness around him ripples and he's gone. His magic along with him.

47

MELODY

Caryan's sudden absence makes me snap out of it, leaving me cold. Empty. Shuddering.

I step away from Riven without another word. Without another glance. I slink through the crowd, too restless to think. *What the hell just happened?* I feel feverish, as if my skin is too tight for what slumbers in my veins. As if *something* almost tore me open. Almost left me fractured. *They.* Caryan and Riven.

When I swallow, my throat is still raw from Caryan…

The tattoo on my wrist burns painfully as I push further through the crowd of revelers, dancing and drinking wine from each other's mouths. I pray they didn't see what just happened. But no one pays me any attention, or so much as looks at me, too absorbed with each other, and I allow myself a shudder of relief.

Hells, what have I done?

Behind me, Riven is following, but slower, because people are either too dazed or too drunk to make way for him. A few startle out of their spell in sudden fear of him, falling to a knee, making obeisances.

I start to run. Air. I need air. And space. And silence.

Finally, reality sets back in. I ignore the thrill that runs through me at the sheer lunacy of what I'm about to do. Sobering me up. I'm going to run away. I'm scared. So fucking scared. But a life in shackles again—I cannot.

I push through more drunk fae, too aware that Riven is still following me. Still too aware of what we'd just done. Of the heat that's still in my body, burning my insides. Of my restless heartbeat. The touch of his fingers between my legs, lingering.

I run even faster, diving into a labyrinth of small streets and alleyways packed with stands where fae are selling cherry wine and spiced bread. I eventually shake Riven by taking a sharp turn left, then right.

When I glance back, he's no longer there.

I dash on, letting my strange talent guide me to the ruins. It's terrifyingly easy. It scared me before, back with Lyrian. But no longer.

When I reach the huge gate I run even faster, throwing all my newly won strength and speed into my movements. I skitter between the dark silhouettes of the ancient, carved columns I glimpsed on our ride here.

Someone grabs my arm.

I'm caught and pushed hard against a crumbling wall. I flinch, my eyes wide, my breath short and fast from running. I swivel and stare into Riven's eyes. They seem to burn in the darkness like dying stars, simmering with rage.

"You're trying to run," he snarls.

"No, I wanted to find the library," I lie quickly.

"Liar!"

I freeze when I feel talons instead of his nails pressing into my skin, too similar to those of the men in my room that night. *What the hell?*

For a moment I'm too scared to deny that I wanted to run; the words die on my tongue. *He knows.* And he caught me just like the first time in the woods. Or the second time in the Fortress. But he's never looked so furious before. So intimidating. So unhinged.

"You just happened to conveniently leave out the part where my mother ran from *Caryan*," I throw back at him, right into his face.

"Who told you?"

"Does it matter?"

He bares his teeth. "I never told you because it'd have just made you try to run again. But it seems no matter what I do, you run anyways." His hand closes around my throat then, talons grazing my skin, on the verge of drawing blood. "I warned you."

"Please…" I whisper, suddenly terrified. I wonder how far his vow to never hurt me goes. How much he *can* do.

"Please what?" he asks in a cruel voice that reminds me how he made Lyrian cower and grovel with merely words and a point of his fingers. So different from his usual self. Hell, when he's like this, it doesn't take much to imagine why he's Caryan's right hand. Because he's just as lethal. Just as deadly.

"Please don't…"

He pushes me against the wall again, pinning my body with his, my wrists held captive above my head. But this is so different from before. He is so different.

"Don't what?" he mocks, leaning into me.

I can't find words. I know he's still wild.

He grabs my chin, the talons gone. Then he kisses me.

It isn't pretty kissing. It's carnal, possessive, and brutal. He kisses me with his body, his teeth, his one hand still gripping me in a chokehold, opening my jaw. He snarls as I bite his lower lip so hard I taste his blood in my mouth.

But he pulls back, glowering down at me.

Good. Because I don't want him to be like this with me. Not him. The rudeness, the brutality of it… It breaks my tiny human heart, and I want him to see this.

"Traitor."

A male voice behind us makes Riven whip around, his blood still dripping over his chin. I scan the darkness around us but find no one.

Then a flicker in my peripheral vision. A shadow, moving.

My head snaps up and I find a figure with membrane wings rending the night like a creature out of a nightmare. *Nefarians.* Three more of them squatting on columns, still partly hidden by the dark. I realize that they used their wings to shield themselves, to blend with the darkness so thoroughly neither of us noticed them.

"I'd hoped you wouldn't be here, Riven. And I'm sorry that *this* complicates things even further," the man closest to us drawls. He lands smoothly on the column above us with one mighty flap of his wings. "I'm sorry that she has to die. But you know she must."

"Touch a hair on her head and yours will roll," Riven growls back, in a voice I've never heard him use before. He pushes himself in front of me, keeping me behind him against the pillar.

"Have you forgotten our ties? They run deep, whether you want it or not," another Nefarian hisses from above, his voice echoing from the ruins.

"I do not care about our ties. You heard me. It was a last warning," Riven snarls back.

The men exchange a glance before they step further out of the shadows.

"They're going to attack, right now," I whisper, not sure it will change anything if Riven knows, but I see it clearly in their auras.

Riven doesn't wait. A wall of dark flames shoots up, surrounding us, a burning tornado reaching far up into the sky, leaving us unharmed in its middle.

But harsh, bluish-tinted wind slams into us from all sides, dousing the flames.

My senses are not fast enough to witness Riven's shift. Huge membraned wings engulf me a second later, as he pushes himself off the ground and up into the air, me in his arms. Then he spreads them wide, and we are flying.

Riven pulls me against him and spears for the city.

"They're coming. They're close," I say in his ear, loud against the air whipping past.

The Nefarians have recovered and black wings beat hard as they try to catch up. Too quickly, driven by a stream of wind-magic that brings them closer and closer, lilac magic bristling at their fingertips.

My eyes widen as Riven's magic twists around us in a dark fire to shield us once again—and fails. Fails because of the arrow protruding from his shoulder. An arrow made of a black, thrumming metal that makes the fae part of me recoil and hiss. Hells, it went right through him.

Riven spreads his wings wide, at the same moment he presses me against him, to shield me from more arrows. A roar rips from him when they strike his legs, his wings, his back, burning holes in skin and flesh. I feel the impact, feel his powerful body barking in agony. Those beautiful, powerful wings. Shredded.

"Riven…" I breathe. Fear grips my heart and squeezes it tight. Fear, not for me, but for him.

"I've had worse. Now hold on tight," he growls, but I see the pain searing his aura.

Then we're falling.

I close my eyes as we hit the ground, sand and gravel flying all around us, filling my mouth, my lungs as we keep skidding. But I'm not hurt. Because Riven's under me, I realize with a cold shock, his wings and back taking the collision.

In a heartbeat, he's pushed me off him and jumped to his feet, keeping me behind him as the three Nefarians land in a crouch in front of us. Riven again spreads his shredded wings to shield me from them. Horror roils in my gut. I can only guess how much this must hurt him. The scent of his blood fills the air as it leaks out of him, seeping into the sand, the vicious arrows protruding out of his flesh in all angles. Too many to count.

"Step aside, Riven. You know too well the arrows have nullified your magic," the first one says. He's as tall as Riven and just as muscular, with sun-tanned skin and black hair. Now, in the low light, I can make out harsh features and the swirls of black ink that stretch over his collarbones and up to his cheeks like war paint. "And your healing along with it… even if you're *cursed*. Step aside and I'll let you live."

"That's not going to happen," Riven retorts, unfazed. His breathing comes in uneven rasps as he unsheathes one long sword from his back.

The man laughs. "You're in no state to fight. You're only

drawing the inevitable out. Step aside, and I promise I'll make it quick. She won't feel a thing. This is not about you. We will let you live, I swear."

"Keep dreaming, Adriel," Riven retorts with a snarl.

"You know, sometimes dreams come true," the warrior drawls, then raises his hand at the same moment Riven throws a dagger he must have kept hidden in his sleeve.

The wave of building, lilac magic collapses the instant the black blade buries itself in Adriel's heart.

The warrior's eyes widen in disbelief, and he staggers backwards. "Nefarian steel… how?"

"You forget that nightmares are dreams too. And you just walked right into one," Riven rasps.

"Blood runs thicker than water. We're family, Riven," the man says, his breath coming in sharp, dying rasps.

Riven only lifts the mighty sword in his hand. "Blood alone doesn't make family. Love and loyalty do." Then he looks at the two others. "*Caryan's* never going to let you leave."

With this warning, he charges. The other two Nefarians lift their hands almost simultaneously. I freeze as a wall of wind slams into Riven, hurling him meters through the air. I watch with cold horror as he's driven against the wall of a building, so hard it gives way and starts to crumble.

Blinding pain flares behind my ribs. All that talking had been only to stall. To buy us time. Buy *me* time. Riven charging with that sword against their magic—was to keep them focused on him instead of me.

Suddenly, there are screams *everywhere,* bright as daylight, ripping me back to reality. I hadn't realized where we landed. Now my eyes find the empty dais to my left. The crowd has scattered, retreated to the shadows, forming a semicircle around us.

Right as a breathtaking, tanned figure plummets from the sky, landing gracefully on her long, muscular legs right between the two Nefarians. She eases into a slight crouch, as if ready to jump at any moment. Her taloned hands are curled by her side, her two huge, leathery wings tucked in tight; her long, midnight-black hair dancing on a phantom wind.

Her purple eyes, brighter and much more aqueous than Riven's, focus on me with lethal intention.

Nefarians. The word hisses through the crowd, the smell of fear tingeing the air.

I glance back to the collapsed building, and my heart threatens to fall apart. *Let him be alive. Please. Let him be alive.* I won't allow any other option.

Then I pivot on my heels and run.

I sprint towards a tiny alleyway, praying that it's too narrow for their wings. It saved me once.

But a moment later talons dig into my arm, shredding skin. A scream rips from me as I'm hurtled to the ground again, one of the Nefarians on me. I draw Riven's dagger and aim for his neck, the only part, save for his hands and head, that isn't covered in hard, scaly armor.

But before the blade can find his skin, he starts to scream, the sound unlike anything I've ever heard before.

He lets go of me, stumbling back, spasming, his face torn in horror as every bone in his body seems to break into tiny pieces… and then even tinier ones.

He falls to his knees, then slumps headfirst into the sand in front of me, his screams subsiding to a strange kind of howling.

A shadow falls over me, and I know he's here long before I manage to draw my eyes to him. Before I hear his growl, so visceral, so deep it roils in my bones, shakes my soul. "She. Is. Mine."

Even the Nefarian's howls fall silent at that. Not because he's dead, but because of the effect of Caryan's voice. At the pure hatred that drips from him. At the primal dominance and aggression.

Restless shadows twine around the buildings, hissing and snarling, coming in a never-ending river off his shoulders and gathering, denser and denser around us until the air is so tight it is hard to breathe.

"I'm going to kill your companions, but you—I'm not yet done with you." Caryan's growl gives way to a silent coldness, one that is more frightening than anything he could have done.

Eventually, I look up to him, his eyes black as his shadows, which reach out and lift up the Nefarian. His head lolls, his whole body a wobbly mass, and I realize he has been fragmented from the inside. He moans in pain at being moved, a sound animalistic and foreign and guttural.

"Oh no, you will not faint. I will not allow that. You will feel this until I decide to let you drift into oblivion for touching her like that," Caryan says. "But before that, I'm going to heal you and do what I just did over and over again."

Gods, help me, but I've never been more afraid of him than now.

I gasp as the shadows around the Nefarian grow tighter, squeezing his already shattered insides. The Nefarian's eyes roll to me, silently begging me to help him. I'm too shocked to make a sound.

Caryan's gaze eventually settles on me.

I have the good sense not to pull away this time when he reaches for my arm. It's bleeding, the laceration deeper than I thought. I barely feel it though.

My heart stumbles when I glance back at his face. If I thought Caryan couldn't get any angrier, I was wrong. There's pure death in his eyes as he takes in my wounds.

"Stretch out your arm," he orders in a voice bereft of anything. It's like an abyss. Endless and black.

I do as he says, and he brings his wrist to his teeth, slicing his whole artery along the length, his blood gushing out. He drips it over my mangled flesh and I clench my teeth as the deep wounds start to knit back together.

"Riven," I whisper, trying hard to block out the groans of the Nefarian, still writhing in the grip of Caryan's shadows. I think I'm going to be sick right here. "He... Please, we need to look for him," I squeeze out. It takes all I have left to look into Caryan's eyes again.

"He is alive," Caryan says.

Alive. I allow myself to breathe again.

"Move," Caryan orders me, and I do, fighting hard to ignore the sounds of the tortured Nefarian behind us as I try to keep up with Caryan's pace.

When we step out of the seclusion of the alleyway, I no longer recognize the place. All fae have retreated further to the shadows as if they might blend into them. Fear is palpable, as if the very air and the wind consist of it. But in the middle of the place, Caryan's magic is wavering in a churning, black circle, keeping the fae out and the Nefarians in.

I briefly hesitate as we reach it, the whirling dark, bristling magic swirling up into the air before me like a wall of black smoke, streaked with chained lightning.

Caryan glances at me and, somehow, this suddenly feels like a test.

I will not be afraid.

With a deep breath, I step through. The magic bites me, but it doesn't shatter me, doesn't burn me to ashes as I'm sure it would most others foolish enough to try.

The two remaining Nefarians kneel on the ground, the sight so similar to the fauns last night it quickly robs my breath. Two men, the woman with Riven's eyes in the middle. They are flanked by Ronin and Kyrith. In a group behind them, I spot the priestess, Sarynx, and a few other fae I recognize from the celebrations at the Fortress.

I nearly cry when I see Riven walking through that circle. His wings are gone, so are the arrows, his armor is torn in parts, but he's alive and breathing… no longer bleeding. His eyes lock on mine for a second before he looks at Caryan.

With a snap of Caryan's fingers, the whole, huge wall of magic pulls back into him. It's a terrifying sight, but everyone suddenly comes back into view. The fae who tried to hide in the shadows step closer, drawn to the violence the same way a moth is drawn to a flame.

This is going to be an execution.

A statement. Exactly what Caryan promised them.

"We will end this tonight," Caryan says, his voice echoing through the ancient town.

I glimpse something in my peripheral vision. Sarynx. Her aura is a thread of panic laced with the ugly, gaudy green of betrayal, gleaming bright like a beacon, catching my eye even within the sea of fear and fury.

Her. It was her, all the time. How could I not have felt it? Seen it? She wanted to get rid of me so badly. Badly enough to have me dead. I even said it to her face, that Caryan never drank her blood. So he wouldn't have known.

Caryan follows my gaze. Sarynx's eyes widen as she finds both of us looking at her. Then she turns on her heels and runs. Only to be caught by vines of black magic, ensnaring her ankles and dragging her back on her stomach over the ground.

She thrashes and screams as Caryan's shadows pull her through the sand, tearing her gown and her skin, until she ends up in a bloody bundle to his feet.

Her green eyes briefly find mine before they look up to Caryan, pure pain shimmering in her utterly beautiful face. "I just wanted her gone. I wanted her to escape. It would have been for the better. For all of us," she says, her voice a heartbreaking plea.

And no matter how much I dislike her, no matter that she tried to kill me, I can't bring myself to hate her enough to want her dead.

She's speaking the truth, of course she is. She did want me gone… not *necessarily* dead. I see her love for Caryan, her bottomless desperation that drove her to do the things she did.

"Please, Caryan," she starts again.

There is no warning as he leans forward and lifts her by her slender neck like he once held Lyrian. A chill rakes down my spine.

His teeth sink into her flesh. Rude. Careless. He spits her blood out, as if it was poisonous, and I wonder whether he can, indeed, taste it in her blood—the betrayal, her envy. Whether the emotions of its owner tinge the flavor.

By the way his face contorts, it must.

"You were behind it. Only you," he says.

Sarynx still dangles limp from his hand, her face a mask of pain. "I did it for *us*, but for her too. I never really wanted her dead," she whispers to him. Truth, blue and resonating in her aura. "But most of all—I did it for you."

"Please, let her live," I say.

Again, her eyes flit back to me, surprised, before Caryan's darkness engulfs her like a swarm. It's over in less than a second.

All that is left of Sarynx sifts down between his fingers.

My heart can't comprehend what I just saw. It beats so violently like it has a chance to escape my chest, to abandon my body.

Without sparing another glance at her leftovers, Caryan walks towards the Nefarians, stopping in front of the woman. Their leader.

"Caryan," she hisses, flashing her row of sharp teeth up at him. Wanton, feral pride in her face, in her whole posture, even kneeling on the ground with her hands tied. I admire her courage.

"Shiera. What a surprise to see you," Caryan drawls, his power pressing against my skin, prowling through the city in a wave as he looks down at her. "I must say, I thought you dead and gone."

Shiera just laughs, haughty and breathless. "I have a gift for you, Caryan. It's fastened to my belt."

Caryan glances at Ronin, who steps forward and unties something big and dark dangling from a holster around her hip. It's a metal object—the point of a massive, oversized arrow.

"I brought something for you as a reminder that *we're* not."

Ronin presents it to Caryan.

Caryan looks down at the arrowhead in Ronin's palm, a vicious, deep snarl escaping his throat. Another prickling rumble of power follows in its wake, a thundering sound like two boulders colliding. Everyone in the crowd takes a step back, gasping for air as Caryan's power comes crushing down like a wave. I too, briefly struggle to breathe before it eases.

"Remember this? Gatilla's arrow. This is how you were brought down in the first place, angel," Shiera snarls, obviously satisfied with his reaction, the slant of a smile tearing her full lips. I wonder whether she's just gone mad or whether the knowledge that she's going to die anyway makes her that bold.

Caryan just says, "I will bring you down. All of you."

"All of us? I doubt that," she hisses right back, turning to look at Riven.

He's gone utterly still, his gaze trained on the woman like a weapon. But a streak of sharp red pierces through his aura like a spear. *Pain.* Searing and hot. He hasn't bothered to veil it.

"The exception makes the rule," Caryan responds coolly.

His shadows form around Shiera, yanking her body up to him, her right arm close, outstretched, her wrist turned upwards like an offering. A knife appears in his hand, conjured like his shadows. He cuts deeply along her extended arm, then he licks the blade.

When he's done, he turns his attention to the other Nefarian, repeating the same procedure with him. Caryan's eyes briefly flick to Riven, and I know that he's seen what the man saw at the ruins the way Caryan's gaze flits on to me and stays there for a heartbeat. Riven, kissing me. What I said to him, about my mother.

"Didn't find what you were looking for in there, angel?" Shiera snarls, spitting at his feet.

Caryan just lazily draws his head back to her, as if she's nothing but a nuisance. "I do not need to. That you came here, willing to sacrifice your lives, shows me that you're running out of hope. I will wait. Wait until the last scraps of that hope have whittled down to the marrow of despair. Then I will come for you."

He turns his back to her, then pauses, as if he just remembered something. "I promised my people a celebration tonight. Well, you are going to be the spectacle. Think of your third man—your lover, your *mate*, was he—while you burn and burn and burn. Know that I broke every tiny bone in his body into pieces and that I shall keep him that way until the day I come for the rest of you."

His gaze goes back to Riven then, who still stands unmoved, his face unreadable but his aura still burning alive with pain. "Kill them, Riven. Slowly."

I dig my nails so deep into the palms of my hands that I draw blood. I can see Riven wants to disobey the command, and briefly, I wonder why. But all he does is incline his chin in a nod. His eyes flick to me one last time, and I can barely stand the torment in them before he walks up to Shiera.

"I hope this sacrifice was worth it," she whispers very quietly to him. A private comment.

"I can only say the same to you. Goodbye, Shiera," Riven retorts. There's no kindness in his face—the immovable mask of the Dark Lord's right hand.

Then, on his silent command, I watch black flames start to eat away their clothes. My stomach turns over, my heart can't take it. I turn away before it starts to burn their skin, slowly as Caryan ordered. I wait for their screams, but they don't make a single sound.

I flinch when, after a felt eternity, I feel a gentle hand on my healed arm.

Riven.

He guides me away, back to the horses. Ronin and Kyrith flank us. They mount their steeds and ride back to the Fortress with us. I hold on to Stormhunter's mane the whole time, clinging to his reassuring warmth underneath my cold body.

I can't stop shivering and don't, even when I'm long back in Riven's quarters, in front of the fireplace, the flames for once red, as if, after what he'd just been forced to do, Riven couldn't stand the sight of his magic anymore.

Eventually, he joins me, standing next to me looking down into the flames.

"You loved her," I say quietly into the laden silence between us.

His face is unbearably sad when he looks at me. "I did. Once."

"You... you are a Nefarian too," I breathe.

"Half. I'm half-elf, half-Nefarian." His answer sounds only tired. He turns away and sinks onto the sofa, leaning his head back, closing his eyes.

After a while, I get up and curl next to him. "What... what about your wings?" I whisper.

He looks down at me, his remarkable eyes serene.

I push, "You will be able to fly again." I don't say it like a question, because *no* is not an option. I know he loves flying. I would if I had wings.

He gently runs his hand over my cheek and his fingers come away wet. "I will, my little love. They will heal," he says and finally, for the first time after this horrible night, I feel like I can breathe again.

As his fingers bury themselves in my hair, drawing lazy circles, I allow my eyes to drift shut.

"Thank you for saving me tonight," I murmur before I drift into oblivion.

MELODY

I wake up to find Riven standing in front of the fireplace. His torso naked, his back facing me. My blood freezes in my veins at the sight of the strange ornament of scars and ink that have been carved into his skin. A circle, like the sun, filled and rimmed with wild, arcane symbols.

"It's a list, written in the demonic language," he says, slowly turning to me, having somehow guessed that I am awake. His face is calm, but his eyes are damning.

"Who...?"

"Who did this to me? Someone who reveled in having power over me."

I feel a wildness running through me at the chilled tone in his voice, at the darkness that starts to teem all around him, threatening to form wings and talons. It couldn't have been Gatilla, or he would have said her name. Nor Caryan. No, Riven *loves* him.

"You said you were a slave too," I whisper.

"Yes. This happened before Gatilla enslaved me. It was the king of Palisandre," he confirms, his eyes shining. He lifts the glass in his hand with unearthly grace and takes a long sip. "I'm sorry, I didn't think you would wake up. You slept so soundly, and I like to... stay close, selfish as it is. I certainly didn't mean to startle you with this gloomy sight."

"You didn't," I breathe. I sit up, wrapping my arms around my legs. "Why? Why did he do that to you?"

He flashes me a smile, but it's not the kind that warms my heart. "A mood. A deep hatred against my kin. An open display of power over me. Or maybe... maybe he was just afraid."

"Afraid of what?"

"Afraid of me. Of my powers. Afraid of the king I might become."

I let that settle in before I ask quietly, "And what does it say?"

"It's a contract."

"A contract?" I echo, my eyes wide. "About what?"

"A name for every life he spared in exchange for me and my power. I told you that I was born in Khalix, in the desert lands on the third continent far east. My kin still live there."

"The Nefarians, you mean?"

"Yes. It's actually a secret, you know. Few are aware that a lot of the Nefarians stayed behind after the Demon Wars. They were allowed to stay because of that contract."

"Those people tonight..." My mouth goes dry and my heart aches from everything he just told me.

"This group broke with the leader of Khalix soon after my *agreement*. They left and became renegades, hiding in the Black Forest. It was their decision—what happened tonight. But, yes, I grew up with them before I have been ordered to Palisandre. That bargain on my back holds their names too. Such a waste of life." He says the last part almost angrily before he catches himself.

He puts his glass away and strolls closer, sinking down in front of me. He is paler than ever, if that is even possible, and for a second, he looks strangely fragile, the way his eyes dart over my face almost vigilantly.

I think about what we did before, about what happened between us, in Niavara. How unrestrained he'd been as his infamous self-control slipped for once. Then about the way he kissed me at the ruins and whether he meant to be so cruel. Whether it meant anything at all...

He's so different now.

I stretch out my hand to take his, squeezing his fingers. He frowns at our hands entwined as if this is something alien to him.

"But why did the king of Palisandre want that contract?" I ask, still not understanding fully.

"He wanted my power. He wanted me bound for his purposes. He offered me that bargain when I was still a young man, barely grown up. And I accepted because saying no was not an option."

Everything lies in his eyes, in his aura. Everything he's not saying out loud. He became that man's slave to save his people. His kingdom.

His honeyed breath brushes my hair as he says, "But one day I will go back for him."

I shudder at the cold fury lacing his words. At the quiet sort of light that shines in his eyes. "You will kill him?"

"No, death would be too merciful," he says, his tone liquid in a way that sends a chill all down my neck. "There are other, much more inventive ways to *end* a life." His gaze softens as he takes me in. "Such a gory subject after such a terrible night. Forgive me."

I look down. "I'm sorry I ran. It's my fault."

"*None* of this is your fault, Melody," he corrects, the anger in his voice makes me startle.

"He killed Sarynx. His lover. He killed her so easily." *Caryan.* I don't know why I say it. I don't know why it matters so much.

"Angels do not feel the way we do," Riven answers carefully before he brushes a strand of hair out of my face. "Some say they cannot love."

I glance at him, my heart suddenly tight. "And do you believe it—that Caryan can't love?"

He looks away at that and rises. "I hope it's not true."

49

MELODY

I wake up in Riven's bed in the morning. He must have carried me there after I fell asleep again. When I turn, I find him sleeping right next to me, his torso still naked, his dark hair disheveled. His face is free of the strain I saw on him last night. Of the pain. The honesty. All the horrors of the past.

I shudder against what I'd seen last night—that act of unspeakable brutality and cruelty, etched into his back forever. That anyone could have done this to him—it makes me sick to my very bones. And angry.

I turn to the side to watch him for a while, then get up as quietly as possible. I shower in my room and change into fresh clothes before I join Nidaw in the kitchen.

To my surprise, everything is as always: loud, hectic, the servants chatting with each other. Everly throws me an apologetic glance over the kitchen isles while everyone is busy preparing piles of unreal-looking food.

There will be more celebrations tonight.

I don't know what I expected, but not that everything would continue as if nothing had happened. Obviously, none of them has heard about the attack last night in Niavara. Or the executions. Or maybe they just don't care. Maybe it's part of their nature, after all. I think of the way their eyes shine when they see blood and shudder.

I'm nervous though. Agitated. On edge. Caryan saw everything in Sarynx's and Shiera's blood. That I wanted to escape. I don't know what that means for me. Whether there will be consequences. I guess all I can do is wait.

$$\supset \cdot \subset$$

I'm tense all day, part of me waiting for Ronin or Kyrith to come get me and throw me into the dungeon. But nothing happens.

Later, Nidaw comes to me to put me in the bath and get me ready for the night shift as usual. But this time, the mood in the bath is different as I enter. The sirens seem looser, grinning and smiling, chatting with each other while they wash and dry me. Then they start to press their golden hands down my body as some sort of decoration before they paint flowers on my cheeks and around my eyes, over my temples, and up to my eyebrows, matching similar artwork on their own skins.

When I cast a questioning glance toward Nidaw, she says, "Tonight, the new moon cycle started. We all are allowed to dress up while we serve, to celebrate too."

"Magnolia, wisteria, violets, and snowdrops," a siren with slightly greenish hair declares, giving me a wide smile of her small teeth before Nidaw waves her off.

They chuckle like children with a secret while they scatter out of the room. I envy them for their lightheartedness. I know that I've never been that way.

"Before you came, they said you look like an elf from the Enchanted Forest," Nidaw explains when they're gone, smiling to herself while she braids strands of my hair and entwines them with each other in a beautiful but complicated pattern, the rest of my hair falling loose. Then she starts to weave in some gold and silver filaments again.

"The Enchanted Forest?" I ask out of politeness. I don't want to spoil her mood.

"Yes. They find the elves from there the most beautiful," she answers, her hands gently combing strands away from my neck. Her smile is warm when she meets my eyes in the mirror, as if she senses my restlessness.

"The High Lord Riven is from there," she adds before she releases me, but not without another long, knowing glance toward me. And I can't help but think how little they know about Riven and his past; that they probably don't know the truth.

Then I wonder how much they talk about me and him. Again, I think of his lips on mine last night, his hand in my hair, on my neck. The way he...

"Where are the angels from?" I ask to distract myself.

Nidaw stiffens slightly, but then rolls her tiny shoulders as if to shake off some tension. "We don't know. They just fell from the sky one day." She starts to apply some more gold dust on my cheeks with a furry brush.

Finally, she touches the tip of my nose with her finger. "We also say the angels are made of stardust. That's why they're so beautiful. And now, it's time to leave, my little fairy girl," she says, ushering me out.

☽ * ☾

It's the same as all the other nights of the celebrations save for last night. All the high lords are present in the ballroom, as fauns with impressive, scimitar-like horns tipped with gold and silver carry huge bowls with dark flames around. Some fae burn incense that emits a heavy smoke. It seems to take the edge off everything, and guests gather around to inhale it, their eyes glazing a little.

I occasionally watch Riven, who is lounging in one of the seats with a dramatic flair. He looks so aloof, so untouchable, so otherworldly and cold and infinitely amused it's hard to believe that he can be different; *is* different, for that matter. Or is he, really? Or is this, between us, just another game? Am I just a game for him?

A lot of women of all kinds—horned, hooved, winged—are gathered around him, throwing him long, longing glances, laughing and joking while they pass smaller pots around, holding the same incense as the larger ones. Their pupils widen after they have inhaled their share, their bodies becoming lax and their movements slower, lazier.

Twice I meet Riven's eyes. His fingers glide back down the naked, silver-colored spine of a lavender-skinned, emerald-winged pixie, who has propped her head in his lap while he sips from a golden goblet, the liquid in it tingeing his remarkable eyes red.

My heart aches.

As if last night never happened.

I avert my gaze quickly when I spot Caryan with another breathtakingly beautiful elf woman with long, dark hair next to him. Her hand rests on his arm as she laughs about something. I wonder whether she's the woman from last night, from the celebrations. But I shake the thought off.

Yet it's hard to look away for long. They're the most beautiful couple in the room, as if their presence drinks all the light from the other glorious creatures around them. And for a second, I find it hard to breathe.

At that very moment, Caryan looks over to me, as if he's sensed me watching, sensed my discomfort. I stare back too long, my eyes wide, before I snap out of it and flee into the kitchen.

$$\supset * \subset$$

The last rays of sun dip the terrace in a mystical gleam before they pull back and the fiery ball almost disappears behind the bluish peaks of the mountains undulating in the distance. I chew on a piece of honey-spiced bread I sneaked from the chef before I slinked out of the kitchen unnoticed to watch the sunset.

Caryan comes striding out. He looks over at me as if, again, sensing my presence. As if he knew I was here all along.

"I'm sorry—I was just taking my five-minute break," I say hastily, jumping to my feet to run back inside. Run from him.

"Stay." An order. Cold.

I slowly sink back onto the marble balustrade where I've been sitting, hidden in the shade, the stone comfortingly warm under my body. Maybe the only warmth I'd get for a long while. I take a deep breath.

Have it out now.

Because I need to know, and because diplomacy has never been my strong point, I ask, "Are you going to throw me into the dungeon?" I ran around all day feeling like I was living on borrowed time. And I'm tired of waiting.

"What if I do?"

"I would offer you another bargain," I say quietly. I thought about that during the long shift today. But there is nothing else I can offer that he could want from me, nothing he doesn't already have.

"Would you?" he asks, stepping closer.

It's the threat in his tone that makes my head snap up. I find it hard to meet his eyes though after last night.

They're dangerous, and I try hard not to remember how his magic felt in my mouth. How *he* felt…

The cold way he looked at me while he did it.

The man my mother ran from.

The man who killed his lover without a moment's hesitation.

My treacherous heart skips a few beats, and I look down again. "Please don't. I never saw a sunset until I came here, never felt the sun on my skin." Because it was *always* raining. Panic makes speaking hard, but no matter how hard I fight it, my past pushes back. Unwanted. Lyrian. The bunker. My cell. The cold. The darkness. The endless nights, locked away and chained, all alone with my dark, desperate thoughts and only fear to keep me company.

But that time still ravages me, and will probably always, in some moments. A fissure, a crack, running through my soul.

"My lord…" A purring voice behind him makes me jolt up. It's the dark-haired elf. "Oh, *servant*," she says when she sees me, her eyes narrowing. "Since you're already here, why not bring me some raspberry wine with rose petals."

409

I glance at her, briefly repulsed by the haunting similarity in our appearances. She's wearing a breathtaking blue dress that reveals more than it hides, fluttering around her perfect body. For another bizarre second, she reminds me too much of Sarynx, the eagerness in her eyes, the awe when she looks at Caryan.

I just nod, not trusting my voice. I slither past them and inside, returning outside a few minutes later with her order. The woman doesn't so much as glance at me when she takes the drink. Neither does Caryan, again entrenched in a conversation with several other fae who have formed a semicircle around them. In the distance, I make out Riven, a beautiful purple-haired pixie woman by his side this time, also lost in conversation. More people have gathered on the terrace now that the sun has set.

Caryan didn't give me an answer. I glance one last time up to the beautiful sky, trying to memorize everything, the stars so close they look as if you could pluck them from the firmament like silver berries, then I return inside. Nobody notices me sneaking away and out of the ballroom, heading for the bathrooms before anyone can see the tears streaming down my cheeks.

I shouldn't cry. But all I can think is why Caryan couldn't just have let the worm eat me. Didn't Riven warn me that fae don't *feel* the way humans do?

I suppress more tears.

I'm tired. Just so tired, and my panic is more present than ever, swamping me. I want to spray cold water onto my face, but then remember the flowers on my cheeks. Those beautiful flowers the servants painted on me. Such a stark contrast to all the violence, my dark thoughts.

I wipe the tears away and gather myself. I need to go back, or Nidaw will notice my absence and chide me. I straighten my dress and step back out into the twilight of the corridor before I walk back to the kitchen.

My hands are still shaking when I start to line up glasses on a tray, and one slips through my fingers. Shards fill the sink, and I cut myself as I fish them out.

410

I'm an idiot, cutting myself again.

I curse quietly when Nidaw steps next to me, handing me a clean kitchen towel to wrap around the cut. When she asks me whether I'm alright, I can't look at her. Can't look at her pitying face without starting to cry again.

So I just nod, quietly promising to clean up the mess. Nidaw shoos me away and tells me to go to a healer to have the cut seen to.

I don't, but I'm glad to have been let go. I venture through the darkness, my breathing easing a little in the quiet of the halls. In one of the patios I pause.

I climb onto the rim of the marble fountain, dangling my bare feet in the cool water while I press the kitchen towel hard on the cut, willing it to heal. I close my eyes for a moment, listening to the soothing splatter of water.

"There you are."

No other voice has ever had that effect on me. And never will, I know. The deep, melodious tone like a cruel mocking in my ears, a perverse mirror of the ridiculous, cruel beauty of his face.

Caryan. He snuck up so quietly I didn't hear a thing. But then, I'm only a half-elf-something, so why the hell would I?

I have never fit in anywhere, not in the human world, and sure as hell not here.

I bite the inside of my cheek, not able to look at him. Knowing I'm being unacceptably rude for a slave, ignoring my master or owner or whatever the word for this fucked-up relationship is. Knowing too well he won't let such behavior pass and that it certainly won't help my cause.

"You're hurt," he says, no softness in his voice now.

"Just a cut," I murmur, trying to twist further away from him.

He steps up behind me. "Let me see it." His voice is commanding but I don't move.

"So bossy?" I ask instead, knowing I'm overstepping.

He snarls his response. "Show me. That's an order."

As if on cue, a ripple of power slithers along my bones, but I ignore that too. How can I explain that I feel unable to turn around, to look at him, to face him without starting to cry again?

I freeze when I feel his hands in my hair. His fingers brush against my neck before he pulls my head back just as he leans in, exposing my throat, his lips right next to my ear.

My pulse skyrockets.

His voice is a quiet growl that shouldn't affect me the way it does. "Ignore me one more time, and I will show you exactly how *bossy* I can be."

I slowly turn then, taking my feet out of the water one by one and sliding around so I'm facing him. I keep my head trained on the jasmine bushes behind him. He grabs my arm, unwrapping the kitchen towel, and I suck in a sharp breath as a pain I haven't felt until now jolts through me. Maybe the cut is deeper than I thought. From the look of the blood-soaked kitchen towel, it probably is.

"You weren't going to the healers, were you? As Nidaw told you to." His tone is another growl, his fingers holding my delicate wrist like a vise. I know I'm going to have bruises tomorrow.

How the hell does he know everything? He must have overheard it. Probably smelled my blood and trailed my scent.

"It's not so bad," I retort between my teeth, sharply. I shouldn't talk to him that way, shouldn't push it further. But I'm just so angry. Partly from the pain, partly at myself, at them, at Lyrian and Riven and my mother and everyone else on this planet, or the other, or however this place works.

I just want to be left alone. I just want some peace.

"It *is* bad, given that you are surrounded by blood-sucking creatures. You act carelessly when you choose to ignore *every warning* I give you," he hisses back, even angrier than I am. "And where is Riven? He should have accompanied you."

"I thought the threat was over. And I can walk on my own, without a babysitter. As you know, I'm not a child anymore." Hells, I don't know what's gotten into me.

Caryan's eyes shift, a horizon darkening. "You're not? But you're behaving like one just now."

His words hurt, hit me harder than they should. Maybe this is why I snap, "Yeah? Maybe I'll stop when you stop treating me like one."

I shouldn't have said that. Definitely shouldn't use that tone. Shouldn't bare my teeth and glower up at him the way I do. But the alternative is breaking down and crying. And I'm not sure I would ever get back up again.

His eyes morph into a blazing amber, his teeth bared right back at me. "You want me to stop? Then I will—"

Before I know what he's doing, he's wrenched my bleeding wrist between us, closer to his lips. Then he… licks it. No teeth, just his tongue, running along the inside of my wrist like the flame of a lighter. I hold perfectly still, mesmerized by the sight of his mouth on my flesh.

He closes his eyes, as if he's enjoying it. For the first time, I have the chance to watch him closely, without a rush, without the full weight of his attention, without it being forbidden.

He's so supernaturally beautiful. So beautiful I probably wouldn't even fight it if he killed me right now, just for the sake of watching him a little longer.

The slight mauve of his eyelids, feathery, dark, long lashes. His ears… those perfectly, strange arched ears I find I want to touch as desperately as those wings that are hidden again.

My eyes wander back to his delirious lips. To those cruel, perfect lips and strong, long fingers around my wrist. The sight shifts me.

I know I shouldn't be feeling this way. I should hate him for what he almost did at the maze. What he did last night. What he's no doubt going to do.

I gasp when he starts to gently suck at the cut. At the stream of his dark power that emanates from where his mouth lies on my skin and flows into my body, an exchange for the blood running out of me into him. And again, it's no longer that bristling current, but milder. My own body responding to it, as if it's made for this.

Coming awake. My own blood singing to his. Sharpening every sense of myself in all the wrong ways.

Yet a tiny part in me suddenly startles when I think of the faun chef, Arbor, and what he swore to me in the kitchen. About all my moments alone with Riven. A cold shiver goes through me because that tiny part is terrified of what happens if Caryan sees this.

But then Caryan opens his eyes again, and they're a hypnotic alloy of gold and red. And yet another, absurd, stupid, dark part of me feels a deep satisfaction when I should probably be frightened. No, I should definitely be frightened. But right now, I can't bring myself to be.

He lifts his lips away from me eventually. His thumb grazes my healed skin one last time, gently, before he lets me go.

When I can't stand the intensity of his eyes any longer, I look down again, at my wrist, at the unharmed skin there, and whisper a breathless, "Thank you."

"My pleasure," he says, his voice a timbre that unravels me completely.

I shake my head, trying to return to sobriety, to find that earlier anger I want to use like a shield. But there is none, as if he has sucked it out of me. I feel drunk on *him*.

I grapple for any clear thought, for words, as I ask, "What did you see in my blood this time?"

To my great surprise, I find a look of frustration on his face.

"Nothing," he answers eventually.

"Why?"

"I don't know. It might be that you didn't give me permission," he muses, as if to himself.

"What? How?" I blurt out.

He frowns and I can see him debating whether to give me an answer. I didn't really do anything before. It was just a tiny part of myself begging my blood not to reveal itself. It was barely more than a thought. But then, when I broke through those wards, my body did it all on its own accord too. It didn't feel hard, but rather, *natural*.

Caryan says, "We call it shielding. The ability to shield oneself against magical invasions of all forms." I'm not sure I trust my ears when he adds, "I've heard of this happening, but never witnessed it firsthand when it came to my magic and abilities." He doesn't sound angry though, but rather intrigued. His eyes are crystal clear as they seem to take in every inch of me then. As if he can find the answer somewhere in my face. As if I'm a mystery, a riddle to solve.

"So… you never met anyone who could shield themselves from your magic?" I repeat, not sure I heard him right.

"No, I have not. This is *interesting*." He holds out a hand to me. "Come. I wanted to show you something before you cut your hand."

I stare at his outstretched hand just like on that night when he found and saved me in that maze. I surprise myself by gently putting mine in his. He keeps holding it as he leads me back into a dark corridor and then further along into another one I've never seen before. Steps lead down to a massive door that unlocks on his silent command, opening out into another vast garden, even bigger than the one we were in yesterday.

The smell of oranges and lemons and persimmons suddenly hangs thick in the air, emanating from the huge, ripe fruits on the trees above my head. Caryan leads me through hip-high flowers in all shades of the rainbow, crystal dust shimmering on their petals. I can still see everything perfectly clearly, although there's no source of light anywhere close.

"Night vision," he explains, as if he's read the thoughts from my face. "All fae have it," he adds.

He gently guides me into a meadow under huge trees that shouldn't be able to grow in these conditions. Their roots are huge, sprawled around them in waves like some sort of strange legs.

"Milkwood." Caryan again answers my silent question. "They remind me of home, so I had them planted here. They can move, not far, but a little if they want."

"Home?" I ask.

His eyes darken a touch and his voice becomes deep and raw.

A ripple goes over his aura. I'm not sure, but it might be nostalgia. "What I remember of home, that is."

"You don't remember much?"

I watch the soft blue in his irises leaking into the gold-red whirl as he keeps looking at the trees.

I can't read his tone when he says, "I am old. When you reach my age, you lose a lot of things in the process, but sometimes fragments remain. One of them is the memory of those trees."

Again he laces his fingers with mine and leads me on through those endless, unreal gardens, through a patch of forest so dense that shadows disappear before we reach a clearing. And I have the feeling I've stepped into a living painting.

There are so many different hues and shades, so many flowers and bushes and trees; fat grapes of wisteria winding along low branches, wild blackberries and raspberries glistening in-between like jewels adorned with thorns.

Caryan lets go of my hand and sprawls so casually in the silvery silk-soft grass that for a moment, I just stare. Stare at the picture in front of me, at the beauty of him, a creature so undeniable fairy. His skin milk-white, his hair black like ink, moonlight threading through it, touching his devastatingly beautiful face with those sharp, pointed ears, as he lies there, strangely relaxed as if no one was watching him, surrounded by impossible nature.

And I know that one day I'm going to paint this scene. One day, *if* I ever feel confident enough to capture his otherworldly grace, the alabaster hue of his skin and the way his veins shimmer through. I stay a moment longer, trying to memorize every detail, every facet, before I match him, lying down on my back, close but not too close.

"This is what I wanted to show you," he says over the wild song of frogs and cicadas, one arm tucked behind his head; with the other, he's pointing to the stars. "Starfall. Tonight is the peak of the equinox. It's the time when the stars rain from the sky."

Indeed, as if having waited for his words, stars do begin to fall, leaving long, glittering trails like silver fireworks, each one longer and brighter than the last.

"In the human world, we believe you can make a wish for every shooting star you see," I say quietly. Not that I've ever seen one so big and so close. Not when it had always been raining at Lyrian's.

"Then I think you can make a lot of wishes tonight," he answers darkly.

"I think I do need a lot," I admit.

His gaze wanders over me before he looks back up. We lie there for a long time. I turn on my side, carefully stretching my fingers toward his right hand. He's so close I could touch him. And a part of me wants to. A dark part of me wants to feel his power again, his energy, his magic. *Under* my skin.

Despite all that happened last night. Despite what he is, in his very essence.

Maybe because of it.

Heat flushes my face, along with a shiver.

I hear him turning his head to me, hear the grass rustling at his movement.

"Nidaw said angels are made of stardust," I whisper.

To my surprise, he laughs quietly, a sound like black velvet and soft as water. Startling. Alluring. I look at him, spellbound.

He raises his brows in question when he notices my gaze.

"You can laugh."

"I have not, in a long time," he admits after a while, his gaze lingering on my face. "But we're not—made of stardust."

I'm still looking at his skin, which seems to glisten in the dark, and at my fingers so close to his, when something slithers over his arm again—the same black and gold I saw the other night in his kitchen. I don't pull my hand back, but watch, mesmerized, as those foreign symbols and tattoos sneak up over his wrists and fingers, gliding around the area where my hand is closest to his as if they are curious.

And somehow I have the feeling that it is *alive*. A *living* tattoo. Something with a pulse, almost like the bargain on my wrist.

"It's dark magic," Caryan says. "Old runes. Gatilla gave them to me."

I look up to meet his eyes again, but they are veiled by something I can't grasp. It might be melancholy, but I'm not sure.

Then he gets up in such a smooth, powerful movement that all I can do is watch with awe. He takes a few steps away, his powerful back to me. I get up too, briefly afraid that I've said something wrong, but then he returns to me.

He lifts his hand to my cheek, tracing the flowers there before he says, "You were crying. Before, at the festivities."

He saw it. I want to look away, but he holds my chin gently, studying my face like a painting.

His voice falls low, and I don't trust my ears when he murmurs, "You are even more beautiful when you cry."

My breath catches in my throat. I wonder how it is that a lot of the things he says sound like a compliment and a threat at the same time. I don't know what to make of the way his eyes drink in my face. How he kept looking at me the same cold and indifferent way he's looking at me now while he pushed himself between my lips. Cruelly. Aloof. As if he's pondering how far he wants to let himself go.

But his expression doesn't match his tone when he says, "Do not believe that I don't know how much you fear being locked away again."

"Does that mean you won't?"

"I do not want to. That doesn't mean I'm not going to if I have to."

"Cool." I look down at my naked feet in the grass.

"But I do not like to see you sad," he adds, immune to my sarcasm.

I peer up at the silvery stars, my chest tight. "How will this work? You keep me forever?"

To my huge surprise, he asks back, "What is it that you would rather do?"

"I don't know. Have a house by the sea one day. Maybe a dog. A simple life. Freedom."

"Freedom can easily turn into aimlessness," he retorts, and I expect a joke.

418

But when I glance back at him, I find his gaze unusually soft. Knowing.

"You think I can't live on my own?"

"Do you want to?"

I look away. "Honestly, I've never really thought about it."

I've been too busy surviving. Running. Escaping. Fighting. There had been no place for *want*. When I again glance back at him, I see that he already knows all those things. It makes me feel naked.

"That doesn't mean I want to live a life in shackles," I snap.

"Some perceive the boundaries of an enclosure as safety because outside looms the wild," he counters.

"Yeah? Who? Sheep?" I snap.

"For one."

"Well, I'm not a sheep."

His callous lips tear into an almost smile as he leans into my space. "No. What are you then?"

Indignation lifts my chin. "You tell me."

"Bold. Daring. Valorous. Audacious. Enigmatic. Rebellious."

"Lovely—" I seethe.

"Very. And a lot of other things, but most importantly, as unique to this world as I am. Which might change your perspective in time. You might find that you come to like your enclosure."

"Sounds more like a foregone conclusion than a possibility."

"I've just seen too much in my long life."

"Well, if I am a sheep, what are you? The shepherd?"

"In a sense."

"A shepherd with a penchant for very public displays of vengeance," I say, a touch too sharply.

I see his eyes change into those hues that tell me his uncharacteristic lenity is running out. I should stop, because I might regret it. But regret is something for my future self, always has been.

"Justice is not merciful," he retorts coolly.

Something in me snaps. "Those fauns were innocent."

He catches my throat too fast. "I have come to believe that you are no sheep. That I have, indeed, found a wolf in the midst of lowly cattle. But a wolf with a weakness nonetheless. It's your ridiculously soft, half-human heart speaking. It's this very heart you owe that mark to. To your fragile little feelings."

"You make it sound as if it's something bad."

"They make you weak," he seethes.

"At least I still have feelings—or I think I'd feel dead inside," I bite out.

He lets go of me, but lifts my arm, holding my newly tattooed wrist up between us, wrenching me close. "Then tell me, does it *feel* good that I can make you do anything I want?"

I still. My fury is gone in an instant. Only my heart still beats, and my skin still feels. "Can't you anyways?" I ask quietly.

I wonder what this is between us. His gaze once again drops to my lips and down my body, filled with a mixture of disgust and hunger. The same dark thing that made him do what he did to me last night. And it terrifies me. Because I know he has the power to destroy me on more than one level.

But even more terrifying is the thought that I know I would let him. That I would let him do *anything*, bargain or no.

I know he can sense it. Feel it. Read it in my eyes.

Hells, he knows, by the way the look in his eyes turns ravenous.

But just as I think he will go too far, that he will lose control, he says, "I could adapt my methods of governance in time."

He lets go abruptly, taking a step back from me. My body, my mind, still reel. The words hang in the air. He looks away, as if he didn't want to acknowledge what he just said.

Only eventually, he breaks the silence once more. "You already learned that you are the last silver elf and what happened to your kind. You will be hunted. You're never going to be safe out there."

"And I would be with you?"

"As safe as you can be," he retorts, again unfazed by my sarcasm.

I don't like his answer at all.

He startles me all over when he says, "I wanted to discuss the terms of our bargain."

"Terms?"

"There is a war coming. I need your gift—to find lost things."

My blood turns to ice, and I retreat a step. There it is, finally. "I won't—"

"Not people, not like Lyrian made you do," he interrupts me, and I know that this is what he saw in my blood. One of the many things. Those terrible things I did. "Objects. Relics. Find three of them for me, and I will free you from that bargain. And if freedom is still what you want by then, we can see about that too."

"A contract, then?" I ask, confused. Not yet sure about their rules.

"A promise. I will stick to it if you fulfill your side."

MELODY

Caryan walks back without waiting for my answer. I follow him quietly through the nocturnal lushness. My mind is wild. I don't know what to think. I will get rid of that bargain on my wrist.

Yet at the same time, there is a hollowness in me, as if everything that just happened—the way he drank my blood, the way he showed me the garden and told me a shard about himself—as if this all has served only one purpose.

Yet, why ask? Why, if he could just force me to? Because he needs three relics, or more, and the bargain on my wrist counts only for one? Freedom. He said we could talk about my freedom.

I follow him back inside. It sends an entirely different kind of fear through me when I notice that we are heading to his private rooms.

The flame-eyed face at the door greets him, then addresses me simply as "Melody" before it closes shut behind us.

I stand there like I did two days ago, strangely lost in the huge rooms, my arms wrapped around myself while Caryan strides toward the kitchen, just as the last time after he saved me from that sand worm.

I quietly go after him, reluctant to enter, nervous to be alone with him as I watch him pouring two drinks over ice. The memory of what happened the last time— all those dark things he said to me— still runs vivid in my blood. *Or shall I promise you that there is nowhere in existence you could run that I would not find you. That there is nothing I would not do to save you. That I would rip apart every world, every dream and every nightmare for you. I would even rip apart the hells.*

I take my glass wordlessly and down it in one go. I'm not sure what it is, but it's sharp and burns like a whiskey, numbing my senses. *Good.*

"I guess I'm nervous," I say with a shy smile and put the empty glass back down on the counter.

Caryan just keeps watching me in that unnatural way of the fae—barely moving, impossibly patient.

I finally ask, "You never get nervous, right?"

"No," he says, clearly not knowing where I'm going with it.

I point at my glass. "Can I have one more? Please?"

His gaze says no, but then he puts his glass down and pushes it over to me. I grab it, drinking more.

Eventually, the alcohol shows its effect, and I feel a little bit calmer, bolder. Bold enough to ask one of the many questions that ravage my mind.

Let's start with the simple one.

"What does Kalleandara's prophecy say exactly?"

Caryan walks over to the open window, his muscled back turned to me. After a while he answers, "As I said—there is a war coming. And you, with your talent, could change its outcome."

It's true. Everly said the same. I can see that in Caryan's aura too, but that's not all. And I already know it only has to be true *enough.*

"There's more to it." I follow him, stopping a little behind him, not daring to get too close. "It says that I will end the blight, right?"

He licks his teeth while he keeps looking up at the stars. "Prophecies say a lot of things. Things I do not necessarily believe in."

"They say Kalleandara's the most powerful oracle."

"She is. That doesn't make her predictions any more or any less real."

"But a lot of people believe it does," I push.

He says nothing.

"Is the blight the war?"

"It refers to the *outcome* of the war," he clarifies somberly.

"Are my talents the reason the Nefarians want me dead?"

"In a sense," he admits. Ambiguously. An answer that is none. Fuck him.

I know I surprise him when I ask, "What are the relics?"

He angles his head at that while his eyes scrutinize my face, as if his decision whether to tell me more depends on something he finds or doesn't find there. "It is bound magic. The elves bound magic to relics back then to hide it away from the world under Gatilla's reign."

"Why do you want them?" I ask.

He turns fully to me, a sad half smile on his lips, his eyes pitch black so his pupils are gone. There is no light left in them, not even the golden circlet that normally surrounds his irises. Briefly, the sight of him like this terrifies me. He looks like a demon. "To win this war."

I shake my head. "No. You don't need them to win the war."

He takes a step towards me. "And you can suddenly predict the future?"

"No, I can just see in your aura that you don't believe you need them."

"Then I would have just lied to you, wouldn't I?" His voice has dropped dangerously low; his smile tears into something lopsided.

He takes another step and I involuntarily take one back.

"Which I can't," he reminds me, that smile spreading into a terrifying grin as I try to read his aura, searching it for the truth, but it's veiled again.

"It seems I'm not the only one who can shield herself," I say, my eyes never straying from his, although everything in me locks up.

Heat enters his gaze, but for some reason it doesn't make him look warmer, or softer, just even more frightening. Something's wrong here.

"I learned to do that early on, in the young days of this world. I just happen to be negligent from time to time. At least where you are concerned, it seems." he says slowly, aloofly, too lightly, as if it is all just a game we're playing.

"How?" He must have taught Riven too.

"Oh, my little girl, I know so much more about magic than this world itself will ever understand. But I think you learned that already," he purrs, and gods help me, his magic flares up under my skin, the same mixture of velvet and leashed lightning, as if to remind me of last night. I try my best to ignore it.

"Why do you really want them?"

"So no one else can find them."

I shake my head. "Not true."

He snorts incredulously. "All the things you seem to know."

"You want all the power for yourself," I say with cold realization.

"Do you know what happens if that power falls into the wrong hands?"

"And yours are the *right* ones?"

He cocks his head, then straightens. "It's an old song—history, always repeating itself. There will be war again. There will be a new king, but none of them will lead this world to glory. He will just scorch its soil again. All monarchs are blinded by their insatiable greed. All of them turn decadent, all of them fall. And people, they are like cattle. Obedient until panicked. Rabid when they turn desperate. Look at the human world, thoroughly raped and destroyed."

"So the Nefarians want me dead to prevent you from getting this *magic*."

His eyes flash in a warning, along with his fangs when he says, "Some will want you dead to try to dethrone me. Others will hunt you down to have you find those relics for them."

I don't like the direction this is headed.

"I might not tell them."

As a test, I throw my talent out and ask for the relics, but nothing answers me. *Strange.* A vague image of a flute appears in my mind, but no direction, nothing about its whereabouts.

I don't tell Caryan though. Not now, not here. Not when my freedom depends on it.

Not as that strange echo of a smile, like a ghost, brushes his lips again.

He says, "They won't ask as nicely as I do."

Again, I wonder why he does—ask so nicely. I saw what he did to Sarynx so easily. What he would have done to those fauns had I not intervened. What he did, and probably is *still* doing, to the Nefarian warrior in some dark torture chamber.

"You said the blight is the outcome of the war. So—what *is* the outcome of the war?"

"It depends. As I said, I do not believe much in prophecies."

"That's not an answer," I whisper.

Shadows rip from his strong shoulders, teeming around his head and body and wrists, curling over the floor between us.

"What happens if you find the relics with my help? And what happens if you don't?"

He stills as he watches me. His eyes again go black like the space between planets. The space that eats stars and worlds and universes. They seem to drink all the light from the room, like his shadows. Drink life itself.

"And here I was, thinking that I've already established that the second option is obsolete," he says, unbearably gentle as he comes for me.

I stumble backwards, banging into the kitchen chair behind me.

"But you might need some more convincing."

"Were you the same way with my mother? Is this why she ran from you?" The words tumble out of me. Too sharp to veil my fear underneath. "Did you threaten to torture her too if she didn't help you?"

He pauses briefly, surprised. "No. I didn't. Your mother didn't have any of your talents."

"Why... why did she run from you then?" My voice breaks as

I brace myself for his answer. My blood runs cold like water when none comes. "What? Too cruel to tell me?"

"Perhaps," he admits, but his voice is suddenly rough. His shadows, hovering.

"Tell me anyway," I say, holding my ground.

He turns his head away, as if considering. Then he says, "Your mother ran and hid, not only from me, but from a lot of other people as well."

I instinctively retreat another step, and this time he doesn't follow me. "Why?"

He frowns. "Because of you."

"Because of Kalleandara's prophecy. Because of my talents."

"Yes."

"But Sarynx…" I make myself say her name, although my ribs feel too tight to suck down another breath. "Sarynx said my mother had been hiding in the human world from you. *Because* of you."

My heart almost stops when he says, "It is true."

"Why?" I scowl at him when he says nothing. "*Tell* me," I push.

Nothing could have prepared me for his next words. "Because she wanted to sell you."

"What? To who?"

"To a few powerful people. Kings and queens."

"But I thought she was in the human world."

"She was hiding there, yes. Though she planned on returning one day…"

"Once she sold me, you mean?" I feel strangely detached, as if we were talking about the wheather.

"Yes," he says gravely.

I swallow hard. "Why… why did she want to sell me? And what did she want in return? Money?" I spit out the last word. Gods, I want to know what I'd been worth.

"It's more complex than that. Your mother was an outcast, because of a few things she did in the past. You were her only chance to redeem herself. To buy back her freedom. Her safety."

I don't know what I'm feeling anymore. The woman I believed

had loved me. She would have sold me like some object. Like Lyrian.

"But it never got to that. Because Lyrian found her," I add quietly.

Caryan says softly, "Not exactly. It was she who went to Lyrian when she found out she was pregnant with you. It was Lyrian who managed the negotiations for her."

Negotiations… about me. About who'd buy me.

My throat feels dry, my heart too heavy. I take a deep breath, trying to somehow wrap my head around that. "Why Lyrian?" I whisper. "Of all people, why would anyone seek out Lyrian out of their own free will?"

"For one, because he was powerful enough to shield his existence from everyone through the magic he harvested. Even from me. And because he was not always that evil. The stolen magic corrupted his soul over time."

I look down at my feet. "Who… who killed my parents?"

"Your grandfather, Regus. The right hand of the king of Palisandre."

My head flies up. "What? He killed his own daughter? How? Why?"

"They weren't exactly on the best terms. And as for how—your mother was negligent. Arrogant. She stepped out of Lyrian's magic shields. That is when he found her. Lyrian fled with you while your grandfather *interrogated* your father and her," Caryan explains somberly.

"How do you know?" I ask before I can take it back. The words fall almost soundlessly. I'm not sure I really want to know.

Caryan's eyes glitter otherworldly as he says, "Because I found him afterward. But he could not give me the answer I was looking for."

My mouth feels dry. "Is he… still alive? My grandfather?" *Murderous* grandfather.

"He is. Although some people say he lost his mind."

"Lost his mind after you… released him?" I ask, not knowing why.

"It depends on who you ask," is all he retorts. I glance away, sucking in a deep breath while I try to detangle the mess of my thoughts. The mess of my feelings.

"So Lyrian kept me. But... at his house, he said he kept me for *you*. Why?" I ask, my mind still reeling, confused. I know so little, and all I can do is puzzle together the pieces. Lyrian, not always a monster. My own mother, trying to sell me to save herself. And well... the rest.

Caryan keeps watching me through his long lashes, his eyes gray, unreadable again. "In this world, people are superstitious. As you already know, there are seers and other oracles who give prophecies all the time. He received one that said you were meant for me, and he was to hand you over if he wished to be kept alive."

Meant for me. I don't like the sound of it at all, but I don't find the sharp response I wish to throw into his face. Telling him that I'm not meant for anyone, in any sense. Not after everything he just told me. I just look away instead, grinding my teeth so hard they hurt. My eyes probe through the room while I try to process everything he just revealed.

Caryan gives me time. Waiting. I know he's watching me closely. Know he can hear the uneven beat of my heart.

After a long moment, I ask, "Did my mother... did she get pregnant on purpose?"

"Fae rarely get pregnant. It's not a thing you can plan on."

I nod, not knowing if that fact makes it any better. "But if she was going to sell me anyway, and already had bidders... why not to you?" I sure as hells can't look at him while I say it.

"I wasn't yet the king I am now. I could not offer her what so many others could."

I swallow hard. My mother. The woman I had dreamed up so many nights alone in the darkness. I know Caryan's words should hurt, but they don't. All this information should rattle something in me, but for some reason, it doesn't.

Where I maybe should be heartbroken, there is just numbness. A void. An absence.

I take a deep breath and then I move on, as I always do. I have to.

I say with a bravado I do not feel, "You know, after all that gloomy talk I think I need another drink."

I slink past him, walking around the kitchen island to avoid his path, heading straight for the fridge. I open it, looking for that bottle—whiskey. I find it and pour more into one of the tumblers.

Caryan remains standing on the other side, his expression unreadable. Cold.

I watch him over the rim of my glass, wiping my mouth after I've downed another glass.

"Is it wise to get that drunk?"

"I don't know. Is it wise to keep whiskey in a fridge?" I ask back.

He runs his tongue over his teeth. "We fae do have different palates. I like it that way. The opposite goes for little girls."

I raise my brows at him. "You don't like them cold?"

His upper lip curls back, annoyed. "I don't like them drunk, for obvious reasons."

"As you just said—I'm a little girl and reckless and audacious and... right, enigmatic. And you have no feelings anyway. So I guess this is what reckless, oversensitive little girls my age do when they want to have some fun. Or as you'd put it in that elaborate way of yours, *I might have a tendency toward volatility at the worst possible of moments.*"

I'm drunk. There's no other way I'd have just snapped at him like that. Mocked him like that. But a part of me is threatened to drown in desperation if I didn't.

I'm going to need to find three relics for him. Relics that don't call to me on top of that. But even if I manage to find them, even if he gives me my freedom, I'll be safe nowhere. I'm not foolish enough to think that I'm safe with him either, now or ever.

He licks his lips, and I hate that I follow the movement of his tongue. He retorts dryly, "*This* hardly looks like fun."

Something unholy flickers in his eyes, but he doesn't intervene when I refill my glass another time and drink some more.

I secretly fight against the burning in my throat, like hot water, but force it down anyway. Then I give him an innocent look. "No? It could be, you know."

I fill the second glass and shove it, the way he did before, glad it slides elegantly over to him as if I planned it that way all along.

"That is, if you decide to let go for once." I shrug, trying to say it as nonchalantly as I can. Hells, I'm drunk.

"You don't want me to let go, believe me." His voice has dropped, but I opt to ignore the warning in it.

"Maybe I do." I lean against the counter, looking him in the eye while sipping some more, although it already feels too much.

He doesn't reach for his glass, just watches me in that stoic, serene manner of his. But his eyes flicker again, some deep purple entering the gray. It reminds me of Riven.

"So what now?"

"What do you mean *what now*?" he echoes sharply.

"Will you just stand there and watch me getting hammered?" I take another sip of the sharp liquid and then I walk around the island, stopping right before him.

I try not to think of how tall and intimidating he is as I hold my glass out to him, a daring smile on my lips.

What the hell is wrong with me? Am I flirting with death? Winged death, that is. A very, very bad idea. Yet part of me wants to go further. Feels it like a pull under my skin. I want to see how far I can go and what will happen if I cross that line. I want to know why he treats me differently than all the others. There must be a reason for it, I know it in my soul.

I want to find out. Tonight. Maybe I'd come too close to death too often over the last few days.

He stands unmoved, like a man made of stone.

"Kyrith said that you don't have any sense of humor. Now I get it," I push.

"Kyrith would never dare."

"Doesn't mean it's not true."

He just glowers at me, and it takes everything to keep my face blank.

"Good. Since *you* don't want it," I say, deciding to empty his glass, hoping it will numb me sufficiently.

I'm about to reach for the full one still sitting on the counter when he grabs my wrist. The very wrist his lips had been on just an hour ago. When I saw that gold in his eyes that I know, deep in my bones, means something more.

I felt it back then in that dungeon, and felt it at the fountain, clearer than ever. Something that horrifies him. Something *about me.*

I know it. It isn't just in my imagination. It's a clue. A lead.

He says with a growl, "That's enough."

I try to wrench free, but he holds me.

"You say that very often, you know?"

His eyes flare. "I mean it."

"I'm not a girl anymore."

"You are a *slave*," he says, baring his fangs. "My slave, that is." His voice is sibilant. I feel the leashed rage underneath like a pulse.

"Yes, I know I'm *your* slave," I reply, unfazed, right into his face, looking deep into those surreal eyes as if I might drown in them. His absurdly stunning face. The face that has the lethal, gentle beauty of snow.

I want to say *you could have me, you know. You could have everything* if you just say it, and I hate that.

I hate that I'm his slave.

Hate that he doesn't let on anything.

I tear free from his grip and sink onto my knees. "Is this how you want your slave, *my lord? Your Highness?*" The mocking sounds bad, even to my ears.

He goes utterly still. I glance up at him, daring the gold in his eyes to return. Or the blue. *Anything.* But instead, the violet-gray only darkens. A storm is gathering, ready to break loose. I have no clue what I'm doing when I put my hands on his pants. When I let my fingers glide upward to undo his belt.

His hands close around my wrists again, stopping me like he did at that party.

The way he says "Get up" feels like a slap. No. *Worse.* A part of me wishes he would just slap me.

"Isn't that what you did last night?" I taunt.

There it is—a flicker of that furious red that announces doom. Finally. I almost feel triumphant.

"Get up, Melody."

Again, he looks like he's restraining himself. I feel it, the tension. Fight it when he yanks me up as if I weigh nothing. When he holds me tight as I try to wriggle free again. I hiss at him, baring my teeth the way I did at the fountain. More red is bleeding into his irises now, and I feel some revolting satisfaction in having finally pushed him over the brink. At least there's that. Just a little more, I know.

"That's enough now, Melody. I warn you." His voice is laced with a growl, the silken menace unmistakably announcing coming violence.

"Yeah? I think you should just discipline me," I whisper right into his achingly beautiful face. I've probably gone insane. But a dark part of me is sick of these rules. Sick of being told what to do. Sick of all the selective truths and no one telling me what's really going on.

For a sliver of a second, I think he will—discipline me. That I'll pay for this when he says, "This is the last time I'm warning you."

He lets go of me, but his whole unholy essence whispers around me, sizzling in the air, remnants of power flickering along my veins.

I let out a cold laugh. "I see. Yet you didn't seem too repulsed by a little girl like me sitting on your lap at the party."

"You have no idea what you're talking about."

"Is it because I'm talking back?"

"Hold your insolent tongue!"

"The tongue you—"

His fingers are around my neck again, harder this time. I find myself pushed against that counter before my mind can catch up with his speed, his momentum. He's standing between my legs, his teeth mere inches away from my lips, so close we would be sharing breath if he let me breathe.

I meet his stare, those eyes burning right into my innermost being.

Hold your tongue. Your *insolent* tongue. I'd laugh at his choice of words if it didn't hurt so much. But the hell would I show him.

Just then his fingers ease slightly. I draw in a breath and hiss, "Ah, I forgot that you only like *real women.*"

He shoves me even harder against the counter. So hard my head smacks against the cupboard, his body pinning me, grinding me against the stone, his shadows crawling up my skin. He's all animal now, his eyes not gray but a bottomless black as his free hand slams into the cupboard next to me so hard the material splinters. So close I can feel the whisper of air on my face, his hand only missing me by an inch.

I swallow hard as I stare at his hand next to my head, swathed in midnight smoke.

All I wanted was to push him, even if it meant that I made him angry, and now I'm terrified.

I feel myself struggling for air, his fingers digging too deep into my neck. A little tighter and he could just snap it. Tears I can no longer hold back fill my eyes while I look up at the all-consuming blackness in his.

Just then, like in the desert, something silvery flares up all around me, swirling around his shadows. I stare as it glistens and gleams, Caryan's magic reacting to it—his shadows twining and untwining all around us, laced by that silver, sparkling light. I've never seen anything more beautiful, as if the night and the stars had changed their shapes just to dance with each other.

Caryan holds me a moment longer before he lets me go. His eyes, like mine, focus on the strange light curling around his darkness.

When I look down at myself, I find my skin alight with it. The magic streams out of me, trailing off me like smoke infused with stardust and liquid moonlight.

For a second, I think I'm imagining things. That I just drank too much.

This can't be real.

But then Caryan's eyes glide to mine, and I find them as silver as the magic, as if some of it has just melded with his very being. The fury in them is gone, and too much lies in them now. I see my own surprise mirrored there, caution, pride and… admiration.

He goes to step away from me, but I dig my fingers into his shirt, burying my head in his chest like I did two nights ago. My head is spinning too fast to allow any clear thought, the floor wonky under my feet, unreliable. The whole room swims as I turn my head to the side. The light, *my* light, is still everywhere, flickering over the high ceiling and the walls, still curling in the air like smoke, now brushing up against Caryan's magic, teasingly, almost playfully… and his answering, carefully, curiously.

I'm still staring at *our* magic as he gently lifts me up. He carries me, and I let him. My light fades until only remnants of it flicker through the air like fireflies, before they wink out, my skin white and pale again, only his shadows still brushing around me like the gentlest of touches.

I barely register another door opening into darkness before Caryan lowers me onto cool, incredibly soft pillows. Then he's over me, laying me down, bracing himself on one arm above me.

"Please don't leave now," I whisper. He hesitates. Our eyes lock.

Then I feel him pulling back and my heart sinks.

But he just walks around the bed and lies down on the other side.

I turn to him in the dark, looking at the soft blue stars that now dance in his eyes, all the blackness dissolved, as if it was never there in the first place. I feel his hand gently stroking my hair and close my eyes. His scent, which clings to his sheets, engulfs me like a soothing lullaby.

I'm not sure I hear right when he murmurs, "You look like a child when you're afraid," more to himself than to me.

But I'm already asleep.

51

RIVEN

Riven shoves away the girl who has started to open his pants, getting up when the scent of Melody's blood drifts over to him, cutting through all the other smells, as distinct as a beacon of light in a starless night.

He follows the scent back to the kitchen, and then, spotting servants sweeping up a mess of glass shards, trails it back outside into the corridor. Vanella, the dark-haired elf, comes sauntering through the darkness. A red gown made of translucent chiffon slides over her body, the front cut so deep it reveals her belly button, that piece of fabric only held into place by golden fibulas. Her face is schooled in a mask of pure triumph. Not a day has gone by, and she's already replaced Sarynx. Riven would almost believe the act if it weren't for the hard lines around her fluorescent-colored lips.

"Where's Caryan?" he asks her.

"Don't worry, your king is safe, as is your little slave girl. Or as safe as she can be, I guess. I just saw him sucking her blood on the patio. It looked really... intense." She curls a strand of her silken hair around her finger as she rolls the last word, batting her long, green lashes up at him. She laughs bright as a bell when she notices Riven's clenched jaw.

He tries to pass her, but she blocks his way.

"I wouldn't go and watch that if I were you."

"And why would that be?" he growls down at her.

She cuts him a slashing grin that doesn't suit her. It's a little bit too desperate, just like her dress. "Do you think no one else notices how you two are looking at her? It gets kind of boring, though, to watch the display of your depraved tastes."

Riven scrutinizes his nails, but his voice is cold with a warning as he drawls, "You better not forget who you're talking to, and all the more, who you're talking *about*."

Flames flare up on her skin, enough to bite and hurt, but not to burn. Yet.

For a moment, Vanella looks truly afraid as she stares at the flames licking at her. Flames that could eat everything, even stone. She falls to her knees, pressing her forehead against the ground. "Forgive me, I forgot myself for a moment, my lord."

"Indeed you did."

Riven pulls his magic back with a snip of his fingers. "I'd be careful if I were you, Vanella," he says, straightening the sleeves of his shirt. "I know you feel triumphant now Sarynx is finally gone. But you do not seem to realize that he's already as bored with you as he was with her. And it's a dangerous thing—to lose Caryan's interest."

He steps past her and walks toward that patio where Melody's and Caryan's scents linger, although they are already gone. Only drops of her blood shimmer on the ground, silvery in the moonlight, the scent heavy in the air. And yes—Vanella wasn't lying—there are *other* scents too.

He takes a moment there, in the quiet, watching bats cutting through the night catching prey, before he slowly walks back to the party, to the girl with the silver imprints on her lavender skin who's still waiting.

MELODY

I wake up in a bed that's not mine. I'm alone.

I get up and walk past the open terrace door, the warm wind caressing my naked shoulders. I follow the faint sound of rushing water while I fight hard not to remember snippets of what happened before.

I'm dead sober again, and I suppose my fae blood might process alcohol faster. Or maybe it's magic, but my head feels clearer than ever. I don't even have a hangover, although it's still the deepest night outside.

Maybe it's just the few hours of soundless, deep sleep like I haven't had in years.

Not the sleep brought on by exhaustion, but calm, safe slumber.

Absurdly enough, I felt safe when Caryan lay down next to me, watching me in the dark.

Light from a single candle that flickers on the ground dips the bathroom into a warm, restless twilight while my bare feet soundlessly pad closer. There is a bath like the one Nidaw always puts me in. A huge round pool, embedded in the floor, marble steps leading into the water. The ceiling is open and you can see the stars.

Caryan's in the bath, his arms and upper body out of the water. His head is leaned back, his throat exposed, and the magnificent wings I dream of sinking my fingers into are spread wide out behind him, a velvet black in the absence of light, soaked from the steaming water.

He must have summoned them, or however *that* works.

I pause, taking in the scene—him in such a vulnerable, private state. His face, stripped of its usual, lush austerity.

He doesn't stir, doesn't open his eyes.

Could it really be that he hasn't heard me approaching? Hasn't smelled me?

My eyes take in every inch of him, but rest on a huge scar that runs from the left side of his chest down over his navel to his right hip. I spot magical runes there, but they're not moving like the rest of his tattoo. They look damaged, brutally maimed by whatever weapon and whatever cruel hand tried to cut him open from his heart down, as if to saw him in half.

"Pretty?"

I jolt. When I glance up, I find him suddenly watching me.

"Who... who did that to you?" I whisper with a kind of cold shock.

"You wouldn't want to know that," he says dryly, stating a fact, but his eyes shift back into a sonorous blue at my tone.

I draw closer, too aware of his nakedness. Of my... of whatever happened between us. Was it real? My *magic*, dancing and playing with his? I pray he can't see the heat in my face, yet I know he can hear my galloping heartbeat. Sense all the other things that give my nervousness away.

"I see you're sober again."

I pull back my shoulders and hold his gaze. "Who did that to you?" I ask again.

"Did that to you, *Your Highness*," he corrects me. I don't know whether he's joking.

"Who did that to you, *master?*"

His eyes darken slightly at that, but not from anger. "Does it matter?"

"It does to me."

He raises his brows at my tone. "Let's just say a lot of people have tried to kill me along the way, but not even a Nefarian sword could do it."

My mouth goes dry at the ambiguity in his tone. At the insinuation. What must life be like when so many people want to murder you? "You... I thought you were immortal."

"I am. But a lot of people have pondered the dreadful question of how to succeed in killing me regardless, and tested their theories, as you can see."

"But—they failed," I whisper still staring at the damaged runes. Such violence it makes me sick. Makes it hard to breathe.

"Well, isn't that the most interesting question? How to succeed." His tone falls to a dark timbre, as if challenging me.

I reflexively shake my head. "Why would it be?" It's not at all a question.

He seems surprised by the conviction in my tone. "Do you want to come in?" he asks instead, to cover it, to make me blush even more violently. His eyes are ambiguous and sparkling; so is his tone.

Is that—an offer? Or another game?

I stand there like the girl I still am, unaware of the rules of this world. He was right. I'm no woman. A woman would shrug her clothes off and get in. Maybe just take what she wants. But... what *do* I want? Again, that dreadful question. *Want.*

My throat gets dry as I push the thought down. My gaze falls to my feet while I wrap my arms around myself, shaking my head as an answer.

"Then would you mind handing me the towel over there?" he asks, his voice deep and elegant. Another question, not an order to a slave.

I obey and grab an immensely huge towel I suppose can dry his wings off too, before walking over to the steps, keeping my head trained on the tiles.

I want to bend and place it down at the edge of the pool, but he says, "Bring it over here." An order this time.

My head jerks up. He's right opposite me now, all of him even more striking up close.

I want to open my mouth, to decline, but instead, I keep watching the faint amusement in his face, biting down my lip.

"So bold, so sassy—and now so shy." His tone is lilting. Vicious.

I feel shame and heat, and so much more, slither down my spine.

I cast a glance over my shoulder as if to calculate how fast I can possibly make it out of here.

He just laughs, coolly, as if he's read my thoughts again. "The door won't let you out. And you don't want to push your luck any more tonight, believe me."

"The door likes me," I reply.

He raises his brows, watching me with predatory intent. "Does it now?"

"It will let me go."

He smiles at that, but to himself this time. I've never seen him really smile, and it affects me. It's a thing of savage, dark beauty. It makes his face so handsome I can barely stand the sight. But I can't look away either, and I know that, for some reason, he's in a strangely mild mood.

The smile fades when he says, "The whole Fortress is an extension of me."

My heart jumps at the revelation. What does that mean? That *he* likes me? That the door really won't let me out? That the door was only nice to me, only showed me the library because *he* wanted to show me? And if so, why?

"Now be a good girl and bring me the towel," he repeats somberly, power rippling unmistakably around the edges of the room and over me—a bittersweet resonance in my bones. His darkness, like a song something in my veins wants to answer.

With a last glance toward the door I obey, my bare feet stepping one step down into the water, then another one and another one, until water starts to claim my dress, steam clouds my face, and I'm in it up to my ribs.

Caryan pushes himself away from the edge then, drawing closer to me. I wait, mortified, my heart beating so violently I must be shaking from it alone.

I look down at the water, then at his wings slowly being pulled through it behind him with every step he takes with that unnerving grace. He stops in front of me, the darkness and the water hiding his lower body from me—that marvel of muscle and power.

A shiver of premonition goes through me when he takes the towel from my hand and carelessly throws it aside before he closes the last distance between us.

The world stops. Only to return faster and clearer than ever when his fingers trace an invisible line over my cheek, over the flowers that might be still there.

I shudder against the touch as his fingers move down to my neck where he bruised me before.

His voice is quiet when he says, "I didn't mean to hold you that hard, Melody."

Melody. My name is like a beautiful song from his mouth. A chant that runs along my skin.

"It doesn't matter."

I know it was the wrong thing to say when he grabs my chin and makes me meet his gaze. "It *does* matter. But sometimes I forget how delicate you are. How vulnerable. How breakable."

I don't know what to say, disarmed by the honesty in his eyes. Instead, I reach out and run my fingers over his wings. They are as incredibly soft under my skin, just as I dreamed them to be, those feathers like silk, so soft and fluffy I want to wrap myself in them.

His eyelids flutter when I stretch up and, ever so gently, run my fingers over them, tracing the mighty muscles of his wing arches under the feathers. He shivers under my touch. When I look at his face again, a golden fire burns in his eyes.

Raw and aching.

When I look around, I find the water has turned into a gleaming, silvery pool of liquid starlight. Black magic spreads in its middle, its inky vines brushing up against me. Above us, I find the same tiny little sparks of silver fire in the air, whirling like snowflakes around curls of shadow light, playing around my cheeks and through my hair like the gentlest of breezes.

I glance back at Caryan's face, only to find his irises again a molten silver, surrounded by darkness, like a star lost in the universe.

"This... you're doing this," I whisper, awestruck. Yet there is a hollow echo of disappointment in my bones I can't deny. That I could even think something so beautiful could be *mine*. Could come from *me*.

"No. This is all you," he says back. When he notices my gaze, he adds, the same admiration I saw before in his face now lying in his voice, "You are the one allowing it to do this. I could not, even if I wanted to."

He stretches his hands out at that, and the silver magic, *my* silver magic, curls around his fingers like a snake, seemingly of its own will, gliding along his fingers and around his wrist, intertwining with his shadows, dancing over his mighty wings.

I put my hand against his, palm against palm, shuddering against the effect of being so close to him. Against that spark deep inside I feel every time he is near. The silvery lights burn even brighter as our bodies touch, as if my skin on his intensifies it.

I say, "But you... your magic triggers it."

"It amplifies it," he corrects darkly and, indeed, my light fades when I pull my hand back, when I'm no longer touching him.

"You will learn to call it on your own," he says.

I glance down at myself, at the slightest shimmer of stardust still glistening over my skin. "Your magic, it's... calling mine," I say, wondering whether this can be true. But I can feel it. I feel *him* everywhere, more acutely than ever, as if a part of him is running along the inside of my veins, dark and velvety, singing and humming.

Darkness, calling light.

He lifts his chin, his irises pitch black, rimmed only by that silver circle.

"As I told you, you and I are unique to this world."

With that he pushes me against the edge, wings splayed wide behind him, making me feel incredibly small. His thumb grazes my lips then, his own lips so close to mine as he whispers, "Tell me what you *want*, Melody, and I will give it to you."

Everything. I want to have *everything*, and yet I'm terrified of it.

I don't say anything when he lifts me, his hands on my butt. I shiver when I feel him hard against my belly, pushing. I spread my legs for him as he runs his hand up my bare thigh. Further and further, pushing the seam of my dress up and slipping past my underwear, his magic like dew and midnight, twining around me, lacing with cascades of stardust that flow out of me.

"Tell me to stop and I will," he whispers against my lips, but I just shake my head.

I gasp when his fingers glide between my legs, and into me, while at the same time he sinks his teeth into my neck. My body starts to melt away from within. From his talented fingers that feel too huge, while I feel too small, too tight. From the overwhelming sensation of him inside me, pushing, sucking, drinking in my very essence. From his hard body against mine, hot and hard under my flat palms. From our entwined magic, burning together through every inch of my body.

It feels elemental.

It's too much, and not enough. My skin is too tight, every part feels raw. Aching.

He pulls back then, his gold and silver eyes never leaving mine as his fingers glide a little deeper. It's more intimate than being touched like that—the way he's looking at me. I arch against him, my nails digging into his flesh as his fingers go even deeper than I thought possible.

I gasp as my thoughts splinter. As I rip apart and shatter.

It feels like a relief and not. It's not enough. It leaves me trembling and strangely empty.

I lower my eyes, self-conscious of what we'd just done. Of what he has done to me and made me do.

My skin still gleams otherworldly. My very blood is still burning, ablaze. I'm suddenly too aware of a part of me that wants more. Wants and wants and wants.

Another is terrified.

I whisper, "Please let me go," into his shoulder.

He keeps me locked against the edge, one hand still around my neck. I startle as I read the same desire in his absurdly silvery eyes when I look up and search them.

Panic floods me, swamps me when he doesn't move. "You promised," I whisper too quietly. "You promised to let me go."

"I promised to stop," he replies sternly, so darkly it makes my blood freeze. "Nothing more."

My innermost being turns into liquid fear so overwhelming it makes me shake in his hands. His eyes have darkened into a beaten gold I'm drowning in.

He won't. Won't let me go. He will make me stay. Will...

"Please don't..." My lips shape the words against his skin. My palms push against his chest as if I could do anything against him. "You said I should tell you what I want—I want to leave. Please."

I've never hated a word more. But it's all I can do.

His fingers loosen from my neck, from my thigh. He lets me go. I don't dare breathe as I slip past him, past his mighty wings that brush against my naked skin like a last caress I barely feel.

As soon as my feet meet the solid ground, my whole body dripping wet, I storm through his living room. The door swings open to let me go, as if already awaiting my departure.

53

RIVEN

Late at night, Riven slips out of the embrace of the naked bodies sprawled all over the floor around him. He collects his clothes from where they tumbled to the ground after he finished with the silver-backed woman and she led him to the ballroom, where the celebrations had taken quite a different turn. Even those acrobatic, magnificent dancers joined the mingling of flesh and lust and lush insobriety.

He trails down the familiar route he could probably find with closed eyes, sleepwalking along the corridor to Caryan's private quarters.

"It is always a pleasure, Lord Riven," the face in the wall greets him before he enters.

The scent of Melody and Caryan hits him in the back of his throat with its intensity. There are so many facets—arousal, blood, desperation—he finds them hard to detangle. It's worry that drives him into the kitchen and on into the bedroom, where Melody's scent is the strongest.

He pauses in the doorway and stares at the ruffled silken sheets, drenched with Caryan's and her irresistible scents.

"She is gone." Caryan's voice sounds from behind him, making him spin around on his heels.

Caryan stands on the terrace, his huge wings stretched out to dry them in the hot wind, the landscape outside entrenched in permanent summer. Fae don't feel cold the way humans do, so Riven supposes the increased heat of late has something to do with Melody. It's turned hotter since she's been here, but maybe it's just in his mind. His wild mind, still drunk from too much sex and fig wine—and there, Caryan's and Melody's scents, lingering on his skin as if part of his own, on his tongue, on his lips.

Abyss, he can taste them there.

"What happened?"

Caryan turns at the rawness in Riven's voice, and what he's no doubt sensing over the bond too. The angel is so breathtakingly beautiful that the sight of him renders Riven speechless. It's so rare to see Caryan with his wings out and only a few have ever seen him for what he truly is and have survived the encounter with the last fallen angel.

"She got drunk and fell asleep," Caryan offers, his voice carrying no emotion at all.

Riven stalks over to the kitchen, to the two empty glasses and the almost empty bottle next to it. He grabs it and pours the rest into one of the glasses, then drinks it in one go to dull the edge his whole self has whetted itself into since last night.

It doesn't help at all that their scents are still riding him a bit hard.

At that very moment, the wind shifts, wafting another wave of arousal mixed with unmistakable fear from the bathroom. A mockery, thrown right into his face.

Riven bares his teeth against it, against what it does to him and his own senses.

It is insane.

Caryan and he have had women together over the years, yet it has never felt this way before. Last night it took all his self-control not to rip Melody's clothes off and take her while Caryan claimed her lips, her mouth, her breasts...

Abyss, her soft skin, her scent, the way she felt under his hands when she came. And the sight of Caryan as he fucked her lips. The way he looked down at her while he did it, his eyes morphing into that gold…

So beautiful. So alluring. So tantalizing. So fatal.

Riven tilts his head back and runs a hand through his hair, trying to ground himself again, to release some of the tension even the orgy couldn't assuage.

In vain.

"Go on. Ask. I can feel it all over you," Caryan demands coolly, his eyes black and reflective like polished onyx flecked with gold, revealing nothing.

"Have you…?" Riven lifts his chin towards the bathroom again, still trying to make sense of what he is smelling. Sex, yes. But the fear and desperation and blood and tears don't match the arousal.

A sudden shudder runs through him. Did Caryan…

No. His instinct tells him that he wouldn't, because so far, Caryan has been uniquely lenient toward her. But then, didn't Riven say himself that Caryan could be cruel? Was cruel before, as was the nature of the angels—their mercilessness? One of the reasons they were hunted down to extinction. Destroyers of worlds, some called them, for their ability to jump from world to world—or to eliminate one for that matter if they deemed it necessary.

Riven has never considered his friend, his brother, to be unnecessarily cruel. But if Melody's effect on Caryan was even a shard of the effect she had on Riven, he might just have taken her against her will.

"There are more interesting things than bedding a mortal girl," Caryan says with a snarl, as if he felt Riven's thoughts.

"I thought… forgive me, Caryan, but…" Riven hesitates, unsure whether pushing would be wise. Hells, their scents make thinking hard. What is wrong with him? But last night changed him in a way he hasn't yet deciphered. Whatever happened, it altered something in his very core, tied his soul to Caryan even tighter, but to Melody too.

"But what?" Caryan's voice cuts through the air.

"I thought she would... mean something to you. Something beyond her heritage," Riven adds.

"Don't be ridiculous." Another snarl, revealing fangs.

"I saw the gold in your eyes when you looked at her last night."

Caryan pivots toward him, pupils flaring, those mighty wings spreading even wider. For a moment, Riven thinks Caryan will come for him. But Caryan's face turns cold. He tucks his wings back in, rolling his shoulders once as if to rid himself of invisible tension before they disappear as if they had never been there.

Even Caryan's tone changes, becoming conciliatory. "Do not fool yourself. It has something to do with the prophecy." He turns back to the city then. "Tell her we're leaving tomorrow to find the first relic. I think she's ready."

Riven starts to speak, but Caryan cuts him off, not yet finished. "I want you to stay here. I'll take Kyrith and Ronin."

Riven keeps his voice solemn. "Why not me?"

"Because I need you here to reign while I'm gone."

He stiffens at the unspoken words. *I need you here to reign... in case I don't return.*

"Caryan—"

"Find her and tell her."

"Please, Caryan—" Riven tries one last time, sudden desperation clawing at him, cutting through all the insobriety.

"Leave me now. I need to prepare for tomorrow."

It's an order wrapped up in a truism, yet there's nothing Riven can do to fight it as Caryan's power forces him out.

Nothing other than obey.

54

MELODY

Riven finds me in my room. He enters, his eyes fastening on me in my soaked dress.

"I want to be alone," I say, hating that my voice is still shaking slightly.

"What happened?" he asks, too gently. It tells me that I must look like a mess.

"Why would you care?" I snap, and his eyes flare open. I glimpse a wave of fury, immediately smothered by *hurt*. Why the hell is he hurt? It was he who kissed me last night. He who... He who behaved tonight as if nothing ever happened. He who spent his evening with another woman. *Or women, for that matter.*

I'd gone back to being a slave, just as I predicted. I knew, yet...

I straighten my shoulders with as much dignity as I can muster. "I thought babysitting was over now that Sarynx is dead. I think you can go."

"I cannot. I have the order to watch you," he counters roughly, his eyes straying from me.

I feel a sting in my heart before it sinks. Watching him, all of a sudden I feel extremely tired. Tired of all the rules of this world. Tired of all the unbendable orders. Tired of people trying to murder me, for fuck's sake. Tired of being controlled, of not being told the truth but only shards and pieces of it. Tired of pity and protection, of my own weakness. Of my own fucking feelings.

"I *want* to be alone," I repeat.

"I am not to leave this room," he retorts unfazed.

I can see that he doesn't like it at all. It hurts.

Finally, he remembers to veil his aura or cares enough to. *Good.* Because I'm tired of that too—of reading everything in other people's auras. I wonder how others go through life when they don't see everything openly. It must be a relief, not to care for once.

"Very well, then make yourself at home," I hiss and I wriggle out of my dress right in front of his eyes. I hold his gaze while I do, while the piece of fabric glides over my breasts and down my belly.

Eventually, he averts his gaze.

I hate how my heart aches when he turns away. Whatever he might have told me before, I'm not beautiful *enough.* Not interesting *enough.*

I try to shake the image of that pixie woman out of my mind and how his hand glided up and down her painted back.

On a snap of his fingers, a chair appears, and he sits down on it. His gaze only returns to me when I'm fully dressed again in my slave attire. *Fitting.*

I slump down onto my bed, my body turned away from his as I curl up under the blanket.

"You're going to leave tomorrow morning." Riven's voice drifts through the room.

"What?" I whip my head to him.

His features are grave, his eyes muted, his achingly beautiful face solemn. If I didn't know better, I'd say he looks torn, his pale fingers curling around the wooden armrests of the chair as if he'd like to strangle it.

"Caryan's going to set out with you tomorrow to hunt for the relics."

"You're not coming with us?" I ask, despite myself.

He shakes his head only once.

I turn away again so he cannot see the tears rising in my eyes.

My heart sinks when I spot Kyrith standing next to Ronin in the corridor to the throne room the next morning. I quickly look away when I hear Caryan striding closer, keeping my head down as I follow them towards the dungeon, then out through a door to the right. There are two cars in a room that looks more like some kind of monster den than a garage, with a black tunnel leading deeper into the bowels of the Fortress. I'm not sure, but I think I catch the scent of carrion wafting over from it. My gaze snaps back to the cars. They're weird-looking cars, but *cars*. Black, sleek, monstrous things.

"Demons," Ronin explains simply, indicating the vehicles.

"Careful, princess, or they'll try to take a bite out of you," Kyrith drawls as he passes me. "They might just like your scent a little bit too much."

If I didn't know they can't lie, I would think they were joking.

I ignore him, though, not keen on another encounter with him. I still don't even dare to look toward Caryan—not after last night— and only briefly glance at Ronin as he opens the car door for me.

I'm glad when Caryan gets in with Kyrith, and Ronin and I take the other car.

We leave the Fortress and the machines—or *demons*—almost fly over the uneven, stony ground with breathtaking speed, soundless as hawks on a hunt.

I find myself looking out the window, surprised that I'm strangely excited to see more of this world. I should probably be terrified, given my last encounter with the worm and all the possible *new* horrors waiting for me, but I'm not. Maybe it's the knowledge that Caryan is here to protect us, or just the power of my curiosity that's getting the better of me.

I haven't seen much, not of the human world nor of this one, and suddenly I long to know more, dangerous or not.

The desert seems to stretch out endlessly. After a while, the hard, rocky ground and stones under us disappear altogether and fade into a red and white ocean of sand meandering in waves into the distance. The car under us seems to shift too, now soaring just above the ground rather than moving on wheels. It drifts along the dunes like a ship going with the tide.

I have the window open. Strange, new smells fill my nose, the warm, arid wind ruffles my and Ronin's hair.

Twice, we pause for a break, only short moments before we go on.

The light eventually shifts into darkness, so I curl up on the huge seat—the interior larger than any car I've ever been in and close my eyes.

🌒 🌘

I wake up when we stop. It's day again, only different. The warm, desert sun has morphed into a silvery light that seems to be reflected by snow-covered mountains rising up far in the distance. When we get out of the cars, I smell the snow of their peaks, the cold arctic and unforgiving like a promise, although it's still warm. I look around to find the desert has vanished, and we are in a strange land of transition. The orange has ebbed out from under us, giving way to a mirthless gray ground where nothing grows.

A soulless stretch of land, as if it belongs to no one and nothing.

They don't tell me anything, and I don't dare to ask, as we leave the cars behind and start to walk. I'm wedged in the middle, Ronin behind me, Caryan leading and Kyrith in front of me, shooting me occasional glances, as if he doesn't trust me. But his hostility towards me is gone, at least for now. I can see as much in his aura. I guess I should be grateful.

Suddenly, I feel a cool prickle over my whole body, as if I've stepped through a curtain of water. And behind it, green grows everywhere, omnipresent and overwhelming. A grassland stretching out so far only the horizon is the limit. There are so many shades of green, I only manage to name a few of them—verdigris, emerald, terre verte, celadon—and others I've never seen.

We make our way through the hip-high grass when I freeze in my tracks. A pristine forest with ancient trees appears out of nowhere, towering up right in front of us. I blink. Hells, it wasn't there seconds ago. The air is now scented with moss and flowers and spicy barks. Huge birds with colorful bills circle above.

We walk straight toward it, yet the closer we get, the more the trees come into focus. They form a kind of wall, the forest a fortress in itself.

I can't detect a way in.

Caryan strides ahead unperturbed, his dark hair whipping in the wind as he steps up to the towering tree line. My eyes widen as some of the highest, oldest trees start to bend slightly as if they're bowing to him. I watch spellbound as Caryan stretches out his pale arm, palms open toward those trees like an offering, and a silver flame springs from his hand.

A spark of *my* magic. *My flame.* I can feel it even from a distance. I remember how his eyes shone silvery the other night as my magic ran through him and his through me. Something he took from me, I can feel it. I can't help the sting of betrayal.

"The light of the moon and the stars. We do remember that light from a time where only ageless darkness ruled." An echoing, eerie voice calls from the forest, booming over the meadow, as if the whole forest is speaking together as one, a sound of power and knowledge thundering over us.

"Then you do remember what vow is bound to that light and bend to it," Caryan answers, his voice strangely magnified so it, too, echoes over the canopy.

The two massive trees bend further down, their barks creaking. I suck in a sharp breath as their branches become like massive whips, ready to be unleashed.

Caryan doesn't retreat an inch. Unfazed. Unruffled.

"We cannot say we welcome your sight, angel," the forest's voice booms again, shaking so menacingly that all the birds disappear and even the wind falls quiet.

"The sentiment is mutual, yet here we are, and I once again remind you of the vow you once took."

"Not to you, Lord of Darkness."

"I am here... and the one who carries the light." Caryan's voice has gained an edge.

The forest's voice sounds once more. "Then tell us, dark angel—are you here as a wanderer of the worlds or as a destroyer of the worlds?"

Destroyer of the worlds. The words reverberate along my body, followed by another rumble of that strange power the forest seems to hold, as if it wants to brush up against Caryan's own. A threat, I realize. The forest is *afraid.*

My heart stutters when Caryan says, "That depends entirely on your answer. I demand free passage. Grant me it, and you can rest assured that I mean no harm."

"Tell us one more thing—what is it that you desire, angel?"

The sound of Caryan's chuckle runs over my skin like ice-water. An eerie sound, cold and arctic. "Oh, at least one thing jumps to mind."

One thing. Only then do I remember that fae can't lie and that this is probably just a clever way to avoid an honest answer. A dark part of me wonders what he's hiding, what he would have said.

"And will you find it in my forest?" the voice demands.

"I don't think so. But enough of this. I ask one last time for leave to pass to the Silver Mountains and then back. For me and my party." Caryan's voice is somber again and ancient, like the forest itself.

"Your party..." the trees echo. Wind comes up, brushing over us. "Ronin the Witcher and Kyrith, the white mountain lion of Palisandre. You will also be allowed to pass freely if you mean no harm." This time the threat in the forest's voice is unmistakable before it dies, only to start anew. "And you—daughter of light and silvery blood, queen of the Kingdom of Two Moons." I swear the gush of wind turns into a gentle breeze that runs through my hair. "We have long yearned to meet you."

Queen? *Of the Kingdom of the Two Moons*—Caryan's kingdom. I flinch. That must be a mistake.

Ronin and Kyrith turn to me, genuine surprise and confusion

shining on their faces, their gazes darting from me to Caryan. Caryan has turned too, his eyes that gleaming amber as he watches me, and unreadable. But he doesn't say anything, so I swallow and say quickly, "I'm no queen."

"Come to me," is all the forest retorts, and a sudden gust of wind pushes me forward.

I walk closer to the edge, to where Caryan stands, careful not to look at him again. The largest and oldest of the trees bends down, one huge branch dangling closer, as if to reach out. When I stretch out my hand, it brushes ever so gently against it—a rustle of velvety foliage against my skin before the massive tree straightens up again. My heart races.

"Remember through shadows and darkness we grow," the forest says, "reaching light through the long night." A final warning.

I gasp as all the trees step aside then, opening a passage between thick columns of silvery bark. I feel Caryan still watching me as he steps forward. I follow after him.

As soon as we enter, the exotic sing-song of birds and frogs envelops us, louder and clearer inside, as if the trees and high canopy contain the jungle's heart melody. We walk on over plush, soft, mossy ground where breathtaking fluorescent flowers bloom.

Caryan doesn't seem to pay any attention to the beauty around us, and I can't shake off the feeling that he's been here before. He's old, he said. So old. *Angel—destroyer of worlds.* The forest was afraid that Caryan had come to harm it.

I watch his strong back under his black shirt, the way he moves so soundlessly and elegantly through the humid thicket. The way the light filters through the leaves and touches his hair, turning it into liquid night.

I tremble as the memory of last night comes crashing through my mind. What he said about my mother. The way he was when he showed me the stars. The sensation of his fingers on my skin, the way they glided up between my legs. His scent and power, engulfing me. Flooding me.

Him, so close.

So unleashed. So… irresistible.

The absurd softness of his magnificent wings. How he shuddered and seemed to hold his breath when I touched them as if *I* was making him feel that way.

How his and my magic—*our* magic—danced with each other in the dark.

You will learn to call it on your own.

My magic… I have magic. That thought still feels surreal. I look at my hands, my white skin that shone silver as his magic thrummed along my core, calling it.

I swallow. He and I together—so beautiful it was heartbreaking. Something that was meant to be, almost impossible to stop once it started, terrifying in its force. Ravishing. Devastating.

A cold shudder licks down my spine, vying with the heat that surges through my veins once more, whether I want it or not.

Hells, last night I was so close to giving in. To surrender to it. To this strange lure. Now that I know what it does, it's even harder to ignore.

I promised to stop. Nothing more. Caryan's serene words cut through my mind. They should rattle me awake. Scare me.

He's cruel. He's dangerous. *Destroyer of the worlds,* that's what the forest called him. I'm nothing but a slave to him. Mean nothing to him. I'm a pastime. A tool.

I saw what he did to his lovers. Did so easily.

And yet, that doesn't prevent me from feeling raw. Feverish and restless.

I let out a breath as something under my skin starts to undulate along my bones. Something that wants out, that wants to be released, to burn and burn and burn, just like that night in Niavara.

I shove it down, down, down, and lock it away.

I let my hair fall into my face while I pray none of their fae senses will detect my shame and arousal. And if they do, hopefully, they'll blame it on something else.

As if the forest has heard my wish, a gentle breeze comes up from the side, wafting my scent past us, and I murmur a quiet thank you to the kind magic.

When I glance back, I find both Kyrith and Ronin looking around, as if they don't trust the paradise around us for a second. Their eyes dart from tree to tree as if, behind every one of them, an enemy squats. For once, they're unusually oblivious to me.

"Is it... dangerous here?" I ask, so quietly I doubt anyone hears.

But Caryan's ears pick it up, although he's walking a good five yards ahead. He answers without turning. "For some."

"Why?"

He pauses then, waiting for me to catch up to him, and I shiver once more when I enter the halo of his scent, his power. Not yet ready for it again.

He steps behind me. "Close your eyes," he orders, and I ignore the prickle under my skin. The deep timbre of his voice. "Now listen. With all your senses."

I do.

"Tell me what you hear. What you *feel*."

His words brush against that fragile spot in me, but I fight them. Instead, I focus on my surroundings. There's a rustle to my left, a silent crack as if someone has stepped on undergrowth, then the faintest rhythm of footsteps further up ahead.

"People. Moving," I whisper. "Hiding."

"Use all your senses," he murmurs against my neck. So close. "What do you smell?"

Him. A storm. The scent of midnight and lightning. "Blossoming flowers. Leaves. Wet bark. And mold."

"*More*," he whispers just like that night in the throne room. And gods help me, but heat flushes my entire system, pooling in my core. "Imagine pulling back layers and see what comes up."

I do and—startle. "Something sweet, like fruit. Salt—no, sweat." I open my eyes and look at him over my shoulder.

He just asks, his clarion eyes on me, "What kind of sweat?"

I try again. "Not elf. More... tart. Smoky maybe, as if they're sitting close to a fire. And something like a river, wet stones, and algae."

I'm surprised by what I've just said. Maybe it's utter nonsense, but Caryan looks down at me and says, "Good. That river smell is typical of nymphs and sirens. The campfire smell is dryads. Nymphs would never go close to a fire, neither would sirens, but dryads cook over blue fire. The tartness tells you that they're tense, so does the salt. They're excited, sweating." He looks toward the trees as if he knows that the people behind them can hear every word he's said.

Then his gaze comes back to me. "You have to train your senses. It can be vital," is all I get before he walks on, and I have to jog to catch up to him.

"Who are they?"

"The folk of the Emerald Forest. Dryads and fauns, a lot of other creatures too," he says, his amber eyes trained on the path ahead again, as if he expects a trap somewhere.

Darkness falls suddenly, like a curtain, the sun no longer blinking through the high canopy, right as we reach a small, milky brook, glistening in the twilight.

"We will spend the night here," Caryan declares.

Kyrith still doesn't seem to feel comfortable, but Ronin is content enough to sit down with his back against a tree, stretching out his long legs, allowing a sigh to escape from his throat. Only then do I realize that none of them has slept.

My stomach growls, reminding me that I haven't eaten a thing in hours. I ignore it and choose a mossy spot to curl up, turning away from the others.

MELODY

I wake up with small, cool, sticky fingers in my hair, on my face, and on the bare skin of my arms. Huge, round turquoise eyes blink back at me before a slick finger wanders against my lips. Behind this creature—female, I think—another one squats, gesturing for me to get up. Then those bluish and webbed hands grab mine and guide me along the brook, along another path that must have just opened up because it wasn't there when I fell asleep.

When I cast a glance back, I see all three of the fae lords sleeping so soundly, not one stirs. I wonder whether the forest emanates some magic to make them sleep so deeply. My eyes rest on Caryan a moment too long. But seeing him so unguarded…

They tug at my sleeves and usher me on.

As soon as we are far enough away, the tiny little women start to giggle and pull me, more impatiently now, up to a clearing in the forest, where white moonlight meets the shimmering surface of a steaming pool.

The creatures dig at my clothes like Nidaw's sirens, and I allow them to undress me and lead me into the water. The women or not-women—I'm not too sure since they don't look too human—are naked themselves and seemingly unbothered by it. They reach almost up to my hips, but their bodies look like mine, with breasts and bellies, only their lower part is sleek like a frog's, and small, round horns sprout out of their heads. Their eyes are larger, too, their lips full, and rows of tiny, sharp siren teeth shine at me when they smile.

When I glance up, I meet more eyes gleaming green in the dark. Emerald-skinned women my size, with hair in all sorts of impossible colors and graceful gazelle horns sprouting from the midst of it, step out, pearls and twigs braided into the strands. They're also naked, save for bows and arrows around their backs.

They glare at me curiously and bow when a pale woman steps out of the dark after them. She has long, wavy, white hair that falls around her lush, curvaceous body, reaching down to her ankles. She glides into the water so she sits opposite me, her hair floating like white seaweed in the stream, matching the strange whiteness of her eyes.

White horns spiraling like those of a kudu, but only half the length, protrude from her head, beautifully curved and coming to a sharp end. A circlet of gold, wild vines, peonies, and pearls rests around them, completing a regal and frightening image.

"Soak yourself. This is healing water from the holy springs. It will wash away a lot of things. It will also leave you rested and well." Her voice is clear as a bell, her words tinged by the slightest hint of a hiss. "I'm Calianthe, queen of the Emerald Forest," she explains before I can thank her or ask who she is. "And those are my daughters."

She gestures to the green-skinned women, some of whom have brought food and a goblet made of stone that holds some water with herbs in it, which they lay gently next to me on a flat stone.

"Eat," the queen orders.

I'm too hungry and thirsty to care whether I'm being rude, so I grab the goblet and down it, then take a fruit similar to a fig, the flesh so ripe and sweet it drips over my chin like honey when I take a bite.

I swallow, then ask, "Why are you so kind to me?"

"Your soul is tied to someone dear to me. Your paths will cross."

"Who?" I ask carefully, not sure what to do with this information.

Calianthe glides closer to me, so close her long hair brushes against me underwater like smooth, slick tendrils of kelp. "She was the one who changed the course of fate, Melody. You should have been her daughter. A daughter of light as you are."

"Pardon? I'm not sure I understand."

"We do not only believe in blood, but in the stars too. In the bonds that are written in the stars, you still are hers, only she didn't bear you into this world."

Calianthe lifts a pale hand out of the water and another stony goblet appears in it, filled with the same liquid as before. She holds it out to me. "Drink. You need it."

"Thank you," I mumble shyly.

A few of the little, blue-skinned women step closer and put a crown of fluorescent flowers on my head. I mumble another thank you, and they jump away, giggling.

"How do you know about the bonds? About fate?" I ask after I've emptied the new goblet too.

"We do know parts. There are some of us gifted with the eye. Seers, as we call them," the beautiful queen answers.

"And how—how can you alter fate?"

Calianthe looks down at the water, then back at me, but the softness in her stunning eyes has given way to sorrow. "You can't always but remember—it's all about choice. I need to leave you now. Just don't forget that, when you're lost in the darkness, the darkness is a part of you too—" She seems to hesitate, as if struggling with herself. "Your fate might have changed that day, young one, but it still might change ours too. It all depends."

"Depends on what?" I ask, suddenly impatient. I'm fed up with all these cryptic hints and warnings.

She frowns at my tone before she catches herself and the perfect planes of her face smooth out again. Her pale eyes focus on mine with new intensity. "We cannot exist in total darkness. Your mother knew that too. She came here to search for the same thing you're looking for now. One of the three relics that is hidden here."

"She wanted the flute?"

"She wanted to *destroy* the flute," Calianthe hisses. "It corrupts the body and soul with darkness."

I swallow. "And why didn't my mother find it?"

"Because *he* came, and she fled," the queen whispers with a glance behind me.

Before I can ask more questions, she vanishes. One moment she is there, the next she's gone, together with everyone else. Only the fruits on the stone are still there, glistening in their syrup.

A rustle behind me startles me. When I turn, I find Caryan between the trees, his eyes black as the forest without the moon. I know I only heard him because he let me.

He looks at the flower crown on my head, then at the fruit, but says nothing.

I glide away from him, to where the queen sat, as he steps up to the spring. He seems to sense my fear and pauses at the edge, his face unreadable.

I glance down at the tattoo on my wrist. "What you want me to find... I can't... I can't feel it," I admit. I'd been too afraid to voice it, but he'd find out sooner or later. "It's never been that way before."

He squats down, touching the water with one hand, and I watch the tattoo on his skin slithering down as if it wants to touch the water too. He keeps his hand there, and I feel his magic mingling with the magic in the spring, his body drawing from it, while he looks back at me.

I don't realize I'm holding my breath until he says, "The elves wove a spell around the relics before they hid them away. You have to get close in order to feel them."

I allow myself a shudder of relief. "My mother searched for it," I say then.

His eyes flicker, but he retorts, "She did."

"And then you came, and she ran."

"The queen talks too much," he observes darkly.

"How did she know where to look for it if she didn't have my talent?"

"She found a book," he says.

"Where is it now?"

"She destroyed it."

This makes me pause. "She... my mother didn't want you to find them, the relics, did she?"

His eyes are blacker than ever when he finally says, "She most certainly didn't."

The words hang between us. He closes his eyes and retracts his hand out of the water, clenching his teeth as if he's suddenly in pain without the soothing magic of the spring.

I want to probe further, but an image hits me so hard I'd have stumbled if I wasn't drifting in the water. I see a woman with a heavy black sword in her hand, silvery flames dancing along its blade as she plunges it into Caryan's body, before drawing it up, tearing through his belly, splitting his ribcage right up to his heart...

What the hell? Where did that come from?

"My mother... she did that to you. Your scar," I whisper, suddenly sick and breathless.

Caryan opens his eyes again, and I'm surprised that they're now holding the pale blue color of the spring. Surprised at the cool way he says, "Yes. She did."

"She... she *tried to cut you in half.*" The scar I saw, the maimed runes. My voice breaks. I'm still trying to get that image out of my mind. Still trying to somehow wrap my head around the unspeakable violence.

But I can't.

"Maybe she should have, to see whether it would have killed me," he answers. The serenity in his words alarms me. *He means it. Means it with his whole being.* I feel it somewhere deep inside me, along with a jolt of seeping, agonizing pain that isn't in me and at the same time is.

"You—you are hurt," I say, my eyes instinctively searching for a wound that's causing his pain, but I find none.

He frowns at me before he puts his hand back into the water, the pain I just felt subsiding instantly.

"The runes. The destroyed runes on your body," I gather, the knowledge suddenly there, just like that gory scene before. *He's in constant pain because of my own mother.*

"Yes. They never heal. Even the healer couldn't restore them because they are old. Older than I am."

He looks tired as he says the words, and I sense the burden of his endless existence like a dead weight on my shoulders. Along with the searing pain he carries constantly, I realize, an echo of it still reverberating in my own body.

"This water soothes it," I whisper.

He frowns again, irritated, before he relents. "Yes."

"It's the same water that..." I can't bring myself to say it after last night, so he does it for me.

"The same water that runs through my court, yes. It's water from the seven rivers, laden with healing magic."

Suddenly, I'm aware that the only reason he doesn't come in is that I'm there. "You can... you can come in," I say quietly. "I'll get out."

"It's alright," he says.

I get up anyway, ignoring every instinct to cover myself when I step out of the water naked. He doesn't look at me, though, keeping his gaze politely away to give me privacy until I've wriggled wet into my clothes. I want to walk back to the others to give him some space in return, but suddenly the idea of being alone with Kyrith and Ronin doesn't feel too appealing, so I settle down on the stone next to the fruit.

"You want one?" I ask, offering a piece to him.

"Eat. You need it."

"You do eat, don't you? Generally, I mean. You have a kitchen." The words tumble out before I can take them back. *Apart from drinking blood,* I want to add but don't.

466

"We do, but we can go for a long time without food," he says, but gods damn me if he isn't looking at me with a sudden hunger that startles my heart into an uneven beat. It reminds me of the voracity of a predator.

But it's gone in a heartbeat, and his face shifts back into its usual, bored austerity.

My heart still races, though, as I look down at my hands.

I shove the piece of fruit into my mouth, looking away as he strips down, only looking back when I hear him sliding into the pool. And hells, I know it's wrong, but I can't resist. Can't resist seeing him, seeing more of that body the water hid from me that night, as if it's a secret I crave to learn about, despite every better judgment.

I want to see more of that tattoo that's much larger than the tiny tails I saw running over his fingers and wrists when he touched the water. There's no denying that it's marvelous. There are so many symbols shifting and intermingling, gold and black, it's hard to make out a single one, especially from a distance.

And the rest of him…

My mouth goes dry. The rest of him is utterly beautiful too. I can't help but stare, admire the defined muscles of his too-perfect body, no doubt honed by hundreds of years of fighting.

The sight of his naked skin changes me all over. Violently. He's a pure angel, his absurd beauty a brute force of nature, hitting me in the back of my throat.

He catches me looking.

I feel myself blushing deeply. "I'm sorry," I murmur and quickly look away, but the aftertaste stays, humming in my blood like a burning longing. A longing for what we did and didn't do in that hot water. To distract myself I ask, "Where do we go from here?" I don't dare to look at him again, afraid of what I'll find in his eyes, what he will find in mine.

"We will try to get closer."

"Closer to where?"

"You tell me," he retorts, unperturbed. So sure of me I blush all over.

But this sense of surety seems to spark something in me, because suddenly, the image of that flute fills my mind again. This time it comes into clearer focus, and I can make out details. It's frozen by eternities of snow, surrounded by relentless storms.

Instinctively, I turn my head to the mountains I glimpsed in the distance. "It's on one of the mountains. Buried under a glacier," I say, knowing in my blood it's true. As true as if I placed the flute there myself, the relentless ever-cold shielding it from being tracked down, the Emerald Forest like another ring, isolating it. "Someone was very careful to hide it away from the world."

"Clearly," he agrees. For a moment, we just look at each other. His eyes are dangerous though.

"Why did my mother not want you to have the relics?"

"Maybe she wanted them for herself," he offers. I watch him very closely. His aura is veiled behind that mist again.

"Why?" I ask to test him.

"Because this is what power-hungry people want—more power. Your mother, as you already know, was a very ambitious woman."

I freeze. His face is still blank as he delivers the twisted truth.

"You said if I wanted truths you would give them to me," I whisper, more hurt, more betrayed than I should feel. "Calianthe said my mother wanted to destroy the flute. So *no one* could have it."

"The truth has many faces, Melody," he retorts, not at all surprised that the relic is a flute. So he knew this already. "But did she really? Want to destroy the flute—so no one else could have it?"

"She couldn't lie, could she?" I ask.

"No. But in order to consume the flute's magic, she would have had to destroy the flute indeed. In one way or the other."

"Calianthe said the magic corrupts the mind and soul with darkness."

His eyes flash. "It's *stolen* magic. Impossibly powerful, stolen magic. Of course, it corrupts anyone who's not its owner. Anyone who wasn't made to hold so much."

I startle. "Stolen… I thought the high elves bound their magic to the artifacts. Out of their free will."

He just looks down at the water, his eyes reflecting its milky surface like a mirror.

"So you would allow the magic to corrupt you? What does it mean? That it drives you mad? Or kills you?"

He lifts his head, but he doesn't answer me. I scrutinize his face. It's so dangerously blank. There's so much he's not telling me. I feel it. *Know it.* Know it from a dark thing shimmering inside me, black and velvety and streaked with starlight. Something like a ribbon of pure night. Before I know what I'm doing, I yank at it.

And tumble.

Something in me opens up then. A connection. A door to another world through which I just slipped. Purest night engulfs me, dewy on my skin. *What is this?*

I take another step in and a heavy weight settles on me, in me, old and archaic the further I probe into the foreign blackness. A weight amplified by the thousands of years that lay on my shoulders, so strong it takes everything to fight it.

What is this?

I'm still trying to get to this *feeling* I can sense, hidden within all this darkness that threatens to pull me down, consume me, suffocate me. Crush me. It gets worse the more I fight it. Yet I keep probing further into the darkness, trying to reach for the silver light that shimmers on the horizon like the evening star. But every time I'm close, it seems to slip away again, just out of reach. As if it's not ready to be seen, acknowledged, recognized yet.

I shake my head, then realize that, to get to its core—to the darkness's black heart—I must immerse myself in it first. To understand it, grasp it, face it.

Without another thought, I plunge in, headfirst, and down. The darkness changes then. It turns into an abyss, vast and endless. It gently pulls me along when I let it, when I no longer fight it.

The blackness starts whispering to me then, whispering its secrets.

Desperation. Heaviness. Years and years and years passing by. I can make out blurred scenes, faces, people, voices.

"Stop it!" Caryan's voice is like a slash laced with ice, somewhere, cutting through all of it.

I startle, meeting his gaze, wide-eyed, as he growls in a way that makes every instinct in me scream.

"Whatever it is you are doing, let it go. This is not your mind."

Not your mind.

As if on cue, walls of adamantine onyx slam down in front of me, a black phantom wind pushing me out of that black sea. I'm hurled ashore, the brute force of it so strong, so powerful, I briefly sway like before, or would if I were standing.

The blackness still hums through me, though—fatigue. Exhaustion. Bone-grinding, never-ending weariness that permeates everything, only fought off and kept at bay by cast-iron will. But glimmering within it, there's still that silver star I glimpsed, the only guiding lantern in this ocean of blackness.

A rush of water tells me that Caryan has left the pool. When I glance at him, he's already wearing his clothes again, his hair perfectly dry. I'm still on the ground, still waiting for those dark feelings to ebb out of me. Still shaking, I realize.

When he steps in front of me, I ask, "What... what was that?"

"Nothing pretty."

I look up at him, my eyes trained on his as I get up. All warmth has leaked out of his expression.

"I saw that. But what was it?" My voice is sharp.

He licks his teeth, his upper lip curling slightly back. "Let it go."

"No. You said *not your mind.* It was *your* mind," I blaze on, the truth hitting me while the words tumble out. I had been *in* his mind. Is that part of my talent too? To be able to flit into his mind? It scares me.

"You keep overstepping boundaries. You've continued to push your luck since the moment you came here." He bares his teeth now, those frightening fangs.

I don't retreat an inch. "Well, you probably should have put a lid on it from the very start. It's a bit too late now. And if you didn't like me in there, why didn't you kick me out straight away? I didn't ask for it. I didn't ask to be... *sucked* into your mind, to see all that terrifying, never-ending blackness." My words come out breathless. Suffocated. Directly into his face, that is now mere inches away.

A black flame springs to life in his eyes then. His voice is lethally calm when he says, "Do you think I liked it? Being torn from sleep by witnessing your panic and diffuse fear night after night? Wading through this... necropolis of your feelings day after day, year after year? When I wasn't able to distinguish your recalled pain from a real threat, or whether it was just your nightmares again."

I have no words for what he just told me. He has been in my mind. For *years*.

Not just when he drank my blood. He... for *years*...

"Why...why didn't you lock me out if you hated it so much?" I try to sound angry but fail. If anything, I sound broken and miserable. Hurt. Embarrassed. Lost.

"Because I—" He starts, but catches himself, the words reverberating in me anyway, as if his mind continues to speak to me. *Because I didn't want to.*

Instead, teeth flashing with every word, he says, "Because that is not how *this* works."

"What do you mean by *this*?"

"This conversation is over," he growls back.

He turns when I grab his wrist. He stares at my hand on him, then back at me.

I know he could just pull free, send me stumbling, but he doesn't. Instead a growl works its way up his throat, so menacing it takes all my will not to flinch. To run. His eyes are a black wildfire, his lips are fully pulled back from his teeth now, but I don't let go. I flash mine right back, ready to rip into his flesh.

As if he could read my mind he seethes, "I dare you!" His eyes glitter dangerously.

"It is you who wants something from me. Tell me what *this* is. Why? How is this possible? How could you *see*... me?"

"You think you have a choice." He laughs, but there is no humor in the sound. "Do you really still believe that I need to be polite and ask? I could force you to reveal the location, break you, and leave you shattered when I'm done. It wouldn't even take much. I see it all over you, in your eyes. You are so tender a breeze startles you."

Every single word feels like the stab of a knife plunging into my soul. He leans closer, towering over me, speaking right into me, his breath mingling with mine, brushing my lips.

"Then why not just get it over with? Why bother?"

I try to ignore his dark power gathering around me, swirling and pulsing like a dark storm. My own magic is cowering and frightened.

"You would be useless to me broken. And you were too many nights on the brink already." He says it ravenously, cruelly, his eyes on my lips.

"Why do you know that?" I push. My eyes are searching his for *anything*. Warmth. Truth. Malice.

"A bond, born into our bones," he spits as if the sheer words disgust him.

A *bond*. I don't know what to do with this information. What to feel. "But... why? What kind of bond?"

"Oh no, it is your turn. You're going to lead me to the flute. *Now*."

"No. It's dangerous," I say, ignoring his magic sizzling through the air around us. But that artifact is suddenly *whispering* to me, right into my heart. A warning. It's warning me about its cataclysmic magic, its sinister nature. Its unholy power.

"I will not ask again," Caryan says.

I feel the last string of his patience snapping. I make myself look at him regardless. He's gone utterly still, only his power licks along my skin like hungry flames.

"Its magic," I say, "is not from this world." I shake my head, retreating as the flute keeps whispering to me in its foreign yet familiar tongue, clearer now that I'm close to it. "It might kill you. It should be destroyed."

"Careful. I might just have the same thought about you." At that, he turns on his heels and walks away.

"It says that only death is waiting up there, Caryan!" I call after him, my voice coming more desperate than ever.

At the sound of his name, he pauses and turns to look at me.

"Oh, I've been waiting to meet death for a long time," he says. And I shudder at the bottomless pitch that yawns in his eyes. A reflection of what I just waded through. An ageless dark. "Let's see what it has to say."

On that, he strides away.

56

MELODY

As we march on through the forest, Kyrith complains several times about food. I can't shake the feeling that he's glancing frequently in my direction, as if I'm the answer to his hunger.

I try to watch my steps. The forest has turned into a treacherous swamp, and it has become hard to find solid ground and not sink knee-deep into the insidious bog. Dead trees thrust upward on stretches of solid grassy land in between, cutting through the veil of mist like spears. Silence coats everything like a heavy blanket.

It's as if the green paradise from hours before has been eradicated. Even the frogs have gone still a long while ago. Nothing lives here. Well, nothing *good*, because I can feel a sinister presence hovering close, can smell death and decay. As we probe on, I can't fight the dawning sensation that it's been purposely made that way—dangerous and deadly—for all who want to cross. And that the only reason we don't find our end here is because of Queen Calianthe, who fears Caryan's wrath.

My eyes snare on a piece of blanched wood that protrudes out of the soil, and a cold shudder rakes through me. Not wood... *bone.* A human-like ribcage.

The silence grows even more oppressive, doing nothing to distract me from the gaping void in my very being, where just a few hours before there was that connection to Caryan's mind. Only with it severed do I realize that it has always been there. Something dark and velvety, laced deep with my soul, buried in my very core. When I reach out to it now, those walls are still locked into place. Cold.

A bond…

A bond. We share a *bond*.

I still can't wrap my head around that.

But whatever it does, with it suddenly blocked, all that's left in its wake is my own aching heart and a sudden heaviness in my bones. As if, without it, a part of me is as good as dead. Just like this swamp.

I don't know why all that darkness I saw in his mind affects me so much either. Why it makes breathing difficult. And all those things he said to me before. *Do you think I liked it? Being torn from sleep by witnessing your panic and diffuse fear night after night? Wading through this… necropolis of your feelings day after day, year after year. When I wasn't able to distinguish your recalled pain from a real threat, or whether it was just your nightmares again.*

How could he know? How is that possible? How could he *feel* me, even in a different world? For years?

As we go on, my body grows heavier and heavier, my steps slower. Sluggish. Sweat runs down my body in rivulets, and my clothes are drenched from the unrelenting heat and humidity so thick you could cut it with a knife.

Caryan's set an unforgiving pace. Ronin and Kyrith seem to have no trouble matching it. And I try to keep up as well as I can, yet I become tired, my half-human body exhausted. Drained. My throat aches from thirst and my head is dizzy.

In the early afternoon, the swamp suddenly ends, the dead trees reaching up like a rampart, pieces of bones thrown in between, their peaks sharp like teeth, forming a kind of fence. In its middle, a gate appears rippling out of nothing.

We step through.

Before me, a rough meadow stretches out towards roiling, grassless hills, a thin path cutting through them like a scar, leading up to the mountains.

"We should pause here," Ronin says. It's the first time I've heard him speak since we left the Fortress.

Caryan shakes his head. "No. We will go on and set up camp further up."

"But… we need rest," Ronin says with a significant glance toward me.

Suddenly, I know the witcher's asking Caryan on my behalf, as if he can sense the exhaustion in me. There is no denying that I'm tired to my very core. Over the last two hours, Caryan has set an even more brutal pace, and after we crossed that bog I more or less stumbled along rather than walked. It touches me… that Ronin cares.

"We don't," Caryan cuts him off.

"But—"

Caryan whips to him, fangs bared. "You heard me."

Ronin nods once, clenching his teeth. Kyrith snarls quietly but doesn't say anything either.

The hike up takes forever. I drag myself along, up and up until my feet hurt and I'm so tired that I feel like I'm sleepwalking. A dense, strange fog has come up, cold and eerie, as if it wants to suffocate us. Voices and laughter cut through it like ghosts. I stagger a few times, my steps becoming heavier and heavier the further we climb. On one occasion, Ronin catches me before I can hit the hard ground. Caryan only turns once before he walks on.

The next time I stumble, I barely manage to get back up, my legs and arms are feeling that weak. The cold fog feels like it's creeping under my skin, draining the life out of me. Deep down, I know it's not natural. It makes me slow, so slow and dizzy.

Death. This is the death the flute warned me about. Not Caryan's but—

My death.

I stumble one more time and then darkness envelops me.

BLAIR

Blair has summoned her phantom wyvern, holding on to its barbed skin and glimmering rainbow scales while she circles the landscape at the border to Caryan's lands, where the wall of his wards is thinnest. The only downside of wards—they can only span over so much distance before they weaken. Blair could risk flying through the curtain of his magic and probably come away more or less unharmed.

But she doesn't want to.

He would instantly know about it.

She sighs and banks left as she, Aurora, and Sofya keep patrolling along the edges of the Emerald Forest. But its canopy is so thick they can sense nothing. This damn forest is like a shield, impossible to tell who prowls through it.

But Caryan isn't what Blair's looking for, even if her mothers believe it is what they are doing day in and day out. Why they have traveled these circles for the whole of last week—flying over and over above the trees until Blair's limbs were so stiff from cold and exhaustion she could barely move when they finally returned to the inn at the crossroads. The inn is the only place you can get a bed and decent food, that connects the harbor—the doorway to the elven kingdom of Palisandre in the east; Avandal, the city of the healers in the north; and Niavara in the south. A strange patch of land that

Calianthe, the queen of the Emerald Forest, granted Caryan back then to make it possible to travel by foot or horse from his kingdom to Avandal.

Before, you could only reach Avandal by ship, or you had to cross Calianthe's forest, full of her murderous dryads, monstrous flesh-eating trees, and other creatures Blair isn't sure anyone has ever seen and left the forest alive to talk about.

But then—the myths must come from somewhere, right?

What Calianthe received from Caryan in return, Blair has no idea. But Calinathe's cruelty and cunning easily match Caryan's own, so Blair figures Caryan must have given her something that would amplify her power.

No, in truth, Blair's looking for that spot marked on the blacksmith's map. She studied it over and over every night, when her mothers were already safe and sound asleep. She's looking for that godsdamn marker. The place of power.

Hells, she has no intention of ever going against Caryan. Certainly not with her mothers in tow. They would be dead in an instant. No, she has a different plan.

Blair takes one last turn on her wyvern before she signals the other two witches to veer and follow her back to the inn. It's so fucking cold up here, and Blair craves some spiced beer and a fire to warm her boots.

But halfway, she suddenly spurs her wyvern into a sharp descent.

There it is, finally, the crossing of three tiny brooks that she's been searching for all this time. The marker on her map. Finally. There, beneath the fog.

Her wyvern's claws touch the lush, high grass, her huge wings still spread, ready to take off any second. Blair slides down, and her mount pushes herself protectively between her and the forest, her massive head rearing to throw a vigilant glance towards the wall-like trees to their right. A breeze comes up in answer. A warning.

The air down here is treacherously soft, caressing, so much

warmer than up there, filled with the foreign fragrances of the forest. *Dangerous* fragrances, Blair corrects herself.

"I know, I don't like it here either," Blair admits as her wyvern gives a warning screech.

"What is this about, Blair?" Aurora's wyvern touches the ground nearby. Her mother jumps from her bluish wyvern—Vyren—and comes walking towards Blair, her gaze also trained on the forest, as if she expects an arrow to fly at them at any second.

Sofya, on her prickly, grayish hell of a beast—Tharox—follows last. Yes, well, her mothers named their half-solid mounts. It seems that Blair's the only one who could never bring herself to name her wyvern. *Never get too attached.* Her credo. That's probably why she never did. As if her wyvern felt her thoughts, she roars again but Blair ignores her.

With another grounding, deep breath she faces her mothers, pulling the crumpled map from her saddlebag. Her faeish heart suddenly beats unusually fast and her hands tremble when she says, "We can leave the fae world. Here." She taps a silver nail on the three lines painted on the map, running like veins through the landscape, only to join right here, the drawing in the map resembling a star. "It's a place of power. Three tiny arms of the healing springs from Avandal. It should be enough for us to open a portal to the human world—"

"We cannot, Blair. We should return to the inn," Aurora cuts her off sharply.

Blair's face falls, and her stomach tightens from an unknown terror. "We *have* to leave. We can just go. Leave this all behind us. You would like it there. There's so much to see."

Aurora's beautiful face stays hard. Blair's gaze darts to Sofya in a silent plea. But only sorrow and regret shine on her mother's stunning face. Sofya will always do what Aurora says, no matter whether Blair is their leader.

Blair's heart sinks, back down, down, down into that bottomless pit. "We will die if we don't leave," she pleads, her voice trembling with all the desperation that haunts her every night, every day, every breathing second, for fuck's sake.

"We are to find the girl," Aurora counters sternly.

"Fuck that girl. We can just leave. We can have a life. A *real* life. Do you know how that feels?" Blair asks.

Aurora steps up to her, and Blair closes her eyes as her mother's still-cool hand rests on her cheek. Part of her expected a slap, yet her mothers have never hurt her in any way. Not then, not now.

"My beautiful witchling, we cannot. This is bigger than us." Her mother's voice is as gentle as it was when she sometimes sang to Blair at night, when Blair was still a child and couldn't sleep. She hasn't heard that voice in a long time. "You have a responsibility, Blair. One you cannot just turn your back on."

"The Abyss knows we're entitled to our freedom," Blair says, her eyes flying open, her teeth clenched.

"There's a reason you were brought to Caryan, Blair. A reason for all that pain. I know it. All your suffering, it was not for nothing."

Blair can feel her stomach bottom out. *They knew. They always knew.*

"Who told you?" she hisses.

"Oh darling, no one. Everyone could see the way you looked at him."

"It's because of that *fling* that Perenilla says I committed treason," Blair grinds out.

She expects Aurora to be disgusted. To step back, or hurt her finally, for the first time. Take it out on her,

But her mother's face stays unbearably soft, so understanding Blair feels something in her cracking open to bleed all over.

"Then find a way out, Blair. I know fate brought you to him and to that girl. I know that you're meant for something else. Something *more*."

"To be queen," Blair spits, but her mother shakes her head.

"No. You are meant for more than even this. You are meant to change the world. You have a bond with that girl, I can feel it. There is a reason for everything, Blair. A reason you never brought her here. You cannot deliver her up to Perenilla."

"You and Sofya will die if I don't bring her to Perenilla." Blair's eyes fill with all the unshed tears she's been saving. But they just well up there and do not fall. Not here. Not in the fae world. That she's able to produce tears in the first place should scare her, because no fae can.

"Then so will it be, if this is our fate," Aurora says, so easily Blair wants to grab her and shake some sense into her.

Again, her eyes go to Sofya, looking for support, but the blonde witch just watches silently.

"You will find a way, Blair. You always found a way. And I know that this is not the end. Not for us, not for you," Aurora says.

"You cannot know that," Blair seethes with sudden fury.

"Yes, my beautiful darling. I can *feel* it. Our time has not yet come. Find a way and let us no longer speak about it."

With that, Aurora pulls her hand back. But the echo of her warmth stays, even when Blair stalks back to her wyvern. The creature is restless, snapping the air with her vicious teeth as they soar higher and higher, until Blair can make herself believe it's just the wind stinging in her eyes and nothing else.

An hour later, they open the battered door of the inn, entering the dimly lit room. The smell of food and fire fills the warm air, welcoming their stiff bones. Blair and her mothers are wearing strong magic on their bodies to camouflage themselves as simple elves, hiding from the crowd with their combat clothes and their daggers and swords. Not to mention their innate weapons—silver nails and canines. It would wreak havoc if witches showed up here, outside of their territory. Blair, Aurora, and Sofya would have to kill every guest at the inn.

A prospect Blair wouldn't have minded only a year ago.

But since she's been to the human world, she's changed. She knows it, but she isn't ready to tell Aurora or Sofya that much. Not when it won't matter anyway.

Not after what just happened.

She quietly nurses her beer, tucked in a dark corner of the shady inn, boots close to the fire.

"I kept my ears open. No trace of elves or a witcher, for that matter," Sofya says, the blonde beauty putting a plate laden with a heavy piece of what looks and smells deliciously like roasted piglet in the middle of the table, interrupting Blair's brooding.

Her fair-haired mother pretends they are still set on doing Perenilla's bidding. Aurora too meant what she said—both of them behave like nothing ever happened and will continue to do so until their last breath. Well, trust her mothers when they decide on something.

Fine, they can have it their way. But Blair isn't fine. Not even close. They know. They are ready to die, for fuck's sake. For this world, for her fucking mistakes.

They fucking refused to come with her to safety.

"Word would have spread if someone spotted them." Aurora hums her agreement, as if they were talking about the fucking weather in fucking Palisandre. Both witches just joined Blair at her table as if it were theirs. Aurora takes out her hunting knife and starts to elegantly cut off a neat piece of juicy meat. Aurora always reminds Blair of a high elf, the way she carries herself, speaks, and even eats.

"Still not hungry?" she asks, her groomed eyebrows raising at Blair.

Blair gives an animalistic snarl as an answer, huddling deeper into her corner.

"I've never known her to be so quiet," Aurora says to Sofya as she puts a delicious-looking piece of roasted piglet into her mouth with a fork.

"I've never known her not to be hungry," Sofya replies, tearing off a huge piece of meat with her fingers and nails and stuffing it into her mouth, unbothered by the pink meat juice dripping over her elegant chin.

It has always been like this—Aurora the lady, while Sofya and

Blair ripped into the meat with their nails and teeth like animals, and Aurora playfully chiding them for their lack of etiquette.

It is so engrained into Blair she almost waits for it to happen.

But her mothers continue to eat in silence. Blair can't help but watch the large piece of meat disappearing too quickly in front of her eyes and her empty stomach. The smell of it makes her mouth water and her belly twists with hunger. Fuck witches and their appetites.

Blair reaches out and slices off a fat-dripping piece, her nails going through it like a knife through warm butter.

Sofya's shrill laughter fills the room. "I knew it."

Blair cuts her a sharp glance but goes for another chunk of meat. She might be brooding, but she is also starved.

"You are brutes," Aurora sighs theatrically.

Blair bares her teeth at both of them, Sofya flashing her an innocent grin in return.

Aurora says, "At least you *could* do better, Blair. It's not like I didn't try to teach you *some* manners." *There we go.*

"That would imply that I *want* to do better," Blair retorts dryly, struggling to keep a treacherous smile from her face despite her anger.

"If it were up to you, Aurora, Blair would run around with a patrician countenance, demanding powdered pearls and kelpie-caviar." Sofya swipes to her aid, ruffling Blair's hair before she plucks another piece of meat from the bone.

Aurora rolls her eyes in playful annoyance. "Good then that you taught her how to roll in the dirt to camouflage her scent."

"I like to think that I balanced all those lessons in decorum and grace. And—that was definitely one of her favorites. I remember how she came home one day, covered from head to toe in boar shit," Sofya says, a vicious smile on her face at the memory of it. "And how she screamed like a skewered pig because you put her straight into the bathtub and scrubbed it off."

"I didn't scream like a skewered pig," Blair mutters under her breath.

"Oh yes, you did. It took forever to get it out of your hair. We used up all the lavender soap," Aurora reminds her sourly, crossing her trained arms.

"Oh, that precious lavender soap. Aurora will never forgive you this, Blair."

Blair grumbles, "Soap's overrated anyway."

But the witches no longer listen. When Blair looks up, she catches Sofya and Aurora sharing a long, warm look. Lost in memories. Blair tries to swallow the lump in her stomach, heavy as lead and burning like acid. How she missed this—moments like this, just the three of them being together like a normal family. As they had been back then in that hut in the woods where they'd lived when Blair was still a child. Before they had to return to Gatilla's court.

"What about another round of ale to patch things up?" Blair asks. Not expecting an answer, she gets up to fetch some more honey-sweetened and cinnamon-spiced beer. A handful of moments later she returns, putting the three jugs on the table before she slides back onto the bench.

Aurora and Sofya seem to have finished eating, so she helps herself to the bone, sucking the meat off it before cracking it open.

"I remember it took three baths a day for a week to get the scent off her and out of that hut," Aurora adds with a sigh, picking up the conversation after taking a hearty swallow of her ale.

"I was so proud. No one could smell me," Blair retorts, still chewing.

"No, Blair. Because you were a moving pile of feces," Aurora chides.

"Old gods help me, I still remember that dwarf walking past her on that market one day and muttering that she smelled like an arsewipe," Sofya burst out, laughing so hard she barely gets the words out. Almost spitting her ale all over the table.

Blair joins in and both sit there, tears running down their cheeks from laughing so hard. When Blair almost slides off the bench, even Aurora can't hold back her smile.

Blair tries to memorize their faces then. Every line and expression, frozen in smiles, their eyes glistening.

How long had it been since they laughed like this? Bantered like this? This is how she wants to remember them.

It might be the last time she sees them, and she wants to keep them in her heart.

Forever. Shining.

Because someone has to die, and it won't be her mothers. She would make sure of that.

After Aurora and Sofya go to the room they rented upstairs—a simple thing with filthy sheets that stink of rancid, unwashed low folk and simple elves—Blair returns downstairs to give them, and herself, a moment of privacy.

She hasn't spent this much time alone with Aurora and Sofya since she was a child. It felt good, in a way, to say goodbye like this. Although it breaks her heart. A heart she's not supposed to have.

But since she made her decision, her mind feels clearer. She is more focused.

She steps out to look up into the night sky, sipping listlessly from some too-sweet, mulled wine, wondering whether the seer might have been purposely vague. About Caryan and Melody coming here. And *when.* Blair would give it another two days before she tried to get more information. Tried to find out whether something might have changed Caryan's course of action. Went back to that scrawny seer and dragged her through the dirt until she gave her a better answer.

If Caryan still wants to go to the holy mountain Silas, the only path is right through Calianthe's murderous forest. Blair hasn't told her mothers, though—about Silas. She's been vague about their mission, just mentioning that Caryan wants to find the relics and that they are somewhere around the Emerald Forest.

And if all that bullshit the seer's brabbled about—about Blair's fate being linked to Melody's—is true, well then, something is supposed to happen. *Soon.*

Or Blair is going to make something happen, because she is fucking running out of time.

Perenilla wants an outcome, *soon.*

She takes another sip when her ears pick up some peddlers talk. One mentions having seen four people—no doubt elves clad in armor, one swears—stepping out of the magical curtain, coming from the lands of the two moons, and walking straight up to the Emerald Forest.

She turns her head to the two fauns with ram horns that curl down around their faces, and then walks upstairs, ignoring the lingering smell of sex and sweat. The two witches are already asleep, naked, entwined in one bed. Blair opens the drawer of an old, wooden desk and gently takes out a blank sheet of paper, then she heads back downstairs.

She finds one of the fauns still there, leaning against the wall of the inn when she returns. "Greetings. I was wondering—if you could write something for me?" She fumbles for some gold and pulls it out from a purse around her belt, holding it up between them.

The merchant understands. Blair can't lie, but he can write something *for* her. The content doesn't have to be true—it is one way to circumvent having to tell the truth.

"What do you need me to write?" he asks.

"*I went alone. Don't come looking for me. It is the only way. If you're reading this, I'm dead. I'm sorry. Thank you for everything.*"

The merchant takes out a feather and some ink and makes quick work of it.

He hands her the letter but holds on to the paper when she reaches for it. "I hope this is not true," he says in an accent that tells her he's been living in Akribea for a good while. Tells her that he must be old if he remembers the good life there.

"Why do you care?"

"You remind me of my daughter."

"My horns?" Blair asks—she has none—and he huffs a laugh.

"No. The fierce determination in your eyes."

He lets go of the paper at that. She hands the golden coins over to him, but he doesn't take them.

"Keep it, girl. You need it more than I do."

"You're wrong. Where I'm going, I won't need it anymore, old man," she drawls. When he still doesn't reach for the coins, she throws them in front of his hooves in the dirt and goes back inside, stepping up the creaky, old wooden steps.

She leaves the letter open on the wooden desk. Then she kneels in front of her still-sleeping mothers, takes out some silver moonstone dust she got from the blacksmith, places it in her open palm, and blows it into the witches' faces.

A potion. It will make them sleep for two or three days straight. Blair plans to be long gone by then, in one way or the other.

She quietly sneaks down, paying the innkeeper three solid gold coins and telling him that her two companions got ill, and that she's setting out to find a healer and some herbs, and that they should not be disturbed.

The tired-looking low elf only nods, and Blair ventures out. The merchant and the gold are gone into the night, and Blair walks down the road alone.

MELODY

I shiver constantly. The cold is so deep, so severe, so uncompromising, I know I won't escape it. It's going to claim me. They've conjured layers of clothes for me—anoraks from the human world and a blanket of fur. I have no idea where they came from. Caryan's magic maybe, but I no longer care. My head is dizzy, as if wrapped in a layer of snow, my teeth won't stop chattering.

I feel tired, too tired to walk on. I don't realize I've tumbled again, barely feeling the icy snow that seeps in everywhere, but hands lift me and carry me, soft wings brushing against my cheeks, shielding me from the worst.

I hardly register how they set up a tent. When I open my eyes again, I realize that it is huge, with beds and a massive wooden table in the middle. Three fires burn in iron bowls that are scattered all over. I'm lying next to the biggest one, wrapped up like a bundle.

Slowly, so slowly, my senses return. I blink a few times, finding Caryan watching me. His eyes are storm-dark again and unyielding, like his aura as he's crouching next to me on the ground.

"Drink," he says serenely, handing me a steaming cup.

I try, but my fingers are so cold I can barely close them around it. I want to lie down again. To close my eyes, just for a second…

"Drink, Melody."

A rumble of power jolts through me, so hard it hurts, as if

something is burning its way through the inside of my skin. I take a sip, trying hard not to spill any liquid. Then my eyes drift shut again.

I barely hear Ronin's voice when he enters the tent and a waft of cold swipes in. "It must be close."

I told them in the forest what I'd seen. I tried to describe the shape of the peaks and the formation of rocks and ice so they might find it without me having to climb up all the way. I know Caryan could have demanded that I show him through my blood, maybe could have forced me to show him as he said. When Kyrith, and then Ronin, once suggested that he should, he growled at them. That shut the topic down quickly.

I can't shake the feeling that he's avoiding it for a reason beyond my comprehension.

Maybe it's because he didn't see anything in my blood the last time. Maybe because of something else entirely. Maybe it's because he doesn't want me close... doesn't want to feel this connection again.

My thoughts have become indistinct and slow. All I can think of is the cold, so deep and raw it's as if it is eating me from the inside.

"You might want to go and check yourself—" Ronin says, but Caryan pivots around, snapping his teeth at him. Ronin steps back, hands raised defensively in front of him.

I feel someone lifting my head, a body sliding under the layers of blankets and jackets and pressing up against me, wings folding over me as soft as the snow outside. I'm asleep again, drifting in and out of nightmarish sequences when there's a sound like an avalanche. A cracking of stone and snow, screeching and hissing.

Inhuman and terrifying.

BLAIR

The seer had been right. They have been headed to Silas, the holy mountain. Blair once overheard Ciellara mentioning the range of those mountains, Silas the highest peak in their midst, covered in eternal snow, and haunted by blizzards. The moon elf Ciellara read about them in a book. She said it was a place where you only found doom. Wicked and cursed and not holy at all.

Blair commanded her phantom wyvern to circle over the area until she spotted a tiny flicker through the dense snowstorm. A tent with fires inside.

She cursed under her breath, her fingers so numb she had trouble holding on to her wyvern, even with fur-lined gauntlets on. She made the beast perch on a nearby rock before she slumped off, bracing herself against the bitter, unnatural cold. Undiluted, raw, ancient magic, eating away at her own.

Even a witch wouldn't last long up here.

No wonder those crazy high elves chose this spot to hide a relic. No one halfway sane would come here.

Now she's wading through the hip-high snow, planning her attack.

Four elves, the peddler said. They sure looked like elves from a distance.

One must be Melody. One Caryan himself. The other one that

pain-in-the-ass warrior Kyrith. The last of them the witcher Blair has heard only stories of. Witchers—eerie half-breeds rumored to be the secret offspring of witches. Since the coven allows no male offspring, boys are usually killed at birth by their mothers. But some, those who aren't dispatched... well, they say they become witchers. Destined to be natural witch hunters with senses no one knows much about, turning against the very mothers who abandoned them.

But who knew? Rumors were often a lot of bullshit.

But Caryan hasn't brought Riven, Blair's sure. He would have left Riven behind to rule. The breathtaking, silver-tongued elf has always been the one Caryan trusts. But thankfully, he isn't here... Blair isn't too keen on another encounter with him. For one because she can't look at his smug face without the constant wish to smash her fist into it. Not that she would succeed in this endeavor. Riven's magic is one of the most powerful Blair's ever witnessed. Gods, she's seen him lay a whole town to ash without so much as lifting a finger.

Not that his absence will do anything to change the odds.

An angel, a blood-sucking elf, and a blood-sucking witcher against a witch... hells, not good. She licks her canines. They are so cold her tongue almost sticks to the silver, and she has to peel it back off with a hiss as she crouches low and watches the tent.

Yep, she's seen better odds and better days. But all she needs to do is kill the girl.

Or die trying, which is the far more likely scenario. But it's the only thing Blair can do to save her sorry ass. To make amends. To save Aurora and Sofya too.

She figures it doesn't matter either way whether she dies or not. Her mothers will be safe. That's all that matters.

She stretches out her hands and pulls off the gauntlets, snarling against the cold that instantly starts to gnaw at her skin.

A silvery green light dances in the storm as she summons the illusion of two huge wyverns—similar to the ones Aurora and Sofya ride, drawing deep into her magic. She's too far away from Perenilla to channel from the reservoir, so she needs to use her own. It won't last long here, though, in this strange, ancient cold—and definitely won't be enough to keep up a fight with three different kinds of monsters—but it will be enough for a distraction.

And a distraction is all she needs.

The two beasts roar like real ones when she sends them toward the tent. Then she jumps on her wyvern and follows them, drawing the long Nefarian sword from her back.

Melody

Ronin and Kyrith storm outside, and Caryan follows.

The noise and his sudden absence startle me, briefly bringing back some life in me. I manage to get up when the tent is sliced open, and a woman with long, fiery-red hair enters, the point of her long, black sword trained on my neck.

The woman Lyrian wanted me to find. The woman from the bar in the human world.

She snarls at me, silver canines reflecting the fire as the sword tip presses into my skin. I feel the sting, the metal digging, biting my flesh, and taste the coppery smell of blood in the air. All the while, I hold the woman's amber eyes, as clear and beautiful as Ronin's.

I wait for her to increase the pressure a touch more, to plunge the sword through my throat.

But the woman hisses once, like a cat, and then lowers the sword. "A life debt," is all she has time to snarl before Caryan's fingers close around her neck, his other hand grabbing the sword around the blade, not caring that it cuts into his flesh as he frees it from her hand. He tosses it, and it slithers somewhere into the tent.

"Blair, it was a mistake to come here," he says, and his teeth rip into her flesh.

61

BLAIR

Blair's vision blurs. Pain. Searing pain shoots through her. Caryan's teeth tear her flesh so savagely, so brutally, she cries out. Her whole body burns from an invisible fire.

Her silver nails dig into his hand around her throat. A ridiculous effort to loosen the grip of an angel. She's lifted into the air. She kicks wildly, trying to fight. But her power and magic are draining out of her and into Caryan with every sip he takes.

Blair pulls her lips into a tormented smile. Somehow it feels fitting that she will perish by Caryan's cruel hand, the same way her aunt died. Drunk to a husk.

As if that missing piece of their triangle finally snapped into place.

"Stop! Please!"

A faint female voice sounds behind her, carrying all the horror Blair doesn't feel.

"Please, don't kill her!" the voice starts again, closer.

Her scent wafts over to Blair then—the scent of the sweet human world Blair dreams about. A life where she could have…

Why the hell is this girl pleading for her?

Melody. The ridiculous, soft-hearted creature. *Well, look who's talking. Pot, kettle, black*, that dark voice in Blair's mind whispers.

Caryan's eyes turn to the girl, but he doesn't stop drinking. And

Blair knows he won't. Not until she's dry and brittle. He's an angel, always has been. They have no heart, have no mercy, and it's alright.

When Blair blinks again, the girl is no longer there.

Caryan lets go of Blair so quickly she meets the ground hard.

Groaning and cursing, she makes it to her feet, not willing to glance at the blood that's soaked into her clothes. Instead, she stares at the open tent flap fluttering in the wind.

Where the hell is Caryan? And what the fuck happened? Where is the girl?

Blair moves, hissing as every tiny movement sends a wave of agonizing pain through the wound on her neck and all down her body. Leaving a bloody imprint of her hand on the wall of the tent, she stumbles outside.

She fights on through the knee-deep snow, flakes the size of walnuts whirling all around her, accompanied by hail that needles her ravaged skin. She falls to her knees, panting hard, darkness wavering at her periphery as she spots two figures, barely more than sentinels in the dark. The whirlwind of flakes so thick they look unreal.

Behind her, Blair smells the other two high lords, who must have returned after having realized the phantom creatures she sent were nothing but a distraction. They halt next to her, all three of them gazing at the girl.

The girl who's standing at the very edge of an icy cliff, shivering so badly she can barely keep herself upright.

Only yards away, Caryan. He's gone still as stone.

"Let her live. Let her live or I'll jump."

The wind carries the girl's voice over. Blair, despite the pain, lifts her head. *Why? Why fight for me? Again. And blackmailing Caryan... She's got some balls. Crazy half-human.*

"Come back, Melody!" Caryan's voice is like a sword, cutting through the whirlwind, his eyes gleaming in the storm like two wildfires bundled into marbles. All Gatilla's monster, no trace of the man Blair sometimes lay with in all those lonely hours. But even he doesn't dare move.

"Promise you won't hurt her," the girl says again, swaying slightly.

Blair curses silently. One wrong move and she will fall, plunge to certain death.

"Come. Back," Caryan repeats, his voice dead as stone.

"No. Promise—or I'll jump. You won't be fast enough to catch me. Not in this storm. And from this height, not even you'll be able to bring me back," she says, every word cut off by her chattering teeth.

Caryan snarls, his wings spread, ready to launch himself at her. But… he doesn't. Even he doesn't dare.

Blair holds her breath. Because Melody's right—not even the angel will be able to bring her back if she falls. And from the fierce determination in Melody's eyes, Blair knows she means every word. She will jump.

For a strange moment, everything around Caryan has grown as still as he. The storm subsides, snowflakes drifting softly through the air as even the wind has fallen silent, as if it, too, listens to Caryan's words, deep and vicious as he says, "I promise."

The girl nods, as if to herself. And, as if she's just been holding out long enough for this, she collapses.

Caryan is already there, catching her body and carrying her back to the tent in his arms, not once looking toward Blair as he strides past. *Of course not.*

Blair doesn't fight when Ronin and Kyrith grab her arms, the first one as madly beautiful as she remembers him, the second the same rugged-looking bastard. A scream rips from her throat as they wrench her up and the wound on her neck is torn open all over.

"Fun's over, witch," Kyrith croons. The white-haired idiot has the nerve to smirk at her, his eyes glistening with a dark kind of enjoyment.

"Fuck off, you shithead," she snarls. That earns her a snap of his vampire teeth right into her face, way too close to her shredded throat. Not that Blair can do anything in Ronin's relentless grip other than pull her lips back.

It is pretty much the last thing she masters before everything grows dark around her and she falls into oblivion.

Blair's curled next to one of the fires, hands tied behind her back with iron chains when she awakes.

The first thing she notices is that she feels different. Empty— the steadying, ever-present hum in her veins, her magic... gone.

She lies like that for a while, with her eyes closed, half dead, her mind straining for some leftovers somewhere inside her that Caryan might have overlooked.

But there's nothing. Not a single ember is left to stir when she calls to her power.

It's all gone. She's a witch without magic.

A witch without magic and no coven to return to.

She's as good as dead. Her body is nothing but a strange, lifeless shell without it. Weaker than any lesser fae.

She listens to the howling outside, hoping that Aurora and Sofya have returned to Perenilla by now. It's all Blair could do for them—make sure they're safe.

She doesn't know how long she lies there, drifting in and out of sleep, unanchored, without the grounding power of her magic, before she feels brave enough to finally open her eyes.

Gods, her body is like a deadweight without magic. How the hells can humans move like this? Her head feels like it's about to burst, her lips parched, her whole body aching for water. But the wound at her neck at least seems to have closed up because the thirst is worse than the pain when she manages to lift her head. The good news is that her fae healing is still working. Even with her magic gone.

She should be thankful she's still breathing, but all she wishes for is death.

Her vision blurs a few times. She fights against grinding nausea before she summons enough of her strength to sit up and lean against one of the wooden posts that hold the huge tent up. The room—it's more a room than a tent—swims in front of her eyes before it slowly solidifies.

Blair's jar unhinges at the picture before her. She's only ever seen Caryan with his wings on the battlefield, never any other time. To see him now—the cruel, ruthless angel she knows—sitting with his wings folded around the unconscious girl in his arms is... definitely something new.

Not something she thought she'd ever see.

When she eventually tears her gaze away from the angel to take in more of her surroundings, she finds Kyrith scowling at her from a corner next to one of the fires. The red-haired witcher is behind him, stretched out on a bed, his back turned to the room, obviously sleeping.

"Do you think Perenilla is going to send more witches?"

It takes Blair a solid minute to realize that Caryan's question is directed toward her. Her voice comes out cracked when she answers truthfully, "I don't know. All I do know is that she sent me here, but I guess you know all that already."

He ripped everything from her blood. Hells, all her miserable memories. All the darkness he caused. Splendid, now he knows what a pathetic piece of a mess she's become because of him.

"That was not my question," he counters.

Now his eyes find hers and she can't help but marvel at the bright starlight blue she's never seen before, not even when they screwed at Gatilla's court, his eyes always a glistening black then.

"Why did she send you here? What did she hope you would achieve?"

"She wants that... girl," she snaps. "And because you and I fucked, I had to obey, in case you missed that tiny little detail in my blood."

He ignores her provoking tone. "She wouldn't really have believed you could retrieve Melody from me. I wonder why she sent you then."

Blair clenches her teeth. "Oh, she also wants me dead. She counted on you finishing the job, so she doesn't have to make her own hands dirty. Wouldn't look good, you know. Politics..."

She tries not to flinch as his power brushes up against her—

that writhing, living monstrosity. So achingly familiar. That power that just imbibed her own.

"Your mothers believe you have a bond with her," Caryan muses quietly, as if flipping through the pages of her mind all over again while he looks down at the girl in his lap. Gods, her lips are blue.

Blair startles. *Caryan wouldn't hurt them, would he?* "You know how they are. Very superstitious," she answers evasively.

His vicious growl makes every hair on her body stand up. "The seer said the same to you. That your fates are linked. What does that mean?"

Blair makes herself hold his gaze. "I know as much as you. Go consult that seer yourself and try to throttle more answers out of her."

"Careful, Blair, there is a good chance your mothers are still at that inn." *Fucker.*

"True, but I doubt you want to spare one of your lackeys to track them down right now," she croons back, throwing a significant look at the girl. Not showing any of the panic she's feeling. Panic that threatens to tear her apart. "You're running out of time—she's halfway dead."

"She will recover," he answers, as if he needs to convince himself.

Blair lets out a hoarse laugh. "Sure, the way corpses recover. But you can bring her back, so it's not too bad, right? I mean, when she kicks the bucket."

Caryan says nothing, but it's the way his jaw is working. Blair's eyebrows shoot up. "Oh, wait… you can't. Is it because she's a half-human and your necromancy thing doesn't work on her? Or because you're not sure she'd accept your lovely *I-bind-you-to-me-in-a-way-like-you-just-have-to-do-everything-I-say-from-now-on-but-hey-you-can-live-that-a-problem-for-you* contract."

"Careful, Blair. I could just finish what I started," he growls, his eyes shimmering with unspent cruelty.

As if he'd just been waiting for this moment Kyrith gets up, too eager to shed her blood, Blair knows.

"Really, Caryan—you'd let that little elf sucker finish me?" Blair asks, but her eyes hold Kyrith's as he comes for her. She forces a cold grin onto her lips and turns her head fully to the elf. "If you want a brawl, fine. But at least take the shackles off me and do it the real way. Or are you afraid I might chop off your favorite part this time?"

"Watch it, bitch!" Kyrith crosses the room so fast she expects him to crash into her.

But when she blinks, she finds the warrior feet away, glowering, ties of dark magic restraining him.

Her grin widens and she clicks her tongue. "Look who just put his dog on a leash."

"Don't make me regret not killing you, Blair." Caryan's voice is low, his eyes pouring night when he looks at her. *Gods, how many songs did he ruin for her?*

Blair shrugs it off, in vain. "It wasn't my choice. I didn't beg for anything. Do it if you feel like it."

Caryan's gaze lingers. "Why didn't you kill her?"

"I don't know. Maybe I didn't feel like it," she chirps lightly. "Can I have some water now? I'm parched."

"Where did you get *this* from?" Kyrith holds up the black Nefarian sword.

"Let me think—oh yes—*why-don't-you-go-and-fuck-yourself!*"

"I'll torture it out of you, witch," Kyrith snarls.

"Yeah? You better keep rolling your eyes like that—maybe you'll find a brain back there," Blair hisses back. "Besides, just ask your master. He'll tell you if he thinks you worthy."

Kyrith snarls, but she trains her gaze back on Caryan, batting her lashes.

"Water? Pleeease?"

Just then, the girl stirs, and Caryan's gaze goes back to her, ignoring Blair.

"Oh, great. Yeah, just ignore the witch you used to fuck all night," she snaps, shaking her head and regretting it instantly because it hurts.

Kyrith saunters over, glaring down at her, a water bottle conjured in his hand. He makes a show of slowly unscrewing it and bringing it to his lips, taking a hearty swig.

He grins when he catches her staring, smacking his lips. "Oh, where are my manners? You're thirsty too." The bastard cocks his head, a grin on his face. "Want some? Hm, why not try *May I have some water, please, oh my great high lord*, witch, and see how that goes," he purrs. "Or why not see to some of my needs? It's been a while up here without a woman."

"I'd rather bite off my own tongue and swallow it," she snarls.

"I wasn't talking about your loose tongue. Word has it you spread your legs for anyone," he snarls right back. "I guess, even for a Nefarian, if that sword you carried is anything to go by."

"Maybe I had one for dinner—because that's what I do. I slice pathetic men open and drink their blood as soon as I've used them for my needs. So, yes, take off these shackles and see what I can do. You fit right into the mold."

"You know, Blair, you were average with your magic back then, but now, without your magic, you're nothing." Kyrith flashes his teeth, knowing the blow hurt.

She flashes hers right back. "Oh, shut it. I still wear heels bigger than your dick, neck-pricker, with or without magic."

"Enough of this. Go and do what I asked, Kyrith. I'm tired of your juvenile antics," Caryan cuts in, another silent command laced with power following his words.

Kyrith curls his lips back in Blair's direction before he obeys and leaves, unable to ignore the direct order.

With him gone, silence falls over the tent, only the howling outside and the crackling of the fire remaining. Blair's gaze wanders to the sleeping witcher on the bed, then glides back to the girl in Caryan's arms.

She's so pale, pale as the snow outside. Her lips are no longer blue, but almost as colorless as the rest of her.

The girl who saved her life. Twice. Blair shouldn't care. She tells herself that she doesn't care. That she wouldn't like to tear the girl to shreds because of the way Caryan's looking at her.

Gods, it fucking hurts to see the angel after so many years, and the first thing he does is rip her throat out and cradle that half-human in his arms like she means something to him.

Good. Let Melody die and be gone. Caryan deserves this.

But despite it all, Blair finds herself saying, "You know where we are, right? What Silas does? This cold—it's not a normal cold. It's raw, ancient magic, Caryan. Fighting anyone who tries to come closer. Killing *everyone* who stays too long."

He looks at her, and Blair continues. "She will die on you, whether you want it or not. Soon. Your own magic can barely stand it. Silas's magic is draining you, too." She juts her chin toward the sleeping witcher in the corner. She knows the witcher would never have fallen asleep if it weren't for the magic burning him out. "I wasn't kidding when I said before that she's barely alive. Not much longer and she'll be dead. You need to take her out of this magic if you want to prevent that."

Caryan ignores her, looking back down at the girl.

Blair's eyes turn to slits. "She has barely any pulse left. She's only half-fae. She can't stand this cold. She's *going* to die." Her words are sharp, trying to reach the angel. It's the least she can do for the girl.

Caryan's lips curl back in a warning, his eyes holding the promise of violence before he says calmly, "I know she will die."

Ice-cold bastard.

"Is it really worth it, the relics? She can get you the other ones too, but not if she dies—you know it, and I know it too. She's more useful to you alive than dead!"

Blair's voice has risen an octave before he cuts her off, his voice grave, his black eyes burning into her. "I need to wait for the storm to subside. As long as it is like this, I can't fly with her. I wouldn't be fast enough. It would be too cold."

Blair starts at what she sees then, what her witch instincts pick up in his tone.

Pain. There's pain in Caryan's voice, in his face, in his power

502

even, so clear and bright it's unmistakable. Not once in all those years, not even when he was in hellish physical pain, had Blair seen him as much as flinch. But right now—*he's suffering.*

What the hell? Why?

She'd ponder this later… if there's a later for her. For now, she says, "Give her your blood."

"I can't," he growls back between clenched teeth.

"Do it or she'll die," Blair hisses back unperturbed. He says nothing, and she lets out a snort. "Too fine to give an ordinary girl your blood? Or is it because she's Ciellara's daughter? Are you afraid people will learn about it and mock you for it?"

Abyss, how long she'd itched to finally shout at him.

His snarl runs over her skin, throbbing in her still-wounded neck. "Don't be so ridiculous, Blair."

"Then don't fuck around and do it!"

"As I said, I can't," he repeats in a way that raises the hair on Blair's arms.

"Why?" *Why indeed?* She can't pinpoint the pain she's feeling in him, can't find the source.

But he doesn't give her an answer. Blair wants to give him a biting rant full of expletives but the girl would die. *Is going to die.* Blair notices her fading heartbeat.

"She doesn't have long, Caryan," she says one more time, somberly, knowing he knows it too.

He seems to hesitate, but then he gently bends Melody's head back, the way one would give water to an unconscious person. He brings his teeth to his wrist, slicing along his vein, so a spring flood of blood comes gushing out. He holds it against her closed lips, the blood dripping over her chin and neck.

Melody gasps, her lips parting ever so slightly, and the blood flows into her mouth.

Her brown eyes flare open as the magic—Caryan's magic—violently pulls her back to life.

"More," he says when Melody tries to wriggle free, realizing what is happening.

Her eyes widen with horror, but Caryan only forces his wrist harder against her lips, forces more blood into her mouth, willing her to swallow.

She does, clearly despite herself. Blair feels Caryan's magic flaring up in the girl, then Melody's body goes limp again. But she is no longer unconscious. Her lavender eyelids flutter, and Blair watches with a mixture of fascination and terror as the girl starts to shake her head again, mumbling and whining, as if caught in the middle of a terrifying nightmare.

Caryan watches her too, looking even more pained than before, but not surprised. Blair wonders what the girl's seeing. From her pleading and whimpering, it can't be anything good.

"Wake her up," Blair demands, but Caryan just says, "I can't."

It stays like that for hours. Occasionally, Melody whispers some words or a scream cuts through the tent, sending the red-haired warrior startling up from sleep before Melody falls back into that restless semi-slumber.

Blair loses track of time herself, the blue magic eating away at her too, making her tired and woozy. Her healing throat burns, as every layer of skin slowly starts to knit itself back together, her agony catalyzed by her aching, tormenting thirst that lets her, too, drift in and out of sleep.

When she comes to the next time, amber eyes like her own—but with slitted pupils—watch her, embedded in a face she's seen before. A beautiful face, almost feminine. Then she feels a bottle at her lips, and water flows into her mouth. She's so grateful she wants to cry. She closes her eyes and gulps it down until the bottle is empty.

"More?" the gentle voice asks, and she just nods.

The red-haired witcher brings another bottle and holds it to her lips, and she downs this one too.

Just then, the tent door flaps open and Kyrith strides in, over to Caryan, who's sitting in the exact same position he's been sitting over the last hours, the girl still in his arms, wrapped in his wings, fighting invisible demons. Kyrith watches her for a second, then

Caryan, in a way that tells Blair he has never seen Caryan like this either. That he's *worried.*

Then he clears his throat, the exhaustion obvious. "I haven't found anything. But the storm has abated. We might be able to make it up to the peak, Caryan."

Caryan looks at him, then stands, the girl still in his arms. "No. We return to the Fortress. You go by foot, take the witch with you. I'll take Melody myself. I'll meet you there," he says, not explaining more before leaving the tent.

The witch. That's all Blair's become. But had she expected anything else?

Maybe.

Through the flapping door, Blair sees Caryan spread his wings and jump from the cliff, soaring up in the sky.

BLAIR, TWO YEARS BEFORE GATILLA'S DEATH

There was nothing left. Nothing but piles and piles of bodies and scorched soil and wafting ashes. The rain had slowed to a drizzle as night had fallen. Her aunt had long retreated to the amethyst tower, as soon as she'd seen the outcome of the battle, along with one coven to protect her.

Caryan had killed them all. All their enemies.

Blair stood there, unmoved for hours, at the cliff's edge, watching. Watching Caryan and his never-faltering magic. Watching him fight and kill. Now she watched him walking between the corpses and smoldering ashes.

He knelt beside a body in the mud, his black wings carefully lifted above the ground. He didn't look up when her wyvern landed next to him and she dismounted, her boots sinking into the mass of flesh and mud.

He was dripping blood from a cut on his wrist into the open mouth of a soldier. A white-haired soldier, his features sharp and vaguely familiar. Blair watched with a kind of cold horror as the soldier opened his eyes, his former blue irises tinged red.

Kyrith, the mountain lion of Palisandre.

"I will make you an offer." Caryan's voice was calm, and the not-so-dead Kyrith tilted his head as if to listen. Like an animated puppet. "Swear yourself to me, and I will bring you back from the dead."

Blair's heart stopped for a beat, with awe, with dread, with horror—she wasn't yet sure—as the dead nodded.

She didn't wait. She just ran. Her body was exhausted. Drained. Close to a collapse, but the shock made her fast and strong. Behind her she could hear her wyvern take flight, while her feet flew over the scorched soil, over steaming cinders and debris and death.

She wasn't sure, but she might have started crying. Or maybe it was just the rain.

She fell. At some point, her legs just gave out, and she landed face-first in the dirt. Then gentle claws lifted her and carried her away, up and up and up. Away from the blood. From the carnage. To a clearing surrounded by a beckoning abyss where wildflowers bloomed. Away from death himself, until the soothing scent of moss and camphor filled her nose and she could see the stars above her.

Her phantom wyvern lay down next to her, her long, deadly tail protectively curled around Blair while she just lay there like a corpse.

She lost her sense of time. It was deep into the night when her wyvern stirred and Caryan landed next to her. He stood in the clearing like a statue. The moonlight dancing over his head and gilding his wings made it look like he wore a crooked halo over his head.

Broken in the middle.

As if two horns protruded out of it.

He shifted and the illusion vanished.

Blair sat up. She found herself scanning him for injuries, knowing he had none. "You... you killed Kyrith, only to bring him back." She got to her feet and met him halfway. "He knew. That's why he didn't kill me," she pushed on. Her words flushed out. They needed out. The truth. Finally.

Caryan just stood there, unmoved, and waited.

"You promised my aunt an army. You... a doomed fae army." She spit the words out, still unable to fully wrap her head around what she'd seen. Impossible. Necromancy was impossible. But then, so was Caryan. He was a necromancer. And he would bring them all back.

"You wanted the reservoir's magic to grow that army," she continued.

When he still said nothing, Blair turned her head to the side, to her wyvern who was watching Caryan carefully, her daggertail swishing restlessly.

"You... did you kill Riven too?"

"No, Riven accepted the pact without losing his life." Caryan's voice was smooth as polished glass when he finally spoke.

Blair scrunched up her face. It should have made things better, but somehow it didn't. That Riven accepted this. Knew of his fate and still chose it.

"Why? Tell me why, Caryan."

"Does it feel good to be shackled, Blair?" was all he asked back.

"What do you want? To march that army over the whole planet?"

"I thought this is what you feared most—to lose the ones you loved. There is no more death. This way, war can't bring more death."

She let this sink in.

"You made monsters, right? They drink blood. They need to be controlled." She saw it in their faces. That wildness. That feral stare and hunger. And fangs. Kyrith grew fangs before she left.

"Like me. Like you. I will control them until they learn."

"They are—abominations." She started to scream, her voice reverberating from the high peaks, being thrown back at her like a mocking echo.

Caryan just waited, his perfect face so blank. So empty. His eyes were as black as the gaps between stars.

"Say it, Blair. Say what you think I am. Come. For once. Be

508

brave enough to voice it." He stepped closer, his black wings huge and vast behind him, blocking out the moonlight, a shadow falling over her. "Say it," he said again. Calm. He was so fucking, eerily calm.

"This… where will this lead?"

"The world thirsts for dominance. Always has. Always will."

"And my cruel aunt on the throne?"

"That throne could just as easily be yours."

She shook her head. "This is against everything we know. Everything I believe in. Against tradition."

"Tradition is the illusion of permanence, Blair."

She took a step back. He followed. They danced like that through the dark.

"This… this destroys every rule of the natural. Disrupts the order of things. The balance of nature and magic."

"Believe me when I say those rules were destroyed long, long ago."

She did believe him, although she couldn't understand what exactly he was saying. Wasn't sure she wanted to.

But there, in the moonlight, he looked more ancient and timeless than ever.

She whispered, "This is… bad. Wrong."

They stopped at the edge of the cliff, the abyss yawning around them.

"Maybe I'm not the villain you think I am, Blair."

Blair gazed down into the darkness. Such an irony that her aunt was afraid of heights. And slept with an angel. Such an irony that her aunt built a tower like Windscar, made for creatures born into the storm, yet she couldn't even bear entering the platform, couldn't bear looking out a window. Never rode a wyvern.

Blair kept her gaze to her right, staring down into the bottomless pit. She wondered how it would feel to tumble into it. Down, down, down.

Caryan's words reached her at last, and she leveled her gaze at him. He wasn't just beautiful. He was horrifying and otherworldly and more than vaguely threatening.

He was a dark king. Eternal and almighty. She felt his power roiling in her soul, endlessly.

"Maybe you're much worse," she breathed.

"Or maybe you made me yours."

"You're a monster," she breathed.

"It takes a monster to destroy a monster."

Her aunt. Did he mean her aunt? She didn't want to know. Didn't want any of this.

She shook her head and finally touched him. She longed for him. Burned for him. Whatever he was—is—she always would.

She stepped closer and whispered against his chest. "When's a monster not a monster?" He stiffened, but said nothing until she raised her chin to him and breathed, "When you love it."

63

RIVEN

Riven's heart jumps in his chest when his ears pick up the sound of a car traveling far across the desert. He steps out onto the balcony and watches the cloud of dust trailing behind it.

One car. Only one.

No flare of Caryan's power to announce the king's return. Something is wrong, he's felt it over the last few days.

His mouth is dry by the time Ronin and Kyrith, faces grave, enter the throne hall, dragging Blair, Gatilla's niece, in iron cuffs behind them. Ronin stays with Riven while Kyrith takes the witch to the dungeon. The red-haired witcher tells Riven everything that happened. They suspect that Caryan flew to the Emerald Forest to Queen Calianthe as soon as the snow stopped because Melody had fallen into a strange state of nightmares. This was three days ago. They haven't heard anything since.

"Calianthe hates Caryan. She might—" Riven starts.

Ronin grabs Riven's shoulder as he runs his fingers through his hair. "Caryan wouldn't have taken Melody there if he thought she would."

"You can't know that," Riven snarls, too agitated to rein in his temper.

Ronin regards him, his hazel eyes clarion and his voice that soothing, ever-calm melody. "I do. I've never seen Caryan like that before. He carried her in his arms, Riven, the whole time, as soon as we set foot on the holy mountain. Melody was slowly dying from what we thought was just the cold. She couldn't stay, so he shielded her with his wings. Caryan held her the whole time, not once leaving her side. He left with her as soon as the storm was over, not once looking for the relic."

Riven watches Ronin's face closely; the witcher is obviously as unable to make sense of it as Riven himself. Ronin also tells him about Blair, who tried to kill Melody, but, in the end, for some reason they haven't yet learned, decided against it.

Eventually, Ronin mentions what Melody did when Caryan wanted to kill the witch—that she threatened to jump from a cliff— her threat based on the very knowledge Riven shared with her on her first night here, not thinking she would ever use it against Caryan.

Damn, this girl.

When Ronin has finished, Riven nods, thanking his friend and mumbling an excuse to leave before Kyrith comes back from the dungeon. He hasn't got the stomach to deal with Kyrith, who, according to Ronin, has been raging on and on all the way back here.

His private quarters are calm, so unsettlingly calm. Riven walks over to the marble bar and pours himself a glass of raspberry wine before slumping down on his bed, closing his eyes to the scent of Melody that still hangs in the sheets.

She almost died.

Caryan almost let her die.

And now none of them knows where in the Abyss's name Caryan has gone. They are probably lost in the Emerald Forest, at the mercy of Queen Calianthe, famous for telling her nymphs and dryads to greet every stranger with an arrow to the heart before asking any questions… and never to take prisoners.

Caryan could easily raze the Enchanted Forest to the ground, that's not the problem. The problem is that there's no way he could protect Melody while he did it.

Riven sits up, eyes wide, a snarl coming from his throat as he hurls the glass against the wall. Shards rain down and ruby liquid scatters, the drops as red and thick as blood, staining the sofa below. He should never have let Caryan go alone with her. He should have stood up to him.

He gets up and walks out, striding straight to the dungeon.

He finds the witch sitting with her head low, leaning against the wall. Now, with her fire-hair bleached like old bone and her shredded, bloodencrusted clothes, she looks more like a noon wraith, safe for those menacing silver nails glowing in the dark.

"My, my... isn't it the beautiful elven prince, Riven? Or should I say the arrogant prick?" she asks without looking up, having either sensed or smelled him since he's stepped soundlessly out of the dark. "Tell me—did Caryan leave you here out of fear you might break a manicured nail, or are you just the most useless of his lapdogs?"

"No wonder Caryan grew tired of your mouth. It's quite big and a bit filthy," Riven counters coolly, crossing his arms.

She hisses at him, the two silver canines catching what little light is down here, vying with her deadly claws.

Riven looks right back at her, flashing a grin that shows his fangs.

"What do you want, Riven? Free me and have some fun. Lonely up there, isn't it? Have you ever fucked a witch?"

"No thanks."

She stands up and steps closer, her fingers closing around the iron bars. Her full lips purr, "I saw the way you used to look at me."

He picks an invisible flick of dust from his shirt. "Yeah? With aversion and slight nausea?"

"You're an arrogant asshole," she snarls.

He ignores her. "Why didn't you kill the girl?"

"Why don't you bring me some decent food to start with?"

"You can have water."

"Fuck you."

"Now I see why you seem to like the human world so much. A penchant for their language" he says. "And other… *amenities*."

"Something we have in common, don't we, princeling? A certain… *weakness* for them, am I right?" she shoots back.

"How do you know?" he asks dryly.

She makes a show of looking up at the ceiling. "Melody's scent clings to you—of her… you know." She waves a hand. "And it's not just the worry about your darling king Caryan that brought you down here to me, I take it."

"Well, I just wonder—do the other witches know how much you enjoyed yourself in the human world, Blair Alaric?" Riven counters.

Her gaze shoots back to him, her eyes narrowed. "How do *you* know what I did and didn't do in the human world?"

Riven's heard about Blair kicking up quite some dust there. He answers smoothly, "I'm Caryan's right hand. It's my job to know a lot of things."

She looks away from him, offering her beautiful profile. Her jaw is a hard line, working.

He expects another sharp retort, but instead, she just shrugs tiredly. "It no longer matters, any of it, does it? So there's no reason to pretend I'm not terribly thirsty and hungry."

"Like you'd ever drop that hard façade, Blair, and reveal a feeling creature beneath."

"Humans call it badass—and yes, I'm tired of games, believe it or not. Although not of *all* games…" Her amber eyes are deep with hunger. A hunger Riven doesn't want to contemplate too closely— her appetite has little to do with eroticism. Rather, it's as if she wants to break open his bones for marrow and contemplates the fastest way to do it.

"Why didn't you kill her?" he asks again, a bottle of water appearing in his hand.

He hands it to her through the bars, and lets her drink. She gulps the water down as if she can barely do it fast enough. Hells, that bastard Kyrith probably left her without water for days.

"More?" he asks, handing her another full bottle he's conjured up. She downs this, too, then he throws her an apple.

She frowns at it.

"It's not poisoned."

"Huh, funny one, aren't you? Definitely too much time at the court in Palisandre," she says, taking a hearty bite, letting him, once again, see her silver, enlarged fae canines and what she'd gladly do to his throat and other parts.

Riven looks down to his fingernails, bored by her games.

"You know—those fangs suit you, princeling," she eventually says, not one part of the apple left. "They give you an edge." She steps closer again, her clawed fingers twirling around the bars once more. "I like men with an edge."

Her voice is a seductive purr that has no doubt lured many men into her bed… and to certain death.

"Is that why you slept with Caryan? Or was it to outdo your lovely Aunt Gatilla?"

She pouts her coral lips. "It's nothing like fucking a high elf, and I've been with some. He's dangerous, and he lets you feel it. With him, you never feel safe," she whispers, an erotic timbre in her voice that crawls under Riven's skin whether he likes it or not. Her amber eyes flare. She knows.

"That's a good thing?" he asks indifferently.

"A thing some women like," she says, tilting her head, her long hair grazing her hip as she does.

If he didn't like the way she looked at him before, he certainly doesn't like it now.

"That might be why Melody feels so… attracted to him."

"Who isn't?"

"Oh no, don't pretend you're not bothered by that." Blair's eyes flare and her eyes turn vicious. "Or I could tell you how he made her kneel and beg while he—"

Riven's hand shoots out and grabs the witch's neck between the bars, so hard she makes a choking sound. He steps close, so close he can see the tiny speckles of silver in the amber of her irises.

"Enough of the games now. Tell me why you didn't kill her." His voice is a growl—letting her see that side of him. He loosens his fingers just enough to let her catch her breath to answer, only to realize that he mistook her laughter as gagging. *Insane creature.* "Tell me or I'll hurt you."

"Maybe I'd like that," she whispers back. The witch has the nerve to underline her words with a grin.

Riven's nails turn into dark claws as he wills them to, digging into her neck until blood leaks.

The witch's laugh stops, but her eyes turn hollow. "*Interesting.* Go ahead. Hurt me. I have nothing left to lose anyway."

Riven lets go of her then, pulling his hand away, stained with her blood. She straightens too, bringing her fingers to her bleeding neck, looking at the crimson on her fingertips before her eyes turn back to him.

"What are you? You're not *just* a high elf." She squints at him as if seeing him for the very first time.

"I asked you a question first." Riven makes a show of licking her blood off his fingers.

She holds his stare, then says, to his surprise, "Perenilla knows I didn't help Gatilla when you and Caryan killed her." The words hang between them. "I lost my coven. I can't return. She's already made my life hell in the last few years. But now the fun's really over."

"You could fight her," Riven says quietly.

She shakes her head. "No. Caryan took my magic." She looks at her hands—once such cruel, powerful tools, which now are supposed to be just... hands. It's hard to believe it.

"Do you want to know a secret, little vampling? One my sisters would decorate the ground with my innards for? I'd have traded my magic without a second thought just to be like *them*..." she says, self-forgotten, still looking at her hands, as if seeing them for the first time. "Just to be like one of those ridiculous mortals." She huffs a laugh. "And now, the dark irony is that I ended up having neither.

I'm a toothless monster." She frowns at herself before her eyes focus back on him. "The girl, Melody—she shouldn't have stopped him when he wanted to kill me," she adds, and for once, Riven reads the exhaustion on her face.

"Why *didn't* you intervene, Blair? When we killed Gatilla?" he asks with true interest.

It's a question that has long burned in his mind. Caryan killed every witch present, Riven and Kyrith hunted the fleeing ones down, but not Blair. There just wasn't the time after Ciellara slit him open with that sword. In that moment, Blair, who had just been standing aside, watching with a face empty of everything, turned and jumped out of a window, her phantom wyvern flying by, carrying her away.

Riven doesn't know what Caryan would have done if she had stayed. Whether he would have killed her too for idly standing by, or whether he would have offered her to join his court.

Maybe this is why Blair fled. Because she had not had the courage to let herself find out.

She says, "You first."

"I'm a half-blood. My mother was a Nefarian." Have it out. Let her know what he is.

She stares at him. "Do the others know? I mean, like, do the people of this kingdom know? Or Palisandre? Gatilla never knew."

"This is another question, I suppose."

She nods slowly, to herself. Then she says quietly, an unusual frown on her face, "I don't know why I didn't fight for her. Or for Caryan, for that matter."

"You do, deep down," he says, but she shakes her head vehemently. Yet pain flits across her features.

When she looks back up at him it is gone though, her gaze focused once again. "I didn't kill Melody because she spared my life in the human world. She warned me that Lyrian was coming for me. She helped me escape by leading his lackeys away. I figured I owed her." She pauses and shakes her head again, that frown deepening. "And now she's saved my life once more."

She opens her mouth again, as if to say something else, but catches herself, and says instead, "If you want to do me a favor, tell Caryan to make it quick and painless. I know he listens to you, lordling. I've suffered enough."

With that she turns her back on him and steps into the darkness, returning to the spot on the floor.

64

MELODY

Magic hums through me, scalding hot, pushing the cold back. It burns. The cold, not the hot. Two different forms of magic, clashing in my body like two mighty, fanged, and taloned beasts, one blue and one golden, both as ancient and raw as the other. The gold startles my heart back to life, shielding it from the cold that wants to make it stop.

I blink to life, looking up into the familiar, breathtaking, golden eyes. The same magic reflected there that's in my heart now, swamping every part of me like a dam that has broken, filling everything, where before there was only a shy trickle.

Then the cold sweeps back in, claiming me again.

The pain. The agony, slamming into me.

But that isn't the worst of it.

The worst are the nightmares, feeling so vivid, so real. As if I'm witnessing everything myself.

I'm on a battlefield, looking down on an army full of glorious elven warriors in shining white and gold armor, mighty black wings on my back pushing me on, keeping me above them. Razor-sharp instincts make me dodge the arrows that sing past my ears, my reflexes so fast that I can see them flying by like doves in the sky.

Then there is magic. Dark, agonizing, black shackles invisible to observers, cutting deep into my flesh, leaving imaginary wounds that feel so real I clench my teeth against the pain.

The scene jumps, and I'm on the same battlefield again.

Where that gorgeous army was before, there's only fire and corpses, the smell of blood so overwhelming, so omnipresent, tingeing everything, that I feel myself cry out in pain. A sound my unconscious mind registers, echoing somewhere outside the walls of this dream. But I stay there—I, the ancient creature with black wings don't cry out, but instead plummet from the sky, the long, blue-glinting sword in hand, cutting through more bodies, as if the blade is an extension of my body.

I will myself to stop. I fight it, but I can't. The magic that once enslaved me is a force in my blood, sending excruciating pain down those shackles as if they were liquid iron, trying to melt into my flesh and soul.

I whine, plead for the magic to stop, but this is not me, not the creature with wings who slays warrior after warrior until the chopping sound turns to a hum and a mist of blood drenches everything so profoundly and devastatingly I know I'll never get rid of it.

The scene jumps once again and blood's running down my throat, thick and delicious, sparked with power that melts with the golden force in my veins, while the eyes in front of me lose their shine. Yet I drink on until the heart of the man whose wrist I'm holding in my hands—no, not *my* hands, but elegant and strong and violent ones—stops, his body a dead weight falling to my feet once I let go.

No. No! I'm no killer. I didn't do this!

I...

A bedroom. A woman with long, deep-red hair sprawled around her over silken cushions like a puddle of blood. Her head bedded on her arms, her naked body sweat-slicked like my own, the smell of sex heavy in the air. I watch the woman beneath me, wanting to get up, wanting to crush her throat with my bare hands, but I don't, knowing those shackles of enslaving magic will prevent it, will cut so deep. Knowing I will pay if I so much as try, knowing it is better to play along. Give her what she wants. He—*I*—sit up when it's over. But the woman slides closer, leaning over my muscled back that's familiar and is not mine, her deep-red fingernails scratching over my chest, her lips whispering, "That was a hell of a ride, Caryan, but I am not done yet." And he—no, *I*—turn, obedient, pushing that beautiful woman back down onto the bed while I keep looking into those cold eyes I hate so deeply, so fiercely that the hatred eats away at me. I whisper in a deep, lilting voice that costs me, "Oh, I will make you beg this time."

Darkness.

Pain. Hellish pain jolts through me. It goes on and on and on while magic claws and bites into my skin, black magic lacing with the gold of my own. I want to die. I just want to die, not knowing how to hold on any longer but not knowing how to escape either.

There's nothing I can do other than bear it while the pain lasts forever, leaving me gritting my teeth, straining against the iron shackles that bind me to the table I'm lying on. The red-haired woman from the bedroom is bent over me, guiding a knife carved from bones and inked with blackness over and over into my flesh.

Snap.

Music. Naked bodies everywhere. Gold. Smoke of foreign herbs, intoxicating my senses. A woman over me, straddling me—*him*, the angel. Her body glides up and down, her sensual mouth parted, a moan escaping. I—he, the angel—leans his head back, glancing over, and there's Riven.

"Riven. Riven!" I scream, or at least I think I do. But he doesn't look at me, doesn't react at all, his beautiful face a mask of anguish, his violet eyes so terrifyingly empty as he kneels over the same red-haired woman I just... *Riven! Riven!*

More blood.

Blood in my throat blocks my screams. Humming in my bloodstream as it seeps in, power coming along with it, the heat of it the only feeling left in me. The woman whose blood is running down my throat is already dead, her body chalk-white without the vital fluid. I feel nothing when I look at my own naked body—the perfectly defined muscles of a man—then at all the other naked bodies around me. They are not only naked—they are *dead*. *I* killed them. I stare, repulsed by the horrors, but the body I'm in takes it all in, unfazed.

Taking life means nothing to him. Never has. Never will.

The darkness swooshes back in, and I'm grateful for the break, grateful for the change of scene.

Riven. Naked. So utterly beautiful, his eyes no longer so empty, so hollow, so dead inside.

I feel a jolt of relief. I—not the body I'm still in—to see him like that. The body I'm in, bristling with golden and black power so endless, so immense there are no words for it, no boundaries. But the relief is short-lived because Riven's eyes—those beautiful, violet eyes—are wide with pain because of what I have just said, I realize as they come into clearer focus.

"You can't, Caryan. There must be a way…" he whispers.

Don't cry. Please don't cry I want to say as he falls to his knees, resting his forehead against my thigh.

Cut. Darkness.

Riven again, but dressed, no longer naked but in a half-sheer shirt gaping open almost to his navel, revealing his muscled chest as he lounges on a sofa with his usual dramatic flair. But the nonchalance of his posture doesn't match his eyes, which are trained on *Melody* before me on the floor. My voice reacts to a thing Kyrith said before a sharp command down that bond forces Kyrith into submission.

Yet my own gaze strides back to the girl, taking in the fine features of her face, her delicate body. The unpointed ears. Those deep, brown eyes are so wild and lost when they glance up at me, knowing she shouldn't, holding mine a touch too long before she looks away again, down at her hands. Her rush of fear is so strong it's palpable, so real it's as if he—*I*—am feeling it myself as a resonance in my veins.

Yet it's those eyes that have arrested me ever since. Everything is so open in them, as if I could look right into her innermost being.

Those eyes that make me want to touch her. Make me want to…

I, the angel, lean forward to her and whisper, "Come here," watching how the girl shakily gets up, confusion and terror all over her; again the reflection of it in my own body—the sensation of feelings so strange, like a long-forgotten memory.

Curious.

Unnerving.

I say, *Amuse me,* just to see what the girl will do, what it would do to myself.

The effect of her blood in me when I tasted her in that dungeon still haunts me.

Ciellara's daughter—no, *I*—I'm looking at myself kneeling over Caryan through Caryan's eyes. The thought dawns in my mind before it slips away again; before I slip away again into that memory. She kneels over me, and my golden magic flares up like a flame in an unexpected gust of wind when she touches me. Melody's body singeing my skin where her thigh brushes against mine, twin to the flame her hands leave on my chest. He—I—clench my teeth, fighting the instinct to push her off, to throw her back into that dungeon.

To have her so close is pure agony; letting her stay only prolongs it.

Her smell is everywhere—this permeating smell of lilacs, woods, and vanilla, evoking the memory of the taste of her blood. It's like physical pain not to drink her in again. To see more of the memories in her blood, even if they are heartbreaking.

I want to, though. I want to see *everything* of her. Taste her. Consume every inch of her. Own her.

What is this? The thought cuts through me… no, through *his* memory—not for the first time.

Nemesis: that's what she is. His—no, *mine*—my personal nemesis.

I clench my fingers to fists when Melody's full lips brush ever so gently over my skin.

The need to touch her, to taste her—to just *take* her—

I can no longer keep my hands to myself. More wildfire of

magic erupts when he—I— touch her, so intense it's soul-burning. Her skin is like silk under my fingers. Her full lips. Her elegant face up so close. Her scent mixed with fear, trepidation, and arousal. Her eyes again, so wide, so open, so deep, overflowing with everything.

Those eyes. They undo me. Haunt me.

Make me want to do all sorts of things to her. *Dark things.*

It needs to stop. Stop right now, or...

The angel grabs her slender wrists, barely forcing the words out. "That's enough."

The picture dissolves once more like a waft of smoke, spilling into tendrils of nothingness, and I'm in a throne hall, a different sort of agonizing, hellish pain striking me like lightning when the whip comes down on my back once more, splitting skin open, the iron end digging deep through flesh and into bones and magic.

Riven in my peripheral vision; his face a solid mask of pain as he watches me.

The crack of the whip stops, and that red-haired woman gets up, strolling closer, her cruel face looking at me with a half sneer that holds no amusement. Gatilla.

"You disobeyed me, Caryan. Now kneel."

"No."

"Kneel or the punishment will be worse, angel."

"I will not kneel, Gatilla. Not even in front of you."

The invisible shackles of dark magic pull tighter, cutting flesh, and I bare my teeth. It's all pain. There's no distinction anymore, yet I remain standing, my magic fighting hers. The red-haired woman steps even closer and cups my cheek with her silver-clawed hand. Sweat has gathered on her forehead, though, from the strain as she tries to push me to my knees. In vain.

Her voice drops low, only for me to hear as she leans in. "You're disobeying me in front of everyone, Caryan. I cannot let that pass, you know that."

Only then does the audience in that hall become clear. The room, full of women and bristling, dark power and glimmering, amber eyes. The witch pulls back and claps her hands, an axe appearing in them.

"I will take your wings, angel, for this disobedience," she declares, loud again. Then she swings the axe, and unspeakable pain sears through my back.

I scream, instead of the angel, who just endures the pain. I scream and scream and scream.

Light. There is light when I open my eyes. Arms still hold me, and I turn to the side just in time to vomit. Not that I have anything in me, but those pictures, the sight of the dead wings, severed from Caryan's body, that pain prickling through my own…

MELODY

I retch some more, sweat covering my whole body, but the hands around me don't let go. I wipe saliva away before I dare to look up into Caryan's eyes, the gold-rimmed black in them slowly shifting into a grayish blue like a misty morning.

A rustle makes him look up from me as Calianthe, accompanied by armed, sinister-looking dryads, enters the clearing. I blink, and arrows come into clear focus, the sinews of their bows strung tight, all of them aimed at us. The queen's head is raised high as she strides up to us. A semi-transparent gown of white fabric flows down her body, making her look like a flower in the wind.

"Caryan," she says in a royal tone.

"Calianthe." Caryan returns her greeting, unfazed.

"One might bow his head to a queen, if not fall on a knee."

"One might do the same to a king," he retorts coolly.

Her snow-white eyes shift to me then, narrowing to slits before she lifts her hand. The women lower their bows. "What have you done?"

"She is on the verge of death. She needs to rest. She needs warmth. My Fortress is too far," he says.

Calianthe nods once before she gestures to her right. Another corridor between the trees opens up. I barely register how they undress me, how they put me into the hot water, the spring's magic burning me from the inside out, chasing off the last remnants of that bluish magic.

Slowly, so slowly, reality returns, and I start to notice the warble of birds in the trees and the buttery light that falls in columns between the heavy trunks, the green so intense it looks like a dream.

A good dream. A peaceful dream.

I want to hold on to it as long as I can.

When I look up, I find Caryan sitting in the shade next to me at the water's edge, watching me motionlessly. The angel with his black wings and his short, black hair rustling in the mild breeze in the midst of that incredibly beautiful greenery—it looks like a page torn out of a fairytale book. One where the characters live happily ever after and vanquish all evil.

It makes my heart ache.

I never want to leave. This is a better world, a good world.

Only after a while do I realize that this is no longer a dream. That I'm in my body again, the healing water prickling deep inside me.

I look down, trying to calm my swirling thoughts. How long has Caryan been sitting here? How long have I been unconscious, entrenched in those nightmares I thought would never stop; and which I'm still untangling? How long has it been since the snowfields I thought I would never escape?

Then I notice that I'm naked, remembering vaguely that someone undressed me. It isn't a dream anymore. Caryan is real. His wings are still there, stretched out behind him, feathers ruffled by a breeze, shielded by the shadows and the huge vines that dangle from the columns of those trees.

He is real. He...

I feel tears in my eyes before I swallow them down.

"How are you feeling?" he asks. His face is stern, his eyes shadowed. I sense that it's a careful question.

"Alright," I answer, maybe too lightly, because he growls at me, "Don't lie to me."

Despite his tone, I wade closer, silently praying that the mineral water will hide most of my naked body. I don't know where it comes from, this sudden need to touch him, but I stretch out my hand, brushing my fingers over one velvety wing. He tenses at the touch but doesn't move.

"There were nightmares," I say, more to myself than to him, as I let the soft feathers run through my fingers. I can't shake off the feeling that he's holding his breath. "I saw you. I mean, I *was* you, I think. And in one of them, a red-haired woman, she—"

"She cut off my wings." He finishes the sentence for me. His tone is dispassionate, his eyes adamantine, yet weary.

The confirmation takes my breath away. To know that they weren't just nightmares, but what I feared they were: his past.

I look down again, the memories of all that violence still vivid in my mind. All the pain this man in front of me has endured. And caused.

He stands, and I have the feeling he wants to get away from me.

He pauses at the edge of the pool, looking down at me. "I had to give you my blood because you were dying. I didn't want to, but I had no choice." His voice is raw, his eyes bereft of any color, any light, his jaw hard, as if he's angry. "What you saw weren't dreams. They were scenes of my life."

"But your wings—" I say.

Maybe I should be repulsed by what I saw, by the things he did. A part of me is, but my compassion is stronger. Right now, there's nothing else I want to do but touch him again, hold him. What he had to undergo, whatever he is, whatever he was... no one deserves that. It should have broken him, but it didn't.

"They grew back. It took a long time, but they grew back," he says, his voice cold like the relentless, merciless ice on that mountain. "Rest. We will leave when you're ready." He turns to go.

I watch him, guilt roiling in my belly. "Did you—did you find the flute?"

He pauses and I spot his wings twitching as he rolls his shoulders, as if to ease his tension. He doesn't turn to me when he says, "No. I didn't."

There is nothing in his voice. It's as empty as a void. It sends me into a freefall, tumbling down a dark abyss. I failed. I disappointed him. I messed up—my chance for freedom disappearing along with it—for what it's ever been worth.

$$) * ($$

Caryan barely looks at me on our hike back through that forest. His wings have disappeared again as if they were never there at all.

I'm keeping my head down as blurred memories of those nightmarish scenes push back to the surface. I can hear screams, voices begging for mercy where there had been none. The faint tinge of blood fills my nose, snippets of faces and people flaring through me. But the scenes are scrappy, no longer so clear, no longer so intense. More like an old film whose reel has been damaged, jumping randomly, the images awash and hazy, the sound disrupted. Once, something hits me, so absurdly vivid I don't notice a root on the ground and stumble over it. Caryan grabs my arm before I fall.

"I'm sorry," I whisper, pressing a hand against my forehead, only to find it cold and sweaty.

"It will be better in a few days. This is the aftermath," he says.

I can't look at him. I have the feeling he doesn't want me to anyway.

It's very strange to witness *everything* a person has done firsthand. It's so intimate I can't find words for it. I can feel that he hates it, though, feel his distaste so clearly in my body, as if it's my own emotion resonating through every fiber. His disgust is so strong, so much deeper than mine was when I learned he had seen scenes of *my* life the same way.

But then again, there's nothing interesting about my life. Nothing but panic attacks, the pain when Kayne and Hunter beat me up. A short life of despair and solitude—*everything* a feeble shadow of his. My demons, the joke of my life.

He must have secretly laughed about me.

I barely register that we've left the forest, barely feel the brush of the invisible curtain and the shift of energy when we enter his kingdom again. One car is still there, the doors open as if waiting for us to get in.

Caryan drives and I curl up on the seat next to him, occasionally glancing at him from beneath my hair. His marvelous face is a mask of stoicism, but I can see the tendrils of anger that twine around his aura, suffocating everything like thorny vines. Can feel the anger as a prickle on the underside of my skin, again as if it's *in* me.

Anger and hate and disgust so deep it burns my soul.

He hates me for my failure, and is probably disgusted by me. For trespassing into his life, not that I had any choice.

He doesn't so much as glance at me once the whole drive. Not when we stop for tiny breaks, not when we eventually reach the Fortress. He just steps into the shadows as soon as we've walked up the stairs from the garage, leaving me alone in the corridor, as if he can't bear to spend another second with me.

***

The Fortress is quiet without the celebrations, and I wonder how long we've been gone. It feels like an eternity. I slowly walk back to my room, not meeting anyone on my way. I take a long, hot shower before putting on some fresh clothes and climbing into bed.

But as soon as I close my eyes, there are pictures, clearer in the silence of night—a different kind of hell and anguish once again.

I get up and only then notice a set of paints and some sketchpads and canvases next to a fresh palette and an array of brushes. A tiny card in beautiful handwriting says:

Stay wild, moonchild.
Welcome back, Riven.

I stare at the card, tracing the swift, elegant letters with my finger before a quiet tear falls onto the paper.

I've never received such a gift from anyone. Not once in my life.

I stay still for a while, the sudden warmth in my chest like a shield against those dark and evil flashbacks that are still prowling through me. Then I get up, carefully unwrap the colors, and start to paint.

66

RIVEN

Riven finds Caryan in the ring in the arena, his powerful upper body naked and sweat-slicked as he dodges relentless, night-misted punches from Arien, one of the few shadow-shifters Riven's ever caught sight of—they are so rare. Feared for their ability to turn into liquid night without giving themselves away by smell or sound— and their relentless speed—their reflexes are even faster than those of high elves. They are a dangerous, lurking species who, as far as Riven knows, can also breathe underwater like mermaids. Arien is not a creature Riven would trust for a second if he wasn't blood-sworn to Caryan, yet he has become the best spy Riven's ever met.

The shadow-shifter launches for another attack, Arien's lithe body—muscle, covered thick with ornaments, white skin glinting through them as fluorescent as the moon over the waves—shooting forward. His hair, already sticking to his forehand, is the deepest blue, like the coldest part of the sea, the color matching eyes that are trained on Caryan with unrelenting focus.

Seeing Caryan and Arien fight isn't something one would easily forget. Their motions are an avalanche of blocks and attacks so fast even Riven's vision has trouble following. Only the mist that permanently envelops the shadow-shifter betrays his moves.

Arien dodges a blow from Caryan before he sidesteps, then vanishes only to reappear to Caryan's left, his fist already going for

Caryan's face when the arch of a black wing manifests out of nowhere and hits the shadow-shifter right in the face.

He goes down, so slack Riven knows it's a knockout.

Caryan sneers, his breath still coming slowly. No wonder the elves killed the angels. *They are frightening.*

At Caryan's feet, the shadow-shifter comes to, coughing hard but grinning at Caryan as he gets up, wiping blood from his lips. "I didn't see that coming," Arien says, true surprise ringing in his voice.

"Me neither," Riven agrees.

The shadow-shifter turns, still grinning, his teeth covered in blood.

"We're done, thank you, Arien," Caryan says.

The shifter nods once before he grabs one of the towels and steps out of the ring. Another step and he's gone altogether.

In the ring, Caryan spreads his fingers along with his wings.

"I thought you had a long journey," Riven says, sauntering closer, one hand in his pocket.

"I needed to stretch my legs."

"Well, clearly more than just your legs." Riven pauses beside the ring. "Wound a little tight?"

Caryan shoots him a flashing glance. Riven keeps his mocking expression, although he is not the least bit as relaxed as he pretends to be.

They were gone too long. Ten solid days.

"Want to join me for another round?" Caryan asks.

"You know I prefer weapons or magic over hand-on-hand combat anytime. Less chance to get an armpit full of sweat," Riven sneers.

"You can use your magic," Caryan offers.

Riven raises his brows. "You're really up for it, aren't you? And will you use your *skills?*"

"I'll play fair. Only my body, no magic."

"Don't complain when I singe your eyebrows," Riven says forcefully, shrugging off his shirt.

The corner of Caryan's lips lifts ever so slightly, but Riven's unable to say whether it's to flash his teeth or a hint of humor.

They fight like they mean it. Riven only survives the rounds without a knockout like Arien because he uses the same talent the shadow-shifter displayed—to become shadow, stepping in and out of the darkness.

Riven doesn't hold back though. He fights with all his anger, his claws, his speed. Caryan lets him work it off, he knows.

It doesn't spare him from a punch to his jaw so hard he'd have lost all his teeth if he were human. A flash of dark flames springs to life all over his skin, turning Riven briefly into nothing but shadowfire. Only this keeps Caryan from landing a second blow.

Riven pivots, steps into darkness, and lands a flame-laced kick into Caryan's back.

The angel clenches his teeth, snarling.

"You wanted it," Riven chides, wiping sweat from his forehead with his arm, challenging Caryan to counter with his magic.

But the angel doesn't. As with Arien, he shoots out his wings to knock Riven out, but he becomes darkness again, throwing a fist right into Caryan's face, a move the angel blocks with his lightning-fast reflexes, putting an elbow up between them to deflect Riven's hand while he lands a blow right into Riven's face. The impact hurts—revenge for the kick to his back.

Riven barely avoids another similar strike as shadowfire flares up on Caryan's wings before Caryan can block it with his magic.

For a sliver of a second, the angel with black wings burning with dark fire looks like a god from hell.

Gloriously vengeful.

"Now we're even," Riven says, both hands up, palms open, breathing hard, willing his flames out before they can singe the feathers of Caryan's wings. Not that Riven would allow them to truly harm Caryan, no matter how furious he still is. He'd only let them sizzle a little on the outside; knowing too well how sensitive Caryan's wings are—he might as well be singeing Caryan's balls.

Caryan bares his teeth nonetheless, snapping at him, living onyx dancing in his eyes. "You cheated," he snarls, his tone lethal.

"You said I could use my magic. And you were the one who used his wings, or they would have been off limits," Riven says quickly between breaths.

Caryan glances at his wings—not a feather has been even slightly singed—then nods in acceptance of Riven's truce.

Two water bottles appear out of nowhere in their hands—a gift from Caryan—and Riven watches with some satisfaction how Caryan gulps down his as quickly as he does.

"Good to see that I can still make you sweat harder than Arien," Riven drawls.

Caryan just raises a brow.

"So…" Riven starts again, grabbing a towel and wiping his wet torso with it. "I take it you didn't get what you were looking for, or I'd have found you screwing one of those gorgeous elves rather than working it off here."

"Elves *you* passed the time with, as I've heard," Caryan replies.

Riven shrugs. "One has to pass the time. Turns out being king is not quite as fun as it looks."

Caryan just says, "I need a bath," and steps out of the ring and is gone.

Riven follows him, entering Caryan's private bathroom a split second later, watching Caryan undress fully and slide into the hot water. Caryan's wings are gone, the angel leaning against the edge of the bath with his head back and his eyes closed.

On a snap of Riven's fingers, a siren enters, bowing her head. Nodding when Riven tells her to bring two glasses of honeyed wine. She serves them before retreating as quietly as she came.

Caryan doesn't touch his glass, doesn't so much as open his eyes once. Riven watches him, trying to make sense of everything Kyrith, Ronin, and that witch have told him.

The way Caryan carried Melody in her arms, shielded her with his wings. It would make sense that he didn't want to lose the girl who's the key to the artifacts. Or the key to his death. But the rest

535

doesn't fit. The way he didn't leave her side to go looking for that relic, but held her in his arms the whole time, trying to keep her warm while life leaked out of her by the minute.

The way Ronin said Caryan hesitated to give her his blood.

That also makes no sense. Caryan gave his blood to all of them—to all of the people who lived again because of him, who he offered the curse to, and who now inhabit his kingdom. His whole army exists only because Caryan gave his blood to every single one of them, no matter whether they were elf, faun, or any other fae.

Riven might have been able to believe that Caryan was too fine to give his blood to a half-mortal—or to a half-mortal who was Ciellara's daughter, for that matter—if Caryan hadn't watched over her the way Ronin and Kyrith said he did.

"Do you want to tell me what's going on?" Riven asks when he grows impatient with the silence. It's one of the things he has to handle about a true immortal—Caryan's confounded patience.

Caryan opens his eyes, still black as the sky on a moonless night. "I made a mistake."

"In what regard?"

Caryan just closes his eyes again.

"What, Caryan? A mistake how—in bringing her to that mountain? Not considering that the mountain she told you about is the *cursed* holy mountain, and she's a half-mortal, and that its raw magic would kill her?" Riven can't hide his temper anymore, his anger.

Caryan meets his eyes over the steaming bath while Riven's voice echoes from the walls, unusually sharp and loud.

"Or in flying back to the Emerald Forest with her, to Queen Calianthe, so that now everyone in all of Palisandre knows that you have her and that they will hunt for her even harder?"

Caryan stares at him with the stillness of a predator, his face unreadable. The Caryan Riven knew would have lashed him, shown him the ropes. But all he does is answer, "She knows better than that. Or I will burn down her forest."

Riven shakes his head, then presses, "Why not just sacrifice her for the relic? She could have led you there with your blood in her veins, could have stayed alive long enough for you to retrieve the relic. Is that what you regret? Your mistake—letting her live? Is that what you mean? Or is your main concern that *dead* she couldn't lead you to the other two relics?"

"It was a long night, Riven and I am tired," Caryan says but Riven's not yet done. Not this time.

"Tired in the sense that you finally decided that you want to die, Caryan? Is this why she is so important? Because if so, letting us know about it would be the least you could do." Riven bares his teeth, flashing them at Caryan, waiting, daring him to answer. To react.

But all Caryan does is angle his head slightly and look at him.

After a long silence, Caryan asks, "How long have you known that you are in love with her?"

Riven doesn't know what to say.

Caryan gets up and climbs the stairs out of the bath, turning his back on Riven. "My mistake was believing, no matter what I told you, that I could avoid the inevitable, Riven. But apparently, even I cannot. Stay as long as you like, but then leave. And don't follow me this time."

It's an order Riven feels in his bones. Unable to follow Caryan, all he can do is watch him go.

MELODY

The next day, a knock at the door wakes me when the sun is already up.

Nidaw enters, her frustration giving way to worry when she spots me still in bed.

"I'm sorry, I must have overslept," I say, quickly wriggling out of the mess of sweat-soaked sheets and getting up.

Nidaw's eyes rest on the wall I was painting the whole night.

Caryan with golden eyes.

"You're very good at that, you know," Nidaw says while I brush my teeth.

I say nothing, spit, wash my face, and follow Nidaw outside, deciding the shower has to wait. My hair's a mess and I try to tame it with my fingers while I walk to the kitchen.

The day unfolds as if I was never gone. Except the tasks are harder. There is more scrubbing needed than ever, although the floors look clean, but I don't question my orders. There are still occasional visions of Caryan's past; the sudden hush of whispers or laughter or screams, but every time I look up, there's no one around.

While I work the brush over the tiles, my mind wanders back to all the images I've seen.

All that Caryan did.

Then my mind drifts to the flame-haired woman in the tent,

the memory of her more like a dream than anything real. I vaguely remember that she held a sword to my throat. The woman I'd saved from Lyrian had come to kill me. A woman with silver teeth and claws.

But—why didn't she? Why did she decide to let Caryan take her and almost kill her instead? Caryan knew the woman. I heard him saying her name—Blair, or something like that—but everything's so blurred, I'm not sure.

The day is over, the palace quiet and empty, and only after a while do I realize that the absence I'm feeling comes from Caryan's physical absence. I don't know how, but I sense he's far away, clearer than ever before. And that *bond* within me—where it had been a shy, black idea of something… now it's a swirling, velvety dark orbit, forged into the night, a whirlwind of black, streaked with silvery stars. When I mentally brush up against it, it morphs into a bridge, silken and half-solid, as if woven of black mist, leading deeper into the blackness. A gust of night-kissed magic comes up. An offer. I mentally stumble back, not even daring to get close again. Not after Caryan's reaction the last time I did.

I snap out of it, the rooms and reality coming back into harsh focus. Suddenly restless, I find myself venturing toward Riven's rooms, but when I ask the head next to his door, it tells me that Riven has also left.

"For how long?"

"I am not sure, my lady," the head answers.

I swear remorse laces its voice. I remember what Caryan told me about the door, about the whole Fortress being and acting like an extension of him and his wishes.

"Where did they go?"

The blue eyes flicker to life once more. "I can't tell you, my lady."

I sigh, wondering how long I could possibly lead a conversation with a door before I would reasonably be considered crazy.

To hell with it. I can't bring myself to walk back to my barren, lonely room to be alone with those *flashbacks*, so I slide down to the floor and lean the back of my head against the wall, savoring its coolness.

"Do you know whether he's still angry with me?" I ask into the night.

The blue flames next to my face return. "Why would my lord be angry with you?"

"Because I failed him. I disappointed him." *I fucked up our bargain.*

"I do not think it is you he is disappointed in, my lady. And not you with whom he is angry."

I frown. Caryan said something similar to me once.

"But—who then?"

"With whom are you angry when there is no one else to blame?"

"With myself," I say quietly, as if it's the answer to a riddle. I'm not sure what to do with this realization though.

"Correct. Do not forget that, my lady, for whatever happens in the future."

I mumble my thanks, although I'm not sure that any of it was an answer to my question.

When I glance up, I flinch. Ronin's standing there, silent as a shadow, his arms crossed in front of his chest. He watches me curiously.

"You know where they went, don't you?" I ask, breaking the silence.

"Does it matter?"

It's an honest question, I realize. One that holds no mocking.

"You miss him," the witcher gathers.

I startle like a deer. "Who?" I ask, covering it.

"Both," he says.

"Can you read auras too?"

The hint of a smile comes to his lips, genuine. "In a sense," he admits.

"Tell me what you see in me. Please," I say, suddenly curious.

"You do know everything I *sense* already yourself," he says, not unkindly. Again, just a fact. "Which is rare, but I assume that comes along with our... talent."

I watch him. "It feels strange, when someone can read who you are," I admit. Again, that smile. "I can only agree."

"I misjudged you, you know," he adds after a moment of silence.

"In what sense?"

"I thought you crueler, but you are more soft-hearted than I estimated."

I don't know what to do with this. His tone tells me nothing either.

"And that is good or bad?" I probe.

"Neither. It just changes things. Or might, in the future."

"Why?"

He takes a deep breath, looking up at the ceiling. His amber eyes brighten when they settle back on me. "Isn't it ironic that they say people who can't love are dangerous? But then, on the other hand, the gravest crimes in this world, we commit for the one we love."

With this, he turns and disappears back into the darkness. I know he's staying close, yet all the way back to my room I can neither feel nor hear nor smell him.

His words left me with a strange sensation in my body.

Back in my quarters, I look at my painting for too long, before I fall asleep, imagining that Caryan is watching me like he did that night in his room.

MELODY

They are away for a week.

I paint a lot, adding a new detail every night, breathing more life into the painting. Sometimes it's the curves of his lips. The shade of his skin, his eyelids. The arch of his ears or the way his hair curls around them. Sometimes the speckles in the gold, the veins of his irises.

In the afternoon of the seventh day, I feel the Fortress come alive with his power again, and I know he's back. As if his energy affects my very being, too, I feel more alive than I did the whole of the past week.

As if I'd been sleepwalking and now have woken up to the real world again.

Once Nidaw informs us that there will be a gathering to welcome the high lords back, I can barely hide my nerves at the prospect of seeing Caryan and Riven again.

The latter crosses my path as I'm on the way back from my room to shower and change into fresh clothes. I run toward him when I see him, not caring what anyone else will think. Not caring what he thinks.

But he sweeps me up into his arms and holds me for a long while.

"I missed you," I whisper when he lets me go and gently puts me back down on the ground.

I haven't seen him since we left for the mountains. His eyes are as stunning and soft as ever, but I can't help but notice that he looks paler, if such a thing is even possible with his skin already as white as mine.

"I missed you too, my sweet, sweet little villain," he says. His hand brushes my cheek ever so briefly before I hear servants behind us come streaming out of the kitchen. He gives me a gentle smile. "Later, then."

$$\supset * \complement$$

The gathering is quieter than the parties. There are just a few already familiar faces I recognize, and the mood is somehow more official, although there is still a lot of exposed skin—fae don't seem to mind that in general, I should know that by now.

I spot Riven joining in a little later, in his usual opulent evening attire. Caryan's accompanied by that breathtaking, dark-haired elf woman, who doesn't once leave his side. He doesn't look at me, though, not for the whole evening, while in return, I can't help but notice the possessive way the woman touches him and stands close whenever she can.

It's only deep into the night, when the sun has long set and there are only a few people remaining, that I spot Caryan walking out onto the terrace alone.

"Elderberry wine with lavender ice. Your favorite," I say quietly when I step up to him.

He regards me distantly, as if he has totally forgotten about me.

"I added a splash of lime. I think you'll like it," I add with a shy smile that dies on my face when he keeps looking at me in that serene way. I let my gaze drop to my hands when he eventually takes the glass from me, avoiding touching my fingers.

"You were gone so long," I add, my voice a whisper.

"I was."

I glance up at him again, at his stone-gray eyes. Reverent and cold.

I want to say *I missed you*, but suddenly I can't find the words. I want to ask *Did something happen?*, but this too dies on my tongue when he says, "You should lower your eyes."

I say nothing, just quietly step away, not daring to look up at him again, my heart aching from a phantom pain, pulsing so hard I feel it wants to break my ribs and rip free of my chest.

☽ ✳ ☾

Later, after my shift, the celebrations are still in full swing. I meander down the halls, the music echoing through them. When I hear someone singing eerily, hauntingly, I briefly think it's coming from the throne room, but then realize the sound is traveling up from the dungeon. A modern song, just a weird interpretation. *Kiss me hard before you go.*

I stop, consider, and then—fuck it—head down. Down to the prison, to the clammy cold, fragrant with mold. I pause in front of a cell, only to find the woman with the formerly wine-red hair there.

She's still alive. The woman who tried to kill me, only to spare my life. So Caryan kept his promise.

We stare at each other from a distance. She looks so different now, her hair white as freshly fallen snow. She's slimmer, too, I realize with a kind of shock. Her torn clothes hang on her. And cold, her cherry-red lips are tinged blue.

"Look at you, Caryan's little pet," she snarls, getting up from the ground and walking closer to the bars before easing into a crouch again, as if she's too weak to stand.

"What happened to you?" I whisper.

She looks feral, the way her amber eyes rove over my exposed flesh, filling up with hunger. Her skinniness does nothing to hide the starved killer beneath.

"I could ask you the same. You reek of desperation," she hisses.

Before she can say more, I turn around and run up the stairs. I head to the kitchen, and when no one's looking, grab everything I can find—a tiny apple tart, raisin bread, a duck leg, plums—all leftovers from the celebration. I stuff them into a kitchen towel and run back to the dungeon.

She's still crouching in the very same spot. I fight my fear and step up to her, putting the towel with the food on the ground so she can choose.

"What do you want, human?" she spits, but her eyes stay on the presented things.

"Nothing."

"Nothing in the world is free, especially not kindness. What do you want?"

I frown, then shake my head. "You're starving. Eat. I can get more tomorrow. And eat quickly before someone comes looking for me."

"This is not how this works," she says, and I can see that she doesn't trust me. *Fae rules.*

"Well, then tell me your name."

Her eyes widen for a sliver of a moment. "Blair."

"Now eat, Blair," I say.

She goes for the duck leg first. I watch with a kind of horrified fascination as she devours it almost whole. She eats the whole piece in less than a minute, bones included. When all the food is gone, she leans her head back, color creeping back into her skin.

"You look like Gatilla," I say quietly.

It's clearly the wrong thing to say because she bares her teeth at me. I see hate in her aura, a second too late. Hate. And jealousy. Pain. Disgust. Fear. Envy. Horror.

"How would you know, little human, huh?"

"I saw it, in Caryan's blood," I answer quietly.

She lets out a hissing sound. "Do I look like my aunt, huh? With my hair bleached and white and barren." She spits the words out, her face torn with fury and pain. She *hates* it—her new look.

"I'm sorry," I say quietly, meaning it with my whole heart. She looks away. "But it's rather beautiful, you know," I add.

Her head snaps back to me. "Spare me your dewy-eyed sentiment, little liar."

"It's true. You look like a moonmaiden."

"Shouldn't you be fucking off or something?"

"At least you don't look like your aunt anymore. Maybe it is a new start," I try.

She stills before her eyes glower at me with all the fury I just saw scorching her soul. "Why would I not want to look like my aunt? I loved her."

I shake my head. "No. You didn't. You just told yourself that you loved her, but deep down, you hated her," I say before I can think better of it.

She flexes her clawed fingers. "Is that a challenge?"

"No, I'm sorry." I shake my head, regretting my words.

"Are you? Shove your psycho-tips up your human ass until they shine out of your mouth. I call that reversed bullshit deep-throat," Blair growls, slamming her hands against the bars. "Now you better run back to your master before Caryan starts to miss his breakable little toy."

"I'm *not* his toy," I retort with a sudden anger that surprises me.

As if she felt it, she croons, her eyes shining wildly, "No? Should I call you his *lover?* Or rather mistress? Or slut?"

I raise my chin. "I've been called worse, but that's not what I am."

She huffs a laugh, an eerie sound, thrown back by the walls. "No? Are you not? Tell me you haven't yet opened your legs for him. Tell me that you make the exception and are the one who isn't under his clean thumb."

"You're jealous of me," I say to my surprise, but it shines clearly over all the other emotions, lacing with her anger. How could anyone looking like her be jealous of *me?*

She bares her teeth, the canines as long as Caryan's fangs, but silver and slimmer.

We look at each other.

"You love him…" I gather, reading her aura like an open book. Caryan. She loves *Caryan.* I try to understand what I see there, and how that goes along with what I know. "I thought he was your aunt's lover." That's what Riven told me. What I saw in Caryan's memories.

"My aunt's *slave*," she seethes, her pale fingers with long silver claws—which match her canines—twining around the bars as if she'd like to grind them like old bones and come for me.

"He broke your heart," I say quietly. I can see that she's hurting, so much. Her aura, bleeding sorrow.

"I don't have a little, breakable, human heart, girl. Let me out and I prove it to you."

"That's not true. You care. I can see it. That's why you spared me, right? Even though a part of you wants me dead."

"Clearly, a mistake. Now make way, or I swear I'll try to rip these bars apart and come for you."

I lift my chin and straighten my shoulders. "Keep going with your threats, but we both know that if you could, you'd have done so by now."

She snarls. "Bold. But I'd really suggest you fuck off now."

I take a deep breath, not moving a muscle. But oh hells, she's terrifying, even behind bars. If her gaze could kill me, I'd be long dead. I do my best to ignore it and to hold my voice steady as I say, "If you were at Gatilla's court, you must have known my mother." I saw her in Caryan's memory, my mother; my features so unmistakably hers. It hurt, to see how much I look like her. The woman who gave me away, who wanted to sell me. She stood in the crowd when Gatilla cut off Caryan's wings.

"Oh yes, I *did* know your mother," Blair snaps, disgust tingeing every word.

I take another deep breath. "Why did she try to kill Caryan? And when?"

Blair's head perks up, and she narrows her eyes before a cruel smile spreads over her face. "So many questions, little clueless one," she taunts, clearly enjoying that she has something over me.

"What did she do at Gatilla's court?" I probe on, ignoring her mocking.

"Why not ask your master?"

I swallow down my anger at her remark. "He won't tell me."

"Huh. That's how he does things," she muses, almost to herself.

"Please, Blair. I saw so many things in his blood, so many bits and pieces, but they make no sense to me. I need to know more."

Blair's eyes go briefly unfocused before they fasten on me again. "Very well then, it's not like I have anywhere to be. Your mother was an outcast. She came to Gatillas's court because my aunt offered her refuge in exchange for Caryan's runes. Your mother painted them for her. She and Gatilla were best friends—"

"What?" I breathe but Blair holds up a silver-clawed finger. "Nuh, nuh, nuh, don't you dare spoil the moment. I'm not done yet. They were best friends, or so it seemed. But, in truth, your mother came to infiltrate my aunt's court and destroy her."

Blair makes a pause while I don't dare breathe.

Then she says, "Your mother had guts. And she was good at what she did—so good no one suspected a thing while she secretly sided with Riven and Caryan." Blair lets out a sad, choked laugh. "Even I didn't see it coming. But Ciellara was the one who helped free Caryan from Gatilla's shackles in the first place. She worked on him for months, right under Gatilla's nose, yet even my aunt didn't feel it. Didn't realize that she tampered his runes, made them able to cut through her leash."

I startle. Those magical shackles I felt when I was in Caryan's body, in his memories.

"But why did she do it? Help him in the first place, only to turn against him?" I ask.

Blair gives me a look as if I should know these things. "Because everyone wanted to get rid of my aunt, she was that bad. And your mother did the math. She helped Caryan, who was strong enough to kill Gatilla, but he was also severely wounded and weakened from that fight with her. I guess your mother just saw a chance and tried her luck."

"But... why?"

Blair snorts and rolls her eyes as if I'm truly stupid. "*Why* what? Why she wanted to kill him? Because he already was the most powerful fae. With Gatilla's magic... well, he became what he is today. Unmatched in power. I guess she killed one monster but realized she unleashed another."

"And he still wants more," I say quietly. "He still wants those relics. He said he needs them for the war." Blair smirks at me, and for a moment, she looks so human despite her beauty, it's startling. Then she says lightly, "Of course he does." Too late do I realize that she's being ironic.

"You don't believe that?"

She shrugs. "I just believe in what I know."

She doesn't say more. After a moment I grow restless. "Calianthe also said it corrupts the mind and soul of the person who claims it."

Blair throws me an endlessly bored look. "And?"

"He still wants it."

"What is it *you* want, little confused human?" she drawls with a sigh, tilting her head back, peering at the ceiling and the bats who have gathered there as if she was contemplating whether to snatch one as dessert. "Other than riding my last nerve?"

"I just want to do the right thing," I whisper.

She laughs at that, truly laughs, throwing her head back. "Huh. That's adorable and the funniest thing I've heard in a long time. Heartwarming, really. You just made my day."

"Everyone here seems to love Caryan as a king. They... adore him," I say carefully, ignoring the barb.

Her gaze cuts through me. "And you don't. Was he mean to you, little human?"

I take a deep breath. "I think he can be dangerous. *Is* dangerous."

Her face changes as she takes me in, as if seeing me in a different light. "You're an interesting little creature," she murmurs, seemingly more to herself again. "I must say, you do not have much of your mother. *Yet*." The last word sounds like a warning.

"You haven't answered my question," I say.

"You haven't asked one," she says back, her tone like a knife.

I grind my teeth and make myself ask, "Is Caryan bad?"

Blair's eyes rove over me again, from head to toe. I wonder what she's thinking. Her aura is a mess of too many hues, too many streaks, like the palette of an artist after finishing a painting. Messy.

Then her eyes snare on my wrist, on the tattoo there. "I think it doesn't matter anymore when you were stupid enough to bind a part of your soul to him. I hate to say it, but you're already doomed."

"He promised me freedom in exchange for three relics."

Her bleached eyebrows rise high before she cackles again. "You truly are adorable. You do know it is all about semantics in our world? Freedom might indeed mean that he lets you walk out of his Fortress as a free woman. But—" she shrugs demonstratively, "It could also mean you find your freedom in death."

For a second I don't know how to breathe. She just turns her back on me, walking to the other end of the cell, slumping down against the wall.

A second later, I hear someone behind me and whip around. Ronin stands there. He's approached silently, and briefly, I'm stricken by the similarity to Blair—his hair is the same, coppery red that hers used to be, his eyes hold the same amber. Only his pupils are like that of a cat's.

"I've been looking for you," he says, and I think I hear a touch of remorse in his voice, see it mirrored in his aura. "The Dark Lord sends for you."

69

MELODY

I slowly walk to Caryan's quarters, Ronin silently accompanying me.

"My lady," the door greets me as it swings open.

Ronin waits until I step in, then walks away. The door closes behind me with a thud. I can't help the feeling of being locked in.

I pause there, my ears and my instinct straining for Caryan. My gaze falls on a huge, black sword leaning against the wall. The very same sword Blair held to my throat on the mountain. So similar to the one my mother tried to split Caryan in half with. Next to it on the floor, still huge but so much smaller than the sword, is the black arrowhead the Nefarian woman threatened Caryan with.

I tear my gaze away from them and venture deeper into his apartment.

I find Caryan in the room to my left, standing with his back to me in front of the window, hidden by darkness.

"Come here," he says without turning.

I slowly cross the distance. When he finally turns to me, his expression holds the same bleak coldness I found in his mind, mirrored in his eyes. His aura is unreadable.

Something about him is wrong, I know. I *feel* it, in me.

"I want you to take off your clothes," he says.

My blood ices over. My heartbeat suddenly thunders in my ears. I step away from him.

He follows.

I bite my lips, not daring to make a sound as his power enshrouds me. Not that gentle kind hum that caressed my skin the previous times, but bristling and prickling, biting my flesh and underneath it like a writhing, raging creature. As if it wants to crawl into me.

I can feel my magic flaring, trying to push it away, silver light running under my skin. But his magic just closes its fangs around it, biting deep into my magic's flesh until my magic succumbs, holding very, very still.

"Do I have to say it again?" His voice is laced with impatience. Coldness. His power, a merciless prickling that licks up to my wrists, harsh and scolding. A mixture of lightning and dark fire. He has been angry before, but I have never seen him like this. So *cold*. So inhuman.

My throat tightens as I say very quietly, "I... I don't know how to... how to do *this*. I've never done it before." I barely force the words out.

He lets out a derisive snort, almost a snarl, that slithers over my raw skin and makes me want to curl up in shame.

I flinch when he grabs my chin again, tilting my head back.

"No, you do not. Apparently," he says, though his voice is not mocking, but tender. Tender like a bruise.

I try to rein in my thundering heartbeat, my trembling, but fail when he runs his hand along my collarbone, pushing my wide shirt off my shoulder. "Now, take that off."

I do. And just like the night after he saved me from that worm, I hold it in front of me, as if it could shield me. Protect me.

"All your clothes," he says.

My pants. My underwear.

I can't. I shake my head. "Please, Caryan—"

"That was an order." His words are relentless.

He will keep me in his bedroom. Caryan's whore, they called me. I didn't want to listen. No, I didn't dare to.

I whisper before I can think, "Please. Please don't do this. Not tonight. Please give me some time," I beg with all I have.

I press my hands against his chest, more reflex than anything as he steps up to me, his power engulfing me once more. His hand finds my cheek, his fingers caressing me so tenderly I close my eyes, suppressing tears. He leans in and I shudder when I feel his breath on my neck, right over my pulse. My heartbeat flutters under his lips.

His voice is impossibly gentle when he murmurs, "This is not about sex."

My eyes fly open, up to his, simmering clear and bright like a hellish flame; bottomless. I'm not sure what I find in his face. But I know I don't like it. He looks almost pained, and my heartbeat stutters into an even faster, violent beat.

Instinctively, I try to wrench free, but he just yanks me close, between his legs. His shadows pushing me against the wall, twining around my limbs, my ribs, my throat.

"Do not fight me. You're a liability like this." He spits the words at me, like an insult.

"Like what?" I manage to snap at him.

"Weak. Defenseless."

My throat tightens. I had it all wrong. He's not going to make me stay for the night. He's going to do what Gatilla did to him, over and over. What I saw in his mind. The pain I felt like my own.

"You're going to chain me to an altar and rape me?" My voice comes out all wrong, my breathing too fast, matching my galloping heartbeat.

He looks like I've slapped him. "I would never do any of those things."

"But I saw what—"

"What you saw was me chained to an altar and her inking the tattoos in my flesh," he cuts me off. "And sequences of me and her in the bedroom. Those were two entirely different things."

"And you're not going to do *that*?" I'm proud to manage to speak the words, to deliver them with some sarcasm, although a part of me is falling apart.

His expression darkens. "No. Because of the bond between us,

553

I can give you some of my power without having to mend it with your flesh. This process is going to hurt, but you will get used to it," he says. Cold, dead horror slices through me, splitting me in half. Consuming me.

"No. Please, no! I don't want that," I bare my teeth as his magic again comes for me.

"I will not allow you to die on me!" His voice is suddenly a primal growl that comes from somewhere deep in his throat.

And I know he has long made the decision. There is nothing I can do as the shackles pull tighter, his magic swamping me, invading every part of me. Bristling and biting, searing me from the inside. A burning like nothing I've ever felt before.

I shake my head as tears well in my eyes. "I fucking trusted you!" I scream as he steps up to me once again, the magic a thousand times worse when our bodies touch, amplified as if I'm a wildfire and he is gasoline. "I don't want your evil magic!"

"Do not fight me, Melody. I have to," he snarls into me.

But hells, I *am* fighting him, his damn, dark magic. Kicking and biting and clawing at him, my teeth finding flesh and ripping until I taste blood. My magic desperately scratching and straining against his magic, but he's too much. His magic is too much. Way too powerful. I sensed it the first time in the desert. *He* is endless.

My vision blurs as his power shoots and runs through me so wildly that I become pain. Just pain, as everything disintegrates.

My body turns numb.

Silent tears stream down my face. I can no longer hold them back, no matter how hard I'm trying.

My body, my very soul, are aching from *this*. From what he's doing to me, the crack deepens every second it goes on. A pain beyond something physical but so deep I don't know where it starts and where it ends. Shadows and crackling lightning flaring under my skin, becoming so painful, so elemental as it tears my innermost being apart.

I will survive. I survived Lyrian, I will survive this too.

It's those thoughts I cling to that tether me, that don't make me lose my mind. My sanity.

It's all-consuming, the pain, breaking more than just my heart. Shredding everything in their path.

My senses barely remember how I ended up on his bed—the bed I slept in, feeling so safe, his scent lingering like a callous mocking. But when the pain finally subsides, he's above me. His body is so heavy and huge over mine. Only hard muscles, pressing me deep into the sheets, his hand holding my wrists over my head.

Somewhere I register that I'm shivering under him like mad, worse than I did on that mountain when I was fighting the cold. Now I'm sweat-slicked and feverish.

Eventually, he lets go of me and sets my body free.

I curl up on my side, my fingers digging so hard into the sheets they turn bone white.

I know he's watching me, standing in the dark at the foot of the bed. Looking down on me. But I don't dare glance at him.

My heart is still beating, despite the fact that it feels like it's been shattered so thoroughly, and I almost wonder if magic alone makes it beat on.

My whole body aches from what he has done. Every part of me feels sore, every inch ravished, violated, broken.

And empty.

I watch his white, powerful body when he turns his back to me and walks out of the room. I must have torn his shirt, because it lies next to me on the bed, discarded, shredded.

The silence that follows closes in on me. The emptiness as soon as he left me.

I get up, the ground under my feet unreliable. I look down at myself, still in my pants and my bra, yet I couldn't feel more naked. More bare. More alien. As if this isn't me I'm looking at, but someone else. It's only then that my eyes rest on my wrist—there's still the tattoo of my bargain, but it looks different. Ornaments and runes spread around it now, rimmed with black and gold tendrils, shifting.

Runes. Those are runes from *his* body. I touch them, and as if on cue, a wave of darkness shudders through me, rattling me so deeply I pull my hand back from my skin, eyes wide. But the new, dark force keeps undulating along my bones, filling the emptiness in me.

What the hell?

Slowly, so slowly, I follow him to the living room.

Caryan stands in front of the open window. His back is still to me. He's watching the stars.

My gaze goes to my shirt on the floor. Like an article that belongs to another person. How long did his magic run through me like a wildfire? Burn me from the inside out? It felt like months, years, but it might only have been moments.

I snatch up my shirt and wriggle it over my head. Then, before he can turn to me, I run. Toward the door, toward the carved head I've spoken to so many times.

The blueish flames in its eye sockets jump to life.

"Please, please let me go."

The flames are smaller, as if muted. As if sad, it says quietly, "I cannot, my lady."

Tears start to stream down my face again. I sink onto the ground, my fingers splayed against the door. "Please... he will hurt me." *Hurt me even more.*

I know he won't stop until he's done. Not when he made his decision.

"I cannot disobey the wishes of my lord, my lady." I swear the words are tinged with regret as the flames die.

I turn and spot Caryan in the doorway, his eyes crimson with my blood. I drop my gaze to the floor. I didn't realize that he bit me. I bring my hands to my lips, finding blood there. I have the vague memory of sinking my teeth into his shoulder to stifle my cry as his magic shot and ran wild through me.

I wish I could recoil into myself, melt into the wall.

Instead, I get up and turn to him. Still avoiding looking into his eyes, I repeat the same words I've just said to the door, my voice sounding foreign to me. "Please let me go."

I watch him come closer, his bare feet moving soundlessly over the ashy wood. He pauses a yard away from me. "I'm not yet done."

I flinch at the sound of his voice. So deep. So raw.

The truth resonates within me, in every fiber, writhing along my bones and curling around my soul. I can feel his mind again, his decision as if it was my own. Feel this dark... *bond,* as he called it. This dark thing between us. Stronger than it has ever been. He will do this again and again. He only survived because he was an angel. I can't get through this again. I'm only a half-elf. I won't survive.

Or maybe I will, but it will be a broken survival. Shattered.

"Let. Me. Go."

"I cannot."

Fear renders me speechless. Fear so deep it is bottomless. It paralyzes me.

I can't breathe.

I can't think as he comes for me again.

And somehow, this is far worse than with Lyrian. Because Caryan is a force of nature. Nothing can stop him. I didn't understand it fully, not really. But I do now, having learned it the hard way.

My gaze goes to the runes on his body, to the tattoo shifting over his chiseled, hard muscles that pressed against me just moments ago.

The runes on his chest, shifting, moving. *Alive.*

And I suddenly *know* their meaning. I can make out every individual character within the ornaments they're embedded in. I can *read* the power they hold. The deep, raw, ancient magic that has been formed into symbols and bound by ink and blood. Almost as powerful as the flute I did not find.

I can make out those my mother tried to destroy. She picked the most powerful of them. The sad irony doesn't escape me. I wonder whether she felt the same before she tried to kill him. Whether she felt so helpless, so lost, as desperate as I?

"Do not—"

The words die in my throat as Caryan stretches out his hand, running his knuckles over my cheek, his magic curling around him like dark flames made of smoke. Tender, gentle, as it had been in so many other moments.

"I cannot let you die, do you understand?"

I shake my head, unable to find my voice.

He clenches his teeth, his eyes flickering. "You almost died on me on that mountain because you're so weak. So fragile. I cannot allow this. I cannot let you live in a world as dangerous and cruel as this one, defenseless as you are."

"You said my magic showed. That I would learn. That it would become stronger. We can wait." My voice sounds strained, shaky. Pleading. Desperate.

"It can take a century for a fae to fully develop their power. War is coming. I do not have the luxury of time. Forgive me."

His hand runs along my neck, down to my collarbone. So gentle I feel sick.

Then, without a warning, it starts again. I clench my teeth as his magic again laces with my bones. Shatters me from the inside, just to create me anew.

Again, I fight him. I try to kick him, to push him. His magic only drives me into the wall once again, his body against mine again. I bite him again, sink my teeth into his throat until I taste blood, my nails shredding his skin as his unholy power eats me from within.

Something in me opens its eyes then. My magic, but no longer. My magic, laced with his, woven together, streaks of silver and black. I can feel it, his magic running along mine, interlaced, melded together, but *mine* now. I can feel the runes on my wrist, powerful, and my new magic drawing from them.

It surges in answer through my veins, through my blood. Flaring through my fingers right into his chest. Undiluted, silvery light laced with his blackness and lightning. Stronger than ever. *A monstrosity.*

His eyes widen. He staggers back from me, clenching his teeth, flashing them at me in pain. Then he looks down at my hands still on his chest, burning away his skin. I can see his ribcage opening, his bones shining through. His beating heart.

The sight almost tears me apart. Makes me sick to my stomach. The expression on his face is even worse.

No anger. No hate. No fury.

No. For a second, I think the corners of his mouth lift into the faintest hint of a smile.

I pull my hands back. Horrified at myself. By what I just did.

I never wanted that.

But just like that, his skin, his bones, everything starts to knit itself back together. Slowly, but healing already.

I won't have long.

My fingers close around the hilt of the black sword.

With a last glance at him, I run. But not towards the door, but toward the window.

I spread my arms and—

Jump.

Falling, I swallow the pearl Arbor gave me.

MELODY

Freefall. The ground comes into focus too quickly. My heart, leaping into my throat. *Fuck, fuck, fuck.* The pearl—it doesn't work! It was supposed to allow me to fly. Maybe I should have asked how quickly it would work.

I fall and fall. It feels so much like I always imagined it would when I stood on that cliff, those grayish swells waltzing underneath.

I watch the hard rock passing me by in a blur, the stony, unforgiving, desert ground that will be my grave already waiting.

I don't even blink when something catches me and lifts me three seconds before I collide with the ground.

No, nothing *catches* me. *Something* catches the wind.

I turn my head and stare at the pair of beautiful, lavender moth wings protruding from my back, shedding sparkling dust every time they move. They beat of their own accord, as if they are sentient.

Not long, Arbor warned me. They won't last long.

"To the town," I beg them because I don't know what else to do. I'll find a horse and then go north, as Sarynx said. I pray that the spell will last long enough and not run out in the middle of the desert.

The wings beat hard, lifting me up and up in the air, shedding more glittery sparks into the night.

Just then something blots out the blood moon. My head snaps

up, and my stomach plummets. Something gargantuan. A... *dragon*. Above me is a *dragon* with four horns protruding from his head, an immensely huge, leathery body, and a deadly, black Morningstar as a tail.

Its gleaming golden eyes find me. Then it dives for me with teeth the size of my forearm bared. Terror seizes my throat and my heart lurches.

"Back to the Fortress!" I scream at the wings, and they beat harder than ever, pitching upwards. The beast rushes past, jaw snapping shut, those teeth passing so close to my arm I could touch them.

But the stream of air produced by the dragon's massive, leathery wings whips me further up, hurling me through the night like a butterfly in a storm.

The dragon lets out a frustrated screech, and then banks, coming for me again. I stare at it diving toward me, my heart hammering like mad while my tiny wings shed more and more stardust.

"Faster!" I beg them.

The dragon surges up from below, its deadly mouth in direct line with my body.

Three seconds away.

Two.

One.

I'm dinner.

My wings disappear without a warning.

I'm in free fall again. Darkness swooshes around me as the ground rises to meet me once again. Air rushes past me as I plummet toward my certain death. Above me, I hear the click of those massive teeth as they rip into nothing but air.

I hit the ground. Hard.

I brace for the impact with my elbows, shielding my head. Searing pain shoots through my knees and a scream rips from my throat. I blink, fighting to keep from blacking out. My bones sing. I try to move my limbs, one by one, my toes, my fingers. Everything hurts like hell, but nothing seems to be broken.

I dare to glance down between my hands. *A terrace.* I've landed on one of the many terraces.

Above me, the beast screeches again, and I scramble to my feet, grab the sword that landed somewhere next to me, and sprint toward the door. I feel wards as I splay my fingers against the metal of the door, cool and smooth like an invisible wall of ice. The tattoo on my wrist warms and the wards ripple briefly before they let me through. Stunned, I tumble inside. *The tattoo did this.* It works like a key.

I try to catch my breath while my eyes scan the room, my fist closed tight around the hilt of the sword. Kyrith's scent invades my nostrils, and I panic briefly before I realize that I'm in his room. He's not here, but everything smells of him.

I cross the vast room in a few strides but stop at a table where various weapons and scabbards are neatly laid out, polished and honed to perfection. I grab a leathery, black scabbard, sling it over my shoulders, and sheathe the sword between my shoulder blades. Then I head for the door and rip it open. Again it's the new tattoo that opens it before I have to break through those wards, saving me precious time. I need to get out of the Fortress. I need to get away before Caryan recovers.

I clamp down on my desperation, my fear of what will happen if Caryan finds me. *He won't,* I cut my spiraling thoughts off. *I'll be long gone. End of story.* I don't allow myself to think of another option.

I stagger into a corridor and run.

I know my way. And for some miraculous reason, like on my first night, not a single soul crosses my way as I sprint through the Western quarters.

I don't know what would happen if someone did. I'm glad I don't have to let myself find out, with that strange new force still thrashing and roaring under my skin, all too eager to shred and rip and burn.

I shove it down and cross the patio to the kitchen.

I'm still shaking, flinching at every sound that travels through the endless corridors, every sense in me alert. My heartbeat; feverish.

Then footsteps. Long strides. Coming close. Too close, too fast.

My eyes scan the corridor, desperately trying to find somewhere to hide, but there are only smooth, cold walls and the door to Riven's quarters to my right.

Just then Riven cuts around the corner. His eyes widen when he takes me in.

I just stare back at him, backing down when he nears. He looks disheveled and drunk, his hair irreverent, and the kohl under his eyes slightly smeared, but his eyes are sober.

"Melody, what..." His voice is breathless and tinged with worry as he looks at me.

I just shake my head, unable to speak, unable to form words.

He must see the horror in my gaze, because his face changes, hardening as he gestures to his quarters. The door swings open.

I follow him in. My sword is by his throat before he can react.

His purple eyes are wide, and he swallows against the blade, but they focus on me with new intensity. "Melody, please..."

But his words are not about the sword, I realize, but about my bruises. He reaches out to me, wanting to run his fingers over them. "Melody—"

"How do I get out? I'm sure there is some secret tunnel or something," I cut him off, angling the sword as a reminder and he lowers his arm. I suspect Caryan's magic somehow prevents my talent from working *inside* the Fortress.

His brows rise as his eyes find the marks on my wrist. The tattoo, now adorned with some of Caryan's runes. He looks back at me, the light in his eyes dimmed by shock. "This is a part of Caryan's tattoo. How did you...?"

"It doesn't matter. Tell me how I get out," I hiss, more animal than human, making the blade cut ever so slightly into his skin. My heart is hammering so hard it makes me sick. But with those monsters prowling outside, I can't just break through the wards again, and there's no chance I will manage to fight the soldiers guarding the stables.

Riven clenches his teeth and sucks in a sharp breath in response.

But the rest of him makes no move to fight me. I know he could if he wanted to. And that he would probably win—new magic in my veins or not. I don't allow myself to even think what it would do to me if Riven hurt me.

But he just looks like I've slapped him awake.

"An escape," I remind him. "A hidden pathway. *Anything*."

"I'm afraid there isn't," Riven says quietly, those startling eyes somber behind his thick, long lashes.

Panic grabs me by the throat. "Are you sure?" I ask with all the menace I can muster.

"As sure as I can be." Riven takes a step backward, but I hold the blade steady.

We move like that through the room until he sinks onto the edge of a low, velvet daybed, and I stand before him, the blade still at his throat.

"Don't fuck with me," I warn. "Or I might slice your throat."

"What a tempting challenge," he has the nerve to counter.

"I'm dead serious," I snarl.

He looks up at me before leaning back against the cushions, closing his eyes. He says, words full of self-mockery, "Do it, if you feel like spilling a little blue blood tonight."

That's all.

"You're drunk," I hiss.

"Oh yes, indeed, my beautiful darling," he replies, his violet eyes on me.

"What is the best way out?"

He stays silent. I realize the reason he doesn't answer is that he can't lie and that he doesn't want to tell me the truth. I lean forward and bring the blade to his throat once again, angling it so the sharp point bites into his skin, drawing blood.

"Tell me, Riven."

"Or what?" To my horror, he grabs my wrist too fast and leans in.

He's caught me. And I let him, forgetting about his speed. I'm a fucking fool.

My chest closes in on my stupid heart, my lungs; my thoughts running wild.

As if Riven can read every single one of them, he lets go of me.

"You... let me go," I breathe, not trusting it.

"As you said, I must be drunk," he replies nonchalantly.

The way he looks at me shocks me into silence though. I can't stand it, can't stand that he can read my terror, smell it, sense it.

"If you want to help me, then tell me how I get out of here."

"You already know how... because you left the Fortress that way, along with Caryan and the others," he answers, and now I understand. He can't tell me directly even if he wants to. Because something has changed between Caryan and him. Caryan *forbade* it.

We stare at each other.

"Don't dare try to stop me," I warn.

"I wouldn't, and you know it." He covers his eyes with a long-fingered hand before he whispers, "Maybe you should just cut my throat after all."

"Don't be so dramatic," I snap.

He reaches out to me again, the traces of silver in his face catching the low light as he pulls me toward him, despite the threat of the sword. Then he kisses me, hard yet gentle, careful not to touch any of my bruises.

He pulls back too quickly, breathless, his eyes roving over every inch of me. "Did Caryan...?"

I timidly shake my head.

"But your skin, those bruises..." he replies, his eyes gleaming with rage.

"He didn't rape me," I answer truthfully. "He... forced his magic into me and gave me these runes."

"Melody—"

"I have to leave." I pull back and head for the door.

I say, "Please... be careful," before, with a last glance at him, I slip out of the room.

My heart breaks, and I know the bravest thing I ever did is run.

BLAIR

Blair stares at the wall, sitting in the exact same spot since Melody left.

Food. The girl brought her food. An act of kindness. Wasted on her. It doesn't matter whether Blair will starve to death down here while she's waiting for her execution, but that her belly no longer aches from hunger feels good, she can't deny that.

She licks her teeth, ignoring the cold of the unforgiving stone seeping through her torn clothes and into her bones. She can feel Caryan, even down here. He is in *everything* around her. It's his magic that built the Fortress, his magic that still writhes and hisses through the stone. Being so close to it—it's torment enough for a lifetime. Oh, how much Blair would like to think he keeps her because Caryan still cares on some level. But it's a lie. The only reason she's still breathing is that Melody wrought a promise from him.

Not that this means anything. Melody doesn't yet know enough of their rules. Or maybe she had just been too weak by then, on that mountain.

But Blair knows Caryan will keep her only until things have cooled down a bit. Until the girl has forgotten about her. And then, sooner or later, one of his lapdogs will come down here to snap her neck. Caryan's in no rush. He will wait. It could be weeks from now, or months. He is patient and it's not like Blair can do any harm.

Or maybe... maybe he would just let her starve to death. Not that it matters, how she dies.

Blair's mind drifts back to her mothers. They will be alright. They *must* be. She slices off the thought, and pushes back the ugly fear that threatens to grab her by the throat.

No, she won't allow it.

She wrenches her thoughts back to the present, and they snare on Melody again. That weird half-human *thing*. Caryan's latest pet. She reeked of desperation when she came down here before. She smelled of salt, too, which told Blair that she'd been crying.

She came to ask about her mother, so Caryan, the cruel bastard, has told her shit. Of course. Had he told her *anything*?

Blair snorts, leaning her head back against the cold stone, her white hair falling around her body, bereft of pigments, as if magic had made her hair shine. Now, gone, she's half a corpse.

A moonmaiden. A kind thing to say. Blair hates it, the girl's kindness. It makes her want to be kind back. But kindness is weakness, and if she got weak, she would break for good. *Do you think Caryan is bad?* That's what Melody also asked her. *I think he is dangerous.*

Funny how that little creature had more sense than Blair ever had. It doesn't make Blair like her more. No, not at all.

But she's thought about it, oh yes. Melody's question struck deep. Is Caryan bad? No. She loved him.

But then, didn't she say exactly that to the blacksmith— warning him, about Caryan?

She'd been so blind. Blind with love. Perenilla had been right, all Blair wanted was to be at his side. She'd never really thought about anything beyond that.

And avoided thinking of him at all after they split up.

What if she'd overlooked something essential?

She laughs, quietly to herself, like a lunatic. There is no stopping Caryan anyway. There is no one in this fucking world who could stop him. Not even with all their forces aligned. She'd seen him on that battlefield, and that was before he broke her aunt's chains and consumed all her magic.

And once he found those relics...

She looks up when she hears someone running. Fast. A second later, the girl appears, Blair's black sword strapped down her spine. Her eyes are feral, her breath coming fast and uneven. There are bruises on her wrists and around her neck.

"I'm going to run," she says. "You can come with me if you promise not to hurt me."

Crazy little thing indeed. Blair smiles with her teeth to hide her surprise. "I knew you were a bad idea the moment I saw you."

"I don't have time for this. You want to come or not?"

"Sure," Blair says and gets up. "I like bad ideas. I just doubt that you can open that door."

"I think I can."

Blair watches Melody drawing closer, her eyes coming to rest on some of what looks like Caryan's runes on her wrist. *What the fuck?* How did those runes end up on *her* body? And what is that in their middle? A fucking *bargain.*

Melody puts her hands on the wall next to the door. The runes on her arm start to gleam, and the bars begin to dissolve as if they were never there.

"How the hell did you get Caryan's magic?" Blair snarls, torn between fascination and, yep, bone-eating jealousy.

"Long story. Later. Let's run," the girl says. She's already turned on her heels, sprinting towards the stairs.

For a second, Blair contemplates grabbing her. Dragging her back to Caryan. What would he do? Maybe he'd take her back if she'd delivered his precious half-human up to him on a silver platter. But where the hell *is* Caryan?

And no, Caryan would probably kill her anyway, the girl wouldn't change that. So Blair follows, for now.

They run. The girl seems to know her way around the Fortress. Yet as soon as they leave the claustrophobic staircase to the dungeon, Blair can't help but stare at the breathtaking architecture, the perfect mixture of the fae and human world. When Ronin and Kyrith brought her here, she'd been half dead, but now the lightness and splendor hit her like a blow as they dash down a vast corridor.

"Do you actually have a plan?" Blair asks.

"Cars. There were cars," Melody says, pushing against a door and bolting down stairs.

They reach an empty hall that looks almost like a cave, something hewn in stone, not necessarily by anything with hands, Blair notes.

"Fuck, where are they?" Melody mutters, because there is no trace of cars.

Blair looks down on her nails. "Fuck is always my favorite option, although you're not exactly my type."

"There's a tunnel. They must be in there somewhere." The girl ignores her and runs towards that black, cavernous mouth of a hole in the wall.

"Whoa, wait a second, firecracker! Maybe we should contemplate finding another way," Blair suggests as the faintest hint of carrion reaches her nose.

"It's the only way," the girl shoots back and slinks into the dark. *Great.*

Blair stalks after her. Darkness envelops her, so pristine that even her night vision is useless. Hells, it's so much like Caryan's deadly power it makes Blair's skin itch and crawl.

"That's for sure not the only way—" Blair starts, blurting into the cloud of darkness while she keeps her hands out so she won't hit the wall headfirst.

"It is if you don't want to end up eaten by a sand worm," Melody says from somewhere close by. "Or fight our way through the soldiers who guard the stables."

Point taken. Caryan's guards are skilled, and cursed; and Blair in her miserable state is too weak for a fight. Not to mention the half-human, probably more hindrance than help.

"Where *is* Caryan?" Blair asks as the darkness around them shifts, swallowing them whole before it tears slightly, like pushing through a veil until they can see outlines again. What the fuck is this? It's as if this was a living thing.

"Close," the girl retorts, walking ahead, her voice pressed.

"Are these bones?" Blair asks with a frown, kicking aside a skeleton that looks very much like a human ribcage. *Interesting.*

Melody casts a glance at the mortal remnants before her eyes dart to Blair's.

Blair starts to cackle. "You have no idea where this is leading, huh?"

"I want to get out. And survive," Melody snaps back, but her eyes shine quite wildly, and she smells of despair.

"What happened?" Blair asks again. "You reek of Caryan's blood, and you obviously have some of his runes on your wrist." Not to mention the bruises there and on her throat. "I'd say good sex, but sadly for you, you don't smell of sex," Blair adds when the girl stays silent.

Melody pauses as if she's heard something and puts a finger to her lips. Just then, Blair hears it too. A faint rumble, as if something big is moving their way.

Fast.

"I asked you a question," Blair hisses. Threat or no, she would not be shushed. By anyone. "And I'm better not ignored," she adds, just to make that very clear.

"As I said, long story," the girl whispers back, still staring toward the source of the noise. She's unsheathed the sword from her back and eased into a fighting stance, but that sword is almost too heavy for her human body.

"I like long stories, especially if I'm not to slit that person's throat," Blair croons.

The girl cuts her a glance, her tone sharp. "Is that a threat?"

Blair flashes her teeth at her in a saccharine smile. "Did it sound like a compliment to you?"

"I think we have bigger problems right now. Later. Let's get out first," is all Blair gets in return. The tone in Melody's voice makes her blood boil.

"Oh no, not later. I want to know what you did exactly before I take another step."

Melody turns to her fully. "Yeah, then, you know what, turn around and crawl back into your cell if you liked it so much."

For a second, Blair's speechless. Not sure whether to admire the girl's courage or throttle her. It's not every day someone dares to speak like that to a witch. But it's also the girl Caryan's obsessed with, so Blair's rage wins, flashing red in front of her eyes.

She grabs Melody's slender throat, her other hand closed around Melody's hand still holding the hilt of the long sword. She pushes the girl against the ragged stone before she can so much as blink.

"Watch your tongue, human, or I'll rip it out and eat it as dessert," Blair drawls slowly, her teeth mere inches from Melody's neck, hot blood pulsating underneath in a too-fast rhythm. All it would take is to sink her teeth in to taste it. Hells, it smells delicious.

Another rumble shakes the cave, sending tiny stones and debris raining down on them. It's followed by a snort that must belong to a massive beast by the way it travels along the halls.

Blair's head reflexively snaps towards the sound. A mistake, because just like in the human world, that nasty little thing comes for her. Melody's knee slams into Blair's solar plexus, and gods help her, she struggles for breath like a pathetic youngling. The human pushes her off, and just because Blair is weak, she lands on her fucking ass.

"You're going to pay for that," Blair seethes between breaths.

"Good, make me. But first, let's get the fuck out of here. Alive," the girl snaps back, her tone laced with temper. Her gaze probes the darkness that has started to move again around them, like a cloud of pure blackness. As if it wants to hide them within. *Weird.*

"Tell me what happened, right now," Blair demands, getting back to her feet, swallowing the bile in her mouth that's threatening to rise—the aftermath from the blow. "Or I swear I'm going to convince you that you just freed your worst nightmare."

The girl glances at her, and it must be something in Blair's tone because her face falls. And once her façade is gone, she suddenly looks terribly tired and young. Even her eyes have taken on that haunted quality again. As if Caryan indeed shattered an intrinsic piece of her and beneath the surface is nothing but a fissure, yawning, running deep.

It reminds Blair too much of herself.

"I... I don't know what happened," Melody starts. "All I remember is that Caryan forced his magic into me, and my magic somehow... Caryan's hurt. But not for long. Is that enough for now?" The girl's tone is neutral, but her eyes are pleading.

Blair just stares at her. So Caryan gave her some of his runes—purposely. Why in the damn hells? Because he wants those relics, of course. But... when in the Abyss's name did he tattoo them into her? Because Blair sure as death didn't spot that rune on her a little more than two hours ago. And how? And where did he get that magical ink from?

The girl holds out her hand. A truce. An offering.

Blair snarls at it, but Melody doesn't pull it back.

"Please, Blair, I need you. I need your help," she says, and for some inexplicable reason, Blair finds herself taking her hand.

"For now," she warns.

Melody only nods, and both of them stare down into the darkness as the sound of very heavy steps ghost through the halls once more, followed by a scratching sound, as if something hard carves the stone. Something gigantic, with more than two legs. Maybe horns.

"What kind of cars did you see exactly down here?" Blair asks, eyeing the cave walls around them again and not liking the sheer dimension of it *at all*.

"Ronin said they were demons," Melody admits, her eyes alert, her heartbeat even faster than before.

Blair twists to her. "Demons? Are you fucking kidding me? We should run the other way, right now!"

Melody only shakes her head, her face set and limned with icy determination. "And go right back to the Fortress? No. I won't. That's not an option."

"But being eaten by a monster is?"

Before Blair can grab her, the mad woman has sprinted off again, surprisingly fast and nimble, right towards the suspicious noise. Blair throws a last glance back, and then—to hells with it—follows her.

But just like that, another wave of darkness erupts right in front of them, swallowing them whole, so thick they can barely breathe. Unnatural. It makes every hair on Blair's body rise in answer. Something pushes and probes against her in the shade, fading as it realizes she has no magic in her. Then a gush, like water but insubstantial, rushes around them. When Blair blinks again, she finds herself in a huge hall.

Or rather, what *once* was a hall, ages ago. Marble columns still flank it, but the stone already has cracks and fissures, and the ceiling has started to sink and collapse in places. Melody lands next to her, looking equally scared.

As Blair glances down, she realizes the ground between her feet is strewn with bones. Bleached piles of more bones stretch up to their left and right, gracing the walls like some macabre fashion, and rising high, glimmering in the shade. Cows, fae, humans, and who-the-fuck knows what else. It's a damn cemetery.

And something ate them all and spat them out here.

"Tunnels, over there!" Melody says, pointing a finger towards three holes on the other side of the bed of bones.

"Wait! Can we, for a second, wait and think?" Blair starts.

"And what? Wait for whatever prowls these halls to come and find us?" Melody shoots back over a shoulder. She's already dashed right into the cemetery, sinking hip-deep in the macabre sea of death, pushing her way through with hands and feet.

Blair follows. Both of them work through it, wading through sharp bits and treacherous forms, clawing their way through it with mainly their hands and pure iron will towards the tunnels. Three of them, gaping like black mouths ready to devour them whole. Blair doesn't even want to imagine the creature whose claws ripped into the stone to build them. Maybe the same one who uses these halls as its lair. Maybe different ones. Everyone knows Caryan's kingdom is haunted by demons from the nine hells.

When they finally reach them, panting, sweat streaming down their bodies in rivers, Melody casts a glance back at Blair. "Which one?"

Blair brushes her hair back out of her face and sniffs the air. "The bad news is—all of them reek of blood."

"And the good news?"

"The right one reeks of *old* blood."

The moment they dive into the right one, another rumble shakes the cave, so strong they both stumble, landing on all fours. Blair curses as the hard stones cut her palms but falls silent as she looks up.

Right into two huge golden eyes, embedded in a scaly head.

"The dragon," Melody whispers from beside her.

"No. That's not a dragon."

"Well, it damn well looks like a dragon to me," Melody shoots back.

Blair shakes her head. "No, the color of the scales is not right. Nor are the horns." Its scales have the shiny quality of Blair's wyvern. So do the horns. But there are four of them instead of two. Massive and curled, protruding left and right out of his head, scratching against the ceiling. "Dragons only have two horns," she explains.

"Well, maybe anything a little more helpful, Blair?"

"Those aren't just demons. Those are Trochetian horses. Shape-shifting demons, in the form of a dragon," Blair explains, suppressing the shiver that runs down her spine. Fuck, she's only ever heard rumors about them. "A creature from the Abyss, and fucking deadly if you're not his owner. They're rare and utterly lethal."

"Their diet doesn't, by any chance, happen to exclude half-humans and witches?"

"Not that I know of," Blair whispers, ignoring her heartbeat that's started to skyrocket.

"Anything else that might help our cause?"

"Well, they obey their owner, so you might just pray Caryan shows up here to save us," she drawls sarcastically.

Melody scowls at her before she pushes to her feet. "Run, Blair! Now!"

At that, Blair startles to her feet too, and they bolt back the way they came, the dragon so close on their heels its hot breath warms the tunnel, carrying the unmistakable scent of flesh and carrion.

"If it fucking likes fried food, we're dead," Blair pants through her gritted teeth. Her weak body protests against the strain, but she pushes even harder as large, utterly deadly teeth snap shut behind her, missing her by mere inches.

"What?" Melody throws her a glance, eyes wide at the teeth right behind Blair.

"They can breathe fire," Blair throws back. "We're gonna end up as fucking barbecue."

"Not today," Melody has the nerve to snarl back.

Just before the darkness swallows them again as if it wanted to protect them. It spits them out a moment later, throwing them right back into the cavernous hall and the sea of bones, saving them from the unmistakable heat that has started to emanate from the demon's mouth.

"Left tunnel!" Blair screams.

They skitter over the bones, half crawling, half running. Sharp edges cut open their skins, drawing blood as they push towards the leftmost tunnel.

"I think we shook him," Blair pants between her teeth, right as another dragon—a green one—comes shooting out of the middle tunnel right behind them. It wants to launch itself at them, but it, too, is slowed by all the bones, skittering awkwardly towards them over the slippery surface.

Blair stares at it for a moment too long before she catches herself and starts to push on. But something holds her back.

"Fuck," she curses under her breath. "My leg got stuck in a ribcage." She pulls and pulls, but her ankle has snared, interlocking with the other bones. *Game over.*

"Run. Use me as bait and get out!" she shouts to Melody, meaning it.

But the half-human turns around and, hells, is coming back for her. Again.

Blair bares her teeth. "Save your fucking, miserable life," Blair snarls as the girl grabs her arm, trying to drag Blair out.

The demon skitters closer, its teeth snapping for Melody.

She draws the Nefarian's sword again. "Good, you want to eat us? Then earn it," she spits at the monster.

The demon lets out an irritated hiss, its eerie eyes fixed on the black, thrumming metal in Melody's hand. Unsure whether to strike or not.

"Get up, Blair!" Melody orders as the demon starts to perform some strange, serpentine movement Blair knows all too well.

"Get the fuck away, girl! It's going to burn us!" Blair screams as the demon's tongue starts to curl. "Leave me!"

But Melody just grabs her arm harder and pulls with impressive strength.

Blair slams her hands over her ears, and her whole body locks up as demonic fire blasts towards her, singing every patch of exposed skin. It feels like it goes on forever, but there's no excruciating pain incinerating every cell of her being.

When Blair glances up, she finds the blue blast roaring over her head and illuminating the whole cave—and Abyss fuck her—she's lying flat on her belly like a stranded fish. And in front of her, having fallen backward as she dragged Blair out, is Melody, breathing hard, her eyes wide, her hair plastered to her face from heat and sweat.

The ringing in Blair's ears stops, along with the stream of fire. All that remains is a surreal moment of total silence before the beast rears his head, realizing they are still alive and not fried. Then it comes for them, swinging its massive head, its jaws locking with an audible *click,* slamming shut right over Blair's head.

Blair blinks a few times as the air saws out of her.

Melody stands, the sword right at the demon's eye. "Think twice," she says, her voice impressive with contempt.

The beast blinks and Blair suppresses a sound as saliva drips from its mouth and lands on her shoulder.

All three of them startle as another growl sounds, the entire mountain shaking with the impact as the other demon pushes itself through the cave mouth and comes towards them. The green demon pulls his head back slightly, as if passing on a meal to make room for the even bigger predator.

Blair swallows against her dried-out throat. The other demon found them—the gargantuan monster they'd encountered in the tunnel. Horror coils through her and settles somewhere deep in her stomach. Here, in the hall, it looks even bigger. Bluish scales seem to shimmer on their own when he moves, his body so heavy and huge the bones crush to dust under its weight.

Instinct makes Blair press herself even deeper into the bones, as if she somehow can make herself smaller. Invisible. A motion born out of primal fear and despair and the knowledge that she's lying here like some pathetic weakling with her magic gone.

The demon pauses in front of them, crouching low, sniffing them. Another blast of steam washes over them as it exhales, the temperature soaring in answer. But, Abyss, Melody just stands there, looking the bluish behemoth right in the eye, unfazed by the size of its bared teeth.

"Don't," she says, her head raised high, her voice pure command. Almost like Caryan's.

The irony of it doesn't escape Blair. But the demon halts, his eyes blinking slowly as if he, too, is surprised by her not running and screaming.

Melody pulls up her sleeve and holds the arm with the runes up to him. "You recognize this, don't you?" she probes on, in the same unforgiving tone.

And, Abyss help them, Blair finds herself actually holding her breath as the demon angles his head, one huge, golden eye fastening on that tattoo. It blinks once.

Melody's voice is strained but firm as she continues. "You obey your owner. I am your owner. I carry his markings and his magic."

The two demons—dragons, whatever—exchange a glance, a silent communication between them. The blue one growls again, lower and more viciously. The green one retreats another step, not taking its hungry eyes off Blair yet.

"Help me. Please," Melody says, still looking at the blue demon. "We don't have much time," she adds, as if the creature can understand her. As if it was *sentient,* and not just a hungry beast. But it cocks his head, considering her words.

"Keep going. I take it as a good sign that they haven't eaten us yet," Blair bleats.

Melody shoots her an exasperated look.

The greenish one growls again, and another waft of steam and hot breath blows Blair's hair back. The bluish one swishes its massive tail once in warning, before it bends its impossibly large head down to Melody. Blair stares as its snout touches her body, so frail, so tiny compared to the monster next to her.

But Melody doesn't retreat. Doesn't even flinch. She just stands there and, eventually, lifts her free hand and lays it against the leathery skin, right between its flaring nostrils.

Blair's throat has dried out by the time Melody says with a jerk of her chin, "Come, Blair, let's go. Get on his back."

"What? Are you mad? No fucking way."

"Come on, Blair," she says again.

Blair watches with rapt fascination as Melody, indeed, starts climbing up the dragon's back. At another snort from the greenish one, Blair gets to her feet, too, and with one last glance at the blue dragon, climbs onto its back and slips into a scaled dip behind Melody.

For a moment, grief slices through Blair like a sword dipped in fire. *Her beautiful wyvern.* Without her magic, she will never ride on her again. Never taste the wind in her heart, let the coldness rip all around her, never scream along with her beast into the storm. Her beast, her friend. Her *family*. Real or not real.

"Are you alright?"

Her head snaps up as Melody turns to her, as if she felt Blair's shift.

"I'm riding on a fucking demon instead of dying by its teeth. I'd say I couldn't be better right now," Blair snarls back.

Melody twists back to the front, just as the demon turns its massive body and starts to run towards the tunnel it just came from in a lizard-like motion. Melody and Blair reflexively crouch close to his back as the dragon slithers back into the narrow tunnel, shaking loose more stones and rocks, his massive wings tucked in tight. Melody's holding on to two spikes that have sprouted out of his back, and Blair can't do anything other than cling to her slender body.

They cut through the darkness that now seems to make way for them. Night shimmers at the end of the tunnel—the light of the stars, Blair realizes, thrown into the endless darkness.

The tunnel ends in an abyss, and the dragon plummets before it throws out its impossible wings and they are airborne.

72

RIVEN

Riven knows she's gone.

He feels it in his bones. Her absence is beyond something physical. Her scent, the memory of her silken skin like a brand tattooed on his mind.

He can't think about the bruises on her body, not to mention the other things he picked up in her scent. Not without wanting to set the whole Fortress on fire.

He slowly wanders through the halls when he can't stand the seclusion of his room any longer. He drifts through the empty spaces and, without noticing it, winds up in her room.

He looks up. Black wings are dancing in the wind that streams in through the open window. Caryan stands there in the dark, as if he was born out of it, his white skin the only contrast. He doesn't look at Riven. His gaze rests on the wall opposite her bed, where Melody had painted him, with his golden eyes so realistic it takes Riven's breath away.

Riven stands there for an age, not trusting his voice or his own body next to Caryan. Not after what Caryan did to her.

Finally, Caryan turns his head and looks at Riven for a very long time, his eyes black as his magic swathes around his wings and shoulders.

Eventually, Kyrith teleports into the room, his green eyes

narrowed to slits. "The girl and the witch are gone. I can't find them anywhere."

But Caryan continues looking at Riven. *He knows.* Caryan knows already. But why isn't he following her?

The angel turns and, without a word, vanishes through the window. Only then does the smell of angelic blood hit Riven like a solid blow. Drops of it shimmering like dark ink where Caryan stood.

The realization hits Riven like another blow, aimed at his ribs. Caryan can't follow her, or he would have already. Because he is *wounded.*

Dread sluices through Riven then, raw and ugly. Whatever Melody did, she harmed him, with her magic. Badly enough that even Caryan's runes and the curse can't heal him instantly; her magic obviously weakening his.

The last time he saw Caryan bleed like this, the wound had been caused by Ciellara. Melody's mother. By her light magic.

The only magic that could stop a creature like Caryan.

73

MELODY

We fly for most of the night, the wind up here no longer warm but icy and cutting under my thin clothes. We sit wedged between the huge, dark scales of the dragon, soaring high over desert lands.

And as I look down, I wonder whether past events robbed me of my primal fear of heights, because I find it strangely beautiful and peaceful up here.

As if nothing could touch me.

Blair behind me stays silent the whole time, and there is only the boom of the dragon's powerful wings under the stars and my own, wild thoughts.

I hold on tight when the dragon suddenly soars higher, closer to the moons and towards the clouds that have gathered over the ocean. A storm, ready to break loose. When they part, I spot outlines of an ivory city perched on the coast, surrounded by houses, safely enclosed by massive walls. A huge tower protrudes from its middle like a warning, a fire burning on its top so big I can see it from here. The city, so much larger than Niavara.

A real city.

"What is this?" I ask Blair, twisting around to look at her.

She still looks bad. Pale and thin now, her muscles protruding, her face sharp and angular, accentuating her piercing, golden eyes. Her long, white hair streams unbound behind her as if she's underwater. Her torn clothes hang on her, some scraps that must have been a red cloak once, now soaked with blood, fluttering in the wind like a flame. How she survived Caryan's prison… it must be her fae blood, because right now, she looks more dead than alive save for the fire in her eyes.

Those eyes zero in on me, and I can see the hunger guttering in them, reminding me that she is still a predator. And that a part of her would love to see me die.

Preferably violently.

She drawls, "It's Avander. A harbor town, where Caryan's fleet lies. Like Niavara, Caryan rebuilt it from elven ruins."

Indeed, as the clouds below us part further, I spot huge ships anchored all around, surrounding the town and the coast. Hundreds of them, their silvery sails tinted bone white beneath the moonlight. And on them, two moons, one white and one gleaming red, with black, angelic wings spread out in the back.

Caryan's signet. The Kingdom of the Two Moons.

I feel a twist in my stomach. "I didn't realize his kingdom was that huge," I whisper, more to myself, but with her acute hearing, of course Blair heard me. I instantly regret it, because she lets out a cruel laugh.

"What did you think it was? A Fortress in the middle of the desert, a tiny desert town, and nothing else? That's just where he *lives*. A tactical move, obviously. The desert, roamed by demons, is impossibly hard to cross if you don't have wings. Not to mention all those creatures that haunt it."

Obviously. Creatures like a sand worm.

Blair is right, I *should* know. But still, her words cut deep, and I'm not prepared. I'm still so naïve, thinking the glimpse I got of the fae world over the last two months is all there is.

But it has just been a tiny shard. I only saw what Caryan *wanted* me to see.

The dragon banks hard to the right, and Blair lets out a sharp hiss, as if she's burned herself.

"What is it?"

"Can't you feel it? It's his wall. Caryan's warded the kingdom and sealed it with spells. We have to fly north to the end of his shields." She bares her silver canines against the invisible force.

I frown as I, too, feel a slight brimming in the air, brushing up against me as the dragon veers sharp to the left so that we're now flying parallel to the coast, keeping the city at our back, before he suddenly descends.

"Caryan indeed warded his kingdom. You will have to break through, little one. A temporary hole will be enough."

I flinch, not because of the rapid descent that makes my stomach shoot up, but because of the voice that suddenly sounded *in* my head. A deep, foreign voice. *What the fuck?*

I get a rumble under me as an answer. My mind tries to catch up as the realization hits me. The dragon, demon, whatever just... talked to me. *In my thoughts.*

"I did, indeed. Now hold on," he warns.

I obey out of sheer reflex as he spreads his massive wings wide to slow our rapid drop before his colossal claws dig into the soil under us, his weight making the whole ground shake.

"Why can you talk to me? And I to you?" I ask back in my mind, following the direction his voice came from. At its end, there is a connection, like a bridge, or a thread. Something dark blue, shimmering like his scales. Something I can reach out to just as I once reached out to Caryan's bond.

"Yes, this is me. Or us, if you will. We have a bond now," he explains patiently.

Riven once explained that fae have bonds.

"You are a fae too," the dragon chimes in, cutting off my train of thought, as if he could hear it. *"I can."*

"That's... weird."

"Lock me out if you don't like it," he grumbles back. *"Or I can read every one of your thoughts. It can become rather tiresome."*

"Lock you out how?"

"By focusing on pushing me out and then sealing that bond with walls or the like. But for now, get off and break through his ward, little

one. *Time is of the essence. My former master will not be stalled for much longer.*"

He bends one leg so I can slip off his back easily. My knees buckle slightly, though, my whole body stiff from the long flight, the cold, and exhaustion.

I jump as his huge snout, with very impressive teeth, nudge me towards the edge of the cliff, to where the desert meets the ocean. Hells, one of his beautiful, curled horns is almost as long as my leg, not to mention those teeth.

"*I won't hurt you,*" he says after a scoff that sounded suspiciously like a laugh.

"*Wait—you're the one who tried to eat me a couple of hours ago, right?*"

"*The very one,*" he says without a shred of remorse. "*But I won't try that again, I promise.*"

Until you change your mind, I think. Nothing has prepared me for the bone-shaking growl that comes from him. I stare at him, wide-eyed.

"*A bond is a sacred thing. You think I accept that easily, or broke my old one, for that matter?*" Before I can answer he continues, "*Besides—you can hardly blame me for trying to snatch you out of the air if you looked like a perfect midnight snack with your glowing wings.*"

"*Then it's a good thing that they are gone.*"

"*Definitely. A pixie is far more delectable than an elf,*" he counters and I can't tell whether this is a joke.

"*Reassuring, really,*" I grind out, rubbing my bare arms, still not trusting it. As if he felt it, his mood turns somber. Hells... I can feel that in my body.

"*I am serious, little one. Things changed.*"

"*Because I'm wearing Caryan's tattoo?*" I ask. I just have to know. He scoffs, blueish smoke coming out of his nostrils and I stagger back.

"*No. The tattoo does not matter, neither does Caryan's magic in your veins. I accepted the bond because you earned my respect. It is not every day that someone is brave enough to threaten one of my kind.*"

"The last one was Caryan," I think automatically before I can stop it.

"Yes, the last one was Caryan, and no one after him," he confirms. *"And—I never ate someone I bonded before."*

"Encouraging. There's always a first time," I bite out.

He scoffs again and a wave of amusement washes through me at that.

I bonded a demon. A demon *with humor*.

"Yes, I am a demon with humor. Still more common than a half-elf around here, I assure you," he snaps back into my head.

Of course he heard.

"Lock me out if you don't want me to listen," he reminds me again before I get another nudge with his snout, pushing me further towards the cliff.

"And grumpy," I add, stepping up to where the wall of magic waits, invisible to the eye but all the more deadly. So close I can clearly feel the traits of its even deadlier creator. A tiny part of its essence now flows through me too.

"A tiny hole will be enough," the demon rumbles, as if there was no easier thing in the world.

I draw in a sharp breath while I try to remember what I did the last time I broke out of Caryan's Fortress. Back then, my body acted of its own accord. But this here... this is much, much stronger. I can feel a complicated pattern, like a thousand different strands of magic intricately woven together and pulled tight. Sealed with bristling spells.

Way more complicated than the shields of the Fortress. Much stronger. Like a current that would rip me away and draw me under if I so much as tried to find a way in.

"Of course it is stronger. It is the wall that seals his kingdom," the demon snarls into my mind.

"Not helpful," I shoot back.

"You broke out once."

Right, I can do this. I take a deep breath and lift my hands, my magic probing up against *this*.

"Want to tell me what the fuck we're doing, human? Wasting precious time?" Blair's voice behind me makes me startle. She's jumped off the demon's back, too, and approached, silently as a ghost.

The demon's warning growl fills the air, followed by his words in my mind. *"I do not trust her. I never did."*

"So, you two go back a long way?"

"Define long when you are ageless," he snaps, but his sharpness is not directed at me, I know. *"But definitively too long for my taste."*

I turn to Blair. "The demon wants me to break through that wall," I explain.

"Are you kidding me? We have to fly north. No one can break through a fucking wall, certainly not you."

"Of course she wants to go north. And deliver you up to her witches on a silver plate," the demon growls in my mind.

"I must at least try," I say.

Her white eyebrows shoot up, and she scrunches up her face. "Wait a second—did you just say *it* wants you to?"

He, the demon, snarls, and it makes my bones vibrate.

"Yeah, he told me to try," I say, turning back to the wall.

"Are you trying to tell me that you can fucking *speak* with Caryan's demon?"

"Formerly Caryan's demon," the demon corrects in my mind. *"Now concentrate, Melody."*

I just nod, focusing on the deadly cascade of magic before me, running down in a stream. Something that knows no end and no beginning.

"That's impossible," Blair snaps.

"The only impossible thing is her. Tell her that," the demon growls, and I can feel his fury.

"Demons do not bond with weaklings," she says into my back. "They incinerate them for fun. Or snack on them."

My head shoots to her before I can help it, and I find myself glowering. "Are you calling me pathetic?"

Blair shrugs, but I can see her aura belying her nonchalance.

Pure, yellow envy shines there like a weird form of beacon in the night. "Weak. Annoying. Helpless. Pathetic. Just stating the obvious."

"You know what, Blair? Fuck you."

She wants to jump at me, I can see her muscles tensing, preparing, but a snap of the demon's teeth makes her change her mind last minute.

He pulls his upper lip back, exposing the full length of teeth the size of my arm. *"Tell her I will incinerate her for fun if she doesn't shut her mouth,"* he says to me.

"I think your body language is quite convincing," I retort, because her amber eyes widen, darting between me and the demon.

She is still slightly crouched, her fingers with her deadly nails spread but frozen in motion. Only her lip curls back, exposing her silver teeth. "If he cares so much for you, tell him that what he's asking you to do is practically suicide. The wall incinerates *everything*. We need to fly west. Then sharp north. Cut over the Emerald Forest and then cross the ocean from there, at the outskirts of Caryan's kingdom." The demon snaps his teeth at her in warning.

"Not happening. Witches prowl those territories, and Queen Calianthe will likely try to shoot us down before asking who we are," the demon shoots back. *It is a trap. Or the witch is mad. Or both. Ignore the witch and focus on that wall, little one. I know you can do it."*

Blair glowers at the demon, then she says to me. "We're losing critical time. If we wait here, we lose our advantage. Caryan is an angel. As soon as he's recovered, he'll just open up a portal and jump there, wait for us, and we're doomed. Let's go *now*."

"Tell the witch that he will be faster regardless. There is no way I can fly fast enough to arrive at the border before him. Breaking through the wall is our only chance."

"He says that this is our only chance," I repeat loudly for her.

Her eyes turn to vicious slits as they stay on the demon. "Yeah, maybe he wants you roasted. A late form of revenge against his former master. What a glorious payback."

"Tell her I will devour her if she says anything like that again."

"I need to at least try," is all I retort—to both of them, exasperated—before I turn back to the wall.

I lift my hands. The wall's magic reaches out to me, while mine desperately tries to find a loose thread. Something to start with.

I think I scream as the magic suddenly seeps into me, so like Caryan's before, ready to kill me, burn me from the inside.

The next time I blink to my senses, I'm lying on the ground, my mouth tasting like ash.

The demon's remarkable golden eyes focus on me, and I swear I can feel his relief swamping me. Relief that I'm still breathing.

"That went well. Great you're still alive. I thought I was going to have to fight that demon over your roasted barbecued corpse," Blair snarls, and my head jerks up to her. "Let's get north, whatever your newfound pet says. We're running out of time."

My eyes find the demon's again. *"It's too strong. She's right. I'm so sorry."*

"Do not be sorry. But try again," he pushes. *"I know you can do it."*

I swallow hard. My arms tremble from the strain as I push myself to my knees. It feels so much like what Caryan did to me... I think that part. I didn't mean to think it *loud*, but the demon heard me.

His voice in my mind is gentler than I ever thought possible. *"I know, little one. But this time you can control it. This is our only chance."*

It's the sudden desperation I hear and feel, as if it was my own and yet not. Different. Tinged by a wave of remorse and regret that has me get up and step to the wall again.

This time, as the whitish fire invades me, I'm prepared. My own magic dodges the attack in time, diving right into the labyrinth of bristling, deadly power before the magic can sink its talons and teeth into me. I feel the wall's magic turning around, giving chase. Flickering and biting threads of magic, designed to kill spear through me while I hunt for a way out.

It hurts, unlike anything I ever felt before. Something eating away at me, burning hot and arctic cold at the same time. I fall to my knees, but I keep my hands in that current.

Cold water splashes over me, and I jolt awake. I can feel it coming off me as steam, I'm burning *that* hot. When I blink, I find that I'm held by talons, immersed fully in the flood of the ocean.

I gasp for air, and the demon pulls me up again before gently carrying me back to the spot where Blair's settled down with her back against a rock. The first silvery light of dawn graces the horizon.

"What happened?" I ask.

"You—"

"You almost turned into a torch." Blair's answer comes faster, but her voice is unusually flat.

The demon shoots her a glare, huffing steam, but she keeps looking straight at me.

"I'm so sorry... we should go. Blair's right," I manage to grind out, my voice coming out shaky. Strained. My whole being feels like I'm more dead than alive.

"Sure, I've been right. But it's too late by now. You fucking doomed us. He will be here soon." Blair jumps to her feet, looking up at the sky, at the hint of sun. "I will get a swift death, but as for your demon here... I'm not so sure Caryan will make it quick. He doesn't take well to treason. And you..." Her gaze settles back on me, her lips pulling into a cruel smile. "I hope your little attempt to escape was worth it because it'll probably be the last time you've seen daylight in a long time."

I don't know what to do with this sudden desperation. This time it is mine, mingling with that of the demon. The flood of both of our emotions united is gripping me so hard I can barely breathe.

The demon behind me growls, but Blair just laughs. "What, lizard? Don't like me to state what's going to happen? I know him too well. Melody at least deserves to know. And you, breaking that bond to him..."

"An execution?" My head snaps to the demon and he blinks once.

"I'm sorry, little one."

"No. I will make two more bargains. That won't happen," I say out loud, keeping my voice from breaking.

Blair just laughs harder. "Oh, I'm sure he's in no mood for bargains this time." She turns away at that, and I can see her heavily scarred back through her torn clothes. Just so much pain and a life ending like this.

I glance back to the demon who keeps looking at me with his head hung low. *"Tell me he's not going to kill you. I don't even... fuck, I don't even know your name."*

He lifts his chin at that.

"I'm Aravanach'lach'kaniss Kahir'ach Manazhsss. Son of the nine hells. Abyss' born. Forged and hatched by the nine fires at the beginning of the days. And it's been my honor."

Tears begin to fill my eyes. *"Tell me there's another way."*

"I cannot, little one. The witch is right."

"But why? Why do it then when you knew? Why help us?" I scream at him mentally. I feel the sudden wish to destroy something. Anything. To shred and rip.

Something in me rises. Something dark and lethal, silvery and black, rearing its mighty head as tears start rolling down my cheeks. Blair's right. I'm pathetic. And weak, for fuck's sake.

"You are not. I do not bond pathetic people. And I am never wrong."

"Well, you were this time," I bite out. *"I should have never asked for your help. I doomed us both."*

He lifts his head, towering over me. *"I am ancient. I have never made a mistake before, and I did not make one now. Maybe you are not strong enough now, but you will be. I know it. And everything has a time to die. Maybe mine has come. And I will go with pride, because I served you, even if only for a short time. But never stop believing in yourself. You were born out of light. Never succumb to the darkness."*

The pride that washes through me makes me sick to my bones. He *is* proud of me. Why?

I can no longer hold his soft stare. I shake my head and turn away, marching back to that wall.

Oh no, if Caryan was going to kill them both, I would die first. But he won't get what he wants. I will not yield. I will not serve on my knees the way he wants me to and watch all my friends die. I'd rather be dead myself.

"Little one! Don't!"

I slam down a mental wall just as the demon told me to and block his voice out. Then I hurl myself against the warded wall. Back into that labyrinth of wards and spells.

I scream. I know that, somewhere, I'm screaming as the magic starts to take me apart. But then this new magic in me answers. Surges. Something laced with utter darkness, with fangs and talons, so like the ones of that wall. Talons that lash back and teeth that snap and rip and shred… and I let it. Let it run wildly like a monster on the hunt. Somewhere lightning strikes as I let it tear those threads apart, bit by bit by bit. Layer by layer by layer.

Let it rip everything to ribbons.

And suddenly, I can see it—a hole. Blue as the morning sky. Air streaming through. Salty, beautiful air that cools my burning, steaming body. My molten bones and marrow. My ruined soul.

Oblivion.

Cool, soothing oblivion. It feels like flying again.

"Good you're back," the demon's voice greets me. I blink as my senses return slowly.

My clothes are drenched in water, I realize, and I'm shivering. Blair's silver nails are digging into my shoulders, piercing my leathers to keep me seated on the dragon's back.

"You made it. I told you I make no mistakes," he says with no small amount of self-righteousness.

"Don't be so modest," I manage to grind out.

"Demons were not born to be modest, my little one."

"Just so you know, I'm going to call you Aris because there's no way I'll ever be able to pronounce your full name," I say quietly, remembering the way he said it into my mind, full of hisses and snarls. Guttural, foreign sounds only a dragon, or demon, can make.

"Aris? You are aware that I am one of the biggest, deadliest demons

of the nine hells?" he grumbles but over the bond, I can feel that he likes it.

"You might want to hold on on your own," Blair snarls from behind me. "The smell of your blood is rather distracting."

She lets go of my shoulders, and I grind my teeth against the wounds her nails have left. Then I dig my nails into Aris' scales. *We made it.* The high of that fact swamps my blood. I could cry. All three of us would *live.* We are free. When I twist around, I find the ivory city still perched on the cliff, the wall we just broke through invisible to the eye.

I turn back to look ahead, just in time to see a volley of magical arrows spearing for us. The demon banks hard, lifting his wing to take the brunt. His bone-shaking roar fills the night as his wing is shredded. I feel the blinding pain through the bond, ripping through me.

I scream.

More arrows come flying.

Arrows made of bristling, lilac magic.

They strike his legs, his neck.

I glance up, only to find a squadron of membrane-winged warriors above us, blotting out the sun. *Nefarians.*

Then, we're falling.

74

RIVEN

Hard, cold wind whips Riven's black hair, whining through the high peaks of the mountains around them. Slick icy rain batters their skins, their clothes long soaked through, their breaths coming in clouds.

Ronin's leaning against the stone, a little sheltered from the weather, his amber eyes closed—the witcher's probably meditating. Riven just stands there and looks into the curtain of relentless rain, glad that Kyrith went in the opposite direction, or he would have to listen to his constant grumbling.

He's nervous. On edge. There is no denying that he has been since Melody disappeared two days ago. They never found the demon, only eyewitnesses claimed to have seen them flying over Avander, Caryan's harbor town. A dragon, they whispered.

Abyss, when Riven directed Melody down to their den, he assumed the demons were out hunting and guarding the Fortress and she, astute as she is, would find the one way out through the tunnels where the sacred spring ran through. The underground river would have taken her directly to Niavara. It was the only direct way out of the Fortress. Never had he dreamed Melody would encounter Caryan's Trochetian horses or he would never have sent her there. They were utterly deadly.

But to learn that Melody and the witch had not been killed but that Melody instead *bonded* with one of Caryan's monsters…

The green demon told Caryan what happened.

Riven briefly closes his eyes, baring his teeth against the cold. When Caryan told them about it, Riven expected that Melody and Blair would fly west and then up to Avandal, crossing the Emerald Forest. But they must have gone north instead. The Abyss, how did they manage to tear through Caryan's wards?

Hells, Riven never deemed it possible Melody could just break through that wall.

And what lies beyond it… the fae gap. The Black Forest. Palisandre. None of the options sound good. And now she is Abyss knows where. And he doesn't even want to think about the murderous witch she freed. And what that meant.

His fault. All of it.

His only hope is that Blair spoke true—that with or without Melody in tow, she could not return to her coven. But Riven fears the day he learns the witches have Melody.

Or that Palisandre has her.

Or—

He doesn't allow himself to think it—the last possibility. That they are, indeed, already dead. No, she is not, or he would feel it. She would not die. Fate would not allow that.

Riven tilts his head back and lets the rain pelt his face, the water run under his clothes as lightning cracks above, splitting the air. Black lightning, followed by thunder that threatens to crush this world. Caryan's magic, raging.

He takes a deep breath. *What has he done?*

What had he been thinking when he let her go that night? But he hadn't been thinking. All he saw were her bruised lips, her winter-white skin ashen, her feral stare. The scent of utter despair on her. An intrinsic part of Riven has just snapped at the remnants of what Caryan must have done to her.

But his hands were tied. Telling her how to escape had been the only way.

But he doomed her nonetheless.

He hasn't spoken to Caryan since that night. He can't without going for Caryan's throat. He takes another long breath, massaging his temples to let the fury and tension ebb out of him. A futile endeavor. He hasn't slept the last two nights. Hasn't so much as touched a glass of water or food.

The witcher opens one eye, throwing him a long, knowing look.

Riven ignores him and studies the entrance of the cave before him. The halls of the grand oracle, leading right down to the chasm. Into the very core of raw magic that holds this world together.

A couple of minutes ago, Caryan walked between the two slabs of rock that mark the entrance to the most powerful oracle the fae world has ever known. And disappeared.

They are on an island, shielded from the rest of the world. Only a handful have ever made it here in the last decades. The dense fogs on and around the island are murderous, tongues whisper. Part of a territory that's believed to belong to the dead and the kings of the underworld, their sentinels hunting all the living souls.

The remaining, lucky ones who made it here alive barely survived receiving their prophecies after that. Consulting the great oracle is dangerous, as Kalleandara is known to be moody.

But the oracle is the only way to find out whether Melody is still alive.

Riven casts Ronin another glance before he decides to walk in. The witcher has been expecting his decision, and has probably read it in him with a talent similar to Melody's, yet he doesn't try to stop Riven.

He *must* go. He needs to know. And—whatever horrors await Caryan, Riven is going share them with him, too. *To whatever end,* Riven swore the day he accepted the blood oath. Or... maybe Caryan would just kill him for what he did. For the betrayal.

And maybe Riven deserves it.

He follows a narrow path that winds through the darkness. Stalagmites and shimmering crystals sprout out of the ground, some so tall they stretch like columns up to the top. Then the path gives way to a platform tiled with ancient, polished stone, a black abyss beckoning to his left and right.

The Chasm. Never-ending darkness, a room between worlds, between space and time. Something Caryan could step in and out of.

Riven walks on, fighting his growing unease as an unfamiliar power starts to vibrate through his bones, pushing up against his magic, as if to examine him. When he spots the raw blue column of light that flows like a waterfall from the top of the cave down to the Abyss, he stops. The platform ends right there.

A naked woman seems to float in the stream of rushing magic. Her hair is spread wide as if she is underwater. The same raw magic fills her eyes, making them blaze. In front of her stands Caryan. Riven pauses in the shadows. He can't help but shiver at the column of light so strong that ancient tongues called it soul-eater. No one survives touching it, and Riven watches with icy horror as the woman seems to float closer to Caryan.

"Caryan," she says. "My fallen angel. What an honor to see you again."

"Oracle," Caryan retorts coldly.

"Tell me, why are you here once more, wanderer of worlds? What is your desire to know?"

"You know very well why I am here," Caryan says, his voice close to a snarl. Riven stills. No one speaks like that to any oracle— and lives.

But Kalleandara only scrutinizes him. "Yes, I do. I can sense the rage in you—this is interesting."

"*Interesting*? You dared to shackle me with a bond."

A bond? What bond? Riven freezes inwardly.

"It was never meant to *shackle* you, Caryan."

"Spare me your lies. Angels have no mates. Never had. How dare you bind me to another creature like some fettered animal?"

"They have now," the oracle retorts unperturbed.

Riven holds his breath, his heartbeat strangely fast. Melody... Caryan's mate?

"Break the bond!"

"I cannot. You made that decision yourself, Caryan. A long

while back. When you gave a promise to Meanara of Avandal. When you swore a blood oath to never harm her unborn child. You bound yourself to that child."

"That child *died*," Caryan growls. "My oath died along with it."

"No, it did not. She ceased to exist before she lived. In that world, in that time, back then. But her life and that oath you gave her are still written in the stars, even if she was not born by her true mother, but by another woman years later, Caryan. You brought this upon yourself, by your choice."

"It was a dirty trick you played on me."

"Not a trick. You gave that oath, Caryan. It is now written in the stars too."

"I never asked for the bond!"

"And yet I see that you forged it."

Caryan lets out a snarl. The walls shake with his dark power in response, yet the oracle doesn't retreat an inch. It's terrifying to watch. And riveting to witness a stand-off between two of the most powerful creatures this world has ever seen.

"Do not challenge me. You forced me to forge it. Just another of your ploys." Caryan's voice has lost all its warmth, laced with nothing but disdain and a lethal promise.

Riven braces himself again. Hells, no one has ever dared to speak to an oracle like this. Or survived if they have.

But again the oracle just cocks her head, the river of her hair flowing all around her in undulating waves. "No, Caryan, I did not do that either. Again, it was your decision not to sacrifice her. It was your decision to give her your blood and seal what has always been there."

"That is a barefaced lie. You knew I wouldn't let her die."

"It is no lie. Yes, I knew, but it was still always up to you. I gave you a choice and you chose."

"I never chose a mating bond!"

"And yet she still lives. You could have severed that bond, Caryan, instead of just damaging it."

Riven clenches his teeth against the relief swamping him, despite everything he just learned. She *lives*. She *is* still alive. For some reason, it is all that matters. The news is enough that he can breathe again.

Caryan seethes, "She still lives because I still need her. But if you think you turned me into a fae by having me enslaved by another creature, you are wrong. I am not fae and will never be. A mating bond is not going to change that fact."

Again, the walls shake at every word, stones falling into the nothingness. There's no sound when they hit the ground because the caverns are endless, and depthless. Those who stumble are doomed to forever fall through never-ending layers of darkness.

"Only time will show."

"Do not be delusional, old woman. Time is going to prove that I will end her once I get what I need. That you and your prophecies signify nothing because you have long since lost your power. I have altered the course of fate a million times before, and this time it will be no different, even if you think you gained the upper hand with your little gimmick."

The oracle steps closer, one long, slender leg out of the blue, rushing column of pure, undiluted light. Her body is half made of pure, blue light herself, part insubstantial, part solid, but enough for Riven to watch how she leans even further out and puts a hand on Caryan's cheek.

Riven freezes, holding his breath for what is inevitably going to come next. But... nothing happens when she touches Caryan.

Caryan's skin is miraculously unharmed. "Oh, my dear fallen angel, so full of ancient rage. You still deem me cruel. You still think this is a power play. It is interesting that you cannot see that I tried to do you a favor when I weaved in that bond with her."

Riven stills by the words. As a part of him, in him, fractures. So it is true, all of it. Melody is Caryan's mate, and he forged the bond already. Riven feels as if the ground has been pulled from under his feet, as if part of his soul has just been shattered thoroughly.

The laugh that works up Caryan's throat holds nothing human. No warmth. No life.

It is as empty as the look in his eyes.

"You've always had a bizarre idea of favors and an even more grotesque idea of cruelty."

"Maybe you just believe me a monster, unwilling to see that I am not."

"A monster recognizes another when it sees it. Shackling a half-mortal girl to someone like me is a callous thing to do, even for you."

"Maybe. Maybe not. But letting you live on without any feelings at all, angel—wouldn't that have been just another testimony of my alleged cruelty? I can only imagine how dull everything must be without any emotions at all. I felt your world-weariness, your lethargy. And I merely answered your wish—I gave you a way to end your blighted existence if you wish, or let you live, truly live, for one."

Riven frowns at the change of her tone. At the sudden sadness in her face, the gentleness in her eyes. What is going on between them? Caryan must have known her for a long, long while then. But nothing Riven sees makes sense.

"Truly *live?*" Caryan makes a vicious hissing sound as he pulls out of her grasp, his own eyes hard and cold like star-flecked onyx. Shadows have gathered all around him, swirling all around the column of light. "All I've felt is her pain and despair since the day she was born."

"For now, sadly. Yes. But that made you want to find her all the more. How many days did you try to track her down? How many nights did you spend with her so she would not be all alone?"

Caryan's hand shoots out, curling around the oracle's throat. "In her *dreams,* because you would not let me find her in *reality,*" he spits. "You would not tell me where she was. Before you cut me off from her entirely for years. She was still a child, alone with that monster."

What are they talking about? Caryan... visiting Melody in her dreams? But the oracle just frowns down at him, her voice soft and tinged by compassion. "I know it drove you out of your mind to feel her misery, her despair, day after day, night after night, Caryan. I swear, I could not prevent that. I would have, if I could. But giving her another fate would have required powers even beyond my ken. Lyrian shielded her from you and not even I could do anything against it."

"Liar!"

"It's no lie, Caryan. But despite it all, haven't you felt more alive than ever before?"

"Where is she?"

"I cannot tell you."

"*Where is she?*" Caryan's response is an animalistic, primal groan full of pain and fury. His teeth are bared, his eyes as blazing as the oracle's.

Riven watches with horror as the energy starts to peel away the skin of Caryan's hand, bit by bit, until bare bone shimmers through. It reaches a point where Riven thinks he's going to hurl the contents of his stomach up, but Caryan still doesn't let go of her.

The oracle just shakes her head, regret limning her otherworldly features. "You will find her when the time is ripe. Now let go, you're only hurting yourself."

"I will accept that," Caryan grunts. "Tell me."

The halls start to shake and rumble, the very stone they are hewn out of cracking open like split skin, and Caryan's power erupts. For a second, everything is dipped in absolute darkness before her light rips through it, blasting the cloud of darkness away like a sun, so bright it burns Riven's eyes. Caryan's magic lashes back and, for a second, the two forces swirl around each other in a deadly tornado, the two of them still in the middle. Untouched. Unruffled.

"Do not fight me, Caryan. For I am fate, and you have been fighting me all your life. It's time that you accept that not even you can erase fate from this world." The oracle's voice is still soft, despite the violent collision of their magic ravaging the halls and shaking its fundaments.

"Do not tempt me, Kalleandara. I might just prove you wrong and end you once and for all. Now tell me where she is!"

"I cannot. You made her run from you."

"Do not chide me, old woman. Tell me where she is!"

"You tell me—why did you fight so hard against her when you finally found her, Caryan?"

"How dare you ask that, since it was you who planned it this way all along? She's going to be my weakness. A ridiculous half-mortal you chose, not even a full fae. But I'm not going to be your puppet. Never was, never will be. She won't change a thing."

"I never expected you to be, Caryan. But there has to be a balance in the world. All things need a balance, even you. Someone breakable for someone unbreakable."

With these words she grabs his hand, prying open his grasp with impossible strength. At the same time, her blueish light flares, extinguishing the blackness like a blanket thrown over flames.

"You aren't stronger than me, Caryan. Not even you. Not here, so close to the source of all creation. And now stop." She's still holding his hand—only bones now, attached to an arm, Caryan's limb held together by magic alone—and no matter how Caryan fights against her, she is stronger.

She twists his hand effortlessly, and out of the column of light; his skin immediately starting to knit itself back together.

"I will make you pay for this," Caryan growls, still fighting the oracle's tight grip with all his force. Teeth bared and clenched, he says, "You made me—you created an abomination and now you are afraid of it."

"Not afraid, Caryan. Yes, I made you, angel. But I could never be afraid, because I love you, regardless of what you are. I always have, and I will until the very end, whatever this might be."

"Then you're an abomination too."

"I am and I am not. The same way I am alive and not. But tell me one last thing—what sort of monster does it make you, that you decided to give her some of your power so she will stand a chance in your world?"

"I did it because she would be even more of a hindrance without it."

"We always know the truth, Caryan, even if we keep telling ourselves lies. Find your other half, angel, and heal that wound inside you. Because a broken bond is a wound, and this is what weakens you, as well as her. Until next time, my angel."

With that, she steps back into the column and just disappears.

Riven resists the impulse to run when Caryan turns and spots him standing there. He stands his ground when Caryan slowly walks toward him, eyes black again, shadows teeming everywhere around him, crawling up the walls.

"You saw that. Witnessed that."

"I was afraid you wouldn't return," Riven answers truthfully, trying as hard as he can to swallow the lump of roiling dread and pain as Caryan stops in front of him. "She was—*is*—your... mate." The words tumble out of him.

Caryan's voice is calm when he says, "I know you thought that she was your mate, Riven. You still think she is."

Riven doesn't know how to respond. To the truth that shatters his heart all over, the pain in every fiber, livid.

"How long have you known?" He barely forces the words out.

"I suspected it the day she was born. I knew it the first time I tasted her blood."

"Why did you never tell me?"

"Maybe I wanted it to be you, Riven." With that, Caryan passes him, but Riven catches his arm and holds him back.

Caryan angles his head, a snarl on his lips.

"You love her," Riven says, tired of lies. Tired of holding back. But it is true. All this time, he thought that Caryan had changed. The gold in Caryan's eyes. It all makes sense now.

"Do not mistake a mating bond for love."

Riven shakes his head. "You keep telling yourself that, but it's not true! I know you have feelings for her beyond that bond."

"Let go, Riven, or you'll see how little I care about any of you."

Talons form on Riven's fingers, digging deep into Caryan's

arm. His voice has dropped to a growl. "You gave her your power. You *decided* to do that. I thought it just happened by accident, but you… the oracle said you did that out of your own free will, so she'd have a chance."

"Let go!"

"No."

Caryan stares at him, snapping his teeth. Then he says, his voice low and lethal, "Don't believe everything an oracle says. I did so to give her *some* power in this world so she could find those relics for me. I hurt her in the process, as badly as Gatilla hurt me when she gave those runes to me, and I did not care. I would have gone on and on if she hadn't wounded me."

"She is your mate. You wouldn't."

"I don't care what she is other than a liability."

Riven shakes his head. "I know what you are. I know that you care, Caryan. I know you."

He doesn't see Caryan's punch coming. It shatters his ribs, piercing his lungs. Riven lets go and crouches into a ball, hissing against the devastating pain.

Caryan just looks down at him coldly. "If you knew me indeed, you would know that I do not forgive betrayal."

"I did not betray you, Caryan," Riven hisses between clenched teeth.

"Did you not? I do not need to slice open your veins and look into your blood to know that you let her go. That *you* told her to go to the demons."

Riven says nothing, because he can't. He can't even breathe with his ribs shattered. Caryan might just end him here.

And it is alright.

But eventually, Caryan lifts his eyes and strides toward the cave's mouth.

ACKNOWLEDGMENTS

Thank you to my husband, Hans-Otto, for being the gentlest, best person in my whole world. Thank you for supporting me in every way and for being the best source of inspiration a writer could ever have—book-husband, boyfriend, mate. Thank you for holding my hand and believing in me, even when I didn't believe in myself, and for walking through the darkest days and nights with me. You taught me what love is. You taught me to live life. You keep teaching me how to live every day you spend with me. You are my brightest light. You are the most intelligent man I've ever met—and the kindest, loveliest, best! Thank you for choosing me. I'm thankful that I can trust you. Thank you for sharing your life with me and for all the things only you and I know.

An author's manuscript is like an unpolished diamond. It is beautiful but it only truly shines when passed over to very talented hands and keen eyes and those are yours, Mom. Thank you for your endless support and critical mind, for your ideas, for your enthusiasm. For the hours you spent reading my drafts and going back and forth over scenes. You are the best editor one could ever wish for! Seriously, you should contemplate going out there and helping other people with their books, because you have a natural talent in making a story shine. Thank you for reading Harry Potter to my brother and me every night. Thank you for your love. Thank you for being such a beautiful person and a light in my life that shines like the sun. It means the world to me!

Thank you, my beautiful aunt, Sylvia, who was and *is* always there for me. Who bought me all those fantasy books I spent hours reading. Magical stories where dwarfs caught dragons with coconuts. It was you who invented stories yourself starting with the (creepy) witch doll which scared but, yes, also fascinated me. Who made a dragon out of a sponge so I could take it with me into the bathtub every night. Who took me for walks when I was a kid and told me stories about our secret path into the forest only we knew. Thank you for taking me in as if I was your own. Thank you for being in my life, Sylvie. I don't know where I would be without you and your endless love. You are in my heart like a star. Ever burning.

Thank you to my other beautiful aunt, Gloria. I owe you so much. It was you who read my first real book, Still Strangers, back then and loved it so much. You who said I should go out there and embark on my self-publishing journey. You who set spark to this idea. Thank you for being in my life!

Thank you, Louis Greenberg, for working on this with me and working your wonders. You are a painter with words and the book wouldn't be what it is without you! Thank you, Shannon Cave, for doing the best possible. For your eagle eyes and relentless focus on all the things that tried hard to slip past even my eyes only to be mercilessly pointed out by you—thank you so much!

Thank you, Elina Vaysbeyn, for helping me through all of this, teaching me how the business works and, well, supporting me along the way and holding my hand. You're brilliant. I would be nowhere without your expertise. And I'm so happy I found a friend, too and once I have that farm you come visit!

Thank you to Reece-Alexander Norris-Paterson for all the endless hours you and I spent on that astonishing cover. I love, love, love it! You're a genius! And another friend I made along the way.

Thank you to my agent Mel Berger, who took a chance on me when I was still so young. Who worked on so many books with me and never stopped believing in me. Thank you, Mel! And also, thank you, Ty. I know this book is also a little bit your baby, so fingers crossed that it turns into a success. I love your ideas and thank you for answering endless streams of emails.

Thank you, Basti Prenner, for the beautiful artwork you created! The map is wonderful! You are incredibly talented! Thank you also, Lauren (lady labyrinth), for creating the beautiful illustrations in my book.

Thank you Lorna Reid for the last touches.

And a big, big thank you to every reader and every blogger out there who has taken a chance on me—I love you. And I mean this with all my heart because this is only possible because of you. Some books and some characters stayed with me throughout the years, became a source of strength or inspiration, or simply changed my perspective on things or maybe even life itself. Some taught me things about love or made me believe in the good things again. I always hoped that one day my characters would mean something to others. Something good. That the stories I write bring you some joy or stay with you. Thank you for reading! Big hug. The world is brighter with some magic in it.

Thank you to my lovely little dachsie, Audrey. Thank you for your kind heart and sweet, sweet soul. You are such a beautiful little being and I am so grateful to have you in my life. Thank you, Emmi, you will always be in our hearts and never forgotten. Thank you for walking a part of the way with us. We love you.

And lastly, because again, you are my beginning and my end, my partner in crime, my best friend, my world—you are my mate— thank you again, Hans-Otto. You are in every hero, every villain, every bad boy I write (whatever that means for you ☺).

Made in the USA
Middletown, DE
12 April 2025

74175860R00368